MELODY JACKSON
DRAGONS' HOPE

MELODY JACKSON
DRAGONS' HOPE

Isles of Vivet Transbladasia

Galdania

Calest

Rodan

Oktar
Ocean

GALDANIAN
PROTECTORATES

Dragon
Territory

Amael

Cover Design: Fiona Jayde Media
Map drawn by Renee Hougey

Printed in the United States of America

2018—First Edition

ISBN-13: 9781548958831

melodyjackson.weebly.com
facebook.com/melodyjacksonauthor
melodyjacksonauthor@gmail.com

To my book dragons, who helped this story find its wings

KAIDEN

A smarter person, Kaiden was certain, might have considered the consequences of their actions *before* rushing into a burning building.

Fortunately, he wasn't that smart.

At the first helpless cry, his feet were already moving forward down the dusty street, abandoning their prior mission in favor of this one. Panic seeped through the air around him like a disease, slow and infectious with its reaching fingers wrapping tight around the townspeople. Tearing off the thin coat he'd gotten back in Galdania, he ducked through the open door, his ears tuning to catch the sounds of a small child amidst the crackle and creaking of burning boards.

Kaiden peered through the gathering smoke and scanned the rooms before him, picking out the shadows of a staircase leading to an upper level. A muffled cry confirmed his suspicion, all caution abandoned as he hauled his way up, shielding his mouth and nose with the coat.

It all happened so fast. In what felt like an instant, he had the terrified, trapped child up in his arms, smoke slipping into his lungs as he shielded the child, instead, with his jacket. The logical side of his mind was shut off, silenced like his hearing while submerged underwater until he was back out on the street, breathing the now too light air as he passed the child over to its frightened mother. A burning tickle built in his throat with every breath.

Now that the danger was past, his lungs set about expelling the unwanted substance filling his chest, hands pressed to his knees as he coughed out the remains of the smoke. People – ones who were no longer strangers, his mind reminded him – were watching him with equal expressions of shock and awe, as if he'd just turned into a dragon before their very eyes. In a way, that must have been what it seemed like, to them.

It was only then, as their shock hit *him* with the clarity of what he'd done, that he realized his mistake – and the consequences. Despite the grateful look on the child's face, and the mother's relieved terror, everyone else would be putting the pieces together, from the way they looked at him. A farmer he faintly recognized opened her mouth to question him, just as the mother breathed a postponed 'Thank you'. Even if they didn't identify him directly, it was a small enough town. Word would travel fast. No sane person would run into a burning building to save a stranger's child. And even if they did, they wouldn't come out unscathed.

The looks in their eyes hit him like a galloping horse. He had to leave, and *now*. Already the awe was dissolving to fear, the mother's eyes apologetically guarded as she held her child closer to her. Even though most Calestans weren't opposed to the existence of Gifted, the consequences of associating with one had grown far larger lately than they had been just months ago.

If he had the breath for it, he would have cursed to himself. Though he couldn't seem to summon his gift at will anymore, it apparently didn't stop it from protecting him from things like this. As unpleasant as the gritty air in his lungs still felt, it wouldn't, or possibly couldn't, cause any lasting harm.

"I'm afraid...I can't offer you a reward," the mother whispered, eyes downturned as she cradled her child. Before Kaiden could reply, she lifted her eyes to meet his, mournfully grateful. "We haven't any money..."

"I don't need money," Kaiden breathed out, watching the onlookers' expressions changing from skepticism to something far more dangerous. Meeting the woman's eyes made his chest ache with recognition, the pressure eased only by the relief and gratitude that flooded through her eyes. She bowed her head.

"Thank you."

The whispered words were more of a reward than he could have ever asked for.

"S...Sir?"

He was already turned to go when a small hand caught his – his breath catching in his chest for a moment as it always seemed to at any kind of touch. The hand – soft and surprisingly steady – folded something small and round into the dip of his palm. "I...I want you t' have this," the boy rasped, some of the smoke probably caught in his own lungs. Kaiden wished his gift could extend to others; he'd take the boy's discomfort away in a moment. But he would be alright, Kaiden reassured himself, looking back to meet the boy's bright brown eyes. Dark hair tousled as it was, a thin nightshirt rumpled at one shoulder, it made a different memory tug at Kaiden for a moment, aching in his previously satisfied chest.

"It's for luck," the boy whispered, looking down in quiet awe at Kaiden's hand. A smile tipped up the corners of his mouth. "Though y' don't seem like y' need that."

For a second, Kaiden held his breath, the smaller hand cupped over his, fingers curled, a reverent understanding in the child's eyes. A peace he hadn't felt in far too long relaxed his shoulders as that smile bloomed further up the soot-smudged cheeks in front of him, the boy lifting hopeful, misty eyes up to Kaiden's face. "Thank you."

He could have closed his eyes and lived there forever, in that moment of peace. All dark memories banished, something anew and oh so precious created in a moment the younger of them couldn't even fathom. The words echoed in his head like a reply, though he kept them to himself as he matched the smile, as much as he dared, and gave the barest nod to the boy. "Thank *you*."

The light in the boy's eye was enough to keep the smile lingering even as Kaiden was forced to turn, the tiny treasure tucked tight in his palm as he strode out of the square. With any luck, the observers' awe and grudging respect would keep them from calling the authorities right away. They all knew what happened to those in possession of Gifts – and those who turned a blind eye to them.

Possession. As if this was something people could give and take away, rather than an inherent blessing – or a curse.

Safely out of sight, Kaiden looked down at the stone the boy had given him -- oblong, dull in its grey, ordinary hue, but with a river of blue running straight through the middle -- and smiled. For once, his mind felt simply, blessedly clear as he made his way through twisting streets, back to Resenya's side. It was as if there was...a *light* inside him as he walked away, steps barely seeming to connect with the ground despite the inevitability of what he now had to do.

Resenya rumbled a quiet hello as he ducked into her hiding place. The deep green dragon had disguised herself in one of the many littered alleys in the town, Ru'ach herself shielding it from human eyes, or so she said. Kaiden ran a gentle hand along his dragon's flank, some part of him still aching from this new, unfamiliar softness. More than anything, he didn't want to leave it.

But the family he'd stayed with here wouldn't be safe if he continued to stick around, after the stunt he'd just pulled. He couldn't say goodbye, or even explain why he'd left, lest he get them wrapped up in his mess.

A part of him whispered, as it had before, that he shouldn't have involved *anyone*. But his supplies had only stretched so far, even with his harsh rationing, and with no money to his name, he'd had to find work to support his search these past few months. This family, as almost all others had before, had practically insisted he stay with them, on top of the pay for helping on their farm. What else was he supposed to do? Declining hadn't exactly worked before.

Guilt was still too often of a companion for him for it to not come crawling back at the thought, though, as he swung a heavy leg up and over Resenya's side, clearing a lump from his throat. The dull spark he was so used to trickled back even just with that motion, scraping at him as he quietly gave Resenya the order to take off – and resisted the unbearable urge to shut his eyes. It was always there, no matter how much worse it would make this whole experience. As if not seeing what would happen could somehow convince his mind that it wasn't there. That it wasn't going to happen, again.

He could have *done* something. He could have...been smarter, or something like that. Though the family he'd been staying with hadn't known about his gifts, there was still always a chance they could get into trouble now, for their association with him.

If they had *known,* his mind insisted on adding, *they wouldn't have let you stay anyway.*

The little boy he'd saved should be safe, he hoped, along with his mother, but at times it came down to the particular official of the town as to their leniency in other matters. Though the family could plead ignorance, and truthfully, without one of the Empress' interrogators, they might not be believed. And individual officials tended to prefer making the judgment themselves rather than calling in a higher authority to undermine them.

It didn't matter, though, Kaiden thought as his stomach lurched inside him; as if it, most of all, would have preferred they stay on the ground. He'd spent long enough in this town as it was, fooling himself into thinking he might find a clue somewhere to his siblings' whereabouts if he kept looking rather than moving on. Ten towns in and none of them had even an inkling of who he was.

It should have been a relief. No matter where he went here, no one knew what he'd done. No one knew the burdens he carried around, and no one ever had to.

They'll be alright, he tried to assure himself against the winds picking up from Resenya's ascent. *They have to be.*

Some of the towns he'd hardly spent a few days in, for one reason or another. All of them had given him no answers. This latest one, though, he'd tried a little harder, dug a little deeper into whatever he could find, all as an excuse to stay. There was little need to pretend on that matter anymore.

Anonymity was his blessing and his curse. No one knowing him made it easier to relax, when he could, no specific way to act constantly whispering in his mind. But it also made finding any information about his family about as impossible than finding a diamond ring in a back-alley scrap pile. Of course they didn't know his family. He was nothing, a Gifted child from people who weren't even looking for him.

What if even *they* didn't want him?

His stomach had dropped out the moment Resenya left the ground, leaving him empty and more anxious than in a battle. Tension threaded through his muscles, tight as a tailor's sewing. The twisting, sweating sensation taking hold of him grew almost too strong to ignore.

This, too, was why he'd lingered so long. Running once again from a truth he didn't want to face. Even if he found his family, his record was anything but admirable. And he had a *gift*. What made him think they would even take him back?

When they crested the buildings, leaving gaping onlookers and dusty reds and blues far below them, Kaiden's fingers dug tightly into Resenya's spines, enough to draw a low warning from the green dragon's throat. Though the motion was instinctive and near-impossible to fight, his knuckles turning whiter than snowy mountains, he whispered an apology to her anyway. As much as he'd rather die than admit it, flying wasn't easy for him. It reminded him too much of another time, a different place he hardly remembered, yet haunted him all the same. The moment his feet left the ground, control tore away from him like a sharp knife from a child's grasp. Breath trapped in his throat, refusing to enter his lungs as he fought against it. He fought so *hard* against it...

As Resenya banked for their turn, Jade's breeze-like touch from her seat behind him was the only thing that kept him off the verge of utter panic, his thoughts cut apart by the terror slowly coursing through him. Though shutting his eyes only dizzied him further, he *had* to do it, to keep his mouth from crying out and betraying him. Every previous journey he'd taken in the air dulled in his mind once again in comparison to what he felt now. It was a cycle that he couldn't escape, a paralyzing punch to his emotions that left him reeling every time. Frozen, yet writhing inside at the panic slithering slowly and inevitably through him. Another reason he hadn't wanted to leave. Another excuse to hide from the pain.

Jaw locked to keep the past where it belonged, Kaiden forced his eyes back open to meet the sky surrounding them. How small his previous awe seemed now, in the face of this gaping monster he dealt with so often. He hadn't even had a chance to prepare for the onslaught this time, and not even the spark of previous relief could keep memory's claws from him for very long, as they sunk sharp lengths into his skin.

A hand closing around his throat.

Jerking his head, Kaiden fought against the image, swallowing against the burning, phantom pain coursing through his shoulders as he focused his gaze on the soft spines that his white-capped knuckles now perfectly matched.

A tap on the shoulder choked out the rest of his thoughts. On instinct, his body tensed for a blow, even as a cheerful voice shattered any of his expectations.

"Don't worry." Like sunshine flooding through a dark room, Jade's voice slipped through the fog in his ears. "I won't let you fall."

He would have let a laugh fall if he had any strength for it. If that's what she thought he was worried about...well, she was only half right. And that half was a thin ghost of instinct, a shadow to the real fear burrowing its way into him, numbing him slowly from the inside out.

He'd enjoyed being in that town, with that family, more than he would have liked to admit. Under pretense of searching for more information, he'd extended his stay long enough to learn the names of his hosts and each of their children – and just how desperately they needed help. Even with so little to their name, they'd *insisted* on giving him food and a bed, never knowing how little he deserved either of them. The mother was playfully stern about it, and so he'd given in to appease her.

Though he was perfectly content to sleep in the stables – when he did sleep, anyway – the little boy of the house had been more than overjoyed to have Kaiden in his room.

That was one thing he'd had to decline, and come up with an apt excuse for. He didn't want to scare the child with his sleepless habits, with how bad they had been of late. Even when he slept, he couldn't seem to escape his troubles any longer.

The thought brought him right back to the present, and the unbearable knot his gut was twisting itself into. Flying always seemed to sour anything that had been in his stomach when he dared to attempt it.

And this high up, his mind was free to imagine far too many possibilities, none of which eased his mind in the slightest. Belatedly, he turned his mind back to Jade's statement. Desperate to keep himself from spiraling, he resorted to the response least likely to dig into his conscience.

Falling. Yes, because *that's* obviously what he was worried about, this high up on the back of a dragon he barely remembered, talking to an imaginary friend. Who would have known?

Swallowing back a sudden surge of emotion, he gave a brief shake of his head. The sarcasm always dissipated when it was directed at Jade. Even if he tried, even if his mind was screaming that he *should* be mad – though never at her – he couldn't bring himself to respond that way.

Her claims were seeming more and more real as the days went on. He was just too stubborn to accept them.

Maybe she is just a coping mechanism, his mind suggested for only the ninetieth time.

But she couldn't be, with how she acted. Right? She had to be right, because he certainly wasn't. They were both in big trouble if neither of them were smart.

And she *was* right. There was no part of himself that could ever, ever love any bit of him as much as she did.

"How much farther?" he found himself saying in long-overdue response, the dull ache dimming his voice as he directed the question mostly at the scales of his dragon. Jade's hand shifted to rest on his, a silent reassurance he hadn't the strength to push away.

She was far too gentle with him, even now. *Especially* now. He knew what he'd done, knew...the consequences of his actions. They tore him apart, no matter how much she tried to hold him together.

"It shouldn't be too much longer to Milea."

"Milea." He breathed it like a prayer, the kind you made to ward off evil – if you believed in those things. Though his mind held an empty hole in place of the name, he knew exactly what it was. Where he had been heading all along.

A phantom ache flooded his shoulder, pain jerking through his senses like a delayed reaction. He blinked against it, even as it made his stomach roll and twist in on itself, as if fighting to pull away from what tormented him. His hearing was fuzzy, a distant, fickle thing swinging between whispered memories and whipping winds, both far too close to his ears. Digging his fingernails into his palms, which usually reoriented him, did nothing in this state.

If Jade replied, he couldn't hear it. Numbness spread through him instead, a steadiness filled with dread as the phantom feelings slipped away, slowly. His only way to cope.

Somehow, the calm terror was always far worse than the shaky, sweaty one. It lingered even once his memory changed views, when he could *feel* the ground beneath his feet and all but convince himself that it was real, that the terror was over.

But that meant everything else was real, too. The snippets of memory he couldn't grasp, sharpened to painful clarity by his acceptance of them. A door creaking open more than just a crack, to reveal the whole truth, before he shut it again, terrified.

This was how it always went. Occasionally catching bits of what Jade said – she tried telling him stories, sometimes, to distract him – and managing to nod to make it seem like he was listening. Burning his gaze into the shifting, reflective scales of Resenya's neck, as if they could make the sky around him disappear.

The worst part was, it wasn't about what he *saw*, or even what he didn't see. Shutting his eyes made his stomach lurch, but it couldn't change the images flashing before his mind. It couldn't make his jaw relax, couldn't even bring a false sense of security when his entire being was *convinced* by the mere action of leaving the ground that something was irreparably wrong. There was no escape. No way down, or out, or away from the burning, building *pain* he tried so hard to shove down. Compounding in its many forms until it seared his eyes – the worst kind of weakness.

Going home wasn't going to help any of this. Going back to that place, the very same building...what did he expect to find there? An answer? Hope?

What a bitter irony that would be.

Still, like a tidal wave threatening to engulf him, there was only one way to stay afloat. Riding the waves, feeling every emotion of it as clearly as water soaking into his skin. Mere inches from the very thing that could destroy him.

Turn back. Turn back.

He couldn't, as much as his mind screamed it. As the waves grew larger and the sound drowned out everything else, as it shook him so desperately he felt like he would shatter. It hurt so badly to keep himself together.

The waves stilled. He hadn't even realized he'd closed his eyes until Jade's hand wrapped around his, gentle, urging him with his name. Forcing himself to look, he took in a sight that had never in his life looked so welcoming.

Trees.

Dull and haggard like everything else in this forsaken land – the bark drier and sharper than any other he'd seen, branches furling out in sickly, leaf-starved coils – he'd never seen something so lovely. The roots extended deep into the ground – the *ground* – in a desperate

14

search for any drop of water, and while the grass around it was far from any shade of green, he could already imagine it whispering around his feet, surrounded by blessedly hard earth.

Resenya set down with a click of her claws, folding her wings back above her as she rumbled something in his direction. Sometimes, he thought he could understand what she said – when he wasn't barely holding on to reality. It seemed like he should be able to.

Right now, though, the message seemed clear even to him. Peeling his fingers away from their stranglehold on her spines, he shifted to slide down off her back. Despite the relief spreading through him, his knees still crumpled beneath him once he touched the ground. Jade was beside him in a minute, her hand settled on his arm as he bent his head down, drawing in deep breaths to stave off the dizziness now reeling through him. He had to fight hard not to claw at his aching throat.

"It's okay," Jade murmured. Her hand kept him from slipping back into the memories.

"I'm fine," his lips whispered of their own accord, repeating the words until they sounded like a mantra. Like the aftershock from an earthquake, the pain coursed through him all over again, the room he pictured suddenly seeming even more *real* now that he was safe. Now that the terror was over.

"I know. Shh."

Jade's arms, wrapping softly around him, nearly pulled free the sob lodged tight in his throat. He rocked on his knees to relieve some of the ache and fought down a wince. It made no sense to him, breaking down now. Shouldn't he be relieved, rather than feeling sick and shaky that it was finally over?

Jade understood. She always understood, even when he couldn't put it in words. When all he could do was sit there, paralyzed, and choke out sounds that shouldn't be sobs, too shaken by a mere memory to stand on his feet.

It wasn't a surprise she'd been with him all of his life. It would take a lifetime to understand a single thing about him.

As the panic slowly released its hold, his mouth no longer denying the truth even a blind person could see, his mind began to rearrange itself, putting pieces back where they belonged. Back in the dark where he never had to see them.

"Look at me, Butterfly?"

It hurt to lift his eyes, to banish the alternate version of her words playing through his head as he met her gaze. Her hand, gently lifting to cup his cheek, helped drive it away.

15

"It's okay to have fears," Jade said. Far too kindly for someone like him. "That's what makes us human." He wanted to laugh at that painful sentiment, even as she continued on. "There's nothing wrong with being sad."

Before his own voice could rebut everything she said, inwardly or otherwise, he shut his eyes. Cringing at his own slipping control, he forced together a careful reply, his mind pressing back against the shadows.

"I don't want to...remember."

Shame flooded in with the words, that deep internal voice flaying him for his weakness. Jade just rocked him gently, closing her eyes. "I know. Shh. Sometimes we have to remember the bad to remember the good."

He might have tried to laugh, but it came out more like a sob. The *good*? Was there- *could* there even be anything 'good' about what he'd seen?

Despite his wishes, everything she did and he tried to do, the voice only seemed to grow louder in his mind, taunting him for every breath. Trying to forget. Wishing he could somehow change things. He squeezed his arms tight enough to dig into the skin, reflexively cringing at his own reaction.

Before he could tighten his hold further, desperate to prove his point, Jade's hands gently took his, repositioning them so they were around her instead. "You can hold on as tight as you need. I won't break."

The irony of everything, the softness of her words, was what ended up breaking him. A noise like a whimper escaping his throat, he pressed himself against her, as close as he dared to, tightening his arms around her. Though the voice continued to tear him down, and rightfully so, having her there was a relief that he was too desperate not to cling to.

Continuing to rock him, Jade hummed a little off-key tune, the vibrations rumbling in his ears. Though he knew she'd seen it plenty, more than she should have, he did his best to bury his distress, hiding the dampness of his lashes behind closed eyes. Part of him still felt trapped in the memory, helpless and terrified in a way he couldn't shake. The other part strained to keep a hold on his emotions before they broke. He couldn't afford that right now.

"Let's make camp," Jade suggested after a long while, as he knew she would. It still made his shoulders fall a little, as she explained that they could go into town later. *When he was ready*, since he wasn't now. When he stopped being such a coward.

16

She didn't say any of that, of course, but she didn't have to. His mind was good enough at supplying such things already.

Eventually, with plenty of small, deep breaths and a lot of steeling himself, he was steady enough to at least let go of Jade. His throat raw, as if he'd been crying, he stopped himself from brushing at his eyes.

Aware of Jade quietly studying him, he averted his gaze. The voice's words seemed embedded into his mind now, heavy reminders that he didn't want to think about. The Bane, and everything he'd done, all rushing back once more to weigh him down. Leaving his friends. Betraying them. *Using* them. The countless lives he'd taken or ruined by his own stupidity and greed. His chest ached with it all as he dragged a finger through the grass, attempting to distract himself.

Somehow, though, he managed to pull himself up after what seemed like an eternity, with Jade's prompting, and set up camp. Something dulled further in him when he lit a fire by traditional means, another example of his weakness. Though his gift hadn't stopped protecting him, he couldn't bring himself to actually *do* anything with it. It made the voices inside him scream so much louder, flames and terrified voices crashing through his mind until he could barely move.

Settling down in front of the blaze, he let his eyes follow the flames as they crackled and hungrily licked at the wood. Like the scenes crackling through his mind like dying embers. A reminder of his failure.

Something touched his leg. Blinking down, Kaiden was surprised to see a tiny pink creature nudge and crawl into his lap, curling up with a contented hum. But, Resenya was the only dragon he'd brought with him, wasn't she?

Ril. The name came to his mind like he always should have known it – and maybe he should have. For a moment, he saw through different eyes, tracking the dragon's journey to get to him. A quick glance at the saddlebag near him confirmed the story, the open flap and spilled crumbs undeniable. Though kit dragons *usually* ate insects and the like, some had developed a taste or even preference for other food. Of course the one that followed him across two separate countries would be one of those.

Kaiden stared down at the creature, who gave a little hiccup as she blinked up at him. A tiny pink dragon, curled up in his lap. He almost wanted to laugh. He'd killed people, lied to them, betrayed them, failed them over and over. And yet, to this small creature in his lap, he was nothing but a warm place to sleep.

A teasing thought poked at the edge of his mind, startling him. There was a warmth and affection to it that he didn't expect, that silenced the echo of his laugh. It did know. And it just didn't care.

That thought only made him feel worse. At least with Jade, there was still a reason why she stayed around. She wasn't just naive and hopeful like so many others were. Assuming he was some good and kind person just because he still knew how to smile in all the right ways.

As if this entire thing was normal, Jade came over and retrieved some of the food still left in the bag, holding it out to him. Though he had little appetite at the moment, Kaiden made sure to take it anyway, looking it over in an attempt to avoid what she would eventually, as always, ask. Ril's eyes widened, tiny blue pools that followed the food held almost too close to her. Her tiny nose twitched. Maybe she would eat it before he had a chance to.

Lightly, Jade nudged his hand. "Go on."

Though it felt like ash in his mouth, Kaiden forced himself to obey, careful not to choke on what she'd offered. Ril's protesting trill wasn't enough to keep memories and mental reprimands from filling his mind, guilt still churning inside him until he felt sure he wouldn't be able to keep anything down.

"What's the matter, Butterfly?"

Maybe this was why Jade hadn't yet mentioned the stowaway. He stuck a larger bite into his mouth, avoiding her question. Ril's ears drooped, her tiny gaze following a falling crumb as it landed on the ground.

Jade raised her eyebrows. "That's not getting you out of it, you know."

Considering how little he'd actually swallowed, there wasn't much room left in his mouth. Kaiden stuffed another piece in anyway, shrugging a shoulder as he chewed . *For the moment, it is.*

"You're putting me off." Jade chuckled. "Shame on you."

He couldn't decide whether Ril's answering squeak was in agreement or indignation. Though he didn't have the energy to deny the accusation, a faint smile tugged at the corner of his mouth, as his eyes sought the grass.

"I see." Teasingly, Jade grinned. "I'm abandoned for the food!"

And the dragon, Kaiden thought. Ril turned around with a tiny huff, settling better in his lap to stare at him. Though he now had the capacity to speak, Kaiden remained silent. The weight of everything was still far too heavy on his chest to carry normally.

Lightly, Jade nudged his arm, watching him. At his lack of reply, she leaned her head against his shoulder, her voice gentle. "Do you just not want to say it aloud?"

Why did she have to be so good at this? Part of him hated it, some days. It meant there was so little he could actually hide away. And yet, part of him ached to give in and let go like she wanted, let it all spill out in the broken, dirtied mess that it was. But he couldn't. He had to be strong, now, since he'd failed before.

Ril made a noise of dismay deep in her chest, tiny forehead wrinkling as much as it was capable of as she pressed closer against his shirt. An answer slipped from his lips, Jade's words drawing a speck of truth to the surface.

"I miss them."

He lowered his head, nearly cringing at the admittance. It wasn't what he'd meant to say, or something he should have ever voiced. They were all far better off without him, after all. There was a very, very good reason he left Galdania, and no one's fault but his own that he'd had to.

Ril's whine only made him feel worse. He'd left without her, too. Though even without their bond, he could feel her rumbly annoyance, as if the mere thought of him being *able* to leave her and not having her follow was just ridiculous. Maybe, it was.

"Your family or your friends?" Jade asked.

Once again, she knew too well what he was thinking. Holding back a wince, he shook his head before more of his secrets could slip out. "Family."

Jade rested her head against him, her words more sure than he could ever be. "We'll find them. I promise."

Ril hummed in what sounded like agreement. Breathing in a quiet sigh, he nodded, since there was nothing else he *could* do, currently. At least...his siblings didn't know what he'd done, or any of his secrets, really. His stomach twisted itself in ugly knots as he remembered what it'd felt like, realizing someone else knew about his...scars. It was just another reason to leave, rather than face the truth.

And yet, as much as he longed to find his siblings, a part of him still wished he hadn't left, either. Though it hurt, constantly remembering what he'd done, and why they were better off without him, they were his friends, too, and he didn't think that would ever change. It was part of what made the whole thing so painful.

A deeper sigh escaped as he drew his knees up to his chest, resting his arms on them. With a squeak of dismay, Ril hopped into the air and flitted to his shoulder, tugging gently on a piece of his hair.

All this was silly to think about anymore, anyway. They were probably *glad* he had left, no matter how they pretended to care. He'd seen the hurt in their eyes, far more often than he'd liked to admit. He knew what he'd done – and how irredeemable it was. No words could heal those wounds, no matter how they tried. As much as they might attempt to deny it, it was far, far better that he'd left. They'd see. They probably did, even now, not having to see him and remember all the things he'd done.

In time, they'd be grateful. They wouldn't even try to get him back, if they were smart. There was absolutely no reason to miss him, after all.

LENA

Dagging idiot.

With a satisfying *crack*, my staff hit its mark as surely as the words flying through my mind. My straw-filled opponent reeled backward, nearly toppled by the force of my frustration. Why did people have to be so, so...*infuriating?*

I punctuated the thought with another sharp blow to the training dummy, the flexible suit I'd had designed hot with sweat, my hair whipping my face in shortened, wild strands. It'd gotten in the way during other sessions, so I'd decided to cut it. Less trouble, and less connection to who I had been, perhaps.

That girl...I didn't even know where she'd gone. She certainly wasn't here, anymore, unless she got transformed in the midst of all my anger. Some days it was far worse, like today, when everything burned in my veins and not even a scream could let it out. I had to be too dignified to scream.

Or so I said.

Too many people looked to me, nowadays. I'd had to throw off so much of who I was, and the ease of how quickly that came still shocked me. Looking in the mirror was like looking beneath a dusty mask, the truth that had always been there now in plain light for everyone to see. The fury from everything that had happened, buried for so long. My father's death. The injustice of my former life. The way everyone I had ever cared for had been taken, or hurt, or *broken*.

No, it wasn't alright for me to hide that anymore. Leaders needed to be strong, and Raoul had looked to me to be an advocate. A link between worlds, a Galdanian scorned as so many were, a Calestan born from the injustice I'd seen.

No more. No *more* would I stand for it. No longer was any of this just about me, as if it ever was. I hadn't seen, before, so wrapped up in my grief, but I did now, and I refused to back down from it. These people needed a strong hand to pull them up from despair, and a strong hand couldn't also be trembling. At least, not where they could see.

Still, there were days like today when it all just proved to be too much. A little comment, a look in someone's eye and it all came crumbling back in, threatening to wrap me in the remains of who I had been. Withdrawn and hurting, like a wounded cat that would lash out at any who tried to help it.

But now, I saw, I wasn't the only hurting one. I wasn't the victim of their prejudice; they were *all* affected, in different ways. I couldn't just look after myself anymore.

Despite my attempts at distraction, something still stung my eyes as I struck another blow. Furiously, I blinked it away. If my brother wanted to be an idiot and get himself captured and executed because he couldn't just *lay low* and wait for me, that was his problem, not mine.

And that's why I was out here, beating the gleaming straw out of a training dummy. Because as skilled as I was, there was *nothing* I could do for Caleb. The Empress had shut off all access to the Cities soon after the Bane had failed to show as the 'god' she had promised. Though many Galdanians still followed her, it was clear their devotion wasn't as wholehearted as before, and the Empress was nervous. Caleb had been in the Cities when she'd closed them off, and we still hadn't figured a way to get him out.

Or even what had happened to him.

With my next blow, I loosed another frustrated breath, cracking the staff against the dummy's poorly painted face. I couldn't lose my brother too. Didn't he know that? I'd already lost too many people, too many times. Even Chan had taken Katya and gone back to Calest, to rally the people there – and to get away from the Empress, I imagined. Basil and Olive had stayed in Galdania, and Fern with them, but so soon after losing my father, every absence still made my heart lurch and my eyes sting much fiercer than they should have. They weren't him, but they reminded me of him all the same, as the fact that the last time we'd spoken, I hadn't *known* would be the last. I hadn't gotten a proper goodbye. Not with anyone.

And now Kaiden had done the same. I'd known *that* was coming, and it still stung. I had seen it in his eyes, once he remembered about his siblings. He decided that we were just 'better off' without him, leaving without a word in the middle of the night. I would have panicked if not for the fact that he left a letter – a very unsatisfying one.

"I'm sorry", it had said, followed by a long and unnecessary list of excuses dressed as further apologies. I nearly threw it at the wall for that. Dez had made dismayed noises at the idea, though, so I'd refrained. I'd had enough of 'sorry', both in looks and words. *Sorry about your dad. Sorry about this. Sorry about that.*

Couldn't people just stop being idiots and move on? I had. I'd moved on from crying to anger, and it worked out wonderfully for me. I didn't dwell on the past, or what I messed up. It only clouded my view ahead.

Admittedly, it had taken me a while to read the rest of his letter. It was just...easier to be mad, and pretend I didn't care. Not to wonder what he'd said, and why he'd written a letter *just* to me, a well.

He'd left one for the others, of course, but it had been more...generic. Like telling someone you had stepped out to grab a drink of water, rather than to disappear for *months*. I didn't think any of us had quite forgiven him for it.

I'd gone through the room he'd been staying in after he left, if it could be called that. I'd remembered the tension of the day we rescued him, the knots in my stomach as they laid him out and he barely even moved, paler than was normal even for him. The thoughts flashing in my mind, jumping between what I'd seen and what I saw now. I realized then he'd *known* what would happen to him. He got us out but stayed behind, to help his siblings. He took all that, for them. Just like he'd said.

I'd felt numb, glancing between the others in the room and seeing the same thing written on their faces. For Olive, it was determination, rekindled by a knowledge she'd always secretly held. For Chan, it was a clash of feelings, a rolling storm between disbelief, regret, and something I couldn't quite name.

For me, it was a sense of quiet I couldn't quite understand. Like all the puzzle pieces clicked into place, and I could only stare and wonder why I'd never seen it before.

But he hadn't wanted me to. He hadn't wanted *anyone* to. And maybe, if I hadn't seen them before that day, I would have assumed all the scars were the same. It'd been just a brief glance, before, and one I could never quite recall very well. I was more concerned with dodging the vase he threw at me. Good times.

But sitting there, seeing it all laid out before me, I had no words. My mind pulled pieces into place, forming theories I didn't dare ask about, even later. All I knew in that moment was the boy before me was nothing like he said he was, in any capacity.

This... *this* was the only truth, the only concrete image. A story written in indelible ink, over and over in the lines of his skin. It burned so fiercely it lit up all the other truths and half-truths and made them look dull. And somehow, we'd all missed it.

Somehow, seeing him lying there made it all fall into place. He couldn't hide anything; he was barely aware of us being there, from what I could tell. He barely cried out when Olive cleaned his wounds, and it was a weak, strained sound. He looked so *young*, somehow, gripping the sheets with a mixture of fear and determination flashing across his face. Murmuring names and shuddering at even the smallest touch, the muscles in his jaw tensed to stifle a cry.

I knew his secret. Or, at least, a very important part of it.

I'd helped bring Olive what she needed, since I didn't know how else to help. And I stayed with Kaiden once they were done, holding his hand while he broke down and cried, mumbling incoherently as tears tracked down his cheeks. Olive had given him something to help with the pain, and hopefully help him sleep, but he was still restless for quite a while, drifting off in exhaustion only to wake up in distress an hour or so later, shivering. He'd screamed once when I wasn't there, a chilling, heart-stopping sound, and it had haunted me for nights to come. Even once I got up to investigate, it had continued on despite Olive's best attempts to calm him, cries of terror and something far, far worse, a broken desperation that twisted my own nerves into anxious knots.

I couldn't stand not being there after that, even if I was mostly another set of hands. Despite her usual desire to be alone, Olive seemed grateful for it. Chan knew, of course, but his face always got very dark when he saw any of it. He did his best to keep the others from worrying, and explained why they weren't able to see him. Even if Kaiden wouldn't have minded, it wasn't anything any of us wanted them to see.

I took the time sitting by his bed to think, and think, and think. Pieces of the puzzle still didn't make sense, but the foundation was clear. I could see now, however wrong it was, that he thought he could help by using the Bane. He'd thought he could protect his siblings by keeping everyone distant. He was an idiot, at times, but his intentions were right. He hadn't wanted anyone else to get hurt.

And I understood that sentiment far too well. But I was still going to give him a piece of my mind when he came back.

If he came back.

23

That sobering thought had me stepping back, eyeing my straw opponent from a distance. Where *was* he? He must have gone to find his siblings, but I had no idea where they were. I couldn't very well scour all of Calest in hopes that I might find him. And I had duties to attend to here, anyway. With Sari gone, I had to take care of everything. Raoul oversaw the military aspects of everything, along with Olive, but everything else was up to me.

And all the instruction Sari had left was to wait, and train what Gifted we had to fight against the Empress. Her vagueness could be terribly infuriating.

I should have been out there, helping them. But I had far too much to attend to. Between keeping contact with the other protectorates and making sure mass mutiny or panic didn't break out, I had to train with my own gifts, and keep everyone from falling apart. All while dealing with my own grief.

Needless to say, it didn't leave much time for pleasantries. Or grieving.

A low whistle floated through the air, interrupting my thoughts. "You're almost as intense as Olive."

Rolling my neck, I took a step back and shrugged, still eyeing the toppled dummy. "Have to keep sharp."

Even my words clipped the air, short strokes of the blade I held in my tongue. I tried to keep the edge dulled. It wasn't Basil I was mad at. He was doing his best.

Basil leaned casually against a tree, his hands in his pockets. On his shoulder, his dragon did her best to imitate his whistle, squeaking with what I assumed was laughter when it didn't quite work. "You alright?"

Shoving my bangs from my face, I hid a frown. Though the sharp words I wanted to say sliced through the front of my mind, I held them back. "Fine."

I knew he didn't believe me. I wanted him to. But my lips must have been downturned enough to look concerning, for he pushed away from the tree and came over to stand by me, his eyes sweeping over the fallen dummy. "I bet he deserved it."

A laugh escaped into the air, too harsh and quick against my lungs. Leaning my cheek against my staff planted against the ground, I nodded. "He definitely did."

Basil's smile was slow, but no less infectious. Closing my eyes, I pressed my forehead against the back of my hands and let another small laugh loose. It shook me, unnervingly similar to sorrow, but I pretended the tears were from amusement as I smiled back at him.

"I don't think he'll be getting up anytime soon."

24

Basil chuckled, reaching over to brush something off my sleeve with a small grin. Then, he nodded. "I highly doubt it."

I let silence hang between our smiles for a moment, its shadow looming, but not overwhelming. Blinking, I straightened up, helping him pick the leaves off my sleeves as I explained, "I may have...attacked a tree."

Basil laughed again, and this time my grin split a bit farther as I mimed how my strike had caught the trunk square in the middle, sending a shower of leaves onto me. His tiny dragon snatched one of them from me, growling protectively like I might try to take it back. Despite her obvious concern, I didn't think hoarding leaves was the solution to my problems.

"Seems like it got its revenge, though. Too busy beating up that guy to care?"

A chuckle. "Yeah, I suppose." The grin shrank a bit as I glanced around. "Where are the others?"

Basil glanced the direction I had, shrugging. With a huff, his dragon crawled up onto his head, clutching her leaf close. It was a rather yellow-like color. Maybe she thought it was gold.

"Olive's doing something on her own. And Dailen is helping Raoul." He hesitated, a shadow of sadness crossing his face for a moment before he murmured, "Fern's by herself, again. She didn't want any company."

His words just pulled me down further. Out of everyone, it seemed that Elle's death had affected Fern the worst. She'd retreated farther into her shell, a haunted look settled in her eyes that she didn't seem able to shake.

I blew a strand of hair away from my face, as his dragon chittered unhappily at me. "Any news?"

The slight hesitation before Basil spoke told me enough. I cut him off before he could speak. "Keep me informed. I want to know the minute there's a change."

Pulling off sweat-soaked gloves, I strode away from the field before Basil could protest, or find a way to pull me back with his sweetness. I knew I was being short with everyone, but right now, I didn't care. It was my way of coping with things, and they would just have to deal with it. It was that or have a breakdown, and I wasn't fond of that option.

Besides, I was an unofficial leader now that my father was dead. I was supposed to be curt and commanding, right? Raoul said I needed to show that I was in charge. This was my way.

25

I supposed I could have joined Chan in Calest, but I doubted they would have listened to me. Despite the past few months, I was still too Galdanian to be relatable to Calestans. And I refused to leave my brother, anyway. Or Kaiden, if he decided to come back.

Of course he had to leave in the night, so we couldn't follow after him. It was enough to make me furious, and take out my anger on straw opponents to alleviate some of the building stress.

It still didn't fix my frustration, or the fact that nothing felt right. Though I hated to admit it, I wanted Kaiden back. I felt like I was just starting to understand him – *truly* understand – and then he just...left. With guilty excuses and with little thought to anyone else. And it wasn't like I could track him down and drag him back, either, since he'd been very clear with not stating *where* he'd gone. I didn't have the time to start a countrywide search for someone I cared about, again.

Zarafel watched from the distance, somehow appearing regal even as he lounged. I didn't know if he approved of my coping methods, and frankly, I didn't care. If he tried to lecture me, I'd just shut him out.

Maybe that's why he hadn't tried.

I hadn't gotten used to the dragons just being able to come and go as they wished without anyone's permission. You turned around and they were just...there. Between our dragons and the ones already in the city, there were days you could trip on a scaly tail if you didn't watch your step.

I didn't want to talk about it. I knew I was blocking everyone out. I knew it wasn't healthy. I also knew I couldn't afford to break down and snap at everyone I was trying to reassure.

I made it a point to keep to my room, and turn the other way when I saw a familiar face, or pretend to be busy. They were grieving too, just as I was. They probably needed time for themselves, anyway.

Dez chirped his encouragement from his perch in the tree, his little eyes bright and wide as he let out a whistling tune. I paused to scratch him under his chin. He flapped his tiny wings, his eyes hopeful. With a small sigh, I stepped over and helped him onto my shoulder, where he gave a happy chirp and nuzzled against my neck. It made a smile crack free on my face.

It seemed that kits were more often seen than regular dragons, and they liked to congregate wherever they wished. Sometimes I would find them hiding in a cushion, or under a pile of someone's clothes. They loved warm and soft things, it seemed, and there were definitely occasions in which I had socks go missing, only to find a tiny hoard of them discarded elsewhere.

The living situations didn't allow for as much privacy as I expected. I stayed mostly in my office, since I had one of those, but my rooms seemed to be free game. And as much as I wished to be alone, I couldn't get up the energy to scour the place for all the hideaways and kick the tiny hitchhikers out. Dez would shiver and snuggle next to me when he saw them, though I hoped maybe with time, he would warm back up to his own kind. I couldn't give him as much attention as I used to, especially with the care it took to watch over him.

Zarafel stayed surprisingly close to my quarters, lounging around behind in the shade of the building and refusing to acknowledge that he was guarding me. Somewhere deep down, I appreciated the gesture, and I appreciated even further that he didn't push me on it. Sometimes he still got a guarded and distant look in his eyes, and I'd never had the courage to ask for the story. In time, perhaps, maybe we'd get close enough to share such personal things.

But he was always *there* and available if I needed him. Silently extending the invitation, however I chose to take it. Sometimes I would fly with him, in silence over the forests, in the early lights of dawn, and let the frustration of the previous day roll off of me. Some days he avoided me, and I him, and it worked out wonderfully.

Sometimes I ached to talk to the others, but I still didn't...know what to say. It was easier to hide, and pretend to be busy.

Kaiden wouldn't have let me hide. He would have been getting in trouble so often in one way or another that I'd have to talk with him. Telling lame jokes or distracting me with a little song he made up.

I couldn't quite forgive what he did. Not yet, even if it wasn't his fault. Allowing it to be in any way 'okay' at the moment just felt...wrong. I didn't resent him, but I couldn't accept the result, either.

And I hated to admit how much I cared. Those few weeks had been the most interesting experience, seeing that side of him. It felt like walking on a thin rail, slicked with ice, and hoping I didn't slip and bring us both crashing down, crushing him.

Sometimes, though, he just seemed...lost. When he looked at the world as if he were the glass, and they the rocks that might so easily crush him, shatter him into pieces.

And then there were the days when he acted as if the world was glass, and he was a rock that might break it with too much pressure. When every step he took was like a ghost, as if it would be better if he was simply not noticed.

But it was real, talking with him, and it only left me aching for the pieces to come back together. For him to eventually become whole, and return to us.

That didn't mean he had to leave to do it.

Rubbing my dragon's scaly head, I let out a frustrated breath. *Kaiden, where are you?*

The Dragon Within

II

KAIDEN

He was here.

Despite taking time to rest – which didn't involve sleeping, despite Jade's prodding – his steps felt like that of a ghost when they entered the town. Ril stubbornly stayed on his shoulder until they arrived, coming back to him even when he tried to brush her away. She looked rather put out by the time he gave up, nipping the edge of his shirt with a pointed look. But even with his memory jumbled, he knew it wouldn't be wise to enter a Calestan town with a dragon on his shoulder. Of course he pushed her away.

By the time they reached the entrance, he managed to bribe her into hiding in his jacket with a piece of food. Though he didn't think dragons were capable of such emotions, Ril's look clearly told him she thought he was an idiot for trying to keep her away, or telling her to stay hidden. He could practically hear the sass in his mind, that she knew better than him what she was doing, and had been doing it for longer, thank you very much.

It was an odd sensation, and even if he knew it should be normal – to her – it still wasn't for him. Her presence on his shoulder reminded him of a harsh hand sometimes, more than anything. Intentionally or not, her little claws nicked his skin when he moved too quickly, and the brush of her tail against his back – and the scars that lingered there – didn't much help with his unease.

Resenya remained outside the town, assuring him with a nudge of her head that she would be fine without him, and waiting when he returned. With the many dragon attacks Calest had endured, it wouldn't be wise for her to enter with him, even if she would fit.

Everything in Milea seemed so foreign and yet so *familiar*, twisting in his gut and stealing away his breath before he could even breathe it. Like a million tiny rods pricking his skin, itching his senses with every person he passed, every building that felt more familiar than his own mind. Did they know his family? Had they known *him*?

This was why he'd been stalling. The inevitability of his journey had been looming ever closer, the fear of discovery keeping him pulled away. What if he didn't find anything here? What then?

Perhaps it would have been better to return to one of the other towns, after all.

Before his fear could make him hesitate further, Jade tugged him gently down through the dusty street, his feet numbly following. Every market stall screamed at him, every broken stone under his feet feeling like one from a dream that he had tread many, many times. He could almost imagine, in flashes, the beginning of images that sent his mind reeling, blinked away before he could make any sense of them. The screams of the vendors hawking their wares did nothing for his already uneasy mind.

Calest, as a rule, was not a pleasant place for the lower class. Though some of the towns were more civilized than others, all of them had an air of instability about them, a restlessness that drove people to tightly lock whatever doors they had and watch everyone with an unsure eye. He wasn't unused to this.

And yet *here*, in this town, that feeling seemed to multiply, growing with every step he took. Even the children watched with wary eyes rather than smiles, hungry gazes seeming to calculate if their desperation was worth the risk of being caught stealing.

No one in Calest was kind. But the authorities could be especially cruel, to whomever they chose.

Several times, Kaiden's feet almost fell out from underneath him at what he saw. They seemed far more familiar with this place than he did, weakening as he passed a certain stall, an innocent street leading further into the city. When they reached the square, the stones there edged in darker, unnervingly rust-colored hues, he could barely stand, caught in what felt like a paralyzing trance. Even Jade's gentle nudging couldn't immediately pull him free.

This place...none of it was *right*. None of the towns he'd seen had been this broken. It made Danten look like a pleasant place to live.

This was where he had grown up? In some ways, he should have expected it. In others, he still couldn't believe it. Not that he could fully fathom the complete desolation of the town anyway, after spending weeks in Galdania. It only made his dislike for them grow further. Who was doing something about any of this? Who *would*?

He didn't know how long he sat there, on his knees, staring at that square. Long enough for mud to be kicked in his face, a disgruntled patron shoving past him with a muttered *'Beggars'* before heading on his huffy way.

Veden. The word flew to his mind as easily as his own name, a coil of dread accompanying it. It was a bad idea to come here. Such a bad idea. They were likely to come, and they'd see him, and they'd *know,* somehow, as they must have before for it to happen...

Someone had told them. Somehow, they knew, and they'd take him...and he wouldn't be able to get away, trapped there like he'd done something wrong. He didn't think he had.

He wouldn't be able to get to his siblings. Couldn't get away. Wouldn't know if they... If their father...

"Kaiden." Hushed, gentle, Jade's voice urged him from his trance. Shaking, he pulled himself to his feet with her help, blinking away images as they continued on. People were starting to stare. A part of his mind knew that was never a good thing.

Finally, after making their way across most of the town, everything began to lessen. Noises died down, people grew sparser, and shadows ruled over the darkened alleys that wound away from the main road like serpents waiting for unsuspecting prey. Thankfully, they avoided those, heading down a section more open to the sky, though that didn't seem to be by design. Crumbling half and quarter walls and loose stones were all that remained of what had once been buildings, the uneven, discolored cobbles of the path far too exposed to the elements. Where it was possible, shelters had been constructed in the wreckage, from whatever people could find to use, but even those looked in need of repair.

After so long, so hard trying to find it, and simultaneously dreading the day, he stared at the street that he knew, without anyone telling him, would take him to his house. His childhood home.

His feet stalled at the start of the path, though, knowing something he didn't. Cold dread settled over him, a chill in his bones as he stared down at the familiar cracks in the pavement. Of all the things to recognize, it didn't reassure him. It told him he spent a lot of time indecisive on this path, or watching the ground as he walked. Neither of those boded well.

The chilly air curled around him, stirring the hair on his skin. Wrapping his arms around himself, he rubbed them to generate some of the heat he was missing. Despite the leather of his jacket, the thin and worn material had seen better days. He wore it more as protection for his back than any other part of him, and his arms. Though the scars there were not as awful, and not quite as unusual, it was best to keep whatever weakness he could hidden, especially here.

He could just use his gift to raise his temperature. But any time he opened his fingers to summon it, they trembled, and the heat that seared through him had nothing to do with fire. Memories flashed in burning currents, flickering before his eyes and threatening to make his knees buckle at the phantom pain. He bent and braced his hand on his knee, breathing in hard a few times as if to distill the pain it left. The things he had once done with his gift, he never wanted to do again.

At least he hadn't had to explain any of that in the previous towns he'd visited. It was a welcome feeling, wandering through a place that didn't know his name, or what he'd done. Shopkeepers smiled at him, sometimes casting an inquiring look at the messy, flame-like style of his hair, but he liked it that way. It represented a lack of control and direction, a silent sign that no one understood. He wouldn't have let it grow so disheveled before, or not on a regular basis. It was another element of the thin pride he had, a badge that marked him different. Ridiculous, maybe, or even insane in some cases, but it was worth every look. A reminder that he wasn't the same, anymore.

The other version of him had always looked so put together, so in control. Trying to smirk like he had then left a nasty taste in Kaiden's mouth, as if he'd somehow swallowed something vile with the expression. Walking like he knew everything brought back memories that trailed behind his every step, lingering. And using his gift... well, flames fed on oxygen, and those ones stole his until the world blackened back into those moments, to memories of smoke and fire licking at skin, curling around wood. Burning screams into his mind like a brand.

A small, quiet part of him swore every time he'd never be like that again. An even quieter part wondered if that was really the truth.

And this was why, when it boiled down to it, he'd had to leave Galdania. The memories were too strong. Every moment he caught the damage in their eyes, no matter how it was hidden, it stole his breath away like the flames were still there. Like he was still that person.

But here, at least, he'd been able to meet eyes without shame, and summon smiles that didn't send guilt in violent twists through his gut. Here he'd laughed and made conversation without parts of him breaking inside. Here the pain was far enough away that he'd just pressed it down, deeper, and only suffered when it eventually came screaming out.

Sometimes, it had seemed to be working, when he could look up and smile at Jade without being flooded with a burst of memories. Other times, it'd made the pain worse, and he'd had to duck into alleys out of sight and breathe deeply until it passed, fighting off flashes of memories and voices in his head until he could see properly again. Jade was always there beside him, no matter what.

32

Someone had said he was crazy, once. He wasn't so sure that wasn't true now.

This all would have been so much easier if he just knew where his siblings were. He had known it once, before he lost his memory, but trying to extract that detail now was like sticking his hand in a tank of razor-teethed fish and hoping not get his hand bit off. There was no way to safely search his mind without triggering anything far, far worse. It happened easily enough on its own.

And those were always the hardest moments to hide everything. He'd see a flash of something, hear a word wrong and his hearing faded to static. The past clawed its way into the present, dragging him in until a worried voice asked him why he was shaking. He did his best to hide it, dodging around questions and keeping mostly to himself, but sometimes the memories couldn't be stopped. They came when they wanted and tore away pieces when they left, leaving him raw and bleeding inside. He supposed he deserved it, after everything he had done.

And now, after too long of lingering, he was here. Where the memories were guaranteed to be far worse than any phantom pieces his mind could throw at him. Why did he think this was going to *help* anything?

Because this was his town. His home. Maybe his siblings were around, somewhere. Maybe, at least, someone would have a clue as to where they were.

And if not...

A nudge in the shoulder brought him back to the present. Jade urged him onto the path before him, gently. Taking a breath, he let his foot lift forward onto the cobbled stone. To anyone else, it might have looked like a path to nowhere. The area beyond the town was even more barren than the surrounding area. But he knew there were more homes back there than just his, hidden behind the more put-together shacks lining the streets.

As he passed several of these, he saw children playing with a ball along the cracked paving stones. It only made the cold cling to him tighter, like a hand gripping him and pulling him along. His feet moved, not out of eagerness, but reluctance, scraping against the pavement as he went. This was such a bad idea.

Eventually, the simpler buildings died away, leaving a path up to what looked like a forest, over a hill. Walking up it stole the last of his calm, the cold sealing around his mind with quiet, foreboding whispers.

A shiver ran through him. Jade's hand brushed his arm as his steps stilled just outside the clearing. Slowly, his hand found hers and squeezed it, and she returned the gesture.

Dread curled inside him tighter, capturing his breath so it barely misted the air, his hand instinctively coming up to brush his jaw. He couldn't shake the feeling that the house was growing, towering over him until he was no taller than the grass at his feet.

Seeing it, in front of him, made everything pale in comparison. From the moment he stepped foot on the path, he knew exactly which stones were loose, what pattern they followed, which was the smoothest. The number of times he'd studied these stones, rather than the landscape around him, said terrible things about the creaking building in front of him. Dusty grey and chipped, leaning on porch poles that looked like they'd taken a beating themselves, it was a battered ghost of a world that didn't match anything around it. Yellowed grass waved around the front, as tall as his knees in some places and speckled with tiny bundles of pink petals. Once-whitewashed steps led up to a porch that groaned far too much under his feet. Cringing, his trembling fingers reached for the door handle – and refused to grasp it.

"Do you want me to go first?"

When he didn't reply, Jade stepped in front and entered the house, leaving him to follow with building dread a moment later.

The smell hit him first, old and dusty, choking, smelling faintly of something he couldn't quite name. For a moment, he caught a phantom lantern flickering on the wall, casting an ugly yellow light on the already faded and dusty room. It only made things look more foreboding, the creaking beneath him setting his heart pounding even harder than it did while flying.

Breath refused to come to his lungs, his eyes darting about the space on instinct, and picking up more memories as they did. They tumbled and meshed in a cacophony of sounds in his mind, screams of children both annoyed and terrified, running feet, pounding hearts. Laughing. A sickening feeling crept over him, like a wave cutting off his oxygen and slipping over his mouth, drowning him. He could see them, for the faintest of moments: running across the room like in a game of chase, if not for the truth written deep in their eyes.

"What exactly are we looking for?"

He barely felt his own shrug, the house seeming to reach out and curl invisible hands around him in ever-tightening vises. He became aware of how tightly he was squeezing her hand and mumbled an apology, even as she turned to him with an answering grin and assured him she didn't need it.

But it was more for him, a distraction, maybe, as she stepped further inside and he reluctantly followed. Those hands grew tighter, their presence lingering along his arms as his gaze flicked around the room, spots of memory returning.

"I...don't know. Anything. Clues..." the words almost stuck in his throat, "as to where they might be."

Jade nodded. "Alright. Just a quick look around, then."

The crash of a lamp nearly made him flinch, until he realized it hadn't happened. A dull thud echoed, and an ache he couldn't explain. Heated words seared through his mind, warning him to stay very, very still. Where his gaze caught, Jade moved to investigate, which only made the images grow sharper. His hand brushed his jaw to catch something that wasn't there, the gesture strangely comforting to the throb he felt.

Jade followed his gaze when he stilled, to a locked room at the end of the hall. "You want to go in there?"

His heart pounded with the reply. The very *last* thing he wanted to do right now was go in there. Which meant it was exactly where he'd need to go.

No. No, no, no, no...

Somehow the words must have reached the air, for Jade cut off his panicked thoughts, ever-knowing. "How about you stay here and I'll go look, then?"

Fine. The word repeated through his head in a loop, despite the building panic shouting that it was *not* fine. Nothing was fine.

"Okay."

Jade squeezed his hand. "I'll be right back."

Then, slipping her hand out of his, she walked away. Leaving him alone.

She didn't need to keep assuring him like this, really. It was just... a lot to take in. A lot of puzzle pieces he didn't want to assemble. A lot of truths he might have guessed, or been told, but didn't *know*. Not like you knew your best friend by the sound of their voice, or the exact path to your childhood home.

Without something to hold onto, though, the memories only seemed to grow before him, looming darker and growing stronger, stronger. Everywhere he looked they blurred together, painting a picture he hadn't wanted to see. It was such a bad idea to have come here.

And yet...if it helped him find his siblings, maybe it could be worth it.

Maybe.

Simply hearing about his past – if he could call it that – didn't hurt in comparison to this. He could imagine it far tamer, or not happening at all, despite the reminders carved in his skin. He could tell himself it was his fault, or he should have been stronger, when he didn't *feel* what it was like.

Visceral, gnawing at him like endless rows of sharpened teeth, the terror that his memories had only cast the shadow of before. Pain so harsh it became numb, in the moment, words bleeding out of existence and back in. *Worthless. Pathetic.* Each one of them digging sharper than a jagged knife.

He'd seen some of it before, in dreams. He'd woken up drenched from already fading fear, slipping off his skin like the falsehood it was. It couldn't stick. Not really.

At least in his dreams, not everything was real. It was easier to brush aside, to laugh at the seemingly ridiculous parts because honestly, would that ever happen?

Could it?

Calling his past a nightmare would have been a mercy, because it meant there was something else to wake up to. He'd tried believing that, for years. Instead, his nightmares felt more like a relief, because they would never happen again. They would evaporate like water left out in the sun, only a faint reminder left behind.

Here, there was no such mercy.

There was nothing else to focus on. Nowhere to look that could give him even the slightest reprieve. His head was buried beneath his arms, his breath coming in uneven bursts as he fought to tune everything out. The voices, the shouting, the screams.

Within a few minutes, he found himself sliding down to the floor, hiding a wince as the wood of the wall brushed against his back. It only churned up more memories, his body flinching instinctively from the bombardment. He felt sick down to his very bones.

"*Get up.*" The all-too familiar voice warred with his own thoughts. It shouted at him, louder, until he nearly obeyed. Insults, escalating to a steady stream of profanities as he tried, uselessly, to comply. Pain stinging endlessly through his face.

"*I said, get* up."

And then he was choking, harder than his mind could have imagined. He couldn't swallow the terror, couldn't breathe without sharp pain rushing through him, throbbing in his ribs.

His head ached. The room spun, growing fuzzy until another blow jolted it back into place.

Worthless, the voice spat at him, disgust filling every crack in the tone. *Pathetic,* landing against his skin with far more damage than any fist ever could. *Useless.*

Weak, his mind supplied in a whisper, feeding the memories. *Helpless.*

"Help me," he whispered, though the words never made it to the air.

It was so much more vivid, seeing it *here.* Hearing a crash and feeling the flinch jolt through his spine, his muscles tensing for something he couldn't see coming. A dull crack against his skin, a flash of brightness, and then, just like that, nothing. His hearing slipped away, everything slipping away for the shortest moment before it was back, and he was on the ground without ever realizing it. Being pinned to the wall and realizing with a sickening dread that it wasn't, in fact, a nightmare. It wasn't something he could wrestle his way out of, because that wasn't how this went. He could only stay there, terrified as his air seeped away and his legs kicked helplessly, until he was released in disgust and could gasp from his shaky position on the ground.

It wasn't hard enough for the truth. A dulled blade, even unsheathed, was no preparation for a sharpened one. Words lacked power without details behind them, without meaning to grant a clear image.

And oh, how clear this one was. He bit deep into his lip until it bled. Better there than letting it all out elsewhere. It was always much worse if he cried.

Tears tracked down his cheeks anyway, an inevitable funeral march down his face. He just wanted it all to *stop.*

An unfamiliar, dismayed sound cut through his mind. Ril squirmed her way out of his jacket pocket, pulling herself up to his shoulder and letting out another squeak.

Ril. Shakily, he cupped her against his chest, rubbing a finger against her smooth scales. The thrumming that filtered through him helped anchor him to reality, easing some of the terror. It would return, later, but for now he clung to anything that could get him through. Disjointed thoughts of food and even flying, told in the form of innocently simple pictures.

Ril. He forced his mind to focus on the name, on anything other than the churning, writhing pain that threatened to take ahold of him. Even if he couldn't see her, he *felt* her. He grasped for her flitting thoughts like reaching for a firefly, praying it wouldn't be gone by the time he'd moved.

Ril hadn't been here, before – in these memories. He'd found her in the Mountain – or she'd found *him* – and she'd never left him alone. She had crawled out of his pocket, chirping in dismay, and was now rubbing her tiny, scaled head against his fingers so he felt the ridges, the solidity of her scales.

In a way, he was right about it all. This didn't hurt any worse than it had when he only had suspicions of his past. It just stuck around longer. It clung to him like a leaf on a stick, no longer brushed away with a simple touch. It whispered through the edges of his mind with every word, trying to draw him back to that moment, even as he brushed his hand over Ril's tiny, bumpy back. It sought to continue what had already been started, by making sure he could *never* forget those words.

You'll never amount to anything.

The voice blended with his own, *becoming* his own, until he shut his hands over his ears to try to block it out. It followed, buzzing through him until he was forced to look up, to finish what he had started. Ril made a dismayed sound in her throat.

How true it was, too. What good had he done in his life, since getting out? What had he truly escaped, without making things that much worse? What lives *hadn't* he ruined with his own miseries?

He was right. He's always right.

Was knowing worse, or being taunted with thoughts and ideas of it? Before, he was sure that knowing *couldn't* be more painful. It just couldn't.

And yet, here he was.

Ril's sharp squeak brought him momentarily back to reality, from the burning of the terrible images looping in his mind. Now, more than anything, he wished he could take it back. He didn't *want* these memories. He never had. And yet, he knew they were the key to understanding who he was, somehow. Terrible as they were, dark and terrifying as some of it had been, it had shaped him into who he was. Not knowing that...it was like missing part of his foundation. Like being able to walk without his legs. It wasn't quite...right.

He could recall Jade's explanation, if he tried hard enough. "*There was a man who threatened your family.*"

The pain grew sharper, tearing tears and a breaking laugh from his chest. 'A man.'

You never said who it was.

38

He saw it sometimes, in his nightmares. A shadowy figure, looming and menacing. He'd always just assumed...

But no. Of course it couldn't be that simple. Of course it wouldn't. Those scars, those screams...

He had to shut his eyes, barely getting in a breath. It shuddered through him like he was already crying. Maybe he was.

And the worst part – the *worst* part about the whole thing was he still didn't understand why. He didn't know *why* all this had happened, in the way that it had.

In memories, he didn't have to feel anything. Somehow it made the whole experience that much worse, watching it from what felt like outside of his body, watching the senseless cruelty and the words to which he was far, far too numbed.

Did you ever wonder why it didn't surprise you?

Failure. Coward. Weak. They felt as drilled into his bones as the scars etched into his back. A permanent burden to carry around, whether he wanted to or not.

Footsteps. His head shot up on instinct, body tensed against further contact as the past melded with the present. Ril pushed against his finger with a squeak, unconcerned.

Someone was coming. Someone was always coming. It was why he walked across the floors as if he were a ghost, each motion as silent as a passing breeze. It made every part of him still, the breath of a moment before a storm hit, when no one knew what to expect. When lightning might strike anywhere, anytime, without a single warning.

"Let's go outside to look at these."

The voice shattered his expectations in a way that made him want to collapse – in relief. He forced himself to look up, shakily, to see Jade standing there. She held a stack of papers, smiling in a way that seemed meant to cheer him up – and in another place, probably would have. As it was, he was too busy steadying his turbulent thoughts to reply.

Jade, his mind repeated, as if to solidify it. He'd almost forgotten, with...everything. A word whispered through his mind, an explanation for what seemed unlikely otherwise. *Insane.* Time didn't move normally for insane people. Or they didn't move normally inside it.

Somehow she had his hand, and gently helped him up, his body acting on instinct even as it took him a moment to gain his footing. The house tilted under his feet, a wave of dizziness crashing over him as spots dotted his vision. He could still smell blood, though he was mostly certain it wasn't on him.

More aware of his fragile state than he seemed to be, Jade steadied him. Everything was amplified now, nearly drowning out her voice until he really could imagine he was back in that place, like nothing had changed. Screaming; running about the house with reckless abandon. A doorknob turning. Silence falling heavier than a stone choking the air from a condemned man's neck.

He was aware of every step they took toward the door, of the way they pounded in his ears, in tune with his heartbeat, like a mourner's drum. It followed them all the way to the door, his heart slamming harder in his chest as Jade opened it, half of him expecting to have to face the man that stood just beyond it.

Instead, Jade closed the door behind them, and his breathing grew easier. His hands instinctively rubbed along his arms, as if warding off a chill. Even the sunlight didn't seem real until he felt it on his skin, and heard the click of the door behind him.

He nearly sagged in relief, rubbing his arm and blinking at the sunny ground as if it would dispel the shadows he still felt, right behind him.

"Let's sit over there."

Right, Kaiden thought, a semblance of awareness returning as Jade nodded to a copse of trees, just beyond the property. He was vaguely aware of answering her as she led him over and sat down, but he couldn't hear his reply, his mind drowning again in snippets of memory. A burst of laughter, as bright and warming as the sun. Flame red hair, pulled into braids. Little feet pounding through the grass, playing on a phantom swing, hanging from a sturdy branch. A name in the midst of it, though he couldn't remember what it was.

If he was going to remember all of this, he might as well get something *good* out of it, too.

Kinny was the one who appeared brightest in his mind. Her small, laughing face as she played with the flowers; in the creek; by the house. She always seemed peaceful, when she was on her own.

A word whispered through his mind, the beginning of it barely heard. *Butterfly.*

It took him a moment to realize Jade had spoken, and another more to focus on the papers she was holding out to him.

"Here, Butterfly."

Shaking off further memories, Kaiden sank into the grass across from Jade. He fought off another shudder as he reached for it, his fingers curled too tightly as he read the name at the top.

"Kendel,"

The name flashed through his mind like fire, jerking free more memories that he didn't want to see. This was a correspondence, and

40

one he'd rather not read. But it might give him a clue to his siblings' whereabouts.

"Don't crumple it before reading it."

Part of him wanted to do just that, despite the information. But a different part made him whisper "*I won't,*" and keep reading.

"*Kendel,*
I trust you are doing better than the last time we met."

Without continuing on, he knew exactly who the letter was from, and it made what little food he'd forced down sour in his gut. He needed this information. He also didn't want it.

Damien. Kendel. Kaiden.

His own name almost made him flinch as he read on, the unerringly pleasant tone disguising something far worse beneath it. There was a mention of his mother – a casual inquiry about her health – and talk of business that masqueraded as beneficial, all exchanged in that horrid cordiality that neither of them meant. Pleasantries to distract from the darker side of what every word meant, the mention of seemingly casual affairs. He couldn't even take Damien's subtle warning to his father as any form of satisfaction, knowing from his swiftly-repairing memory just what had become of that.

After a point, even in his mind, he couldn't bring himself to read the rest of it as if it were actually being said aloud, or dare imagine what the exchange would have been like. His traitorous memories filled in the details anyway, making his fingers dig into the parchment as he read through the 'discussion' between his father and Damien, words twisting inside him like they had come alive from the page just to cut him open. The pleasant tone laced through the entirety of the script barely hid the sting of his father's words, even though he skimmed more than fully read those, and hoped there was nothing useful in them. Kendel Dyran had never been very good at 'pleasant'.

"Anything useful?"

He was about to say no; he didn't think he could stomach anymore. It was a painful reminder of things he couldn't change. The words twisted through him enough as is, threatening to take him back to darker memories. Damien, as he already knew, was responsible for a large part of what had happened to him.

But he was only *half* of the story.

Kaiden found his name again, on the page, and was unable to tear his eyes away even as his mind urged him to just move on. The comments he read made his stomach writhe, his mind piecing things together at dizzying, terrifying speeds. Things Jade had said, and he had seen. Her careful comments, and the looks on her face when things had happened to him. A grumpiness that, as she had said, was the result of something much deeper.

It was all there, right in view, if he wanted to reach for it. Enough of the pieces dangled in place to make even the ones that hadn't quite lined up make sense. The things he knew weren't right, and the things that already were.

His past self, he knew, wouldn't want to remember any of this. His present one didn't seem to have a choice.

Determined to keep this costly knowledge from being in vain, he read a step further, skimming until his eyes caught on a number. He let his shaky hands drift to his lap, the words murmuring from his lips.

"An address."

His mind was already turning, thinking on the implications. It was an invitation from Damien – to a temporary meeting place, possibly. But the way he talked about it suggested otherwise.

Jade nodded. "Maybe try there, then?"

She made everything sound so simple. He would have smiled if he had the strength. "Good idea."

Jade gave him a moment to sit in silence, and he didn't know if he was grateful for that or not. His gaze drifted past the trees, to the meadow near the house, dotted with tiny yellow flowers. An ache moved up his throat and settled there, hot tears pricking his eyes as he watched the tall grass bend in the breeze. There was something missing from the whole picture, but he couldn't tell what.

"What are you thinking?"

A sudden desire tugged at him, even as he shook his head in response. It was a terrible idea, and most likely another costly one. And yet the ache in his lungs said otherwise, pulling him back toward the house. He wanted to remember. If he had to know all of this, he wanted to know what else he was missing. It couldn't possibly be any worse, after all. Right?

"I can't help you if you don't tell me."

Shifting, he drew his knees up to his chest, hugging them. His face rested half-hidden behind his arms, the barest of murmurs slipping out that even he couldn't hear.

But her hand, when it settled on his arm, pulled it all free from him. He shut his eyes to stem the crushing tears, forcing out the words so she could hear them. "I miss her."

She breathed out quietly, even as he squeezed his eyes tighter shut. He knew what was missing from the picture, now. And it made the ache increase tenfold.

"I know, Butterfly."

He swallowed slowly to clear his throat. "I wish...I could remember..."

His hushed admittance brought more memories flooding to the surface, as much as he wanted to keep them hidden. His sister. *Kinny.* She should have been here. She shouldn't be gone.

"You will, in time. Some things just take a while."

He nodded for her sake, choking down a broken laugh. It didn't feel that way. It felt like those parts, the ones he might actually want to know, would be lost forever.

Maybe that was because *she* was. Even if he could remember her, she was still *gone*. He would never see her again.

And that, of course, was also his fault.

"How can I help?"

That insane idea took advantage of his hesitancy, gripping him tighter until it squeezed the words from him. "I want to go back in." The words sounded desperate, flooding out as he gripped his own arms. But what more could it hurt, at this point? "I want to remember *something.*"

The last word just solidified the ache. He needed to know more of this, even if it hurt. He needed to remember *her*, and not just in fleeting flashes that never stayed. Not just in nightmares, in brief, terror-flooded memories.

Jade nodded, quietly. "I'll go with you, if that's what you want. Do you want to find her room?"

He nodded, even as it made the pit of pain tighten in his chest. There had to be better memories there. "I don't remember where it is."

"I can help you. I remember the layout of the house, so I know where it is."

Something like relief and a thing far worse than it twisted inside his chest, twining together. "I keep forgetting."

Jade's quiet chuckle calmed his nerves. "That's alright. I'll remember for both of us."

Slowly, he stood to his feet. Walking into the house for a second time, his fingers shaking on the doorknob, was somehow far worse and much better. The echoes seeped through the door even before they entered, whispering in his ear and refusing to be silent as Jade led him upstairs.

At least now, though, he could try to fight it.

The steps creaked. Even his careful steps couldn't stop it – or maybe he wasn't focused enough for it. His hand gripped Jade's and the railing as they ascended, his breath coming quiet in his ears.

43

At the top, she pushed the door on the right open for him, squeezing his hand lightly as she did. His breath caught in his throat as he entered, the memories thick in the air and growing thicker as he brushed his hand along a few of his sister's dust-covered things. The shelf full of 'collectibles' she'd so treasured, rocks and twigs and bits of metal scattered in rows. The closet she hid her surprises for others and little gifts in the back of. The small, too-empty bed, untidily made and left alone for too long of a time. He barely made it over before he sank down on the edge of it, dropping his head in his hands.

She was...gone.

Jade's hand settled on his shoulder. It made the tremors running through them seem even more prominent, his hands damp with the silent tears that fell. He rubbed them to stop it, drawing in a breath as Jade squeezed his shoulder.

A moment later, he stared distantly at the wall, hands folded in front of his lips. His eyes still felt heavy with unshed tears.

"Remember something?"

He almost smiled, but it hurt too much. "Kind of." His gaze moved back to the shelf, and he stood again, reaching over to finger one of the items. A reddish pebble, uneven in shape but smooth to the touch. He rolled it in his palm, squeezing it like it would somehow give up its secrets to him. "Maybe...it will just take time."

Jade tucked her hands into her jacket pockets, replying with a half-smile – just as a different thought took hold of him. On instinct, he palmed the stone and walked out of the room, his eyes searching the hall before he came across a smaller room and pushed his way inside. It should have screamed with memories, but he brushed them away, refusing to linger on how familiar the scuffs on the floor looked and how this bed still had the same blanket used when the occupant was small. Instead, his feet moved to crouch by a small space in the corner and search around the makeshift alcove there, until his fingers brushed over familiar wooden ridges.

A hushed laugh escaped as he withdrew and turned over the set of musical pipes, his fingers settling over at it with a familiarity that burned inside. "It's smaller than I remember."

Jade chuckled. "You were smaller then."

"I know." His thumb rubbed over every mark and scratch in the wood, something like a sigh escaping his lips. "She wanted me to make it."

Jade grinned, and a flicker of relief passed through him that he was remembering it right. Tucking the pipes into his jacket, he turned to the door. "We should go."

44

Even as he said it, his gaze flicked around the room, taking in everything he hadn't wanted to before. All the memories locked inside it, hidden in the thin shavings on the floor and a couple of reddish marks that had never quite cleaned out. He wanted to move, frozen until he forced himself to pull away, Jade following him out.

The memories seemed determined to dog him, though, spilling out through the hallway with sounds that made his ears ring. His hand pressed against the wall on instinct, a noise trying to leave his throat as he wrapped an arm around his stomach.

"You okay, Butterfly?"

Dizziness swept through him. His palm pressed harder against the wood as he paused, voices filtering louder through his head and seeming to make the memories come alive. "Should be."

"'Should be' and 'are' aren't the same things."

He let out a quiet chuckle, even as it made his side burn. "I know."

Jade steadied him, watching him like he might fall over. "Do you need to sit down?"

He hid a wince as best as he could, though a cry still wanted to escape his throat as he sank down against the wall. "Probably." His voice held a strain that didn't seem natural. Locking his jaw to hold back a groan, he shut his eyes. "Probably...would fall otherwise."

"Well, don't do that. You're a butterfly, not a rock."

Even his chuckle sounded labored, a phantom pain running through him and trying to tug another cry from his throat. "I don't know...what's wrong."

"Maybe accessing the memory was too much."

Memory. This didn't *feel* like a memory. It felt real, and exhausting. He was tired of holding back a reaction, but it seemed pointless when there was nothing wrong. As if it wasn't him in this moment crying out, but a different version of him, in another time. "I...guess so."

He didn't realize how tense he was until Jade squeezed his shoulder. "Just try to relax."

He wanted to laugh, but that would have been too painful. His hand settled over his heart as he focused on taking breaths that wouldn't stir imaginary aches in him.

"Just try to breathe slowly. Focus on something else."

He blinked at the wall, seeing spots as he nodded and tried to follow her directions. "Like what?"

"Well, you could think about how fantastic your imaginary-not-imaginary friend is."

She was teasing, but he couldn't help the smile that slid across his face as he closed his eyes, words flowing out in a matching tone. "That shouldn't be hard. I think about that a lot, Beautiful."

He didn't know where the last word came from. But it made her stick out her tongue at him, which in turn made him want to laugh.

"And here I was hoping you wouldn't remember that nickname."

A grin spread across his face, answers slipping out easier than they ever did. "Of course. How could I forget it?" He peeked open an eye at her. "Or at least for long."

Ironic words, given his situation. But it was as if someone else was talking at the moment, anyway, and he was trapped in the past, focusing on just breathing and doing his best not to pass out. Jade scrunched up her face.

"Can't you pick a new one? Something less...pretty?"

His slow shrug seemed evidence to his irregular state, even as he casually replied. "I don't have the brainpower to do that right now."

"Well, later then. I still stick to the fact that it's totally too nice for me." She wrinkled her nose. "I mean, look at this hair!" She gathered a fistful to wave at him.

He let out a sigh that didn't seem entirely false, like both versions of him used it for different purposes. "My memory isn't so great lately, Beautiful. I doubt I'll remember that." He eyed her hair with a solemn nod. "I see what you mean. Your hair is better than beautiful. But it was the best word I could come up with to describe it."

She gave him a look, whacking his arm lightly. "That's not what I meant, and you know it."

Faking a wince, he rubbed his arm. "Ouch. Whack the injured guy, huh?"

Injured...? Even his mind seemed to question it, confusion swirling in his mind as he glanced down at himself. He was perfectly fine. Except he wasn't.

"Just another reason it's unfitting. Beautiful people don't whack their injured best friends!"

He shook his head at her, chuckling. "Well, as I've said before, you'll *always* be beautiful to me."

A heavy sigh. "And I keep saying I'm not. Just something we'll have to agree to disagree on."

"I know." Another soft laugh bubbled in his throat as he slipped his hand into the inside of his jacket, drawing out a pen and paper. He wanted to write this down before it all slipped away.

46

Because it was, he realized. With every moment the invisible pains subsided, the memories grew weaker. Quieter. He wanted to write down what he'd felt, capture it in the simplest of terms for later.

Happy.

The word put an ache in his chest, his hand stilling so it didn't waver across the page. Jade shifted beside him, and he leaned his head against her on instinct, a heaviness stealing back through him.

"What is it, Butterfly?"

Though he wanted to smile, he couldn't muster it. The world returned to steady, weighted on his shoulders, but firm. "Just... everything fading again."

Jade's smile was gentle. "This just proves you can remember. And if you can, you will in time. Maybe just need a bit of help doing so."

A smile broke through, but only for a moment, fading back into something even harder to hold as he shook his head. "Not like that."

"Not like what?"

He shut his eyes, moving his arm to his side. *On my own.*

And he'd known that wouldn't work, right? But he wanted to try anyway. In a way, he *had* done it, but at a price. The thread had come dangerously close to breaking, even if it was now mended again.

"Like that. Obviously it didn't work."

Even his words sounded empty.

"You just need a different strategy, then."

He wanted to laugh, but the sound was far too quiet. "Guess so."

Silence stood between them for a moment. "Good enough to try the stairs again?"

He glanced down at himself. "Only one way to find out."

Jade grinned. "Can lean on me. I'm sturdy."

He didn't need help. Or he shouldn't have. His attempt at a grin came out all wrong as he pushed himself to his feet.

The world tilted funny again. Jade stood up as well, offering her arm. He braced one hand against the wall, one on her. His legs felt wobbly, unsteady.

"Ready?"

No. But he nodded, ignoring the creak in his ears as they moved toward the stairs. It took all of his concentration not to grip her arm too tightly, the whole house seeming to whisper to him again as they went, on top of feeling like he should be bleeding from somewhere. Jade led him down and out of the house, over to the trees again, where he sank to a sitting position and closed his eyes.

<><><>

47

He awoke with a start, sweat coating his tingling skin. For the next hour he slipped in and out of sleep, his body fighting to stay awake though he kept drifting off.

"Let me help you."

The voice that should have been a savior felt more like a threat. And he couldn't fight it well, in this state. He had drained his own energy attempting to hold onto memories, and it wasn't returning. His mind was caught in a dizzying whirl, past and present melding in a loop that muddied his vision, a thousand moments playing out in the span of just one.

He didn't know how long it lasted. All he knew, as memories flew through his head, was what the voice had been trying to tell him all along.

You can't win. Can't win. Can't. Win.

It echoed like the hollow ache inside of him. The memories were too strong. He was too weak. He couldn't hold them, even if he wanted to.

And even if he found his siblings, he wouldn't remember them. Even Kinny he just barely remembered, now, and it had cost him. It made the ache grow and shift into something sharper, deeper. It stole the breath from his lungs and pricked his eyes until they stung. Jade squeezed his hand, yet he had hardly the strength to return the gesture.

Instead, he shoved himself to his feet. He couldn't stay around here much longer. It made memories cling like cobwebs to his mind, barely seen but felt all the same. He knew the address in the letter. It wasn't far.

The busy street he finally stepped back onto drowned out his thoughts. People brushed by him, and he gave a wordless smile to a passing vendor, his mind unfocused on what they said.

Footsteps tore through the air, followed by angry shouts. Some of the passerby turned to watch as a little girl burst into view, dark hair flying around her face as her arms pumped by her side. She ducked and wove under people, navigating the crowd like an obstacle course.

"Stop, thief!"

Behind the girl, several big, angry men followed, one clutching what looked like a very wicked knife. Several townspeople shrank back, but none interfered.

"Daddy!"

The little girl's shout recaptured his attention, just as she barreled into his legs. Two small arms wrapped around him, twisting her around until she was positioned behind him. Kaiden was caught between the urge to look around for who the girl was referring to, and the knife-wielding man that was now moving toward *him*.

The girl heaved in several quick breaths, burying her face against his leg. "I've been looking all over for you!" Fear laced her voice as she tossed a glance over at the men, tugging urgently on his pant leg. "C'mon, we need to go!"

Shock sped through him like an icy blast at what her words meant, followed by a slower wave of understanding. The man with the knife shoved his way through the crowd, hurling names that made Kaiden want to cover the girl's ears. With a wince, she buried her face against him, tightening her grip with a whisper. "Please, Daddy."

The pleading in her voice struck him, even if the last word threw him off again. All he could think of was his siblings, and that man with a knife, and it didn't matter what he had planned to do, or why she was saying it. Instinct kicked in, hard and fierce.

"Thieving little-" The man was almost to them now, something gleaming in his eyes as he continued to hurl a stream of dirty words at both of them. Not only that, but the telltale redness to his eyes and the veins bulging in his face told Kaiden there would be no talking his way out of this.

Surprise flashed briefly across the girl's face when he lifted her off the ground. She ducked her head against his shoulder, peeking one eye back at the men. But Kaiden was already turning, scanning the square for the best exit as he cupped one hand on the girl's head and ran.

III

Joss

Jocelyn Rees had been called a thief and a liar before, but never at the same time. People were either concerned with what she took or what she gave, never both.

She rather liked the sound of it, though. A lying thief. A thieving liar. They sounded more affectionate than boring old 'thief'. Like her father calling her 'you little rascal' long ago.

The man who had been chasing her was far from affectionate, however. He had a knife and towered nearly twice as tall as her, his heavy steps pounding in opposition to hers like the harmony to her heart's melody.

Thud, thud thud. Thud, thud thud.

Except now, maybe she had a chance. Whether it was luck or fate that the fire-haired stranger had fallen for her act, the tight way he held her told him everything she needed to know about him. He'd done this before. Maybe he had a child of his own, and that's what had prompted such a protective response.

But that couldn't be, she realized as she glanced up at him through thick lashes. Despite the stubble on his chin and the creases by his shadowed blue eyes, he wasn't old enough to have a child her age. She'd assumed at first that he was around Jesen's age, but with every glance she stole up at him, she knew this wasn't the case. His hair was a flame-red mess, sticking up slightly in the front, and despite the deep, troubled lines to his face, he couldn't be more than a few years over twenty.

For a brief moment, he glanced down at her, as if to check on her. Joss ducked her eyes, the picture of youth and innocence as she pressed her cheek against his shoulder. The rhythm of his steps was surprisingly smooth, a crease forming in his brow as he tossed a glance behind him. She could see the questions written on his face, but he didn't ask them yet. He kept his breathing even, slipping through alleyways and dodging down streets you wouldn't know about unless you grew up in the town. Joss was surprised. She had taken him for some confused, distressed visitor, but maybe this would work to her advantage. She just hadn't expected a Calestan to help her.

Self-conscious, Joss shut her eyes and pretended it was because she was scared, her heart pounding a quick rhythm that opposed his. Maybe he hadn't seen her eyes. She'd been quick and kept them hidden; it was habit by this point. The moment anyone caught sight of the shifting color – 'unholy', 'cursed', her mind echoed every time – they turned her away. It was why she stayed on the run, stealing bits of kindness where she could and coin purses when she couldn't. And yet somewhere in the back of her mind, there was always a voice wondering if someday, someone wouldn't mind. If maybe, when they saw what she was, they wouldn't turn her away.

The gem of her latest catch, pressed against her side in her dress pocket and safely hidden where its dazzling surface wouldn't give her away, said otherwise. She hadn't planned to take that, too, but she had been desperate, and it had kept calling to her, whispering to *get out while you can,* until she finally gave in. And ran.

Hanging on that distracting thought, Joss wondered what she might find in this stranger's pockets, if she could reach them. He eyed everything like it was confusing and unfamiliar, yet navigated the streets with an ease even greater than her own. She made a mental note of the path they had taken, planning to study it later when she got a chance.

If she got a chance.

As the sounds of footsteps behind them died away, leaving only the slowly increasing rhythm of the stranger's heart beating and his feet against the ground – too soft a sound for the boots he wore – she should have felt relieved. Instead, she was even more on edge, waiting for the moment when he would discover her secret.

Checking behind them one last time, the stranger turned a corner and slowed, a quiet breath out the only sign of his exertion. Joss saw the crease creep back into his brow, stronger, as he shifted her against him and strolled down the street. No one bothered with these alleyways in the daytime. Ducking under an awning of what used to be a shop, he situated them out of view of the streets and sat down, shifting her to face him.

Jumping down from his lap, Joss did her best not to catch his eyes. Her hands sought to make sure the necklace was still in her pocket, while her mind worked out what to do. Those men were still looking for her, and this stranger seemed to know his way around. But if he found out who she was – *what* she was, he'd stop helping her.

Mind made up, Joss spun toward him, a bright grin on her face as she met his gaze, abandoning her frightened act like an unwanted coat. "Wow, you really know your way around here, huh?" Before he could so much as open his mouth, she did a quick glance around, letting out a whistle and nodding. "This might do for now. Those men will still be after us for a while, but at least we can rest."

Her heart pounded as she looked back to take in the man's reaction, smiling easily. He *could* just turn her in and not deal with the trouble of all this. Maybe that's what he'd intended from the beginning. Why else would he 'help' her?

Searching his eyes, though, Joss had the odd thought yet again that he must be from somewhere else, by the way he looked at her, brow furrowed only in what seemed like concentration. She waited for the realization, for the look of disgust or disdain that would soon change the lines of his face.

Instead, he just looked confused, like he'd gotten lost somewhere and nothing looked familiar, but should have.

"Uh...hello?" She waved a hand in front of his face, ignoring the way her heart still fluttered furiously against her chest. "Fire Man?"

Awareness snapped through his eyes, and she nearly cringed, more words running off her tongue in a nervous, pressing tone. "Look, I'm sorry I fooled you." *Not really.* "But they're going to be after you now, too." She wrinkled her brow, thoughts clicking in her mind that he should have already *known* that, yet he helped her anyway. "Why'd you help me, anyway?"

His brow was still creased, like she was a puzzle he couldn't figure out. Like he couldn't comprehend her words, or wasn't hearing them. "Why'd you call me your dad?"

Because you seemed gullible and lost. "You...kinda look like him."

He gave his head a quick shake, like he was clearing it, and glanced around. "Where are your parents?"

"I have none." Something fought to crawl into her tone, and she shoved it down. "Not anymore."

Why was she telling him this, anyway? Why was she telling him *any* of this?

"You know what I am, right?" It wasn't fake emotion choking her throat now, trying to cling to her words. "You're...you're from here?"

His brow furrowed more, his eyes glancing her over slowly. "Yeah?"

Something inside her wanted to laugh, and shatter at the same time. She shouldn't have asked more than one question. "And you don't...care?"

He looked even more confused. She wanted to curl into the shadow of it and become invisible, a blind spot she could hide in so he'd never notice.

"About what you are?"

She tamed the tremble from the edge of her voice, giving a swift nod.

At this rate, he was going to have permanent lines in his brow. "Why would that matter?"

He said it as if asking why it mattered that cats had claws, like she was a kitten instead of a mountain lion. She couldn't speak for a moment, blinking at him and waiting for things to change. Waiting for him to say it was a joke. *Waiting.*

Instead, he got to his feet, brushing dust off the front of his pants, and offered her a smile. "I should get you home."

"I don't have a home." It came out swiftly, her tongue numbed enough by the rest of the conversation that the words spilled out without protest.

He seemed to consider that for a moment, then nodded. "Okay. Well, you can stick with me until you find one."

"You don't have a home either?"

Though he let out a chuckle, his head dropped slightly, something flicking through his gaze as he shook his head. "No. Not really."

"So you're looking for one, too?"

He shrugged a shoulder, a faint smile on his face. "Sort of."

Joss never felt uncomfortable stealing kindness from people. It was a tool, a lever she moved by playing a game and fooling everyone. It was what she should have done with him, too. But even though she had told him the truth, he was still here. It was something she couldn't wrap her mind around.

"Well, I could always use a bodyguard," she admitted, nearly returning the smile. But she couldn't bring herself to accept his offer, even when he bent to pick her up again. The touch was still too gentle; she squirmed until he set her back down, taking several steps away and avoiding the look of concern in his eyes.

"I think you're confused," she said, a high note of fear rising too close to her tone, in the back of her throat. "You don't want to be around me. Even if you have to be, or should be. You shouldn't *want* to." Another step away. The tattered fabric of her dress brushed against a fallen support beam, the bump of wood against her legs enough to still her. "You know what I am. Stop acting like you don't."

He was still looking at her too kindly, a look that could melt even the hardest steel if she wasn't careful. It was all just an act. It *had* to be an act.

"I'm not going to hurt you."

Though she screwed her eyes shut, words still burst from her lips. "Just turn me in already. Tell them what I am. You're a good enough pretender, you can probably convince them I just...duped you." The word slid thick off her throat, a hot sting lingering near her eyes. "That I just...used my...my..."

Her voice wavered too much to say more. She'd walked right into a trap and was now caught, unable to move. She felt him step toward her, bend down until he was at her level. He was studying her, probably with a glint in his eyes now that she couldn't see, planning whatever he intended to do with her.

"I'm not going to hurt you," he repeated instead, softer than a murmur. Quiet, not only in volume, but tone, as if she might break if he wasn't careful enough. "Promise."

She shouldn't have believed him. But when she felt his hand on her arm, her eyes opened on their own, her body tensed to move. A tingle spread through her small frame, almost enough to make her gasp. Warmth flooded her arm, stirring the power in her own blood.

"You're Gifted," she murmured, looking up into his eyes as if she might find her answers there. Things were starting to make sense, in some ways. Why he didn't leave, if he knew what she was.

But then she drew away, brushing aside the disappointment as the warmth faded. "You still shouldn't be around me."

Even the few of his kind she'd encountered wanted nothing to do with her. They claimed her power was a shadow, a curse, that she must have done something wrong or altered it – *twisted* it. As if she had the ability to misshape what Fate had given her. She heard stories about her people, cautionary tales about the Isles and the strange beings that lurked there. They claimed their power was unholy, a kind that made the regular Gifted look tame. Like her people were monsters with claws they had formed themselves from their powers.

And yet this strange flame-haired man did not seem to make that connection. Maybe he was still confused, though he didn't move away. Joss wet her lips when he didn't respond, forcing the words out. "My power isn't like yours."

He lifted a shoulder, a shrug that seemed to pull a bit of weariness from his eyes. "I don't mind."

When she found the strength to answer, it was little more than a whisper. A warning. "I'm...trouble."

"Well then, Trouble." As he stood, his lips tipped up in a small smile. "I'm Kaiden."

SARI

Sari did not get nervous. When one was bonded to an all-powerful being like Ru'ach, one tended to see the bigger picture better than most.

But now, with Ru'ach so close and so far away from her, it was easier for that feeling to creep in. It had been bothering her since Ru'ach had first made her decision, worming its way under her skin and refusing to leave her alone.

It was a good thing she wasn't around the others. They only saw her as calm and collected; they didn't need to know the truth. How, deep down, she was more terrified than all of them.

Usually, Ru'ach's unshakeable calm was what gave her peace, and confidence. But their bond was stretched thin with Ru'ach in disguise, and it reminded Sari too strongly of things she'd rather forget. She *liked* being calm, and in control. She liked forgetting who she'd been, and how she'd gotten here. How little she was without Ru'ach, and how helpless she'd be again if she left.

That scared part of her liked to bring up how real that might become, if this didn't go well. Ru'ach cared dearly for her brother; Sari knew this better than she knew her own name. She would do whatever it took to attempt to convince him, as futile as they both knew it would be. Love was blind, or maybe, it just saw second chances even where no one else would.

Parts of Ru'ach's past still confused her, though she never dared ask about them. As wholly as Ru'ach knew Sari's mind, Sari knew she would never understand to the same extent. Ru'ach had lived too long, and seen too many things, that Sari's mind wouldn't be able to handle it all.

It was why this arrangement worked between them, where it never worked with the Bane. One took everything to use as it pleased; the other offered a partnership. Ru'ach had never forced her will on Sari, and she never would.

And that's why it was important that this all went well. The dragons had to choose to listen to her, rather than Shedim. From what Ru'ach said, that would be more complicated than it seemed.

There were many things in her life that Sari knew, for a fact, were not myths. The Bane. Ru'ach. The ability to bond more deeply with a dragon than most knew.

And this. An entire kingdom of dragons, living just beneath the Empress' nose. Far enough from her Cities for her not to care, but watching, and waiting. Galdanians knew to venture there was foolishness – to them, the dragons in the wild lands were as entirely feral to cruelly clever as the ones that fought in the arenas. Since Shedim's banishment, they had managed to live in peace.

It was only a matter of time, then, before Shedim returned to stir up trouble.

Ru'ach had told her, upon their reunion, just what Shedim was likely to do. It was partly why Sari went to find her first, before going after the Bane. Now that Shedim knew where his sister was, he would do anything he could to defeat her. Since humans were too fragile to manipulate, most of the time, he'd sought out the dragons, instead. Though most Galdanians knew the stories, how the dragons had retreated when the Empress came to power, few likely remembered just how close by they still were.

But Shedim knew, and his influence over them could be very dangerous. It was Shedim's presence in Calest that slowly corrupted the dragons there, and given the chance, he would do the same here, to turn them against Ru'ach. The number of dragons living just outside of the Empress' territory made that a terrifying prospect.

It was also part of why the dragons had left in the first place, to escape possible corruption. But by closing off their minds to the Bane, they also made it far harder for Ru'ach to convince them to fight against the Empress, too. Her word over her brother's, in a way. They couldn't be as easily corrupted, but they wouldn't remember Ru'ach, either, or why they should listen to her.

Not only did Ru'ach have to stop her brother from converting all of them, but she had to get them to open back up again, to care enough to fight. They didn't stand a chance otherwise.

She could see it, as clearly as if it was her own fears. The dragons, turning against Ru'ach. Ruining her...

Sari shook off the memories with a shudder. Ru'ach lay sleeping beside her, purple-scaled eyes closed, and Sari savored the warmth while she was able to. Soon, Ru'ach would be gone, and she would have to fight through the day on her own.

Another involuntary shudder passed through her at the thought. Was she so weak that she couldn't face her demons on her own? The others she'd lived with did it, effortlessly.

And they thought *her* the strong one. They couldn't have been further from the truth.

Without Ru'ach's constant presence in her mind – her energy directed elsewhere, and with good reason – Sari felt the weight of her life upon her shoulders. She wondered, as she often did, how things might have gone if she had just...left. If she hadn't accepted Ru'ach's help. Hadn't have offered her life in exchange.

She would have been downright miserable. Trapped on a slaver's boat far from the continent, tossed overboard, living as a pirate...

No. Sari shook her head, momentarily amused by the image. She could not imagine herself as a pirate. Though she was born in the Isles, she was no more fit for that than a fish. She never would have survived in that life.

She understood, too, why the dragons had retreated. Despite Ru'ach's explanation that the dragons had closed themselves off, and that it wasn't a good thing, Sari couldn't help but long for the simplicity of it all. Forgetting all of their problems.

Ru'ach had warned her against this. It wasn't good for her to be so exposed to these dragons. Their ideals, however good the intentions, could infect her if she wasn't careful.

Dragons were more sensitive to the push and pull of spiritual energies. Shedim couldn't touch human minds without wrecking and eventually killing them, but dragons were far stronger, if not insusceptible. They wouldn't die from it, but they *could* decide to go rampant and destroy what they found. It was possible that they would lay destruction to the rebels and accomplish the Empress' work without even intending to. Or, perhaps, the Bane had a more sinister plan.

Either way, the end goal would surely be to take down Ru'ach, however he thought to accomplish that. Regaining his old form, or finding a dragon willing to give him control. He was patient and would bide his time.

It wasn't surprising that Shedim left the Gifted that lived amidst the dragons alone. Despite their own closed-off nature, the dragons protected those humans with their lives, and murdering them would have tipped the dragons off to Shedim's true nature.

Those humans, the lucky few, were the only ones who had managed to live with the dragons, so far. Children who had gone missing, refugees considered desperate enough to choose possible suicide over living, by handing themselves over to the dragons. To most Galdanians, dragons were little more than feral beasts, unless tamed and collared. They were too ignorant to see the truth, even if they wished to. If the dragons were not treated as overgrown, scaled cats, to be fed and accessorized and paraded around like a symbol, then they were seen as bloodthirsty and thoughtless, other than their instinct to kill. It was this that prompted the creation of the arenas, and the sport which funded the underground of Galdania's society.

Most of those dragons had grown up in captivity, or forced into it, and didn't know to shield themselves from the Bane. A stubborn few knew, and fought anyway. Though Sari had hardly interacted with the dragon herself, Zarafel had once known her friend quite well, and was one of the few who chose to remember, and fight it.

Even he had been forced to give up something, though. The dragons' strong connection to Ru'ach had allowed them to manifest and enhance gifts in many forms, like the ability to breathe fire that so many dragons were proud of. But that connection was too easily tampered with, by someone as strong as Shedim, and only the truly foolish dared to leave it open. These often became tools of the Empress, wielded by the secret force of Gifted she kept in her employ. Sari wondered how that had panned out for her, now that her credibility was shaken. Some, she knew, would continue to follow her anyway. Others they may be able to draw to a different side, with their faith in her weakened.

As Ru'ach stretched, smiling at Sari as much as a dragon could, Sari fought the impulsive spike of her heartbeat.

It was *time*.

KAIDEN

As the little girl – Joss, she said her name was – bounced alongside him, holding his hand and chatting as if she truly did know him from any other person, Kaiden's mind wandered far away.

A tug on his arm drew him back to reality. The little girl was looking at him with a frown, her eyes a deep purple in the dim light, like a cat's eye. He had the oddest suspicion that he should have known the significance of that, but it wouldn't come to mind.

What did it matter, anyway? She was a child, and obviously a scared one, despite how brightly she kept up her act. He knew firsthand how hard it was to survive in Calest.

"I said, we gotta get outta sight. We can sleep under the stars for tonight."

He felt in a middle of a dream, letting the little girl pull him along, out of the city. Apparently it wouldn't be safe to sleep there, now that he was harboring a little criminal.

What had she done, anyway?

When they woke the next morning – not that he "slept" much – Kaiden packed up camp while Joss hummed to herself, something bright in her hands that wasn't there before. He stared at it, eyes wide.

"Where did you get that?"

A mischievous grin sparkled on Joss' face. "I stole it."

She said it as nonchalantly as if she'd just taken a walk, rolling the apple along the back of her shoulders and catching it before it hit the ground. Before he could stop her, or insist she give it back, she crunched her teeth into it, eyeing him the whole time as if she knew what his plan was.

"You can't..." He ran a hand through his hair. "You... you need to..."

"Give it back?" Her grin widened as she extended it to him, the white inner flesh bright with juice. "I don't think they're going to like that very much."

"But that's... wrong." The last word fell as lamely off his tongue as he knew it sounded.

The little girl's eyes went hard, then, something angry flashing behind them. "Oh please, don't tell me *you've* never stolen from anyone before. You'd rather starve than eat?"

Before he could answer, she shoved another apple at him from the depths of her pocket, her eyes carrying an angry spark to them. He looked at the fruit in his hand, words dying on his tongue the moment he opened his mouth.

"If you don't eat it, I'm going to make a fuss," she grumbled, her eyes too narrowed and hard for such a small girl as she sat in the grass just past the boundary of the town, glaring at a nearby rock. "And I don't think you want that."

It sounded like a childish taunt, but she knew as well as he did that unwanted attention could be very dangerous, especially in this town. He sat down on the ground next to her, curling his fingers around the fruit to hide the light tremble in them. "I'm not hungry."

She turned an annoyed look his way. "Yeah, and I'm a flying dragon." She hunched her knees up to her chest, wrapping her arms around them with a huff and planting her chin on them. After a long moment of glaring at the ground, she muttered, "I need my bodyguard healthy, you know. Otherwise what use will you be to me?"

He couldn't help a smile at that, setting the fruit aside to wrap an arm around her. She smacked it away with a hard stare, her eyes still angry and far too cold for one so young. Her eyes penetrated his, staring into their depths as if searching for something. When she finally spoke, her words were hissed, as if he had somehow hurt her.

59

"Why don't you care about yourself? You have no money, so you must live on the streets. But you won't even get food for yourself." She poked him in the ribs, a slight, annoyed scowl on her face. "I'm just using you to get what I want. Yet you don't even care. I give you food and you don't even touch it. Do you know how hard I worked to get that?" Frowning, she dropped her head back onto her arms with a growl. "What's your deal, anyway? No one in their right mind would do any of that."

It was kind of fascinating, how this little girl had suddenly transformed from sweet and innocent to hard, weathered, like a stone left too long in a storm. She swung back and forth between her acts as if she couldn't decide which would hold his attention more, eyeing him like he might stab her in the back when no one was looking.

The girl scowled and buried her chin further in her arms, staring at the cobbled stone. "You'd better at least get some money soon or somethin', Bodyguard, so this will be at least partially worth my while."

As she spoke, she fished into his pocket – as she had at least twice already – a disappointed sigh escaping her lips as she caught his inquisitive gaze. "Just checking. Again," she added pointedly, as if it was his fault that his pocket was empty.

It amused him, how she seemed to think if she kept doing that, she'd find piles of treasure, like he was just hiding his obvious wealth from her, and she'd weasel it out of him eventually. The thought almost made him laugh, looking down at his ratty brown coat and the worn, dirty edges of his clothes. How could she think he had anything of value on him?

Ril chose this moment to squeak in Joss' direction, in what sounded like indignation. Her eyes widened as she looked at the bag. "What?"

Kaiden feigned ignorance, raising an eyebrow at her. "Still surprised at how little I have?"

Joss frowned, poking at his bag. Another squeak made her jump back. "Bodyguard."

He shrugged a shoulder, secretly enjoying her cautious surprise at his now wriggling bag – and Ril's mental protests to being prodded. "Yes?"

"Is your bag s'posed to move like that?" She squinted at it. "Like somethin's alive in there?"

He shrugged again, plucking a blade of grass to rub between his fingers. "Is that unusual?"

She narrowed her eyes, directing a poke into his side this time. "I'm not an idiot. I was just seein' if you knew." Eyeing the bag, she muttered to herself, in words too quiet for him to hear.

Then she turned her pointed frown at his untouched fruit. "I worked hard to steal that, so you'd better eat it."

The words sounded suspiciously like a threat. Blowing out a breath, he gave in and picked it back up. He almost didn't even taste it as he took a bite, though.

Ril poked her head out and squeaked loudly at Joss, which almost made her fall backward. It was as close to an insult as the dragon ever got. Kaiden had to hide his smile.

Frowning, Joss stood to her feet. "Never liked dragons anyway." She brushed grass off her dress, huffing at him. "So where're we goin'?"

Taking a moment longer to think, and get confirmation from Jade, Kaiden pulled himself to his feet. "Where do you want to go?"

She narrowed her eyes at him. "That's not what I asked."

"Hm." Slipping his hands in his pockets, Kaiden headed away from the town, glancing back just to make sure she followed. "You don't have anywhere you need to be? Any parents?"

Her gaze darkened, arms folded over her chest. "Nowhere but away from here." She kicked at a small rock before adding, in a mutter, "I told you I don't have any."

"You sure?" He glanced down at her, ignoring Ril's displeased rumblings at being ignored. "You didn't just run away?"

"*Yes.*" She snapped the word out harshly enough to make him pause. He still wasn't quite sure he believed her, though.

"I thought that was just part of the act."

Joss muttered to herself, hands shoved in her armpits as she stomped along behind him. "Yes. It was all just a big ploy to steal your food. Which you don't have. You caught me."

Without thinking, he reached over to ruffle her hair, catching only air and a nasty glare instead.

"Well, if you were wanting to leave anyway, I guess you can stick with me for now."

Joss clasped her hands and traipsed along beside him, peeking up at Ril any time the tiny dragon poked her head out. They seemed to be having a game, in which Ril couldn't decide whether or not she trusted this small child.

"S'pose it depends on where you're goin'."

Kaiden gestured to the field in front of them. "Keriax."

Joss drew up short. "Whoa. What business do you have there?"

"A personal kind."

Joss let out a laugh, though it sounded unsettled. "Touchy." She rubbed a hand into her unruly locks, then set out a bit of a grin. "Well, you're going to need help."

"I won't."

"You *will*," she sing-songed, walking on her tiptoes. "I happen to know that town better than the back of my hand, and you walk around everywhere like you don't know what the ground even is."

Kaiden frowned. "I don't need help."

"Surrrrre. You just want to help me. I see." She nodded her head in an exaggerated way, sarcasm coating her tongue. "Just decided to adopt an orphan out of the goodness of your heart, huh?"

When he didn't answer, she narrowed her eyes at the path ahead of him, her voice growing harsh. "No one is *kind* in this country. No one is going to help you, Bodyguard, so you better be glad my price isn't steep." She cast another look at Ril, which only seemed to make her grumpier. "I'm hungry."

"We just ate."

"No, *you* just ate. I snacked, and even if I *had* ate, I'm still hungry." She shifted her gaze over as if daring him to deny it.

With a sigh, Kaiden turned in the direction of the town, handing her a roll from his pack. Joss eyed it for a moment before greedily stuffing pieces of it into her mouth, barely chewing before she inhaled the rest. She eyed him again, at his look. "*What?*"

"Nothing." It unsettled him to see how starved the girl was, in a place that, though not prosperous, should not be *this* lacking in food. Dagged Uppers.

"You're a really weird bodyguard, you know that?" Eyes still flattened to slits, Joss stuffed her hands in her armpits, glaring at the road ahead. "Why'd you have to go and do somethin' like that, anyway?"

"Like what?"

"Bein' *decent*," she scowled, and he couldn't tell if it was a good thing or not. "No one's decent in Calest, or even just okay. There's the baker, and th' old lady who makes candles, but they'd still turn you out if you're too different." She narrowed her eyes at him again. "But *you* didn't."

"Did you *want* me to?"

Joss let out a most annoyed sigh, tucking her arms closer against her and rubbing them. "No."

Kaiden was confused, but he left it at that.

"What d'y 'spect to find in Keriax, anyway?"

My siblings. A clue. "A house."

62

She raised an eyebrow at him, more in disbelief than anything. A spark started in her eyes, shoulders less tense. A more interested tone filled her words. "A house, huh? Interesting." A grin spread across her lips, filled with scheming. "So you *are* a thief."

"No!" Kaiden exclaimed, maybe too loudly. Joss laughed, throwing her arms across her chest like she was twice her size and walking backward.

"Then what, Fire Man? You want to *live* there?"

Dagens, no, Kaiden thought. He'd had enough of Calest to last a lifetime. "I'm trying to find my siblings."

"And how are you doing that?"

Whether from loneliness or manipulation, he found the truth spilling out again, as easily as if she'd coaxed it from him. "I'm going to break into the house."

Joss laughed. It was a merry sound, from such a small girl. "*You?*"

One part of him wanted to be offended. He knew how to pick locks, at least. He didn't know *why*, but it'd gotten the job done before, so he hadn't questioned it. As if reading his mind, Joss cocked her eyebrows. "You know breaking in is about more than the lock, right? You have to be stealthy. You have to be...not you."

He could have sworn he saw her nose wrinkle as she glanced down at his shirt. "You know what I mean."

He didn't, but it was better to pretend to. Joss let a moment of silence pass by, then continued on with her idea. "I mean, if you *really* want to break into somewhere, you're going to need help." The twinkle in her eye told him exactly what she was thinking.

"No."

Joss pouted, falling back into step by him instead of walking backwards, seeming done with her pointed inspection. "But you haven't even heard my plan."

"If it involves you, it's not happening."

She huffed. "Even if I'm just a distraction?"

"Who says I need a distraction?"

She rolled her eyes, giving him a look like, *"Look at you."* "Your hair sticks out. Your clothes stick out. *You* stick out. You're going to need a distraction." A bright grin flashed across her face, her eyes twinkling with the sudden adventure. "Unless you want to *be* the distraction."

He frowned, even as the idea started turning in his mind. He shook his head. "I need to see what's in there."

Joss laughed. "*You* need to get in, but *I'm* the one with the skills for it. I can slip in windows. I can find exactly what you're looking for."

63

"I don't know what I'm looking for."

Joss shrugged. "I usually start with the jewelry box."

He stopped, turning her to face him better. She made a brief face at being handled.

"I'm not stealing from them."

Joss raised a cynical, disbelieving eyebrow. "You just want to look around?" she said dryly.

With a frustrated breath, he let her go. She settled in the grass, halting their progress, before asking, "What *do* you want from them?"

He settled in the grass beside her. Out of the corner of his eye, he saw Jade collapse into the grass on his other side and get comfortable on her back, staring at the sky. "Information," he answered Joss. For some reason, it was incredibly easy to talk to this girl. Scarily easy.

Joss looked up at him with a grin, as if predicting his thoughts. "It's my charm," she explained teasingly. A moment later, she grew serious again. "What kind of information?"

"Important information," he answered swiftly, cutting off the rest of her curiosity. "Why are you doing this?"

Joss shrugged, taking a moment to trace her fingers over his arm before answering. "The way I see it...you saved my life, whether it was your decision in the first place or not. So I figure I owe you."

Ghosts of a shiver crept over his arm at her touch. Noticing this, she paused, eying the reaction, and lightened her strokes.

He drew in a breath, steadying himself. "You don't owe me anything."

A faint smile crossed her lips. "I owe a lot of people a lot of things. If I can't make it up to them, 'least I can make it up to you." She shrugged her shoulders in a way that seemed to dwarf her face, a carefree smile hiding whatever truth lay beneath. That was alright, though. He didn't have any desire to pry.

"I can find it for you, you know. Papers, or whatever you need."

He shook his head, his mind made up. "I need to see it for myself."

There was an exhalation that might have been a sigh, and a resigned nod. She looked up at him, trailing a glance down his face to his clothes, the slightest wrinkle at the corner of her nose that she seemed to be trying to fight off. "Then you're going to need a disguise."

IV

BASIL

For once in his life, Basil wished he could just be *useful*.

Even when he was younger, it had always been Olive helping everyone. Olive, learning to scout for raiders. Skinning a rabbit with her own knife. Outdoing him in every skill and every way.

And now it was Olive, bringing them together. Training the Gifted in the city, not just in the use of their gifts, but in fighting, as well.

With Sari gone, and Kaiden, and Chan, they were hardly holding together as is. Lena had the world on her shoulders. Fern carried her world on hers.

They were instructed to train the Gifted, which always only gave Basil a bitter reminder. His gift wasn't useful. He wasn't the one they needed. He never was.

Basil missed Kaiden.

Basil got squeamish at the sight of blood. He *hated* killing things. He couldn't figure out how to climb up a tree or scale a wall like Olive did, even with everyone saying it 'should be easier' with his long limbs. The things he could do, she always did better. More gracefully.

No one ever minded that he wasn't like her, or said he should be able to do things better because they were the same age, or he was bigger, or technically older by a few seconds. His mother said he was just different, and was more than happy to have someone help her in the kitchen, or patch up things around the house.

Basil never minded, either, or tried not to. He knew Olive was better because she put everything she had into what she did. She trained more than she spoke, was always on the lookout, and always had some tool if not her knife on hand, and about a dozen more possible things she could use assessed around her.

Basil had asked her about it, once, and her process made his head hurt. He was far more likely to look for a way of escape, or check if everyone was alright, than look for what he could use to knock someone's head in.

But some days, like today, he wished he had her bravery. Her steady words and unflinching resolve. Basil had always preferred to play the captive, not the hero, in any of their games. At the best, he might help them out on whatever mission they had planned out, if it was really necessary. He knew he couldn't match her, or even come close, if they went toe to toe. Even when Olive tried to get him to take on a bigger role, he always turned it down.

In the Mountain, too, he'd preferred to stay on the sidelines. He'd said before that he had just been the light so they could find Olive. She was who they needed. He was just...useless.

It seemed a bitter irony, then, that their scenario actually came true. He'd never minded having to stay in a tree the whole time they played, watching Olive and one of their cousins 'fight' and knowing that if nothing else, he'd come down when their mother called for dinner. But being captured *with* someone else...that had never happened before. Suddenly, he was still forced into being a hero, and failed miserably at it. He couldn't protect anyone. He *hadn't*. So what made Olive think he'd be any good at this, either?

She'd prodded him several times now, sometimes twice in one day, to talk to Fern. So here he was – sitting in the kitchen while she flitted around like a sugar-covered dragon – remaining absolutely silent.

Basil had always been able to read expressions better than most. It was a talent he never acknowledged and only sometimes classified as a gift. He knew when others were hiding things, even if he wasn't certain what – though most of the time, he at least had a clue. Expressions, he learned, were just layers of emotion concealing others beneath them.

And Fern was definitely concealing things. *All* of his friends were, in one way or another. For as well as he could see it on their faces, though, Basil had never been able to imitate it.

He didn't like to acknowledge it either. Just because he knew everyone's secrets didn't mean he had to give them away. He didn't want to become the reason they put on more masks, to hide from him.

And he didn't know *all* their secrets, anyway. Since his capture, especially...it hadn't quite been the same. He'd second-guessed himself, and obviously hadn't been able to figure out what was going on with Kaiden. Some observational skills he had, there.

Fern, though...he didn't think he'd ever be able to mistake the look she had in her eyes. It was like looking in a mirror, if he let himself admit it. Except Fern was doing her best to keep hers hidden. Basil's slipped out whether he wanted it to or not.

The knot in his stomach tightened at the thought. He wasn't ready to talk about this yet. He didn't want to acknowledge that it'd actually...happened. That there were things he hadn't been able to stop. But if he didn't, things were only going to get worse, for all of them.

If Fern seemed alright, then the others would pretend to be, too, for her sake. She was the innocent one, still chattering away at anything she saw and baking cakes as if the world would end if she didn't. Her hair was in pigtails today; her blue, pink and yellow patched dress splotched with flour and frosting. If he didn't look past any of it, it would seem like nothing about her had changed.

Sometimes he thought he was the only one he could see her truthfully. It was so obvious, in the subtlest ways, that it ended up painful when he did.

But every time he'd come in here, to try to talk to her, his mind had failed him. His tongue went along with whatever inane chatter she spouted and let her drag him over to taste what she made – and, inevitably, to help clean up the mess.

He couldn't bring himself to do it. She looked too *happy*, if he didn't think about it. He didn't want to be responsible for taking the smile off her face. Didn't want to make her go back, and face that.

But if he didn't, she'd push it away until, somehow or another, she'd be able to keep it out of sight, while it slowly ate away at her from the inside.

Basil rubbed a hand through his hair, not at all surprised to find a cloud of flour coming with it. Fern covered her mouth, a little grin peeking out the sides of it anyway. "Oops."

Instead of playing along, or pretending to scold her, Basil lowered his hand to study her. Maybe, somehow, he could just communicate it through a look, rather than actually having to speak. It hadn't worked before, but that didn't mean he couldn't try, right?

Fern whirled away, her voice growing louder as her hands went up in the air. "The cake!" She said it as if she'd forgotten about her project, when Basil knew she had just put it in far too recently to be concerned about it.

"Fern." He sighed, some of it slipping out with her name. *There's something I need to tell you.*

She turned back to him with a too-bright grin, eyes dancing in the light. "It'll be done soon, don't worry! Hold your patience!"

Sometimes he wondered if she made strange comments just so people would focus on those. It was hard to tell, with her. "I'm not...worried about the cake."

"Then what?" She stuck her hands on her hips. "You sure look worried about *somethin'*."

Yeah. You. Basil shook his head, holding back another sigh. "I'm just tired."

67

She cocked her head at him. "You don't look tired. You slept in so long, the sun was wonderin' where you'd gone!"

He couldn't help a faint smile at that, even if it was bittersweet.

Just tell her, Basil. Tell her.

He'd already failed them too much, these past few weeks. He saw what they hid and just...let it slide. Lena looked like she needed a hug, and he'd been afraid of getting his head bitten off if he gave her one. She hid all her worries behind a brittle and bitter anger, fragile as it was. What was the worst that would happen? He'd get yelled at? That never bothered him.

Olive fought dragons and had sustained more injuries than he could count, in the course of their lives. It made his hesitation seem even more cowardly, with how little he had to lose in comparison.

But being imprisoned had sapped away the small bit of bravery he thought he had. It reminded him, more than anything, of just how useless he was. Day in and day out. What could he do, really? Light up a room? That wasn't useful when you were trapped. He wasn't clever, or resourceful, or sly enough to even *attempt* breaking out. He'd just had to sit, and wait, as he always did, for someone to come rescue him.

Except that time, it had actually cost him something. It had cost his friends something terrible, something he couldn't even take a part of. Their captors had tested him, as they had for all of them, and basically determined that he had no value, except to use against others.

He didn't want to ask what they'd done with Fern. He didn't want to know, and further bear that guilt. If he'd just...tried a little more. Put an effort into being smart. Maybe, *maybe*, he could have helped them.

But thinking about it made all his thoughts funnel down into a very dark place, where even his light couldn't do any good.

"Basil!"

He was jerked back to the present by Fern's exasperated cry, though her eyes looked concerned. "You didn't hear a word I said, did you?"

Now, even more than ever, he could see the burden in her eyes, and he couldn't bear it. Everyone thought of her as the young one, innocent and hopefully still carefree. They never saw that she was a lot older, inside. A *lot* older. She'd been the oldest in her family, once. Basil knew how that felt.

Before he could think about it too much, he reached out to take her hands, sticky and colorful as they were, and draw her closer. She looked surprised, something else flashing across her face as she let him guide her.

"It's alright to talk about it, you know. Right?"

Fern blinked at him, quickly shaking her head. "Talk about what?"

He had to smile, even though it hurt inside. He waited until the expression in her eyes shifted, and she tried to pull away from him.

"Umm. My cake is going to burn if I don't…"

"Fern." Closing his eyes for a brief moment, he drew in a breath for courage. "What happened, when we were captured…"

"Yeah, I don't really want to talk about that, thanks." Unsuccessfully, she tried to pull her hand away again.

Basil met her eyes for a long moment, his voice subdued. "Neither do I," he admitted.

"Great! Then we can just-"

"But we *need* to." He stressed the word gently, squeezing her hands lightly and holding back a quiet sigh. Her hands looked even smaller, cradled in his. "You can't keep pushing it away."

She shook her head again, her eyes brightened with something other than happiness. "No. No."

"It's not okay to keep hiding it." He drew in a breath, the words spilling from his mouth like a burden released, an ache he'd carried for way too long. "It's not helping me, either. I don't…even know what happened to you. And with how my mind works, I think not knowing is far worse."

She swallowed, staring down at their hands and blinking for a long moment. Her lip started to quiver, no matter how she bit down on it.

Basil drew her closer until he could wrap his arms around her, closing his eyes with a quiet sigh. "I'm sorry," he whispered, and forced himself to add on, "I should have talked to you sooner."

Fern rubbed a fist over her eyes, hiccuping a shaky breath. "Y…You have frosting on you."

He squeezed her lightly, until a sound like a whimper escaped her throat. Her fingers curled tight in his shirt, unsteady.

"It's alright. I've got you."

"You…d-don't have to worry about me, Basil." She took in a shaky breath. "I can take care of…myself."

"I can't," Basil managed to admit, feeling something well in his eyes. There it was, the truth laid bare even for him to see. *I can't.*

He'd been putting this off because he had been afraid, and he still was. He didn't want to think about that time, or what he might have missed. Didn't want to think about Elle, or Fern, or how utterly useless he was.

Fern rubbed his back gently with a flour-covered hand, biting her lip to hide its tremble. "It's alright," she whispered, as a choking sound fought to leave his throat. "It's ok…okay."

Her voice nearly caught, too, and he pulled her closer, as tight as he dared. He heard the sounds trapped in her throat, too, that she tried to swallow down.

It wasn't okay. It couldn't be. Not without Elle. The hole she left, that everyone danced around, couldn't be that easily filled.

"It's not."

Neither of them were okay. *None* of them were. They walked around wearing mouths painted with smiles while the truth festered underneath. They lied and hid and fought it, ran from it, and those were never going to make anything better.

Olive would have said it was perfectly normal. Everything was perfectly normal to be messed up after what they'd gone through. But now, Basil thought it just another reason never to tell anyone.

Which was, of course, exactly what he needed to do. To acknowledge that hiding things wasn't going to work and force them to face it, to get through it.

But doing so was not as easy as saying it, when it required him to start being honest, too.

Fern whimpered against him, eyes screwed tightly shut. "I'm okay," she insisted, even as her voice held a note of breaking.

This, as Basil knew, and had for a while, was the real problem. They were all trying so *hard* to seem alright, that they could just move on as if none of it ever happened, and everything would be fine. Lena was hurting. Kaiden was gone, and so was Sari. Even Chan had left to help out in Calest. *Some*one had to pull them all together before they completely fell to pieces.

And Olive had never been the kind to bother much with feelings. It was why she kept urging him to do this, rather than do it herself. Fern was the first – and supposedly easiest – step. She was the only one who could never quite hide the shine to her eyes, the unsteadiness lurking beneath her voice as she animatedly chatted on. It had gotten better in the last month, which was why Olive kept pushing him. If even she could force it all down, they might end letting themselves believe they all were fine.

Basil couldn't do it any longer. He couldn't keep watching his friends press together masks from whatever bits they could gather and talk as if they were still close, while the gap between them just widened farther with their unspoken pain.

He never had the bravery to speak up about it, though. This is what happened when he did. Any moment now, Fern would probably use this opportunity to distract him from what he was trying to say, and he wouldn't have the strength to push it aside and keep going. It hurt too much. Losing her just hurt too much. It took all the words away from him, every time.

"Are you okay?" came Fern's quiet voice.

No, he wanted to say. *No, I'm not.*

The truth, really, that he didn't want to admit to himself, was that *he* didn't want to do this. In his mind, he framed it as being Fern's disappointment. Fern's sadness. *Fern's* breaking down. The reason he didn't want to talk. The reason he never had.

His throat ached at the thought. At not only stealing that smile from her face, but knowing exactly what it would do to his.

There was no way to talk about it without bringing up burdens *he'd* also tried to push aside. Without remembering things he wanted to just forget.

There was also no one else who *knew* what had happened, like she did.

I'm not like them, Basil wanted to shout, shaking his head in response to his friend. *I know you don't need help. I know you'd get through it okay. But I can't.*

I can't...

In the most bared form of the truth, this was why he'd been stalling. As much as Olive tried to tell him, and he let himself believe that Fern was the one who needed this, it wasn't actually true. Fern would find a way through. Fern had always been strong even through her sadness.

It was Basil who was still breaking apart, day by day. Piece by piece.

Fern would take her sorrows and fill them with sunshine. Olive let hers out with a sword. Chan sealed them away to contemplate later. Lena lashed out. Kaiden lied.

Basil just...broke.

He couldn't do it. Hadn't been able to, since her death. It terrified him to think about, not just that day, but how it affected everyone else. How they let the shadows' presence be known, but never actually let it out. How he sometimes felt he might scream if he couldn't talk to *someone* about her. He understood they were in the middle of a war. He understood they had their own ways of handling it. But he couldn't...he just couldn't keep going like this. Holding it in was going to tear him apart.

Elle would have talked with him. That was the part that hurt the worst. Elle would have understood, and bore the burden of their hurt without trying to make it better. Letting it out instead of making him shove it back in. She never shied away from truth, no matter how ugly it was.

Though his voice was moments from breaking, he forced himself to reply. "Are *you*?"

Fern's glance strayed away, a grin creeping up her mouth. "Well, of course! And once I have my cake, I'll-"

"Fern." He nudged her head back toward him, so she had to meet his gaze. Her eyes shone far too innocently to be convincing.

Drawing in a breath, Basil shook his head again. "I'm not okay." The words whispered from his throat, and he cleared it to speak better, looking away. "I don't think you are, either."

Fern turned her head too, her lip caught between her teeth as she blinked over at the oven, which she might actually have to check on soon.

Basil drew in a deep breath, blinking at the ceiling to keep the emotion in his eyes from spilling out. He'd nearly had to shut off this part of his brain when they were captured. The number of people that had been innocent and still imprisoned like them made his skin crawl. Very few of them ever made it out alive, if at all.

His mind tripped on a fact, then, that made him choke. *Elle hadn't.*

He couldn't stop thinking about the people in those cells. Of how wrong it was that they were there, still, and he was here. Of the fact that no one else *knew*, and no one would understand what it had been like. Olive was pragmatic, and perfectly capable of seeing both sides of whatever she wished, but it still wasn't the same. Not without seeing it. Not without *knowing*.

He couldn't keep doing this; maybe Olive had seen that. He'd tried talking to Katya about it, once, and upset her so much that Chan was silently seething for a week. *How could he say such things?*

How could he *not*? They all wanted to pretend it never happened. Fern wanted to act like she was a child again. Olive still carried herself as if they were under Damien's command, and that she had to protect her twin, no matter what. Lena kept a brittle and bitter anger out as a flimsy excuse to keep others away from her hurt. Dailen had just gotten...withdrawn, more and more. He stayed with the dragons more than people, and never wanted to talk.

Basil blinked back the moisture gathering in his eyes. This wouldn't work if he broke down crying. He couldn't help Fern if he couldn't keep control of his own emotions. She'd make it all about him, and he'd let her, and nothing would be addressed.

"You can't...pretend it didn't happen," he managed to whisper, the words heavy and aching in his mouth. Like a plea it seemed only he could hear, no matter how he tried.

Fern sat and watched him with a timid nod, her hands drawn close in on her lap. For a moment, she looked paler, and smaller, with her hair limp from dirt and her eyes so, so young. It scared her to talk about it. He understood that. He also knew it was the only way for them to heal.

But watching her, with that haunted look in her eyes, he couldn't bring himself to take it further. Her hands were subconsciously rubbing her arms, a shiver running through her. He took them in his again, gently, and made sure her eyes met his.

"If you need to talk about it," he said quietly, finally, "I'm here."

FERN

Fern really liked making cake.

It was one thing she remembered from her mother – or sort of. As rare a treat as it was, her mother had always tried to make anything she could into 'cake', in one way or another.

The only problem with that was Fern could never remember the exact ingredients, or even the amounts. The kitchen always turned into a flour-filled, sugary mess that Nitl did nothing to fix. He'd sit by a failed lump of frosting and greedily lick it until she shooed him away. Basil teased, and was probably right, that this was why the 'little' dragon was so chubby.

But she didn't mind making a mess, and it reminded her of trying to help her mother. So she kept at it, and tried to keep the dragons from eating *too* much sugar. It made them kind of hyper.

None of this, of course, had anything to do with what Basil was trying to say. But dragons, as it turned out, really liked cake, and that was where her mind chose to go, flitting around the topic she should be focused on.

Basil still had frosting on him, she noted silently, as her eyes tracked over the spots of color she'd smudged on his worn grey shirt. He kept his clothes so neat, usually, using a vest or whatever he had to hide any stains, or rips from unexpected 'adventures'. She always felt a silly thrill of pride at being the reason his outfit wasn't immaculate. Chan just cleaned off whatever mess she left on him -- and part of hers, too. For the most part, Basil left them alone, kept just out of sight like a secret reminder.

His offer hung heavy in the air, still avoided.

Fern held back a hard sigh. She *liked* pretending she was younger, and less aware of the gravity of everyone's smiles. It made everyone's grins soften and their words get a little calmer for the time, if only a little. Cake, she found, brought everyone together.

Nitl, though, preferred to eat everything *before* it was ready. Right now he sat on the counter with his face covered in flour, a tiny pink tongue coming out to lick the frosting sitting on his nose. Yesterday it had been the eggs, and she'd had to chase him all over the city to properly scold him.

For the most part, though, Fern stuck to making cake. It was relatively difficult to mess that up *too* badly, with so many basic ingredients. The one time she had tried to make muffins, Fern had sworn she saw horror on Basil's face before he tried to eat it.

He hadn't exactly chewed the bite, but he hadn't spit it out, either. Or, at least, not where she could see it.

Nitl enjoyed her offerings no matter how cooked or uncooked they were. He'd even eat vegetables if they were overcooked. Somehow she wondered how she'd gotten so lucky, or if he, too, was just playing along to appease her.

She wondered if he would still eat *burnt* cake. Probably.

But this – whatever *it* was – was obviously bothering Basil, and she couldn't bring herself to leave him there for too long, so visibly troubled.

Fern drew in a breath before it could be stolen from her. Everyone else was content to let her handle this in her own way. They let her have her games, their pretenses. They never even tried to look past it, and she never invited them to. It helped them, she thought, being able to convince themselves that at least *some*one was still okay. That she was still a child, still carefree, still able to laugh and bounce around without the threat of a panic attack looming in every shadow, every corner. That her needy desire for company wasn't from fear of facing the dark by herself.

Everyone, that was, except for Basil.

The problem, as it always had been with them, was that Fern was too old for all of this, and never old enough. Fifteen years felt like an eternity when you grew up the way she did, and yet by that comparison, Chan must have been ageless.

Yet years, Fern had learned better than most in her own short few, passed differently for different people. One entire cycle of life could feel like the snap of a man's fingers, or the blink of a child's eye. It could stretch as far as the endless forests by her old home, further than the oceans she'd never dared get near, as slow as the breath taken before an anticipated moment. They were fluid, influenced by the spin of a person's thoughts and what their eyes perceived of the world, stretched by impatience, shortened by dread. Pushed and pulled by the threads of emotions that tied everyone together. Weighed down by knowledge, buoyed by ignorance. Bliss, some called it. Naivety was the more logical term.

And yet even those were subjective to the whims of thought and feeling. It was how, when two people went through the same things, their explanation of events could still be so unique.

All in all, Fern's fifteen years felt more like fifty, no matter how little she liked to admit it to herself. Sometimes she was sure a part of her must still be trapped in that prison – endlessly losing time to something out of her control.

The same part she knew Basil must have, and kept avoiding. The broken pieces of themselves that no one else could see, or understand. The ones they *should* talk about, and would, sooner or later.

Smiles were heavier, she knew, when they were weighed down by experience. The past was a ball and chain slipping along behind her, a quiet clink of chains she ignored and fought futilely against. It wasn't enough, to her, to smile as *if* she didn't have a care in the world. More than anything in the world, all Fern wanted to do was have the ability to smile *like* that again, like she was five years old and could still smell her mother's cooking wafting in from an open kitchen, the bright, raucous laughter of too many bodies and pattering feet, the bubbling of a creek that marked the most dangerous possibility in their lives.

A broken toy. A skinned knee. Those were her biggest concerns, then.

But knowledge, Fern knew too well, was the one thing you could never return. No matter how it was purchased, no matter the cost or whether it was even welcome, knowledge was a weight you could never shake off your shoulders.

She never asked to be captured. She never asked to be shown things no fifteen year old should have to worry about. She never wanted to have parts of her that she had to hide away, too scared to face them. She didn't want to hear the echo of her own screams.

Neither did Basil. She could see it on his face, if she looked. Which was why she never did.

If she really wanted to, she *could* smile for them, as she had been doing. She could do what she'd seen so many before her do and bottle it all up until it made her chest ache. Let the emotions stretch her chest out to make room for them and hold them tight, deep enough that she could lift the corners of her lips again as if nothing was wrong.

But Fern had never felt old enough or wise enough for such things. Even with her fifteen eternities hanging behind her, she was still just a child, and children were allowed to cry, weren't they? Children didn't have to know what was going on. Children didn't have to hold the world together for anyone else's sake.

Not all the time, at least.

Fern's biggest secret was that she hadn't been a child for a very long time. Maybe, in her own way, she was still pretending. But to her, it felt more like she'd been split into two, like that first day her world had burned down, a part of her had died as well, a solemn ghost that now kept watch but never interfered. A soul no longer bound by time, and therefore ageless. Unaffected by earthly whims and fickle feelings. Tired by the weight of all it had seen and felt.

A part of her, though, still clung to her childhood. That side was the one that had screamed and shook and collapsed into the grass that horrid day as if the world was wracked with earthquakes instead of fire, keeping her on her knees. She'd stayed there for several hours, she'd been told, and fought anyone who tried to tear her away.

"Just a child," they all said. *Just a child.*

But the truth, hidden beneath everything else, was that child who fell into the grass had never left. She was still there, another soul trapped by a past that she simply couldn't accept. Skipping and bouncing around as if she hadn't a care in the world, for she *hadn't.*

That was the person Basil was trying to find, and fix. The one she never wanted him to see.

Only the older part of her was able to grieve everything she had lost, and she hid it where no one could see.

Now, it seemed, that child had slipped away, the last echoes of a life she had tried so hard to hold onto. It had gotten harder during their capture, seeing Basil's face and all the other despairing ones in their prison. Wondering if she would ever see the light again. Wondering if she had ever truly seen it.

Imprisonment did things to an individual, and in the clutches of the Empress, that had only intensified.

Fern could still remember the night her father had returned from his imprisonment – a petty way to try to stifle protests on the selfish laws inflicted by the Council. There was a light in his eyes that hadn't been there, a harder one that only seemed to fill him with more determination to make things right.

Fern thought her light must have broken, because she couldn't figure out where it had gone. It seemed so foolish now, clinging to childish memories just for the sake of forgetting. Of pretending that everything was alright, and her parents were going to come along soon and make everything better, sweep her up with a kiss on the forehead and say 'I'm proud of you'.

It seemed foolish because it obviously wasn't helping. Basil saw past it. He *needed* to see past it.

She imagined he might feel somewhat like this, too.

Which was why, of course, he'd brought this to her. Why he was waiting for the words she had never, and told herself she would never, say. She wouldn't be a burden to them. Wouldn't add to their troubles.

Only Chan had seen past it, back then, and he was kind enough never to mention it. Perhaps he had considered the burden in her eyes to have just been grief, rather than something much deeper. If he recognized it later, he didn't say a word.

Basil, on the other hand, *wanted* the truth, and she just...wasn't sure she could give it to him. Fern *liked* being a child. She knew the rest of them hadn't had easy lives, even at her age.

But she had. *She*, at first, had at least been happy. She had something to run back and hide in. She'd never expected the dragons to ever reach her hometown; none of them had. They'd lived in an ignorant bliss that ended up destroying them all.

And yet that's exactly what she sought out, now. A dangerous form of denial that promised a measure of peace, for a while.

She wouldn't admit it, even to Basil, but that innocent denial had been already slipping away, anyway. She'd found out, during their capture, that sometimes her bright light only made the darkness more painful. Those had been bad days. She didn't like it when people yelled at her. But her shoulders were still young and strong, and her ears always open. It was amazing, sometimes, just how much having someone to cry on helped in a place like that.

But listening to their own sorrows aged her by eons, their experiences seeping in with her own knowledge and stretching it until she was sure she had lived through all of their pain with them. It didn't change the situation, but it made the burden just a little easier to bear. Knowing, understanding looks were less painful than smiles, and they made her terror a little bit lesser.

Basil was the only one too caught in the mire of that prison to ever return the looks. His were swallowed by the darkness, dimmed as if their very existence was tied to the girl in his cell with him. Basil knew, Fern thought, about her secret even back then. He knew, deep down, that he didn't have to worry about her.

Elle, on the other hand...

Fern squeezed her eyes shut tight enough to hurt. How was there so little difference between them, in how long they had drawn breath on this world? Elle had seemed miles away and eons apart from her, born of a different world that Fern didn't understand the time system of. She was like a mother, a sprite, an old, tired being trapped in the body of a youthful girl. Her smiles were sunshine and her eyes shadows from their light, the mists spilling out stories of a life Fern couldn't even begin to comprehend. Her weariness was more in the mind than it ever was in her body, in the looks she cast at those around her. As if she wished she could use what was left of her little energy to take their burdens from them.

Fern's smiles were fireworks. Elle's were gentle sunshine. The quiet, assuring kind that let you know at least for the moment, in the warmth of its embrace, that the world was alright. Nothing cold could penetrate its thick skin.

Older, and wiser, and yet far more frail. Basil had seen it, as always. It was a wonder he hadn't challenged Damien himself for even considering putting her on their team. Putting her in danger.

Fern was a spark that didn't dare to shine; Elle was a sun that had been alive for far too long and had slowly, inevitably, died out. Time didn't differentiate between the two of them, choosing to sweep one away while the other was allowed to escape.

She knew how badly it had to eat at Basil. She knew he'd blame himself, because it was so *easy* to. Attempting to justify what had happened by claiming that if you'd just...if you'd just done *something*, things would have been better.

She'd felt that way about her family, too.

Why me? Fern's mind still wondered, most days. *Why did I get to survive? Why not them?*

In the depths of her soul, she understood why – and she hated it. Because she was special. Because she was needed, and they were not. Because all the good intentions in the world couldn't save every soul that got trapped in the path of a wildfire. They would all burn. No one had enough arms to keep everyone safe, no matter how they tried.

And oh, how they tried.

Basil wanted her to grow up. He *needed* her to, really. She could see it in his eyes, as much as he'd never admit it. Fern's siblings had looked at her like that a lot.

He knew, more than any of the others, what she'd been through. He knew you couldn't go through it without it changing you, and aging you. He would never buy her child act, no matter how much she wanted to cling to it.

And yet, she knew this wouldn't be easy for him to talk about, either. It had taken him so long just to get these few words out, and now he was looking at her like he might break apart if she pushed him aside one more time.

She'd been stalling long enough. It was time to fix things.

He'd been brave, daring to say it. She could be brave, too, and tell him the truth.

"Okay."

V

KAIDEN

Kaiden surveyed himself in the dirty piece of mirror that Joss had found. He looked like an entirely different person. Joss had succeeded in disguising him, that was for sure. His bright hair was capped inside a black hat, a matching jacket paired with soft black pants. He didn't even want to ask where she'd gotten them from. They didn't have time to be picky.

Joss looked him over appraisingly, then grinned, giving him a thumbs up. She was dressed in a faded purple coat with matching gloves, which stuck out on Calest's dull streets. She'd 'found' Kaiden a pair of similar, black ones, but he would have rather kept his hands in his pockets than wear them. After Joss explaining with an eyeroll that he kind of needed his hands to pick the lock, he agreed to wear them, but not until it was absolutely necessary. The nights were much cooler, even for early summer, but for some reason the gloves felt...stifling. His hands felt trapped, encased in a thick fabric like that.

Maybe it had something to do with his gifts. If worst came to worst and he had to use them like this, he would just burn through the gloves anyway.

The plan was simple. Joss would stand watch and pretend to be a lost little rich girl if anyone came by, steering them away from the house. They had a code word for if something went wrong, though Joss seemed confident in her abilities. Thefts weren't uncommon in Calest, and as long as the guards didn't find out, no one should be after them if they were discovered. Or so he hoped.

If it was any consolation, as Joss had said, they were both already wanted.

So far, no one was out at night. Joss had wisely chosen the hours before the lower class came out to roam, when respectable people were just heading home and lights had not yet been put out. Still, he felt nervous as he stepped up to the door, retrieving the lockpicks from his jacket. Damien was dead, according to Lena, and by the looks of it, he hadn't been to this house in quite some time. But what if he'd left a guard, or someone else was there?

Well, there was no going back now. The gloves, despite his reservations, were on his hands, and the pick was in the lock. Jade leaned against the wall, humming offkey as she usually did and studying her nails.

It wasn't difficult to figure out the lock, which just brought another question to his mind as he turned the handle, and was rewarded with a nearly soundless opening.

"How...do I even know how to do that?"

Pushing away from the wall, Jade followed him into the house with a nonchalant shrug. "Eh. You taught yourself how, once upon a time."

Used to her statements as he was, this one made him stop, directing a look at her like he might have heard her wrong. "Why would I do that?"

"Psh, why wouldn't you?" She motioned to the door. "I think that speaks for itself."

The way she said it, he would have thought he was a thief before, or something equally underhanded. "But why would I *need* to do that?"

"You spent the majority of your time around people like Damien. Why wouldn't you need to know how?"

Her statement didn't make him feel any better. Rubbing a hand against his forehead – and nearly forgetting the hat sitting there – he glanced around the nearly dark room. It felt oddly familiar, for some reason. "Alright."

Jade waited beside him for a moment. "So where to, Captain?"

It was enough to shake him out of his musing. Half-grinning at the title, he shrugged. "Exploring, I guess."

Following him into the next room, Jade grinned. "Fancy."

He chuckled, but it sounded breathless and empty as his eyes took in his surroundings, and recognition crashed onto him like a relentless wave. His fingers gripped the doorframe as his memory filled in the missing pieces, the voices, the people that would be sitting there...

Jade's hand rested on his shoulder. He tried to stop his mind, but it continued connecting pieces until his fingernails were digging into the wood, his knees stiff so they wouldn't shake. "I think...I've been here before."

Jade nodded, squeezing his shoulder gently. "Take your time."

Shifting to flatten his hand against the wall, he returned the nod, moving through the room as carefully as he could. Each step brought back memories, tugging at him and stinging his face. He did his best not to tense up.

He still had to look around, though every glance brought back another moment. A too-polite smile. A feeling of dread. Nowhere to hide.

Any time he tried to stop, voices scolded him. Hiding a cringe, he carried on, shutting back a sudden onset of tears. When his fingers touched the adjacent doorframe, he expelled a breath of relief, gripping it for support. He knew beyond the room would not be much better, but he would take any bit of false hope he could. He couldn't bear to look at this scene any longer.

After a moment, Jade's voice broke the silence. "What exactly are we looking for? 'Cause I can look for you."

"The...same thing as before." It came out more of a question, and he released a quiet laugh at his obvious weakness. "Something...about where he might have them."

He was slipping. The memories tightened around him like a vise, a second skin that froze him in place, strangling him. Damien. This was Damien's house, and he was looking for information about his siblings. Kinny. She had been here before, too. He could still remember...

"Alright. How about you sit and I will look?"

Once again, the implications were enough to make him cringe, but his body was too weak to fight it anymore. He knew his breath was already coming quicker, a little too irregularly for the situation. With a nod, he sank down onto the couch, trapping his face in his hands. "Okay."

The quiet admission broke him. His shoulders threatened to shake, but he held them firm, balling his hands into fists and shutting his eyes tightly. He wouldn't let it win. He couldn't...

Flinching, he tugged his sleeves into his hands to have something to hold. His cheek stung like it had been struck. A whimper rose to his throat; swallowing it down was like inhaling fire. It streaked down his face, burning in liquid rivers as he gave in and pressed his face into his arms with a quiet sob. Somehow, being on the floor felt more assuring, and he slid down until his knees touched his chin, hunching over them. He was small again, small and very scared. Each sob choked his throat, burning almost as badly as the tears down his face, and his chest constricted as he tried to sear them back in. Each one was painful, a reminder and a warning that terrified him. A sharp gasp in his mind, and a familiar growl. His sister. They were going to hurt his *sister*.

A tongue clicked, the sound shattering the silence. A voice like polished wood, smooth and straight, cut through the space that should have been occupied by pain, throwing his instincts off.

"Now, Kendel, that's no way for company to behave."

There was almost amusement in the tone, and relief washed over him at the realization that he hadn't been hit. It occurred to him for a fleeting moment that this wasn't actually happening, but it felt so real, it might have been. He could see the man calmly restraining his father's raised hand, his sister watching them fearlessly in her little white dress, unaware.

"Don't tell me how to raise my kids, Damien."

A shudder ran down his spine at the low voice, unpleasantly familiar. The suit-wearing man he knew far too well nodded, though there was a smile on his face that Kaiden had never liked. A moment later, he was reminded why.

"I wouldn't dream of it," Damien replied coolly, his gaze flicking back to Kinny. *"But there are simpler ways."*

Kinny wasn't supposed to be here. She was supposed to be with him, in the other room, safe from this conversation. She'd wandered off without him, curious as she was at such a young age, and he'd not been fast enough to stop her.

Before his gut plunged, Kaiden heard it: a scream cut back before it reached the air.

"Don't touch her."

At a nod from Damien, one of the other men dragged Kinny from the room, a heavy hand on Kaiden's arm holding him back. His heart pounded in his ears as he fought against it.

"Stay quiet and do what you're told," the same low voice snapped in his ears, the grip on his arm tightening. But he kept trying to fight against it, desperation and stubbornness burning fiercely in him, flooding through his veins.

Damien waved a hand, dismissing them both. *"Step out of line again,"* he said calmly, with the same air of indifference, *"and you won't be the only one punished."*

Kaiden fell still, even as a slow smile spread across the man's face. He nodded to the man holding Kaiden captive.

"As I said. He can be trained."

Pain in his face, nearly jerking him back to the present. He felt himself stagger, back against the rough arms holding him like vises. The same smooth clicking noise filled his ears.

"Karah wouldn't be pleased."

The other man stopped, then, a wild light still burning in his eyes that he then turned on Damien. His voice more of a snarl than anything. *"Are you threatening me?"*

"I have no need to threaten you, if you are so scared of a small child."

83

Cursing and a violent crash that he couldn't stop himself from flinching at. Damien stood indifferent, calm even as he brushed at a chip of what used to be a plate with his foot. *"That will need to be repaired."*

"He's pathetic," Kendel spat, his chest heaving. *"He'll never amount to anything."*

"No," Damien agreed. *"Not in your hands, he won't."*

Shaken, Kaiden dropped to his knees away from the two men, working on not hyperventilating and drawing too much attention to himself. Tears stung the corner of his eyes, though he refused to let them fall until the room started tilting. The panic of knowing his sister was elsewhere, alone, terrified him more than anything. And if he tried anything, *she* would be the one hurt.

Kaiden felt sickness rolling deep in his stomach. His heart pounded too hard to argue, his mind whirling over what the man had said. Eventually, Damien's eyes returned to him, as if he was an afterthought, dismissed as much as the words that left his mouth.

Opening his eyes made the memories painful, but leaving them shut made them real. He could hear everything, even smell the subtle aromas of whatever his father and Damien had been drinking. He could picture a small, innocent child creeping in to 'play' in the room, the raised eyebrow and the look of fury at her entrance. He remembered what it felt like, the terror for her and the determination to keep her safe. Shoving himself out in front of her, defying his father with the look in his eyes. The fear when they took her away, and he couldn't do anything about it.

Someone sighed and sat down beside him, breaking the spell. "Hey."

Swallowing back another cry and hugging himself tighter, he shifted his arm just enough that one eye could peek out at Jade. When he did, she smiled, waving a little like to be reassuring. "Just me, your friendly neighborhood imaginary person. What do you say we ditch this place?"

Harsh voices flashed through his mind even before he could reply, reprimanding him for the idea. He couldn't even handle a little time in the past, or face what had happened so many years ago.

No, he couldn't. Jade extended her hand, and despite the voices screaming at him, he took it. The pain was phantom now, wisps of memory slipping in and out and wavering as she helped him to his feet. He still felt shaky, his breath catching at the contact, but it was better than sitting there, helpless.

"We'll just go as quickly as possible. 'Kay?"

With anyone else, he would have felt shamed. He could still feel the moisture at the edge of his eyes, the redness that told exactly what had happened. How he'd broken down crying in an old house because he was scared of his own shadow, from the past.

It took him a moment to realize he hadn't replied, and another to nod his consent to her, a twinge still running through his chest. Rubbing his eyes again, he focused on his breathing as Jade led him back out of the house, a bit quicker than they'd come in.

He'd feel it later, the guilt of his weakness, but at the moment he just felt...worn. Stretched thin between too many memories, several of which still threatened to tip him back over into grief. Knowing was one thing, but seeing...always made things so much more real.

He didn't stop rubbing his eyes, intermittently, until they were back outside. Jade took a deep breath and grinned. "Ah, much better. Outside is always better."

The best he could offer was a faint nod, half a smile pulling at the side of his mouth.

Jade motioned at the grass. "Want to sit?"

With a quiet breath out, he nodded, letting the smile fall. "Probably should."

Even his voice sounded a little like someone had run a bunch of pebbles over it. As she smiled at him, he shifted down to the grass, expelling a quiet sigh and letting his head fall in his hands. By the rustle of grass and familiar rubbing sound, Jade had sat across from him, running her palms over her knees. "You okay?"

He let a laugh out, quiet as it was, and nodded. But the images were coming back again, his arms tensing against his chest as he held back a cry, rubbing his fingers into his eyes.

"Just breathe," she murmured, and he couldn't. Holding himself together even as his breath caught and nearly shattered into a thousand, choking pieces, moisture stung his eyes worse than any cut could.

I failed her.

"Don't sound okay, Butterfly."

His laugh broke into a million shuddering pieces at the end, piercing breaths that seared almost as much as the tears that started down his cheeks. *I'm scared.*

She wrapped her arms around him, carefully, and he thought it was the only thing that kept him from completely shattering. Leaning into the touch for support as he slowly broke down.

I'm sorry, Kinny...

He could picture it sharply, vividly. He could see the fear and feel his heart lurch, the sting across his cheek nothing compared to the low, pulsing ache that sat hand in hand with terror as they took her away.

"If you act out again..."

He didn't even know what he'd done. He'd tried to help her, and failed, and she was the one to pay for it. He couldn't handle it.

I'm sorry. I'm sorry.

"I'm here." Jade's voice soothed him through the emptiness. "It's all over now. Shh."

And yet he couldn't stop crying, even as he forced his arms to wrap around her, slowly, as close as he dared. "Too much." He pressed his face against her shoulder, his voice wavering, unsteady. "Too clear." Another shuddering breath rocked him as he closed his eyes.

"I know, Butterfly. But they're just memories. You're alright now."

She squeezed him gently, and he returned the gesture, twisting the sob in his throat so it couldn't come out. His eyes burned. Kinny wasn't alright. The pain was sharp, eating at like acid as he squeezed her back again, burying his face further into her shoulder.

"I'm sorry. I'm sorry..."

The words were empty, and yet he repeated them, nearly choking as he rocked her and held back a sob. It tried to force itself out of him anyway, ugly and tangled in its endless grief.

I'm sorry. I tried. I failed.

The last admission hurt worst of all, the present breaking to give way to the past, his body trembling with fear, and guilt. They'd taken his sister away, and he didn't know where. He couldn't protect her. Even now, he was failing her.

"You don't have to say sorry to me, Kaiden." Jade's voice was too soft for the pain he felt. "I don't need apologies. It's alright."

Even his breath shuddered like it might break, racking his body as he drew air in. "I tried." Hoarse and whispering. "I tried..."

"I know, Butterfly. I know." She was as close as possible now, curled around him as if to hide him from everything. It only made him break down even more, her breath so near and her voice so soft as if to say *"It's okay."*

And it wasn't. Not by a long shot. But since he was breaking apart anyway, he gave into it, pulling closer to her and letting the quiet storm out. "I couldn't...I tried to help her." His voice shattered against the words like the rocks in a current. "I tried..."

But he could have, then. He must have been able to. He was six years old again, rocking himself in a corner of the room and hoping they couldn't hear him. Pretending Kinny was there, so he could comfort her, his chest burning with the effort of not crying. He was failing.

"I told you he could be trained."

Tears slipped out anyway, his body shaking with fear as he pulled himself tighter into a ball. He couldn't let them see his weakness. He didn't know what he'd done wrong, but he wouldn't let his sister suffer for it.

His stomach was rolling, a twinge running through from where he'd been hit, and refused to move past that moment. He was too afraid that they would come back, and Kinny would be in trouble. His father wouldn't understand if he saw him trembling on the floor like this.

"I couldn't stop it." Pain filled his chest, his lip wobbling as he opened his eyes.

Jade's eyes were gentle and sad as she nodded, brushing the bangs from his eyes. "I know, kid. We can't stop everything. We're only human."

He forced what might have passed for a smile to distract from the burning in his chest, his eyes still bright with tears. "I don't know why..."

"Don't know why what?"

Tears slipped out again as he let his eyes fall, his shoulders trembling. "Why I couldn't stop it." *What I did wrong.* "Why it happened." His words trembled, but he pushed them out anyway, bravely despite the onset of tears choking his voice. "Why...why they..."

His eyes slipped closed again as he choked out a quiet sob. There it was, shattering his world all over again. It had been so much easier when he only knew, had the knowledge of it. When it was a collection of facts rather than reality. A piece of himself he didn't have to access, a scar of memories long forgotten. "It's...harder when I can see it."

Jade nodded, her hair brushing against him. "It's always harder when you can see it."

He was still small, in his mind, and endlessly shattering at the news that his life had fallen apart. If it was ever whole to begin with. That quiet ache in his chest had been ripped open and was now bleeding everywhere, openly, staining his skin with memories he could never unlive. Vivid shots of a life full of scars and pain, the broken pieces of himself he'd lost along the road to where he was.

"I wish I didn't remember it."

Her breath was quiet, as was her nod. "Try thinking of something else, then."

That was hard to do when his chest was aching and his eyes kept spilling tears. But he nodded anyway, forcing out shaky words from his broken chest. "Did you...find anything?"

Jade shook her head. "Not here, no."

His eyes were red and throbbed, and yet he rubbed them more, as if somehow it would allow him to unsee what he had. She smiled at him, in that simple way she always did. Like there was nothing to it but a gentle invitation for him to do the same. Yet his always came out lopsided, or hiding tears, or completely false.

Still, as much as it hurt, he tried to imitate hers. Tried to push past everything that had been weighing him down like she did, a quiet declaration that things would be better.

"Aha, he smiles! Much better."

His eyes felt sad as he dropped his gaze, letting a quiet chuckle answer for him. "Do I really smile so little?"

He saw the answer even before he heard it in her chuckle, even quieter than his. "Yeah. Haven't really been smiling much for a couple of years now."

A couple...but it seemed like much longer. A lifetime, perhaps. He didn't know if he had ever truly smiled, without there being more to it.

His mind tugged him back to the past again, and memories that only made him ache more. A group he'd cared for; gotten too close to. The way everything darkened after they were gone, like a curtain pulled over the sun. A couple years...or a lot more.

"It isn't your fault," Jade continued quietly. "You've not had much to smile about."

The thought wasn't very reassuring. If anything, it made the ache grow even more. With his memory open as it was, he remembered his old team, years ago. The ones he'd grown close ...and lost. That had been when he'd really stopped smiling.

A part of him wondered what it would have been like. If he hadn't been Blaze. If he'd...found a way around it. There was always a way around it. He hadn't smiled as Blaze because he hadn't wanted to. He'd been trying to protect himself, throwing up a shield so no one could get to him. And he knew why.

It hurt, knowing there had been a way around it. But he had been too damaged to take it, and too shattered now to attempt it. Even now, he wanted to curl into a ball and hide before anything worse could happen. Before he could be hurt again, or hurt anyone else.

"Just let me know when you want to leave."

Hanging on to the distraction, he nodded, lifting his head and pushing himself to his feet. "Probably should." Taking a breath, he glanced around. "Should go find Joss, anyway."

Getting to her feet, Jade nodded, slipping into step beside him. "Alright. Lead the way then, Captain."

SARI

This hadn't gone to plan. As much as Ru'ach tried to convince her it was alright, the human part of her was terrified. Shedim really knew what he was doing.

When they had arrived at their destination, Shedim had already been there, invalidating everything Ru'ach said, even before they'd gotten there. It'd been their word against his, and he had been there longer.

Not by much, though. The fact that he was a child, still, was both to their advantage and disadvantage. Dragons were, by nature, wise. But they gave up a part of that when they chose to put away their powers and suppressed them.

Now, they were torn apart. Nothing had worked out right. And Sari had heard it in her mind, as clearly as if her friend was there. They had to leave.

Without Ru'ach.

How had it all gone so *wrong*?

The others needed the dragons, and she would bring them. More than ever now, they needed them. To train everyone. They needed *urgency*. But it had been hard to convince them to join her, and it had come at a cost. It had been a struggle just to get them to allow her in, and even then, Sari knew she was not entirely welcome. Many of the dragons had terrible scars from humans, mental as well as physical. And Shedim had been playing them much as he had the humans, eons before, this time to turn them against the humans. Convincing them they could take their land back. That they *deserved* it.

They were so much smarter than humans. But now, with the knowledge of their power – and both deities – obscured, it had been her word against his, and she had the misfortune of appearing Galdanian, whereas he was a small, helpless boy. Ru'ach had appealed to the dragons, and their sense of decency, but the guard on their minds was too strong, leaving them locked in a checkmate, until Shedim had grown impatient.

Sari looked around at the chaos around her, the result of their fight to convince the dragons. It was hard to imagine so much had happened because of a small child.

Sari was reminded of another day she was left gasping for breath, soaked through with water that bit at her skin, and wondering if she would make it out alive.

Tossed in a ship hold, where her mother had been murdered. Ru'ach was still weak then, not yet recovered from her long-ago battle with her brother. She saw the sorrow heavy in her friend's eyes.

And now?

Ru'ach wasn't here. Yes, things definitely did not go to plan.

Sari couldn't stop wringing her hands in her silky skirt, feeling as if the weight of the world had come crushing in and sucked her far, far down. The dragons *knew* now – Ru'ach had convinced them. But at what cost?

It was such a terribly, terribly risky move. She recalled the conversation with Zarafel, one Ru'ach had initiated, and his gruff take on the entire thing. Sari wished he'd come with, but he refused to leave his companion's side. And just as well. If nothing else, Lena needed the protection still, from herself, and her self-destructive thoughts.

The dragons cast wary glances at her, and yet still they followed, some too proud, some wary. Galdanians, of course, were the ones who had given so many of them scars, and these dragons did not possess the additional knowledge Ru'ach had first imparted on them.

As many times as Sari had heard it explained, both aloud and in her head, it was quite the concept to grasp. Long before humans were aware, Ru'ach and Shedim had taught the dragons how to be *more*. How to use the energies of their newly formed world for their good. She hadn't wished to summon the Essence, and trap it there with them. But the rift created from the siblings' fight separated them from the spirit realm forever.

She hadn't meant to destroy their home. No matter how she tried to convince them it was Shedim's doing, they wouldn't believe her. But they must have also been hesitant to believe Shedim, because they'd listened long enough to make him impatient. He'd corrupted the ones he was able, amassing a small army, but it had also served the purpose of swaying the ones he was unable to corrupt to Ru'ach's side.

Now Ru'ach was gone, though, 'talking' with her brother. Distracting him and holding him at bay until Sari and the dragons escaped, to join the others and protect them. That's what they were doing now: traveling back to the city.

She would follow shortly, Ru'ach had said, but the detachment still made Sari jump. She hadn't felt *calm* since Ru'ach had pulled away from her. A small, nagging part of her whispered what she never dared think: *What if she didn't come back?*

It was 'to avoid detection', she said. What if she was simply tired of Sari?

She scrubbed a hand over her face. Now she really knew she was tired, to be doubting her dearest friend. Human minds were such fickle things. Sari often wondered what it was like, not being burdened by them. In the spirit realm, where this had all began.

But what if she *didn't* return? Sari was forced to confront it, as a viable option. What if she decided that 'for their good', they would have to *stay* detached?

Sari knew, if she thought about it, that Ru'ach was still there. But it made her antsy, not being able to sense her friend. Wondering what she was doing, and why. She felt the bond still tethered at the back of her mind, if she looked hard enough. What if it just...snapped?

There were other dragons wishing to bond with her, but none of them would ever be the same as Ru'ach. Never.

Since they had followed Shedim out of Galdania, all the way out here, Ru'ach had grown increasingly more concerned. And her prediction had been right. Shedim *had* been amassing an army. One of dragons. And they hadn't manage to sway all of them to their side. Many, Shedim had managed to corrupt.

Sari marveled, at times, how strong their bond could remain even over such distances. She assumed it was the same with Shedim, though to a different extent. The dragons had been growing restless, according to Ru'ach, and it would only take Shedim a while of manipulation before he would turn those he had swayed to his side against the humans. By baring their souls in physical bodies, the dragons had left themselves vulnerable.

It was why, though no one thought about it, only the dragons in Calest ever truly went 'feral'. The Bane's return to Galdania would stir up an unrest unlike any the people had seen in years. The Empress, however, had to know how dire it was. She was the one to hold the secrets her people had no knowledge of. She had to know how dangerous it was, letting Shedim get so close to the other dragons.

And now, he was not working with her anymore. He would continue amassing an army and lay siege to Galdania, bit by agonizing bit, until nothing was left but ashes and rotting corpses.

Gods forbid Shedim ever discovered the truth about gifts. At the moment, he would only attack those he could reach, such as the Empress' Gifted, for her defiance of his beliefs.

Sari felt the sorrow from her friend. The desire to save her people, and the ache to give her life for theirs. She had to pull strongly on their bond, to discourage it. It was something she rarely did before.

"We need you," she murmured, overwhelmed by a moment of vulnerability. "*I* need you."

Ru'ach was pulling away, disentangling her control bit by bit, leaving Sari feeling more and more exposed. *No.*

"*I won't abandon you, she're.*" Whether from the past or present, Ru'ach's voice sought to soothe her. "*I promise.*"

And then, she was gone.

Sari had never felt more afraid in her life. Ru'ach was gone, and she...she was as terrified as a small child. She didn't dare test what abilities she still had, or attempt much without the familiar cloak of comfort she felt all along.

Was this what it was like, for them? She looked around at the wide, scared eyes of the Gifted who had been staying with the dragons, and knew that yes, this was exactly the truth. It terrified her.

What chance did they have, without Ru'ach? Everything seemed simple through her eyes, but like this... they were stumbling infants trying to carry swords.

A whimper fought to free itself from her throat, locked in there for so long it felt dry and dusty. Tears from the past burned her eyes with their phantom presence, her mind reshaping the room into the shifting, swaying hull of a ship.

Was she really so weak, still? Could she even bring herself to get to her knees, fight past the waves of nausea building in her not only from the tossing sea, but the events of what she'd seen?

There, next to her, lay a dragon. Bloodied, bruised, a faint purple glint in the light as her massive chest heaved, and hitched in a painful breath. Tired, once-brilliant eyes opened to meet Sari's, dull and quiet with an aching sorrow she couldn't understand.

Help me. It was said as a plea of her own, to this wondrous being, though a part of her knew the dragon should be the one saying it.

But dragons were so...powerful, and one like this, Sari knew must have a special level of power. Surely she could get them out of this.

But no, she looked...dejected. Eyes drifting down to the boards beneath them, she gave another chest-rattling sigh, seeming to sink further down. Her scaly face was pressed flat against the ship's deck, her posture proclaiming her defeat.

Sari didn't understand it, then. She didn't know just what the dragon had sacrificed.

By this point, Sari wasn't even certain of her age. Her link with Ru'ach kept her from aging, but she traveled around so frequently that few ever seemed to notice anything unusual. This jaunt with Damien and his Gifted was the longest she'd spent with a group, and aside from the few 'ageless' comments she seemed to get, no one found it strange.

Humans were odd, when it came to things they just wanted to accept. They made it make sense, in their minds, to justify any oddity.

Sari released a quiet, heavy laugh. Everything felt so much...dimmer without Ru'ach's presence constantly with her. She knew her dragon wasn't gone, simply away, but a small part of her still questioned it. *Is she? You had a fight. Perhaps she decided she was done with you.*

No. Sari couldn't accept that, no matter how much sense it made. Ru'ach wouldn't abandon her like that. She just wouldn't.

A small wave of peace washed over her, and faded, leaving only a lingering echo of what she never should have forgotten. She was Saria e'Denan and she would not be afraid. She had a companion stronger than fear, even if she herself was not that strong.

Still, the images lingered like spiderwebs clinging to the entrance of a room, cobs she had to brush away before they could stick and frighten her. She remembered her sister, taken years earlier. The fear she felt every day, soul-deep, any time a ship came into the harbor.

She should have known. She should have *known* they weren't just there to trade. But they had her father by the throat, and then he was dead, his blood spilling out across the white sands as the winds whipped furiously at her dress and hair, obscuring and drying her tears. She couldn't move, paralyzed as they dragged her away, and gutted her mother for good measure, leaving Sari wholly, undeniably alone.

Now, in the present, none of it had gone to plan. Sari had to draw in breath slowly to stop herself from hyperventilating, focused on the task at hand.

Going back. Without Ru'ach.

But that was alright, right? She *said* it would be alright. It had to be. Ru'ach would always be okay. There was nothing Shedim could do...

Unless Ru'ach did it to herself, voluntarily. But Sari couldn't believe that Ru'ach would abandon her people like that.

For the moment, she needed to get the dragons *away*, and quickly. The battle had gone terribly, and she felt the fury bristling through the barely amicable beasts, the jagged scars more prominent in the light,

93

their flashing teeth baring sharp snarls at the sky. At the one who had betrayed them, not just once, but twice.

Sari knew of the stories, more than any human ever did. How Shedim had tried everything to destroy what Ru'ach cared for, out of revenge. She had given him a second chance, and it had backfired. Some of the dragons still did not look on her kindly for that.

But all that seemed to be forgotten, for the moment, the grave wrong of what Shedim had done far outweighing any hesitance from the dragons. In a way, Shedim had helped them, though she doubted that to have been his plan.

Leaving Ru'ach had been the hardest part. Sari imagined Zarafel here, lips bared in an ugly, scarred snarl as he fought for his people. She remembered before, through Ru'ach's memories, the impetuous and passionate youth he'd been.

Dragons lived for centuries. A human's life was a mere breath to them, a blink of their ageless eyes. Only Ru'ach outlived them, and this was probably what garnered their respect of her.

Dragons surrounded Sari, of all colors and sizes. Waiting for her to lead them away. For a moment, she felt frozen, plagued with fears that were usually gentled by Ru'ach, or swept away altogether. Entirely irrational fears, the likes of which she hadn't felt in a long time.

"But what if I hit my head and drown in the tub, Papa?"

Her eyes had been so solemn, dark and serious as she looked up at her papa, everything about him aged in grey and wisdom. He had laughed, but it was a gentle sound, the kind used to frighten away monsters under her bed. He rested his large hand on her small head, and she waited.

"I'll be with you," he murmured, as way of explanation.

And then, she had understood. She would not fall because her papa was there. He would protect her.

Not anymore.

And now, with Ru'ach gone, too, would she fall apart? Was she little more than a doll stitched from torn rags, fraying, torn at the seams and held together only by a loving hand? Perhaps without Ru'ach's presence, she would be nothing, a limp and broken shred of cloth, the stuffing ripped from her.

Sari's dreams were morbid, without Ru'ach. She remembered very little from her life before, save what Ru'ach told her. It might have been a year, or a century.

Would she lose this now, too?

It didn't matter, she decided as she faced the waiting dragons. They had to warn the others, now, and prepare for the upcoming battle ahead.

Even with a note, though, Sari didn't think any sort of warning would prepare them for this.

VI

KAIDEN

Spending so long in the past had rubbed him raw, like sandpaper scraped too long across his soul. Now that he was out, the ache had given way to irritation, mostly at himself.

"Did you find anything?"

He shouldn't have frowned at Joss, but he couldn't help it. He felt something pricking at him that he couldn't deny, the fire flickering under his bones.

"No."

Joss gave him a look, huffing through her nose. "Touchy. I was fine, thank you." She turned away, then stood up, walking away. "I'm going to go look for food."

"Don't steal it," he muttered, even as she made a face at him.

In truth, though everyone he knew would disapprove of his behavior, and he *had* been rather rude, he just wanted to be alone. Expelling a long breath, he dropped back against the stone wall in the alley Joss had met him in, feeling the roughness scrape against his uneven skin.

"So that's it. That was all...for nothing. There's no information about them, anywhere."

Though he knew he was being dramatic, at the moment, it didn't matter. Jade, however, cocked an eyebrow at him in that way she seemed so fond of, as if everything that just came out of his mouth was stupid.

Maybe it was.

"You really are just wanting to be negative today, aren't you? Alright, I can play along." She made her voice squeaky and dejected, which he hoped wasn't an imitation of him. "Woe is me! We have checked one location and it's obvious there is absolutely no evidence anywhere on the planet with their location!" She made a face, her voice normal again. "I'll get right on finding that hermit cave."

Her sarcasm didn't help his mood, nor did her joke. She'd teased him once before, when he hadn't wanted to follow through with this, that he could run away instead and live alone in the mountains somewhere. Not that it was actually an option. Rubbing his face to disguise a frown, he muttered his response. "Not that I have any *idea* where it is."

"Lucky for you," came Jade's unbothered reply, "I'm sitting right here - an entire depository of knowledge, quite a bit of it about you, your past and Damien. Super convenient, right? Even more convenient, this depository of knowledge only has to be asked and she'll give you everything you want to know, free of charge." With a teasing grin, she cupped her hands under her chin, the picture of innocence again. "Isn't that nice of her?"

His shoulders fell of their own accord, though whether they were releasing or bending under the weight of a burden, he wasn't sure. His answer came out too quiet, following a sigh. "Yeah. I forgot."

And he had, of course. For as much as Jade told him about himself, things still slipped away far too easily. Some days he was sure he had forgotten his own name for a moment, a different one flitting through his mind and memories. He shook it aside the best he could, focusing on Jade's answering chuckle.

"It's a good thing I am annoyingly persistent in reminding you then, huh?"

Reluctantly, he nodded, adding under his breath, "Not that it seems to do much good."

"Come on then, Grumpy." Hopping to her feet, Jade held out her hand. "I'll show you where, as long as you promise to stop beating yourself up over forgetting my usefulness. I happen to be very forgettable, you know."

To hide his frown, he scrubbed his palms over his face again. "Fine."

"Hmm." Tapping her lips with her free hand, Jade studied him. "That doesn't seem very convincing. I am still getting a distinctly grumpy-at-self vibe from you."

He really hated how right she was sometimes. It was easier to hide those things, or pretend they didn't exist. It was easier to frown when no one else was around – easier to deal with what he'd done.

"The deal is simple," Jade declared, as if they had decided on a plan that she was now confirming. "I will take you to learn about your siblings as long as you stop thinking about yourself so much. That includes self-incriminating thoughts." Lightly, she nudged his shoulder with her fist. "If it helps, you can think about me and how utterly strange I am. I'm told that's a topic that can take days to work out."

97

Self-incriminating. She said it like a joke, or something he should brush aside, but he couldn't. He wouldn't. He couldn't stop thinking 'self-incriminating' thoughts because they were true, and deserved. His mind made sure to remind him of that.

Still, he did his best to tease back, even as her first words simply drew him back into that same frame of mind, stealing the conviction from his voice. "You make me sound like I'm selfish and self-absorbed."

Too quiet. It came out as a question, disguised as a joke. Before she could comment on it, or he could dwell too long on it, he glanced up at her, summoning a half-smile. "But I guess that works."

If Jade noticed the shift, she didn't comment on it, continuing on in her matter-of-fact, teasing way. "Hey now, drowning in thoughts about how bad you are can be just as rotten as self-righteousness, and totally as damaging. As your best friend, it's important I help you kick these habits as quickly as possible." Her tone light again, she shrugged, returning his smile with a grin. "I thought so. Thinking about my weirdness works every time."

In answer, he gave her another half smile, choosing to go the same route she had. "It does give me a lot to think about."

Whether or not she caught the note of teasing, she chuckled. "Well, you can focus on that if you feel like it and it helps. My strange qualities run deep." With a wink, she motioned away from the path. "This way."

Though he followed her in silence, his one-sided smile grew. *It might.*

But first, he would have to find Joss. And possibly bail her out from another theft.

BASIL

Basil had never seen so many dragons in his life.

They *filled* the skies. It was as if all the birds in the world had decided to migrate at the same time. All sizes, all colors. Descending outside of their city.

And among them, in the front, was Sari. Her face looked ragged, from lack of sleep, perhaps, and the front of her deep purple dress was torn. Though there was something off about her eyes, she smiled anyway, and dipped the same graceful nod that Basil remembered.

Basil had never liked Damien much. Olive had said they should respect him, since he saved them, but he could tell she didn't much admire him, either.

Sari, however...he was drawn to something about her. The age on her face seemed to blur in his mind, for a moment seeming no different than the first day he'd met her.

It was the best day of his life. Or the beginning of a better one.

He remembered it all with too much clarity. How close he'd come to getting them both killed. How willing Olive had been to step in and how frozen his tongue felt, unwilling to bear any of the bravery he so wished to take up. It was his excuse, and his greatest shame. One he let follow him even now, as he failed to do anything of value.

There was a reason Damien had chosen Olive. It was Basil's theory that he wouldn't have been chosen at all, if it wasn't for her. Without a word, it was clear in her sharp eyes that if Damien wanted her, he'd have to bring Basil, too.

Extra weight. Useless hands.

He'd *tried* to fight. He'd tried to find some other application for his gift, but there were none to be had. He could dim Blaze's fire, much to his disapproval. He could make his hands glow, and delight Fern, who was hardly into her formative years at that point. But that was about it.

Fern stood by his side, most of the redness gone from her eyes. They had talked for a long time, and walked around, until Qui brought him the news. Fern craned her head up at the sky, rubbing her nose and squeezing his hand tighter.

He saw the uncertainty in her eyes, still, and the way she bit her lip every so often to keep it from wavering. He knew how hard it was for her, pretending to be normal. Letting that ache back in, as she subtly leaned into him and cuddled Nitl closer to her.

Sari was back, and Basil didn't know what to think of that. There was something weary to her eyes, so unlike her usual expression. He could only recall two other times he'd seen her look like that. And neither of them had been good.

Basil knew, even if the others didn't, that Sari blamed herself for the deaths. For Gigi and the others, for bringing them into it. She understood the burden of bearing guilt that shouldn't have been yours, but was close enough that your instinct was just to shoulder it, before it fell on someone else.

Their dragons were near the front, watching the newcomers with glittering eyes that Basil couldn't interpret. Why were there so many dragons?

Sari didn't offer explanations, and somehow, none were asked of her. She simply held a hand in the air, as she often did, and people fell silent and let her walk away.

Raoul stood to meet her, his feet spread in a wide, confident stance, Lena frowning by his side. She looked regal in her ruby dress, swept over one shoulder and draping nearly to the ground, and the effortless elegance draped over her like the finest cloak, enhanced by the glint of the jewels by her ears and neck. She looked every bit a ruler, with Zarafel standing guard by her, and Dez on her shoulder. Her two white knights.

Their dragons, Basil realized, had been waiting for this. Whether they could smell the other dragons or perhaps just sense them, here they were. Perell stood at attention, his golden head raised to view the newcomers. Qui hummed by him knowingly, silver wings displacing the air beside them.

And standing close to Sari were... *Gifted*. The kind that inspired a sense of awe in Basil, who looked every bit the heroes they were expected to be. She'd even managed to gather Jayn and his people, bringing along those who were willing and ready to learn.

Along with everything else, though, she also brought grave news.

Ru'ach could no longer protect them. Sari kept her eyes lowered for longer than necessary, something flickering in her eyes as she spoke. She took a breath, shoulders pulled back, eyes lifting as some of the old light in her face returned.

Shedim had failed to sway the dragons to his side. This should have been a cause for victory. Instead, Sari looked distressed, beneath everything.

"There are still dragons coming, to attack." Sari averted her eyes. "Though they haven't intentionally turned against us, they have been...corrupted, by the Bane."

Basil's veins went cold. *Corrupted*, like the dragons in Calest. He'd been told their dragons were immune, by blocking off that access, but he had still seen the damage a corrupted dragon could do.

And now there was an army of them, coming to attack.

It made the mass of dragons in front of them still seem like too few. People gaped from the streets, and out of windows, children pausing in their play to crane their heads up at the mighty beasts. Murmurs went through the crowds at her words, uncertainty in the air. The dragons Sari had with her clearly weren't corrupted, but what did that mean?

"Some of the dragons...grew lenient while they were away. The Bane's proximity made it far easier for it to corrupt them, despite their best efforts." Sari seemed reluctant to continue. "Ru'ach created a distraction, for the rest to get away. She is doing her best to hold back the Bane, but...he has many dragons under his control, too. With Ru'ach preoccupied, he will send the corrupted ones here, to attack."

100

Her eyes turned solemn as they swept over everyone. "We must prepare to defend this place. The Gifted who stayed with the dragons will stand with you, and train those they can to hone their gifts." Looking like she might say more, she hesitated, though it was gone after a moment.

Though the people still looked unsure, in the presence of so many dragons and in light of such unsettling news, they slowly nodded. The dragons, however reluctantly, had also come to aid them in furthering those with Gifts. Though Sari looked as if she wished to say more, she didn't seem to dare, with so many eyes on her.

Basil could tell Sari wasn't telling the full truth, though. She kept her eyes averted a moment too long before she continued. "Even those of you without gifts may have a chance to help. Dragons carry with them a reserve of the Essence, which flows through all things. With this many of them in one place, it may stir up gifts where there were none before."

Basil could tell Sari was lying, but what could he say? Did he confront someone he'd admired for most of his life and tell her she wasn't being truthful?

But *what* was she hiding, and *why*? He waited until she finished giving instructions and let Raoul take charge of the situation, leaving Fern to fawn over the many dragons as he followed Sari away from the crowds.

"Why so...many?"

She raised a perfectly arched brow. "Can you really have too many dragons?"

He thought she was joking. It turned out, she wasn't.

"You're keeping something from them."

A flash of something almost like guilt filled her eyes – an unusual look for Sari. "From us," he clarified, pressing the words just slightly. He was beginning to have enough of all the secrets.

"They cannot know," she murmured, gaze drifting away. "Not yet."

Her uncertainty was worrying, her hand nearly fidgeting with the sleeve of her dress before she forced it to stop, giving him a smile. Her calm seemed shattered, not a piece of it in the same place as usual.

"I need to," he surprised himself by saying, his tone the even and confident one. Sari nodded, nearly looking worried before she brushed it aside.

"Let us find your sister."

Though Basil was surprised, he went along with her anyway, his confusion growing when Sari gathered each of his available team members in turn – save for Lena and Chan – and ushered them somewhere far from listening ears.

Olive looked nearly annoyed at the interruption – or from the secrets she surely knew were being held from her. Fern was cuddling an armful of kit dragons, asking timidly if they could come along and lighting up with joy when Sari allowed it. Dailen, too, was with all of the dragons, seeming practically in heaven until Sari pulled him away.

They all waited, Sari's nervousness seeming to infect all of them as she shifted on her feet, watching them.

"All humans have the potential for Gifts," she said simply, "like anyone might learn to play an instrument or use a sword with fluid grace. It is simply the ones in which talent has already been awakened that you refer to as 'Gifted'."

Dailen dropped the stone he'd been playing with, the only sound from all of them. Basil was sure his mouth must be hanging open, even as he touched his lips and found it wasn't. Olive looked more annoyed, if that was possible, the lines of her shoulders hard and stiff as she eyed Sari. Fern cocked her head, confused. Dailen fumbled with the stone and dropped it again, nervous and flustered.

"You mean to say," Olive eventually said, to most of their surprise, "that *any* of the people in this city could develop Gifts? And you kept this information from them?"

He was surprised at how much bitterness touched her tone, as much as he couldn't blame her for it. He knew how furious his twin had been when their parents attempted to convince her her gift wasn't real, to keep her safe. Unfortunately for them, Olive was too stubborn to let that happen, and promptly learned to strengthen her gift until she was able to put on a display they couldn't ignore. Basil had just stifled his light, or hid his hands in his pockets if they were nearby. He didn't want them worrying more than they already did, especially knowing how valid their concerns were. As careful as Olive was, and as furious that they didn't trust her, there was always a chance that someone might notice, and then...

Olive was waving her hand in a quiet rant, silently seething beneath it all as she finished. "*Why?*"

Sari looked far too nervous to be dealing with an irate Olive, without either of their usual calm. "It *can't* slip out, *she're*. If the Bane were to find out..." She wrung her hands in front of her, face crumpling in worry for a moment. "Right now, it is believed that some humans are just...born with gifts, and others are not. So far, this has kept the Bane from simply laying waste to everything it sees. It only attacks those with gifts. That gives us a severe advantage, and an opportunity to protect those without them." She didn't seem able to dismiss the worry, or even wish to, her forehead creased in distress. "Imagine attempting to keep a secret that only one person in the entire world does not know. The chances of it slipping out...it was too great." Her voice grew hushed, defeated, as if she knew Olive was right, but tried anyway. Her gaze lowered. "I am sorry. I did not know another way."

Olive was unsettlingly quiet, eyeing her with arms folded. "What's done is done," she said eventually, words clipped to the shortest beats possible. "Don't expect me to keep any more secrets that might save lives."

Sari pulled in a slow, unsteady breath as Olive started to leave. "It would have been too much, all at once." Her tone was more pleading than anything, as if asking Olive to agree with her. "The dragons, the Bane..."

"Perhaps." Olive paused, a hand on the nearest building as she looked back at Sari. For a moment, her eyes lost some of their hardness, replaced with a pinch in her brow from Sari's posture. Slowly, she lowered her tone, until it was less accusing. "If you don't know how best to do something, ask. I recall someone rather wise telling me that more than once." Something different passed through her eyes for a moment before she continued walking. "Come find me later. We'll work it out."

Sari drew herself up at Olive's words, brushing stray dark hairs from her face. The confused hope on her face was something Basil didn't think he'd ever seen before. It was replaced by a light of gratitude, gently smoothing the lines in her face until she nearly looked normal.

"I am sorry. I...do not quite feel myself." She looked away, not seeming to want to meet their eyes. "It was a long journey. I think I shall retire to a room, until I feel better."

With that, she turned to walk away, leaving Basil reeling from all the information. He didn't even need proof *or* his lie-detecting skills to know she wasn't lying. It soured in his gut the way the truth always did when you didn't wish to face it. Her news only served to confirm, with a heavy relief and bitterness, what he'd always known. He wasn't *special*. He wasn't powerful. He'd just, by accident, stumbled upon something anyone else might easily find with some small measure of skill. Luck, even.

It was a horrid way to think of it. But it didn't stop his insides from twisting with tension at the thought.

This was not a battle they would win easily. It was one they must keep secret. An entire city full of exiles, keeping a secret that could destroy the world. It was a very, very risky move.

Dailen, too, seemed caught in a mix of brooding and contemplation over the news. On one hand, Basil knew he was overjoyed to see all the dragons – Basil had spoken with the boy more than any of the others had, feeling a kindredness with him that he couldn't with any of the others, least of all his sister. But he also saw the depths of the sadness and the twisted ache on his face, the questions plaguing and haunting his mind. *"Why?"*

Why?

And he knew, even without saying, that Sari wouldn't be able to answer it. That his questions were, indeed, unknowable.

Why would have to wait until Ru'ach arrived. And none of them knew when that would be.

Ru'ach knew the secret. Despite Sari's explanation that the dragons could not yet unmask themselves, she claimed that *any* of them could have and use Gifts.

It was a matter of belief, when it came down to it.

Though Basil didn't doubt the validity of her statement, he felt for all of those it slighted. The ones like him who would take it the same way as, if he would simply take control and *try*, he could be as good as Olive.

It comes with practice, she had told him time and again, always in that slightly admonishing big-sister tone. Never mind that he was older by a manner of minutes.

It still left him reeling. *Anyone could use Gifts.*

Basil couldn't even remember when or why his gift manifested. Or, he did, and felt childish for it. The first night that Olive had pushed him beneath the cupboard in the stairs, voice laced with dangerous urgency, and told him to stay very, very quiet. She was supposed to stay, too, but Olive never listened when danger was involved.

He felt afraid without her there, in the dark and alone with his thoughts. And then it happened. A brief flicker of light, seemingly from nowhere but his own hands.

Olive explained hers as simply as selecting a tool from her arsenal. As he thought about it, Olive had always had an uncanny knack for finding berries and other things where he had looked, and not found any. They liked her.

Basil's gift was more a manifestation of his fear, though Olive assured him that it was helpful when they needed light and she didn't want the smoke from a fire. She'd asked if he could make it warmer,

104

long ago, but he didn't...know, and with that hesitation, it only flickered and dimmed.

Chan wished for a storm, and it had come. Fern grew up surrounded by flowers she seemed able to conjure on her own after her family's death. A reminder of them, she said. They'd sprung up on the graves of her parents and her siblings, faster than should have been possible. According to Chan, Damien hadn't planned to bother with her, until he pointed that out.

And Dailen...no one truly knew what had happened with him, and no one would say if they did. Though Basil wondered if Lena's gift had come about in a similar way, he didn't dare ask.

Why was it, then, that so few had gifts? Sari explained it as a balance, between ability and belief. As children, imagination ran rampant, but unfocused, and their minds couldn't fully grasp the scope that things were not only possible, but could be honed. Children who claimed to dance with fairies and brought home unusually bright flowers in a dry season were far more likely to manifest gifts. It was yet another reason why so few of the Uppers seemed to possess them, or not that they knew. The Empress, by instilling fear in everything, inadvertently tightened the chokehold around the few who did possess the skill.

Basil knew Kaiden would never tell, but he was also aware that Kaiden had held his gift longer than any of them. He wondered what it had been like, in his childhood. What fancies made him dream of being able to control fire, or what horrors.

Despite everyone being capable of them, however, Gifts could not be commanded to manifest. It worked better as a natural revelation, than a forced one.

Basil nearly tripped over a dragon's tail as he walked, stunned for a moment before he remembered just how many of them there were now. The dragon gave him a haughty look, but said nothing. From his shoulder, Qui rumbled an equally unpleasant reply, her feather-tipped tail curling protectively around Basil's neck. It tickled his skin, even as he wondered just where the tiny dragon had heard those words before, to be able to repeat them.

As always, whenever he was feeling uncertain, and overwhelmed, Basil sought out Olive. She usually spent her free time training, and today was no exception. Except this time...she wasn't alone.

Leaving a boy not much younger than them to watch and try to control the flickering cloud in his hand, Olive walked over to greet him. "I didn't expect to see you here," she said in amusement.

Basil looked around at the small gathering, all ages of people focused on different things. Some sat in meditative poses, eyes closed. Other stared in concentration at an outstretched palm or fist, as if willing something to happen. A few's eyes were lit with delight and a measure of tension as the spark of something unnatural flickered in their hand, or at their feet, or simply in front of them. One older woman watched the sky as if she expected something to fall in front of her at any moment.

At his expression, Olive raised an eyebrow. "They may not all have bought it, but," she nodded to the group, "there's always the few who are willing to believe even when it doesn't make much sense." Her eyes softened for a moment, as she looked back at him. "Give them a nudge, and they'll learn how to fly. Right?"

Instead of meeting her eyes, Basil kept his on the group. An elderly man with his hands held out as if in prayer opened his eyes, something old and warm filling them at the fire that glowed from his palms like embers.

"They may not be the strongest," Olive murmured, "but they have something much more valuable. Hope." She took in a breath. "With any luck, that will spread to the others, even before they learn the truth."

A crash behind them drew Olive's attention back, as she hastened to help a young girl who was soaked from the waist up.

Basil sat away from the group and stared at his hands, hesitantly conjuring up the glow in them, the light from within that seemed to make his hands look – well, ghostly. It was part of the reason he kept it hidden, though the unnaturalness of it was obscured when the glow was bright enough.

It was laughable to think he'd have ever been of any use in battle. He hated killing things, enough so that his hesitation had cost Fern more than one bout against sparring opponents, when Damien let them try their hand together. The most he'd ever managed to do was blind a man once, and that was purely an accident, triggered by the surprise he felt at their sudden appearance.

Even Fern could do more than he had, if she felt strongly enough. Olive showed her how to use her plants not only for tactical advantage, but to choke or at the very least, ensnare enemies. Basil's were only fooled once, and shielded their eyes past that point. Plus, it was hard not to accidentally blind his teammates in the process, too.

A small head poked over his shoulder. If he weren't used to such intrusions by this point, Basil might have jumped. The blond-haired boy looked down at his hands with round eyes, probably ready to run away shouting at the sight.

"Your hands glow!"

Basil looked up at the kid, hardly more than eight or nine, it seemed, and managed a small smile. "Yeah. They do."

The boy's eyes rounded further, lit by the glow like it mesmerized him. "Can I try?"

Basil was going to explain that wasn't how it worked, when the boy just reached down and plunged his hands into the white glow like scooping up water. He lifted them out with a laugh, and Basil could only stare, as the light trickled like water through the boy's fingers, dripping back into the rest of Basil's. The boy's face was giddy with glee.

"Whoa!" A little girl with similarly colored hair had joined them, soft mouth open with awe as she stared at her brother's glittering hand. "How'd you do that?"

The boy puffed out his chest proudly, though his foot kicked at the dirt in an almost shy way. "He showed me," He said, pointing at Basil.

The girl looked at the light and pouted. "Mei, you can't just take his powers!"

"I wasn't *taking* them. I was just using them!"

"But he needs them!" The pout from her lower lip extended further. "He can't fight bad people without it!"

Huffing a quiet laugh, Basil reached out to play with the boy's hair with faintly glowing fingers. "It's nothing special," he murmured, though a low, peaceful warmth settled in his chest at their words.

The little girl was hugging a kit dragon like one might hug a stuffed doll, though the poor thing kept squirming so not to poke her with its spikes. She didn't seem to mind. "What else can y' do?"

"*Nothing*," Basil wanted to say, but instead, he found his mouth lifting to the side. "I've been told I tell the best stories."

Both children plopped themselves in his lap unexpectedly, another breath whooshing from Basil's lungs as he resettled both himself and his thoughts. "Once upon a time, there was a very lovely little girl..."

The girl in question's ears got adorably pink as the story went on and he made it clear who he was talking about, describing everything about her like one might talk of a princess and hesitantly using his light to illustrate his points, or manipulating it to create outlines and images, though he wasn't very good at holding those. More children began to gather around, shyly, some enthusiastically, a chubby-cheeked toddler throwing her hands around his neck with a happy laugh.

"Can we do things like that, too?" one of the boys inquired at one point, his mouth open in awe.

Basil wondered how many times these children had been told their dreams were possible. That they really *could* fly and harness clouds into the shapes of bunny rabbits and make flowers grow that were colored like rainbows, if they wished. Sari said they didn't have enough control or development to cause mischief, so why shouldn't he tell them?

At his nod, the awe became more prominent, spreading in a wave of excitement through them all. He added them to the story, cast as fairies in a world not much different from their own, and let them be the heroes for once. He found himself getting more ambitious with his gift, attempting things he never had before because it made the children smile. His light was bright and weird and flickered a lot, but they didn't seem to care, watching with rapt attention as he brought the story to life.

When he was finished, they ran away to tell their friends and families. Basil couldn't wipe the smile from his face, though he wondered if it was worth anything. Even if they did manage to control magic, what then? Surely children weren't what Sari had in mind for her grand army.

But maybe, just maybe, they could be the seed of hope that would slowly but surely spread amongst the others, encouraging those who might have otherwise thought it possible. Children had such simple thoughts and ways of viewing the world – perhaps they could explain, to their loved ones, what grownups would only botch with non-fanciful terms and great spoonfuls of practicality. Too old. Too young. Too busy. Too weak. *Too...*

It hit Basil like something had struck the knot in his chest, the one he had refused to acknowledge for too long. Too what? He was too *what*?

Too...scared. He didn't *want* to see what potential his gift had. He didn't want it to be used for harm. Better to leave it worthless, and hidden, aching inside him like a dream he'd never quite reach.

What did he want to do? It seemed silly to put it in words, even though he'd seen the kids' eyes widen in awe at the effect of his storytelling. He just wanted to delight people. Put a smile on their faces.

And that's when he realized what his role could be. Olive had mentioned that she was only working with the ones who had already approached her. But what about the ones that were still hesitant? The ones who had that hope, deep down, but had smothered it somewhere in their lifetime, putting aside their dreams in the face of what the world had thrown at them?

Basil didn't often think Olive and he were similar at all, despite being twins, but she must have been watching him, for she came over once she'd dismissed the Gifted-in-training to go get food, bringing up the same idea he'd had. Even before she finished, he was nodding his head in agreement. She looked away, the first spark of uncertainty crossing her face.

"I...wouldn't know how to find those, though. I'm happy to help them, once they're ready." Olive had always seemed to have a better understanding of gifts in general than most, Basil mused. "But I only helped these ones because they asked." She paused. "Do you think you could...find more...?"

He rarely heard such hesitation in her tone. Olive was such a go-getter, a get up and do it sort of person, that she rarely stopped to look at peoples' emotions, and he knew it did bother her sometimes. He knew she in part blamed herself for all the things she never noticed with Kaiden, even if she'd never say it. She knew, just as Talon had, what Kaiden's injuries had been, and what they were from, but she never said a word. It wasn't her secret to tell, she said.

And now, this was out of her comfort zone. So she was asking Basil. For once, he felt a thrill of excitement. He could *help*.

It would be a large task. With so many people...Olive suggested he focus on the ones who expressed direct interest in channeling gifts. If he could discover what was holding them back, she said, Olive would assess the potential of those interested – and at times, those who weren't. She had a knack, not unlike Damien's, of spotting talent in people. She had never pushed him in his, perhaps because of his hesitation.

No more. Today, he would finally do something.

VII

KAIDEN

Joss wasn't as hard to find as Kaiden might have imagined. He knew, despite his warning, exactly where she would be, and the cry of *"Thief!"* ringing through the street seemed more like a beacon to guide him than a potential mistake.

While he looked around for where she might have gone, something small slipped up beside him, grudgingly handing him a roll. "We should get out of here."

Holding back a sigh, Kaiden lifted Joss into his arms, handing it back. The stubbornness gave way to surprise, just for a moment, before she pressed her face against him, frowning.

"You like to make things difficult for me, huh?" he said under his breath as he ducked into a maze of alleys so they weren't seen.

"Says the man who's always too *nice* in a country where bein' that only gets you robbed or killed," she muttered back.

Instead of answering, Kaiden held her closer, pretending it was to keep her hidden as he slipped out of the town. He took a brief amount of comfort in imagining she was someone else, and he hadn't failed after all.

Joss had stayed silent after that, squirming only once they were out to be let down, and frowning even as she held his hand, "so you don't fall into a creek or somethin'."

"I know where I'm going better than you do."

She tipped an eyebrow up at him, skeptically. "And yet you *still* look like you don't even know what the ground is."

Free from the danger of others' eyes, Ril flew out from her bag with what sounded like a huff, nestling on his shoulder. Kaiden managed a faint smile.

"I used to live here. A long time ago."

Joss eyed his dragon like she might spit fire at her, even though kit dragons didn't have that ability anymore. "Where're we goin', anyway?" she asked instead.

Kaiden glanced briefly at Jade and took in a breath, even as the answer touched his lips. The name of their destination rang through his mind without anyone saying it. Flashes of memory tingled his skin as he took it in, and remembered. That other name, the one he'd tried to forget. Memories that still made him flinch. A cold, stilling feeling creeping even through his thoughts.

He knew the place far too well. He just couldn't remember why.

They were going back to the Mountain.

<><><>

Kaiden and Jade stood together in an office, inside the Mountain, his skin racing with goosebumps. It hadn't taken them long to get there and he'd left Joss near the entrance, in case this went as badly as his last attempt to gather information. He could see everything too clearly, at the fringe of his memory, but didn't dare reach for it. He let the bit that he needed float to the front of his mind, guiding his steps.

Damien.

The name prickled his skin again. His feet moved of their own accord, bringing him softly over to a desk he knew he'd stood before many times. He could envision it all, if he wanted to.

"Oh."

Glancing over, Jade smiled a bit at him, though he wondered what she was hiding behind it. He knew this office didn't hold good memories, and yet he sank down into the chair and cautiously opened a drawer, drawing out the papers inside.

"Probably is something in here somewhere," Jade said.

His finger ran lightly over the tabs numbering the pages, scanning the names on them. A small black journal beneath it all caught his attention, and his breath. "Yeah. Probably."

While Jade glanced a few of the other pages over, he reached for the journal. Though something told him he didn't want to read it, *everything* about this room was already sending warning vibes to his mind. And he had to know where his siblings were, even if he hated it.

Shoulders tensed, he ran his thumb over the pages and cracked open the journal.

"Dyran," the header read, centered on the page.

This was what he was looking for. But instead of feeling triumphant, his stomach dropped like a hot stone, sinking further as he noted the name before it. The date dotting the top of the page in bold, neat letters. Damien's handwriting was casual, but professional, a brief log of facts presented as if the entire thing was a story.

"The experiment went better than expected."

He nearly stopped right there, one part of him shutting the journal and hiding it away while the other continued to stare at the words until they burned into his mind. Until the details told him everything he needed to see.

This wasn't about his siblings, after all.

His breath caught as he continued reading, feeling everything else fade around him as he did. Stomach turning, his muscles tightened until his fingers left marks on the pages. But he couldn't tear himself away.

"Though I knew from the beginning that the boy was resilient, it was much more of a delight to see everything play out before me. Even when he could barely stand, he would still give so much for his siblings, just to spare them pain.

It makes him a perfect candidate for this plan."

The room spun, tilting him before it finally deposited him upright again, a sick feeling knocked loose in his stomach.

"As for the girl: though I cannot say I was surprised by the results, I was nonetheless disappointed that my theory was proven true. I had hoped the strength her brother possesses might have run through her veins as well."

Something caught in his throat that he couldn't dislodge. The edges of memories crept through his thoughts, whispering facts about his sister against his skin until it prickled, a sense of dread flooding through him.

"The girl lacks his resilience. Perhaps if she tried harder, she could have succeeded. At this point, though, I am not sure she shall ever reach that potential again, or anything near it. The ordeal has broken her spirit, rather than strengthened it. In regards to her abilities, she is all but worthless to me."

His fingers had gone white. As he tried to process what he was reading and line it up with what he saw in his head, his hands shook. A mournful sound attempted to escape his lips, but was locked in his throat.

Damien had done this. Damien had hurt her.

"In a way, however, I have already prepared for this situation. Though her gifts may never be useful on the level I desire, she still holds a strong attachment for her brother. Perhaps with similar, but less intense persuasion, I may yet unlock the secret to her abilities.

"If nothing else, she will make wonderful leverage against the boy. She is so fragile, at this point, that I do believe a simple threat against her may crush the spark of rebellion in his eyes before it even begins. His weakness lies in his attachment to her, and I intend to use that to my full advantage."

His whole body was shaking now, eyes closing in an attempt to block out the flood of red filling his vision and the cries filtering through it. Whitened knuckles gripped the pages, inches away from tearing them out. He wanted to burn the whole book – the whole *room*. As he let it all sink in and then forced himself to read on, a sea of emotion flooded his body, stirring deeper and deeper in him in a clash of rage and grief.

Eventually, one won out. The memories grew louder, rising shouts and echoing pains searing through him. For a moment, he couldn't breathe, his lungs seemingly on fire for what little pulling in oxygen did for them. He remembered the pain, a muddling in his head and several voices he couldn't place, some taunting, some pleading. He remembered thinking he was dying, crumpling under a rain of it with the thought that he wouldn't be able to get back to them. The blind terror and the relentless, crushing blows, shoving him down until he couldn't get back up.

Tears still managed to escape in an angry sort of sob once he was finished reading. Thinking back on what Jade had explained to him didn't help, either. She'd said he had *protected* them. This wasn't protecting anyone. Had anything like this happened to his other siblings, too? Or just Kinny?

The journal slipped from his hands, falling open on the floor as he curled his arms over his head in a desperate attempt to protect himself. Hunched over so his face was mostly hidden, he just barely saw Jade bend to pick up the journal. Once she was done reading the entry, she rested a hand on his shoulder.

"You didn't...tell me about...that," he choked out, feeling the words burn his throat.

"I didn't know, Butterfly." Quietly, Jade moved closer and settled her other hand on the back of his head, sitting on the desk. "I'm not all knowing. I'm sorry."

"I know." He choked on a sob, desperate and strangled in his chest. "I didn't know..." Anguish twisted in his chest, making his lips tremble. He pressed them tightly together, biting down when that didn't work and flinching at the coppery tang of blood flooding his mouth.

Jade sank down so she was crouched by the chair, reaching up to squeeze his arm lightly. "I know. But he's gone now. The horror is over.

Now you're looking for the rest of your family, so you can be reunited with them. This is a new chapter."

Despite the gentleness to her tone, he couldn't stop the cry that broke from his throat, tears stinging his eyes as they fell.

I failed. It rang in his head, over and over, a dull, echoing chime by this point. So many times, in so many ways. He'd failed his sister, failed his siblings...failed himself.

He couldn't help it. The emotion had built up too strongly, and there was no one around to hear it. It escaped in harsh, gasping bursts, a mixture of anguish fueled by anger and devastation. Tears felt like fire on his cheeks, burning, stealing his breath before it even filled his lungs. He had sworn he would protect her, and he'd failed. *Miserably.* He'd failed so miserably, he had become the cause of her hurt.

And he'd never even known. Not to this extent. He wouldn't have been able to live with that. He would have found some way to fix it. He would have...

He didn't know what he would have done. But he for sure wouldn't have put up with everything Damien put them through. He would have found some way around it. Whatever it took.

Instead, Kinny was now dead, and he was no closer to finding his other siblings. This wasn't how it was supposed to go. Not at all.

Though it felt like it would never end, and the ache still remained in his chest, eventually his tears ran out, and his lungs felt too tired to do more than shudder. Wiping a shaking hand over the moisture lingering on his cheeks, he slowly unfolded himself to sit up straighter, staring at the wall.

Smiling slightly, Jade reached up to ruffle his hair. He tried to return the look, but his mouth didn't want to cooperate very well. Letting his gaze shift around them, he remembered where they were, and how little use any of that had been.

At least I know, now. But was that really a good thing? It still twisted his insides at the mere thought. Damien had used *him* against his sister, and he hadn't even been aware enough to protect her. Damien had broken her, as he'd tried to break Kaiden. And he hadn't been able to do a thing about it.

Smiling, Jade followed his gaze. "Don't worry. I'll help you with it."

"Thanks." The word scratched his throat, raw and aching from his meltdown. A shaky sigh broke from him as he glanced at the pile he'd been going through. "Hopefully there's something...in here."

"We'll find something," Jade said, picking up a stack of papers.

To try to steady himself, Kaiden pulled in a quiet breath, willing it not to make his stomach turn again. "Okay," he managed quietly.

He didn't want to keep looking through things, aware now as he was of how dangerous it might be. But he forced himself to look everything over carefully, jaw so tight it hurt as he scanned through other detailed reports and felt flickers of memories taunt him. Other 'tests' Damien had done, outlining the goal and every single reaction it created. They weren't all about him, either, though the ones about his friends were blessedly calmer, for the most part. Fern hadn't reacted well to mental manipulation, though that didn't surprise him. As Damien liked to reiterate, the tests were 'a necessary trial', meant to assess how well they could stand against mental attack – like from the Bane.

Though he hardly remembered it, for the most part, it still unnerved him how much Damien had seen. By whatever means, he had reports not only on any mission they had gone on, but what happened before and after them, whether or not it was of pertinence. He had detailed analyses of each of his teammates, most of which Kaiden set aside, unwilling to pry. He couldn't stop himself from staring, though, at the names that followed after the most familiar ones. Gissina Gilford. Lilianne Retters. Rafe Tomassi.

Gigi...

He still shouldn't have read it. But something told him that even if he did remember them again, he wouldn't know these things. And this was probably his only chance to learn more about them. He hoped his future self would be grateful for it.

If it didn't make his stomach twist up so much inside, he might have kept those papers. But the thought of owning anything Damien had written, and reliving any of that, made him more than nauseous. So he read through what he could, finding his mouth tipping up at times or his chest stinging despite his pale remembrance of them.

Reluctantly, and yet relievedly, he set the pile of papers aside. He could almost imagine them now, even if he couldn't recall the past. It was stubbornly trapped, or perhaps destroyed, blocked by the Bane with only dark memories when he searched. In the case of Gigi and the others, that meant reliving their deaths over and over, in shattered fragments that made it hard to breathe.

At least while he was wasting time, Jade was going through what was probably far more important papers, and not getting distracted by them. Eventually, as he started on a stack that had nothing to do with his team, she held out a page to him. "Here."

A tiny flare of hope sparked in his chest as he took it. He knew there had to be *some*thing in here. Right?

Luckily for them, Damien liked to brag, despite calling it mere 'observation' in his reports. The papers Jade had found apparently had to do with the threats Damien had made against him, regarding his siblings, and his reactions to them. And at the end: a description of where he was keeping them.

Kaiden felt his shoulders sag in relief, the corner of his mouth twitching toward a smile. Though he couldn't quite manage it, he hoped it showed enough in his eyes.

Jade grinned, her voice teasingly haughty. "I know, I know, I'm great."

The tiniest laugh shook his chest. Leaning back in his seat, he closed his eyes, soaking it all in. "Yeah. You are."

Joss

He told her not to wander far.

Of course, Joss didn't listen.

Honestly, did he *really* expect her to just stay put and not explore this hidden fortress of a mountain while he was off looking for his information? Though he'd informed her that there was nothing worth stealing here, that was practically an invitation of its own. As intimidating as the Mountain was, it was also awe-inspiring, and thus obviously filled with treasures he just didn't want her to have.

Turned out, though, he wasn't lying. Instead of being a mystical and wonder-filled trove, the place looked upended in most places, like someone had left in an awful hurry and swept everything into a disarray that only pretended to be clean. Maybe a wild animal had attacked while no one was around, stealing all the food. That would be a tragedy.

She'd seen Kaiden's eyes grow distant when they approached the mighty structure, as if in remembrance. The lines between his eyes had furrowed as he surveyed it, drawing in the barest of breaths before he'd started inside, holding her hand. She would have snatched it back, but she'd imagined he needed it, so she'd allowed it.

"Wait here," he'd said almost automatically, as if she was a creature to order around. The thought made Joss bristle. She was only a child by *his* country's standards, and would hardly be treated as one back home. They would have had her working with a crew by this point, rising up the ranks and earning her place there.

She couldn't just stay put. Something down here was calling to her, something she couldn't ignore.

Kaiden hadn't been lying either when he said it was big. Scarily big. Even with her navigational skills, the tunnels all looked too confusing and similar, winding their way into the dark like flickering snakes. And they echoed all the same.

She was in awe of the painted walls, though, the way it looked like blood dripping down in places, and liquid gold in others. Rivers of murky blue and a purple she imagined her eyes to be like, though she knew it was far prettier than she could ever look.

Joss couldn't stop staring in awe. How did such a wonderful place have such a boring name as 'The Mountain'?

"It used to be a volcano," Kaiden had murmured, only further improving her opinion of it. *"Don't go far. The tunnels can get very confusing."*

And then he'd turned to walk away. Joss had frowned at that. *"Why can't I come with you?"*

There had been a flicker of something in his eyes – guilt? Sorrow? – before he shook his head. *"Too dangerous."*

Well, *that* was the flimsiest excuse she'd ever heard of. Kaiden tried to get his dragon to stay with her. Joss fought against that.

Why had Kaiden ever left this place? Had he forgotten it? Where were all the people?

Joss thought it would be quite lovely to live here, in a cave of wonders that no one could find you in, where every new wall was a different kind of masterpiece. She wandered so far the colors began to run together, playing stories in her mind until she couldn't remember which way she'd come from, or if she'd even come at all. Perhaps she'd always been here, and never should leave.

The thought made her stomach both twist up and bubble with a laugh. She was lost. The great Jocelyn Rees, thief and law-escaper extraordinaire, outwitted by a mere cave.

Kaiden would come find her, right? He had to know this place, to get himself out. Surely he'd find her, too.

What *was* he doing here, anyway? Maybe she should get up and search for him.

But maybe not. He didn't seem like he wanted to be disturbed, most of the time. She might end up further lost if she did.

Her fingers slipped to the chain still around her neck, the trinket she'd stolen earlier. If it was worth anything, and she could find someone to sell it to, she could buy all the food she wanted when she got out.

But...this arrangement with Kaiden worked, for now. Just until she found a buyer for her necklace.

Content with her lostness for the moment, Joss dropped down against a sunset-colored wall and popped open her sack, taking out the food she'd snitched from Kaiden's bag. She hoped he wouldn't be upset with her for stealing it, though he hardly seemed to notice. And he ate so little on his own; *someone* had to keep it from going bad.

It still didn't satisfy her gnawing hunger, as much as she'd never acknowledge it. She devoured an apple and spent a long time licking her fingers, getting every little drop of juice from them. The rumble in her stomach only seemed to grow deeper at the presence of a little food, like the warmth reminded her of just how little of her actually felt full.

Huddling her knees to her chest, Joss made a face, doing her best to ignore the pangs in her gut. If Kaiden were here, she could swipe more food from him.

Lucky for her, Joss wasn't the sort to rely solely on anyone else. Though she probably should have saved it for later, she reached in again to retrieve a pastry she'd snatched from one of the market stalls, while Kaiden wasn't looking.

Once again, she contemplated just looking for him in the Mountain, but she didn't have the courage. *"Don't go far,"* he'd said, in a way that implied it was important.

Well, now she knew why.

Something rustled behind the rock near her. Joss eyed it warily, wondering what sort of monsters lurked in this cave. Maybe this was why Kaiden hadn't come back.

A tiny ball of wings and scales peeked out, big black eyes latching onto Joss' food. It let out a curious chirring noise, flapping at the air.

Joss wrinkled her nose at the tiny dragon's squeaky hello. She'd never much liked kit dragons. They were too...babyish. Especially this one.

Giving her its best approximation of a pout, the dragon shuffled closer, blinking beady eyes.

Kit dragons liked human food just a little too much, in her opinion. Weren't they supposed to eat bugs and stuff? Why couldn't they leave her in peace? Even on the Isles, they'd seemed determined to dog her, food or none. But never as much as here.

Fingers still sticky with pastry, Joss narrowed her eyes at it. She never cared for anything that tried to steal her food. There was no hunger in its eyes, only want, and Joss resented that. The same way an Upper would complain as to the quality of their food while disdainfully tossing the remains in the trash.

Joss hated when people wasted food. The only thing she hated more was anything trying to take hers away.

"Go away. Shoo." Joss flicked her hand toward the dragon with a warning gesture. Its ears drooped.

Oh no. She wasn't falling for *that* trick.

"Go pester someone else." Shoving a piece of the pastry in her mouth, she waved at the tunnel she'd come from. "Go find my bodyguard and bother him. He could use it."

The kit, undeterred, flitted forward with eager eyes, soon joined by several others. One kit dragon and then another peeked at her hesitantly, and then happily, flying up with joyous chirps to try settling on her head.

One solid look from her and they wilted, a small swat at the air enough to make them drop back down, eyes wide and hurt pools she was forced to look at. She was *not* letting a kit dragon have her food, of all creatures.

And she was not desperate enough to ask one for directions. She didn't want to end up even *more* lost.

Kit dragons were useless. They probably knew the way out of here, on their own, but asking them for directions was like asking an Upper's kid where she could find merillyium. The answer would be entirely too vague, nonexistent, or unaware of what she actually meant. Even though it was the entire reason they were filthy rich in the first place. Stupid Galdanians and their love for shiny things. Stupid greedy Uppers who bargained with them. Even those that knew how much suffering went into mining the material just didn't care. Joss considered herself very lucky to have ended up a thief, rather than trapped working in mines.

From the depths of Joss' bag, Ril pouted, assigned by Kaiden as what Joss hoped wasn't supposed to be her guard. That was his job, not his dragon's. Though she liked him, she never said she liked his dragons.

And given the little unhappy noises and restlessness of the kit dragon, Ril didn't like her either. She almost seemed in distress, and more frustrated for being so.

Joss settled down with her food to think, frowning at the kits as if it were their fault. If only they were intelligent enough to communicate, or Joss could trust them. Maybe they *could* have helped her out.

A tiny hopeful squeak echoed through the empty air. Ears pricked slightly, eyes lifted from their downcast angle to see her response, the tiniest of the kits looked at her with big, round eyes, the others following suit.

If dragons could pout, that was what these were doing. And Joss was not having any of it.

Go get your own food, she tried to convey in a scowl, tearing another chunk off with her teeth. The kit's ears drooped as it slowly turned away.

Before she had to resort to more forceful means, however, an unearthly shriek filled the tunnel.

A small black shadow swooped in to steal her food. On instinct, Joss smacked it, *hard.* The thing let out a pitiful shriek, flopping onto the ground on its back. Would nothing leave her alone here?

Joss eyed the creature cautiously as she tore another bite off her pastry. With wings in place of arms and a body that said starving whelp more than chubby baby, it looked too sinister to be a kit dragon. It dug ugly grey wings into the ground with taloned tips to support itself, a low hiss coming from its throat.

The kits scattered in fear, and Joss felt a small measure of gratitude toward the strange creature. She nodded to it grudgingly, as it turned to face her now, cocking its head at an unpleasant angle.

"Mineeeee," it shrieked again, baring needle-sharp fangs at her.

Joss clocked it on the head with her shoe. The creature, which she realized now was a wyvern, howled in pain and shifted away, letting out a low hiss.

"You are *not* getting my food," Joss said sternly.

It let out a harsh, desperate whine, eyes darting back greedily to the food in her hands as it moved closer. Joss almost felt bad for it, if she looked too closely. Hungry or not, it wasn't getting any of her food.

The kits peeked cautiously from behind rocks and each other, and Joss narrowed her eyes at them. The wyvern clicked its teeth anxiously, talons scraping the floor as it wavered indecisively, letting out a loud wail.

Anyone else would have chased the creature and scolded it for its behavior. But Joss couldn't help but be delighted, and partially fascinated, by the way it staked out its territory, a sort of reptilian hiss escaping its fanged mouth as it stretched its wings wide and made a curious growling noise in its throat. The message was clear, and the kits were timid enough to heed it.

Kit dragons were nice and all, but this thing... Joss felt like it actually understood. her. It was raised as harshly as she was, shunned for being different, and brash, fighting hard just to get the same things that others could easily.

Kit dragons were cuddly. This thing was savage, and she loved it.

Though right now, the wyvern looked pitiful, whimper-screeching as its beady black eyes flicked between her and the food, somehow pleading and demanding all at once. She almost felt bad for it. It seemed...more desperate than its companion. Like food wasn't just a pleasure, but something it had been deprived of. She almost gave up a piece for it. But then it would never leave.

The wyvern turned to her and shrieked its usual demand. Joss thought it sounded rather similar to a toddler crying for a favorite toy.

"*Mineeeeee.*"

Joss tore a corner off her food and shoved it stubbornly in her mouth. "Do you know the way out of here?"

The creature's eyes flicked between her mouth and the rest of the food, hungrily. "*Minnneeee...?*"

Narrowing her eyes, Joss studied the creature. Kit dragons, in her experience, weren't that clever. But this beast looked hungry, and Joss knew just what hunger could do for your motivation.

"If you help me out of here, I might give you a piece."

Would she really, though? Give up some of her food to this...thing? *Could* she?

A black tongue forked from the wyvern's mouth, briefly, before it let out another, lower hiss. "*Minnnneeee...*"

Joss stood with a frown, gesturing to the passages. "Only once you help me out."

"*Minnnneee?*" the wvyern screeched.

Suppressing an impatient noise, Joss nodded. "*If* you help me get out."

The wyvern shrieked. Joss began to doubt it had any idea what she was saying.

But what choice did she have, really? It was impossible to tell how much time had passed, down here, and she didn't want to make her bodyguard worry. She had to do something.

Mind made up, Joss ripped off a piece of her roll, grudgingly tossing it to the creature. It snatched it up in one gulp, eyes wild with a fierce, desperate gleam Joss recognized all too well.

The thing blinked at her, letting out a satisfied screech. A part of her felt grumpy for giving her food away. But the rational part argued she'd just steal more from Kaiden. He'd been really useful like that, so far.

"There's more where that came from," she nodded to the bread, the wyvern's head following her actions, "if you'll help me get out of here."

The wyvern must have been smarter than she gave it credit for, for it eyed the two passages before them with a calculating, ravenous look. It blinked once, then twice, head cocking as if it were listening for something, and then with a beat of its wings, it was back in the air, eyeing her food again.

Joss narrowed her eyes at the beast. It let out a low hiss, something that sounded strangely human, but turned and swept away down one of the passages, letting out a calling cry.

Taking her time, Joss brushed dust off her dress and followed, eyeing the passages for any sign of familiarity. They *all* looked familiar, since they were all the same.

It wasn't until after a few minutes that she even realized there was someone else following the wyvern. Or, she thought, some*things*, all of them tiny and scaly and glinting with bright colors and hopeful, eager eyes. Kit dragons.

"Go away," she called back, waving her hands toward them. The kits chirped, almost as one, and followed after them.

Joss fixed them with the most annoyed glare she could. Their eyes got big and round and far too pitiful again.

"Manipulators," Joss muttered resentfully, turning to continue out of the tunnel. Not a yes, but not a no, either.

It didn't matter how little you liked kit dragons. It didn't make you impervious to their charms.

She huffed out a sigh. The kits followed her in a colorful rainbow of wings and scales.

Maybe they were lost, too. Joss doubted it, but it gave her a reason to justify the tiny trail of creatures following her. The wyvern glanced back at them with a distaste Joss quite agreed with, and screeched. But the kits didn't seem deterred.

She wouldn't feed them, though, no matter how much they begged. She'd squash a particularly big bug with a rock and toss it to them, but that was it. She did, however, make sure to give her wyvern some. It gulped it down greedily in one choked breath.

How long had it been here, starved and trapped?

The wyvern stretched a nervous look back at its followers, screeching at Joss in a question. She shrugged. The wyvern continued on, though Joss noted with some peculiarity that it seemed to stay closer to her than before.

For all she knew, she was getting further lost. But the wyvern definitely possessed some intelligence, if only the kind the starving had, for it stopped every so often and eyed her with expectant, beady eyes. She dropped a few crumbs, which disappeared quicker than she could say 'kits'.

After a while, though, she refused to give it more. The wyvern could be leading her in circles, clever little thing, thriving off the crumbs she dropped for it. It screeched at her, showing rows of hooked teeth, but she refused to give in, and so it grudgingly continued on, chittering and making dissatisfied clicking noises as it went.

Soon, a glint of light filled the end of the tunnel – the promise of an exit. Suppressing a grin, Joss tossed a chunk of bread to the wyvern. It promptly choked the whole thing down, letting out something between a whine and a moan.

She was surprised to find she didn't want to leave the odd creature behind. It didn't demand anything further now, satisfied in the way a starving orphan is grateful to have anything to fill their stomach, meager as it had been. But the glint of hunger was still there, all the same.

Joss hesitated. What would Kaiden think of her bringing back a wyvern? He'd been fairly accepting of just about everything else; could it really do much harm?

When a dragon tried to nest in her hair, she impatiently brushed it aside. The kits were still near her, the smallest of them, its head only about the size of her fist, looking up with a mix of adoring and pleading.

They had nothing to offer, really. And yet Joss found herself unable to say no to them, either. The wyvern settled on a rock shelf near her, and shifted subtly closer at the sounds. It made her like the strange creature even more. It would like her Isles.

Maybe one day, she would go back. Somehow.

With an unhappy sigh, she opened the saddlebag she'd swiped, gesturing with a few impatient fingers. Happy trills answered as the kits flew into it, their colors vanishing under the musty brown.

"But you *can't* move, alright?" Joss warned, frowning down at the creatures.

The wyvern, however, she let fly near her, watching it. Several times it seemed as if it might land, but it would drift away again before she could react, back to arms' length away. Joss wanted it to come closer. She hesitantly reached out to its mind, feeling a garble of feelings and static. Kit dragons were entirely too happy, like there was nothing to worry about in the world. Not this creature.

She didn't need that sort of false positivity. But she did have an idea of who else could benefit from it.

At this point, she didn't even need the wyvern to follow her, or bribe him. But she didn't like the idea of just leaving the thing there, alone. Kaiden could get them all food, right?

Besides, a cohort would be terribly helpful in her line of work. He could serve as a distraction while she snatched food, or frighten people off with his screeching. Maybe she didn't need her bodyguard anymore, after all.

The moment she thought it, her stomach twisted in uncomfortable knots. Usually, when Joss conned someone, she only stuck with them as long as was beneficial to her.

But what if that angry butcher came back? Or she ran into the jeweler she'd put out of business? Having a bodyguard was far more essential than Joss had previously considered. And he didn't seem to have much to do other than feed her, so it worked out.

She was just grumpy because he wasn't taking care of himself right. He'd get this haunted look in his eye that she didn't like, sometimes that lingered long after he'd woken up. That was the real reason she stuck around.

She didn't want him to leave. Besides, he needed someone to make sure he took care of himself. He'd obviously grown up used to being hungry, but didn't like to steal.

How was she going to explain *this* to him?

"*Hey, Bodyguard, I got followed by a bunch of kit dragons and they won't leave me alone. Surprise!*"

Maybe they would do him good. He couldn't look so upset with a bunch of cute tiny dragons around, could he?

Joss didn't get it. Even back home, stealing had just been...a part of life. Her parents had only sent her away because it wasn't *their* part of life.

That and the fact that she could make shadows do weird things. They weren't very fond of that. Even the dragons rejected her because of that. Was it any wonder Joss didn't like them?

No one understood her powers; they were all scared of them. Even the ones with gifts of their own were scared of hers. They called them unnatural.

Kaiden didn't seem scared of her. Though Joss doubted he understood enough, from the looks in his eyes, that didn't matter. He didn't need to know, anyway.

She liked the wyvern more because it was a thief, just like her. You could see it in the beady eyes, the shifty, subtle steps it took. It stole to survive. Just like her.

That, of course, did *not* mean she was going to let it have her food, no matter how it dug its talons into her shoulder. It could steal Kaiden's, for all she cared. He never ate much anyway.

She gave the wyvern a light smack on the back of its scaled head. It blinked beady, betrayed eyes at her.

"*Minnnneeee,*" it wailed.

"*Mine*," Joss hissed back, holding the remaining pastry so tightly that crumbs slipped between her fingers. The wyvern watched them drop with a mixture of horror and longing.

Or, at least, that's what it appeared like to Joss. Anyone she'd ever known who saw a wyvern said they weren't very bright. Their expression never changed; they never said anything but '*Mine*'. They were greedy, desperate little thieves.

Was it any wonder Joss got along so well with it?

"You don't have a name, do you? Other than 'Mine'," she said, rolling her eyes. "And that would get annoying to call you." The wyvern blinked at her, nipping at her fingers. Little rascal.

Joss laughed. "I know. I'll call *you* the rascal, and then whenever they blame me, I can point to you instead!"

The creature bit her again when she tried to stroke it. But it didn't draw blood, so Joss didn't mind.

"Joss!"

At least *one* of them had managed not to get lost. Stowing a grin, Joss headed down the rest of the tunnel, toward the sound of her bodyguard's voice.

The cool air felt like bliss on her lungs as she emerged into the open, the already-dimming sun telling her just how long she'd been lost. Kaiden stood by himself nearby, something gripped tight enough in his hand to wrinkle it. It didn't surprise her to see that he was talking to himself, again. Or, as he'd put it, to his imaginary friend.

His expression slipped to relief when he saw her, though something far heavier still lurked behind his eyes. His voice came out a little too quiet. "I thought I told you not to wander."

In response, Joss wrinkled her nose. "Okay, *Dad*." Huffing, she crossed her arms over her chest. "Rascal helped me get out."

She saw the question in his eyes as they slipped to the wyvern perched on her shoulder, with some surprise.

"Why do you have...?"

"He's my friend. This is Rascal."

Kaiden stared at the wyvern for a moment, until it screeched. Joss could have sworn she saw a shudder run through him, though she almost doubted it was because of that.

"Aw, he doesn't bite. See? He's friendly! Touch him!"

Though Kaiden frowned, he reached out to touch the wyvern, who promptly bit him. He pulled back sharply, looking over at Joss.

"That's just how he says hello." She grinned. "He likes you."

"Well, I don't like it," he muttered, shifting his arms over his chest. Something volatile flickered through his eyes. "Wyverns aren't friendly."

"Says *you*," Joss retorted, reaching up to pet its head. It bit her finger in response. Kaiden gave her a look.

"Just...keep it away from me," he said, almost less of a statement and more of a question as he started walking away.

Joss frowned at her finger. It wasn't like it had drawn blood. "He's just hungry," she defended. "As am I. Can we get some food?"

Kaiden sighed. He looked exhausted, just enough not to notice her bulging bag, apparently. Joss kept waiting for him to say something. Instead, he was worryingly quiet.

Joss frowned, but no words seemed to come to her mind. The look on his face was so...solemn. Mourning. He drew in a breath, collecting his face into a smile.

"I found my siblings."

"Really?" Joss' eyes lit up, her head moving to peer behind him as if they'd be right there.

He shook his head. "Not here. But I know *where* they are." He rubbed the back of his head. "It's not far."

"Well, what are we waiting around here for? Come on!"

A quiet, heavy sigh escaped his lips, softening the anguish to something more hidden. He shook his head.

"Why not?"

"Later," he whispered, and it was then Joss realized why he hadn't been speaking normally. His voice sounded raw, like he'd been...crying?

Joss was supremely uncomfortable with this revelation. She did not like crying.

"You don't look good, Bodyguard."

"I'm fine," he insisted, a weak laugh leaving his lips. "Maybe I'm just hungry, too."

Joss eyed him skeptically, nodding. "Yeah. You never do seem to eat anything."

Kaiden nodded, a faraway look on his face for a brief instance as he drew in a breath. He didn't look hungry. "I guess not."

He *guessed* not. Joss couldn't understand him. He was obviously hungry, not like any of the Uppers who always had their bellies full. And yet he never filled his, as if the idea of actually caring for himself was ludicrous.

"Tell you what." She made her voice as stern as possible, even as he smiled. Or tried to, at least. "How about you give me your money and I'll go get us some food?"

Kaiden withdrew a few coins, the surfaces clinking as he sorted through them with his palm. "I don't have a lot..."

"I'll make it work," Joss said quickly, grinning. "You look like you could use a nap."

He closed his hand around the money, his eyes looking like they wanted to do the same. He shook his head.

"Yes, you *do*. Don't make me get your imaginary friend to scold you."

The startled look on his face was worth it. "I don't have..."

Unimpressed, Joss looked down at where his free hand was half-curled in the air. "Look, I didn't say I was judging. I was just saying she'd agree with me."

Kaiden's eyes flicked to the side briefly, before he could stop himself, and he valiantly fought a grimace. "I'm fine."

Joss waved her hand dismissively. Rascal screeched in agreement.

"In either case, you need food and I most certainly need food, so! Are you coming or not?"

He hesitated, eyeing the wyvern. "I don't like those things."

"Yes, well, Rascal doesn't like you either, so the feeling's mutual. But that doesn't matter! What matters is *food*." She scooped the coins from his hand before he could protest. "Look! I'm even going to buy it, like a civilized individual. Aren't you proud of me?"

She wasn't prepared for his nod; she was joking, after all. But he looked all too serious for a moment before he realized, and his brow creased in skepticism. "Hm."

"Don't look at me like that. Rascal stays! He'll keep an eye on me, so I don't steal anything."

Kaiden sank down to the soft ground beneath them, nodding as if he hadn't even heard her. Disguising her alarm, Joss dropped into his lap, slipping her bag off and setting it aside so the kits wouldn't squirm against him.

It looked like she *wasn't* going to buy food. That would be ridiculous But she still had part of another roll left that she'd been saving.

"Here," she said, holding out the last of it to him. "You need it."

Kaiden pushed it away, and she stuck it right back, even more stubborn.

"Eat it."

His expression was so twisted with torment for a moment that she almost felt bad. Letting out a little sigh, she lowered her tone. "Please?"

After closing his eyes for a moment, he nodded again. She didn't like the way his voice got quiet, or that he looked like he might be sick. "Okay."

Though he took the pastry from her, he made no attempt to put it in his mouth. Sighing, Joss settled better in his lap, frowning at Rascal. She hoped the worry didn't seep through in her voice. "Okay. I'm going to make an executive decision and say you need to sleep. You look awful," she added pointedly, giving him a once-over.

Kaiden nodded, his grip on the pastry tightening until a few crumbs escaped. Rascal snatched them up greedily, then retreated to a corner to hiss at them.

Joss slipped off her bodyguard's lap to start setting up camp, hiding her worry from him. Whatever had happened in the Mountain...it must have been worse than usual for him to look like that.

Nearby, the saddlebag squirmed more than usual. Joss gave it a light whack with her heel. "Hush, you."

An indignant squeak answered her. Kaiden looked up. "Joss...?"

She was caught, red-handed. Red-footed, if that was a thing.

"Rascal's acting up," she said too quickly. Kaiden's brow creased, looking to where the wyvern had been. Luckily, her new friend was no longer in sight.

"That didn't..."

The bag continued to squirm, more insistently this time. Kaiden reached over to investigate, looping the latch free.

At least seven – or was it nine? Joss hadn't really counted – tiny kit dragons came spilling or flying out in a mixed rainbow, landing in a tumble and bumping into each other. Several instantly flew to his shoulder, though he brushed them off in bewilderment.

"Wow, hey, look at that." Joss gave him her best innocent grin. "Stowaways."

VIII

Dailen

Dailen hopped across another stone on the glittery pond, a grin lifting his cheeks as something splashed behind him. He was delighted to see the tiny dragon he'd found attempting to follow him.

Baby dragons were definitely his favorite.

He loved having so many dragons around. It felt so...*right*, like Ashalee was smiling down on him. Like he'd finally done something worth smiling about.

The tiny parade of dragons continued to follow him, no matter what he did. Kit dragons, it turned out, didn't care or weren't aware of his feelings about them. Damien had always assigned him to help with the dragons, since he was otherwise useless. It felt like a punishment.

But they just wouldn't leave him *alone*. No matter what he did, the kits stuck with him, hid in his clothes, refused to leave. Eventually he'd just...given up. Ashalee would have let them stay. He learned all their names, just like she would have.

It was bittersweet, having them around. But he'd never gotten along well with the other humans, anyway, and as much as he hated to admit it...he was lonely. Terribly lonely.

Dailen had always loved dragons, before. Ever since his sister had found a book at the abandoned library, its illustrations glittering with ink in colors he'd never even seen before, the fascination quickly took hold of both of them. She would make up stories from the words they couldn't read, and act out dramatic scenes in the living room of their house.

Not anymore.

Still, Dailen couldn't hide the spark of delight in his chest at the sight before him. *Dragons.* Hundreds, if not thousands of them, all roaming around and lazing in the city. It was clearer now than it'd ever been before that this was *meant* to happen. Unlike his home, the city had been designed for just this purpose. It was why the archways towered far above and the streets were wider than ever would be necessary, even the buildings carefully designed with sweeping ceilings and tall towers to accommodate them. Dragons were always meant to live there, with them. Dailen wondered what had driven them away.

And yet, he could feel it, if he reached out enough. The reason why.

Still, there was a bitter tang to everything, a sharpness to the sadness. Though there were a million dragons all around him, the one person he loved most wasn't there with him to see it.

Ashalee would have loved this. It was almost enough to make him sink to the grass and just stay there, as if it were too good to be real. Instead, he moved one foot forward, right after the other, with a deep breath in, and reached out to touch one of the dragons sleeping across the stream.

Can you hear me? he murmured in his mind, closing his eyes. He'd not been able to make a true connection with a dragon. Not since...

Well. He supposed it was a punishment to himself, since he couldn't save her. He wasn't allowed to use his gifts, since they had failed him. It hurt, anyway, thinking about it. They turned to ash in his mind, a fire he couldn't put out, no matter how he tried.

But now, he had a choice. A chance to make a difference, for once.

Dragons always made him feel...close to Ashalee. Like a part of her was still there, living on through their spirits. She joked sometimes that she had the spirit of a dragon. He still had the picture book she'd drawn in from years ago. He kept it safely hidden, where no one could see it.

Ashalee would have loved this. He was fulfilling both of their dreams, by standing here in front of so many, each color even more vibrant than the now-faded illustrations in their book.

The dragon in question didn't stir, deep silver scales glinting in the light as its chest slowly rose and fell. Dailen sat back, quietly, wondering why he even tried.

He couldn't explain why he was still so distant from the dragons, despite enjoying seeing them. Ashalee had never had the chance to see one in real life, until it was too late. It was like a part of him had just closed off after her death.

In a way, he supposed he blamed the dragons. It was a terrible balance, staying around them because of his sister, but secretly despising them because they'd taken her away from him. Loving them because she had, and hating them because she was gone. He still remembered the night he'd broke down, screaming at them and demanding to know why they would do it.

But of course, the dragons wouldn't respond. Though Dailen knew, deep down, that they *could*, and he could communicate with them, he didn't want to believe it. He preferred to leave them distant, like oblivious creatures that he couldn't blame for their actions.

It was easier not to get hurt that way.

He supposed this was why he stayed around the kit dragons. Ashalee had imagined so many designs for them, and they were all so wrong, it made him want to laugh. They brought up less memories, and never pried for his own. He got many scattered thoughts about food and flying and their favorite hiding holes, but they didn't look at him like the larger ones would, as if they *knew*, and were silently judging him. Or nudging him to open a connection, like the ones in the Mountain had.

The thing Dailen would never tell anyone was that he was still terrified of dragons. He didn't blame them anymore, though perhaps he should have, but he feared every time they opened their mouths, as impossible as it was, that flames would come bursting forth.

He should have *been* there. He should have been able to help her.

He was jumpy for so long after, whenever there was a dragon around. And yet he forced himself to interact with them, and make his peace, and find a way to move on. It was what Ashalee would have wanted.

Now, here, all these years later, Dailen had never felt like he belonged as much as he did with the dragons. The feeling of *right*ness was so amplified, he thought it might smother him. This is where he belonged. He could almost imagine Ashalee sitting there, wheeling around in her chair and laughing at the dragons' antics, her eyes lit up with shafts of sunlight as she stroked them and told them stories in her warm, magical voice.

Ashalee had always seemed to him like the magic one of them. Like she could conjure it from the air, just by asking. She found delight in the smallest things, the sprout of a green shoot, or the dying seeds of a puffbud as it blew in the breeze. The autumn colors, and the twinkling brook that she tried to imitate, humming and chatting to it as she drew the wide, swooping curves.

Dailen had done his best to find whatever he could to make paints for her, painstakingly crushing up flower buds and the shells of beetles and juice from berries to let her continue her art. She was confined to her chair, by the world, but it could never confine her spirit. Though Dailen still missed his family, the dragons became his family away from home. He hadn't been able to face his parents since Ashalee's death. Especially when it was his fault. The whole village had loved Ashalee. And he was supposed to protect her.

It was his dagging gift that had gotten in the way. He had run back home as fast as he could, when he heard of the attack, but it didn't matter. She had told him to go, when Damien asked earlier. Had she *known*? She'd always been stubborn and independent, and he had failed her.

Ashalee had always been more than just his adopted sister. She was his cheerleader, his confidant, his closest friend. She filled him with a fire and passion he never knew he could have. You couldn't help but be caught up in her enthusiasm, when she started going on about dragon eggs with a sparkle in her eyes and asked you whether you thought they would glitter in the sun, or whether dragons liked to eat anything other than what the stories said.

Turned out, they did like human food. Although they never seemed very fond of his soup. He couldn't ever seem to make it quite like she did.

Nothing was quite the same without her. More than anything, if he let himself admit it, this was the reason why he'd stopped using his gift. It was a cruel reminder of what they shared, and only he was left with.

When Ashalee had died...it was like that fire had gone out in him.

Even Dailen's gift might not have shown up if it weren't for Ashalee. It had happened quite by accident. Ashalee had said, jokingly, how cool it would be if he could *breathe* fire, and though the idea of that quite frankly terrified Dailen, it made him wonder. And then there it was, in his hands, like it had been summoned by the power of her wish. The delight on her face was clear, even as they both knew how closely it needed to be hidden.

Dailen's parents wouldn't have worried. Dailen never did anything reckless enough to be found out.

He still never told them.

Dailen had never been as important, in Damien's eyes, and so he was allowed to roam as he pleased. He spent his time gathering the small dragons and teaching them tricks, and talking with them. He wished he could send one back to Ashalee. Damien told him no.

It was a wonder he had been allowed to write home, after Damien had recruited him. Though Dailen did begin to wonder, after a while, if they ever actually reached them. Ashalee's letters always seemed a touch too...fake. Too cheery. And then they just stopped coming.

And then it happened. There was a fire in his town, and Damien wouldn't let him go. He *could* have done something, and he wasn't brave enough for it.

Could he ever use his gifts again? He'd asked himself this question a handful of times, and the answer was always the same. It hurt too much.

And yet the dragons made it seem so easy. Urging, and assuring him that they would help. They would share most of the burden. He wouldn't have to feel the guilt and sting of carrying around the very thing that had failed him.

Though it hadn't been his fault, he didn't deserve to bear such a privilege anymore. He was useless, without her, and it felt fitting that would occur naturally, too. When asked why he wouldn't use his gift, he simply lied, and said, "I don't have it."

They left him to his grief, until it faded, and still his answer didn't change. And yet, Damien didn't turn him out. It was never a threat, or even a question. He simply let Dailen cope, and assured him that in due time, it would return.

Damien let him come and go, as long as he kept quiet. Dailen knew quite clearly that Damien was aware of where he lived.

He was too ashamed to go home, anyway. What would his parents say? It was easier just not to face them. Did he miss them? Of course. Would he go home, one day? Maybe. But for right now...the idea bothered him too much to consider.

Rescuing Dez had been his one big step of bravery since then. Damien was disappointed in him, but had to keep him, considering all he knew. Dailen suspected his knack for dragons had something to do with it.

Dailen did, in a way, consider himself a bit of an expert on dragons. When he couldn't bring himself to confront humans, the dragons were always there, and unbearably lonely.

Just like him.

Even before any of this, Dailen had never been very good with a sword, or even with talking. Basil had tried to strike up conversation with him, multiple times, but Dailen always ended up feeling guilty. Like they would blame him for what he'd done.

Though he'd never tell anyone, either, he admired Blaze, and his handle on his fire. He watched him walk into burning buildings and carry out small children, absorb the heat from the flames until his skin glowed faintly, warm to the touch, and the fire died to embers.

Dailen still worried about being made fun of, if he did use his gift. Blaze was fluent, elegant with his flames, tossing them around as if their existence was as normal as breathing. Dailen's only flickered and sputtered and coughed out a meager existence, more smoke than blaze. No pun intended.

Perhaps that's why he was Blaze, and Dailen was just...Dailen. Smoke, dissipating in the air. Poof.

Just like his gift.

He didn't know how to explain it, either. It wasn't *like* Blaze's fire, in any noticeable way. It was a lot more...volatile. A lot more explosive and fumy and filled with thick, choking smoke.

His Gift had become a manifestation of his greatest nightmare. He'd always wondered what would happen if it *did* reach out and choke someone. Would he be able to live with himself?

Turned out, he couldn't.

It seemed so stupid now, with her gone. A child's game, playing with powers he didn't understand, and apparently, couldn't control. Even if it wasn't the cause of his pain, it *was* a reminder, and it choked him up every time.

He couldn't use his gift. He couldn't face the dragons, and their gentle urging. So he relegated them as large, scaly cats in his mind and pretended as if that was all they had ever been.

Sometimes, Dailen still wished he could have his own dragon again. But then he remembered they were all his friends, and that was a million times better.

Well. All except Spike, aptly named because of the ice-colored spikes running down his back, layered like a horse's mane. The dragon had never given him a name, unlike the others, and so Dailen had come up with one. He knew now the dragon hated it.

Sometimes the other Gifted would still go flying with him. But none of them seemed to appreciate the dragons quite like he did, or understand what they were trying to say. The patient and majestic beasts were like adults letting a child lead them around, knowing full well they were going the complete wrong way and would likely take twice as long to get there, if they even arrived.

But Dailen couldn't fault them. There were many things Dailen had *known* before his new life, but not understood how it worked, or what exactly it entailed. Like the fact that dragons could communicate mentally and still be closed off to their gifts, and other influences. Most of the Gifted were wary of bonding too strongly with their dragons, in case they became corrupted.

That was a silly notion, but they didn't know any better. Dailen hadn't, either, until the dragons explained it to them. Dragons knew so much more about the world and how it worked than humans. They had even helped him with his gifts, before Ashalee's death.

Why couldn't he have saved her? He knew he was afraid, and couldn't get it to work right, but he had *tried*. He had tried so hard, and it still wasn't enough. What use was his Gift if he couldn't help anyone with it?

Well. He still had no intention of using his gift, no matter what they said. No matter *who* tried to convince him.

Letting out a sigh, Dailen dropped down on his back in the grass, closing his eyes as it pillowed his body like a green cloud. Despite what some might have thought, he wasn't invisible. He'd heard Sari's explanations, and he knew what came next. Sari had always known, somehow, that he still had his gift, though she never ratted him out for it. Perhaps she'd always known all humans had them, and that was why.

Ashalee could have had one. The thought made his chest tighten up more, a million questions bursting in his mind. Why? Why did they go to some people, and not others? Why *him?*

Sari would come and try to convince him to use his, he knew. It was only a matter of time. Which was why he was hiding out with the dragons, avoiding any responsibility they might try to give him.

Couldn't they just leave him be? Living was hard enough without his best friend. No one else had ever understood him the way she did, and he already knew no one else ever would. He wasn't useful. He had no gift. He didn't want to be dragged into this.

Distracted, Dailen ran a hand through the grass. He didn't think he'd ever get over how much greener it was here, quite literally, than in Calest.

As if sensing his need for company, the dragons scattered around slowly gathered near him, the youngest chirring their happiness as they curled small serpentine bodies next to him. He looked past them, to the one proud mother who was guarding her egg, watching the younger dragons as if to protect them. Given their immortal lives, and especially hiding away, Dailen assumed, dragons didn't lay very many eggs. He considered it a rare privilege to be able to see one, and even more so when the mother had allowed him to touch it, and tell it stories. The dragons always seemed to understand his loneliness, and aptitude for dealing with it. Maybe they just wanted to cheer him up. Maybe they honestly thought he could be of help to them.

Whatever the reason, he went to see the egg whenever he could.

The ruby mother, whose name Dailen had no idea of, shifted aside so he could better see it. Sitting up, Dailen scooted closer to the egg, brushing a hand against it with an expression of awe. It was smooth and shiny, and yet indented in places like a pattern was etched into the sky blue shell.

Dragon eggs, he noticed, were as varied as the dragons themselves. As if an artist dipped their brush in so many paints that they all blended together, red and silver streaking in amidst blues and golds, all

135

glinting like paint drying in the sun. Some had scales that were opalescent, or brilliant deep colors like the shifting depths of the sea.

Dailen's own dragon, a bright yellow beauty named Suvien, had gone very silent since Dailen had stopped communicating with him. It hurt too much. Losing Ashalee made him want to retreat into himself and cut off all communication with everyone. And it didn't seem right to treat his dragon as if there had never been anything between them. He deserved better than that.

And yet, he couldn't help but stay around these dragons, as long as he could, for Ashalee's sake. Because she wasn't able to be the one sitting here, telling stories to the dragons and singing in her lovely voice. Because she wasn't alive to see their scales glint in the sun, and hear the deep rumble of satisfaction in their throats when you found just the right spot to stroke them. Dragon scales, it seemed, though impenetrable armor, were still more sensitive in places than others, or more malleable. Dailen wondered if dragons ever got itches, and imagined them scratching themselves like overgrown dogs.

Now here he was, in the midst of *hundreds* of dragons, and the one person who most wished to see it wasn't there with him.

He withdrew a crumpled page, the last drawing Ashalee had ever made for him. He had asked Chan for a special solution to keep it from dying with age.

There. A bright-eyed dragon, head alert and golden scales glittering. It was as if she had grown up amongst them all his life, and simply drew what she had seen.

"I had a sister," he whispered, opening up to a story that he hadn't told in years. His lips didn't even tremble as he spoke, innumerable pairs of slitted eyes centered on him. He looked down at his lap, fiddling with the cloth, and the dragon egg beneath it. It didn't quite cover the surface. "She loved magic. She loved stories. She loved...dragons."

JOSS

Joss didn't want to sleep. As much as she wouldn't admit it to him, she was still worried about her bodyguard. Despite the kit dragons curled up next to him, one snoring lazily on its back, three tangled in a mess of colorful tails and scales, he still sat there with a distant look on his face, something raw on his face like it had been torn open to show the emotion beneath.

Not knowing what else to do, Joss crawled over and huddled in his lap again. It had to pass soon, right?

After a long moment, he slipped his arms around her, his head resting on hers. He murmured a name in her hair, and it was then reality settled in, and knocked Joss like a blow to the gut. She...reminded him of someone. This was why he was so kind to her. It all made *sense*.

Joss shut her eyes to stem the tears she felt glistening there. She *knew* now that he wasn't thinking of her. But she also knew he needed it. She'd stick around until he found his siblings, and then he'd be okay. Right?

As if in response, Kaiden held her closer, and she shrunk further against him, soaking up the warmth that was never meant for her.

"Do you like the stars?"

Her voice sounded so tiny, whispered like that. She felt him look up, the distraction seeming to work for a moment.

"They tell such pretty stories," Joss continued on, hoping he couldn't hear the choked aspect to her tone as she pointed up. "See? That one looks like a snake, if you connect it right. It ate a dragon egg and died after the dragon hatched." She sniffled, rubbing her sleeve along her nose and trying not to shiver. "Those two were siblings, until the one got jealous and killed the other."

"Such lovely stories you tell," he muttered, though his tone didn't sound as fractured. His grip was calmer, too, if still tight.

"I didn't make them up. Don't you know the star stories? Reign taught them to me."

Kaiden stayed quiet again, lost in the sky. Joss drew in a breath.

"What are they like?" she found herself asking, softly. She had to know, even as it killed her to see him like this.

When he swallowed, head lowering, she thought she had crossed a line.

"I don't know," he admitted, barely a whisper. "I don't remember them."

Joss peeked up at him, watching his throat bob. His chin was scratchy and his hair was getting floppy, rather than sticking out all funny. He needed to cut it. And clean his face.

"You...don't?"

He shut his eyes, shaking his head. Though his voice got louder, it wasn't as in control. "I'll find out soon."

"Did you run away? When you were little?"

His eyes shut painfully tight, and she regretted the question. "No."

Since Joss didn't feel okay asking anything else of him, she just settled closer against him, playing with the necklace she'd carried with her. It felt like a millstone around her neck, sometimes. "My parents didn't want me," she admitted. She was surprised her own voice didn't break. But the pain didn't seem as strong now, in light of his. She added a half-shrug, rubbing a thumb over the glittering gem. "'Cause I'm special and all."

She knew he'd hear the hidden edge to her tone, and understand it. He nodded, his arms around her tightening just slightly.

"But it's okay," Joss continued, letting out a laugh she didn't feel. "Reign took good enough care with me. Taught me to live. I got away once I could." She squeezed the jewel until it dug into her hand, the painful pressure and prick grounding her. "Wasn't much of a home."

"I grew up by the docks," he whispered, his voice a faint ghost of the truth. He looked down at his hands, and the tiny scars there. "Carried shipments, and things..."

"I stole from those," Joss piped up cheerfully, and then wondered if she shouldn't have. She dug a dirty nail into the gem until it might crack. "Only...once..."

She could have sworn she heard a low rumble in his throat, like the hidden depths of a laugh. "Of course you did."

Joss wanted to frown, even though there was nothing funny about it. "What's that supposed to mean?"

Half a smile tilted his lips. He settled back against the tree better, holding her carefully so he could look at her. "I mean, it's no wonder, because you're such a thief." His finger touched the necklace – she'd forgot she had it out – and she nearly jumped.

Was he mad? He didn't look it, and she didn't understand. Surely he didn't approve of her actions. He must be *really* out of it.

"It's hard growing up here," he said quietly, in a voice that spoke of far too much experience. His fingers touched hers, around the gem. "Between the way...everything is run, and how people treat you."

"Hey." Joss pulled away with a frown, her hand closing around the jewel as if to protect it. "I didn't say I need pity. I got along just fine on my own." She stopped. "Get. I *get* along fine. Without any help. I'll always get along."

"I know. You're resilient."

Resilient. It was one of those words that sounded all stuck-up, like she was some tree that stood tall in a storm, not because it was strong, but because it had to. Like she scraped by because there was no other option, rather than it being one of her many skills.

And yet, he made it sound like a strength.

"How did you survive, anyway?" she wanted to know, turning to frown at him. "You don't take care of yourself."

His gaze slanted away, and Joss held in a noisy breath for upsetting him again.

"I...didn't."

She squinted at him. "You might not be bright, Bodyguard, but you certainly don't look dead."

A half-smile lifted his lips. "On my own, I mean," he murmured, something faraway to his eyes again. "I...wouldn't have."

"Of course you wouldn't," Joss teased, using his prior words against him. "That's why you have me."

His smile shouldn't have softened like it did. He shouldn't have been thinking of her as something permanent in his life. Someone better would be that, like his siblings. He deserved it. He deserved...more than her. "I know."

It wasn't the answer she was expecting, and she wasn't sure she wanted it. On one hand, it made her happy to know she was needed, but on the other...it made her expendable. Once he had someone better, he'd move on. It didn't matter what he thought of her.

"Anyway." She poked him with the pastry. "You *still* need to eat."

To her relief, he finally took it, breaking off a piece for her and then sticking it in his mouth. She watched him first, to make sure he actually finished it, then nudged him with the other piece. "*All* of it."

"Yes, mother," he teased, though there was the faintest flicker to his eyes. A soft sigh escaped his lips, though it didn't sound entirely unhappy. It was as if he was murmuring *Thank you,* and so with a little smile and a shrug, she sent back her reply. *You're welcome.*

The kit dragons beside him stirred at the smell of food. Joss tossed them a few tiny crumbs just so he wouldn't feed them instead. From the corner, Rascal glared at them. He was like a cat, Joss mused, with sharper talons and wings instead of paws.

One of the tiniest kits hopped onto her lap, and she was delighted to see Kaiden pet it, an almost smile on his face. There was no denying to herself that she wanted him to be happy, no matter what happened. This was why she'd wait until he was home. Maybe just before. Then she didn't have to see the joy on his face, from no longer needing her.

She shivered harder, so he would notice, and he shifted her so he could build a small fire, although he did it in the normal way, still slightly fumbling with it. Joss didn't feel right asking him about it, or the slightest shake to his hands as he lit it. He let out an unsteady breath when he was done, and smiled at her.

It made her feel way too warm inside, like he was the source of the heat instead of the fire, a hearth in a cozy home.

Home. She hated assigning that word to anyone. Because when home was a person, rather than a place, they could leave you. A house would never leave you. You could leave *it*, but it wouldn't just get up and walk away from you. People had a nasty tendency to do that, and they took all your possessions with them when they did. All the time you put into them. All the love you stored in their hands. Each piece of your heart that was now irreparably gone, and wasn't going to come back.

It didn't matter how many people left, either. You could get over losing a home, with time. You didn't get over losing a person. Joss still missed Reign, even with everything he'd done to her. She missed everyone. She *hated* it.

Kaiden's eyes seemed clearer, now, though she couldn't miss the way his free hand was curled tight, like it was wrapped around an invisible hand. She wondered if his imaginary friend would leave him, once he was okay again. She seemed to do him a lot of good.

Though he didn't want to sleep, she insisted on it, claiming that they both would feel better in the morning. She volunteered to take the first watch, even though she knew Rascal was nocturnal and would watch over them. He seemed too tired to argue, and with a glance at the rocks next to him, he let out a quiet sigh, nodding in acceptance.

Joss made him a nice little bed, and determined to at least buy him something small before she left. As a thank you, or a farewell, she supposed. Maybe she'd do that tonight. Buying, not stealing. Just as he would.

The kit dragons curled around his sleeping body in a way even Joss had to admit was rather adorable. She knew he didn't like people seeing his nightmares. But Joss had always been far more afraid of daytime terrors than night ones. Ones that could actually hurt her, rather than dissipate into smoke when she opened her eyes, or morph into some odd multicolored flower with dripping fangs. Dreams were just too weird to terrify her, most of the time.

If anything, it hurt to see him tense up, shivers running through him that had nothing to do with the cold, his jaw clenched hard and his eyes tight with creases, a choked cry locked behind his lips. She heard him call out, and sob, and whisper names she didn't recognize. Pleas. Murmurs that sounded like a dying man's last wish.

Joss huddled next to the dying fire and watched him quietly, wishing there was something she could do. The shadows danced in playful images, influenced by her mind to be gentler and less scary, as if

140

it would help him. Luckily, his distress only lasted for a few minutes, before he seemed to sink into a dreamless sleep, his breathing evening out. It was then that Joss crawled under her own thin blanket, the fire curling sleepily with smoke, Rascal's eyes slitted but watching over them, and fell asleep.

LENA

Nothing was going according to plan.

I couldn't tell anyone else about it, either. It was too risky, and in some ways, selfish. Raoul's people wouldn't understand. Basil would, but he still couldn't help. None of them could.

Still, I had to *try*, didn't I? I wasn't just going to let my brother fall to the same fate as my dad. The Empress was struggling for control since the Bane's disappearance. She couldn't have found him out yet, then. She'd have a hard enough time controlling her own people.

There had to still be a chance.

Besides, they were all too preoccupied with Sari's reappearance – which was yet another cause for my frustration. Her vague letters updating me on her progress had kept me on edge for weeks, and now she just...showed up, out of nowhere, with legions of *dragons*. Even though Hanen was no longer around, having fled back to his beloved Empress, and Raoul had managed to win most of these citizens' loyalty for me, I was afraid of what Sari's news might do to that bond. Would they even believe her? Would they side with us?

I didn't know. The Empress had played a risky move and now it had backlashed on her, but would it really be enough to sway anyone from their stalwart beliefs? Caleb had said before, in his previous letters, that the number of rebels had been growing. That was, of course, before the Empress cut off all communications from the Cities.

Could I do it? Could I really go back into that place, yet again, and pretend to be one of them? I didn't know *where* Caleb would be, after all. He didn't exactly think it smart to spill the location of his hideout in his letters. I'd have to ask around, and that would require blending in.

For the moment, no travel seemed allowed even between Cities. But I hoped that would all change, soon. The Empress couldn't keep her people separated forever – at the very least, not between Cities. They held to tradition more strongly than their own wits, and with such empty minds, even the ones still loyal were likely to panic at being trapped. No doubt once the Empress concocted a story to appease them, travel would continue as normal.

Raoul kept saying that we should strike the Empress sooner rather than later, while she was vulnerable. But with no information as to the state of affairs – and all attempts to breach the gates proving futile – there was little to do but wait.

And plan.

And now, it turned out, prepare for an attack of our own. All thanks to Sari, and her immortal friend who was supposed to be helping us. While Ru'ach was trying to persuade her psychotic brother not to murder all of the Gifted, Shedim was surely sending the dragons under his control to attack us, while we were vulnerable. According to Sari, that was a necessary risk, if Ru'ach could stop Shedim.

And if she couldn't? Well, then I had to gather an army from this inexperienced group so the same thing didn't happen that had to all the previous cities. If Shedim managed to entirely squash the rebellion here, our chances at stopping the Empress would go from slim to none. Despite Chan's attempts to sway my father's men to our cause, the rest of Calest had already given in to the Empress on the matter of the Gifted. They might attempt to stop her themselves, but they wouldn't work with us.

Expelled a much-needed sigh, I sank my head in my hands. Honing a Gift was not an easy task. In my free time, I still worked on mine, alongside swordplay, and though I could see improvement, it wasn't nearly as much or as quick as I would have liked.

Still, every little bit would count to force my way into Galdania. The more convincing I could be, the better of a chance I stood. At least I had an opening, and inside information. It wasn't an *entirely* foolish plan.

I tried not to think about the fact that I would probably yell at anyone else who attempted it.

From his perch beside me, Dez squeaked. I pretended he was agreeing with me. After all, I'd been thinking this over for months. As in any city filled with airheaded, filthy rich citizens, social gatherings were one of the cornerstone of society – and an easy distraction from whatever the Empress didn't wish them to see. It would make sense, then, that once she had a foothold, she would continue with this trend, for the people's sake. Having grown up in the capital, I couldn't soon forget the semiannual ball held in Aurillea, at the end of every other season. If the Empress continued with this tradition, it would be held in a few short weeks – less than a month away.

My genius plan, of course, was to sneak in and spy on everyone. Provided that the event actually took place, and I wasn't found out, and could keep my act together enough to allay suspicions.

This was another reason I hadn't told anyone of my plans. Even if I could sneak another person in along with me – perhaps they wouldn't be as accepting of a forged invitation as last time, but I had been steadily practicing my mind manipulation skills, if only just for this purpose, and with the Cities in such a state of disarray, perhaps it would still be doable – who would I take? I wouldn't let Basil or Fern get that close to danger again. Olive might flay me alive if I did, and besides, I wasn't *that* selfish. And of course Olive wouldn't come, because she wanted to keep an eye on Basil. Chan was off in Calest with Katya. Dailen seemed to prefer dragon company to human, and he was a terrible liar, anyway. And I wasn't going to trust someone I hardly knew to come along with me.

Sari had her hands full enough as is, with this earth-shattering news she laid on everyone. I knew the truth, already, but I didn't realize we were to the point where it would be common knowledge. It added a new weight to everything.

If I dared admit it to myself, it would have been helpful to have Kaiden here. He was the best liar I knew, and even with his unpredictable states, I felt sure I could get him to go along, if only out of guilt for everything.

But, of course, he wasn't here. So I would be walking into the mouth of the lion alone, praying I didn't have a panic attack and slip up. Perfect plan.

Someone rapped gently on my door. Dez lifted sleepy eyes from his sprawled position on my desk, his mouth stretching in a wide yawn. I squared my shoulders, letting out a breath as I lowered my pencil from the letter I was writing.

"Come in."

It was probably Raoul, wondering what my plan was for the Empress, again. I couldn't get him off my back about it, no matter what I did.

The man who entered the room was decidedly not Raoul. For a moment, I could only stare, as Basil shifted on his feet and gave me a sheepish smile.

"Hey."

Resisting the urge to ask what he was doing, and why he was here, I said instead, "Shouldn't you be playing with the kids?"

Glancing around, Basil moved over, hesitantly sitting on the edge of the bed. His hands fiddled on his lap. "Um..."

"I don't have anything figured out, if that's what you're wondering." It came out too brusque, but he was making me uncomfortable, and I didn't know what to say. "If Raoul sent you."

He looked up, then, and shook his head swiftly. "No one...sent me."

Rather than asking the obvious, I held his gaze, waiting for an explanation. The edge of his mouth wavered, his chest deflating in what looked like a sigh. "How's it going?"

My shoulders sank, caught by surprise. The words spilled out on their own, at his open expression. "Not well."

He nodded, seeming to be waiting for something. He didn't ask any of the things I thought he would.

"What about you?"

Despite the simple shrug, his gaze drifted away. "Normal, I suppose. Which is strange."

I let out a quiet laugh. "Isn't it?" My mind had gone back to my father, and I felt it pulling painfully at the edge of my mouth, as my fingers instinctively brushed against my earring. "I should probably get back to work."

Basil nodded, standing up. "I just wanted to see how you were doing."

"You don't need to worry about me."

Though Basil drew in a breath, nodding slowly, his body language said otherwise. Before he could seem to change his mind, he stepped forward, wrapping me in a soft hug.

It caught me entirely off guard, and made something burning well up in my eyes. Sweet idiot.

"It'll be alright," he murmured, closing his eyes. "We'll be alright."

Any other day, I might have scoffed at his words. But right now, he was right. We needed that optimism. We all needed Basil, more than words could say.

"I miss him," I admitted quietly.

Basil nodded slowly, letting out a breath. "I know. It's okay."

I didn't want him to keep hugging me. I never wanted him to stop.

"Basil." I choked the name out into his shoulder, hushed and hot from the tears threatening to clog my throat. "I don't know what I'm going to do without him."

Basil was quiet for the longest moment, a careful hand skimming against my hair. "He'll come back, Lena," he said quietly.

The laugh that broke from my throat tasted vile on my tongue, twisting my words. "Don't lie to me." A savage bite hid beneath the words, like a coiled viper. "He's *dead*. There's no coming back from that.

Basil hesitated. "Just because... we thought he was before..."

"Stop it. Just *stop*. It's not helping."

Though Basil fell quiet, a crease formed between his brows. "How do you know?"

"That he's gone?" I knew my eyes were too bright, but I met his anyway, pretending they were angry tears. "The Empress executed him. I told you that."

Now Basil looked baffled. "I don't remember you saying..."

"The letter? That Caleb sent? My brother? I don't think he would lie to me, Basil. It's his dad too."

Basil blinked, staring at me for a long moment as his mouth finally fell open. "I...thought you meant Kaiden..."

A broken laugh left my lips. I swiped an arm across my face. "Are you serious? No. I meant my *dad*. Why would I miss Kaiden?"

Basil pushed his lips together, as if debating whether to press it. "I miss him."

"Well, good for you," I snapped, hating how vulnerable I sounded. "Why don't you go figure out where he went, then? Better yet, why don't you join him?" Before he could stop me, I stalked out of the room, swiping the rest of the weakness off my face.

He had to go and bring it up again, didn't he? Why couldn't everyone just assume I'd let it go? We'd almost had a nice moment there, and then he had to go and ruin it by bringing up Kaiden, again.

I certainly didn't miss him. In fact, I wished everyone would stop talking about him. He left us, and excuses or not, it didn't change a thing. He wasn't coming back, and he clearly didn't want to. Just like anyone else I'd ever thought might stay.

Burying my hands in my armpits, I suppressed a shudder. He hadn't left *because* I was different. But he'd left, all the same. The first person in years I'd actually tried to get closer to, and he threw it away like it was nothing, with guilt as his flimsy excuse.

I couldn't do it. I just couldn't. It hurt too much, thinking about it. Why did everyone assume I *wanted* to think about it?

IX

BASIL

It took Basil a long, painful moment to realize Lena wasn't actually mad at *him*, though he knew he had still said the wrong thing. She stood just outside the room with her back to him, shoulders hunched and arms hugging herself so the fabric of her blouse wrinkled considerably. He could almost see the shudder that ran through her, as much as she worked to conceal it. It made him wonder how long she'd been trying to hold all of this in.

"I...I'm sorry." Hesitating, he stepped closer to her, his hands seeking his pockets. "I didn't mean..."

"I know you didn't." Her laugh was quieter, almost bitter. "I overreacted."

Hesitant, he rubbed the back of his neck, then gave in to his instinct and drew her into another careful hug. "I'm sorry."

Rather than return it, she kept her arms circled around herself. "Don't. You're going to sound like Kaiden."

"Is that really so bad?"

In answer, she shoved him off with a scoff, folding arms protectively close to her ribs and focusing her gaze on the thoroughly-beaten dummy she liked to train with, laying battered near her room. He wondered if she ever imagined it as something else, like Olive did.

"It *is* if you're going to run off and abandon your friends. Twice."

"The first time wasn't his fault." Right? "And–"

Lena stuck a hand up to cut him off. "If you try to tell me he *'explained'* in a letter, I might just hit you."

Despite her warning, and his desire not to become a punching bag, Basil went on carefully. "Aren't you...wanting to find your brother? Isn't it kind of the same?"

"That's not the *point!*" Exasperated, Lena threw up her hands and turned as if to stalk away again, then seemed to think better of it. She jabbed a finger in his direction. "You have somewhere to be, don't you?"

"No..."

"Find one." With that, she turned to stride off. "I have things to be doing."

Basil let out a quiet sigh. Nothing ever really changed, did it? He was still here trying to patch up things that couldn't be fixed; comfort people who didn't want it. It was clearer than the night sky that Lena needed it, but she never let him get close enough for it. The best he got was when one of them got injured, and she railed on them for about an hour about how stupid it was of them.

No. He'd done this with Fern; he could do it with Lena. No one else was going to step up and fix things, so he would.

"Lena."

She cast him a slightly longer look than one of disdain, but didn't slow her pace as she headed back into her room. Which wasn't a problem, considering his long legs. *"What?"*

"Did I upset you, somehow?"

She frowned like she couldn't decide whether he was an idiot or just too nice for his own good. "No. I'm fine."

Right. That's why you're death-glaring me and your hands are clenched in fists.

"How can I fix it?"

Slowly her anger dissipated, switching to a sort of resignation and aching. *There.* That's what he was looking for. *That* he could fix.

She rubbed her hands over her face, her voice tilting toward unsteady. "I'm sorry. I'm no good at this. I didn't mean to snap at you." She drew in a ragged breath. "You've always been kind to me, and I can't even...manage a small bit of decency back."

"Hey, that's not true. You saved my life several times."

Dropping her hands, she released a quiet snort. "Yeah. And was an utter jerk while doing it."

Basil shrugged carefully as if in agreement, letting just enough of a smile on his face to seem playful. "You have a point there."

Though Lena frowned, her eyes were almost, *almost* laughing. Looking away, she murmured, "I suppose I do deserve that." As her gaze drifted to the ceiling, she drew in a breath. "Look, I...shouldn't have snapped at you. I just..." She sat back on the bed, her shoulders falling. "It's a lot." Her voice turned numb as she stared at the wall, decorated only with diagrams and various letters. "All of this."

Before he could convince himself not to, Basil tugged her closer, easing her into an enveloping hug. She blinked, trying for a moment to pull away, then went along with it, voice rocky.

"Hey. You already did this to me once."

"And you pushed me away. It wasn't a real hug."

147

She rolled her eyes. "Yeah, well, you weren't being very tactful."

"How was I supposed to know?" Pulling back, he studied her eyes. "I'm not a mind reader."

She held his gaze for a long moment, then dropped it, brushing his arm aside. "Right." Shifting, she pulled her legs up to hug to her chest, taking in a breath. "I'm sorry."

A smile touched his lips again, teasing. "Now *you're* going to sound like Kaiden."

Pulling her legs closer, she looked away. "I'm not...used to this," she whispered. "Having...friends."

The word made Basil smile, though he did his best to hide it. "That's alright."

"No, it's not." Eyes down, she shook her head. "I don't treat anyone right. I tried to hide behind harsh remarks and keep them at bay, because..." Her voice almost caught, as she took in an unsteady breath, blinking hard.

Basil wanted to tell her that it was okay, that she didn't have to say anything. But the war on her face made it clear that this would be good for her, more than anything. And isn't that what he came here to do? Help her?

Maybe all she needed was someone to listen. He could do that.

"You don't know me like you think you do."

"You're right." He nodded. "I know how wonderfully brave you are, but definitely not the full extent of it. There's too much for that."

She swallowed, picking at the edge of the soft, light material of her pants. "No." Staying quiet for a long moment, she eventually shook her head. "No."

With barely a pause for breath, she launched into a story that sounded painful even just to tell, stopping only to control the waver in her voice or regain her calm. Of a girl trying her hardest and doing the best she could in a terrible situation, even if that wasn't what she heard in the words she spoke. It spilled from her like an endless spool of thread, connecting and continuing on until the puzzle that was Lena Montellene began to make more sense. Why she snapped, and hid, and ultimately hurt without ever meaning to.

"All my friends left me," Lena murmured, blinking at her arms. He couldn't miss the way they tensed up to fight off another shiver. A choked laugh rasped from her lips. "Because I was 'different'. Because my father," her voice wavered on the word, teetering precariously before she steadied it, "wasn't Galdanian." Pressing her lips together tightly, she drew in a short breath. "They didn't like that very much."

Even though his chest ached, hearing her explain, Basil made himself stay quiet. He'd known she was hurting, but hearing the details of it just made it that much worse.

"Yeah." She buried the lower half of her face back in her arms, swiping one across her eyes. "So. Now you know."

Her eyes remained down, as if she expected him to yell at her now, or say it made sense why they left. All he wanted to do was hold her close until it erased the look from her eyes. He wanted to ask why she had confided in him, but was afraid of breaking the spell. She'd chosen to be vulnerable, for once, and he wasn't going to question that.

With a soft sigh, her shoulders sagging as if a huge burden had rolled onto them – or possibly off – she rested her head against him. Gently, he squeezed her hand, as her voice drifted quietly through the air.

"Are you going to leave, too?"

It was said so softly, like a breath of air captured in a sigh. As if it had already happened, or was bound to. As if he should just tell her now and spare her the disappointment.

"No."

She laughed, then, a quiet and achy thing. "You will. One way or another I'll push you away." She waved a hand at the empty air. "Already did, with Kaiden."

Her eyes were heavy as they drifted to the ground, her words silenced for a long moment. "Couldn't tell him...I did want him here." She took in a shaky breath. "To stay."

She gripped his hand so tightly it trembled, her bottom lip trapped beneath her teeth in a silent battle for control. Her eyes warred between bright and aching, determination unsteadily pushing it all aside. Shaking her head, hard, she drew in a sharp breath.

She wasn't mad at him, or even, truly, at Kaiden. Not in the ways she made it seem. She deflected it off onto them, and everyone else, because it gave her a way to let it out. But now, as she held his hand tightly enough to turn her knuckles white, the truth couldn't have been clearer. If his eyes had been closed before, after their rescue, then they were now open again, and seeing more than ever. He just wished he knew how he could help.

"Thank you," she eventually whispered, though her eyes were still a battlefield. "Though I don't understand why."

"That's okay." He cupped her hand in both of his, smiling. "You don't have to, for me to want to."

149

That seemed to make her relax, her shoulders falling more as she brushed at the gem of her earring. "I guess that's what friends do, huh?"

Squeezing her hand, he nodded. "Yeah."

KAIDEN

Joss wanted to bring the dragons with them. Kaiden had to reiterate, for the fifth time, why that was a bad idea. Kit dragons were loud and mischievous, and highly noticeable. They wouldn't get anywhere with that many colorful beacons in tow.

Joss protested, and pouted, but Kaiden stayed firm. The last thing he would let happen was Joss getting hurt, after everything he'd already seen.

"Joss," he began, and stopped himself. What could he say to convince her?

"Don't mind me," she answered airily, raising a hand. "I'll just be over here, keeping your pets company."

"Kits aren't pets," he murmured, and stopped at the sly look on her face. "Joss, we *can't* keep them."

"And why not? They're absolutely smitten with you. Look at them." She lifted a tiny blue dragon to his face, curled up in her hands. "How can you say no to that face?"

He looked away pointedly. She knew he couldn't resist for long.

"They look so cute with you. Look, you haven't even pushed them away this time!"

Maybe that was because a part of him *did* remember. Dimly, amidst memories he didn't wish to relive, the familiarity of the kits niggled at his mind. He'd fed them, once, long ago. And now, apparently, they wouldn't leave him alone.

"He's all yours," Joss told the kits cheerfully, petting her wyvern. It shrieked, and the dragons pressed closer to him, one curling its tail around his shoulder. He wasn't going to get rid of them, was he?

When Joss' back was turned, he ran a finger down the blue dragon's spine. A deep-throated hum answered him, the reverberations of it oddly calming.

Joss' grin widened as she looked back at him, her eyes sparkling. She didn't say it, but her expression clearly stated *I knew it.*

Before he could explain, the other dragons joined in with the first, harmonizing in their squeaky way. Joss looked immeasurably proud. "I *told* you they like you."

He set the dragon back down, though it simply plopped down next to him and kept singing. And Joss kept grinning, far too innocently.

"I told them a song might cheer you up."

He couldn't move his hand without brushing tiny scales, which only intensified the hum. "I don't...need dragons."

Joss shrugged in her carefree way. "I know. But they wouldn't leave me alone, and I don't like them, so. I made them flock to you instead." She barely hid a smile as she turned, adding on in a murmur, "They know who is the better of us two, anyway."

Sleepy dragons slowed their humming as they curled against him, one resting against his arm. He could barely move without disturbing them. "Why?"

Joss shrugged again. "As I said. You needed cheering up." She smiled at the pile of feathery tails and shining scales tucked against him. "And I was right."

Eventually, they reached a compromise. As long as they were outside the towns, traveling, the kits could stay. Kaiden tried to ignore the wide grin that spread across Joss' face at her victory. She didn't even *like* kit dragons. He also tried to pretend he didn't see the amused look on Jade's face as she watched the exchange.

One of Joss' stowaways landed on his shoulder, and he was too fed up to brush it away. He settled for fixing Joss with an exasperated look as the dragon sat there, preening itself on him.

She turned her lips up in a grin. "It likes you."

They all like me, Kaiden thought with some discomfort. They acted as though they were drawn to him, for some reason.

A memory slipped free in his mind, as much as he tried to keep it in place. A room filled with dragons, and a boy sitting amongst them, tossing them scraps.

"You have to eat too, you know."

Lil's voice, still too painful in his mind. He saw her sit down next to him, and with a quiet sigh, let the memory carry him away.

"I already ate."

She watched him continue to toss crumbs, amused. Though Lil was by far the analytical one of their group, she was always fascinated by the actions of dragons, and who they were drawn to.

"They like you," she said, an echo of the present.

And he knew why. Dragons were easier to be around, when you couldn't tell anyone your secrets.

Dragons. Once you fed them once, they were your friend for life. Whether or not you formed any other sort of bond, the act of offering them some of what you already needed to survive brought you up to high levels in their books.

Being starving and offering them food, well, that was like giving a poor man gold.

He remembered one particular occasion, when he'd been sitting in the shaded steps by the docks, the events of the day and the low throb of bruises old and new muddling in his mind. It had eaten away his appetite, bit by bit, until he was simply tearing his meager allotment of food into pieces and not eating them.

A kit dragon – not the most unusual sight near the waters, but most likely a stowaway or a captive – peeked out at him. On a whim, he tossed it the crumbs.

Dragons were a funny sort. As little as human food sustained them, save for meat, they seemed to greatly enjoy the taste of it. And to this poor creature, who knew too well the workings of his country, it must have seemed a feast. It had chirped at him in thanks, snatching up the crumbs and humming a little tune.

He never saw the creature again, once it flew away. It was caught, later, and he couldn't say a word even as he *heard* it crying out for him, in a way he couldn't explain, yet couldn't brush aside. He'd not forgotten that dragon.

Even meeting Ril had been a mistake. The tiny dragon had gotten lost from her brood, he assumed, and chirped at him until he picked her up – as he justified to his mind – to keep her quiet. She'd snuggled against him instantly and went to sleep, right in his hands. He hadn't the heart to turn her away. After how close he was to breaking that day...he'd let her be, and kept her a secret.

Poor Ril. If she felt the extent of his emotions...she would be just another one of many that he had hurt. And yet, still, she stayed; the same as Jade did.

Kit dragons were unerringly loyal, and surprisingly smart. Ril had been content to stay in his room, and comfort him when he needed a friend. But she stayed put when he put on his serious face, as if she knew, *This isn't my Kaiden.*

And he wasn't, then, in a way. He was Blaze, and Blaze had his own agenda. His own story. Blaze was a coverup for what Kaiden could never be.

Still, somehow, Ril had stuck with him. Through everything, everywhere he'd gone, she'd tagged along. Other than when he was imprisoned, she was with him. Probably because she knew it would hurt him more if she was potentially in danger.

Ril was smart, and he didn't deserve her.

Now, however, it seemed his past self had cursed him with a hoard of tiny, eager dragons who wouldn't leave him alone. They snuggled in his jacket, on his head, and toyed with the buckles on his boots. He let them be, hoping eventually they'd get bored and leave.

They slipped images into his mind, sometimes, like eager kids trying to show him things. They brought him bugs when he wouldn't eat. They sang to him until he brushed them away.

Dragons, it seemed, never forgot anything.

These dragons, curled around him like he was a warm pillow...they were the same ones from before. Back when the rest of his team was just in training, and the older ones were focused and determined. None of them truly took time to bond with their dragons outside of sparring, and missions.

He'd stopped feeding the kits, after being Blaze, and never went into that part of the Mountain when he could help it. The newer dragons flocked around Fern, presumably following with them on the rescue mission, but the older ones had stayed behind, in the Mountain. Even without proof, Kaiden knew that's what these ones were.

Fate was a funny, cruel thing. It gave him something meant to comfort him, but was still a reminder of his failure.

Still, as much as he wouldn't admit it to Joss, there was something oddly comforting about sitting in a tangled nest of tiny, sleeping dragons. They would forgive any fault if you gave them food, and curl up in your lap like nothing had happened.

Most of all, though, their ease with him was an unfamiliar feeling, and that only made it more relaxing. He didn't have to think, or wonder, or hope he wasn't doing anything wrong. He didn't have to watch what he said or did as long as he didn't step on any tiny tails. And the thrumming noise they made after being petted was as close to therapeutic as he thought a sound could get. It made him wonder why he hadn't taken advantage of it earlier.

There was a *lot* he didn't understand about himself, honestly, and it was frustrating if he tried to think about it for too long. He had bits and shards of memories that bit into him at times, never enough to make anything whole. Moments of Gigi laughing, or his sister's smile, or fire curling around his fingers, licking merrily at an unfortunate bush before him. Flickers of anger, and aching, and a guilt that twisted around him tighter than vines, making it hard to breathe. Just enough to stop him from finding any sort of rest.

The dragons helped with that, briefly. They wouldn't leave him alone, so he let them have their fun, one curled up in his hair while another sat on his shoulder, opposite Ril. The pink dragon was surprisingly gracious to the newcomers, as long as they didn't try to steal her perch.

"Hey, Bodyguard?" Joss interrupted his musing, barely waiting until he looked up to toss something at him. "Catch!"

He looked down at the bread now in his hand, which had definitely not been in his bag the night before. "Did you steal this?"

"Nope!" Joss crowed proudly. Only after he carefully pushed a piece into his mouth did she add, "I stole the money for it."

Kaiden coughed, nearly choking as he pounded his chest to try to expel the dry morsel lodged there, and stared at her in disbelief. Joss rocked on her toes, letting him have his moment of surprise before a wide, innocent grin slipped across her face. "From your pocket, of course."

Jade laughed at her words, in that loud, amused way of hers.

Head bent, hand resting on his knee, Kaiden drew in a deep breath, just composed enough to turn a mostly neutral and yet disapproving stare at her. Joss' eyes twinkled in impish delight, her hands clasped behind her back. "Aren't you proud of me?"

She had him trapped, and he could see she knew it. Instead of answering her, he swept his hand toward her. Joss stilled for half a second before he'd captured her in his lap, his breathing slightly uneven as he rested his chin against her head.

"Now you can't...run away again."

"Hey, whoa there," Joss said, too low to be convincing. "No need to get touchy-feely."

Continuing to recover his breath, Kaiden didn't reply, his chest moving against her back. "That's what you get," he managed to say.

"I should steal your money more often," Joss teased, though there was a funny look on her face. "Your expression was priceless."

Unable to hide a smile, Kaiden shook his head. Joss squirmed, eventually going still in his lap until his hands relaxed. With a triumphant exhale, she slipped free from his arms. "Ha!"

Kaiden just smiled at her, until she cleared her throat and coughed. "Anyway. We're going to see your siblings, right?"

He let her stand in silence for a moment longer, clearly growing uncomfortable, before he nodded, scooping up one of the dragons to place on his shoulder. "Yes." He hoped she couldn't hear how quiet his voice was. "They're not too far from here." He gestured away from the town, eyeing her. "Though I do hope you bought more than just breakfast with that money."

Joss huffed, drawing out the remaining coins to stick in his hand. Kaiden couldn't hold back another smile.

The dragons stayed close by him as they walked, flying around in a squealing game of chase-the-dragon or peeking inquisitively and investigating new 'wonders' that they came across. The smallest of them, a red female he thought of as Ruby, hissed at anything he got too close to, as if it might be dangerous. Her little ears flattened, the spikes on her back rising like hackles as she death-glared a nearby shrub or nipped a branch that brushed its sharp points against him, tiny claws gripping the shoulder of his jacket just tight enough to keep a hold of him, without penetrating skin.

As much as he wouldn't admit it aloud, the kits were starting to grow on him, and maybe make him relax just a little. He knew Joss caught the brief flickers of smiles they pulled from him, as quick as he buried it, and she looked far too smug about it.

A blue kit landed on his shoulder and sneezed. Her eyes went adorably wide, snout twitching as the plant she had investigated tickled another sneeze out of her.

One thing was for sure. Between Joss and all the kit dragons, and Jade's teasing comments, it was by no means a boring trip.

For the moment, Joss seemed content to run on ahead of him, petting her wyvern and getting snapped at. She'd toss him a grin every so often, or fall back to walk by his side and tease the kits, but for the most part, they shared a comfortable silence, broken only by soft footfall and dragon squeaks.

He started assigning names to the kits, if only to keep better track of them. Since he couldn't imagine having nine tiny voices in his head amidst everything else, and kit dragons couldn't exactly speak his language, they would have to make do with his poor naming skills, at the moment. They were the ones who had wanted to tag along, anyway. He didn't asked to be followed by a hoard of tiny kit dragons.

He was gathering quite the collection of stowaways.

Later, when they stopped for another break, Kaiden found himself messing with the music pipes he had saved from his home. Between the dragons' humming and the shards of memories pricking at him, he'd been thinking about them more than usual. He ran a couple careful fingers over their worn, scratched surfaces. They reminded him so much of Kinny.

Joss, who had been digging in his bag for food, furrowed her brow when she saw it. "What's that?"

He wanted to hide it away, to say 'Nothing' and just move on. But he couldn't. She had asked, and he found he couldn't say no. Slowly, his fingers uncurled, revealing the small, child-sized instrument in his palm. As scratched and scarred as he was.

155

Joss' eyes widened in what looked like wonder. "You play music?"

He hadn't been intending on it. But the way her eyes lit up, he nodded, lifting the wood carefully to his lips. Though his mind didn't remember the steps, his fingers did, resting over the ridges with unsettling familiarity as he blew a gentle note from it, the sound echoing softly in the wind.

Joss looked on in awe, settling on the ground with her legs crossed and barely covered by her dress. Her fingers gestured as if on their own, when he stopped. "Again...?"

Holding the pipe more firmly, Kaiden let his eyes drift close as a melody spilled out, just as gentle and lovely as it was in his mind. In that moment, he could have sworn he saw his sister again, twirling in the grass with red braids swaying and a bright, unbreakable smile on her face.

"Dance with me."

It was ridiculous; he couldn't play and dance at the same time. But she laughed and took his free hand anyway, the music managing to stumble from his pipes in an intentional, harmonious pattern as she pulled him in, swaying him around as he continued to gently coax notes from the wood.

"Mama would love it," she whispered.

And just like that, the notes took a solemn turn, slipping to something deeper and far more mournful as he followed the pull of it, his brows drawing together in response. In the dark of his mind, he could see her, the tiredness in her eyes as her smile slowly faded, her strength waning. Kinny growing, and dancing less, and becoming quieter as he played less, until the notes nearly choked his throat to play them. They painted pictures through the air, of pain and beauty and a longing he'd never admit aloud.

He wanted that back. Whatever it was.

Opening his eyes to escape the sight, he saw Joss sitting in rapt distress, her eyes too bright as she cupped her hands to her chest, like the music had struck her as sharply as an arrow. She stayed silent, taking in the softest breath when the notes continued to whistle forth in a magic-less tune from his pipes, now stripped of their joy. Still he continued playing, quieter, even as the notes grew low and haunting, like a funeral dirge.

Joss settled her hands in her lap, her expression quiet as she watched his, as if she could catch sight of the magic that had spilled from it just moments before. But it just felt heavy now, and aching in his throat were tears he could never shed, preventing the magic from coming forth. Changing it, into something he couldn't face. He let it choke out of him to its completion, a little harsh and rusty in the end as if it, too, were dying.

Never again, he heard his mind whisper, an echo of the past. *Never again.*

It had hurt too much, after her death. The music heavy with memories, ones he couldn't even piece together at the moment. For both of their sakes, he lifted the notes to a lighter tune, ignoring the ache in his chest as he blew into the wood, softly. Kinny's favorite song, a journey in and of itself in the rise and ebb of the music, about a traveler and his failures and triumphs. He never found his rest, prompting the song to begin all over again. It felt oddly fitting, for the moment.

Joss looked down at her hands, brows drawn together. She seemed to be contemplating something, and he gave her a moment as he pushed back his own memories, knowing they'd only do more harm than good at this point. There were too many versions, and too many of them painful for him to even wish to know which was real.

The Bane hadn't just taken his memories. It had twisted them, until even he couldn't remember which were real anymore. It was like fire raging through his mind, tearing him apart until all he could do was give in, if only so he didn't have to relive any of it.

If he ever dared, which he didn't anymore, he could brush against them, and remember why they had been buried. Why it had seemed like such a good idea, at the time, and why he'd stopped fighting back. Why he'd let it have its way, so he didn't have to experience any of it again.

His mind was too broken to determine what was the truth anymore. That had been the point, after all. Making him think he should want it, or deserved it, or *needed* it. Whatever it took to break his will.

And no one knew the truth about all of it, anymore. Not even him.

Somehow he knew, even if they did, that it would take more than just words to mend the gaps. He felt Meriador's presence there every so often, offering to help, but who was to say she would truly fix them?

No. For the moment, he had to be content with scraps of memories and pieced-together things he had been told. A name, a smile, a musical instrument. Random jokes and bits of information he didn't know how he had.

Somehow, through all of this, his fingers kept playing. The kit dragons bobbed their heads in delight at the song, humming along softly and trying to squeak in imitation of it. It added a playful echo to the melody, a haunting reminder of the past. Joss sat with her knees too close to her chest, watching the ground as if she, too, was caught somewhere other than the present.

Letting the song drift to an end, he took a breath, and reached to pet one of the dragons' heads. She hummed, pressing into the touch as the other dragons resumed their chirring and happy squeaks.

Joss drew in a lingering breath of her own, her eyes connecting with his for a long moment before a slow smile lifted her lips. "And you say you don't have any skills."

There was still something different about her eyes, but by the way she got to her feet, brushing off a kit dragon that clung to her sleeve, she didn't seem eager to talk about it.

The tiny kit pouted, watching her go. Attempting to smile, Kaiden stroked her head.

"Blue likes you."

Joss stopped, and gave him a funny look. "Is *that* what you're calling her? Remind me not to give you naming privileges, ever. What did you name the other one? Green?"

He scratched the back of his neck, which felt oddly hot. "No."

The dragon in question dropped onto his shoulder, cocking its head at him. He brushed it off, getting a huff in response.

Joss' eyes lit up with a laugh. "You *did*." She leaned back against a tree, tossing her head toward the sky. "Wow."

He couldn't exactly tell her that an evil entity had screwed with his head, and so he didn't feel comfortable linking with a kit dragon's mind in order to know their real name. The colors just...helped.

"I guess I should be glad I'm not your kid, huh? I might have ended up with the name 'Girl' or something." Clearing her throat abruptly, she kicked a heel against the ground. "Which would be silly."

"I don't know their names," he mumbled to the ground. Joss only grinned, one eyebrow lifting higher than the other.

"I thought you didn't *want* to keep them."

He slipped his arms over his chest, not answering. Despite the funny look that kept playing on her face, Joss eventually chuckled, pushing away from the tree.

"Well c'mon, Dragonkeeper," she teased. "We still have a lot of ground to cover."

Though he followed after, Kaiden couldn't help but wonder when she had become the one leading, as if she knew where they were going. The kit dragons gathered close to him, flapping colorful wings in the air as they cheered and tussled with each other. Ruby stayed crouched on his head, hissing at a fly that got too close to them. He buried a smile,

158

slipping the pipes back into his jacket and letting Jade hold his other hand.

The kit dragons made him uncomfortable mostly because of their innocence. They peppered his mind with tiny songs and images of things they'd done, and he'd smile quietly at them, but they could never know his secrets. He saw them waiting, asking patiently. They wouldn't overstep the boundaries he'd set. And yet...he could see they *wanted* to. They'd squeak in delight and try to press images against his mind, and he'd push them away, ignoring the looks on their faces.

Ril never tried to push him. She curled up on his shoulder, protectively, the tip of her tail sometimes brushing against the back of his neck – but never touching his scars – and watched the other kits as if to supervise them. She was sad, he knew, but they already had a bond, and it didn't seem to matter to her if he didn't open it back up for years to come. She would stay by him, all the same.

What did he do to earn such loyalty?

Kaiden rolled a small, uneven stone in his hands and considered the girl chatting with her wyvern. He could leave the kits with her, when he found his siblings. They'd look after her, right?

He didn't understand why he felt such a connection to her. But he wanted to make sure she was taken care of, no matter what happened. He couldn't hide his surprise that she hadn't left already.

The next time Joss asked to stop happened to be conveniently near another of the towns. She took off with little explanation, leaving him alone with his thoughts, and Jade.

His best friend flopped on her back near him, in the grass. "Looks like it's just us again until the kid comes back."

Smiling out of the side of his mouth, Kaiden nodded. Who knew what trouble she'd get up to, wherever she had gone?

Jade nudged him with her foot. Kaiden blinked over at her, confused.

"You looked like you were going to say something." She winked.

Kaiden held back a laugh. "I just said 'Who knows what trouble she'll get up to?'"

Jade grinned. "No, you didn't."

"I...didn't?"

Jade laughed, shaking her head. "No."

Kaiden rubbed the back of his neck slowly and then dropped his hand. "Oh."

Jade looked rather amused. "You just get used to making faces at me, I suppose."

Kaiden dropped his gaze, looking over at the dragons. "I guess I have."

Jade chuckled. "Aww, don't get all sheepish on me. I don't care if you make faces at me." She winked again.

He smiled out of the side of his mouth. It was funny, considering that making faces at the air was...usual, for him. "I know. It's just...odd."

"What about us isn't odd? I mean, I'm your weird imaginary friend that stalks you all over the place and creepily eavesdrops on you and all your friends. I'd say if anyone is odd in this relationship, it's not you, Butterfly."

He chuckled, looking down for a moment and smiling a little wryly. "You're not."

"Am so. I'm probably the weirdest person anyone has ever met, and you know it." She grinned, then paused to think about it. "Or... has never met? You know what I mean."

"I suppose," he teased.

"He 'supposes'." Jade huffed out a breath. "No 'supposing' about it." She reached out to poke his foot.

He arched an eyebrow, high and questioning. Blue stirred from her flopped position over his boot, humming in her sleep.

Jade laughed. "I love when you get sassy. It's adorable." She tossed a blade of grass at him. "Like a kitten or something."

"'Like a kitten,'" he echoed, scrunching up his nose. "Wow. Way to make me sound all cool and clever."

Jade tossed her head back, cracking up. "What can I say? You're like those kittens that try to be all standoffish and sassy, but all you can think is 'Awwww' when you see them. You're even all orangy-reddish!" Sitting up, she reached to mess with his hair.

Ducking his head down, Kaiden rubbed at his hotter-than-usual cheek. Incidentally, the action made it easier for Jade to reach his head. "What's my hair have anything to do with it?"

Jade made it all wild and spikey, looking pleased. "Because the friendliest kittens are often orange. Duh."

"I wouldn't know," he mumbled. "I've never had a cat." At least that he remembered.

Jade laughed. "I know. I haven't either, but I've had friends with them." Turning around, she flopped against him – back leaned against his side and legs spread out in front of her. "If you weren't such a great butterfly, I could call you Kitten."

Though Kaiden pulled his shoulders in, he didn't move away, doing his best to sound more sarcastic than embarrassed. "Please don't. I prefer dogs."

As usual, Jade's laugh was peppy and sparkly. "Yeah, I like Butterfly too much."

Despite everything, he couldn't help smiling at it. "Why do you sound disappointed by that?"

"Because Kitten is another perfectly fantastic nickname. But Butterfly will always take the cake, so no new nicknames today." She patted his arm. "Now *my* nickname on the other hand could totally use changing. You should think up a new one." She made a point to sound all 'casual' about it.

"It makes me sound tiny," he replied, as if 'Butterfly' didn't fit that category, too. Hesitating, he wished again that he could remember *what* her nickname was. "No. I like what it already is."

Jade let out a loud sigh. "But it doesn't fit." She dropped dramatically beside him, puddled in the dirt and leaned against him. "I'm so...weird. I mean, look at me."

"I am," he replied, suppressing a grin at how close she was to the sleeping kit dragons, a tangle of unaware tails and tiny claws, some of them purposefully piled on others. "That's part of why it fits."

Jade made a disgruntled sound. "Fine. But I accept it under protest."

"As long as you accept it," he replied, grinning.

Looking pouty, Jade huffed. Teasingly, he reached over to pat her head.

Jade made a face at him. "Only one of your fabulous hugs can return you to my good graces over this."

He cast a skeptical eye at her. "From that position?"

Jade considered him. "I suppose I should sit up for one. It's hard to hug a puddle."

"Yeah, unless I wanted to get soaking wet. Which wasn't really my plan for today."

In response, Jade sat up with a heavy mock-sigh. "Better?"

"Hmmmm."

Jade huffed. "Well, I can always return to being a puddle."

Nonchalantly, Kaiden shrugged a shoulder. "I never said you had to get up."

"Don't give me any of that. I know how to read between the lines." She poked his forehead.

Kaiden wrinkled it, at her touch. "Between what? The lines on my forehead?"

Jade laughed. "Is that like being a palm reader or something? Weird. No, the ones between 'from this position?' And 'getting wet wasn't my plan for today'."

Kaiden chuckled. "And what would those be?"

"That you wanted me to sit up first."

"Hmmm," he said again, rubbing his chin.

She pouted. "Fine, just don't hug me, then."

He was having trouble keeping a straight face. "Okay."

Dramatically, Jade collapsed back in the dirt, looking mopier than the dragons did when their owners were away. Fighting down a grin, Kaiden rubbed one of the kits' heads, eyeing her teasingly.

But Jade continued to pout, until he wondered if he'd actually upset her. Hesitantly, he nudged her foot, raising an eyebrow at her in question.

To his relief, her eyes still sparkled when she looked up at him, despite the pouting. "Are you going to actually hug me this time, or is this another trick?"

"I think you'd have to sit up to find out."

Jade expelled a long sigh. "I think that sounds like trickery."

Kaiden looked sadly down at the kit dragon, who blinked sleepy, contented eyes at him before rolling over onto her back. "She doesn't believe me."

"If I sit up, then I'd better get a hug," Jade warned, her eyes laughing.

Doing his best to hide his sheepishness, Kaiden wrapped his arms around her. Jade smiled, squeezing him lightly.

"Is this so bad?"

Kaiden stayed there for a moment, holding onto her. and shook his head. "No."

Jade chuckled. "You sure? Maybe my hugs are awful."

He shook his head a little firmer. "No."

She grinned. "No? Weird, I would've thought my hugs at least a little strange." Rocking back on her knees, she threw him a wink.

"Why?"

"Because everything about me is strange, obviously." She shrugged. "I'm a crazy-haired invisible girl. Do I need a better explanation than that?"

Kaiden shook his head. Leaning back on one palm, Jade grinned.

"Well, then I have no good explanation." She reached up to mess with his hair again. Kaiden brushed it back down.

Jade looked insulted at that. "Hey!"

He feigned innocence. "What...?"

162

Jade messed up his hair again. "It looks better like this."

"Does it?"

"Yes," she huffed. "So leave it like that."

"Okay, *mom*."

Jade stuck her tongue out at him. Teasingly, he returned the gesture.

With a laugh, Jade flopped in the grass. "So what happened to your kid?"

Though it caught him off guard for a moment, he tried not to show it. "I don't...know. She sort of just wandered off." *Probably to steal something*, his mind added.

"Maybe you should call her back for dinner." Jade grinned.

Chuckling, Kaiden leaned back against a tree. "And how, exactly, do you expect me to accomplish that?"

"I don't know? Yell into the woods? Rattle the food bag? Shout 'food!'? Or maybe send your tiny clingy dragons after her? Here, dragons, go fetch Kaiden's small child."

Kaiden held back a laugh, eyeing the sleeping dragons. Yawning, Blue rolled over to face him, keeping her eyes closed. The perfect model of a messenger dragon.

"Mm. Not a bad idea," he mused. "Send *them* to pester her instead."

Jade grinned widely. "I thought so. All my ideas are brilliant." Dramatically, she struck a pose, which was made more amusing by her position flopped on the ground.

Kaiden eyed the dragons again, chuckling. "Though, she's not really my child."

Dismissively, Jade waved her hand. "She's close enough."

Wrinkling his nose up, he shook his head. "I highly doubt she sees it that way."

"That's okay. No one knows I am right until I am." She snuggled into the dirt like she intended to sleep there.

His forehead creased. "What is that supposed to mean?"

"Just that being right and being proven right don't usually happen at the same time." She grinned. "The real question is whether or not you can convince the dragons to go get her or not."

Kaiden watched the dragons, scratching the top of Ruby's head. At least she didn't *sleep* in his hair, too. "I doubt it." He was glad the dragons weren't awake to look at him adoringly.

"Well, you might as well try it. It's not like I can ask them."

"No? I figured you could."

"As if they'd listen to me anyway. They'd take one look at me and run away." She wrinkled her nose.

"Why?"

Jade motioned at herself and her hair, which tangled around her upper arms and shoulders and puddled around her head. "'Why', he asks. As if it's not obvious."

"Nope." He couldn't hold back a smile.

Jade sighed. "Well it is."

"I think you're using the fact that I don't remember to try to shape my opinion." He dropped his head in his hands, smiling at her.

Jade grinned back at him. "How so?"

Skeptically, he raised an eyebrow at her.

"That's not an answer, Butterfly."

"It is. It's a silent one. I thought you'd be used to those by now."

"I've always been used to silent answers. Doesn't mean I don't like actual ones."

Rather than respond to that, Kaiden tickled the tiny dragon by him, trying to hide his smile. It just felt natural, teasing her. Like less of an effort on his part and more of a natural response.

Jade flopped an arm over her eyes, so she couldn't see him. He let the smile widen, just a little. Even if he didn't remember much, he knew this was just...right.

When Jade turned her head to look at him, he schooled the smile.

"You don't have to hide it. Not with me." She smiled back at him.

Though he made sure to nod, Kaiden rubbed the base of his neck, looking out at the distance.

"I don't know what I'm going to do with her," he admitted after a moment, blowing out a long breath. "Joss, I mean."

"Keep her, if she wants to stay. I think she likes you, Butterfly."

Kaiden shut his eyes. "She's not my kid. She probably has a family; she's just hungry, and desperate. She won't stick around." His hands curled at his sides, close to fists. *She doesn't need help.*

"If she had a family, Kaiden, she wouldn't be hungry and desperate."

Kaiden let out a quiet breath of a laugh, glancing around. "Here?" He shook his head. Even with his fractured memories, he knew how false the statement was. "I had a family. Have..." he corrected, blinking. It hadn't made everything better.

Jade reached over to take his hand. He squeezed it, and his eyes shut for a moment before he sighed, the tension partially leaking out. "She's not mine," he finally said, quiet.

"I didn't say she was. But I kept you and you aren't mine, either." Shrugging, she grinned a bit.

Kaiden held back a quiet laugh, a hint of a smile playing on his lips. "It's a bit different."

"How so? I found a desperate, sad kid and decided to keep him because he needed someone. You haven't ever been mine, and yet, here we are. It seems the same to me."

He dropped his gaze, trying not to smile. "I don't think she wants that."

"Maybe not yet. But we'll see," Jade said, her tone turning sing-song and almost...smug.

To distract from the other thoughts running through his head, Kaiden raised his eyebrows at her. "You don't make any sense."

"I know. I never have. It's better when I don't make sense." She grinned and shrugged, a flicker of something in her eyes before it disappeared.

Kaiden's lips tipped in a small smile. "I guess so. Probably makes sense to you. Just not to me."

"I rarely make sense to anyone." She pushed hair away from her face, chuckling.

"I doubt I make much sense to most people either."

Looking up at him, she grinned. "You do to me."

Chuckling, he rubbed the back of his neck. Probably not to Joss, though. No wonder she was so eager to be rid of him. She'd said she would be back, but he couldn't help wondering how long it would take before she said that...and didn't return.

"Well, at least one person gets it."

"I've always 'got it'. I've known you a long time, Butterfly."

And that's why you're my best friend, he thought, the fondness slipping back into his smile again as he watched her. No matter what, he knew he'd have her by his side. If the pain of his childhood, faking insanity, shutting everyone else out, hurting those he loved through the influence of an evil entity, and the half-dozen breakdowns he'd had in just this short time hadn't pushed her away, nothing would. It was a comforting relief amidst other thoughts.

Maybe Joss wouldn't come back this time, though. Maybe he should just go on without her, and spare them both a hard farewell.

"Bodyguard?"

Kaiden couldn't hide a smile of relief as Joss scuffed the ground near him, looking down. "Sorry I took off."

Are you? he wondered, raising an eyebrow skeptically. Frowning, she ducked her head.

"I wanted to get away from the dragons," she muttered.

Though he wondered what she had so against the kits, he didn't quite feel like questioning her about it. Instead, he smiled. "Well, you came back just in time. I was about to eat without you."

She narrowed her eyes, fingering the chain still around her neck, he noticed. "You wouldn't."

"It *is* my food," he said smugly, unable to hold back a smile as he held a piece of cheese out to her. "You should be glad I'm sharing it at all."

Her arms stayed tight across her chest as she sat down, snatching it from his hands. She seemed more defensive tonight, and angry, like when he'd first rescued her.

"It should be your price," she muttered, taking a bite and speaking around it, "for enjoying my wonderful presence."

He smiled at her, even as she hunched herself against a tree, eyes narrowed. She seemed angry at him, and he didn't know why.

"You don't have to bring me along," she muttered, eyeing the dragons near her distastefully. "I'll be fine here. You didn't have to wait."

Kaiden rubbed the back of his neck, the words from earlier shriveling on his tongue. *Do you want to come?*

Her eyes met his, accusatory. "Why did you?" It took him a moment to realize what she meant. "Why haven't you just left already?"

He swallowed carefully, unable to read her expression. She was definitely angry, but he wasn't entirely certain yet if it was at him, or just about him. "Do you want me to?"

"I'll be fine," she muttered, turning her body away from him. Lower, she added, "I always am."

Standing up slowly, Kaiden walked over to retrieve a blanket for her. "Either way," he said quietly, "you can sleep here if you'd like."

Along with the blanket, he offered her a little smile. If she wanted to stay, he wouldn't turn her away. But if she wanted to leave, if she'd found something better...

Wordlessly, Joss snatched the blanket from his hands. He could have sworn he saw a shudder cross her frame, just for a moment, before she bunched the fabric around her and turned over, laying so she was facing away from him.

Despite Jade's suggestion that he sleep, too, Kaiden stayed up for a long time with his thoughts. He told himself it was to make sure Joss was okay, and nothing more than that. Though he'd already made up his mind on what he was going to do, that didn't mean he couldn't let this moment linger, in case everything went wrong.

He hoped it didn't. He needed a bit of hope, with all the doubt in his head. It took most of his strength not to think about his siblings, and what they might think of him. What they were like. What was true.

With a quiet sigh, Kaiden let his hoard of kit dragons cuddle closer to him, their tiny chests rising and falling as they snuggled against his outstretched leg and in his lap. Ruby pressed close to his chest near his heart. Closing his eyes, he tipped his head back against a tree and let the past carry him away.

JOSS

When she woke up, her bodyguard was gone. Joss' heart pounded for a moment, as she pinched herself hard enough to make herself yelp. She wasn't dreaming. Where had he gone?

As he usually did in the early morning, Rascal looked very displeased and rather sleepy. She scooped him up anyway, ignoring his half-hearted bite at her finger, and scanned the area.

The previous night came back to her. Her harsh words, now forming a sinking hole in her chest. She shouldn't have taken it out on him. But...

Joss rubbed fists into her eyes, breathing through a shudder. *Reign.* She hadn't expected to run into him, hadn't *wanted* to, even. He'd said he didn't need her. She didn't even know how he'd found her.

He'd said he'd be there for her, and then he wasn't. Joss remembered that night all too clearly, burning in her mind. And yet he was offering now to take her back, claiming it had all been an act.

Everything was an act, in Calest. Sometimes, when Joss heard stories of the Uppers, and Galdanians who liked to hide their emotions behind fanciful masks, she had to hide a laugh. They didn't know what true betrayal looked like, because they could always see it coming. It wasn't the same as being stabbed in the back, and not being able to register the pain until you saw the blood pooling at your feet, staining into your memories.

Kaiden frightened her for that very reason. She'd never seen *this* kind of deception before, and nearly let her guard down to it. Seeing Reign had been a chilly reminder, and a painful opportunity.

"You really think your mark is going to keep you around for long? Jocelyn. You're smarter than that."

She'd helped him find his information. He was probably looking for a good time to ditch her, anyway. Perhaps he felt guilt about leaving her stranded on her own.

167

Joss forced herself to look around the camp again. The kit dragons were still there, she noted, just as she expected. He appeared to have left her the blanket, and a few other supplies, though his bag was gone. How kind.

Just before Joss was about to give up, Rascal screeched at her. There, pinned to the tree Kaiden had been next to, a lone scrap of paper rippled in the wind. She got to her feet, glimpsing the now-obvious footprints leading away from the camp, and tore the paper free, steeling herself for what it might say.

He'd left a note printed neatly on it, a scrawling drawing of a flower of sorts on the other side. Joss stared at it for a moment, temporarily mesmerized. The words said only, "Be back soon," and were accompanied by a doodled picture of him smiling. Joss wanted to laugh and throw it at the same time. There was nothing for her to do now but wait, and think.

What felt like forever later, she heard the approach of his footsteps, and caught a whiff of the steam curling deliciously from whatever he held in his hands. Joss' mouth watered even before he sat down by her, smiling hesitantly. He held it out to her.

She could have cried from happiness. Her mind didn't even register what was in the food, only that it smelled *heavenly* and her stomach was aching in a different way now. She tore into it before it cooled fully, unwilling to stop even to thank him until it was gone. He ate his own quietly, though there was a small look of satisfaction in his eyes as he watched her.

Joss felt something deep and aching prick at her eyes. She didn't deserve *any* of this. She'd thought he was going to leave, and maybe he still would, but she'd still been so harsh toward him. And then he got her food. If she'd even needed any sort of apology, this certainly sufficed.

"You good?" he asked, and it took her a moment to realize he meant hunger-wise. His hand half-extended the rest of his to her. She shouldn't have, but her stomach was crying out. Gently, she pushed it away. "You keep it."

He wrapped it in a cloth, tucking it into his bag. Joss swiped an arm across her face. "It's better warm."

"I can heat it up later," he answered, though there was something faint flickering in his eyes that she couldn't interpret. "We only have a little ways to go, anyway," he said a little too loudly, "and then I'll...be out of your hair. There's a town nearby that..." Pressing his lips together, he stopped.

Joss blinked at him. Out of *her* hair? "You're not a nuisance," she said automatically, and then added a shrug. "I mean, yeah, you can be a little 'woe is me' all of the time, but you have great taste in food. So I'm good." She blinked against the fire threatening to pull tears from her eyes.

Kaiden nodded, his gaze cast away as he contemplated it, like he wasn't sure he believed her. "You're...welcome to do whatever you like," he said, and stood.

But surely not stay with him. That would be unthinkable, wouldn't it? What would she *do*, anyway? Get her life together? Stop stealing? She might as well change her name from Jocelyn Rees. Maybe she'd use the name her mother had wanted for her. If she could still remember it.

It took Joss a moment to scramble to her feet. "You're still my bodyguard, yeah? I need you." She frowned, but decided to go with it. "For now, at least."

Though he didn't say it, she heard the echo in the silence, amidst everything. This was still going to be goodbye. If not right now, then soon. He'd bought her a lovely meal and now he was going to leave. And she would be alone.

His expression was far too quiet, eyes trained on the dirt. Joss swallowed down a sob, even as he nodded. "Alright."

This was good, right? He would be happy. He'd have his siblings, and she'd have Rascal, and...she'd be okay. The gemstone would buy her anything she needed, at least to get on her feet, or she could go back with Reign. Known dangers over new ones. She was far enough away from town that it wouldn't be a concern. She could start over. Have a life.

She didn't...*want* to just 'have a life'. Not without him.

Hugging her arms across her chest, Joss fought a frown. Kaiden was too quiet, and the sparkle of hope in his eyes only made her feel way worse.

"What if they don't like me?" he asked absently, that same odd mix playing in his eyes from before. It took Joss a moment to realize that his focus had shifted.

"Well, they'd be fools not to. You're fantastic. And who wouldn't like that hair?" She ticked the list off on her fingers. "You have great tastes in food, pun completely intended. You play music. You draw." She squinted at him, as if to see his reaction. His expression didn't change. "And you never eat all your food, so there's always more for everyone else. How nice of you is that?"

Though she'd meant the last part sarcastically, his lips tipped up a bit wistfully, and wryly. "I guess so."

"I know so," Joss muttered, looking away to the side. "Anyone would be lucky to have you."

Though he nodded, she could tell he wasn't convinced. That made her grumpy.

Despite his reservations, though, his eyes got achingly hopeful the closer they got to their destination. He even made jokes – too many jokes, in Joss' opinion, although she suspected it might have been from nervousness. He let the kits nestle in his hair, and play with his clothes, and absentmindedly petted them when they snuggled against him. He smiled and said sweet things and even hummed a little, though there was something far-off and unsteady about it.

Joss stayed close by him, feeling the knot in her stomach grow. Despite his best efforts, nothing was going to calm her. If anything, it hurt more than she'd admit, if she looked at his eyes too long. So she teased him with Rascal, and made snarky comments, and did everything she could to avoid acknowledging the pass of time. The grass under their feet grew less prickly, which seemed to surprise them both. Though comparatively, they weren't that far from the last town they'd stopped at, no buildings or civilization of any kind were in sight, in this direction.

And then it happened. Kaiden's feet slowed, just outside a wooded area she was sure he must recognize. He sat down and pulled out food so they could eat, but Joss already knew there was more to it than that, with the way his focus kept wandering.

"Would you...stay here?" he said eventually, his gaze averted. The meaning was clearer than a river when the sun sparkled through it. *I don't want to explain why a tiny thief girl has been following me. And won't leave me alone.*

"Of course," she answered, almost too cheerfully. Something shifted across his face, obscured as always, before he nodded, mustering up a hint of a smile.

"Thank you."

Thank you. A bittersweet end to what had been one of the loveliest dreams she might have ever held. Joss hated that she had gotten attached. She always did.

"No problem," she replied, as she watched him stand back up and walk off, one hand curled at his side in that distinctive way. A boy and his imaginary friend, off to find his old life.

She couldn't bear to see his face when he returned. She just couldn't. Before she could decide otherwise, Joss gathered up what she could and stuffed it in the bag, swiping an arm across her eyes as she took back her blanket, and threw some of his food in, for good measure. He'd understand. He'd left it all there, anyway. Probably didn't need it, now that he was home and all.

Home. That word should not have been like a dagger in her chest. Joss drew in an unsteady breath, leaning back against a particular large rock where Rascal had decided to perch. Maybe she could still wait, for a little bit. Rest up and all. Maybe he'd come back for his things, and...

And *what*? She was just delaying the inevitable, and making the hole larger in her chest. It had already hurt once, with Reign. She should have learned her lesson by now.

With tears in her eyes that she didn't bother to brush away – who was there to see them? – she fingered the gem on her necklace. Her ticket to freedom. Her key, her hope.

The shadows over the campsite shifted, as time went on. She should just leave now, before he came back. But what if his siblings *weren't* there, and he still needed her?

Joss let one of the kit dragons cuddle against her leg, briefly. They would miss him, too. Surely he'd come back for them.

She waited, and *waited*, a good, long time seeming to pass before finally, she allowed it to sink in.

He wasn't coming back. She had known it all along, but it still hurt, deep down. He'd just left his things, and the dragons...and her. Left them all, like they never mattered.

And why would they have? He hadn't chosen any of them. They'd been forced on him, and he was probably glad to be rid of them.

Never mind the burning ache in her chest. It had been there when Reign left, too, even though he had ruined her. She *had* to leave. He wasn't just going to let her stay, and be herself, and...

No one else had ever made her feel like this. There was always a time in which it went wrong, usually around this point. She waited for it, the warning signs, the perfect opportunity, and then she took it. Snatched an Upper's priceless jewelry. Dodged a lengthy lecture for stealing, yet again. Blamed a different child for the disappearances and slipped out with only a twinge of guilt.

She couldn't stay, even if he didn't have anything worth stealing. If anything, that was even more reason for her *not* to stay. Right? What did she have to gain?

Joss looked up at Resenya from where she lay resting a little ways away, eyeing her. "You'll keep him in line." It wasn't a question, or even a command. Just a statement they both knew, and Resenya had no reason to answer. Though the green dragon had come and gone frequently as they traveled, taking off for certain periods of time, she always returned, and stuck by Kaiden.

With a pat on the scales, Joss stepped over the dragon's resting tail. "Good talk. Maybe I'll see you all around sometime."

It was said conversationally, like they were only going a short distance rather than very far.

She debated leaving Kaiden a note, but what good would that do? For all she knew, he would be *glad* that she was gone. No nuisance child to look after. She could steal whatever she wanted now.

She didn't want to see the look in his eyes. She didn't want to read the words on his lips before they were ever said.

She couldn't bear to see him look that way. He already knew her secret, true, but that just made it even more terrifying. What if he *still* left her, later? What if he changed his mind?

She didn't want to face that rejection, ever again.

Besides, he had his family now. He didn't need her sticking around.

And what if he didn't turn her away? What would she even do, then? Pretend to have a normal life? He wasn't just going to let her hang around. He'd try to change her. And when he couldn't...he'd abandon her.

If even her own parents didn't want her, what would ever make her think someone else would?

Never again. *Never again* would she get attached to someone who claimed they cared. It didn't matter what he did. It didn't matter what it looked like, or if he made her forget for a moment that she hadn't always been alone. If he wasn't just *there* and not asking anything from her. Not prying. Not turning her away.

She could do something, to make him let go. She'd sabotaged her own happiness before, or run from it, before it could destroy her.

No. Joss didn't need to spend the rest of her life worrying about a man she'd barely met, anyway. It'd be much better to leave now, before he got back. Before she even had to deal with any of this. There'd be no fear of backing out if she just took off. He had to be expecting it, anyway. It wouldn't hurt either of them.

The stubborn part of her mind shut down any other thoughts, before they could protest. What ifs and hope just got her in dangerous situations, or worse. Better to avoid them all together.

"You look after him, alright?" She frowned at his hoard of kit dragons, who just blinked at her innocently. This showed how desperate she was; looking to *kit dragons* for help.

172

"If you ever leave me, I'll hunt you down," she muttered to Rascal, whose claws dug into her shirt. It was ruined enough anyway, at least. Kind of like her.

Before any of it could hurt more, Joss shouldered her bag, fingering the gem on her necklace. Mind made up, she stepped over the mess of sleeping kits, slipping away into the night like the shadow that she was.

X

LENA

Talking about my past was always a bad idea. It kept threatening to come back now, in burning metal and harsh words whispered in my ear; disdainful looks and a cold wall digging marks into my back.

But I had to tell someone. I couldn't bear to keep seeing my friend like this, like he'd *failed* somehow because of my own shortcomings. Like he, somehow, was to blame.

But locked tight in front of those words were far too many things I still didn't want to let out, attached to shivers I kept swallowing back. It made my throat ache, if I thought too hard about it.

And Basil was silent, for reasons I couldn't decipher. He didn't look disgusted or annoyed at how I handled things. He looked at me as I spoke and nodded as if he understood, somehow – as if in some world, this all made sense and *wasn't* my fault. Sweet, innocent Basil. He always wanted to believe the best of people.

I'd never really...had a friend like that before. Even the few I'd had throughout my childhood were held to as high of standards as I was, and imposed those on me as well. Conversations were as much performances as attending balls and paying homage to the Empress during morning blessings. I always managed to botch them up.

It was too much to bear, this silence. It weighed over us as if promising to break years of heavy chains with a single, empty moment. And though it shouldn't have been, that was terrifying.

You should leave. You really should.

It wasn't going to get better. I wanted to shout it at him, seeing that look settle in his eyes. He couldn't fix this. He just couldn't.

Basil sent me a quiet smile, and I felt sure my mouth would break if I tried to return it. Instead, I pulled my hand away, curling my fingers in tight enough to burn. It was just painful enough to let me focus, and not choke on my words.

I had to say something, *anything* to steer this elsewhere. I couldn't keep going like this.

"How about you?" Though the words burned in my throat, I pushed them out anyway. "How are you doing?"

The look he turned on me then was stripped rawer than I'd ever seen, caught off guard as if he couldn't believe I'd just said those words. It made a part of me want to cringe, wondering what reaction he had expected from me instead. His hand rested against his chest, a shine peeking through it that wasn't there before.

"I'm...okay."

I did my best to give him the kind of smile he would have given me. "You sure?"

His expression wavered, then, like a glass wobbling just on the edge of a table, ready to break. As if there was a weight pushing it down, his head fell, shoulders hunching as he shut his eyes. "No," he whispered.

I wasn't any good at hugging, especially in situations like this. I'd be more liable to punch his arm. But there had to be *something* I could do, to take that look off his face. Reaching over next to me, I plucked Dez off the desk to offer to him.

"Here." I hesitated, but decided to go with it. "Cuddling dragons usually makes me feel better."

He let out a quiet laugh, his lips spread wide in an open-mouthed smile as he swiped a hand over his eyes, but took Dez anyway, holding him close. He got quiet again, his eyes dark and glimmering with something close to mourning.

"They hurt Elle," he whispered, wincing as if the mention of her would provoke a bad reaction in me. After a moment, he relaxed enough to continue, looking down as he stroked Dez and held him as close as he could without hurting the poor dragon. "They nearly killed her when...when we were captured. So many times. It..." He closed his eyes, his voice dropping off in a hush. "It scared me."

Dez nuzzled his cheek against him, eyes still closed. I looked down at my hands, taking in a shaky breath.

"If it helps...you can hug me again."

At the return of his off-guard look, I glanced away. When he didn't respond, I stood to my feet, holding out a hand before I could stop myself. Though he didn't seem to understand what was happening, he took it anyway, and let me pull him quietly up and from the room, still cradling Dez. I dragged him out of the building, through streets with the fewest watching eyes, going even past the edge of town. Dez made sleepy squeaky noises from his little ball in Basil's hand, shifting happily. I wondered where Basil's dragon had gotten off to.

Basil remained silent even once we reached our destination: a hill far enough from the city that we couldn't be seen, but could still see it, from above. I drew in a soft breath, ignoring the twisting in my stomach as I settled down in the soft grass. "I find it calmer to be away from everyone, when my head is too loud."

Basil closed his eyes again, his expression like brittle glass, and I could have sworn I heard his breath hitch painfully. He cradled Dez to his chest, cupping him as close as he could without squashing him.

"It's also a good way to cry without people seeing," I added, quieter.

He almost laughed at that, though his eyes were still aching. I watched him until I couldn't stand it anymore, shoving down my immediate reaction as I slipped my arms lightly around him. It reminded me of too many things I wanted to forget, too sharply. It made me want to jerk away like I was burned, or hit someone because surely, they deserved it. Surely it would let me forget the pain, for a time.

It reminded me of Kaiden's laugh, and his twisted smirk before that. Of all the things I saw in him that I wanted to scream at because I felt the same. It reminded me of Etta, and Cian...and my arms ached just at the thought. Hugging him felt like heartbreak and home, all at once, and I couldn't handle it. It broke my resolve.

Gently, Basil returned my embrace, his eyes concerned. He looked like a boy who held a shattered vase without understanding how it'd broke. Shifting Dez to his shoulder, he turned to hold me better, his chin resting on my shoulder.

Now that the floodgates were open, they wouldn't stop. I hadn't cried on *anyone* like this in so long, but it spilled out now, welling up and choking my breath until my throat ached. I couldn't even hold onto him that tightly, caught in a dizzying spiral of memories.

"*...disgusting. Disgraceful.*"

They were talking about me, and didn't think I could hear it. But I did. I heard every word. I felt every scream locked inside me like a tortured animal as they rooted into my head and tried so hard to split me open, to get me to spill my secrets. I remembered screaming. I remembered my stepfather didn't care. He would get the truth, one way or another.

But there was nothing he could do to me. Nothing, that was, but turn everyone I loved against me.

That wasn't a hard task to accomplish, anyway. Once the news got out that I wasn't 'pure', all my friendships slowly fell away. I wasn't invited to and was even turned away from social events. It wasn't illegal, but I might as well have laid down and rolled in the dirt, for how they now viewed me. Spit on me. Mocked me.

They threatened to do far worse, sometimes, and I never knew if they were serious. Even the men wouldn't be friends with me, and all the animals in the Cities were just as mangy or feral, too much so to be decent company. All but my cat, when I'd still had her.

Even with Kaiden, I'd hid behind everything. I never did anything without a motive, and a plan of action. I wanted to find out his secrets, so I provoked him. Trying to draw him out from behind his mask. It was easy enough to brush off, and he never questioned it.

But with Basil...there was no mistaking the intent behind my actions, and we both knew it. I couldn't pretend I was just trying to get something from him, or didn't actually want to comfort him. I couldn't pretend I didn't care.

And it made me scream inside, holding onto him. It hurt so *much*, being open in a way that had only caused me pain before. In a way that reminded me of every painful memory, and every person who had ever walked away from me. That any moment now, the exact same thing could happen. I could bare my soul and have it ripped to pieces, all over again.

I gripped Basil's shirt tight enough to feel my nails in my palms, holding onto him like a lifeline and trying so, so hard not to shatter into a million separate pieces, even as tears slowly tracked down my cheeks. I couldn't do this. I *didn't*. I pushed people away. I only pretended to care, or not care, and left them guessing.

But I couldn't imagine anything happening to him. I cared about this so much it *hurt*. It hurt so badly, knowing how easily it could be rejected. Misunderstood. Scorned.

What a horrid friend I was. Shoving everyone away just because I was scared. They hadn't left after they knew what I was. They hadn't let me rot in Galdania like I deserved. They had been nothing but supportive, and all I'd done was hurt them.

In theory, I could have kept doing that. But I couldn't bring myself to, seeing his expression. Seeing how cracked open and aching he was, and how little anyone else wanted to help. I knew they had their own issues. I knew I'd failed him, too. But it still made me want to scream that we had allowed this, and left him alone without any support.

I didn't even know how to fix it. But I wanted to try.

So soon after losing my dad, this was terrifying. I wasn't getting anything from this. I wasn't manipulating him or hiding things away. It just *was*, and that...scared me.

Basil didn't say a word, either. There was no push and pull, no wills against each other. No reason to retort, no good excuse to pull away and lock it all in again. He just held me until I thought I would break.

This wasn't just allowing him to touch me, like a moment of weakness. This wasn't something I could brush aside and scowl at, even if I had a good excuse. This wasn't something I could *take back,* unless I actually left and never came back.

Please, I pleaded silently, holding on tighter to him. *Don't let me do that.*

I'd shown him *me,* now, and there was no coming back from that. For the first time in forever, I was allowing myself to have...a friend. One close enough to know the truth, if only a small, important part of it.

He must have realized the weight of the situation by now, the way he closed his eyes and shuddered in the quietest breath.

"I don't know what to do."

You're preaching to the choir, friend. Letting out a hushed laugh, I held him closer, shutting my eyes. "Me neither."

When all your words were filled with lies, silence was the purest truth. As he eventually pulled back and met my eyes, a conversation I'd needed to have for the longest time traveled between us, with silent nods and affirmations and apologies. Promises to answer questions, quieting fears. He asked if this was the truth, and I didn't lie to him.

Somehow, his hand ended up around mine, squeezing it in tight assurance. I returned the gesture, sealing the agreement. This wouldn't be a one-time thing. He held my gaze until I knew there would be no breaking this promise. Not without breaking him, too.

He needed this, just as much as I did. Someone had to start patching things up, and I knew he couldn't do it alone. At least, that's what I told myself, as he offered me the smallest smile and I searched for a way to return it.

Later, I could pretend like today had never happened, if I wanted. I could dismiss it like any other time, go on pretending and hiding and keep my eyes away from his so I didn't see the damage. I'd never actually *said* anything in that promise. But the look in his eyes proved that he knew, and I knew, and he would hold me to it. He wasn't going to let me shove him away again.

I just hoped he knew what he was getting himself into.

KAIDEN

Jade's hand squeezed his gently as he pressed through the underbrush, a tickle of familiarity seeming to whisper against his skin. He had to be on the right track, if Damien's report was true.

He'd asked Joss to stay behind, to watch over her band of strays. In truth, he didn't want to have to explain her presence to his siblings – or the dragons' presence, for that matter. Though kits weren't outlawed like Gifted were, Calest was understandably wary of any kind of dragon, given the events of recent years. Besides, they were likely to cause mischief, and bring up a million questions he didn't want to answer.

It was easier this way. Without Joss, without dragons. Just Jade by his side and his breath held in quiet hope. If it went poorly, no one else had to know. None of his secrets would come out. He could just...move on, as if nothing happened.

The woods in this area were thick – enough so that his clothes almost snagged a couple times on outstretched branches, and though he heard the rustle of wildlife, he couldn't see it. It was no wonder he hadn't been able to find them. Damien knew what he was doing.

There, as he emerged into a clearing. A little house sat by flanked by dark trees, looking entirely out of place with its white boards and clean appearance, far different than what he'd grown up with. It looked like an Upper had cut out their perfect home and pasted it here, in the quiet of an area where it would never be seen.

His steps slowed as he approached the house. The front door swung open, a tall, dark-haired lad in green and grey emerging onto the porch. He took two steps down before Kaiden could force a hushed word out.

"Kelrin?"

The boy stopped and looked him over, a cold warning settled in his narrowed eyes. "That's my name, yes."

For a moment, Kaiden thought Kelrin might have forgotten him. But it hadn't been that long, as far as he knew. He couldn't possibly *not* recognize his own brother. Right?

Something shifted in Kelrin's eyes, almost scornful as he studied him with folded arms. "Yes, I remember you." The impatience had a bite to it, a harsh exasperation that stung too much. Like the words were laughed at him. Scoffed.

It wasn't the sort of welcome he'd expected. But maybe it was one he deserved.

"Are you just going to stand there?" Snapped words temporarily tore Kaiden back to reality. Numbness crept in right after it, dragging him away to another time, another place. Those same dark eyes on another person. A familiar tone as Kelrin's voice continued to lash at him, jerking his focus away from the memory. "What do you want?"

Numb. That was the word for how he felt. Like every word jolted him back, frozen in a time he couldn't remember, but would never forget. Numb, spreading through his fingertips and up into his mind, as if ice had crept inside him and made a home there. Even Jade's hand felt distant, a thin thread keeping him from slipping into the past.

"I...came to see you."

A harsh laugh cut through the air between them, low but dangerously sharp as Kelrin stopped in front of him. "You came to see *me*."

Kaiden nodded toward the house, his voice far too quiet in comparison. "And the girls."

His brother's expression darkened further, something glinting in it as he shifted closer. "You stay away from them."

The low warning gave Kaiden little time to react, shock twisting among other things as he fought to form words. "Wh-"

"You know exactly why. You're just like him, Kaiden." The name was tossed at him like an insult, cutting to the bone. "It's all empty words and then you leave without saying *anything* and expect to just show up again later when you feel like it." With a harsh laugh, Kelrin leaned against the house. "And when you *do* come back, it's only to leave again, the exact same way."

If the previous words had hurt, these were like a knife between the ribs, a slow, expanding pain in his chest delayed by shock and sharpened by the force in which they were said. Kelrin continued to throw words at him, most of them fuzzy to Kaiden's ears despite how they twisted the knife inside him. He thought he may have sunk to the ground, or wished to, his mind absorbing and numbing the words on instinct as other ones started to whisper among them. A different, darker voice, echoing what was said until it made him want to shudder, and forced a reply from his lips.

"Are you done?"

The words sounded hollow in his ears, empty and hushed as the breath in his chest. Kelrin's eyes flickered, like he would have liked to continue, but he folded his arms across his middle with a curt nod, as if Kaiden wasn't worth more effort. The words continued to swirl in Kaiden's head, though, arranging themselves into a coherent and sharp order that struck at him, again and again, deeper with each echo.

You've caused nothing but trouble. You're the reason Mother always worried, and Father was always mad. Didn't you know that? He told me about all the fights you got into. You scared Mother half to death with your reckless 'antics'. Didn't you care about her in the slightest?

A brittle laugh slipped through his mind, bringing pain with it. Kelrin had no idea. He didn't even know the truth. It didn't matter why Kaiden had done what he'd done, or what lies their father had told about him. Kelrin still saw him as a monster.

"But of course you didn't." It had been said as if it was ridiculous to think otherwise. *"He said that's why she stayed sick. She was always worrying about you."*

More lies, but these dug in deeper than he expected. What if part of it was true? What if she hadn't gotten better because of him? Because he was too weak to hide the damage?

"I'm..." He tried to say *sorry*, in response to all the accusations, but it died on his lips when he reached for it. His mind spun in dizzying circles, processing everything that had been said and what he hadn't heard. A weight lodged in his throat, refusing to leave. "Kel, I'm..."

"Sorry?" Kelrin's scornful bark said he wouldn't have believed it anyway. Not that anyone did, or should. "Forget it, Kaiden. You didn't care about leaving before; there's no reason to pretend you do now."

"I didn't..." He swallowed, blinking back a burning in his eyes. "I didn't have...a choice..."

The next laugh made him flinch, harsh as it was. He searched for words to explain, but they turned to ash on his tongue. He couldn't admit what had really happened. Kelrin would never believe him, anyway.

"Sure you didn't." The words were mocking, cutting into him. "Just like Father never did, I'm sure. You're *just like him.*"

"Stop." The word came out too quiet, his hand curling into a fist at his side to stop it from shaking. *I'm nothing like him.*

"If you'd really wanted to help," Kelrin continued, leaning heavier against the house with a frown, "you never would have left." He stopped, dark eyes holding Kaiden's like a dare. Waiting for him to explain.

But he couldn't, because it wouldn't be believed. It would only make Kelrin hate him more, for lying to him. An apology stuck in his throat, but refused to come out. He couldn't keep pleading with everyone to forgive him as if he'd never done anything. He couldn't pretend he didn't care and then turn around and expect them to believe the opposite was true. He'd lied to them, and now he'd lost them.

"I'm sorry."

The words were barely whispered out, a weight that made him ache. Kelrin kept his eyes narrowed, silent for a long moment before he finally replied.

"You really think that's going to make it better?"

The thin layer of ice to his brother's words didn't help. It seeped into the cracks of his mind, taunting him.

"I never forgave him, either." Something dark and bitter crept into the edge of Kelrin's voice, matching his eyes. "So I don't know why you expect this to be any different."

Crumbling. That was the word that whispered through Kaiden's mind as he closed his eyes. He was crumbling, every piece of himself falling away with every word.

I'm sorry, he whispered in his mind, as if that would be enough to make things better. Kelrin had stopped yelling, but his words still echoed through Kaiden's mind, demanding an answer.

I'm sorry. I didn't mean to leave. I didn't have a choice.

"Excuses," his mind mocked, accusing him. And maybe they were. But they were the only thing holding him up at the moment.

The meaning in his brother's words was clear, and even with all his willpower, he couldn't bring himself to meet his dark eyes. They were too familiar, both in their color and the expression they held. A nod was all he could manage, turning his head toward the house. But the request died on his lips before he ever voiced it.

"They're not there. Katana took them out for a walk."

It was a lie, and an obvious one, but the implications were strong. Kaiden moved his head in a slow nod, words stuck in his throat. Echoes still swirled in his head, whispers that fought to trap him in another time.

Each word dug deeper in Kaiden. "Kelrin..."

"No. You don't get to just come back here and lie to me again, *brother.*" The bitterness spread through his voice like acid, eating away any calm in it. "That's all you did, all our lives. You lied to us, you lied to Mom, you lied to Dad. No wonder he was so upset at you all the time." Kelrin spit the words to the side, muttered, but it wasn't quiet enough for Kaiden not to hear. "You deserved it."

"Can I at least...see them?"

Kelrin let out a harsh laugh. "And let you break their hearts again? No. Why *did* you come back, anyway?"

With the memories still fresh on his mind, he had to blink away the impending moisture that the images in his head brought up. "I've been...looking for you."

"*Looking* for us." Kelrin let out another cutting laugh, boring his gaze into his brother. "Do you want to know what happened that night, Kaiden? You *left* us. Mom, Dad, and then you. Except *you* had a choice. And you still left. You and Kinny." He spat out her name as well. "I can't believe you would do that. I was twelve at the time, don't you understand? That's not old enough to take care of a family!"

I had to, Kaiden thought, but kept it to himself. Kelrin kept going.

"Luckily for us, at least *one* of Dad's friends cared. He told us everything, you know. How you ran off and took Kinny with you, with what was left of Dad's money. How you wouldn't be coming back. At least he helped us out. He gave us somewhere to stay. He got me a job, and supplied us with money to get us through." He scoffed. "At least Damien cared."

The words hit him like a dull blow to the chest. Damien. Kelrin thought *Damien* was the hero here.

"I'm not letting you crush their hopes again," Kelrin muttered. "I told them you weren't coming back, and that's final."

"Tell me...what I can do?" The words were starting to sound lifeless on his tongue.

Kelrin let out a harsh laugh. "There's nothing you *can* do. You're Gifted. You're cursed, and that's why you were on the run. You and Kinny. I can't let you back in." The tiniest something flickered behind his eyes, before it hardened back to steel. "I can't let you endanger them."

A feeble whisper was all that left his throat. "He...lied."

"No. *You* lied. You said you'd be here, and then you weren't." He scowled, a dark shadow crossing his face. "Damien said you'd try to make excuses, or give a 'reason' that you'd left."

It was too much. Everything was swirling in a sickeningly black, endless whirl, whispers of the past and his brother's bitter face melding together until he didn't even know if anything was being said.

"I...need a moment."

Without lifting his eyes to catch Kelrin's scornful ones, Kaiden turned and headed back the way he came, barely suppressing a shiver at the parting words tossed at him.

"Don't expect the door to be open when you come back."

"We don't want you," is what he heard in his mind, an echo from before. It had been yelled at him earlier, but he'd been too lost to process it at the time. *"They don't need you. We were better off without you."*

It was hard to tell which words were whose anymore, past voices crowding into his mind until it made him want to flinch.

You're just like him. You're just like him. You're just. Like. Him.

Was he? In some way, was he the same as the man he swore he'd never be like? Kelrin didn't even know about the Bane. What Kaiden had done. Did it really matter if he'd been 'influenced' at the time? It had still been his decision. It hadn't forced him to do anything. He just...hadn't stopped it.

And it was the same way with everything else. He hadn't been made to do anything. He just hadn't done anything to stop it.

Even now, with his memories. He let them torment him because...what? He deserved it? He knew he could fight against them. But he didn't want to.

He was too weak to make his own decisions. He just let others push him into making them for him.

Kaiden stumbled away from the house, barely making it to the trees before he was on his knees. His world crumbled down around him, fracturing into pieces that couldn't be put back together.

They didn't want him. Even his own family didn't want him. Worse, he would only endanger them by trying to stay.

He didn't realize he was shaking until he felt Jade's hand on his arm. "He's right."

A laugh answered him, his imaginary friend rolling her eyes. "Seriously? He's not *right*, Kaiden. He's naive."

No. No, there was more to it. How did he make her see it?

"But..."

She squeezed his arm, gently. "But...?"

He had to drag a slow breath in for air, shutting his eyes and making a fist before he could open them again, trees distant in his vision. "It was still my fault. It won't be safe if I stay."

The words hurt worse than coals in his throat. Jade wrapped her hand lightly around his wrist.

"It might not be safe yet. Not until the Empress is stopped. But that doesn't make this your fault."

A quiet laugh sounded in his mind. Didn't it? Kelrin was right, after all. He *had* left.

"Come on." Jade tugged his arm, gently leading him further away from the house. Tears gathered in his eyes, though he did his best to hold them back.

"Here, Butterfly. Sit down."

Doing so felt like he was crumbling; an apt comparison to how he felt, he supposed. Jade settled beside him on her knees, her hand still lightly on his arm. "It's okay." Her voice was too soft, and doing things to his insides. Pricking his eyes harder. "There's nobody here but us, so there isn't any reason to hide it. Can't be embarrassed by your imaginary friend, right?"

A fierce and shattered laugh fell from his lips, the tears escaping quicker than he could catch them. All he could manage to do was nod.

"It's okay." Jade patted her shoulder. "I've been told I have a very comfy shoulder to cry on."

She tugged him over lightly, and he fell to pieces, shoulders tensing before they just...dropped, his forehead resting against her shoulder.

Everything was falling apart. Without words to distract from it, he joined them, choked and painful sounds slipping from his throat as steadily as tears broke from his eyes. It was gradual, tearing each piece of him into smaller ones until he was nothing but sorrow and failed promises.

"I've got you," Jade whispered, as he broke apart against her.

His family... he'd been searching for so *long* and now...there was nothing. An empty, aching abyss with nothing to fill it. A broken promise, shattered like a glass vase, and him somewhere amidst the pieces.

What now? His world was spiraling out of control, deeper and deeper. He was only half aware of his surroundings, fracturing further with each breath.

And Jade...she was the final piece. It became painfully clear, as he held onto her tighter than he ever should, that she was all he had left. His only chance. His only friend. He'd pushed all the others away.

Jade squeezed him, enough to remind him that she was still there, and he was probably gripping her hand hard enough for it to hurt.

"I'm not going anywhere," she whispered. Another shaky breath from him. "You know me. I'll be annoying you forever. Like, you'll be an old guy and I'll still be hanging around bothering you."

A broken, shaky laugh slipped out, amidst more tears. Jade seemed to realize what was going on.

"I'll keep being goofy and making your life harder. Since obviously you want to laugh at all my awesome lines when you shouldn't." She let out a dramatic sigh, obviously in an attempt to distract him. "I know, so annoying of me."

No. Because those moments, those lines, as she said, were what had held him together since he lost himself. They gave him something else to focus on, and reminded him that he wasn't alone.

A shaky breath left his lips, the world returning to some clarity at her words. Jade. He still had Jade.

"Thank you."

"For being annoying?"

He let a half smile graze his lips, giving a small shrug. Jade laughed.

"Well, sure. I'm very good at annoying people."

"I know."

"It's a talent," she teased.

With the tears subsiding, at least a little, he just felt...tired. So this was it, then. Even his own siblings didn't want him. What point was there in trying, then? What was he supposed to *do* now?

Please. I can't...keep doing this.

Couldn't keep hurting people he cared about. Couldn't keep caring about people he'd hurt. It just ripped him up inside, following the trail of damage he had done. Whether or not it was his fault, he was still the reason it'd happened.

It struck him slowly, like a thorn digging roots into his skin until it reached his heart. Even his *siblings* didn't want him. No one did, and no one ever would. No one except for Jade.

Don't leave me. Please, don't leave me.

"I'm not going anywhere," she promised.

He couldn't do this without her. Not at this point, in this state. His mind was too much of a mess, and the memories were growing and growing, threatening to swallow him whole. Painfully clear, crystal gems of moments, only making his sorrow worse. Kinny. Kellen. Kyra. He could remember them all, and he couldn't *see* them.

What good had he ever done for anyone? All he seemed to do was hurt, wherever he went.

The memories were jumbling together, now, crowded in his too active, agitated mind until they made him want to flinch. Colliding, contradicting images of his brother yelling, his sister crying, and him...leaving. He could picture it, just as Kelrin had said.

They were in danger, because of him. He couldn't stay. Couldn't try to make things right. The only family he remembered, and he couldn't even see them. Jade was speaking and he thought he responded, but the words were numb, buzzing in his ears uncomprehended. He could feel himself breaking down, bit by bit, until Jade pulled him in and he sobbed into her shoulder all over again, choking out broken gasps that shuddered through him like sound waves.

His whole world was breaking, and he clung to her as the only piece still in his grasp.

The darkness threatened to swallow him alive. It was all he could do to remember Jade was still there.

Even Joss just hung around because he could protect her. What bitter irony that was. The only people he could ever protect were strangers.

He couldn't admit to himself that he was crying. Even as the tears spilled down his cheeks, he refused to acknowledge it.

What now? There was nothing. He should just stay here, and...he didn't know. Everything grew white and fuzzy, blended together in his ears until all he heard was static. What good was he to anyone?

The answer threatened to swallow him alive. Everything Kelrin had said was true. And it ate through him like acid.

You're not. You're not worth anything to anyone.

Not helpful, either. Not worth being around, or holding onto. Jade was only here because, well. Even if she *wasn't* imaginary, she was obviously stubborn. She didn't have much reason to leave, either.

As the reality of the situation settled in, he just felt...cold. Sleep was a menace looming overhead, threatening nightmares if he dared to indulge it. Everything, every possible action he could do by this point seemed...pointless.

"Come on, Butterfly. Let's go find Joss."

Even that seemed pointless, when he thought about it. His mind felt raw and ripped open, memories screaming through it that he didn't want to face. The truth, plain and ugly, held back only by the numbness he currently felt.

"Up ya come."

Without Jade, he might have just sat there, for a while. As is, he let her help him to his feet, pulling on a tiny smile when she messed with his hair. He'd have to figure out how to make it normal, so Joss didn't question him when he returned.

"Didja find them?"

Of course Joss was still up, sitting hesitantly and a little worriedly beside the fire as Ril preened herself. Forcing an easiness he didn't feel, he lowered himself down and nodded.

Joss grinned up at him, something brighter than usual sparkling in her eyes. "Well?"

Kaiden let out a quiet chuckle, avoiding the way it scratched in his throat. He cleared it subtly.

Jade flopped down beside him, from where she had been digging in their provisions. "I suggest sleep now, and then we need to go get supplies. We're getting short of stuff."

Jade, always the practical one. He wanted to give her a smile in relief for helping him dodge Joss' question. "Later. For now, we should sleep."

"What are you, my dad?" Though she screwed up her face in teasing disgust, Joss flopped onto her blanket anyway, a smile stretched across her face.

Isn't that what you said? was what played through his mind, though he didn't have the energy to voice it. Instead, he laid down as well, looking into the dark, endless expanse of the sky.

Beside him, Jade rolled onto her side, grinning. "You have to shut your eyes to sleep, you know."

Very funny, Kaiden thought, and fought down the sadness still hanging over him. "Huh. I thought I could just do it with my eyes open."

Even his voice sounded empty, though he knew at the moment he couldn't change that.

"Just give it a try, okay?"

Kaiden shut his eyes, though it was more to disguise the look she was sure to see, and ask about. He didn't need to break down again, with Joss so close.

XI

CHAN

Some days, Chan convinced himself he'd only come back to Calest for the memories. At least those were as bitter as he expected, with just a touch of gentleness. Nothing else was really going to plan.

Calest's council barely humored his attempts to convince them to repeal the law against Gifted. Even with the Empress' now uncertain position, they still hemmed and hawed over the logistics of it all, comparing stats and potential casualties. Though they wouldn't dismiss him outright – he'd recently gotten them to admit interest in the idea – they refused to take any solid action.

Today's meeting, too, had not gone quite how he expected. Though the officials seemed not entirely unyielding on his idea, they still refused to give a definitive answer that he could work with. They hadn't taken the General's death very well, and took the news of his daughter even worse.

He'd spent weeks already in telling them what he knew. Of the Gifted who saved Calestans, risking their lives for no apparent gain. Bringing up, once again, the lack of corrupted dragons in Calest since a Gifted had forced them away. And yet, the Empress had dug her claws deep into their minds, making them hesitate on even the most straightforward decision.

If only he could show them. He had to keep his own Gifts stifled, due to the laws, and was grateful that they wouldn't manifest on their own. But it itched at him all the same, beneath everything.

Calest, unfortunately, was too stubborn to simply be told what to do. They had to be shown, in an undeniable way. But how could he do that without getting himself thrown in prison, or worse?

At least Katya was happier here. It gave him a small measure of satisfaction, watching her slowly relax. Though she had no desire to accompany him to the meetings, she was surprisingly good at keeping Rena in line. And given Calest's experience with dragons, it was better for him to leave her behind, too. Also relieving to know that she wouldn't wreak havoc in his absence.

As Chan strolled down a street that had been silent for years, his mood sombered. Maybe one day, he would bring Katya here with him. Not all the towns that had been attacked by dragons had been saved. In some, the damage had been so great that it was merely abandoned, left as a charred memorial and graveyard for those who hadn't made it out alive.

He'd known, since they'd exposed the Bane, that he would have to return here someday. It had been tugging at him for years. The Empress had locked down Galdania, with their presence there, but now her control was slipping, and with Lena's help and a few mind games, he and Katya had made it out safely.

He knew how tense being there had made her. He didn't like the haunted look on her face anytime someone lifted a hand toward her, or tried to introduce themselves. She grew more and more withdrawn, even though he knew very few of them blamed her. After all, Talon was the one who'd headed the attack that had destroyed their village. At least among Raoul's people, there was no condescension for her dislike of him.

There was still, unfortunately, a difference between Raoul and Hanen's people, in the subtlest ways. Lena said they were a 'little too stuck in their stuck-up ways', and Chan had to agree. Purposefully or not, it reminded him of the Uppers, and the dark memories he shared of that. He knew Katya would never fully be comfortable there.

And someone needed to warn the Calestans, and get them to rise up.

In part, Lena should have been the one to come back with him, to rally her father's people as well. Practically, they knew no amount of respect would convince a city full of Galdanians, ex-City citizens, to follow a band of grubby, desperate Calestans, who they still viewed as...beneath them, even if they weren't denied any of the comforts of the city. He still felt it on the back of his neck, whenever they caught him reading or chatting excitedly about something he'd found. A hint of condescension that seemed bred into the very blood of Galdanians.

So it was best for both of them that they left, and organized the rebellion from a different area. It would have been better to be Lena. But he had made friends with a few of the people there, in their extended stay – scholars who might still listen to them. A desperate revolution would surely seize the chance to move against the Empress, right?

It turned out, he still had a lot to learn about politics and human nature. The Empress had already made her move, sending Talon of all people to Calest to sway the council to her side, against them. Bribe, or threaten, more like. She had managed to convince them of the dangers of the Gifted, to the point that it was written in the law.

Calest didn't stand a chance without the Gifted, though. And with the Empress' handle on things unsteady, he hoped it was only a matter of time before they gave in. As long as it wasn't too late.

With Markus' people, at least he'd had better luck. He had to persuade the rebels not to turn them in, demonstrating how helpful their gifts could be. He didn't like to flaunt his, even in safe places. His gift was...uncomfortable, and they would ask for a demonstration he could never give. He had storms brewing inside him, tugging at him, begging to be let out, to be created. Magic was the extra step that bridged the gateway of time, speeding up what would have already, naturally occurred, whether months from now or years. The right conditions, and you could easily harness a storm.

Now that the Empress was unsteadied, they should be taking the chance to strengthen themselves, say no to her, and fight back.

Instead, they all wanted to live in their safe little holes, away from everyone.

In a way, Chan considered himself lucky for where he'd grown up. If he had to choose anywhere, at least he'd lived somewhere the Uppers would for the most part leave him alone. It was a small victory, in the light of their jobs. But it was better than the docks, so he'd heard.

Or, perhaps, that was simply the town's morbid pretense of optimism, to keep them from losing all hope.

Even before they'd left, he made a habit of revisiting it, as if one day he might walk down the dusty street and find it full and noisy like it once had been.

There were so many memories, hidden in these streets. As terrible as they could be, it made them feel like home, in a way no other place could. It made him feel closer to them, even if he would never see them again.

Tyrel had always been a tiny town. A blip of existence even most Calestans weren't aware of, nestled up in the mountains where rare metals and precious ores lay. It was a town built solely to home the miners who gave their blood and sweat to keep their fragile economy alive. Calest's hardened soil made what little food would grow unsustainable for a large population. Flanked by the ocean on most sides, there was little else to turn to but trade, though most of their resources were scarce and too invaluable to barter away.

Luckily for them, however, Galdanians had an addiction to glittering things. And that was one thing Galdania's land did not flow freely with, as much as they sought after such treasures.

Unfortunately, the balance was never quite fair. When what one party gained was purely out of greed, and the other a necessity for survival, it was far too easy for the lever to be bent further than needed, Galdania demanding a heavy output of metals and jewels in exchange for portions of their food.

Still, the people of Tyrel had taken it on themselves to be proud of their work, no matter how unfair – perhaps to make the workload bearable. They toiled through dangerous conditions and did their best to ensure they could come home at the end of the day. Even with their best efforts, though, the mortality rate was still horrifically high.

Sy had never let him suffer that. Each household had an allotted share to mine each month, in order to keep their lives running. They were given food and shelter, and a promise of protection from outside sources, which was more than many in Calest ever got. Chan had seen boys younger than he forced to take their elders' place, or lose everything. Women were permitted to stay at home, to keep things running smoothly.

He'd been twelve when their father died. Instead of him, though, Sy stepped into his father's role. She wouldn't lose him too, she said.

She never mentioned how much it would hurt to lose her, instead.

Chan always suspected that Damien had a hand in his home's destruction, or if nothing else, knew of the plan, and the attack. But there was never any evidence, just the ashes of an uprising swept beneath an incorporeal rug.

He knew they hadn't survived. The dragons had seen to that. Or, perhaps, Damien had seen to it. Chan had never found enough evidence to either condemn or exonerate him, no matter how he tried. It just struck him as too coincidental that dragons had destroyed his home not long after they tried to stand up for themselves.

Thinking of Damien soured the memories. Not for the first time did he wonder what might have happened had he not shown up. Had Chan stayed, and fought, and...

And what? He didn't truly think he would have stood a chance against the dragons, right? He was young at that time, inexperienced and barely able to leash his gift, let alone use it for any means.

But a part of him still liked to entertain the idea, if only to assume that it could have gone better. His sister might not have died.

Sylen Tiel. One of the bravest women he'd ever known. His mother had died in childbirth, and his father from a cave-in, when he was still young and too naive to truly understand the dangers looming over them.

Everyone in Tyrel was intimately acquainted with loss. There was no 'hope' in their line of work, just whispered prayers that they might somehow do well enough to survive another day. Chan hadn't thought anything would ever change, before Sari showed up.

His stomach twisted at the thought that she might have known, too. But she looked too regretful, too aching for the loss of life. Damien might have tried forcing him to join them. Sari looked stricken that it was the only choice left.

It was pointless to feel guilt that he had survived, because he'd been away. It was fruitless to wonder if Sari had kept him longer, that day, for that very reason.

Chan made it his business to learn anything and everything he could about the world. It was easier to bury his thoughts in books, and let their worlds and their problems consume him, instead. Puzzle out things he *could* fix, even if there was no meaning to them. It always calmed him, being able to solve things.

And yet he liked to walk among the streets of his greatest failure, as a reminder. It sobered him, kept him pressing for goals that he *could* reach. It prompted him to push past his comfort zone and say something to the small girl with bright green hair who'd gone through the same things he had. It gave him patience when his friends handled things differently than he would, and understanding for their actions. It gave him clarity they refused to take, and an opportunity to keep them safe when he was able.

He also read anything he could on the subject of Gifts. Theories and examples that had been recorded, even if most of them were in a false and negative light. He worked with his to make it as strong as he could, so the next time his help was needed...he could give it.

He read up on all that was known of the patterns of the sky, and lightning, and that which was not. More often than not, he turned to fairytales for what scholars were too hesitant to say, the fanciful step between the possible and the impossible. Chan came to think of himself like a bridge between those two worlds: the one in which anything was possible, and the one in which it wasn't. A conduit for the energy required for that change.

Subconscious desires. Chan thought there might be more to it than that, but he would never voice it. But if he truly thought about it, he could remember just where that switch happened, the click from unbelief to belief.

The day his sister walked into a storm, and it nearly swallowed her alive.

They weren't uncommon, in his town, but he still wished, and prayed, and willed the clouds to be lovely for her. He didn't want her to be hurt.

Sy loved thunderstorms. But this one had been too strong, despite her assurances. He could *feel* it in his blood. He felt its power, wishing to tear them apart. But he also knew it could be guided.

Chan wondered sometimes why storms always seemed to come when terrible things happened.

Sari had started training him in secret, not long after his father's death. Once, he used that knowledge to divert a storm, so the worst of it wouldn't hit him and his sister. They reached their destination soaking wet, but Sy just laughed and swung him up into a hug, teasing that they wouldn't need to bathe that night after all.

But it hadn't been a storm to take her from him. It wasn't anything in either of their control. From the new knowledge they had, Chan could now pin the blame on the Empress, if he wished to. But what good would that do?

He just liked the memories. He liked feeling that, if only for a moment, things were normal again. And, he couldn't help but admit, no matter how many times he passed through these empty, lifeless streets, a part of him wished to find his people. As if one day they might simply just be there, where they weren't before.

At least he had Katya, and the rest of his team. Now he had to just do his best to keep them alive, however he could.

KAIDEN

By the time Kaiden woke up, after what little sleep he managed to wrestle from the darkness, he'd almost forgotten what had happened. Pretty much. So he'd failed in the one thing he'd been searching his whole life for. Did it really matter? Did anything?

Maybe this was a sign – the last door slammed in his face. He'd had his chance. He'd botched it at every turn. Why *would* they take him back, anyway? He wouldn't. No one in their right mind would.

How long would it be until Joss realized and left him alone, too?

Well. He supposed before she did, he could make sure she stayed safe. It was the least he could do, to balance out the scales of his actions. He had promised it to her, after all.

But when he glanced over at the blanket where she'd been lying, in easy sight from where he had attempted to sleep, there was no Joss.

Maybe he'd just imagined her, too. It wouldn't be unthinkable, with how crazy he seemed to be. Even without the Bane, there seemed to always be something not quite right with his mind.

Maybe this was all a bad dream. If it was, all he could hope was that he didn't wake up to something even worse.

With *his* luck, though...

Across from him, Jade stirred and let out a yawn, blinking still-sleepy eyes at him. At least she was still here. She hooked an arm under her head and grinned at him. He managed a ghost of a smile back.

Jade yawned again, looking way too comfy for lying in a pile of dirt and leaves. "Is that a 'smile so she doesn't know I'm regretting letting her stay around to annoy me for all eternity' smile?"

His own smile faded as he shook his head, his next breath coming a bit harder in his chest. *No. Never.* She was the only one who'd stuck with him, through everything. He'd never regret that.

Seeing his look, Jade laughed, the sound gentler. "I'm teasing. Obviously you're way too used to my annoying habits to be bothered, what with knowing me literally forever, basically."

All he could manage was a half-shrug, glancing over at the empty blanket where Joss had been laying. *She left, too. Of course she did.*

Jade propped herself up on her elbow, grinning. "So what do you say – head to find some supplies?"

He was about to ask what the point would be, when something attacked him from behind. It shook his shoulders like the world was ending, and he needed to move or be eaten alive.

"Bodyguard!"

Joss? He couldn't decide if relief or confusion was the more prominent emotion as he turned to face her, and slipped her hands off of his shoulders.

The little girl let out a huff, dropping them dramatically at her sides. "C'*mon*, you need to get up! I'm hungry."

There was a whine on the end of the words, though he couldn't ignore the edge of worry he heard mixed in with it. Ril, perched on the girl's shoulders, let out an agreeing chirp.

"Bodyguard." Joss tugged on his arm, as Jade hopped to her feet and tried – unsuccessfully – to shake leaves from her hair. "*Kaiden.*"

Pulling his arm away, he pushed to his feet, breathing out a silent sigh. "I'm *up*."

"Well, *hurry* up!" Joss reached for his arm again, pulling her weight against it. "We can't stay here forever!"

Can't we? Kaiden thought, even as he looked over at where Jade straightened her shirt and stood by him like they were going to start marching, and he was in the lead. "Fine."

Joss continued to tug on his hand and urge him along, as he started in the direction of the town.

Jade glanced around. "No offense to small towns everywhere, but I think we should try a bigger market. We sorta need a lot." She patted the surprisingly empty bag. Kaiden had hardly noticed its contents.

Kaiden let out a sigh. "Alright."

If Joss looked suspicious of his sudden change of heart, she didn't voice it. Kaiden didn't mind walking further, anyway. It gave him time to think. Joss did give him a weird look, though.

Theoretically, it would have been faster to fly. But one of the last things on Kaiden's list of things he'd like to do right now was *fly*, on top of everything else. He wasn't even sure he was holding on to anything stable, at this point. He didn't particularly feel like testing his current state with further mental bombardment.

Ril flew up to rest on his shoulder, letting out a squeak. He brushed her away until she retreated back to Joss, looking very put-out.

Joss let out an exasperated breath. "Why do we have to walk *all* the way to a different town?"

"Because they're more likely to have what we need."

Joss huffed, stroking Ril from where she'd claimed the dragon as her companion. Kaiden didn't mind. "Can I at least get on your back?"

"No." It came out quick, but not harsh, thankfully. Each breath felt heavy in his lungs, every step further from his siblings' house a reminder of the failure pounding into his head. What was he supposed to do now?

Seeing the town – one he'd *been* in before, of all places – was the first thing to bring a thought back clearer into his mind than the previous night's events. As he scanned the crowds, he held onto Joss' hand. "Stay by me."

By his side, Jade laughed. "Aww, are you worried for my safety?"

Though he meant Joss, of course, it was hard to brush away the start of a smile creeping up his face. Funny how easy it seemed to come, now.

"Because if you are," Jade continued, as random townspeople passed through her as if she wasn't even there, "that's super adorable of you, but I don't think it's an issue. Besides, I have *tons* of experience taking care of myself." She tossed him a wink.

Kaiden wiped a hand across his mouth, keeping his gaze straight ahead. Joss squinted up at him.

"Why do you make funny faces all the time?"

Jade tossed her head back in a laugh. Shaking his head, Kaiden shoved his free hand into his pocket, looking up at the sky.

A huffed breath escaped Joss' mouth. "That's not an answer."

As if she knew where they needed to go, Jade suddenly veered off in front of them. Kaiden took it as an excuse to follow her, pretending he didn't hear Joss. He was aware of the face she made at him in return, though, and the muttered comment under her breath.

It was probably a good thing that Jade led the way, as Kaiden almost ran into someone and got a dirty look in response. Joss snickered, though there was an odd look in her eye as she glanced around, slipping subtly closer to Kaiden. There was definitely a reason Kaiden didn't like this town.

Joss gripped his hand tighter as they entered the market, looking around every so often as if they might suddenly be chased for her earlier stunts. She squinted up at him, as if to see if he was similarly bothered. "Are you okay?"

A grin stretched his face. Funny, how normal it felt. "Fine."

Part of his mind didn't even see a reason for any of this. The other focused on keeping an eye on Joss and making sure she didn't get them arrested for theft or something. Even in this state, unentertaining supply shopping would most likely be preferable than getting thrown in jail, again.

As they reached one of the stalls, on the outskirts of the circle, Jade stopped, a wide grin stretching across her face. Her gaze wasn't on the food it sold, though, or even the market in general. Kaiden tried to see what she was looking at.

For a moment, he couldn't believe who he saw. It was just long enough for the person to turn around and catch sight of him, and too late for him to turn and walk away.

XII

Joss

One Hour Earlier...

Joss was torn between worry for her bodyguard and relief that he had come back. If he had looked bad before, in the Mountain, it was nothing compared to this. This...this scared her. Kaiden wouldn't even explain what had happened, and with the state he was in, she was afraid to ask.

Besides, she was still hungry, and she hadn't yet found a buyer for the necklace. She might as well mooch off of him for a while longer, right? Just until she found a buyer. Then she'd leave.

She was terribly worried for him, anyway. He looked like all the light had been sucked from his eyes. Like hope was a tangible thing that had been ripped from him, and all that was left was this gaping hole. Suddenly, Joss was very glad she hadn't left.

Was this really the same man? He looked like he'd lost everything that made him...*him*. Like it had been torn away like old wallpaper, and permanent darkness hung under his eyes instead.

Every time she looked up, Joss was startled by his appearance. He looked like he'd been dragged into death and barely escaped it, or was taken out against his will. Joss began to doubt he'd slept at all.

"Kaiden?" she ventured again, hesitant, as they wandered through the market. His expression scared her. She bit her lip, hard. He hardly looked at her.

"Are you okay?" she whispered, and instantly wished she hadn't. His face became a picture of loss, agony seeping through the cracks there, and his eyes were too bright. He blinked and looked away, an empty smile touching his face.

"Yeah. Of course I am."

Joss couldn't stop her brow from creasing. "Your siblings...?"

"They're not there," he cut in, almost curtly. Drawing in a sharp breath, he added in a mumble, "I lied. I don't have any siblings. I just thought..." Something closed over his expression as he shook his head.

Joss didn't like the hope that crept into her, at that. "Well, you still need to eat."

He let out a laugh that was too close to bitter, a sardonic smile slipping on his face. "Do I?"

Inwardly, Joss tried not to freak out. She'd dealt with this once before, with a friend. One who was contemplating whether or not to jump from the docks. They both knew she couldn't swim.

"Yes," she said, and couldn't hide the tremble to her voice. *She* could lose him, but the world wasn't allowed to. He was too good for it, and they needed him. Someone, out there, needed him.

His expression grew quiet, disguising the sorrow. "I'm sorry," he murmured, his face shadowed in it. Mournful, before he shook it off. "Are you hungry?"

She nodded, if only so he would go look for food. She knew for a guilty fact that there was none left in his pack.

He sighed heavily, and it struck Joss in a worrisome way again. "We can get some food over there. I have money." She held up the gem on her necklace.

He didn't balk as strongly at the mention of it, just halfheartedly shrugging a shoulder and going on his way. Joss hurried after him, slipping a kit dragon out of her bag and dropping it on his shoulder. It blinked sleepily and then curled up next to him, murmuring contently. His shoulders tensed up, for a moment, but he didn't reply.

They had to find someone that he cared for, or who could care for him. Joss would never feel right leaving him like this. Maybe there'd be some rare nice couple in the town, or...

She held to his hand, tightly, and refused to let go, no matter how he tried to brush her away. Eventually he resigned himself to it, wandering through the circle of shops. He scanned everything listlessly, not even bothering to compare the prices and spending his money unwisely. Joss could practically see the shopkeep's eyes lit up with the sum of his greed.

Joss held tight to her necklace, for emergency needs. She didn't feel right butting in and taking over for him, but it was clear he wanted to use all his money, and quickly. To have an excuse, she supposed, as he bought her a nicer dress and some gloves, and Joss got more and more disturbed, as pretty as the gifts were.

This was not what she was thinking by *supplies*.

She had to distract him, drag him away somehow. She swung his hand wildly and shouted and interrupted them, all the while feeling the shopkeep's glare hot and hard on her. Finally, she tugged his hand away, shouting joyfully. "Daddy! Daddy! Look!"

His eyes snapped to her, then, something hard and almost fearful in his eyes for a moment, muscles stiff until he noticed her, and tried to hold her back. Joss broke away and took off running, and for a moment she was afraid he wouldn't follow. But he excused himself from the shop, calling after her. "Joss?"

There was a weary warning in the tone. But she had to do *something*. Taking care to leave herself in sight, just enough, she wove in and out of the crowd, looking back at him and laughing. He was frowning.

By the time he caught up to her, she was holding something from one of the shops and grinning proudly. He couldn't leave unless he wanted to pay for it, and it was far too exorbitant for that.

"Please, Daddy?"

They both knew how little they could afford such a thing, and Kaiden just looked weary. He put a hand on his forehead, almost shaky. "Joss..." he whispered.

She put down the piece, with an apologetic glance at the shopkeep, then tugged on his hand, leading him away. "You okay?"

He looked up then, something definitive crossing his expression. "Fine."

Joss was still worried, but he went back over to the shop they were originally at with much stronger resolve, and Joss waited quietly as he bought actually useful things. At least she had snapped him out of it. Though she was worried the shopkeep might just gut her for wrecking his sale.

Eventually, Joss tugged his hand to urge him away from the shop, but Kaiden stayed put, his brow furrowed on something in the distance. The crowd slipped in and out as a man shouldered his way through to them, politely and out of breath, calling Kaiden's name.

CHAN

Of all the things Chan expected to be doing today, this was not quite one of them.

That didn't mean he was complaining, of course. It just altered his plans a little – or maybe a lot. His findings might have to wait another day, at this rate. At least he'd made contact with the council, and warned them what was to come. Now he just had to hope they would agree to his plan.

Coming back to Calest was bittersweet. Even still, he hadn't been able to stop himself from glancing around everywhere he went, wishing one of the passing faces would recognize him. Wondering if he'd know them, as impossible as the likelihood was. The girl who'd lived across the street. His father's friends, or the cheery older man who ran a bakeshop. Even his sister. He saw the slightest glances, the certain way someone's smile was tipped or a hastily swept mess of blonde hair and his heart stopped, just for a moment.

It wasn't them, and it never would be. Rationally, he *knew* this. But that didn't stop his mind from assuming, and aching with the tiniest hope that maybe, just maybe, when they turned around, he would see blue eyes and a soft grin rather than a harrowed face and eyes he'd definitely never seen before.

Fate had other plans. It was funny how that all worked, usually. If he hadn't been paying this much attention, would today have gone differently? Would he have found out, later, that he had been so *close* and not even realized it?

Chan didn't really know, and at this moment, he couldn't quite bring himself to care. His feet were moving before he could stop them. He heard his own incredulous voice saying the name, knew he must be pushing people aside in the busy square, but none of that mattered. All that mattered was making sure this wasn't some sort of dream he'd conjured up. A trick from fate, rather than a gift.

He didn't know why Kaiden was in this specific town or how Chan had gotten lucky enough to run into him. It seemed a bit of an impossibility, even in such a small country. But here he was, and the relief flooding through Chan was so palpable he could feel it pulsing through him.

Okay, so maybe he'd been hoping for a bit of an impossibility, even if he wouldn't admit it to himself.

Kaiden stood by one of the market stalls, his feet turned away from Chan. His expression was too hard to read in such a wild moment, though that hardly mattered to Chan anyway. It wouldn't matter if he got scowled at and shoved away. He wasn't just going to let him go again.

Even with finding a reason to come back to Calest again, Chan hadn't really let himself admit just how much he'd missed his friend. With everything that had happened, and how much uncertainty usually came with anything having to do with Kaiden, it had been easier not to try to look past the surface – and in some ways, less painful.

But now, having him here again, in reach and not corrupted by some evil entity, Chan didn't think he could stop his feet if he wished to.

Fate, though a harsh mistress, could be quite kind when she wanted to.

To his credit, Kaiden didn't flinch away before Chan could wrap his arms around him, though his own stayed pretty firmly pinned to his sides. It might have been easier not to see what his friend was thinking, but it might not of mattered, either. It certainly didn't at this moment. With his eyes shut, Chan could just as easily imagine whatever he preferred for this situation. For now, it was whatever he wanted it to be.

It was hard to put thoughts into words, sometimes. Sometimes they took a moment, or two, or several hundred before they slipped into place. Sometimes it took years before you could define what you should have known all along. It was the moment of "oh, of course", like discovering you'd lost a set of keys and that's why the doors in front of you wouldn't open.

Sometimes it just took a certain place, a certain word to make the emotion strong enough to name. Whatever the case, it slipped into place now as strongly as if it was shouting in his mind. Having Kaiden back, right now, was like getting a piece of their old team back. And that made all of this worth it.

Chan couldn't put into words the emotions rushing through him. Olive might have understood, but she'd never handled emotions the same way Chan did. He doubted she would feel this bubbling over, all-encompassing joy and relief that his friend was back. He hadn't just lost another person, like so many before.

Suddenly, it was worth it. The bittersweet memories stirring in him ever since he'd entered this town, for the reminder it now was. Memories which were further tainted by the suspicion that Damien hadn't 'helped' him, after all. He'd only made things worse, for everyone involved.

It was yet another reason Chan had found himself looking, wherever he went. After what had happened with his own people – and more recently, what had happened to his friend – he couldn't help but wonder what else he *didn't* know about Damien.

Not for the first time, Chan found himself glad someone else had taken care of him. Whether it had been under the Empress' orders or simply the Bane's doing, the man had deserved to die. Especially now, holding onto Kaiden and remembering just what Damien had done to him, Chan found himself relieved the issue had been taken care of. Had the task been left to him, he wasn't sure what he might have done.

"What are you doing here?"

The words came out incredulous, and he added on, "I just...didn't expect to see you *here*. In the market. I mean, we knew you came here, but not..." He paused, blinking. "I've missed you."

KAIDEN

"I think the appropriate response here is to hug back, Butterfly."

Since he couldn't exactly laugh in response without looking, well, *insane*, Kaiden just gave the barest shake of his head, hoping Chan wouldn't notice. His arms remained glued to his sides, though whether that was from shock or something else, he wasn't quite sure.

"C'mon, the guy obviously wants to hug you. Hug him back." Jade grinned, nudging his arm.

Why? he mouthed, glad Chan's eyes were currently closed.

"Because you were friends." She motioned to Chan. "Go on."

Were. The word settled heavier in his chest than it should have. Another reminder of something he'd messed up. Why was Chan here, anyway? Why did he care?

Jade let out a dramatic sigh in response, shaking her head as Chan pulled back, just enough for Kaiden to read all the things in his face that he hadn't wanted to see.

"Are you...okay?"

Breathless, and just a little too worried. Kaiden forced his mouth up in a convincing curve. "Why wouldn't I be?"

Chan released a quiet breath, as if he didn't seem quite convinced with what he saw. "You're..."

"Handsome? Always. Here? Yeah, I know. It was a surprise to me, too. What are *you* doing here?"

Joss narrowed a frown between them. "And just *who* are you, anyway?"

Chan looked away, letting out a breathless laugh and shaking his head like someone had told him an ironic joke. "Me?" He blinked down at the little girl, and then back at Kaiden questioningly. Joss didn't look happy with his answer.

"He's a friend. I think," Kaiden added. "He might be a secret official in disguise sent to lock you up for all those apples you stole."

Joss did not look amused. "You helped with that, you know. So is he going to lock you up, too?"

"I'm not...going to lock anyone up." It was almost said as a question, as Chan rubbed the back of his head. "I'm a friend."

"Even to thieves?" Joss pressed, turning her skeptical gaze on him.

Chan massaged the back of his neck, clearly uncomfortable. His gaze flicked to Kaiden, questioning.

Joss frowned at him, and kicked Kaiden's shin. "That doesn't answer my question."

"I'm...a friend of Kaiden's," Chan mumbled, tucking his thumbs beneath his shoulders.

Joss continued to squint at him. Kaiden couldn't help a smile, watching them. For some reason, the entire thing struck him as rather funny.

"Katya..." Changing topics, Chan pushed a hand through what little hair he had and let out a laugh. "I've missed you. We all have."

You left, was all Kaiden heard echoing in it. *For good reason.*

"Can you just...ah, stay right here, for a moment? I need to go...let them know..." Mumbling, Chan slid off through the crowd, away from Kaiden.

Beside him, Jade pouted. "Are you ignoring me now?"

"No," he mumbled under his breath, well aware of Joss' watchful eye.

"Am I living up to my annoying title yet?"

Half a smile still lingering on his face, Kaiden shook his head. Joss turned her squinting on him. "What are you doing?"

"Talking to my imaginary friend."

She frowned. "I know you're crazy, but you're not *that* crazy."

Kaiden shrugged a shoulder. Jade laughed. "I guess I'll have to try harder."

Joss shifted closer to him. "So who's that, huh? Is he part of the city watch? I thought you said you didn't have any family."

"I don't."

"Then how come he hugs you like you are?" She wrinkled up her nose.

Kaiden rubbed the back of his neck, half-shrugging. Before he could answer, Chan returned, almost breathless.

"I let them know...they said it'd be fine. We have room for one more person." Chan hesitated. "That is...if you want to come...?"

The dull throb in his chest returned, weighing him down as he took in Chan's posture, and the carefully posed question. As if he expected to just be turned away.

Chan shifted on his feet, fingers tucked in his pockets. "Did you...find your siblings?"

Kaiden settled his arms over his chest, frowning to keep his mouth steady as he looked at the market stalls. This was not a question he wanted to be answering at the moment, especially with Joss' also curious, secretly worried gaze on him.

Chan hesitated. "Look...everyone has missed you, alright? Do you...need help looking for them? I think someone might kill me if I didn't bring you back."

Why do they care? Why was everyone so concerned with trying to keep him around when he didn't want to, and leaving when he wanted them to stay?

"Fine."

Though Chan still looked nervous, he gestured to the stalls. "You can...finish up what you were doing. Katya and I are staying with...a friend of mine. We were going to head back to Galdania soon, actually."

Flying. His chest tightened, his hand curling loosely at his side in a pathetic imitation of holding someone's hand. Jade slipped hers into his, grinning a little.

"Don't worry. Everything will be fine."

Chan continued to ramble on somewhat nervously as Jade squeezed his hand. "Anyway. If we're going to go, we should probably...go."

Jade grinned at him, her attempt to calm him down. "Don't worry. I'll be right there, okay? I can chat the whole way and annoy you so much you won't notice the flying."

Kaiden squeezed her hand back, attempting to stuff down the tension he felt invading his bones. He mumbled under his breath as Chan turned away, looking back at him hesitantly.

"You'll...come back with us, right?"

A smile seemed to spread across his face on its own. "Yeah. Of course."

Joss was looking back and forth between them and frowning, as if she didn't trust either of them. "Aren't you going to introduce me?"

"Oh." Kaiden looked down at her. "Chan, this is the strange little thief that's been following me around and using me as a human shield."

"Bodyguard," Joss grumbled, looking very put out. She crossed her arms over her chest. "And I'm *not* a thief. I told you that." She frowned at Chan. "I don't like you."

Kaiden chuckled, despite how quiet it felt in his throat. "You get used to her after a while."

Chan looked thoroughly bewildered. "You...have a kid?"

After blinking at him for a long moment, Kaiden shook his head. "Stowaway kid. She won't leave me alone."

Joss kicked his ankle sharply. "Hey, I saved *you*, Mister Firehead. You would have starved without me."

Chan looked between the two of them, still confused. "But you...know her?"

"As of two hours ago, yes."

To his credit, Chan took the comment in stride, even if it was completely wrong. Though Joss watched, grinning, she didn't correct them.

"I'm joking," Kaiden added after a moment, though his tone barely betrayed it. "It's been two days."

Chan's brow creased, just for a moment, as if he was aware he was being messed with, but didn't know what to do about it. It sparked a memory, just for a moment, that almost made Kaiden's lips twitch up. Sometimes – as Gigi had helped him discover years ago – Chan was a little too trusting for his own good.

"Okay." Chan seemed to shake the comment off. "So...she's with you, then."

Joss huffed, crossing her arms over her chest. "'She' is called Joss, and she is also hungry."

Chan rubbed the back of his neck, almost looking relieved to have a problem he could solve. "Well...we have food back at the house. Katya's waiting outside the market. She'll be expecting me, soon. Us," he amended, with only a slight crease to his brow. He kept glancing back every so often, as if worried Kaiden would disappear when his back was turned.

I could, if I wanted to, Kaiden thought. *It would be easy enough.*

But what would be the point? All he'd do was hurt someone else, again. Chan already looked like he'd have a permanent furrow to his brow. Joss huffed, tugging along her bag and frowning down at it warningly from time to time, staying close to Kaiden. He let Chan lead, trying to hold back the smile curling his lips. He didn't think it'd help if he made them think he was insane again.

XIII

CHAN

Chan messed with his glasses and thumbed a folded sheet of paper as they walked, anything to keep his hands busy. He glanced back at Kaiden every so often, secretly relieved that his...well, that Joss stayed close by his side. She seemed as worried about him as Chan was, even if she did her best to hide it.

Katya, as usual, stayed silent. The chaos of crowds made her jumpy, and after the second time she'd tried to bolt from one and he'd had to chase after her, panicked that something might happen, but not wanting to scare her, they'd decided it was best if she just avoided them, for the time being. He'd befriended an older woman who lived on the outskirts, and she was more than willing to let Katya stay with her while Chan took care of things. She preferred coming along with him to staying at their house, so they'd come up with a solution.

Chan was glad the younger girl didn't question her, though; Katya actually seemed calm for the moment. If he was braver, he might have held her hand.

Still, it didn't help that Kaiden seemed unfocused, walking through a town like this. It only enhanced the alarm prickling at Chan's skin. But they could deal with that later, once he had them all safe. Right now, he just needed to get them back to Reme's in one piece, and not let Kaiden wander away on him. At least Joss seemed aware of the dangers, and kept him from straying too close to the alleyways.

The one downside to Reme's location was this. Getting there involved a district that was even unfriendlier than other ones.

He couldn't shake the feeling of unease hanging over him, from the entire situation.

A moment too late, Chan stilled. Voices filtered from just out of view, one that was naggingly familiar. An easy laugh, warm and smooth like honey.

Katya shivered, involuntarily, and it clicked. *Talon.* He should have known. The Empress had kept him busy, hunting down Gifted and doing who knew what with them. And he'd been trying to destroy Chan's credibility ever since he got here, by revealing him as Gifted.

Problem was, Chan didn't have a short temper, or a reason to use his gift openly in any way. He wouldn't endanger all his hard work that easily.

"Stay here." Chan moved an arm in front of Kaiden, as if keeping a small child from walking on glass. Despite the fact that no one here knew of his gifts, the fact remained that Gifted were officially outlaws in Calest now, and anyone even drawing suspicion on themselves could get in serious trouble.

Luckily, his friend put up little resistance, dropping down against a crumbling wall with a quiet sigh. Chan's hand strayed to the sword on his belt as he stepped away from the shadows. Though Joss seemed to catch his look, and sent an annoyed one back that said of course she would keep an eye on him, Katya stayed close by his side, as if for support.

"Nice speech you gave today, buddy. Too bad it won't do you any good."

The older boy was standing and grinning at them like only a maniac following another maniac's insane orders would. He was flanked by several other Gifted, the tendrils of their abilities curling around their wrists as thorns or crackling lightning in their hair. One girl had wind whipping around her, dramatically, blowing back the cape stretched over her shoulders.

Katya went stiff against him. Chan fought down the beginning of a frown.

"Good effort at that meeting of yours, Tiel. I really think you might have gotten through to them." Talon flashed him a blinding grin. "Except for, well, the fact that we control the dragons now. *Without* Gifts. You, my friend, are just considered a threat." He cocked his head. "How long do you think it'll be until you give up? How long do you really think it'll be before they see reason and accept her offer?"

Before they're threatened into submission, you mean.

"I won't ever give up," Chan replied. "The Empress isn't a savior, not to this country. *She* is the threat, and it's only for that reason that they bent to her demands."

Talon let out a sigh, flicking a bored finger Katya's way. She flinched. "I was afraid you might say that." Without warning, Katya buckled at the knees with a muffled scream, even when Chan tried to steady her. He turned furious eyes on his former friend.

"What do you *want*?"

Talon grinned at him. "Same thing as you, of course. Peace. Which, at this point, only seems to have one source. Your councilmen bicker and fight over land enough as is; your people live in poverty. Who's to say allying with the Empress won't *help* them?"

Because they'd be giving away their freedom.

Talon clicked his tongue against the roof of his mouth. "Ah, right, I forgot how little you like to talk. No matter. There are other ways."

Katya started screaming in earnest.

"See, the problem is, Tiel, that you're terribly persuasive when you want to be. And right now, I think you do." He let out a fake sigh. "But I can't very well have you ruining the Empress' plan and taking back her control over Calest. I had hoped you might see reason, with time. You can't win this battle anyway. Might as well join the winning side." A glint slipped into his eyes. "But I guess I'll have to mark you as a lost cause. Pity."

A smile curved up his lips, just as Katya went completely weightless against him, a shudder wracking her frame. Talon's eyes were laughing, the scar down his face shifting as he smiled.

"Where's your other friends?" He sounded bored, his gaze drifting around the courtyard. "More Gifted? I know I heard them over there. You can't hide them forever."

He felt Talon pressing against the wall of his mind, knocking in search of weaknesses. But all of Chan's weaknesses slipped away when he had someone to protect. Cradling Katya against him, he narrowed his eyes.

"You're just afraid because you know I'm right."

Talon let his shoulders lift and fall, a hand circling the hilt of his sword. "'Right' is such a funny word. Persuasive, that I'll give you. But right? Far from it."

His smile grew as he watched Katya, nothing human in his eyes. "Give it up, Tiel. Or use your gift to stop me. Either way," he laughed, stepping back, "we both know you can't best me any other way."

Katya shook with sobs, weak against him. Talon smirked.

"*Stop.*" From the shadows, Kaiden stepped forth, cool steel in his voice and in his hands. There was something not quite right to his eyes, like glass that was broken and used as a weapon, distorting the image it reflected. Chan felt his heart sink in his chest, too late to warn him away. Joss, at least, didn't appear next to him.

Kaiden drew his sword in a solid motion, swinging it with a fluid fury that Chan had never seen before. "Leave her alone."

Talon's surprise lasted only a moment before it morphed with his grin, which stretched to his eyes. "You too, hm? Funny, I pegged you as being smarter. Guess that's just another thing everyone was wrong about."

He dodged Kaiden's attack with a nearly perfect arc, an edge of delight playing in his eyes as he took in his new opponent. Grinning widely, he watched as Kaiden's grip faltered, a strangled noise slipping from his throat as his sword slid away. Talon's eyes went wild with delight.

"You...have issues," Kaiden gasped, his legs fighting to hold him up. He made a strange noise in his throat, his grip shaky. Now Talon looked intrigued.

"The great Blaze Montego, not even able to hold his own sword. Guess they were right about the Bane doing a number on you. This is going to be *too* easy."

Chan wanted to move, to help Kaiden as the other boy slowly slipped down, digging his sword into the cobbles as a prop to hold him up. His breath came sharp and choked through the air.

"Don't touch him."

Talon laughed, spreading his arms wide in a gesture of innocence. "I'm not touching anyone, Tiel. Your friends just seem to be caught in the grip of bad memories. What a shame." He tilted his head. "Funny how *you've* now become the impenetrable one."

It would be so easy to wipe the look off his face, if it wouldn't instantly paint a target on his back. Chan would lose all credibility with the Council if they discovered about his gifts.

"What a shame you can't help them. What a shame." Talon drew the words out, his smile widening. "Who would have thought that *you* of all people would be the strong one, hmm? You never thought you could do anything with your gift. Poor Chan. Always buried in a book or looking for help."

That's not true, Chan thought, as an idea began to form in his mind. He couldn't carry both of them at once, or fend the others off, but...

"Why don't you just kill me, if you're so threatened by me?"

Talon made a disapproving noise. "Chan. Unlike the Empress, I see *talent* in you, talent that would serve better not wasted. I'm hoping, of course, that you will change your mind."

Kaiden let out another gasping cry, sounding on the verge of hysterics. Chan bit down a curse.

Talon shook his head again. "Honestly, Tiel. These two? They're not worth it. One's a murderer and quite frankly insane – oh, wait. That applies to both of them, doesn't it?" He tapped his chin. "One of them betrayed – no, that doesn't work either. One of them hurt..." He made a face. "Huh. I guess they're both just as bad, aren't they? No one else would bother to give them the time of day. And yet here you are, contemplating throwing away a perfect opportunity just to ease their suffering. How silly is that?" He let his lips drift into a slow smile. "We'll just have to fix that later. Surely you can see the impossibility of this situation."

From Talon's viewpoint, he could. But there was something Talon didn't know.

"You can't win this fight."

Talon cocked an eyebrow. "Really? It seems I already have. Two down, one to go. Too bad I can't manipulate you as easily as I can them."

Chan wasn't very good with a sword. It never felt right in his hands, the way a book did. His preferred weapon was knowledge. And here, that left him in a standstill. He'd known Talon would be at the meeting; the chances of crossing paths grew the closer he got to the capitol. But now, it seemed he'd have to make a choice.

"Of course, I don't need to, do I?" Talon's smile widened. "All I have to do is threaten them, and you bend as easily as they did. And you claim threats aren't effective." He glanced over at Kaiden, nearly smirking. "Join with us, and I'll let them go. All of this can be our little secret."

Chan tightened his arms around Katya. Talon was right about one thing. There would be no more hiding after this was done. The damage it could potentially do – not to the town itself, but to the reputation he had so painstakingly built – would not be easily undone.

But if Chan had a choice between the world and his friends, he would choose his friends, every time.

Logically, he knew that he *had* stood a chance, before. They were making headway, and he was about to throw that all away. But what else could he do? He couldn't carry both Katya and Kaiden, and neither was in any condition to help him – even if he stopped Talon from tearing apart their minds first.

Chan's blood was boiling from the way Katya had gone stiff against him. He wished he had Lena's gifts, or that he had left her in more capable hands. Anything he could to see what Talon was doing to his friends, how he made her flinch in silence. Kaiden's breathing was too hard to be normal, desperate words spilling almost incoherently off his lips in an endless stream of pleading.

"So weak," Talon murmured, with an inflection that Chan didn't like. "He should have kept the Bane with him. At least then he was useful." Talon's other hand stayed his companions from finishing the job, his smile cruel as he looked at Chan, daring him. "Do it, Tiel." His voice was low. Too low. "Save your friend, and me the trouble of coming up with a charge against you. I might not have power over my sister here, but you..." His grin was cruel. "We both know there's more to you than meets the eye."

Chan refused to look at him, focused instead on Kaiden's quiet breathing. Talon followed his gaze, smiling.

"Oh, he'll be alright. Providing you, you know, fix him." His eyes were laughing now, shifting back to the challenge. "The choice is yours."

It was a thought well accepted that everyone specialized in one gift, and only one. Chan's was storms. Olive's was plant life, of the more vicious kinds. There were varying levels and categories and areas of expertise, ranging from broad and generalized to very specific and highly dangerous. Chan once knew a girl who could suck the air from your lungs with just a breath of her own. Like it was nothing.

But this...this was more than just a challenge. It was a test. Proving what Chan had so foolishly theorized about to Talon, years before. Proving what he'd never dared to voice aloud.

"Go on, Chan," Talon said lowly, his smile too similar to the one years ago. "They're waiting for you."

He couldn't lose his friend again. The life of one over the lives of many...

I'll keep them safe. I promise.

With a breath in, the skies began to darken, Katya's eyes trailing up to watch their progression as she shivered. The sky rumbled in response, pressing against the hold he had on it. Chan remembered what Damien said; leashing this once-caged tiger might be the last thing he ever did. He had seen it many times, played out in many scenarios. The ground cracking beneath their feet. The sky striking them dead with hot white fingertips. The rushing winds tearing them to pieces, without them making a sound. He knew all the scenarios. It prepared him for the worst.

He couldn't control *where* the storm would strike. But he could summon it, all the same. It was dangerous, but that was why he never told anyone about it, making them think the best he could do was summon bolts of electricity and use those.

The storm bucked, and Chan pulled it back, feeling the crash beneath his skin as if the sky was slamming into him. He shuddered, feeling it feed on his energy, his own fading so fast as it crackled into the sky, bright white like phantom roots, crackling, laughing. He watched Talon's expressionless face as he took in his end and didn't say a word. Storms did that to you, when you were staring down the face of them. Chan knew there would be no stopping him now.

Talon had walked right into a trap.

Chan figured Talon had no idea what he was getting into. Most Gifted could only control small clouds, crackles of lightning no bigger than your fingers. They didn't have the capacity to hold a whole storm.

Even Sari hadn't believed him when he said he had storms under his skin. They pulled at him; he knew where they were and where they wanted to appear. He knew how to let them out.

Talon had no idea what he was getting into. He thought by forcing Chan's hand, he would have a reason to arrest him.

He didn't realize he would have to survive first.

Chan let the storm grow to a dangerous level, feeling it crackle and snap beneath his skin as it begged to come out. The muscles in his arms strained with holding back, until even Talon began to look surprised, and nervous.

Joss crept out from behind a wall, her eyes wide. She looked back and forth between them, concern twisting her features.

"Hey, mister?" she said to Chan. "I think your friend can do mind tricks."

The discomfort was clear enough on her face as she knelt beside Kaiden, a shudder running through her as she closed her eyes. He wondered if Talon had loosed some memories for her, too. But she didn't scream, or cry, the slightest tension to her fists the only indicator.

"Stop it," she whispered with eyes closed, and Chan wasn't even sure if she was talking to him, or someone else.

Chan struggled to contain the crackling energy building up in his veins, humming in his fingertips. If he released it now, there was no telling where it would strike. They were too vulnerable, too exposed. Talon seemed to see it too, by the way his smile returned, a dangerous yet wary thing.

Chan summoned the energy begging to surface, with the right touch. Talon's smile faded as he watched the shadow pass over them, stormy and grey, fraught with trouble.

"Well," he said in what almost sounded like an impressed murmur. "It seems the scholar has some fight to him after all. Kill us all, Tiel?" Despite the light, there was real fear in his eyes. "How very unheroic of you."

He could do it. Could he guard them, too? Talon held an invisible knife against their throats, ready to slit it. He knew what the man had

213

done to his own sister. If he made the wrong move...it could kill them all.

Chan was shaking, waves of the storm rolling through him as they barreled out in the only form of release they could find. The wind howled and moaned, and Chan used every last bit of his strength reining it back in. It wouldn't obey, not entirely, but he could siphon some of its power.

People weren't meant to have this sort of influence, Chan thought, as the storm bucked against him like a mad dog straining at its leash. If he released it, there was no telling what it would do.

But the light to his eyes must have been dangerous enough, or Talon cowardly enough. His eyes widened, his lips moving in a silent whisper. He didn't think Chan could contain that much power.

And maybe he couldn't. Already it was drawing off of his energy, feeding so it could grow. He was on the dangerous verge of giving up, the control slipping away through little bolts in his fingers, his hair. Lightning crashed from his fingers into the ground, forcing Talon to back up. Muttering a curse under his breath, he gestured for his followers to retreat.

"You've only doomed yourself, Tiel," he yelled over the storm. "You won't possibly survive this."

Katya crumpled to the ground like a puppet with her strings cut. Kaiden choked on a sob, shielding his head with his hands.

Chan had no idea what he would do now that he had summoned this. He couldn't take in so much energy without releasing it somehow. Already his hands were trembling, bones aching from the strain of so much potential. What could he channel it into?

Chan let loose a smile, though it barely hid the spike of fear he felt inside. The storm was growing far past his control, escaping in gusts of wind through his fingertips. The town wouldn't survive such an attack.

Talon and his friends were gone. Chan's plan had backfired on him, and now they were all in danger. He couldn't contain so much power. He just...couldn't. Talon was right, after all.

He felt the winds whipping around him, dragging his hair in his face. It had grown longer and not been cut, and now stung like tiny lashes against his skin. The winds growled and moaned as they pulled against his restraint, wishing to unleash their wrath on the hapless town.

Already he felt himself crumpling, its energy siphoning the rest of his and leaving him far more distant. Kaiden was silent and still, bent to a knee, clutching his sword with a whitened grip. Katya shuddered, and refused to move.

Perhaps Talon had gotten to his mind, too, for he saw flashes of people in the winds. Sari, with a purple dragon. The outline of an island, all of it a shadow.

Meriador, walking toward him. He could have cried out in relief, even though her expression was mournful.

"*I can help,*" a voice whispered. One that was far too sad and earnest. It reminded him of someone. It reminded him of his sister, begging.

He was so tired. The storm was taking all of his energy, wearing it away, weathering his grip until the rock beneath him would just slip, and the storm rip and rush away in a howl of destruction. He knew, if he let that happen, there would be no going back. He couldn't rein in the storm once it was gone. But he couldn't contain that much energy in him, either. He needed to siphon it, somewhere.

A crack of lightning, striking the ground. The roll of thunder, grumbling at him. He forced the bolt to redirect, and felt a searing pain through his veins. Lightning was far more volatile to absorb. He looked at the spiderwebbed lines running through his skin like cracks, felt their permanence there as he absorbed the effects of it. It hurt with a blinding white pain, but it was worth it, even if he felt like he was going to burst.

He had to channel it, somewhere, before it leapt out on its own. But where? Already his hold was slipping, more and more of the storm leaking out. It fed off of him, an endless cycle of give and take as they played tug-of-war with his lifeforce. He couldn't hold it all in, even if he wanted to.

The storm was slipping. Absorbing its energy might kill him. It *would* kill him, if he let it out. Already he had such a thin hold on its development. He couldn't destroy and create at the same time.

Maybe it wouldn't destroy that much. Maybe it would leave them all safe.

The winds left him with a terrible guilt, though nothing had yet happened. He could picture it anyway, clearer than he ever had before. Buildings torn to shreds. Blood on cobblestones.

This was why he kept to his books, and not to fighting.

See what you've done? Talon's voice, mocking him. Images of the destruction he would cause, if he kept this up. Chan had read far too much on storms not to know how bad of a decision this had been.

"*Let me help,*" the voice whispered again. "*Please?*"

Though it wasn't as if he had much of a choice, Chan let go, bracing for the worst. The storm siphoned away from him, like a hand unfolding his to take the reins. He expected to hear the winds wail, and lightning scream as it tore freely through the air. Instead, it seemed to quiet, slowly, taking his energy with it as some unseen force calmed the monster he had unleashed.

The sudden lack of energy left him dizzy and gasping for breath. Weak at the knees, he sank to the cobbles. Joss looked sad, as she watched the storm with a too-bright light in her eyes.

And somehow, he understood, as the winds began to warp, and vanish, whispering out like the smoky breath of a dying flame. The girl was the only one who stood unafraid, the deep purple of her eyes seeming almost to glow in the flashes of lightning as she pressed her lips together, facing the storm, and held a finger to her mouth, like shushing a child.

His limbs trembled with the aftersurge of adrenaline, even as he watched the storm around him...*vanish*. Winds whispering out, lightning crackling away with the snap of fingers. The girl before him looked centuries older than he, in that moment, aching with a kind of pain he could never hope to understand as she meticulously took apart the storm, stealing its power.

This was why the Isles were considered so dangerous. Not because they had a power that others didn't, but because they knew how to *use* it in a way that, if it wasn't saving your life, was utterly terrifying. Watching a child less than half your age face down a raging storm and calm it down as if it were nothing.

It was a good thing she had stowed away, after all.

The girl's eyes still contained that ache, once the winds were little more than a whisper, hardly louder than the breathing of those around him. Her gaze went to Kaiden, twisted with pain for a moment, and then to Chan, the expression shifting to regret. "I take from others," she whispered, as if in explanation.

He wanted to tell her how good it was, in this case, that she was able to help him. But she looked so sad, and kept lingering with her looks at Kaiden that he didn't dare, for the moment. The storm left him feeling worn and energized at the same time, like he had been stretched out and returned to the same place.

Joss dropped down beside Kaiden, her arms on her knees, looking quite sad and small now. Her hands trembled just barely, though she buried them in her lap. "You care for him a lot, don't you?"

Her whisper gave him pause, though it was only a moment before he was nodding and lowered himself down beside her with a soft breath. "Yeah. I do."

There was something faraway to the girl's eyes, as she belatedly nodded. Then, without a word, she stood, looking to him expectantly.

Chan's eyes widened. "How did you...?"

Joss looked up at him silently, for the heaviest moment. She opened her hand and a tiny storm crackled inside it, smudged grey and thundering dimly in his ears, like a faraway echo.

KATYA

Red as roses.

That was her first thought when she saw the blood, spilling out and blooming across her father's chest like petals. Red as the garden roses, as if they had been painted with his very lifeforce. A knife, sharp and very, very deadly, gleamed in her hand, and she had no idea how it'd gotten there.

She wouldn't have needed a knife to kill them. A distant part of her mind knew this, and laughed bitterly at her own sadism. Theatrics, her brother would have called it. Putting on a show. *Begging for attention.*

She was always begging for attention, in his eyes. Wishing the Empress would see her. Envying anyone who got the chance. Bitterly planning her way to get to the throne.

But now she'd killed them, and though her brother was the younger of them, who would put a murderer in charge of their house? Let alone such an unstable one. Where could they put her?

She was too powerful to kill. Her instinct turned her deadly, like a wild animal, until her brother was convinced she needed to be broken. *It's the only way to fix her*, she remembered him saying. Sadly, as if the very words pained him.

They tortured her. There was no other word for it, and no one to believe her. No one except her brother, who looked at her with pitying glances and held her hand so gently and cleaned her wounds, telling her to just confess. *Confess* it had been her. Her with that knife.

And she imagined it. Her, standing with that bloody, too silver knife, glinting in the deep moonlight. It transferred hands, in her mind, and it was now her brother's eyes that were transfixed with horror as he asked what she had done, and *why*, and whispered that she was going to get them killed.

He blamed her. He had *framed* her. He had put that knife under her pillow and whispered thoughts into her mind until she began to believe him.

It came back, stronger now. The knowledge that it wasn't her, but it *should* have been. His burning jealousy, and what he'd done to her. How helpless she was to stop it.

But who would believe her, when the garden was redder than it should have been and he was the one watching her in horror?

They wouldn't. They never would, no matter how clear the evidence might be. Her brother was too good at what he did. Back then, she usually forgot that.

"Spare her," she remembered him begging the Empress, as if he actually cared. "Just...send her to the Mines."

Just. As if the Mines were a playground rather than a torture site.

And that was the story he told. But the Empress had other plans.

He wanted to keep her close by, to keep an eye on her. To assure she never told a soul.

He wrecked her mind, just before he left. He wanted her to see what he'd accomplished, he said. What he'd been striving toward for so long. Working with the Empress. Going on a mission for her. He was going to bring back the Bane, and she would love him, and give him a personal place in her court. No one would ever know what he'd done.

He needn't have bothered. Her tongue was too stricken to let out a word, and there wasn't anyone around to care if she did. She was mad, the failed daughter of Cloren Isreld, and no one should ever listen to her. It was a wonder the Empress kept her around at all, even for menial work. *If you're good*, her brother said, *maybe she'll be nice.*

I would have liked to use her, she heard the Empress say to him, one day. If he hadn't ruined her mind. Ruined *her*. She was like the old cloth that had once been a shirt, stained and ripped, useful now only for cleaning up messes.

Every so often, he would come, and she never knew if he would be kind or harsh. He said he'd be kind if she only cooperated. She did her best. It wasn't her fault when things fell and broke because her hands wouldn't stop shaking and—

Something clattered. Katya jumped, grabbing the closest hand to her. A little girl looked at her with worry and something far deeper swirling in the depths of her purple, murky eyes. Muddied, like a river stream. She should have known what it meant.

Shh, the girl's eyes seemed to say, though it was gentle and far too familiar as that smile. She looked over at the breaking boy next to her, and it faded.

It hurt Katya, watching him struggle. She knew his demons were many; she saw them clawing through his eyes even when he was convinced no one did. She heard them in his laughs and saw them in the way his chest rose and fell just a little too sharply, a flicker of light in his gaze as he looked away and faced the storm coming upon him.

She didn't understand how he did it. How he faced it all so...bravely, and never fell apart. Not in the way Katya did.

Here, now, with him on the ground between them, *whimpering*, it settled as a sickening realization in her stomach. The truth she'd known all along, and yet had never truly understood.

It wasn't her. It wasn't *she* who was weak, any more than it was he who was stronger. They were both broken, and carried it in different ways, and he held his scars closer to his skin. Hers were lines across her mind, gouges she could never hope to heal.

It hurt her, so badly, to see him being ripped into like that, his breath gasping in his chest in a way that was as familiar to her as the air she breathed. The look of anguish that she *felt* as deeply as the blood in her veins, aching through her. She knew what it felt like to be torn apart.

Chan would fix him. Chan had fixed her, as much as that was possible. Stretching cloth across the gaping chasms and painting it over to look like the ground, guiding her around them. Assuring her what she was missing didn't make her any less.

It hurt worse than anything, and she couldn't cry out *Stop* or *Help him* because the Empress had taken her tongue and her brother had stolen her words, long before that, where they would only come out as a scream. She felt them frozen, sealing her mouth shut so they couldn't come loose and hurt anyone. Her words were *poison*, and that's why he wouldn't let them out. Why he let the Empress take her tongue. Why he was *protecting* her.

She couldn't tell the world her secret.

She could only stare, stricken, and feel the cloth buckle in until she was faced with the gaping hole that was always there, before. If she spoke a word, she would scream. If she reached out to Chan, he would blind her with pain. If she reached out to the other boy, she would poison him with her thoughts. There was no way for her to win, none at all.

This small girl looked at her as if she understood, even if she never could. She reached up with a gentle, so gentle smile and her eyes seemed dark with the depths of survival. A way of escape, if only she could find it.

It broke her, in a way she thought she couldn't be broken further. She knew her friend's pain, and she knew how it was amplified, drawn together and tangled into a mess that he wouldn't be able to escape. She couldn't look at him, couldn't look at *anyone* without damaging them.

And yet this small girl showed no fear. She should have.

Her *brother* had done this. For the first time, Katya wished he might die. She wished something might happen to him, the way it did to everyone he touched. Not for her sake. For everyone he had hurt, and might one day break if he was given the chance.

The small girl reached out her hand, and Katya screamed inside at the touch, but she allowed it anyway, in quiet defiance. Her mind screamed that touching them would cause pain. Touching any of them would harm her, and them, and there would be no end to it.

Touch always caused pain. They had both been taught that.

She knew the same would apply to him. She knew the depths of what he felt. She *felt* it, same as he did. Rejection. Hurt. Fear.

She knew how her brother mixed these, and crushed them in the midst of you, until all you could breathe in was pain and all you could see was blood.

Blood. Blood red roses, blood blooming in a garden, on a moonless night in which a knife still glinted...

It *hurt*, worse than it ever should. She was no stranger to this isolation. She knew it would hurt if she touched anyone. She knew, and endured it anyway, for them.

She didn't want this. She didn't *care* if it hurt. It was...worth it.

Chan had made her feel something, where she didn't think she ever could. Hope? Love? She couldn't name it. It was as subtle as a breeze and just as gentle, entering her lungs in a way that made her relax. It was a soothing, warming presence that cooled her inside and calmed the murmurs in her head.

He was there. He didn't take from her.

And now she couldn't reach him. And that hurt her, more than anything. She couldn't scream here. But she would later, and she would endure it, to cover those holes again. To find a way to move on.

Because she wouldn't go back to that. And as she saw the spark in the boy's eye, from the fire he was burning in, she knew he felt the same. Pain that would soon harden to something far, far deadlier.

She wouldn't be a pawn anymore. She would help bring about the downfall of the Empress, if she could. It was the way it was meant to be.

A part of her was terrified at the thought, and knew she would buckle when it came down to it. But she would try, all the same, and that would be enough, wouldn't it? That was what he did. He was beaten down, again and again, and still raised his bruised cheek from the ground and wiped the blood away, and *stood*. He kept fighting, even when he shouldn't have been able to continue.

How did she ever put it into words? Written ones screamed at her, mocking her until she couldn't stand them anymore. Spoken ones were stolen from her, not even a whisper possible any longer.

She settled for glances, and he didn't understand them. Of course he wouldn't. Why would he? He had no idea just what strength he had. Just how much he was looked up to, and admired. He didn't see the way the others quietly mourned for him, and how their spirits lifted when he was back. How badly they wanted to help him, and how much they wanted to not hurt him.

How could she explain? *How?* She hadn't the strength.

That little voice, the one that whispered to her sometimes, knew the answer. It grew stronger from the girl's look, though it still terrified Katya. It offered true healing, in a way she couldn't comprehend.

One thing Katya knew. They would have to mend gaps to be able to communicate. One way or another, it would not be her words through him, but another's. She sent up a silent prayer for that chance, and could have sworn she saw the girl nod back.

CHAN

Chan's gaze shifted between his two friends. Katya seemed no worse than she usually was, despite her silence. It hurt thinking that was because she was *used* to this.

Kaiden, though, wasn't responding to anything. Chan shot down a flare of panic, shaking his friend's shoulder. They were both eerily quiet, only the slightest whimper an indication of his struggle. He tensed like he might fight back, but went along with it, choking out a raw and broken cry. Chan's heart squeezed sharply at the sound.

Chan turned his attention back to Joss, fighting down the exhaustion still weighing on him.

"How did you do that?"

Joss shifted on her feet, eyes flicking from Kaiden to Chan as she drew in a deep breath, and shrugged. But her eyes said more than she was telling.

I need to know, Chan thought, and drew in a breath of his own. "We'll talk about this later," he said quietly, stepping toward Katya.

Joss' mouth was open in silent protest, but he'd already moved, and Katya shrank back from him. Stunned, Chan stood there for a moment, looking at a girl he hadn't seen in a long time. One more like a frightened mouse than a girl, ready to scream at the slightest touch. He brushed away the fleeting thought that all his progress with her might have been ruined. It made his chest tighten, even as he reminded himself they had been through this before. They could get through it again.

Joss' lips were twisted together tightly, in something close to a frown. She took in an unsteady breath, her fingers crackling for the briefest moment before she brushed it away to only a flicker in her eyes.

Kaiden started sobbing. Joss looked between him and Chan uncomfortably, her brow creased in tiny lines. She shifted on her feet, pressing her lips to hide a frown.

"Jade," Kaiden whispered, his voice fractured. "Please. Jade...?"

The haunted sound to his pleas was cracking Chan's heart. He gave his friend a minute to his sorrow, looking out at the empty streets and drawing in a breath in preparation. Katya shrank further away from him. She stared sightlessly at what remained of the storm, though he could see the agony written on her face.

Joss remained quiet, as if he might scold her for helping him. He thought he sensed a tremble as she stood, waiting to see what he did.

Katya let the girl get near her, and it hurt worse than he would admit. Though her eyes were apologetic, to a degree, she kept her distance anyway, watching Kaiden with fearful, worried eyes. *I'm fine*, her eyes said, though she wouldn't speak the words to him.

After a moment, Chan reached out to his friend, and Kaiden flinched. It hurt to watch, and he drew his hand away on instinct. Kaiden's shoulders tensed, relaxing slowly, forcefully, as he let a breath out.

"Kaiden," he tried to say, and found it came out as a deadly whisper. Like the storm was still controlling his words, trying to infuse them with power.

His friend seemed caught in a trance, trembling, the barest shake of his head the only indication of anything going on, his jaw locked in frozen agony. A low, pained sound rolled through him at Chan's touch.

Taking in an unsteady breath, Chan bent down to move Kaiden's arm away, gently. Maybe he'd been hit by the storm, somehow.

Joss' eyes looked sad. "There's nothing wrong with him there."

Ignoring the cracks in his heart, and the fire sparking out from beneath them, Chan reached an arm around Kaiden's shoulder and pulled him to his feet. He bit down a frown at the sharp intake of breath and the almost whimper slipping past his lips.

Why couldn't he just protect them? All his life, he'd only wanted to live up to his sister's example, and save what lives he could. It was why he joined Sari, to harness the powers he had for good. It's why he stuck with them, through everything. Why he put his all into helping Katya feel even just the least bit less afraid.

But this...this was killing him. Talon knew what he was doing, stranding his friends just out of reach, somewhere he couldn't touch them. Opening wounds he couldn't heal, and forcing him to just watch them bleed and try to cope with it.

"Kaiden," he said again, though there was no response. He wrapped his friend's arm around his shoulder, refusing to acknowledge the shudder that passed through him. Too close to the last time they'd found him. But that couldn't have happened again.

It didn't mean Talon couldn't have brought the pain back, though.

Kaiden tried, feebly, to push him away, a broken whimper slipping past his lips. *"Please."*

The desperation in his voice was tearing him up inside. Chan wanted to do nothing more than hug his friend close and assure him that everything would be alright now. Nothing would hurt him, ever again.

Kaiden bit his lip until it bled, his eyes tightly screwed shut as if to keep from seeing the world, like it was painted in blood and he couldn't bear the sight of it. Katya followed him, but at a distance. Kaiden seemed to accept defeat, letting Chan lead him along.

After a couple steps, he cried out again, louder, biting down on it halfway so it sounded strangled, like from a wounded animal. But he clenched his teeth and kept walking, determination pricking bright in the corner of his eyes as he limped along. Other than old scars, there was nothing Chan could see, though he wouldn't rule it out just yet. He was holding himself together by threads, pools of fear and dread and a shuddering determination muddled in his eyes as he fought not to make a sound.

Chan needed to find a healer. And what if nothing was wrong with him? What then?

What then? He'd have to go on anyway, and hope it faded away.

Kaiden looked up at Chan once, his eyes unseeing of anything real. He looked away just as quickly, half-flinching. Subdued. Though he seemed aware that he wasn't seeing things right, he couldn't seem to stop it. Years of pain etched into his face as he leaned against Chan, favoring his right leg.

Chan felt as if all the masks had been stripped away, and this was what had laid underneath, all that time. A sobering realization.

"Jade," Kaiden whispered again, a sound almost like a groan dragging through his throat. His eyes shut tightly for a moment, to hide a wince as he stilled, his hand slipping to his ribs.

Chan felt down there, instinctively, and Kaiden's muscles flinched as he let out a tight gasp. His eyes seemed to be seeing other things, locking them away behind a grim, pale face as he set his jaw and continued on, only leaning on Chan when he had to.

Chan wanted to touch his mind, but didn't dare. The warning look in Joss' eyes and the quiet terror lurking in Katya's kept him from doing so. Joss' lips pressed into a tighter line.

"Don't hurt him," she murmured, her arms crossing over her chest. "I still need him, you know."

Even her voice was softer, and Chan hated it. He carried the three broken children along after him, until they came in sight of the house.

Reme's eyes widened when she saw Kaiden. "Chan?"

Chan shot Joss a sharp look, upon the opening of her mouth. "He'll be fine. He just had too much to drink."

Reme nodded warily, though she let him carry Kaiden over to the bedroom. "If he makes a mess of my sheets, you'll be the one cleaning it up."

Chan dipped a weary nod, surprised at how tired he felt. He settled Kaiden down on the bed, where he stared sightlessly at the wall. Joss paced the room, eyeing the two of them. Her hands seemed to glow ever-so-often, though she took in a steadying breath to dim it.

Despite the tiredness sinking into his bones, Chan dropped down next to the bed, looking over at Joss. He knew she was aware of what he'd seen, with her hands. Katya was already drifting off against the wall she'd settled against, exhausted by her struggle. Maybe that's all Kaiden needed, too.

What Chan needed, at the moment, was a distraction. And answers.

Joss fidgeted with her balled up fists, as if she knew what he was going to ask. "So, your friend seems nice," she piped up cheerily, smiling too widely at him.

It took Chan a long moment to gather the energy he needed to speak. "You're from the Isles."

Joss flinched, her gaze shooting away like she'd been caught. "Ding ding, we have a winner. Haha." She rubbed the back of her neck, then winced, looking down at her hand. "Kinda hard to hide, with the eyes, huh?" she asked, quieter.

Chan nodded slowly, to regain his voice. "They're more striking, when..."

"Yeah. Striking, like lightning and all that. Danger. Storms. All the bad things." She cleared her throat noisily, attempting a smile. "That was my shot at a pun."

Joss seemed aware that her rambling wasn't distracting him, which only made her more nervous. Chan could hardly focus on one part of her words, shaking his head slowly. "You saved us."

"Haha. Yeah." She kicked at the ground, frowning. "'Saved'."

"What..." He drew in a breath. "What do you mean by that?"

"Nothing. Forget it." She let loose an unsteady laugh, eyes flickering volatilely for a moment before she shut them. "You think being Gifted is bad," she muttered.

"I don't think many understand it," Chan managed to answer truthfully, his tired brain mentally flipping through pages of books he'd read. "Though...I am curious why yours is that much stronger."

She lifted her shoulders in a nervous shrug. "Practice, right? I mean...I am older than I look. Technically." She frowned, kicking her heel against her shin. "Why am I telling you this?"

"Because I'm exhausted and probably won't remember it much anyway...?"

"Oh, you'll remember it alright. That's just regular old exhaustion, 'cept it kicked you in one fell swoop." She lifted her shoulders again, letting them fall. "But..."

Too tired to retort anyway, he gave her a moment. Joss frowned at the ground, rubbing her fingers together. "The Isles are secret for a reason," she finally said, lowly.

"Why...?" he managed to push out, though his voice was growing steadily more and more hushed.

"Because...no one's ready for it." There was a distant look to her eyes for a moment, voice a faraway murmur. She trailed off in a different language, startling after a moment as she seemed to realize, and blinked at him.

"Sorry. That was really out of line." Swallowing, she toyed with her hair. "I...can't tell you much. I wasn't there for that long. Comparatively." A funny smile touched her lips, whisked away after a moment. "Islers tend to stay away from regular people for this very reason. Not that I really had a choice. But what I said was true." She ran all her sentences together, smiling distractedly at him. "I just...take things. If I can. I don't really know...how."

He took the last part to be a lie, but exhaustion was starting to make his head fall to the side, close to Katya. Right. He should get her to a bed, too, and stand up before he fell over. Hopefully by morning, they would all be fine.

XIV

KAIDEN

He tried to stand, but couldn't. His body felt like it was being ripped apart, even the breath in his lungs a struggle to pull in, to steal back from the darkness tearing at him. He couldn't see anyone, anything but white and blinding memories.

"Jade? *Jade...!*" She couldn't have left him, too. "Jade..."

His bones ached like they were made of metal, weighing him down. He was shaking, close to breaking far beyond what even he could piece back together. It was tearing him apart, inch by painstaking inch. This was what his existence would be like, if he was honest. This was why so much of himself was hidden away. Leaving it open would destroy him.

"I can help you, Kaiden."

No. No, he wasn't going to go through that again. He *knew* how badly that went.

But...

"Please."

I don't...want to forget.

Because as painful as it was...it made him who he was. The good *and* the bad. He couldn't just choose one or the other. That wasn't the way it worked.

Help me.

He could have easily turned it down. He could have locked it all away, if he tried. But he *wanted* to remember, and this was the only way.

In time, he could remember. Piece by piece, little by little. It would get better.

He didn't even have a moment to retaliate before his mind was screaming, a wave of pain so sharp it burned, dropping him to his knees. The images came in a furious flow, smacking into him so he couldn't even catch a breath. So *many* memories...

The chaos began to ease, and with it, the pain returned. He was vaguely aware of someone saying his name, but it was also screamed at the same time, and there were so many faces he didn't recognize. A grinning brunette with a bush of curls and the loudest laugh. A fearless blond with a solemn smile. A freckled boy with more creativity than any of them combined. Names, matching up to faces. Gigi. Rafe. Samar.

It was like mourning them all over again.

He remembered, too, things before that. Things after. Chan, hanging out in the background while plans were made, his nose in a book. Olive's determination. Fern's culinary attempts. He remembered Dailen, and laughing in a room full of dragons, a grin too big to be real on his face.

And then he remembered more. Pain so sharp he could barely breathe, dizzying waves of fear and nausea seeking to topple him; words that wouldn't leave his lips despite how desperately he wanted to voice them. Pain from losing them, all over again. Of knowing it was his fault.

He saw his mother, and her gentle smile. He could feel the ghost of her hand on his cheek, achingly close and still so, so far away. Separated by years that she never should have been torn out of, like an unwanted page in a book. He remembered the house, and his siblings. Cutting himself on a knife and marveling at how little it hurt; comparing it to other marks on his arm. The first time he had touched fire and understood that it was one thing in this world that wasn't against him. It had been intended for harm, but it saved him from it. For a time.

Most of all, he could see *her*, now. Where Jade had said she'd been, she was, and now he could *see* it.

Dark rooms and secret breakdowns. The scrape of a knife against wood. Humming, hushed too quickly at the sound of footsteps. A sudden spike in his pulse. He saw it all. He *felt* it all, throbbing like a bruise under his skin.

Amidst it all, swirling like a maelstrom, was what he had already remembered, memories so dark it made him shudder even to touch them. He didn't want those near him again.

"Kaiden."

There it was; that voice. He remembered that, too. Fighting for his life, giving up control, and then...nothing. He woke up in darkness, and it filled his mind as well.

It made him sick, knowing he hadn't had a choice. Maybe this was why he'd fought against it, all this time. Now he saw it all, and he had to make a choice. Did he try to suffer through it on his own? Or did he ask for help?

He'd had enough of suffering, and weakness. Maybe part of weakness was not being able to ask for help, rather than accepting it.

It *hurt*, seeing it all. He couldn't escape it, no matter how much he shut his eyes. It made him burn inside with so many emotions he thought he might explode. The joy wasn't enough to overcome the overwhelming dread and disgust writhing in his chest, both at himself and what he was seeing.

I don't want this, he thought, and knew it wasn't true. Because he knew, too, that this was the only way to get everything else back. That he had to have the bad to get the good. As sad as it was, it was the way life worked. He had it all taken from him, and now it was have it all back, or nothing.

But Meriador's voice was there, gently whispering, and it only made him want to scream further, with what she was suggesting. She wanted him to take it *all*. She wanted him to carry this burden around with him, forever.

He already knew it would destroy him. It had once before.

A spike of fear shot through him at the thought. He couldn't be that again. He *couldn't*. He couldn't snap at them and scream at himself and destroy plants to get rid of the toxic rage boiling inside him, at the injustices. He couldn't put on smiles that ruined his face bit by bit until they were permanent, and that was all that was left of him. Broken, tattered smiles holding together what remained of himself. He couldn't do it. He *couldn't*.

Meriador tried to say *I'll help you*, but he was too caught in his fear to hear it, or want to embrace it. She was already *here*, with him, and he couldn't push her away. She had saved him. She was trying to do it again.

It made him so *sick*, to think of carrying this knowledge again. It made him ache in a way he thought he never could, like tears would permanently make their home in the corner of his eyes, trapped in a place they could never escape and never find release from. It would steal his voice, take away anything that made it okay and leave him with the tattered, broken mess of what he *should* have had.

He didn't want it. He didn't want to hurt them, either. He couldn't go on pretending. He *knew* that. He'd been down that road, and seen what it did to them. Even if there was nothing inherently cruel to what he was doing, they would know. They would be sad. He *couldn't* do that to them.

But it was tearing him apart inside, bit by bit, until he had broken down sobbing somewhere in the depths of his mind, unaware of what was going on around him. Maybe he'd always been alone. Maybe he'd always been *here*, and there was an impostor in his body, living his life. Maybe this was all he'd ever been: *lies*.

Maybe Jade really didn't exist, either. Down here, he didn't know.

He mourned his life, and what it could have been. What it had been. He choked out tears until there were none left to shed, and it began to burn inside him instead, eating him alive. He should let it, right? He should just let this all swallow him and see what became of him. There was no escape. No getting out of this. He might as well throw it all away, if this was going to be his life.

His thoughts terrified him, with how true they seemed. It scared him to think that this was all he could ever be.

He cried until he thought he couldn't cry anymore, and it wracked his body until he thought it might fracture and pieces of himself fell away. He cried until it was quiet, until the storm had become a whisper, a sob, until he had spilled all the tears that had been locked inside of him for so long, they didn't even know how to come out anymore. He'd held it in for *so long*.

I'm ready, a small part of him whispered, and he wondered if it was true. He felt battered, like he'd been in the middle of war and only just now noticed all the damage he'd sustained. He could almost see them, if he looked at himself. Ugly bruises and cuts and fingerprints, all whispering stories and lies to him that he couldn't stomach at the moment. If he had anything to release, he might have. He felt so...empty.

And still, a part of him resisted it. The idea that somehow he was *broken* and could be fixed stirred far too many things in him that he didn't want to face.

It dredged up memories until he thought he might be sick with them, all the things he never wanted to see, and some he thought had never happened. Had they? He didn't know anymore. Everything *hurt*, and Jade...

Jade was gone. Everyone was. He was *alone*, here, and nothing was going to get him out. He would be stuck with this torment, forever.

Someone touched his side, and it sent waves of torment flooding through him like liquid fire. Everything should not hurt this badly, as if he was burning alive. He didn't know what to do with any of it, a scream slowly building behind his lips that he refused to let out, even as it burned and choked him and sent hot tears pricking sharply at his eyes.

He couldn't be here forever. He *couldn't*. Somewhere, he had to know that this wasn't real. But he couldn't distinguish between what was real and what was false when it was all so *present* and seemed so very, very real. It hurt worse than any fire. It stole every bit of him away and tossed it in a maelstrom of emotions and memories, stinging so deeply he couldn't even catch a breath.

He heard his name, distantly, gently, and nearly cried in relief. Meriador again, urging him. Asking him to let her help. He was so desperate, he could do nothing but reach out for her, lest he be swept away.

And then it all became horribly, painfully *real*. Like she had dragged him out of a storm and straight into a fire, burning him alive with the revelations around him. Voices screaming and someone crying and the fire burning, *burning* across his skin, so thick he couldn't even breathe. An agony so complete he couldn't open his mouth in response, forced to watch it slowly tear him apart. He saw, in such clear detail, all of his siblings, and his friends, and what had happened to him. What he had done. He saw with painful clarity the way his little sister smiled, the bright spark to her eyes that he swore he'd never let be put out. He saw it switch to fear as Kinny herded their siblings upstairs and urged them to be very, very quiet. He saw the sadness on their faces as Kaylissa bit back a whimper and buried her face against her older sister.

He felt despair sweep over him like a cold, devouring wave, smothering him. So thick he thought he might choke, or drown, and no one would ever hear him. Like he would just melt into the floor and disappear, and no one would be the wiser. This *weight* pressing down on him, harder and harder with every now-numbing blow...

He felt the pain, fresh and sharp as if it were actually happening, dragging screams from his throat that never actually hit the air. Bone-deep exhaustion and a dread that tore him to pieces, a tremble he couldn't stop for fear he might entirely shatter. He saw himself, curled in a corner and shaking with the intensity of all of it, wishing it would all just *end*.

He felt the numbness, a dreadful aching in his chest like something dear had been torn from him. He saw the smiles for what they were: *empty*, and saw that no one noticed. It worked, for a time.

He felt the grief tugging at him, unraveling him piece by piece as it cycled through each of his teammates – their faces, their laughs, their *smiles* – and they were slowly, painfully torn away. His hands felt the weight of Gigi's body in them, a desperate cry lodged in his throat as he fought his way out of the cave and somehow got them out through sheer willpower and fire, even though his vision was so blurred with tears he couldn't see straight. He remembered collapsing and whispering *Fix her*, and then that was it, she was gone, torn from him with increasing bouts of madness while Damien just *watched*.

He felt that grief slowly hardening around him like a shell until all that could come out was bitter and broken comments, shards of smiles that cut more than they warmed, a spark to his eyes that could ignite a wildfire. He felt the anger, sheathed, leashed, but oh so present, building inside him with every single step. Nothing could touch him. Everything burned.

Everything else began to blur, a confusing mess of things that were far more familiar, interspersed with more pleasant memories that he'd never even felt. Smiles and conversations he'd brushed aside, coldly, because he couldn't handle any more death. He saw himself for what they did, not as he saw things.

And all through it, Meriador remained silent. It made a bitter sort of whimper want to work its way up his throat, that she was subjecting him to this, even though it had been his choice. He'd let her help him one other time. He was letting her do it again now.

But this time hurt far more.

Gently and ever so carefully, she untangled those memories so he could see them for what they truly were. Shock, grief, pain, all melded together and swirling amidst the tiniest bittersweet notes of everything else, only barely lessening the blow.

And in the midst of it, he saw her again. Jade, in all the places he hadn't seen her before. He ached like he never had before, and he felt fuller, as well. As broken and whole as one could be at once, like nothing could touch him, and everything already had.

She waited, questioning, and he let himself simmer in the emotions for a moment longer before he let her pull him through it, biting back a scream at the harsh, abrasive sting of the memories returning to him. *All* of it, all at once.

He chose to focus on Jade, through everything, and let her be his anchor. He clung to *her* with everything he had, until the present slowly, painfully made its way through the cracks and he could *see* her, perched on the edge of his...bed, looking far too grumpy for his liking. *Because of him*, he thought, and amended it. Because of what he'd been through. It all made so much sense now.

Jade.

JOSS

Joss hopped up on the bed, settling beside her bodyguard with a blown out breath. Now that the energy that had been crackling through her and making her hands twitch and her eyes glow was gone, she felt

231

emptier than before, and hated it. Hated how much it always made her long for...something. Something she would and could never have.

This was why they feared her. She was too powerful, on their island. Once the storm was free, it was only a matter of coaxing it gently back into pieces, calming the winds and sending them to gentler places. She tore it apart, bit by bit, and ended it.

It was never quite the same, using the energy from someone else's gift, which is why she chose to just dispose of it, this time. It was easy to see why people called her gift 'cursed' or unnatural, if she used it. Though she might be able to mimic other gifts, it was never quite the same as the original. A shadow of the real thing, since that seemed the only thing she could actually control.

She'd always had a fascination with shadows. Their stories, and possibilities, always overlooked in favor of the 'real' thing. As if they were merely...nothing.

In a way, then, this 'gift' wasn't even hers, was it? Maybe that's why people hated the Isles. Even with her gifts, she was still a thief. It was bitterly fitting.

Joss didn't remember anyone else from her home, or what abilities they had. Maybe they were all just as bad. Maybe hers was the worst, or on the other side of things, the best. She didn't think she'd ever know. All she'd ever been good at was stealing. It made sense that was what her gift would manifest as.

Kaiden didn't wake. His friend sat beside him still, too tired to think straight, the distress on his face stealing away the rest of his energy. He'd led the other girl to a bed and calmed her down while Joss slipped outside to dispose of the excess energy from Chan's gift. She came back in before her absence was ever noticed, though, and now Chan was sitting beside the bed, his forehead drawn in weary lines as he watched Kaiden's pinched, restless expression.

"He needs to sleep it off," Joss said quietly. She rested her hand on Kaiden's chest, and drew it away softly. "He'll be alright."

But she knew also, when he woke, how painful everything would be. How vividly he'd remember, good and bad. It made her ache inside.

After watching Kaiden for an agonizing moment, Chan took her hand and sighed. "You're right. Come on. You look like you're hungry."

Despite her previous resignation, Joss couldn't help a little grin. She knew there was a reason she liked this guy.

Joss let him help her off the bed, out across a hall and into a kitchen that looked like it had seen better days. Which wasn't really uncommon, in Calest.

Chan produced some cheese and chewy bread from somewhere, sinking into a seat across from her at the worn, scratched table. He looked worse than a guy she had once stayed with who had newborn twins. He'd poured tea on the table rather than in his cup and still tried to drink it. Joss had almost felt bad about stealing from him.

Chan, at least, managed to pour them both drinks, though he nursed his like he never wanted it to go away. Sighing, he set down the mug, but kept his hands wrapped around it.

"This was never supposed to happen, you know."

What part? Joss mused. She wondered sometimes why people were so likely to spill their stories to her. Must be part of her charm. Then again, this guy looked like he'd slept even less than she had the one time she'd stowed away with pirates. Sleeping was a little dangerous when you had to worry about someone possibly sticking a knife in your ribs when you turned your back.

Chan rubbed a tired hand over his eyes. "I grew up in a mining town. Nothing spectacular happened there. Everyone knew each other. There were no infected dragons, no one who could manipulate your mind. Nothing like that." He let out a breath of a laugh, his shoulders sagging. "I mean, other than the accidents. Occupational hazards and all." He shook his head, smiling at her. "Why am I telling you all this?"

Because I'm adorable and everyone trusts me? "Because you look like you got trampled by dragons and roasted on a spit for good measure?"

Chan ran a hand through his hair, which stuck up kind of funny from leftover static, holding what of it he could and looking at it. "Is it really that bad?"

"Well. No offense, but I think you need rest way more than the rest of us."

He let his hand fall, eyes quiet. "I'm just worried about them."

"Oh, my bodyguard will be fine. He's already had like two different breakdowns since I met him. Kaiden," she amended, at the tired confusion on Chan's face. A grin slipped onto her lips. "And I don't know this Katy...Cotton...girl very well, but she seems pretty strong. She didn't even call out any random guy's name when she got attacked."

A quiet laugh escaped Chan's throat, though a heavy shadow passed over his face for a moment, like clouds obscuring the sun. Wrapping his hands back around his mug, he sighed. "You think so, huh?"

"Mmhm." Joss smiled at him. "Even if she doesn't, I'd say she's got a pretty good caretaker for now. Anyone who offers food without you asking for it is alright in my book."

Chan reached over to ruffle her hair, messily. "Thanks, kid."

"Eww." Wrinkling her nose, Joss pulled away. "Don't say *that*. It makes you sound a billion times older than me, rather than...however old you are. Thirty or something. Call me Joss, please. Or 'that annoying thief girl'. Just not anything having to do with rascal. That one's taken." She screwed her lips to one side in contemplation.

It was Chan's turn to look appalled, her other words seeming to go right over his head. "I'm not that old."

"You might as well be," Joss teased, standing up and nodding to his mug. "Sittin' up here like a worried dad who can't get any sleep. You're going to keel over into your drink at this point. And then I'll have to help you up so you don't drown." She wrinkled her face up, adding as an afterthought. "At least it's not whiskey."

"I guess that wouldn't be very pleasant." Chan's gaze drifted to the book he'd set next to him, releasing another deep sigh that said *You're probably right.*

"Of course not. Now, as much as I am definitely *not* the caretaker of any of you, I'm going to pretend for a moment that I am and say you need to sleep. Now." She swept up his mug and book before he could protest, nudging his shoulder. "Up, up. No falling asleep on the table."

Though Chan still looked exhausted, the gratitude in his eyes was enough to make it worth it as she shooed him over to the next room. "I'll keep an eye on them, 'kay? I need less sleep because I'm smaller, so I use up less energy." She grinned, ushering him into the room. "Don't worry about it."

Either he was already almost asleep, or he'd decided not to argue, for there wasn't another sound from the bedroom as Joss closed the door behind her. She set the book down by it and grinned, heading back to the kitchen. Though the house itself didn't look like it had anything of value, food was always a valuable commodity. And Joss was starving.

KAIDEN

Kaiden wasn't aware of how much time had passed, if any had. He felt trapped in a million moments, all at once, watching his friends drift by. Watching them die.

The darkness receded, slowly, a shudder running through him as he forced his eyes open. For a moment, he wondered if he was dead. *Nothing* around him was familiar. Kinny had always mused that dying might be more like waking up than anything. Maybe he'd get to see her, then.

Instead, he saw Jade.

An unexpected warmth flooded through his chest as he watched her. *Jade.* He could see her in his mind, now, as if he hadn't truly seen her before. Her goofy grin and bright, sparkly eyes. Tugging him away from his house, doing cartwheels to make him laugh, holding him tighter than he'd ever been held before. Comforting him, when no one else was around. His mother's hugs may have been gentle, and Kinny's were warm, but Jade's made him feel...safe.

Good and bad, it all flooded back at once in a wave that choked every word from his throat. She sat on the edge of his bed, elbows propped on her knees, a grumpier expression on her face than he'd ever remembered seeing before.

Before she noticed he was awake, he sat up slowly and scooted down so he could hug her close, resting his head on her shoulder. Though Jade didn't seem to be expecting it, she shifted to hug him back with a laugh, the grumpiness easing.

"What's that for?"

Does there have to be a reason? Not really. Not when he could actually remember her, for once, rather than just knowing somewhere in the back of his mind that what she said was real. Not when a million tiny things were still playing through his mind to remind him of just what she was to him. Of the fact that he had the best friend in the entire world.

"Nothing, I guess." He let himself smile against her shoulder. "I remember...some."

Jade lifted a hand to ruffle his hair. She really liked doing that, didn't she? "Oh yeah? Like how annoying I can be? Or how weird? Or maybe you remembered that I still owe you from that one bet, which I still regret letting you talk me into, as I am adamantly against betting."

Closing his eyes, he let a laugh escape. "Well, I didn't remember the bet, but thanks for reminding me, Beautiful."

Jade made a face. "Ugh, even worse, you remembered that silly nickname. I keep telling you, my hair is way too insane and I'm way too weird for it."

Yes, he remembered why she said that, now. He also knew why it wasn't true. Why it was actually one of the best nicknames he could have given her. Because 'beautiful' had nothing to do with what she looked like, and everything to do with what she was. A light in a dark room. A spark of laughter in the midst of sadness. An anchor in a storm.

And land never looked so beautiful as when you were drowning.

He reached in and drew out the things that mattered, the ones that would make this ache bearable. He could feel it at the corner of his eyes, stealing his breath. Quieting his voice, as he knew it would.

She was beautiful because she was his friend, through everything. His first friend. His *best* friend.

She was one constant good in his life, a reminder that the dark couldn't be around forever. He couldn't think of anything more beautiful than that.

"I'm far from beautiful, Butterfly. Duh." She plopped her forehead on his shoulder.

So you say, he thought. As she always did. But they both knew, at least now, that there was no changing his mind.

"You gave me a nickname," he said. "I just returned the favor."

"Well, as long as it's just a ridiculous retaliation."

He smiled. "If it lets me keep using it."

Jade let out a huff. "I don't know about that."

"Aww. Why not?"

"Because I think you're still saying it to be sweet and are just agreeing so I stop protesting. Totally not cool."

He stifled a grin. *You see right through me.* "Me? I don't know where you'd get that idea. I said I remember the nickname, not why I gave it to you."

Jade sighed, squeezing him gently. "Fine, you just keep claiming innocence."

He returned the gesture, quietly. "I'm good at that."

"Not as good as you like to think you are." She shook her head, easing back enough to grin at him. "It's nice to be remembered, though. Now you can stop thinking of me as "that random girl who follows me around everywhere for some weird reason"."

"Don't give away my secrets," he replied, smiling back. "It's a lot different remembering than just knowing."

Jade laughed, reaching up to nudge his chin. "Yeah, I know." She pushed her hair out of her face and dropped her hand, rubbing the scars that circled her wrist. "It's a good thing you didn't remember and suddenly realize how annoying I am. But you seem as blind to my annoyance level as always, so I guess that's not changed."

Rather than say what he thought, Kaiden just smiled. This was what they did, after all. The teasing and flippant comments as if everything they did was a coincidence, or a joke. It was nice remembering that wasn't actually the case.

"I guess not."

Jade laughed. "You're too sweet for that, I suppose."

He chuckled. "Says you."

Jade shifted so she could plop herself against his side. "Well, duh. I feel like if anyone should know if you're sweet or not, it's me. Obviously I know you the best of anyone."

"Obviously." And yet, despite knowing him the best, she still never looked at him any differently for any of it. Never thought he was less, or worse, or no longer worth it. It was just another thing about her that was undeniably beautiful.

"No argument, huh? Cool, I'll take it."

"Do I usually argue?"

"Hmmm." She pretended to think about that. "I guess not about that, no."

"Mm."

Jade nudged her shoulder against his. "That sounded suspiciously like sassiness."

"Sass?" He did his best to sound offended. "How is that sass?"

Jade laughed. "Ambiguous answers are nearly always hidden sass."

"They are? I don't think I've ever heard that."

"Well, clearly you never asked my opinion on ambiguous answers, then." She tossed her hair over her shoulder in an exaggerated way, though something else twinkled in her eyes a moment later.

That, right there. It was what he could never quite put into words, or not in a way that made sense. Jokes were easier. Nicknames, too. Their way of saying things without seeming like they were. Because it never mattered how teasing she sounded. If he looked, that something was always still there, no matter what.

One thing he could cling to, no matter what happened. For once, he didn't mind if she was imaginary. She'd never leave him, then.

And if she wasn't? Well...he'd just hope she never did.

"Apparently not."

It must have shown on his face, too, because she cocked her head, studying him. "What's that look?"

One he couldn't explain, or at least...not like this. It was all too new and old all at once, a well-hidden treasure just recently unearthed, the dust not yet brushed off of it despite the familiarity it brought.

Jade smiled at him. "You should know by now, kid, that brushing it off doesn't work so well with me. What is it?"

What was it, exactly? He wasn't quite sure. With all the memories stirred back up in his mind, there were a million different currents with a million different emotions drifting around his head. Sadness, joy, confusion. Everything in between.

Despair. A choking, aching loss...

Sunshine and the delicate yellow petals of daisies. His sister's smile.

Meriador, holding the threads of him close together.

"Do I?" He put on a smile. "I didn't say I remembered everything."

"Ah, a distraction attempt. Also something I am on the expert list of." She set her hand on his arm and squeezed it, waiting.

"You're an expert in a lot of things."

Jade made a face at him. "Hardly. But none of that." She cocked her head again, eyeing him. "Did I say something that sparked a memory or something?"

"Seems like it to me," he said instead, and then shook his head. "No."

"Well, I'm not, and you might as well spill it, because I'll be annoying and keep pestering until you do." She grinned at him.

He grinned back. "You wouldn't want to hear it."

"I wouldn't be pestering if I didn't."

"Mm. I was thinking about how fitting the nickname is." Which, he thought smugly, wasn't even a lie.

In response, Jade wrinkled her nose. "You were thinking I was beautiful so you looked away like 'oh no, change the subject!'? I suppose that's a fairly decent reaction to that thought, though."

He studied the wall. "I told you that you wouldn't want to hear it."

Laughing, Jade lightly bumped his shoulder. "Ha ha. As your best friend, I think I should be given the right to veto ridiculous ideas."

Not this one. Grinning, he nudged hers back. "Is that so?"

"Mm-hm." Jade eyed him. "Are you sure that's what you were thinking, though?"

"Mmhm." He reached over to pet Ril's head, from where she slept next to him.

"I don't think that 'Mmhm' was very convincing. What else was going through that head of yours?"

He released a quiet sigh, the sound consequently infecting his words. "It rarely is." Smiling came a bit harder, even as he tried to shrug it off. "Lots of things."

"Name a few. Name them all. I've got nothing but time." She grinned. "I'm here to listen. It's like, practically my job."

Curling his hand in the blanket beside him, he tried to smile again, closing his eyes. "All of it?"

Jade set her hand on his arm and squeezed. "Just a lot of memories?"

You could say that, he thought as he nodded. "Guess so."

"Anything else? Something specific bothering you?"

Bothering. He supposed that depended on the definition of the word. It was just a little much to take in, all at once. Especially her. How normal this seemed. How...he knew more clearly than ever, every part of who he was. He knew everything that she knew about him, and it never seemed to change her opinion of him.

He didn't understand why she didn't *leave.* Seeing how broken he was. How much *he* had broken. It didn't make any sense to his fragile mind.

"Talk to me, Butterfly. I can't help you if you don't tell me what you need."

To steady himself, he drew in a slow breath. Everything was too unbalanced to think deeply on like this. "Just don't understand it all yet, I guess." *The understatement of the century.* "Too much at once," he shrugged, adding in a mumble, "or something."

"That's okay, Kaiden. It'll take time."

Everything did with him, it seemed. Years and years and more years. And still, even seeing it in a different light, he didn't understand.

Why do you stay around?

"Anything in particular confusing you? I can maybe help clear it up."

Kaiden glanced at the door, smiling to try to regain control of his emotions. "Too much for right now, I think."

Jade nodded. "Okay. How about just another hug, then?"

That, he could definitely do. He held her close, closing his eyes.

"It'll get easier as you sort things out."

Kaiden nodded, breathing out softly. "I know."

She propped her chin on his shoulder. "And you can ask me anything you need or want to. I can help if you need it."

He pressed his face against her shoulder for a moment, nodding. "Thanks."

Jade smiled, and shrugged. "Don't need a thanks."

He almost smiled too, since he did remember that. It didn't make it any less worth saying. "I know."

Jade grinned at him. "Yeah?"

When he nodded, her expression turned teasing. "Hmm. Well, if you know, then how come you said it?"

An exasperated sigh escaped his lips. It was a strange and oddly fitting sound, and didn't ache as much as he thought it might.

Jade fluttered her eyelashes at him, grinning in the most undeniably 'innocent' way possible. Kaiden couldn't stop himself from smiling, even as he shook his head at her antics.

Jade laughed and grinned back. She looked way too pleased with herself. Ruining his moment and then making fun of him. Honestly. He rolled his eyes at her.

Jade only smirked, about as smugly as you could. Shaking his head again, Kaiden reached down to stroke Ril's head instead, as the tiny dragon nuzzled against his leg.

Jade flopped down on her back. "I think I might get in trouble if you don't actually nap at some point."

Kaiden continued to pet Ril, smiling as she lifted her chin so he could rub under it. He didn't want to think about what horrors sleep might bring back. "Yes. Chan will walk in any moment now, see I'm not asleep, and his first reaction will be to look at my invisible friend he doesn't even know exists and scold her for not making me sleep."

"Exactly! And Chan seems like a scary dude to be scolded by, duh. So I'll be sitting here like, unable to defend myself!"

Chanis Tiel: *scary*. If he recalled him more fully, he probably would have burst out laughing. Instead, he nodded, a solemn look coming over his face. "I've seen him scold the dragons before for eating his cake. They were terrified of him for weeks."

Jade tossed her hair sassily. "Exactly. I would hate to have your scary friend be mad at me. It sounds horrible."

"Oh yes. He's *very* scary."

Though he was about to say more, who else walked in but Chan himself, concern digging lines into his brow.

"You're...up?" he asked, looking bewildered for a long, hesitant moment.

Jade looked over and laughed. "Dude, that's sorta creepy timing for him to walk in! All on cue or something."

It took a surprising amount of effort not to laugh too, as if Jade's amusement was infecting him. Blinking up at Chan, he gave the only answer he could think of. "Yes...?"

His mind, however, was already playing a different reply. *No, Chan, I'm just sleepwalking and talking to myself. Obviously.* As subtly as he could, he glanced over at Jade, adjusting his position to be closer to Ril. She did odd things to him, that was for sure.

Chan sat down near the bed, confusion mingling with the concern. "You were just...you couldn't really stand, and you kept calling out this girl's name..." He sat back, combing a hand through his hair, and then dropped it. "I thought you'd still be...out."

Before he could reply, Jade burst out in a laugh so hard she fell off the bottom of the bed. "He mentioned me! He actually did it! Oh my goodness."

Kaiden choked down a laugh of his own, though it kept bubbling up so much he had to disguise it with a couple of coughs. Which, of course, only made Chan look even *more* concerned.

What was wrong with him?

That was probably what Chan was wondering.

From her spot by Chan's side, having slipped into the room at some point, Joss grinned, a twinkle in her eye. "Oh, that's just his imaginary friend. He talks to her a lot. That or himself."

Jade started laughing harder. It *really* wasn't helping his own composure. "I've been found out!" Amidst more laughter, she choked the words out, sprawled on the floor. "Nooo!"

Chan looked between the two of them that he could see, concern taking over his face. "Are you okay?"

Between Jade's loud, wild laughter and Chan's absolute worry for his sanity, Kaiden had to cough out more laughs or risk seeming completely mental for laughing at absolutely nothing. He felt it tug at his throat, prick his eyes, the emotion begging to be released in *some* way. "I just...got something in my throat." Maybe the fact that he had to strain his voice for every word would make the excuse convincing.

"Just laugh, Kaiden, it'll scare the dude less!" Jade sounded breathless from laughter now, and slightly hysterical. "I can't believe he actually came in and *asked about me*. Oh my goodness." She collapsed in laughter all over again.

"Are you sure...?" Chan said, oblivious to all the humor. He looked about ready to get up and – well, Kaiden wasn't sure. Save him from himself, probably. Whatever that entailed.

Joss, in the corner, looked way too smug, probably considering herself the cause of the mayhem. Silly kid.

Kaiden waved his hand, the fake coughs turning into real ones until his throat burned, though he still wanted to laugh. His voice shook. "I'm fine. Fine." He braced a hand against his chest, taking in a breath he hoped wouldn't break into a laugh. "Just...my imaginary friend..."

Jade kept laughing. "Great, just pin it on me. Now he really *will* scold me!"

Chan, however, turned a disapproving look at Joss. Maybe he didn't believe the whole 'insane' theory after all. "I think you need to rest more," he said to Kaiden, his brow creasing up in folds again. "I know..." He let out a slow breath, rubbing a hand across the top of his head and then dropping it, a tired sadness seeping in. "I don't know what all Talon did, to you, but I know it can be...bad."

Katya. Right. This was the absolute worst time to laugh, and yet Kaiden couldn't hold it in any longer. It broke out before he could stop it, and he swiped his arm across his eyes to catch the tears he felt forming there. He didn't want them to turn to something worse. "M...Maybe..."

"I told you he would complain about the lack of sleep! Ha! Poor guy, we made him all worried."

Poor Chan, indeed. He ushered Joss out of the room, probably falsely assuming her to be the cause of the outburst. "If you need..." He hesitated, considering, then shook his head. "If you need anything, just let me know."

How strange it was, laughing without being able to control it. Kaiden laid down to hopefully appease Chan, partially to smother a wide smile in the blankets. "'K...kay." He tried to add 'Thanks', but had to choke it off, along with a louder, harder laugh, in the blankets.

Chan really *was* going to think he'd gone mental now. And maybe, for all he knew, he had.

Still on the floor, Jade laughed. "I'm pretty sure we just scared your friend into believing you're nuts."

Kaiden threw a fake glare over at her, trying to keep at least *his* laughter not too loud. He didn't want it to break out like hers. "No thanks to *someone*."

Jade just started laughing again. Not helping. "It's his fault! He wasn't supposed to come in and *actually* ask about me!"

Kaiden had to grab a pillow to choke his laughter in, tears flowing again from the overwhelm of it all. He wanted to keep them contained, still, before they made him do something he regretted. Ril looked up at him in surprise. "But then he *did*, and you made me look crazy!"

"What was I supposed to do? Not laugh? Yeah, we see how well that worked out for you!"

He raised his head to try to huff at her, amidst laughs. "You weren't supposed to make *me* laugh! You could have tried to hold it in!"

"I don't hold my laughter in! Do you not know me at all?"

"You still made me look crazy!" As odd as it felt to act this way, it was also rather... freeing, and his voice felt less and less like it was going to crack.

Jade changed her tone to sound haughty. "You're the one who found my amusement funny."

"You fell off the bed! How was I *supposed* to react? 'There goes Jade again. Fifth time this week. Don't worry about her! She's completely sane.'"

"True. I'm totally the sane one here. But still! You should be used to my weirdness. Become immune or something!"

"Maybe if I *remembered* you more than in little bits! It's more like 'Did she just...?'" He made the equivalent of Chan's face before continuing. "And then my mind catches up like 'yes, this is completely normal', but by then I've already reacted, so there's no point!"

How strange, hearing himself react so dramatically. It was at once completely foreign and more familiar than his own name.

Kaiden Michael Dyran.

More memories followed the thought. Not all of them were pleasant.

Some of them were fading, though, in light of everything.

Jade settled down on the floor as if she intended to snuggle up on it and stay there. "True enough. Once you remember me in the entirety of my extreme weirdness, it'll be easier to look sane again. After all, you hid my existence for like, ever. Of course, by then everyone could know about me and be scolding me about things! Totally not cool."

"Exactly," he replied, propping himself up to stare at her in what was most definitely serious scolding. "Except to *Chan*, who you probably completely traumatized by making him think I was having a mental breakdown." He dropped back on the sheets staring at the ceiling as he wiped tears from his eyes. "Your fault entirely. Not mine."

"Maybeeee, but you adore me anyway. So you clearly can't be mad because I am your fantastic not-real BFF."

More like 'supposedly not-real', Kaiden mused. "I never said I was mad at you. I just said I'm going to blame you anytime someone looks at me like I'm *mental* now. Obviously."

Briefly, he wondered which of them had been the sassier of the two. He could remember it himself now, if he tried hard enough. But he also knew he didn't have the strength to face more memories yet. His mind still shook with the false ones, trying to brush them aside as the lies they were.

"Well, they definitely will if you keep explaining me as imaginary. Duh. It's not my fault you can't get more creative with your explanations. 'This is my fake imaginary friend that I talk to all the time.' Yeah, people totally won't question that."

"Yes," Kaiden countered, "because saying I have an *invisible* friend that no one but I can see, touch, or hear doesn't make me sound

243

unhinged at *all*." Despite the admonishing shake of his head, he grinned. "And I didn't explain it at all! That was Joss!"

Jade cracked up again. "True enough, I suppose."

Continuing the game, Kaiden let out an exasperated sigh and rolled over to resume petting Ril, who had been watching the two of them like they were an entertaining street act. "What *am* I going to do with her, Ril?" he murmured.

"Keep me around, hopefully." Jade grinned.

"Hmm, I don't know." Keeping the fondness disguised from his voice, Kaiden grinned back. "You've caused *quite* a bit of trouble lately."

Jade laughed. "'Lately'? As if I only just started. I've always been trouble."

"Oh, I know. You're the reason I'm so strange. Probably." He tapped his chin once, thinking.

"Probably? More like I definitely am."

It definitely was strange, in one of the best ways possible. To think that he'd gone from an utter wreck just a few days prior to finally knowing who he was... He had to keep the bemusement off his face. Though he'd known, at least, that he liked jokes, they'd never felt...natural when he tried them. Almost as if he were a different person.

In this, though, Kaiden thought he liked being himself just a little bit more. He let out a laugh. "Well, at least that's one mystery solved."

Jade copied him. "Glad to be of help."

One nice thing about Jade being on the floor: she couldn't see the looks he kept sending her way, or the smiles creeping up his face. Though he managed to keep it wrapped under teasing, his mouth continued to give him away entirely. He liked teasing, as a way of coping.

"Always."

Ril nudged against him, climbing up onto his shirt and nestling there with a contented sigh. He settled back on the bed, carefully. After all, when a tiny dragon curled up on top of you, you didn't move. It was just a rule.

"Take a nap, Butterfly."

Now? He didn't think he could even if he wanted to. And he didn't. "Shush."

Jade laughed. "Shush yourself."

In response, Kaiden stuck out his tongue, even though she couldn't see it. "Yes, *mother*."

Something lightly whacked his foot. "Sleep, kid."

244

Kaiden pulled his foot back to safety, huffing out a breath. "And what if I don't want to?"

Jade sighed, long and drawn out. "It's good for you."

Maybe. But he was also rather enjoying this moment, and didn't want to potentially ruin it by closing his eyes.

"I would have thought being unaware of anything with my eyes closed *was* resting, but nooo, apparently not."

"Actual sleep is better."

"'Actual' sleep, she says." He lifted his head to look at Ril, though she kept her eyes closed. "As if that's not *actual* sleeping. Next thing I know, she's going to tell me that staring at food isn't *actually* eating it."

In truth, he wasn't completely sure where all of this came from. Somewhere in the jumble of dislodged memories, there was probably an answer, but since digging for it could also make things worse, he let it be, pretending that, if nothing else, he was just someone else who really liked jokes.

Jade laughed. "Talking isn't sleeping, either."

Kaiden expelled a noisy sigh. "Finnnnnne. And I suppose you're going to sleep on the floor, then."

"Probably, yeah."

He considered that for a moment. "Just don't get too attached to it."

"Why not?"

"Well, I wasn't exactly planning on leaving you behind because you fell in love with the floor. Or literally got attached to it. That could be a rather sticky situation."

"Ha ha. Very funny."

"What?" He looked over at her innocently. "I'm floored you don't like my pun. I really thought it was ground-breaking."

Laughing, Jade reached up to whack his foot. "You and your puns."

He twisted his face in an expression of mock-hurt. "Yes. I really thought it would sweep you away."

She patted his leg, chuckling. "You keep on believing that, Butterfly."

Huffing, he crossed his arms over his chest. "And here I was finally on fire with a joke, too. I am a connoisseur of puns, after all."

Jade folded her arms behind her head, shaking it. "You've always been on fire, obviously."

Struck by a thought, Kaiden paused to consider his hand, sparking a little flame to life in it. He waited a moment, but no memories swept in to plague him, a grin spreading across his face instead. "Nah. *Now* I'm on fire."

Jade turned her head. "Hmm. Yes, quite literally."

The flame wove between his fingertips at his urging, curling and flickering playfully. A sense of calm spread through him with the motion. "Mmhm. Though that makes you way cooler than me, since fire makes me pretty hot and all."

Jade wrinkled her nose. "I'm not hot nor cool. I'm entirely average."

The fire grew and enveloped his fingers, forming the approximation of shapes when he touched it. "Nah." He couldn't help the little smile that pulled his mouth. "You're fantastic."

Jade made a face at him. "'Fantastic' is way too close to 'awesome' for comfort. And being awesome is way more trouble than it's worth. I'm fine being ordinary, thanks."

He let the fire slip to the other hand, coaxing it into something that resembled a snake. "Not to me," he murmured.

Though he knew the kind of response she'd have, she still stayed quiet for a few minutes. He looked up to meet her eyes, and smiled.

"Crazy Butterfly." But she smiled a little bit back, all the same. "What am I going to do with you, hm?"

He chuckled, letting the fire die down to the smallest spark. "I know, I'm quite a handful."

"Mmhm. A too-sweet-for-your-own-good handful."

Kaiden dropped his gaze, shaking his head. "Not really."

"Don't argue with your best friend. I know what I'm talking about."

"Mmhm," he replied.

Jade stuck her tongue out at him. "I do."

"I wasn't disagreeing with you. I said 'Mmhm', didn't I?"

"It was your tone." She huffed.

"My tone was perfectly normal, thank you. No different from usual."

Jade shoved his foot. He nudged it back, trying not to laugh.

"Don't be bratty."

"I'm never bratty."

"Mmhm."

He pouted, crossing his arms over his chest. Jade laughed.

"What? I agreed with you."

"Nuh-uh. You're making fun of me."

"Why would I do that?"

"Because you're mean."

Jade burst out laughing again, leaning back on her palms. "Mean, huh? Good to know. I suppose mean is better than fantastic."

Kaiden let out a huff. "You're mean *and* fantastic."

"No one is mean and fantastic. Those counteract each other." She made a face at him. "Unless it's *fakely* mean or the meanness is due to a factor beyond their control, or...You know what I mean."

Everything I did, Kaiden mused, even as his mouth spread into a grin at her unintentional pun. "Yes, I do know what you 'mean'. And I guess that 'means' you're just fantastic, then."

"Shush and scoot over." Getting off the floor, Jade waved at him so she could get up next to him. Huffing an exaggerated sigh, he moved over.

Jade flopped on her back on the bed. "I think you need to be monitored better. What happened to sleeping?"

He eyed her. "Yes, Jade, you're doing such a terrible job of monitoring me. *Honestly*." He let a grin slip free. "I don't need sleep."

Jade laughed. "Yes, you do. Thus the needed monitoring."

"Nope." He dropped down on his back, too. "I can just stay awake forever."

"I don't think that's a good idea."

"Why not?" He pushed his lips up in a half-smile. "It sounds like a brilliant plan to me. As all of mine are."

"Because even you need sleep, Butterfly."

"Not that much."

"Yeah, you do." Jade turned her head to see him better. "Don't feel like sleeping?"

"No. Not really."

"In that case, maybe I should distract you." She grinned. "If you aren't going to sleep, we might as well do something fun."

"Like what?"

She shrugged. "Could recount fun memories." She flipped onto her side. "I remember the first time I brought you candy. That was funny."

A small smile spread over his face without his permission. "Yeah?" He hesitated, looking down. "It's all...kind of fuzzy still."

Jade laughed. "Yeah. You got all wide-eyed."

"Well...it wasn't exactly something I was used to. And it kept sticking to my teeth."

"I know. It was cute though." She grinned a bit.

Kaiden nodded, smiling a little bit back. "Yeah. A little." He smiled wider, teasing. "It took like a week to get all of it out."

Jade laughed. "Did you just admit you were cute?"

"No." He looked away. "Obviously."

"It sounded like you did," Jade sang, teasing.

"Well...I didn't."

Jade propped her head on one arm. "Your turn to name a memory, then."

Too many sprung to mind, tiny snippets he had to brush away smiles for. The first time he'd met her. Market trips made bearable with her commentary and faces made at passerby. Sitting by the creek, in small moments of calm before an ever-coming storm. Coming up with names for things, and jokes, and having someone to hold onto when he couldn't hold himself together.

Few of his memories ever ended as well as they began.

"You...um, tried to teach me to cartwheel, once."

Jade tossed her head back as she laughed. "Oh yeah, that was fabulous." She grinned. "Well, not fabulous. More like adorable."

He made a face. "Oh yes. Because me ending up on the floor due to my lack of coordination is adorable."

"No, but your determination is."

Kaiden rubbed the back of his neck, fighting an odd smile. "Your turn."

If she noticed his dodging, she didn't comment on it. "Hmm. When I gave you your nickname."

He cocked a one-sided smile, relaxing slightly as the memory unfolded in his mind. "It's the first time in a while that I actually remember why you chose such a silly one."

"It's not silly."

Slowly, he raised an eyebrow. "You're right. It's perfectly usual to call a guy 'Butterfly'."

Jade faked surprise. "It is?"

He shook his head. "Not in my world."

She laughed. "Yeah, I guess not in mine either. But we aren't exactly normal."

He supposed, given their age at the time, that it might not have been as ridiculous as it seemed. She'd tried to call him 'birdie', and then 'Butterfly' afterward, saying it fit because he wanted to fly away from everything, but couldn't. Like a butterfly in a jar.

It was still a silly nickname.

Jade shifted over to hug him again, closing her eyes when he returned the gesture. After a long moment, she peeled them open again, grinning. "Oops. I'm not the one who's supposed to be falling asleep."

"Obviously you're the one who needs it. Unlike me."

Jade huffed. "I'll nap if you do."

He sighed, making it long and exaggerated. Jade extended her pinky to him.

"Promise you'll at least try to?"

Hooking his pinky around hers, he nodded.

"If nothing else, rest a bit instead."

He supposed, for her sake, he could try. Though he doubted it would do any good.

Seeming satisfied, or too tired to say more, Jade rested her head on his shoulder, closing her eyes.

Despite his own continued hesitation, he eventually closed his eyes too. He only hoped, when the darkness overtook him, that it wouldn't greet him the same way it always did.

XV

Joss

Joss was bored. Chan and his friend had been busy packing things since he woke up – still looking half-tired – and Rascal was being troublesome, so she'd locked him outside until he'd behave. Though Chan had told her to let her bodyguard rest, she couldn't help sneaking back over to his door, pushing it open.

She paused, confused at the sound of his voice. Was he...talking to himself?

When she opened the door, she saw him sitting up and smiling, eyes fixed on the empty air near him as if someone was actually there. Joss' brow creased in concern.

"Are you...okay?"

Confused, and still grinning a bit, Kaiden looked at her. "Yes, I am. Why?"

Joss glanced at the empty space again. "Because you still...have an imaginary friend?" Looking down, she frowned, kicking at the ground with her foot. "I mean. I just thought... you might be okay, now."

Kaiden rubbed the back of his neck, glancing away as he bit his lip. "I've...talked with her before...?" He sounded hesitant and a little sad at the last part.

Before she could reply, though, he blinked over at the air like it had just told him he had sprouted two heads, his mouth falling open a bit. "But you're not... She's not..." Hesitantly, he glanced back over. "I don't understand..."

Trying to hide a frown, Joss hugged her arms to her chest. "It's not...normal to have an imaginary friend if you're...okay."

Rubbing his forehead, Kaiden looked at the wall. "I don't." Pausing, he rubbed the back of his neck, obviously not replying to her. "I guess so." He looked back at Joss. "She's not imaginary."

To hide her concern, Joss gave him a look. Shifting on her feet, she walked over to poke the air. "There's no one there. See?" Kaiden looked away when she did, to hide his face. She sighed. "And yet you still smile as if she just did something hilarious. This really isn't...normal."

Joss rubbed at her neck uncomfortably. Maybe that other man had done more damage to him than she thought.

As she thought it, Joss stiffened at the feeling of air on her ear, like it was blown right into it from a very short distance. Startled, she turned around, looking to Kaiden questioningly. He wasn't close enough to have done it, and the window was closed. Joss didn't like what that implied.

Though he seemed to try to keep it in, a laugh burst from Kaiden's mouth at her reaction. He promptly covered it with his hand, eyes crinkled with mirth.

Joss' bangs blew to the side by the same force as before. Her eyes widened at the thought it cemented in her mind.

Kaiden hid his face in his hands, laughing way too hard and seeming unable to stop. He nodded to the empty air and peeked at Joss with an almost apologetic but still amused grin, hiding his face again. "I told you."

To make sure she wasn't dreaming, Joss rubbed her eyes and cast a wary glance at the air near her. The 'wind' tickled her again. Someone, somehow, was standing next to her.

"Okay. You win." She hesitated, giving her head a quick shake. There was no going back from this. "What's her name?"

Kaiden peeked out between his fingers at the spot beside her, eyes fond and almost shy as he smiled. "Okay, Beautiful." He waited a long moment, a spark of mischief filling his eyes before he looked at Joss. "She hates being called that."

Joss wrinkled her nose at the nickname. "Uh, okay. You still didn't tell me her name...?"

Kaiden tried to look as innocent as he could while still grinning. "I don't know what you're talking about, Jade." He paused, then ducked his head away. "I'm not..."

Joss raised an eyebrow, looking between him and where he was looking. "She doesn't seem to be very happy with you."

"She agrees with you." Dejected, Kaiden flopped on his side like a dead fish, sighing. After a moment, he kicked his foot as if to push away something. "Joss. Make her stop."

Despite trying to hide it, Joss' face screwed up in a very odd way. "Wow. You're weird."

Kaiden waited a beat before replying. "She couldn't possibly be talking to you, Jade. You're far too lovely to be considered weird."

Joss wrinkled her nose. "*You're* weird," she said, pointing at her bodyguard, and then glanced around for where his eyes landed. "I don't know about...you yet."

"It does," Kaiden agreed nonsensically, rolling over to pout at the empty air. Without looking away, he waved at Joss. "You want me to just repeat everything you're saying?"

Joss crossed her arms over her chest in a huff. "You know I can't magically hear her now, right?"

"Exactly! So what do you expect of me?"

Joss shook her head, trying to chuckle. "I think I liked it better when you at least tried to respond to us both."

"Nonsense," Kaiden said without looking at her. "You're not overwhelming, either." He gave Joss a bit of an apologetic grin, looking almost embarrassed for a moment, then went back to his conversation. "You're nothing but wonderful."

With a slight sigh, Joss sat back to watch the odd scene play out.

"I'm always silly," Kaiden said, and pointed at her. "Joss agrees." After a moment, he peeked back at the empty spot. "About what?"

His answers were too vague to get much out of, so Joss leaned her head against the bed and waited for him to be done.

"Nah. Never." Rolling onto his back, Kaiden smiled upside down at his friend, somehow goofy and fond all at once.

"I know." He batted his eyelashes at her, then paused. "Well, you might not be. Or not obviously."

As if suddenly remembering her presence, Kaiden sat up, smiling at Joss. "I could draw her. Then you'd see."

She wondered if he was aware of how insane he seemed right now, even if there *was* someone there. Kaiden made a very sassy face at the empty air.

"Don't worry. I'll make sure to draw your hair like the monster that it is." He reached over to snag a pen and piece of paper from his bag, making a face while his back was turned and glancing at Joss with a teasing grin. Joss watched, amused as he stuck his tongue out and began sketching.

After a moment, he huffed a sigh. "I knew you'd say that." With an unnecessary flourish, he added a very unrealistic flower to the picture, looking smug. Joss stifled a laugh as she watched the drawing take shape, the figure indeed having a rather wild head of hair, from the outline of it.

"So?" Kaiden retorted, apparently uncaring of seeming crazy. "I've worn one of those before. And I'd be the only one who can see it."

"Yeah, why is that, anyway?" Joss looked up at him. "You're the only one who's able to see her...?"

Kaiden wrinkled his face up. "Ew. I don't think she'd want to see that." He shook his head, shooting Joss a tiny bit of a grin.

"I wouldn't want to see what?" She looked down at the emerging portrait, though nothing seemed unusual. "And you still didn't answer my question."

Instead of answering, Kaiden shoved at the air, making a face. "I don't think she'd want to see me period right now." A moment later, he swayed to the side like Jade had retaliated. "I'm not."

Expelling a sigh, Joss dropped her chin in her hands. Kaiden gave the air another sassy look, and then moved the paper high above him, gasping.

"Joss! Keep it out of her reach!"

Despite everything, Joss had to grin. "Why?"

Kaiden stood on the bed so he could hold it higher, brushing the ceiling. "It's my paper! I can do with it what I wish! There's nothing to 'give back'!"

Joss was about to reply when she felt breath tickling her ear again. Blinking at the spot, she rubbed her ear. "What's that for? I know you're not imaginary."

"I don't see how you expect that to work," Kaiden replied in a sing-song way, and then made a face. "She's trying to annoy you."

Joss eyed him over, glancing up at the paper. "I can't get up that high."

"Exactly the point! Jade's short, too, so no one can steal it!"

Joss raised an eyebrow, studying him. "Why are you trying to keep it from her, again?" She poked a finger into his side. "And why are you the only one who can see her? You have some weird invisible-person-seeing vision or something?"

Kaiden made a face at the air. "How...?"

Sighing, Joss waved a hand through the air beside her, surprised to feel...nothing. So...his 'imaginary' friend was a ghost?

Kaiden rubbed the back of his neck, shrugging. "I do..." Then he shook his head.

Joss held back a sigh. "Do you need me to leave you alone with your definitely-not-imaginary-but-who-knows-what-actually friend?"

Though he wasn't looking at her, Kaiden half-smiled and nodded, and then laughed. "No, it's not."

Whether or not it was directed toward her, Joss took that as her cue to leave. It was clear that her bodyguard still had things to sort out, crazy or not. Joss began to wonder just how many times people had messed with his head, or if he was just notorious for hitting it on things. There was definitely *something* she was missing, to make all this make sense. But for the moment, he didn't seem willing to talk about it. Maybe he never would. And she supposed that was alright. It wasn't like she was going to be around forever, anyway. Why did she care what happened to him?

KAIDEN

"You keep saying I'm the wonderful one," Jade was saying, sitting beside him. "I beg to differ."

He felt a little bad about making Joss leave, but...he wasn't exactly used to someone else being privy to their conversations. And Jade rarely stopped talking. Chuckling, Kaiden looked away. "I don't see why you'd say that."

"You never have. But I still will say it, because I mean it. Maybe you'll never be able to fully understand it, but you can at least know I believe it."

Kaiden half-smiled, hoping she could see the gratitude in his eyes. He'd just have to make it up to Joss later, if he could. "Gotta have at least someone who believes in me."

"Well, I'll always be that person. It's practically my job." She winked, nudging his shoulder. "As your imaginary-not-imaginary best friend, one of my most sacred duties is believing in you."

He nudged hers back, half-smiling. "Thanks." After a moment's hesitation, he added, "I don't think I could do it myself."

Looking up, Jade smiled. "There aren't many of us who could do it ourselves. It's a hard thing for anyone to do, let alone someone who's been through all you have. I'm happy to be your positivity for you." She squeezed his hand, tightly. "I see a lot of wonderful things in you, Butterfly. More than I have seen in most, and I've met more people than I care to admit."

Keeping his eyes down, he drew in a breath. "I don't understand why."

She reached over to nudge his chin up lightly, shrugging like to brush something aside. "It would take a long time to explain. But I know you think I've been some sort of saving grace or something else equally as sweet of you to say, and I want you to know it's not been one-sided. You've been a saving grace for me too, in a lot of ways." She smiled, though it seemed heavier for a moment before that vanished. "You've helped me as much or more than I ever helped you."

Quietly, he shook his head. "I don't think that's possible."

A tiny bit of sadness lingered in her eyes. "You don't think it's possible because you don't know..." She hesitated, tracing one of the scars on her arm. "Because you don't know what it's like when I'm not here." She gave him a little smile. "You've done a lot for me, Butterfly. More than I'd ever know how to say or repay."

Not knowing what else to say, he nodded. Jade shifted forward on her knees to hug him.

Hugging her back, Kaiden drew in a quiet breath. "I'm not cut out for any of this."

"I don't think any of us are, Butterfly."

He let out a quiet laugh escape, rubbing a hand into his forehead. "I don't know what I'm thinking. With Joss," he clarified, letting his hand fall. "Can't even... take care of myself..." *How am I supposed to take care of her?*

"I think she's good for you. She reminds you to be happy and responsible. I like her."

He half-smiled back, having little strength for anything else. "I'm not good for her."

"Nah. I don't think that's true. I think you'll be as much good for her as you have been for me – which is a lot."

Looking down, he shrugged. Jade watched him.

"You don't agree?"

He lifted a shoulder and let it fall, something that wasn't quite a smile tugging at his mouth. "I don't really know."

Jade reached up and ruffled his hair. "You'll do fine, kid."

He smiled a bit at her, quiet. "Thanks."

"Sure. If you ever need advice, you can always ask me. Though how on earth I'd be helpful, I don't know. I've never had any kids." She grinned.

With a quiet chuckle, he rubbed his hand against his forehead. "She's still not...my kid."

"Hmm. So you keep insisting."

"Because she's not."

"Well, she isn't anyone else's, and she seems more yours than anybody's, soooo..." She grinned again.

Kaiden's face wrinkled. "That doesn't...make her mine."

"Not yet. But I think if you gave her the option, she might like to be." Shrugging nonchalantly, Jade flopped onto her back.

Taking a slightly unsteady breath, Kaiden rubbed both hands over his face. "I don't know."

"I know." Jade shrugged. "But you'll figure it out."

He shifted over closer to her, subtly. "I hope so."

"You will. I'm sure of it." She winked, grinning. "I'll believe enough for us both."

Smiling a little more, he looked away. "Okay."

Jade grinned, a spark of mischief in her eyes. He raised an eyebrow at her.

"I'm just thinking about how I'm going to get to say 'I told you so' when everything works out perfectly."

Kaiden chuckled. "Hm. So you think, huh?"

"So I know. I'm looking forward to it." She grinned more. "You'll see."

He shook his head, trying to hide a smile. Jade sat up, snatched his notebook and pen suddenly, and set it against her legs, turning it away when he tried to look, so he couldn't see it.

Kaiden huffed, settling back to watch her. She drew for a while, refusing to let him peek. Eventually, though, she handed it to him.

It was a drawing of both of them being their usual oddball selves. Jade was flopped on the floor beside him, one arm looped behind her head as her free hand tried to pick a flower out of her hair – the same flower he'd drawn on her portrait. She was wrinkling her nose at him teasingly while he smiled, eyes sparkling and full of far too much depth for a sketch. Too many secrets. It almost made him uncomfortable to look at, even as his mouth spread into a slow smile. She'd even drawn a butterfly perched on the back of his hand, as if it had actually decided to stop and stay there for a while. Silly Jade.

"For you to keep," Jade said with a smile, and shrugged.

His own smile felt funny on his face, though not in a bad way. "Thanks."

Jade grinned. "I'm just glad you like it."

"Why wouldn't I?" He almost brushed his fingers against it, then decided against it.

Jade chuckled a little. "It's hard to explain. I just am glad you do." She grinned. "Just don't tell anyone it's from me if they ask."

"Yeah, they might flip out just a bit if I told them my 'imaginary' friend drew me a picture." He grinned. "Does that mean I have to pass it off as my own if someone sees it?"

Jade laughed. "Good point. But... Well, if they see it, it might pose another problem – namely that none of them have ever seen this random girl before. Especially since we look like friends in it and we're our current ages. It might raise more questions than "who drew that?", don't you think? I suppose I didn't think it through very well." She grinned apologetically.

A chuckle escaped his lips. "No, that's easy. I just tell them it's my imaginary friend and they think I'm crazy." Semi-teasing, he grinned back. "I have a very vivid imagination."

Jade laughed again. "If you want to explain that to them, sure. Though Joss might give me away now as not-imaginary and then where will I be?"

"I dunno. I rather doubt they're going to believe a young girl who's spent way too much time around a crazy man."

"True enough." She grinned. "So maybe I am safe."

A chuckle left his throat. "I don't know if I should be offended at how readily you agree with that."

"Well. You're the one who said it."

JOSS

"Hey! That's *my* food! Little thieving cake-stealers!"

One of the creatures in question looked up at her with wide, innocent eyes, even as the icing on its nose ruined the facade. The other hissed at her and took a piece as best as it could in its claws. Luckily for them, Calestan cakes were not exactly fluffy enough to crumble very well. 'Cake' was a bit of a misnomer, as far as Joss was concerned. But it was easier to make than the other kinds of pastries she liked, and kept better. Practicality over taste, as usual.

On the counter beside her, Rascal screeched his agreement, standing guard over the bag in case of more intrusion. The blue dragon had the audacity to look hurt as it backed up and chirped. From their lineup above her, the other kits watched unsympathetically, as if it was *her* fault for not giving them some other kind of food.

"Go eat a cricket," Joss scowled, waving them away. "Or whatever else you monsters like. Just leave *my* food alone."

Though Rascal bared his teeth at them for good measure, Joss could have sworn she saw the last dragon look smug as it took off to avoid being smacked with her shoe. It landed a short distance away, continuing to stare her down challengingly.

Rascal screeched. Joss spun just in time to see the very smug green dragon dragging a strip of dried meat away. She grabbed the other end, trying to tug it away, and the dragon's eyes sparkled, its tail flicking behind it as it curled its lips in the approximation of a grin, all without letting go.

Joss didn't appreciate being messed with by tiny, scaly thieves.

Behind her, someone choked on a laugh. Joss turned her head to see Kaiden standing in the doorway, fighting down a smile at the sight before him.

"Oh, good. Bodyguard, get these tiny pests away from me! They're trying to steal my food!"

Ril chirped indignantly from Kaiden's shoulder. He laughed, stroking her chin. "Ril says it's not very nice of you to call them that."

"But they're *stealing* my *food*. What else do I call them?"

Propping a hand on the table, Kaiden eyed her. "Your food, huh? Funny, I thought I was the one who bought it."

Joss narrowed her eyes at the tiny green dragon, who imitated her with a playful growl. Displeased, she growled back.

Kaiden tried to hold down another laugh. She was relieved at least to see a lightness in his eyes, as opposed to the shadows or turmoil that often lurked there. Ril glided down from his shoulder to perch next to the naughtier dragon, chirring her disapproval. The other kit's ears flattened, but it reluctantly let go, sitting back on its haunches with a huff.

Eyeing the teeth marks in the meat, Joss made a face. "*Gross.*"

"What do you have so against the kits, anyway?"

Joss shot a sharp glance at the creatures in question, to disguise her surprise at the question. "It's not just kits," she muttered, stuffing a large piece of bread in her mouth.

Kaiden smiled, reaching over to break a piece off for himself. He slowly raised an eyebrow as he did, as if daring her to challenge him. With a huff, Joss looked away.

"You should probably get your things together," Kaiden said. "I think we're going to leave once Chan is," he paused, looking at the food in his hand, "bread-y."

"Yes, Dad," Joss muttered through a mouthful of crumbs, stifling a groan. "Just give me a moment to locate all the valuables and stuff them in a bag."

The look on Kaiden's face made her burst out laughing. Without another word, she turned away, swiping the rest of the bread from his hand and smirking before leaving the room. As she walked out, she heard him sigh to himself.

"I guess that pun *was* pretty crumby, huh?"

Despite everything, Joss could barely hold back a smile, stuffing another bite in her mouth to disguise it. There was something markedly...different about her bodyguard now, since he'd woken back up. It almost unnerved her. He was just too, too...

Too nice.

That's what it was. Before, she might have fooled herself into believing he was just playing her. And if not, he was a little too beat up to do much against her. It made staying with him seem safe.

She'd only been half joking about the valuables thing. Maybe now it was time to get out. Chan was more than capable of taking care of him on his own.

She should have left already, actually. Chan was still asleep, as far as she knew, along with the other girl, and Kaiden...well, he was probably talking with his imaginary friend again. Maybe this time he really had cracked. Either way, he had help now, right? He *really* didn't need her.

A pang went through her, satisfied only by the wyvern clinging to her back, peeking hungrily at her food. Grudgingly, she broke off a piece, eating part of it before she offered the rest to her new pet. Its low whine soon became a satisfied screech, more like a bird than anything, and quiet enough not to blow out her eardrums.

Why *hadn't* she left? Why couldn't she get herself to do it?

Because...she didn't *want* to leave. A small, stubborn part of her whispered that she *liked* it here, and she should stay. She wanted to stay.

How selfish of her. She knew Kaiden wouldn't turn her away, either. And what then? She'd follow him across the world, wherever he went?

All her excuses were falling away, and yet she still stayed. But there was little reason not to, at this point...right?

XVI

KAIDEN

Kaiden felt as if even his steps were softer, walking out of the kitchen. Chan was busy trying to fit books into a too-small bag, muttering to himself.

He looked up, surprised. "Oh. You're up."

Kaiden managed a smile, a joke teasing at the tip of his tongue, though he held it back. "Thought I should maybe get up before night rolled around."

Chan looked relieved, suddenly, as if seeing Kaiden so relaxed helped him out. "That's a good idea."

Kaiden nodded, glancing around. "Which way did Joss go?"

Chan eyed the door in distrust. "I don't know. She took that...thing out with her."

Kaiden had to suppress a smile at Chan's look. Neither of them had particularly pleasant experience with wyverns.

Remember the one time the dragons started a fight with the wyverns and we had to pull them apart?

It had been a chaotic day. Wyverns usually kept to themselves, but one of the kit dragons had gotten mischievous and tried to track them down. Wyvern screeches echoed far too well in the tunnels.

Though most kit dragons were calm, some were feisty, and a fight had started between the two tiny creatures. It quickly dissolved into chaos.

A million tiny memories skittered across his mind after it, wanting to flit off his tongue.

His eyes must have been flickering with emotion, because Chan looked up from his packing, spectacles perched on his nose. "You okay?"

No, Kaiden wanted to say, because the memories were drowning him again as he watched his friend. Chan, in all forms and times, with a book, laughing at him, staring at him with that disapproving frown. With glasses, without. Worried, concentrated, eyes lit up as he explained something complicated. Subdued, and mourning. He caught a glimpse of himself yelling at Chan and inwardly winced, attempting to brush it aside with a breath.

"Fine."

Though Chan didn't seem convinced, he simply drew in a slow breath, looking over his supplies with a nod. "Right."

With Chan's gaze away, Kaiden squeezed his eyes shut, his hands curling into fists. A million things wanted to scream out of him, and he couldn't let any of them out. So many words crammed close to his tongue that none could escape.

A tiny blue dragon alighted on his shoulder. He relaxed almost automatically with the movement. Prying his eyes open, he forced a smile at it, though it just blinked beady eyes at him and nudged its head against his. He drew in a breath that felt stuck in his chest, unable to move.

"Kaiden." Chan had stood now, and was looking at him in concern, and possibly something else. "You don't...look okay."

Something close to alarm was edging into his voice. Kaiden blinked back over at him, spreading a smile like butter on his face. "Why wouldn't I be?"

And some part of him thought the words should be choked out, brimming with tears and a too-bright smile. He was shaking, he realized, and he couldn't even figure out why.

Chan helped him to a chair, properly alarmed now. "Kaiden?" He whispered the name like he thought Kaiden might be breaking, or dying.

Maybe he was.

The memories had a hold of him again, and he couldn't slip out of their grip. It made it hard to breathe, and not for any particular reason. He couldn't move, trapped in the past. Dragons, fire, playful laughs and sharp words. Shouts of all sorts, dissolving into a screaming match. Flickers of pain, and the sound of skin hitting skin, over and over and...

"Let it go," a voice whispered in his mind. Hushed and gentle, soothing, like the whispering breeze wavering along his skin.

Let it go.

With a shuddering breath, he felt the present return. Chan knelt in front of him looking very worried, and Katya, somehow now beside him, had her eyes closed. Had he just missed her before?

"Let it go," whispered through his mind again, and he realized with a start that it came from her. A small, desperate whisper, as if his mental state would affect her own.

This time when he looked back at Chan, he was pacing like a caged cat, wearing a path in the carpet. Every so often he muttered to himself; then, on seeing Kaiden stand, he shot a sharp look at him.

"I'm bringing you back with me." This time, there was no broaching argument, as if he had already or still might try to reject him. "Someone there should be able to help."

Kaiden was about to ask what he meant when a sharp pain spasmed through his arm. He stared at it, numbly, reminding himself to breathe.

"Let me help you."

Did he really have a choice? Already he could feel himself slipping, further away and deeper into the abyss of his past. He couldn't hear a word going on around him.

"–should get him...to..."

"I'm fine," he managed to say again, and hoped Chan didn't hear the shake to it. Reluctantly, he sank back onto the chair, forcing his memories back into place. "Lost in thought."

"You keep saying that, but I don't believe you." Chan sucked in a sharp breath, distress in his eyes. "What happened?"

Agony might have been a more accurate word, the way Chan's forehead twisted as if he had been the one violently thrown in the past and torn apart for it. He looked like he wanted to speak, like it was killing him not to let free the words lodged in his throat, yet he kept them there, all the same.

Kaiden wondered if he was trying to feel some of the same pain, that way.

Welcome to my life, his thoughts murmured.

"How...how often does that happen?" His words were breathless now, dumbfounded and stilled by certain possibilities.

Kaiden wondered what sort of expression he'd have if he answered, *"Every day."* If that might finally get Chan to stop asking, from pure shock.

"Not that often," were the words he murmured instead, with a halfhearted shrug thrown in. Chan rested back in his chair, inhaling carefully. It took him a long moment to phrase the words Kaiden already knew were coming.

"Are you sure?"

This time he needed a smile, small as it was, and a lighter look to his eyes to be convincing.

"Yes."

Chan's shoulders remained tense, but he slowly nodded, perhaps only partially convinced. But that wasn't Kaiden's problem.

"You can tell me, you know," was the numbed murmur after a moment, Chan's gaze fixed somewhere far away. "I would understand."

Would you? Kaiden would have laughed if it wouldn't be taken wrong. Chan had no idea. None of them did.

Chan continued to look troubled until Kaiden released a slow breath. "I don't exactly know when it's going to hit."

Chan nodded, sitting back slowly as he looked over their supplies, conflicted. "Maybe we should wait a day..."

No. Kaiden stood to his feet, surprised when he didn't topple over. "I'm perfectly alright. See?" He hid behind the false cheer his voice conjured up, reaching for one of Chan's tools. "I've got this handled."

He waved the wooden grip of the tool in the air, a grin spreading across his face. Chan exchanged a look with Katya, drawing in a breath. If he got the joke, there was no acknowledgement.

"Talon really messed with you. It's understandable if-"

"I'm *fine*, okay?" Kaiden snapped. Instantly, he winced, burying the memories that sprang to mind. Chan looked away, nodding quietly.

"It's...good to have you back."

Words choked him, memories crashing in a flood over him. Arguments and harsh words, smirks, mocking laughs disguising what he could never say.

I didn't mean it like that.

He rubbed an arm into his eyes, nearly choking at the influx of memories that followed the action. Sucking in a harsh breath, he pressed his lips together to keep them from trembling. He didn't think he could get words out if he tried.

Someone touched his shoulder. He looked up just in time to see Chan's concerned face before his composure broke, everything spilling out in one endless stream.

"I miss them."

Chan wrapped an arm around his shoulders, and then pulled him close, his brow lined with creases even as he held him.

"Shh." He closed his eyes, tightening his hold for a moment as Kaiden realized he was crying. It flowed out unimpeded, pain and loss mingling in his chest and blurring his vision. He couldn't hold it back, as much as he wanted to, tears soaking his cheeks as he gave in and buried his face in Chan's shoulder.

I missed you, he wanted to choke out, at the same time he wanted to say 'I'm sorry' and couldn't find all the words he needed. He could see them all too clearly. Gigi. Samar. Taisha. Rafe. Lil.

He'd never properly mourned them, with how everything had gone, and now it felt like it might tear him apart, combined with everything else. With seeing them, and *remembering*, and allowing it to affect him.

Chan rubbed a palm over his back, and then hesitated. But the memories were spilling out too strongly for that to bother him at the moment, and Kaiden pressed closer as if to assure him.

It could have all gone so differently. Why hadn't it gone differently? Why had all of *this* had to happen?

It wasn't fair, his mind whispered. It just wasn't.

"They've missed you, too," Chan replied, far too quiet.

Somehow these moments were more painful, watching Gigi laugh as she dumped ice water on him, or Rafe's rare grin that only came out when he thought no one was watching, Lil preoccupied with pretending to scold them all.

They deserved better. They *all* had deserved so much better.

Chan squeezed him tightly, drawing in a breath, and rubbed his hands up Kaiden's arms. "You're okay." He rested his head against Kaiden's, holding him close. "It's over now. Promise."

Kaiden remained tense, eyes aching as he held onto Chan for support. "Sorry," he stuttered, swallowing enough to add, "I didn't...mean to ruin your shirt..."

Chan smiled at him, understanding and gentle, and Kaiden had to scrub an arm into his eyes to stem more tears. "It's okay," he said, squeezing Kaiden's arm lightly. "Really."

He wiped at the rest of the tears, a broken laugh wanting to escape his throat. "I'm fine. I am." Smiling a bit, he leaned back against the wall. "Don't worry about me."

"I always worry," Chan breathed out, assumedly meaning it only for his own ears.

Drawing in a deep breath, Kaiden scrubbed at his eyes once more, folding his arms over his chest. He waited until Chan pulled back, eyes going to the things still strewn out, before letting out the words still burning in his head.

"Can I ask you something?"

When Chan looked over, Kaiden frowned at the carpet. "Why did you stick with me, through all those years? When I wasn't someone worth being around?"

It took Chan a while to respond, a look playing in his eyes as he nodded at the distance. "I've known lots of people like you. People who hide. They always have a reason. I guess I just trusted that yours was good enough to be worth this."

He was quiet a while before responding with the only thing he could think of. "Thank you."

Chan nodded, still smiling too gently for any of this. "You're welcome."

Kaiden copied the gesture, rubbing an arm over his eyes. "So," he finally asked, voice too quiet still. "Ready to leave?"

Chan hesitated, watching him far too seriously for a moment. "Do you need some time first?"

"No." Kaiden looked away, responding too quickly. He could feel Chan's gaze on him, disbelieving.

"You sure?" he prompted.

Gentle. *Too* gentle, like he was actually worth something. Kaiden would have rather been hit than hear that tone of voice. Like he was a fragile thing to be handled with care, a bird with a broken wing to be looked after. He sucked in a breath, disguising it with a smile. "Yeah. You know what, you look busy. I think I'll leave you to...whatever you're doing." He nodded to a broom in the corner. "Wouldn't want to sweep you away from all the fun you're having."

Chan expelled a quiet sigh. Kaiden hid a wince, even though his friend's gaze was still too soft. He looked like he might say something, but shook his head.

Kaiden tightened his hands at his sides, willing himself just to turn and leave.

"Remember Gigi?" was what came out of his mouth instead, a smile warring with the moisture he felt burning in his eyes. The truth that made his bones ache.

Chan looked up, raising his eyebrows in surprise. Kaiden wanted to slam his mouth shut, but the words kept spilling out, like water searching for a crack to slip through.

"I miss her," he whispered. This wasn't the truth he intended to tell, and yet it ached all the same, wanting to come out. Scrubbing at his eyes, he sucked in a breath to disguise the shudder of his chest. "*I missed you*" is what he wanted to transition to, and couldn't manage it.

It was so real, so terrifying to open his mouth and let the truth come out, rusted and creaking from disuse. Dirtied and broken, fragmented pieces of his past.

Chan looked down, nodding. "She was...something special."

"She was nuts," Kaiden choked out in response, through a lump in his throat he was trying to turn into a laugh. "I loved it."

"I know," Chan said just as quietly, with the tiniest tilt up to his mouth. Kaiden scrubbed at his face and swallowed in a deep breath, though his voice still trembled. How did he just...give his secrets away like they were nothing? Like this wasn't anything unusual?

"I...missed you, too."

He hung his head as if the admittance pained him. He couldn't bear to look up at Chan, to see what was lurking in his eyes. He didn't think he'd be able to handle it.

Gently, ever so gently, Chan rested a hand on his shoulder and squeezed. Kaiden gave in, wrapping his arms tightly around Chan and taking in a long breath.

"I'm sorry," he murmured, and though the words were heavy, he knew Chan would understand them. He let his eyes slip shut for a moment, squeezing his friend close, and then pulled away, hands still in fists.

Chan smiled at him in a way that almost made him uncomfortable. He seemed more relaxed, though, as he nodded.

Kaiden rubbed a hand over his nose, scanning the piles. "Anyway." He ignored how scratchy his voice still was. "I should...go get my kid."

He slid his hands into his pockets, tossing Chan a playful, almost wry smile as he rocked back a step, toward the doorframe. He hesitated, turning back. "Let me know when you're ready to go."

Chan nodded, rewarding him with a smile back. It made a weight slip off Kaiden's shoulders, as he drew in a breath. One wrong righted. He slipped his hand into Jade's and squeezed it tightly, giving her a half-smile before calling out loudly, "Joss!"

CHAN

Chan spent far too long trying to fit his last book into his bag. His mind was distracted, playing back the events from what felt like so long ago already. Kaiden, admitting his mistakes and making up for them.

He'd always known it was there, beneath everything. He grew up around too much pain to not recognize it that strongly in others. It was why he never got mad at Blaze, unless he took it too far. He knew how much Kaiden had cared for the others. He knew what the grief had done to him.

But still...having it confirmed was a burden he didn't even realize he had needed lifted. Giving up for the moment, he excused himself to take a walk. It wouldn't do to be so distracted while flying, anyway.

He stepped out the back door and paused. Kaiden was playfully scolding the little thief girl, tiny kit dragons gathered around and on him as he gestured her back toward the house. She looked away from it, hesitant, but eventually followed, a smile slipping on her face once he wasn't looking.

Chan watched them until they disappeared out of sight. His shoulders felt lighter than they had in a while as he settled down on a stone bench. He'd come here often to think, in the months they'd stayed in Calest. Reme was a wonderful host and her own work kept her busy enough that Chan hardly felt like they were intruding. Besides, his work was done here, now, so they could get out of her hair. If the people hadn't listened to his last explanation, they never would.

He gave them a bit of time to themselves, anyway. It was the reason he'd kept himself occupied, with Katya. Kaiden had been through a lot, and from his experience with Katya, he knew that despite anything the younger man might say, this might take a while.

Someone slipped outside beside him and sat down. He smiled at Katya, fighting down a spark of satisfaction as her hand rested against his, and she smiled back. She had come so far since he first met her, and the fact that Talon's manipulation hadn't ruined their connection made him happier than he ever thought he could put into words.

"*Are you okay?*" he whispered to her, still taking care with her thoughts. It had become his automatic question, whenever she sought him out. Just to make sure she was alright, even if she appeared to be.

Katya nodded, curling her hand tightly around his. He did his best to ignore the way it made his chest flutter, just a little. Months prior, she never would have trusted him this wholly. A smile bloomed across his face of its own accord as he breathed out contently.

"*I'm glad.*"

Ever-so-carefully, as she watched the distant clouds, Katya leaned closer to him, dark, braided hair tickling his arm. It had been good for both of them, coming here. With Reme's job keeping her busy, and no one else save for Rena and Lyss around, Katya had more opportunity to relax than elsewhere, and it made him feel warm any time he saw her like this, no fear in her eyes. Content.

Without thinking, he wrapped an arm around her back, squeezing her lightly. She tensed, just slightly, and he felt like biting his tongue. But then she relaxed again, resting her head against him.

He hardly dared breathe, uncertain even as he looked over at her. Like she was a stray animal that had extended its trust to him, he willed his entire frame to still so not to frighten her away. Closing his eyes for a moment, he murmured something inaudible under his breath. One of the few things his sister had taught him, years ago.

Katya looked at him, questioning, as if asking permission from *him*. He had taught her what little sign he had picked up from his childhood, and told her she was free to express herself mentally whenever she wished, but she still often preferred to use wordless conversation, as if what had the least motion or sound was the safest.

He smiled in a way he hoped was assuring, projecting the emotion through their bond too for her peace of mind. She breathed out quietly, watching a nearby bird as she left her head on him. He felt the silence of her *Thank you* reflected back at him.

It made him relax fully again. He had tried his best to communicate in the way that made her most comfortable, even taking to walking in a softer way and avoiding any fast, sudden movements around her. He still remembered how surprised he'd been when she came out one day to watch him spar, and almost picked up a sword herself, despite the fear in her eyes.

Chan brushed his thumb against her hand, lighter than a feather. He'd been worried, at first, to leave her on her own for such long periods. But Katya was good for Rena in a way he never could have imagined, and more than once he had come back from a meeting to find her curled up on the old couch in the living room, Rena pressed close against her.

He'd tried to discover the foods she enjoyed, in an attempt to get her to relax, and encouraged her to try new ones when he could. Between the menial labor he did for various townsfolk, and his help with the rebels, they rarely went hungry, and when they did, it was usually because he worked so late that he simply forgot to eat.

Sometimes he wondered what Katya did when he was gone. She explained to him, eventually, through simple signs and mental words, that she had liked paint, despite how little she had been allowed to use it, and he'd managed to trade what he could one day to get some for her. Not eating for the day was worth it, seeing her face. He'd been so used to hunger before the Mountain that it hardly crossed his mind when he skipped a meal for a day.

Now, he felt even more relaxed about leaving. It had only been a far-out hope, on coming here, that he might run into Kaiden again, but to imagine having left and *just* missing him would have been far worse.

Katya looked up at him, her dark eyes still filled with so many secrets. He squeezed her hand, gently, and smiled at her, as if it might help her say what she was thinking.

"*He needs time,*" she eventually signed to him, hesitating and changing her mind on one of the motions. He'd offered her paper once before, but that only made her hands shake. Any sort of communication, he learned, was still hard for her. He suddenly wished he'd punched Talon when he'd had the chance.

Katya settled back against him with a soft breath, content to sit there for a while. Silence was one of her closest friends, and he had learned to share that with her and cherish it, for the way it calmed the waves he still too-often saw in her eyes. Whatever he could do to balance out the turmoil she'd dealt with for so long.

Maybe, somehow, they could do the same for Kaiden. If he let them.

KAIDEN

Joss stood by a river near the house, fingering a round stone and frowning. Without saying anything, Kaiden sat down next to her, reaching for one himself.

"Someone tried to teach me to skip stones once." He tossed one in the water, and it sank. A wry grin covered his face. "I never really got it."

"I prefer throwing them." She demonstrated, and shrugged. "Feels better." Stooping to pick up another rock, she added, "Was it Jade?" She looked at him with an indiscernible expression. "You two seem very close."

A smile spread across his face at her explanation. "This is why you're my favorite. You're a girl after my own heart." He threw another doomed stone, then stopped, chuckling. "You could say that."

Joss looked around, squinting a little. "She here with you?"

He shook his head. She seemed surprised.

"I thought she went everywhere with you."

"Not everywhere."

Joss folded her arms over her chest, still frowning. "How come you didn't just tell me about her?"

"I...thought..." He hesitated. "I...don't know," he said reluctantly.

"I've seen too many crazy things to be surprised, Bodyguard." She turned her dismay toward the water, watching it. "You seem to like her a lot, at least. She makes you happy."

He thought about what Jade said, though the words stuck in his throat. *You make me happy too.*

Joss heaved a sigh, and another rock. He rubbed his forehead, fighting the urge to bite his lip. "I didn't...have an easy life."

"None of us did, Bodyguard."

"No..." He sighed, the sound pained. "I know, but..." He rubbed his forehead. "She's been with me for a long time. And she's been...my secret and mine alone for all that time. It's not exactly something I tell people about."

Despite everything, Joss arched an eyebrow. "Oh, really? I thought you enjoyed seeming insane."

He choked back a laugh, as much as the past made it sting a little. Joss' brow furrowed, just a little, as if something had occurred to her. "No one?"

He mimicked her, confused. "No one...?"

Joss shifted to pick up another stone. "I mean...you haven't told *anyone*? Not even..." she waved her hand, sighing a little. "I don't know. Your best friend or something?"

"Jade is my best friend."

"Best...*visible* friend." Joss let out a laugh, though there was something different about it. "Wouldn't they be concerned otherwise? Like I was?"

"I've...only told you."

Her expression cleared, blank for a moment. "Oh."

"Jade likes you," he added, grinning. "I was joking about her trying to annoy you."

"I know. You're way too much trouble for her to be worse than you." Her eyes sparkled, just for a moment.

Laughing, Kaiden ruffled her hair. "I think *you're* the troublesome one."

"Mmhm. Sure. You keep on believing that." She wrinkled her nose, smoothing her hair back down.

"I will," Kaiden said smugly, though he could feel the fondness shining through his eyes. Joss turned back to the water, her eyes still distant.

"Joss." He waited until she looked back, hesitating just for a moment. "I like you too. You know that, right? I like having you around."

For a moment, surprise flicked through her eyes, though she quickly hid it. "Well. I guess you're not half bad, either. Only because of the food," she added, though there was still something funny to her grin.

Joss looked away again. Kaiden sighed. "I think Chan wants to leave soon, by the way."

She nodded, but made no other move. Something twisted in his chest as he waited.

Finally, Joss released a slow breath, not looking at him. "Well?"

Even though she couldn't see it, he gave her a little smile. "He gets impatient very easily, you know," he teased.

270

"Guess you shouldn't leave him waiting, then."

Reaching over, he caught hold of her hand, his breath suddenly feeling heavier in his lungs. "You...aren't coming, then."

She shook her head, shifting on her feet. "Better if I don't. I'd just be in the way, stealing your food and scaring off your friends." A little grin touched her face. "See? You've got someone else to look after you now. So my work here's done."

You wouldn't... He couldn't get the words out, feeling something sink in his chest. Joss continued on, matter-of-factly, listing off the reasons she shouldn't come with them.

"...and I don't even like fancy people, anyway. Why would I want to spend that much time around them? Yuck. Besides, I still have this necklace to sell, and..."

He let his eyes drift closed, swallowing against the lump still building in his throat.

JOSS

She was stalling. She should have just *left* already. Hesitation was a trap she'd been caught in before, and should have been smart enough to avoid. Letting other people give her blanks in their sentences so she could fill them with what she wished, falsely assuming and hoping...and letting them go along with her pretense, only to rip it away later with words like, *"I never said I wanted you,"* and *"I was only loaning that to you."* I did it out of pity. I'm fed up with you. I never said this would be *permanent.*

And yet she'd still linger, on doorsteps between two different worlds, hoping she was still hearing things wrong. That somehow their meaning had just gotten muddled, or they'd take it back, or...

"Don't leave."

Swallowing hard, she forced her reluctant eyes to glance back at Kaiden, at his quiet whisper.

"Why?" she asked just as quietly, and watched as his gaze slipped away, rimmed with silver. He shook his head, eyes closing, and Joss stepped away from the creek. "Why, Bodyguard?"

He choked back a breath, and Joss hesitantly moved closer to him. She wanted to hear him say it. She *needed* to know.

"I need you," he whispered, and Joss felt her heart sink. She shook her head.

"No, you don't. You've got someone else to protect you, now. Chan, and all your other friends."

He shook his head, harder, and looked up at her through too-bright eyes. "Don't you want to stay?"

Joss' heart fluttered, though she willed it to stop messing with her. She shifted on her feet, biting her lip. "D'y want me to stay?"

Her accent came out, softer, and she hated it. She sank down to sit by him. Kaiden drew in a quiet breath, looking up at the distance, and nodded. It seemed like he was trying hard not to wince.

Joss turned her gaze away. "You don't sound sure." She hated how her voice started to get hard. "I told you I've been left before."

"I wouldn't," he breathed, and she heard the ache and hurt there, as he squeezed his eyes tighter shut, his composure slipping. "I've messed up before, plenty of times. I don't want to do that again."

Joss glanced at her feet, frowning to feign contemplation. "Why?"

You remind me of someone. Joss waited for it, for the ball to drop. She didn't want to be a replacement. A fill-in, a...substitute. Something temporary he'd always be looking to replace. She didn't want to be a surrogate daughter.

"I like you," he admitted, shaking his head and looking up with a laugh on his lips and a too-bright spark to his eyes, as if the whole thing was silly. "I...don't want you to leave, Joss."

She sat there, indecisive, biting her lip so hard it started to feel numb. "And?" There was still something he wasn't saying.

He lowered his eyes, his hand shifting through the grass. "I know you don't...have to, if you don't want to. But..." He hesitated. "You're welcome to stay with us, if you want."

Did she? How long could she go on pretending, and making excuses for them both, before he admitted the truth?

"Say it," she murmured, almost more to herself. "Just say it."

"I..." He looked almost pained for a moment, drawing his eyes up to meet hers. "I'd really rather you stay, Joss. I like you. I like having you around." His gaze drifted away, quiet. "I can't...really imagine not having you around anymore."

And though she swore she never would, she let the past be the past for a moment, forgetting everyone who had ever failed to catch her when she fell, and took that leap of faith once more. "You promise?"

Closing his eyes, he nodded. "I...can't promise much, but..."

"Well." She rubbed her chin, watching him. "What *can* you promise?"

He looked up with half a smile. "Bad jokes and food?"

"Same as always. Hmm. I'm in." She forced a little grin, hesitantly moving closer to him. "You're...*sure* you're okay with this?"

He smiled at her in a way that made her ache, more than a hug ever could. He didn't even need to say it, but she wanted him to.

Pulling away, she let out a breath. "I've been left before, Bodyguard," she reiterated, barely daring to glance back up.

He nodded, his voice too...soft for any of this. "I won't leave you, Joss."

His hand ended up around hers, squeezing gently but firmly. She saw the ache still wanting to spill from his eyes, hesitantly crawling into his lap. It wouldn't be perfect, not that that's what she was looking for. But it would be real. And that, more than anything, was what mattered most.

"You'll have to put up with the kit dragons," she murmured, resting her head on his chest." "I'm not going to take care of them. And Rascal. He screeches a lot."

His arms wrapped around her carefully, his still-scratchy chin resting on her head. "I think I can manage," he said quietly.

Joss let her eyes close, releasing a soft breath. Despite the memories of Reign, both old and recent, telling her how bad of an idea this still was, she ignored them, relaxing against Kaiden.

"You're like a big, dumb pillow," she mumbled. "But a very cuddly one."

He laughed, hard enough that she could feel it in her chest. Unbidden, a smile spread over her face, as she glanced up at him. "Is your friend going to scold us for taking so long?"

He squeezed her lightly, smiling back. "Oh, definitely."

XVII

OLIVE

"Olivia!"

Olive turned sharply to see Basil running at her, a big grin on his face. Hearing that name, in her opinion, was never a good sign. It took her back in a flash to one particular night, long ago, even if Basil was the only one saying it. She turned to face him, a solemn reprimand written on her face.

But Basil was smiling too broadly to be bothered, or even to notice. "You should come see what Fern's made."

She let a smile of her own slip out, smaller than his, even as her mind continued racing through that night, determined to play it through to the end.

"Tell her I'll be there once I'm done."

"Okay." Still grinning, Basil pet his little dragon, a shine in his eyes. "Don't train forever."

She made herself smile back, even as she heard his voice echo differently in her head, younger and far more panicked.

"Olivia?"

A thrill had run through her, even as her mother's careful warnings filtered in as a voice of reason.

"Keep him safe. Stay down. Don't come looking for us."

They wouldn't know about the dragons until it was too late. She was supposed to take Basil and get to safety, but she couldn't leave them. Not like this.

No one else would be concerned, but Olive was. She'd shaken her twin, hard, to try to get him out of his trance. "We have to *move*."

But Basil had always preferred to hide from pretend pirates than pick up a sword and fight them himself. Olive's older cousins had carved wooden swords for all of them, but Basil always used his as something else. He was much more content to play their prisoner, or damsel in distress, no matter how much they teased him about it.

Olive was the adventurous one. Basil took after their father. Ironically, he worried about everything that wasn't in his control, and nothing that was. Dragon attacks were far from his list of concerns.

It came as no surprise, then, that the supposed raiders attack had him hiding under the stairwell.

"Do you want them to find you?" she hissed. But Basil was frozen with what she could only imagine was fear, and so she softly sighed and pushed him further under the steps in their house, praying to any god that she could think of that he would be safe. "Stay here, then." she said, using her best not-big sister voice. He might have been older, but he didn't act like it.

She forced on a smile, as big as she could manage. "I'll be back soon, alright? I'm going to go find Mamma 'n Papa." Blinking the sudden moisture from her eyes, she gave his arm a tight squeeze and took off running.

Don't come back for us, her mother had warned. *Whatever you do, keep running and keep your brother safe. We'll be fine.*

Against raiders, maybe. Maybe they'd only be captured, and would find a way to escape. But Olive had seen the aftermath of a dragon attack, once. Basil had barely spoken for three days after their friend's village had been destroyed. They'd fled, as always, leaving the smoldering town to fend for itself.

Olive had felt horrid about it. But their father had kept them moving, and he was right to. They all would have died if they'd stayed. Keeping those you loved safe came first, he always said. No matter what. It wasn't worth dying trying to save one or two other people, and leaving your own family grieving.

This definitely wasn't a raider attack. There wouldn't be so much smoke curling in the sky.

And Olive knew what she'd find, when she got out there. But she still had to try. She owed it to them, and Basil.

"Dad!" Cupping her hands to her mouth, and blinking back tears, Olive trekked through the village. "Dad?"

She'd known it was helpless, even as a shudder ran through her entire body at the twisted rubble and acrid fumes, a foggy sheen of smoke making her eyes and lungs burn.

"Dad."

If he was there, he would have responded. Her only other hope was that he'd gotten out alive, and would meet them at the safe zone.

She dashed the moisture from her eyes as she stumbled back to the house, tugging her coat tighter around her. "Basil?"

He was still under the stairs. Relief washed over her even harder than the grief she was fighting back. "Come on," she told him fiercely, swiping an arm across her nose and tugging him to his feet. He curled his hand around hers for a moment, but she shook it off.

"Stay by me," she hissed, in a voice low enough to conceal tears. Taking in a breath, she held his wrist and pulled him along, her expression daring him to say even a single word.

Basil looked back in the direction of the village, of their home as she dragged him. Even without words, they'd always been able to communicate. And the questions written across his face were far too painful to bear.

"We're going to see a pirate ship," she whisper-sang to the rhythm of their feet, dismissing the unsteadiness of her words for the time being. She hoped Basil would join in, but he continued watching the distance behind them, further widening the ache in her throat.

"*Are they dead?*" she felt his eyes asking, searching the shrinking buildings curling with smoke. "*Are they dead? Are they gone? Will we see them again?*"

She lifted her voice louder, even though it might alert raiders or robbers to their presence. But Olive was pretty sure that they would be far away from the dragon attack. Raiders usually knew such things.

Basil whispered along with her song, in a tone so uncertain it almost made her break. Drawing in a deep breath, Olive paused to pretend to cough, to conceal what else ached to come out, and bravely continued on.

When the song ended, they were left with that awful, asking silence again. Eventually, she couldn't bear it, turning to smile at him as bravely as she could.

"Papa will meet us at the safe point, okay? We just have a little while to go."

Her voice wavered too much on the end, but maybe he'd swallow part of it.

They reached the clearing where it was designated the safest to meet, and waited. Olive sat down on a log and tried hard not to fidget, while Basil fingered the remains of a roll he'd been holding and crumbled it between his fingers.

She couldn't stand Basil's dejected face, though she knew no one was coming. Pretending to find a clue, she jumped up with a gasp, letting what she hoped looked like surprise light her features.

"Look! Papa says he found a better spot for us, and he got everyone out! Gram and Annir and Momma, too!"

If there were two things Basil trusted most in the world, it was the word of his sister, and the belief that there was always, always hope. It hurt like daggers to use those both against him, but they couldn't stay there for much longer, or else the raiders *would* find them, eventually. And if she confirmed his fears...well, he might not have acted older, but he *was* definitely bigger. Olive couldn't carry him if he just...gave up. And so, if only to keep her eyes from spilling their burden, she smiled and lied for them both.

Olive pretended they were playing another game, picking a simple yet distracting route for them through the forest, balancing on a log, helping him through a patch of thornwood, climbing up a tree or two. He got scraped and discouraged, but she always helped him back up, and it kept his mind off of everything.

Basil was too gentle a soul to believe ill of his sister. Even as he looked skeptically at a vine she wanted him to use to climb, he'd try it anyway, and fail. His fear was a bigger distraction than anything else, and hope the biggest push spurring him on.

Eventually, they grew tired, and there was no camp in sight. No secret hideaway, no half-formed shelter with footprints leading away. The forest was eerily quiet.

With a soft sigh, Olive set Basil onto a log, presumably to look at his skinned knees. Instead, she tilted his chin up to look at her, making sure his focus shifted once again.

"Bay..." she said softly, afraid of the words. "They're not coming."

Before he could feel betrayed, or confused, Olive continued on, even as the words lodged in her chest and made it hurt."They're...they're gone. They would have met us if they weren't."

Basil was staring at her openly now, slowly shaking his head with every word. It tightened her chest until she could barely breathe. "I had to get you out safely."

"Did you try?" came his whispered words, slicing her deeper. The betrayal and hurt was all there, just as she knew it would be. "Did you look for them?"

The accusation hurt, even more than the truth. "There was no one there, Bay. Everything was in ruins."

"But did you *try*?" He swiped a hand across his own eyes, his voice too gravelly for a boy his age. "Did you search everywhere?"

All the words shriveled and died in her throat, even as they played out in her head. *I couldn't.* There was too much fire, and too little possibility for survival.

Basil got up, hurt shining from his eyes like a candle flame. "They could still be there. We could have helped them."

"*Basil.*" His lack of understanding stripped her raw, deeper and deeper despite how untrue she knew his words to be. "Dad would have wanted me to get you out."

Basil fell silent, scrubbing at his eyes, and Olive sat aching against the log, fighting back her own tears. *You know I didn't have a choice.*

But Basil's hope could be a sharp thing, when he turned it against her. When he pointed his 'truth' in her face and believed it over her own, as wrong as she knew it to be.

"You could have tried..." His voice hitched, in hurt and pain and waning betrayal, slowly being overwhelmed by grief. "You... could have..."

He sunk down to the ground, shuddering, and wrapped his arms tight around himself. Olive moved to touch his shoulder, and he shook it off like hot embers on his skin.

Curling her hand close to her chest, as if she was the one burned, Olive sat back against the log and let him mourn. He would have learned, sooner or later. She shouldn't have kept it from him.

But she'd needed somewhere safe for them to stop. And, if she admitted it, she needed *him*. She'd needed his hope, still, even if it wouldn't help them. She needed to be the only one breaking, to keep them both together. Otherwise, she might have just fallen there and...not gotten up.

She *knew* the results of dragon attacks. There wouldn't be anything left. Anyone, if they had been in the village when it happened. And that thought was enough to shatter the calm she'd always carried so effortlessly. It terrified her.

Rocking on her knees, Olive settled her arms over her churning stomach, taking in an unsteady breath. She couldn't live with herself if she'd destroyed the spark of hope in his eyes.

"Bay..." Her voice nearly cracked, and she wasn't sure she could hold it together much longer. "I'm sorry."

But he wouldn't speak to her, pushing away her attempts to comfort him with a shudder and getting to his feet all on his own. Olive dashed an arm across her eyes, breathing in noisily.

"Uncle...Uncle will know what to do." Her teeth chattered from something that wasn't cold, as she dared a glance over at him. Basil still wouldn't look at her. "Okay? We have to...k-keep moving."

At least they had family, in the next town over. They should be warned of potential danger, anyway, even though dragons rarely attacked two towns in a row. No one understood why. Maybe they were just sadistic and specifically targeted one, for whatever reason.

The grief was souring to something harder and hotter in her chest, and she kept her arms tight across it, as if to keep it in. More than anything, she just wanted to hold Basil's hand, and let it out.

Maybe it was good that he was mad at her. It would keep him going, even if she couldn't.

When they reached the town, hungry and numb from more than just cold, Basil did his best to seem intimidating, and find out where exactly their uncle lived. He stood taller, refusing to let her take point until he absolutely had to. She quietly gathered supplies and information, avoiding the ache they both felt, and thanked the innkeeper that gave them food, in exchange for a little work.

Basil remained silent whenever possible, an entirely normal occurrence which now seemed to loom over them like some sort of threat. She didn't want to lose her brother, too.

"Stop, thief!"

Olive had thought nothing of the cry until she turned, and saw who it was. Basil, his eyes wide with fear as he ran from several much larger, very terrifying-looking men. What had he done? This was why she didn't leave him alone. She shouldn't have let him get mad. She shouldn't have assumed he could take care of himself.

Without a weapon other than her Gift, she felt useless, stuck there watching until she could find a way to help him. Basil tripped, skimming his knees against the paving stones as the objects in question tumbled from his hands. He began to retrieve them with shaky, glowing hands.

Olive's heart dropped in her chest. *Not now, not now.* Basil's hands glowed when he was very nervous, or passionate about something. This couldn't have been a worse time.

"I didn't steal," he stammered to Olive, as she helped him up. "I s-swear..."

"I believe you," she whispered, with her eyes shut tight and arms around him, hopefully concealing and dulling the glow.

Too late. One of the guards tore her arms away, making a disgusted noise at Basil's hands. He was about to call out to his friends when Olive kicked him where it would hurt most, hard, and it turned into a howl of pain instead.

"Run," she whispered to Basil, turning to face the guards. Basil shook his head.

Olive's worst fears flashed before her eyes until her world was shaking. Basil, locked up or executed. Her, unable to help him. Smoke. Flames. Dragons.

"Olive?" His question was quiet, but distressed, and she realized she was barely standing. As they locked cuffs around him and she couldn't even move, paralyzed.

A cooler voice cut through the silence, chilling her bones. An official, from the clean grey suit and shiny red buttons. What did they think he had done, to warrant this?

Olive looked up as a hand fell on her shoulder. A well-dressed man with a calm demeanor and combed blond hair looked down at her.

"Is that your brother?" he murmured. He seemed to be studying her.

Dazed by the moment, Olive nodded, even as she knew how she was sealing their fates. She could already feel the man's hand closing around her shoulder until it hurt, dragging her away with her brother.

The pressure fell away. The man gestured to the guards.

"Release the boy."

Olive was dreaming. She could hardly hear the clink of coins as the man handed them over, the greedy guard pocketing them without protest. Crooking a finger, the man gestured to Basil, who the guard shoved over with a hand between his shoulder blades. Though Basil stumbled, the man caught him, gently, carefully undoing his restraints.

Olive's face still felt bloodless, even as the man kept them both close and Basil slipped his hand into hers with a squeeze and a mournfully apologetic smile.

"I suppose you have a Gift as well, hm?" The man studied her again, his gaze going back to Basil's no longer glowing hands.

Then he was leading them away, and Olive knew she should be afraid, but she wasn't. She had her brother back. She couldn't feel anything but relief.

"Yes, sir," Basil said, peeking up at the man. How quickly he trusted people. "Are you a Gifted?"

In response, the man smiled, waiting until they were out of earshot to respond. "I, unfortunately, am not. But I have been looking for people like you for a very long time." He squeezed Basil's shoulder gently. "How would you like to come work with me? I paid all of your charges with the guards. I would assume neither of you have parents." He raised an eyebrow at them both.

Olive shook her head this time, and the man laughed. He saw how she was answering both questions at the same time, then.

Basil, sweet soul that he was, trusted the man immediately. "Of course we would. You saved my life, sir," he whispered.

The man smiled and waved it off, giving Basil's shoulder a fond squeeze. "Boys like you are a far greater treasure than coins. It's wasteful what they decide to do with you."

Making her voice firm, Olive stepped in. "If you please, *sir*, we need to get back to our family. They will be waiting for us."

There was a glint in the man's eyes that Olive decidedly did not like, even as he smiled amiably. "Ah, yes. You see, children, when I paid off your debt just now, it was under one stipulation. You cannot return to this town, ever."

A stone fell in Olive's gut. He knew. She didn't know how, but he *did*. She hadn't been lying about having family there, and he'd just cut them off from them.

"Our family was killed by dragons," Basil countered, something close to a frown dipping his mouth. "We have no home."

She wanted to kick her brother for his unerring honesty and unwavering trust. At least she hadn't destroyed that in him fully, though perhaps she should have.

But Basil was frowning at her, now, as subtly as possible, and she felt it thud in her chest. No. She *was* the reason he so willingly trusted this man. In defiance of what she'd done.

"He saved my life, Ol," he said quietly. It was hard to tell the meaning behind it.

Olive sighed out silently, looking up at the man. With a single gesture, and a responding smile from him, she pulled him away from her brother. "A word?"

The man's eyes practically shone in delight, answering her words with a murmur. "I knew you had spirit."

Olive twisted the man's wrist, just enough to be painful. He simply smiled, extricating his arm from her grasp and fixing his sleeve. "I will listen to you, child, on one condition. What is your name?"

Olive's eyes narrowed. Names were powerful, in the wrong hands. "Olivia."

If she didn't bare her weakness up front, he would exploit it later. This, she was certain of.

The man waited, patiently. Smiling. Olive pulled him closer with a handshake, lowering her voice like she only did when she was very, very serious.

"You harm one hair on his head and you will have me to answer to."

The man laughed, but the threat was made, and the thorns she let creep out into his palm should have been proof enough. Without a hint of the pain he certainly felt, the man extracted his hand, rubbing it on a handkerchief and smiling.

"Well, Olivia. My name is Damien. It's a pleasure to meet you."

Returning to the present and shaking off the memory with a quiet sigh, Olive cleaned her sword and put it away, stopping to give one of the kit dragons a bit of attention. Hers had never been very...cooperative, which was probably her fault. Olive never found it easy to speak her mind, and that was all kits wanted to do. She'd shut her dragon out long ago, out of preservation. It was too much chatter, all at once.

And without that bond...well, she didn't *forget* him, of course, but Rox seemed much happier with Elle, anyway. Even since her friend's death, Olive and her dragon were more of acquaintances than anything, although sometimes she still felt the longing, a gentle question pressing on her that she still couldn't answer.

Maybe one day. But kits were for delivering messages anyway, right? Or, that had been their intended purpose. And there had always been plenty of those hanging around the Mountain, if you knew where to look. So she hadn't exactly suffered from not having that bond. And though a part of her couldn't deny wanting it to work, it just...wouldn't. It had been hard enough for her to find *one* dragon willing to share a companionable silence. Two, especially in the form of a kit dragon, was pretty much impossible.

But she was content with the bond she and Indigo shared, and so was he, so that was all that mattered. Not every relationship had to involve a lot of talking to be successful.

And for those that did, well, she would leave those to someone more capable, like Basil. She was content to watch, and be his silent support, and he knew what that meant.

Now she really knew she was stalling too long. Shaking her head, Olive suppressed a smile at her dragon's muttered comment, and condolences for being dragged away from her solitude. *"It's not that bad,"* she murmured back, to a sarcastic reply about personal space. Indigo, more than anyone, was probably the most disgruntled about the sudden influx of dragons. He often suggested that when this was all over, they needed to find somewhere far from any more than three people, and just stay there. Although, Olive thought there might be a few more than that. But not too many.

For now, though, she needed to go make sure her friends hadn't blown anything up, or caused any dragon-related chaos. One thing was for certain: the moments between her quiet ones were never dull, and probably never would be.

KAIDEN

Kaiden shifted on his feet, eyeing the dragons. He was far too nervous for this, and his fingers kept straying to his hair as he forced himself to look at Chan. "Can you...not tell them the moment we get back?"

Something quick flashed through Chan's eyes, a tightening that shifted from hurt to remembrance to a quiet understanding in a split second. "Sure."

Kaiden could have exhaled in relief. But he kept it silent, giving Chan what he hoped wasn't too much of a smile as his hand rested on Resenya's side. "Thanks."

Chan stayed silent, nodding after a moment as he looked out at the clearing. Shaking his head, he helped Katya up onto a purple dragon – Lyss, Kaiden recalled – carefully mounting after her. Katya looked too close to calm at seeing him again, only the slightest edge of tension in her eyes despite his own mental reminders of what he'd done to her.

Chan, of course, still noticed, the smallest frown pursing his lips before he shook his head, nudging Lyss forward. Swallowing his own nerves, Kaiden climbed up onto Resenya, brushing away the gentle nudge of her mind until she quit looking at him, a layer of sullenness taking over her expression. This wasn't a trip for fun. It was always the most nerve-wracking for him, first mounting his dragon. That moment of sheer panic rippling over him as his feet left solid ground, leaving him grasping for things that weren't there. To the best of his ability, he willed these away, steeling his bones until he could sit still enough that Joss wouldn't notice a thing.

"It's okay if you're afraid," she said matter-of-factly. In a whisper, as if sharing a secret, she leaned forward to add, "It's my first time, too."

But the grin on Joss' face spoke more of excitement like any reasonable person would have rather than downright terror. It did nothing for his already slick hands, nerves frayed into many separate threads as he pulled a breath in and willed the darkness away. Forcing a grin he didn't feel, he looked back at Joss. "I'm never afraid."

Whether or not she was convinced, he didn't care. Resenya stayed just behind Chan's dragon, growling low in her throat any time Joss tried to speak. The girl swung her legs and stared at her threadbare dress, humming soft in her throat as she eventually rested her head back against Kaiden.

He fought the urge to dig his fingernails deep into Resenya's spines. It was more terrifying now, remembering *everything*. Where before he had been trapped in a morbid desire to know *why* it bothered him so deeply, a curiosity so deep he couldn't shake it, now he knew, and though some of the terror disappeared with that, it also tightened closer to dread as Resenya took off from the ground. He could practically feel the hand latched around his throat, his heart drumming against his chest in a low, dreadful pound as he fought the sensations that were so *wrong*. Joss spoke, and he nodded in response, until she seemed to give up on him.

He could do this, but he didn't *want* to. His mind was achingly open, and Resenya nudged him with gentle, distant murmurs of encouragement and warmth, like a stronger version of the kit dragons. A soothing fire, the gentle rise and fall of someone's chest while deep in sleep. The sun on an empty, flower-dotted field, the blooms waving in the breeze. He clung to these as tightly as he clung to the spines on her neck, forcing himself not to dig his fingernails in. At least Chan was far enough away not to try communicating with him.

"Bodyguard?"

He nearly jumped, and Joss looked chastised, as his heart began to race further. She looked down. "Sorry. I didn't mean..."

It's okay, he thought, and winced when it wouldn't leave his lips. "It's okay," he hedged, grimacing inwardly at the intrusion, and the connection to his mind that his was now *screaming* at. She had access to his head. She had access to his *thoughts*.

Joss fell silent, though, and he didn't have the strength to try to communicate with her further. His mind was raw and cleaner than it had ever been, the memories stark white against his eyes, flashing across his vision. He didn't even know how to defend himself anymore. It nearly made panic rise up in him again. What if...?

He couldn't handle this. He couldn't have everyone and everything just...slipping into his *head*, and seeing things. Messing with them. He couldn't handle it. He *couldn't*.

But he couldn't block it off, either. His mind was terrifyingly open, and he could only go through Meriador to close it. He didn't like to acknowledge that she knew everything about him now, and more disconcertingly, that he had the feeling this wasn't a new thing.

He didn't *want* her getting in. He supposed that might help with learning to put up blocks, but the thought of her seeing any of that...it made him want to break down inside.

From in front of them, Chan's voice broke through his thoughts. "I already told them we're coming."

We're. Kaiden's heart stuck on its beat, until he remember that 'we're' could pertain to Chan and Katya, too. They didn't necessarily know about him. And Chan wouldn't look at him long enough to consider which way it was.

Would they be happy? Disappointed? He didn't want to face any of that at the moment. Every breath, every word sent a million memories spilling over the brink, blinked away before they could drown him. Chan. Sparring. Cakes. Flowers. Yelling matches and shopping trips.

The way Gigi rolled her eyes at everything she didn't like. A teasing grin. A bright smile.

Jade sat backwards on Resenya, facing him, and entertained him with stories to try to keep his mind occupied. It was more terrifying, barely being able to control the memories that slipped deeper into his mind with each second. The moment he'd lock one away, another tumbled free, the endless stream enough to make him want to choke. It had to end, at some point. It had to.

Joss swung her legs and whistled and tried to make conversation with him, occasionally laying her hand on his and giving him a little grin. He forced his best approximation of a smile back, though he couldn't push words past his lips.

Eventually, though, she grew bored, and turned her attention to Chan. Kaiden didn't know if it was her intent, but Joss kept Chan talking the whole time about what kinds of food Galdania had, and if the beds were really made with bird feathers, and whether that was actually comfy or if it made you sneeze all night long. If he was allergic to birds, and what kinds of things he studied, and why he was in Calest. She managed to wear Chan out, and the poor man was too kind not to answer her questions. Kaiden felt immeasurably grateful to her.

Kaiden breathed in deeply and tried to focus on anything but the sweating, terrified ride his mind took him through. The memories were so sharp they *hurt* now, digging deeper and deeper into him with each moment. The sky blacked in and out, memories coming and going and his body numb to all the blows he felt. There was a deep coil of dread in his chest, though his breath was not as ragged even as he felt fingers digging into it, and his heart pounding hard in response. He cast his gaze away and did his best not to focus on it, curling his fingers just closely enough around Resenya's spines not to harm her. He'd done that enough to her, in the past. She had always been so kind to him, and he'd...blocked her out.

Meriador's control kept the memories from tearing him apart, but he still had to bear them. Resenya sent gentle, vague images to his mind, and it wasn't until later he realized he had still blocked her out. But he couldn't let her in, not now, with his head in agony.

By the time they landed, his bones felt made of jelly. Still, Kaiden nearly tumbled off Resenya in his haste to get down, pressing a hand against her for support and reassurance. She lowered herself as close to the ground as she could, sweeping her tail around to be a step of sorts, for which he was very grateful. It took a couple moments of breathing deeply, his head resting against her scales, before he felt steady enough to straighten up. He took a long moment to rub her scales, both to compose himself and to say thank you, and felt a low, gentle rumble from her in response, almost warming him.

He'd wanted to let her in. He really had. And he knew she was aware of this, too. It was just...too much still. His mind felt like it was on fire, overstimulated with memory that was just starting to fade.

He almost jumped when he felt a response in his mind, in a way he couldn't quite put into words. It wasn't words, and yet it went deeper than the kit dragons. He just knew what she meant, as if it was always a part of him. Rubbing her scales again, he tried to summon a half-smile.

Chan helped Katya dismount, keeping her close to him, and then, with a small smile at Kaiden, he gestured them forward. With one final murmur to his dragon, Kaiden pulled away, just as Joss began to whine. "Bodyguarddddd!"

She was over by Chan, huffing at him even once he joined them. A kit dragon landed on his shoulder, and he scratched under its chin until it squeaked in pleasure and rubbed its whole head against him, almost like a cat. He tickled its belly until it squealed, almost falling off of him. A small laugh escaped from his lips.

Chan looked back in surprise, but Kaiden pretended not to notice. He needed this, for the moment. As tired as Chan looked, answering Joss' questions with slower and shorter responses, he needed this time, to pull himself back together. The next time they looked back, he smiled, even as it ached, and gave a little wave. Joss waved happily back.

He didn't know what to say to Chan. He knew how odd it must be, for Chan, and figured he just needed time. To adjust to the oddity.

Joss slipped her hand into Kaiden's, squeezing it with a little grin, but remained mostly silent as they walked, her mouth agape at the lush colors and fresh, sweet air. He couldn't imagine her face when she saw what kind of food Galdanians usually ate.

Eventually, they came upon a small outcropping of tents, circled around a curl of smoke of what used to be a fire, like a war camp. But they didn't stop there. Kaiden wished they would have. They continued on until they reached a wall of stone stretching far above them, lined with parapets and watchtowers and all matters of defense. It was a fortress, and a very elaborate one. Woven, braided blankets with various emblems and dragons hung over the side, sprigs of bright red flowers decorating the corners where all manner of curious statues were carved — dragons, in one corner, and other beasts Kaiden had never seen in others. One of them seemed to be made of fire.

The gate itself, even, was far more decorative than just practical, overlapping and crisscrossing curls of dark metal glinting in the dim light. It gave him a slight feeling of unease he couldn't shake, no matter what he did.

The guards, at least, were not dressed as Kaiden expected them to be. Other than a pop of color on their armor, courtesy of a blood-red flower that appeared made of fire, they looked far more practical than elaborate and fanciful, and their posture was far less stiff when their eyes settled on Chan. They nodded like men paying respect to a general, one of them casting a wary eye at Kaiden before nodding stiffly to Chan. He murmured something Kaiden didn't bother to hear, but it seemed to make the guards relax.

While Chan conversed with the guard, Kaiden glanced down at his friends. Joss was looking around with a bored and pent-up energy, knee bouncing and fingers tapping against his. Jade was grinning by his side, and gave him a wink.

They were ushered forward, and Kaiden released a quiet breath. Joss practically bounded alongside him, whisper-peppering him with questions he had no answers for, and then breaking free from his hold to ask Chan when his answers didn't prove satisfactory.

"I'll show you where you can stay," Chan murmured to Kaiden, a tired smile on his face. "You should rest."

Joss bounced on her toes beside him, in awe of what she was seeing. "Well, *I'm* not tired. Can I see everything?"

Chan smiled, and promised her a tour once he'd shown them where they could sleep. Joss wrinkled her nose, but reluctantly followed.

In the dark, no one should have been about. But a figure whispered across the grass in what looked like an odd mix between a dress and a long robe, the tail of it dragging behind them. Chan's face creased as the figure came closer, pace increasing until they were nearly running, and flung drooping arms around Kaiden.

"I missed you," was whispered against his chest, in a voice he could now recognize as Fern's. Her hold tightened, trembling, desperate. "Don't leave again."

Kaiden couldn't find words to say, as Chan peeled her arms away ever-so-gently, a sad expression softening his face. He lifted her into his arms like one would a child, cradling the back of her head and making quiet *Shh* noises. Kaiden wondered if he ever wanted to be a father.

"She sleepwalks," was the quiet murmur of explanation, as Chan held the girl tighter and closed his eyes. Her whimpers became quiet cries, her fingers tangling tighter in his shirt for a grip as Chan smoothed his thumb over the side of her face, as if to keep her from hearing what plagued her.

"You can go," Chan mouthed over his shoulder, nodding toward the darkly-shadowed buildings. "Lyss can show you."

Katya, despite her earlier trepidation, stayed close by Chan's side, her eyes almost pained as she watched the girl. Jade motioned for Kaiden as well, easing some of his hesitation at following a dragon.

Lyss offered him a wing, to which he shook his head. The last thing he needed to do was break down in the middle of an unfamiliar city on an unfamiliar dragon.

The female didn't seem slighted, however, continuing on her graceful way toward the buildings. Katya stayed close by the dragon's side, one hand on her purple neck, but glanced over at Kaiden through the curtain of her hair when they reached the buildings. She gestured to one of them with a little smile, and he didn't know how to thank her. Her eyes said it wasn't necessary, even as Jade nudged him, and he let it be.

Katya waited until he had opened the door, some deep instinct in him prompting a quick and tense sweep of the room before he allowed himself to relax. It was just a guesthouse, most of the niceties stripped away to leave a home one might expect more in wartime than peace, yet far more secure than anywhere Kaiden had stayed before — other than a prison. The memories prickled over his skin, right at the surface if he wished to access them. For the moment, he let them rest, dropping down onto the surprisingly soft bed and lying back with a quiet sigh. Ril settled playfully on his chest, letting out a delighted trill as she noticed a mirror situated above a simple washbasin and flew over to it.

It felt like home, in a way Kaiden couldn't put into words. Not that it reminded him of home, for that was no longer pleasant to think about. Not that being here made him feel at home. But it felt...right, in a way he wasn't sure he could ever quantify, and was glad no one was around to ask of him.

From her spot on the floor, Joss huffed, arms crossed over her chest. "I wanted to see the city."

"You'll have plenty of time to steal stuff later," Kaiden said dryly, taking in the room. It was so...empty.

He dreaded the thought of facing the others the next day. He just felt so...tired. But his mind was still active and flickering like glowing embers faced with a small breeze. It was the kind of tired that sank into your bones, rather than behind your eyes. The kind that made it where you never wanted to move again.

Jade flopped down beside him goofily. The exhaustion from the day seemed to settle over him like the ache after a workout, easing the tension out of his muscles and quieting the breaths he took. Even still, he knew he wouldn't be able to sleep.

"Whatcha thinkin' about?"

What indeed? What *wasn't* he thinking about, or trying to hold at bay? He suddenly became aware of all the memories, buzzing louder and more insistently in his mind until they threatened to drown him.

"Relax," a voice whispered somewhere in the back of his mind, though he couldn't bring himself to obey it. His breath came quicker in his chest, the room seeming to spiral to some distant place away from his awareness until he was elsewhere, laying on a flat rock with no idea how he got there, and no way to move. Waves curled against the stone, lapping at his feet as they drew ever closer to enveloping him.

XVIII

KAIDEN

"...Is...Is he awake yet?"

A dry voice answered, one his mind told him he should recognize. "Does it look like he is?"

A playful tussle, and a light squeal. Kaiden opened his eyes to catch sight of bright green, whipping across his vision, followed by a soft giggle.

"The kit dragons really like you."

He blinked and caught sight of the tiny bodies curled around him, breathing in sync with his, their plated scales shifting with nearly imperceptible sound.

"I made you tea," the voice said again, hopeful. *Fern?*

Kaiden sat up, and felt like a dragon had stomped on his head. He pressed the heel of his hand into it, drawing in a tight breath. Where was he?

"The sleeping beauty awakes," the other voice murmured, a smile coming into view in the corner of his vision.

Fern squealed, soft arms wrapping around him as she launched herself onto the bed, practically landing right in his empty lap. "I missedyouImissedyouImissedyou!"

He couldn't help the faint, rueful smile that lifted the side of his mouth as he forced his arms to wrap around her too, his mind still buzzing with memories. "I missed you too."

Fern's reply sounded like a sob. "I thought you weren't ever coming back."

And then it hit, full-force. A million images, all with bright green braids and colorful ribbons and dabs of frosting where they shouldn't be. Messy hugs, delighted squeals, hopeful screams. He held her tighter, closing his eyes against what he knew was coming.

The sadness in her eyes. The ache as he pulled away. The one scene he'd seen far too often, even before now: her eyes asking him with all the pain in the world, *Why?*

Why? He'd pushed her away, and for what reason? Because he was scared. Because he was selfish. Because he was...human.

Hugging her made him want to choke. The swell of memories was so thick, so overwhelming that he thought he might drown with a thousand moments crashing over him, good and bad mingled until he couldn't make sense of it.

This is you, it seemed to say, with the bluntness of a blow to the head. Nothing wrong, nothing right. Nothing skewed. Just facts, presented to him as they were.

And still, he couldn't believe it. There was just enough joy to choke out the sorrow, just enough sadness to keep a laugh from bursting from his chest. He just hugged her, swallowed, and prayed he wouldn't fall apart.

He couldn't just fixate on the happy memories. He couldn't pretend any of that never happened. "I'm sorry, Fern."

She let out a mix between a laugh and a sob. "Whatever for?"

He pulled her back, then, just enough to catch a glimpse of her face, even as she scrubbed a hasty hand over her eyes and attempted a tipsy smile. "For not being there for you."

She sank her teeth into her lower lip, bright eyes brighter with tears as it trembled. "Really?" she whispered.

Kaiden closed his eyes, drawing in a shaky breath. "Yes."

Fern played quietly with her hands. "So, what happened to you?"

His chest tightened up at the question. "When?"

She looked almost disappointed in him. "Before you left."

Kaiden drew in a quiet breath. How did he explain... *could* he even explain? He felt Jade's hand squeeze his, gently, and relaxed.

"Were you tortured?" Fern looked at him with earnest, asking eyes, even as the question knocked the breath out of him. No. None of it was torture. He'd been through worse.

But he nodded, for her benefit, and saw understanding filter into her eyes. "Oh. Well, I don't know why they didn't just tell me that before."

A gentle weight touched his shoulder. He looked over just in time to see Olive tug Fern away, ever-so-gently, an indiscernible smile on her face. "Let him rest, Fern," she said quietly. Not a reprimand. A suggestion.

Fern pulled away with a hiccupped breath, scrubbing her hand across her eyes again. "Okay."

Then she slipped off the bed, drying her eyes, breathing in through her nose and gaining her composure as Olive shifted over, that almost-smile still on her face and an eyebrow raised as if to say, *Well?*

What did he have to say? Not enough. Never enough. And especially for her...

"See you later?" Fern asked hopefully.

He nodded, playing along for her sake until Olive ushered her out, gently. She sat across from him, arms folded. Mad.

No, not mad. Furious.

"You thought you could just leave, huh?" The slight quirk to her eyebrow was more emotion than Olive usually output into a conversation. "You thought we wouldn't care." She shook her head, something unreadable filtering her expression. "You're impossible."

Impossible. It felt a fitting word, for the moment. Impossible to deal with. Impossible to love. Impossible to understand.

"Of course we cared," Olive was saying, matter-of-fact, as if speaking to a child that wouldn't understand anything further. She shrugged a shoulder, a frown emerging for a moment before she pulled it back in. "The others might be mad. Fern missed you. Lena's furious." She met his eye. "Nothing's changed, Blaze."

For some reason, the name jolted something deep in him. The fact that she used it so matter-of-factly, as if it were, in fact, interchangeable with his own, and not some terrible persona he adopted.

"You don't remember before, do you?" She cocked her head, an almost smile on her face. Her words softened. "You don't remember that name."

He did, but he could see by her expression that she meant it in a different way. Shifting one knee over the other, Olive took in a soft breath.

"When I first met you, you were nothing like that. You were...hesitant. Worried. I saw it behind your eyes, even more so when Damien claimed you as the leader." Hers trailed down, for a moment, something very quiet about them as she shook her head. "Grief just... changes you. Like it changed me." Her gaze flicked up to his for a moment before dropping away again, as she shifted almost uneasily in her seat. "I didn't...know them all as well as you did. I mean, everyone knew Gigi. It would be hard not to. But...they were *your* team, your friends, and I can't..." She averted her gaze, drawing in a breath, and changed her words. "It was a wonder you went on without them, at all. I can't imagine what I would do if I lost Basil."

He let his eyes drift shut again, trying to stem the flow of memories her words pulled loose. Though he could remember what he did, the motivation behind it was sometimes still too hidden. It was too much to shift around, all at one time. Pretending that he could interpret the actions of his past self.

"It only proves your strength," she continued on hesitantly, as if she might have said too much. Her gaze kept dancing away from his.

"I...knew I would follow you wherever, then." Something tugged at the edge of her mouth, despite her hesitation to lock eyes with him. She seemed almost shy, for the briefest moment, one hand brushing over her knee before she drew in a steadying breath, some of her usual composure returning. "For putting everything else aside, to try to keep us safe. I never held any of that against you." She lifted her head, finally meeting his eyes. "Chan said...you might remember that now, but I thought you should know, either way." With a characteristic half-smile, she stood up, offering him a hand.

Forced to meet her eyes, the weight of her words slowly sinking on him, he swallowed, letting her help him up. She dragged him into a short, firm hug, an almost smile on her face, and then nodded to the door. "You should let Basil know, too."

Kaiden returned the gesture, even as his hands curled in on themselves at his sides to keep from shaking. "I just...need a moment."

Her half-smile returned, far too understanding for his liking. "Sure," she replied, and turned to open the door. After a moment's hesitation, she looked back at him. "Welcome back, Blaze."

He couldn't understand why those words hit so hard, forcing his face to remain calm until she left the room. Once she did, he let out a shaky breath, curling his hand around a bedpost for support. The past kept knocking and then letting itself in without waiting for his permission, swamping him. It was dizzying, reconciling what he'd been with what he pretended to be. Piecing together memories and comparing them to the others' words, knowing just what he had meant and what he hadn't. What he regretted.

He could almost see Meriador again, as she occasionally appeared. Her voice blended with everything else until he couldn't pinpoint where it came from.

"You withdrew because you had to. He didn't give you a choice. He forced you to move on, without a chance to grieve. So you did anyway, in the only way you could."

Kaiden shuddered. It was still a strange feeling, being...himself again and yet not fully remembering the intricacies of it all. His life was a ball of string that had been knotted too many times by naughty kittens—or in his case, likely dragons. He wouldn't have wished it upon anyone if he ever could.

He moved over to the basin, savoring the biting cold of it on his skin for a moment. A handful of cold water in his face and a few deep breaths in, and he felt mostly steady again. His body was still convinced it needed to keep shaking, but he disguised that easily enough with hands in his pockets.

It still hurt, feeling them hug him at all. But it was a distant sort of hurt, and the kind he forced down as strongly as he could, putting on a smile as he let his shoulders relax. Brushing dragons out of his hair, and checking his shoes to make sure they weren't housing a sleeping one, he prepared himself to face his friends. Joss, unsurprisingly, was nowhere in sight, most likely having snuck off to steal something.

He pushed the door open to follow his friends, a grin slipping bright and unbidden on his face. "Well?"

From her spot by the door, Olive sighed as if he had done something exasperating and followed him, though that hint of a smile stayed by the corner of her mouth. At least one of them was alright. Fern's eyes lit up in joy when she saw him.

"Basil!" she called out in singsong, hands cupped around her mouth.

From his seat nearby, the boy in question looked up, eyes widening as he saw them. He stood to his feet. "Kaiden...?"

He hardly breathed the name – far too gentle for what Kaiden expected. Edged with doubt and uncertainty, as if Kaiden might turn him away. It made him want to wince, memories flickering again of a younger boy, just as eager, hopeful, looking at him in the same way. Just moments before the memories would crumple, as he already knew, and his face would turn sad. Kaiden didn't like to see those.

Nodding, he drew in a slight breath as he watched the boy rise, braced for another hug. It didn't come, though, Basil simply standing with his hands in his pockets and a grin blooming slowly on his face, before he reached out and shoved Kaiden's shoulder lightly. "I knew it."

Though it wasn't what he expected, he couldn't help the grin that slipped unbidden on in response, like a past part of him responding in his stead. "Glad to know someone didn't doubt me."

Basil chuckled, but Kaiden didn't miss the brief waver to it, the way his eyes flicked away ever-so-briefly.

"So...what brings you back?" he said instead, only the slightest strain hitching his tone before it calmed down again. "Did you find...?"

"No," Kaiden answered quietly, before the word *family* could run through his mind on an endless loop. He felt his hand wanting to shake again, digging it deep into his pocket before it could be seen. He'd told them why he'd left, at least, and it was mostly true. He wondered if any of them saw past it. Adding a half-shrug, he smiled out of the side of his mouth. "Not yet."

Kaiden knew his friend wanted to ask more, but he also must have seen that Kaiden wouldn't answer, because he let it drop.

"Learn any new jokes?" he asked instead.

Kaiden felt the grin stretch almost painfully across his face. "*Did I?*" He was sure his eyes were dancing, his memories brimming with words that wanted to spill from his lips, all at once. "Nope."

Basil's mouth dropped open for a moment, and then shut it, frowning. "Hey."

Kaiden pushed past him, the grin still foreign on his face. He felt like two separate people, split in two, reacting at the same time in different ways. But this was what they needed. This is what he'd give them.

"Oh!" Fern exclaimed, as if she'd just thought of something. "I made cake!"

Basil laughed. "You always make cake, Fern."

She made a face at him. "Yeah, well, this time it's a *special* cake. It was for one of the dragon's birthdays, but you can have some too." She peeked up at Kaiden, grin almost shy as she twisted her sleeves around her hands. "Since it's a special occasion."

A chuckle passed around the group. Kaiden smiled. "I think that would be pretty foolish of me to turn down."

"It would," Fern agreed seriously, already walking away as if she expected them to follow her. She liked to do that, even back in the Mountain. "Cake is good for the soul."

He couldn't stop the laugh that left his throat, even as she wrinkled up her nose at him for it. "Of course it is."

As they walked through the city, Kaiden kept finding his gaze wandering, taking in the sights. If he wasn't mistaken, there were a lot more dragons here than there had been before.

They sat outside in the sun, which even Kaiden had to admit felt less harsh here than in Calest. It took too long for him to realize that Joss was nowhere in sight. He blamed the sudden onslaught of memories he'd been dealing with.

Fern passed around her cake proudly, which surprisingly looked slightly more put-together than it usually did. Maybe she'd gotten help from someone.

He looked around at his friends as they chatted, taking everything in. They might look at him oddly if he asked about Joss, unless they'd seen her. Maybe she was still hanging out with Chan.

That theory was disproved when Chan came to find them later, Joss definitely not by his side. His eyes immediately went to Kaiden.

"You should go find your kid," he said without preamble, sitting down beside them. Clearing his throat, he focused his gaze on the table, adjusting his glasses. "She's with Lena."

Lena. He didn't have to ask, based on Chan's expression, to know what that meant. Excusing himself, he stood from the table, Ril still on his shoulder, two other dragons protesting his departure. The rest continued playing lazily on the table, tugging teasingly at Basil's hair and trying to steal Chan's glasses, and the cake.

Olive, for some reason, didn't seem that surprised. Basil looked between them questioningly, while Fern cleaned up her mess and played with the kits.

Kaiden cleared his throat, averting his gaze. "I'll be back," he said, and pulled his mouth up in a smile. Before they could ask anything else, he turned to leave. He could practically see the *Good luck* written in Chan's expression as he walked away. Ril, as always, sat loyally on his shoulder, her tail sweeping gently around him like a gesture of support.

He was only just past where his room was located when he heard his name called, his steps stilling as he caught sight of her. Though he couldn't discern her expression from this distance, something in Lena's tone told him she wasn't exactly pleased to see him.

Lena stalked toward him, her eyes alight with too many things he didn't want to name. "You selfish, arrogant, lying, beanheaded..."

Even just her voice brought back a million memories, flickering images he didn't want to see. She certainly had every right to be mad at him.

It didn't stop his slight flinch when she threw a fist into his arm, hard enough to make a more sensitive person yelp. As it was, it still sent a wave across his vision, the throb bringing back a slew of unpleasant memories.

"...dagging idiot," she breathed, barely bothering to stop for breath. "Were you even going to tell me?" She took a step toward him, something flickering through her eyes. "Were you *ever*?"

Looking at her was too painful, and yet he couldn't pull his gaze away, even as she tore into him. Instinctively, he braced himself for another hit that didn't come. Swallowing, he rubbed his arm, wetting his lips. "Tell you what?"

She hit him again, her eyes sharp and hard. "About being back, you dagging idiot. About the kid you brought back, and the fact that everyone else knew you were here *but* me? That I had to hear it from Chan?"

She was practically spitting sparks with her words. Ril squeaked in protest on his shoulder, landing on his head. Lena balled her hands in tight fists, drawing in a deep breath.

"Your kid is a little thief, if you weren't aware." Her eyes were icy. "She's also from the Isles."

Despite having his memory back, Kaiden felt like he was missing something. "So...?"

Lena's face twisted in a tight expression. "You're infuriating," she spat out, and turned to walk away. "I give up."

"L... Wait." He couldn't bring himself to say her name, everything choked up in him enough as is. He couldn't help but feel like he'd lost a terrible battle. "Please...?"

"I don't want excuses," Lena cut in, a laughless sound formed on her lips. "You show up out of nowhere, no warning, no explanation, and I have to hear it from...from a thief that you've come back. So. *Were* you?"

No, he wanted to admit, though it would only make her more furious. Biting his lip, he searched for something else to say, trying to still the memories swirling in his head from seeing her here. Smiling, frowning, crying. His smirk, her anger. Guilt. Hurt. Her intense gaze always on him, searching for something more.

"She's more than a thief," he finally said, subdued.

"Oh, I can see that," Lena replied dryly, a bit of the sharpness returning. "She's 'your' thief or something strange like that. It still doesn't answer my question."

He looked down, his hand brushing his arm. He had a feeling she was talking about more than his reappearance. "I'm s—"

"Say it." Her eyes went cold then, a twitch of something far from a smile on her lips. "I dare you."

"I'm sorry," he choked out anyway, even as he saw the spark start in her eyes again. He didn't know how to explain it, and the ache in his throat was only growing stronger the longer he looked at her. The more he saw, and remembered, just how he'd treated her. "I'm sorry."

Her shoulders were rigid now, making her a statue. An elegant, if cold one. "I didn't ask for an apology," she bit out. "I wanted an explanation."

But how could he give her that, when she'd never believe it?

As he forced himself to meet her eyes, the futility of it all washed over him. Anything he could say in his defense would only sound like an excuse. And she didn't want apologies. So what *could* he say?

Nothing, he realized. Lena, of all of them, wouldn't understand his reasoning. He'd lied to her too many times for his words to have any weight anymore. That, he mused, was the real test here. While he might be able to placate Basil and Fern with ridiculous jokes and wide smiles, Lena had always seen past that. Even when he was still Blaze, she was

297

always prodding, somehow seeing through his cracks to the silvers of truth underneath.

Why was he here, anyway? He wasn't making anything better, obviously. Fake smiles and depthless jokes. Was that all he had to offer? It spun around him in a spiral, dragging him down. His siblings didn't want him, either. Why would they? Why would she?

Lena's eyes went hard, the glint of something sharper underneath at his silence.

"Your kid is in there," she finally muttered, gesturing to a nearby building. Drawing in a breath, an unreadable flicker crossed her face as she brushed past him, tossing him a key he barely caught. Her lips lifted in the cold shape of a smile. "Welcome back, Kaiden."

The words stabbed harder than they should have. He wanted to chase after her, but what would he say? He couldn't apologize. He knew what he'd done, and how he'd hurt her. Words were never going to heal any of that. His lips formed around and choked on words he couldn't say, the desire to find the right words taking hold of him and fleeing in the next moment. A ragged sound left his throat, his arm seeming to throb more than it should have as he rubbed it, trying to push her harsh words from his mind.

Idiot. Shutting his eyes, Kaiden drew in an unsteady breath. She was right, anyway. He didn't know why he even tried. Numbly, he curled his fingers around the key, making his way over to the building Lena had indicated. The world around him felt vaguely fuzzy, like the past was trying to encroach on the present in any way it could. Like he wasn't quite there.

Joss leaned casually against the bars of her prison, her face splitting in a grin when she saw him.

"Your lady friend is scary."

Without a word, Kaiden unlocked the cell and dropped down against the wall outside it, digging deep into the pockets of his jacket.

"Don't worry about me," Joss said with a shrug. "Go talk to your lady friend. Get things figured out."

But what was he supposed to say? His tongue was frozen, throat closed at the thought of trying to face the hurt in her eyes once again.

Having found what he was looking for, Kaiden flipped open a knife, scraping it into a block of wood just a little harder than necessary. Though his hands weren't the steadiest, he kept chipping away at it, roughly, trying to calm his thoughts.

Concern on her face, Joss dropped down beside him. "Bodyguard?"

He said nothing, nicking himself on his knife more times than he cared to count. What did it matter? He hardly felt it, anyway. Even the scrape of the blade drew memories to mind, though he tried to tell himself they would get better. Meriador said they would. His fingers would find their rhythm, as they always did.

"You should go talk to your lady friend," Joss repeated quietly, her brow creasing as she craned her head in the direction Lena had gone. "She seemed awfully upset."

Kaiden bit back a laugh. How did he explain the entirety of what he'd done to a young girl? He just had to try to make it right. Even as he accidentally cut himself harder, with his shaking hands, and pressed a gritty finger to his mouth for a moment out of habit.

Joss' brow furrowed in worry. "What did you do, anyhow?"

His fingers tightened around the wood, agonizing heat flashing through his mind. "I hurt her," he responded, ignoring the tremble to his fingers. Any time the memories got too fierce, he just carved harder, as if he could simply chip them away from him.

Joss frowned, tilting her head as she considered him. "You...?"

A broken laugh escaped his lips. She thought it was ridiculous that he could hurt someone. She couldn't be more wrong.

As if to side with her, a kit dragon peeked its head up, from where Joss had it in her hands. She grinned. "I blamed him for the crime."

Kaiden rubbed at his face, suppressing a shudder at the ache he felt there. He breathed in and imagined there wasn't fire in his chest at the action, hacking away at the wood in his hands until he had...something. It wasn't any good, but that was okay. It would take time. Carefully hewing away the sharp edges, bit by bit, until it was something worth presenting to people.

A rough replica of Lena's dragon, or a dragon, stared back at him. It didn't quite look the same, shaped by his imperfect memories and the images he had flitting around in there. But it was better than nothing.

His life was like that wood. Too easily lit with flames, turned to blackened, smoldering ruin, but capable of something lovely, if he could just chip away at it enough. Maybe. He cut himself too many times, until he was numbed to even the slight prick, but slowly, surely, it began to come together.

Joss sat beside him, looking up at where Lena had gone and then back at him. Her little brow pressed together in a frown as she watched him work. He pushed his emotion into each stroke, rough and sharp, soft and smooth like it was weathered away by the wind.

Everything felt far too heavy as he put his all into honing the carving, chipping away at each piece like all the worthless parts of his life. The bad, unnecessary ones. He used to do this, before, when everything was too overwhelming. He'd carve aimlessly, eyes blurred with tears, hacking at the wood until he'd calmed down. And then he'd slow, movements more purposeful, and bring something worthwhile out of it. It made him feel better for letting it out in such a way.

"I'm okay."

Joss' brow creased in a funny way, even as she stood, tugging gently at his hand. "C'mon. You need to go have a talk with your lady friend."

"She's not..."

Joss gave him a look. "She's a lady, and she's your friend. I'm not dumb."

Chuckling, he got slowly to his feet, letting Joss pull him along as she threatened him sweetly. "Besides, if you don't, I'll tell everyone that you scream like a little boy when you see spiders."

His lips lifted briefly. "Not like a little girl?"

Joss made a face at him again. "Little boys scream just as loud as little girls. And you're a boy, right? So why would you scream like a girl?"

He let the comment slide. "I suppose you're right."

"Of course I am." Joss puffed out her chest. "And you need to go tell your lady friend that you're going to stay here and fix whatever it is you broke."

The smile nearly slipped, but he nodded, reaching down to mess with her hair. She shoved his hand away, but there was a light in her eyes, softening as he stopped. "You have people that care about you, Bodyguard. Some of us aren't that lucky."

He turned to look where Lena had gone, a laugh escaping with his breath. "You're wrong, Joss." With a smile toward her, he folded his hand around hers. "I care for you."

Joss wrinkled her nose, following his gaze briefly before pulling her hand away. "Don't turn this around on me!"

Her warning tone made him smile, despite everything. Huffing, she glanced back where Lena had gone, crossing her arms. "Why are you so stubborn?"

"Because I'm right?"

Put out, she made a face at him. "You won't even give her a chance."

The smile stuck in a way that made his chest ache. "I hurt her, Joss."

"So? Everyone hurts someone at some point in their lives. Even I know that." Her face twisted like she'd just eaten something sour. "But you're never going to fix things by ignoring the problem."

He exhaled a quiet breath. "Since when did you get so wise?"

"Five years," she said simply. Scuffing her foot against the ground, she added after a moment, "You don't usually care for people, on the streets. They'd rather cheat you than do anything for you." She drew in a long, unusually small breath. "And they certainly don't forgive you."

Kaiden pulled her closer, tucking her under her arm. She pouted, but pressed against him for a moment. "So if you're lucky enough to have someone who's willing to stand by you, and offer you a chance to fix things, take it. Don't let it slip away because you messed up. Nothing's ever really broken beyond fixing. It just takes time."

He squeezed her against him, quiet for a moment. She allowed him silence to think, but eventually pulled away, a grin creeping back onto her face. "I'm going to explore this new place of yours. You'd better have talked to her by the time I get back."

He chuckled at the stern look on her face. "Yes, Princess."

She made a face at him and was off, disappearing into the city like the trouble she was. He only hoped he wouldn't have to fix *that* too once he was done.

Forcing himself to move felt like climbing through quicksand. But Joss' words had struck him harder than he expected, and he slowly turned to go find Lena. He just had one other thing to take care of first.

LENA

I did my best to keep the mask of anger on as I headed back to my room, eyes pinned straight ahead. No one questioned me, even as I felt the strings slipping and was sure someone would ask about it.

He'd stayed quiet because he *couldn't* answer my question. It was clear in his eyes.

I just wished he'd told me that himself.

Between everything with Sari and the Gifted, and the anxiety over my own secret plan, I was too on edge for any of this. I didn't have time for his vague answers.

As if he knew what I needed, Zarafel was waiting for me outside my room. Without a word, he lowered himself so I could get on, and then we took off, the wind whipping against my face as we left the city behind for a time.

The wonderful thing about Zarafel was that he didn't need any explanation. Sometimes you just had to get away, and he understood that. He remained silent as we flew, lazily dipping down and arcing around to keep things from being boring. Just enough that I had to hold on tightly, and put some of my focus into that.

When we finally landed, though, and I didn't walk away, he settled down on the ground near me, watching.

"Your human friends are being idiots again, aren't they?"

Expelling a sigh, I leaned my head against his glinting white side. *"When aren't they?"*

"A question I ask myself at least twice a day," Zarafel replied, amused. The fin-like tip of his tail swept against my legs. *"What is it this time?"*

He could have just looked in my head and found out himself, I mused, but chose not to. Sometimes I thought he enjoyed the conversation, as much as he'd never admit it.

Zarafel shifted to his feet, presumably to get me to move, though he would have disguised it as merely stretching. *"Or perhaps I should ask, 'whom'?"*

"All of them," I said teasingly, half a laugh escaping with my breath. The truth lurked far too close to the surface, wishing to wriggle its way out.

"I'm just worried," I amended, sliding down to sit by where he settled – but without touching him, this time. His tail remained rather close to my legs, curled loosely by me. *"About my plan, and...Caleb."*

Zarafel knew the truth, of course, but he never pried. *"And?"*

I frowned, settling my arms over my chest. *"It's a stupid plan."*

"Hm. Perhaps you should get help, then."

I'm trying, I wanted to say, but bit my tongue. *"I'll think about it."*

A rumble sounded from Zarafel's chest, too close to a laugh. I frowned at him.

"I am sorry," he apologized, though he didn't sound it. *"I simply find your dodging around things you don't want to face amusing."*

I shot him a sharp look. *"Says the dragon who will never talk about his own past."*

"If I told you, would you talk with your friends?" Zarafel looked at me down his long snout, continuing with hardly a pause. *"I didn't think so."*

"I would," I answered instead, just to feel the surprise from him in my mind. It was almost closer to discomfort as he shifted, rumbling another sound I'd yet to identity – and he wouldn't explain.

A smile slipped onto my face unbidden as I watched him. *"Would you actually tell me? You seem more hesitant than I am."*

"It's not a pleasant tale, child."

"My life has not been a pleasant tale," I replied, and frowned. *"You're just as afraid as I am, aren't you?"*

Zarafel expelled a rough breath through his nostrils. *"No."*

"Mmhm." I studied him, a thought slipping slowly into my head. *"Is that why...you let me in?"*

He turned his head away, huffing. *"Don't make me regret it."*

"You're as bad as Blaze," I replied, a small, sad smile tugging at my mouth. *"He won't tell me anything."*

"Perhaps he's afraid, too," Zarafel muttered, still not looking at me.

My smile disappeared at the thought. If he was...why did he lie about it? Why did he pretend he just left to find his siblings, as if we weren't able to help him? Why hadn't he *told* me that he'd come back?

The bitter, broken part of me wanted to remain defensive, to keep myself safe. He'd always have secrets, and he was never going to share them with me. Not now that he remembered them. He'd just taunt me by hiding them in his eyes, in plain view, but never explain *why*.

"I wonder sometimes," Zarafel interrupted, resting his head on his claws to see me better, *"how it is that you humans always blind yourselves so wholly to the truths you most want to see."*

For a moment, I could only stare at him, the words striking me far deeper than I'd ever admit. *"I'm not blinding myself,"* I said softly, willing the words to be true.

Zarafel let out a quieter sigh, his entire demeanor subdued as his eyes searched the far distance.

"I met a human I didn't hate, in the arenas. He was put in there to fight, and begged me to just end him quickly." Zarafel shifted his position, practically frowning. *"Instead, I saved his life."*

I'd heard part of this story before, another time when Zarafel was trying to make a point. But I always had a feeling there was more he hadn't said.

"The crowds loved it," he grumbled, as if that was a terrible thing. *"I killed the rest of the dragons, but left him alive. Out of respect for me, he did the same."* Zarafel huffed a laugh. *"Or, simply because he knew he couldn't kill me."* His gaze flicked away, distant for a moment.

"Whatever the reason, they let us both live, for a time. They paired us together, against other dragons, and the crowds grew larger." A stab of pain crossed his face and our mental bond, as hard as he tried to hide it. *"But humans...are fragile. They weren't meant to take such abuse."*

His eyes slipped shut for a long moment. *"It was easier to hate them all, later. For letting it happen. For reminding me, every time I saw their smug faces, what they took from me."* A subdued anger filled his eyes, claws digging subtly in the dirt. *"Even after...your Sari found me. Even after I watched all the humans who weren't the same, by any means."* He huffed out a breath, eyes locking with mine. *"As for*

303

why I let you in, I think I made that rather obvious. You were entertaining to annoy. Are," he added in amusement, flicking the tip of his tail against my leg. In retaliation, I leaned back against his side.

"Hm. I think you just thought I was too fantastic not to make friends with."

"That too," Zarafel replied, not enough teasing in his eyes. Though I could feel the slight tension to him, he didn't move away. *"To come from that place, and still attempt to befriend other humans...that takes strength."*

I drew in a breath, shaking my head. *"I'm sorry about your friend."*

"You're nothing like him," Zarafel said instead, as if I hadn't spoken. *"He was hard and bitter against the world. He never would have been my choice, were there one. But it was that or let him be slaughtered, and he'd endured too much cruelty to give him that."* Zarafel blew a breath through his nose. *"Someone had to try a different approach."*

I stayed quiet for a long moment, pressed quietly against my dragon's side. *"I see."*

"Mm. I knew you would." He shifted his neck around to face me better. *"You're one of the intelligent ones."*

And now I had to prove it, I thought, as much as everything in me twisted not to. Talking to Basil was one thing. Telling Kaiden...

Zarafel shifted onto his feet again, stretching out his wings. *"Think on it,"* he said, and took off again, leaving me alone.

Expelling a sigh, I slipped into my room, trying not to frown. I didn't *want* to think on it. I already knew what it was I had to do. I just...didn't want to do it.

From the nearby end table, Dez chirped a greeting. He wasn't a fan of other dragons, especially the larger ones, though I knew he missed me when I left him alone. I picked him up, setting him on my shoulder, and then stopped. There, on the table, was a carving I had definitely never seen before, and a note with it. Two pictures lay just under that, one large, the other just a smaller, lighter sketch.

The carving was a representation of Dez, contently asleep, the tiny details making him seem almost lifelike. But the pictures, they were what gave me the most pause.

The first was a drawing of Kaiden and I, in the midst of a sparring match as if he'd simply paused mid-stroke to capture it. My body turned away to dodge his sword, blonde hair free around my face and a challenge in my eyes.

And, of course, he had his telltale smirk on, a fierce spark to his eyes as he swung at me. It brought a little smile to my face, remembering those days. If you looked close enough, you could see the enjoyment on both of our faces, a relaxation to our poses despite the verbal war that was certainly going on.

He'd drawn me. He'd drawn *us*, I knew, and yet I couldn't reconcile it with what I saw. There was a fierce angle to the way my shoulder was turned, and yet he'd captured the softness, too, in a way I couldn't put into words. He'd drawn me...as I was, not as I portrayed myself to the world. Same with him, if you knew where to look.

The other picture only cemented it. It was drawn like a second frame, where I missed and his eyes softened just a little, the smugness offset by something softer in his eyes that the drawing version of me couldn't see. And I was...laughing. It was like an outtake on the previous scene, as if the curtain had been pulled back entirely, the extent of our emotions freely shown.

It was ironic, looking between the two pictures now and seeing the softer smile on his face. Eyes fixed on some distant point, as if I might not like to see it. The way the pictures were angled, it looked like he was looking right at me, in the other picture.

I was immeasurably grateful he brought this to my room rather than handed it to me, because I didn't have to suppress my reaction this time. It...caught me off guard, if I dared to admit it. It was so unlike *anything* anyone had ever done for me before. I couldn't even remember the last time someone had given me a gift that truly mattered, other than this one.

It didn't make sense. *None* of it did. The last time someone had tried to apologize to me, it had been with an elaborate bouquet of flowers, and then they had acted like everything was fine between us. This...it wasn't a statement. It was an offering, and I wasn't used to having a choice.

Setting the pictures down, I expelled a breath. I didn't want to face what this might mean, that he would share this so freely with me. Reluctantly, I picked up the note, written in familiarly neat print. It simply said, "*For Lena*," with his name scribbled roughly beneath it, a stark difference to the care put into the other letters.

I stared at the note for a while, unwilling to believe it. Dez examined the carving of himself with wide, curious eyes, squeaking at it hesitantly. I brushed a finger against his head absently, looking the drawing over again.

I hadn't wanted an apology, and this still didn't answer any of my questions, but it did diffuse my frustration more than I wanted. If I let myself admit it, I'd seen more in the reluctance in his eyes than I'd told him.

305

But I still didn't get why he decided to lie about it. The secrets he still kept so deep, despite the fact that I could see the edges of them peeking out.

The same sort of secrets I was keeping, if I'd let myself admit it. Which, of course, I wouldn't.

Still...maybe it would be easier, now. His picture had given me an idea, as I thought back to the earlier days of knowing him. When I'd managed to get the most reaction out of him, positive or not.

It wasn't much, but it was a start. At this point, I would have rather he yelled at me than just...this. Not saying a word, and hiding it because he didn't want me to see.

Well, maybe this would help loosen both of us up. If I was lucky, maybe I could even get him to explain himself.

KAIDEN

Lena wasn't in her room. It was a relief he hadn't been prepared for, as he wrote his brief note and tucked it with the carving in a place she'd easily find it. He still felt restless after, however. Though not as sharp and bitter as before, memories kept tickling his mind, so he went back to his room to draw until they left him alone.

He drew Gigi, for his own sake, until it ached too much to look at. He drew his team, laughing, and he had to redraw a few pictures for the salty stains that ruined them. He drew the dragons, and random snips of memory that wouldn't leave his mind. Chan with his spectacles on, nose-deep in a book. Basil's laugh, and Fern's cheerful, color-splotched face. He drew scenes and objects from his past, anything to get the images to leave him alone. He drew until he could breathe normally again, and at least the smallest part of his burden felt eased.

Carving got out his rawest emotions. Drawing got out the softer ones.

True to her word, Joss came back to check up on him, though she seemed disappointed that he hadn't been able to talk to Lena, and made him promise to do it later. She left soon after, teasingly mentioning the trouble she planned to get into.

Kaiden spent a while longer with his dragons, unwilling to go find any of his friends just yet. They were probably busy, if they'd even want to see him at all. He still saw the hurt he'd caused veiled in their eyes, as much as they tried to deny it. Maybe the distance would help with that.

Eventually, though, there was a knock at his door. Joss never knocked, if she even used the door, and so he dragged himself to his feet, putting on a wide smile as he answered it.

It was Lena standing in front of his door, arms crossed. "Spar with me."

Though he wanted to say no, out of self-preservation, the look in her eyes hardly broached argument. Nodding, he stepped out after her. "I...probably won't be any good."

She flashed him a sharp smile. "I don't mind. I've always beaten you anyway."

Rather than argue, he followed her silently, burying a feeling of unease. Anything too closely related to his time as Blaze was still hard to sort out, with all of the conflicting emotions and lies involved. But if this was what it took for him to make up for everything...so be it. He'd let her hit him again if it would fix things between them.

Lena led him into an unfamiliar building, smaller than the hall in the Mountain, but adequate for their needs. Reluctantly, he took the staff she handed him, shifting into a pose that felt far too natural. It brought back memories of sharp smiles and lashing tongues, anger and frustration poured into something he no longer needed. Like his fire had brought sparks of pain, and screaming, as if the souls of those he'd hurt had been trapped in them.

With hardly any preamble, Lena took her own pose and struck, something like satisfaction glinting in her eyes. Purely from instinct, he blocked her, heart already pounding harder than usual. This wasn't right. He didn't want to hurt her, intentionally or not. But how was he supposed to win otherwise?

"What's the matter, Blaze?" Lena's pointed smirk made him want to shudder. "Too scared to fight back?"

Scared. The word ran through his mind on repeat, laughing at him. Mocking him. Lena struck again, easily, and he dodged away, the wood whistling too close by his skin. At his lack of reply, she frowned, circling him like a dragon eyeing its prey.

"Maybe you're just too good for us," she murmured, her tone intentionally digging at him. "You left because you don't care, and you never did."

I was...scared, his mind whispered, though he couldn't say it aloud. She struck at him faster, and he dodged from fear of being hit.

"Coward," she said slowly, eyes glinting with a challenge. "You're still afraid of being bested by a girl?" She smirked. "Or maybe you're just too weak to fight me."

His grip went slack, his parry clumsy as he stumbled, barely avoiding a second hit. The third, though, connected with his shoulder in a soft crack.

It made his head dizzy, trying to convince himself it was only *on* his skin, and not deeper. He pulled in a sharp breath, eyes flickering as he watched her.

"Why won't you fight back?" Lena demanded, something he couldn't name flitting through her eyes. "I'm not buying into your act," she continued, taking back up her stance, "so you can stop pretending."

At his lack of response, her eyes hardened, her staff moving faster than he remembered as she swung at him again.

"I know you don't care about any of us. I know you only think of yourself, and *that's* why you left." Her expression shifted briefly, as if daring him to deny it. "Why you never think anyone needs to know what you're doing, or why. Why you play games with them and then just *leave* them to pick up the pieces."

His hands turned numb when she struck again, something glinting in her eyes.

"Come on, Kaiden. *Fight me.*"

But he just gripped the wood until his fingers burned, his hands shaking from the exertion. Fights. Yelling. Lena, looking utterly furious. It all swirled in his head a little too close with everything else, the room shifting for a moment to somewhere far different and too familiar.

Something stung his cheek. Imagining her angry face, he winced. Somehow he ended up on his knees, shielding his head.

Lena nudged him with her shoe, sounding almost exasperated. "Get up, Beanhead. It's not that bad."

A shiver rode through him as his body refused, tensing against further retaliation. She had every right to be mad.

Her brow crammed with deep lines, Lena knelt beside him, nudging his shoulder with her hand. "Kaiden?"

"I'm sorry." It slipped out before he could stop it, a whisper that kept repeating itself, desperately.

Shoulders tense, Lena stood back up. "Don't do that again." There was something uncertain to her tone, though he might have imagined it. "I don't want an apology."

What do you want? his mind cried, even though he knew the answer.

The truth. She wants the truth.

But that was the one thing he just couldn't give her. She would mock him. She wouldn't believe him. His words held no weight anymore because of how he had abused them.

There was a loud sigh, and the scrape of boots as she turned to leave the room. He hunched closer to the ground, a strangled noise slipping free from his throat, as much as he tried to stifle it.

She wouldn't believe him. No matter what he said, she wouldn't believe him.

XIX

LENA

None of it worked. I tried to make him mad, to get a real reaction. I hit him where I knew it would hurt the worst, hoping even for a burst of anger or *something*.

Nothing. Not a spark of realness, anywhere. He clung to it like a secret we both knew of, but only he understood. Like he was taunting me with it. His eyes whispered about it, constantly, and it was driving me mad.

I hadn't even intended to hit him. I kept expecting him to block, or scowl at me, or do something. But he just took it without so much as a flinch, as if he expected it. As if he deserved it.

But apologizing for my actions would mean admitting everything, and I couldn't bring myself to do that yet, either. He was...different, since coming back.

No, my mind whispered. Not different. The same, as before. Hiding secrets out in the open, in smiles instead of smirks. It made something uncomfortable twist inside of me, that my same tactics wouldn't even work.

And that meant I had to admit that I had secrets, too, even if he might be lying. I didn't want to bare myself again, after what had happened before.

"Are you okay?"

I'd had a friend, before Etta, who said they'd always be there for me. He looked so earnest all the time that I just...believed him. The disappointment on his face when he'd found out what I was had somehow hurt more than Etta's coldness, as if I had done something wrong to deserve losing them.

I'll always be there, he'd said, and for some dagged reason, I had actually *believed* it. From desperation, most likely, which he'd probably used to his advantage. He'd never minded that I didn't behave like the other children. He said it was brave, and he admired it.

Are you okay?

Any time I heard those words again, even now, I heard them echoed in his voice. He'd had the audacity it to ask even after he knew I was *not* okay, moments before he planned to turn that disappointed face on me and pull away. Unlike Etta, he continued to try to have contact with me after he found out my heritage– as a joke, I guess – but treated it as it were some immense privilege he was bestowing on me. So he could tell his parents he was doing his duty and caring for an ex-Galdanian.

Ex. As if somehow the blood in my veins had decided to rebel and turn purple because of my father's upbringing.

I wondered how stunned they would be to cut our arms open and see our blood ran just as red as the others. That there was no inherent superiority infused in his veins just because his family came from this land.

I wondered how much more appalled he would be to find out just how many of the so-called 'pure' had taints of Calestan blood in them. Long ago, our people had coexisted peacefully. They were all people, same skin, same blood. Why wouldn't they intermarry?

He still asked me that question after my imprisonment, and I almost believed him. How pathetic it was, that I had been so deprived of comfort that I still sought it in him, even knowing how he saw me. He pretended he cared, as if he'd tried to stop them from chaining me up, for nothing I'd done, and that his silence somehow earned back my loyalty. As if it could make up for all the horrid things I'd heard him say about me, when he thought I wasn't around to hear.

He told me, once, that having a friend only in public was better than having none at all. That I might be able to sway people into not shunning me, with his influence. He was too powerful, and arrogant, for them to stand so blatantly against him.

He continued to pretend we were friends, but mocked me if I didn't comply with his wishes. He claimed not to care about my heritage all that much, and yet kept bringing it up, all the same. He'd make crude jokes about my father and then halfheartedly apologize, as if he'd forgotten I was there. And if I did speak up, he'd just say I was too sensitive. As if I should be grateful he was giving me any attention at all, and the comments were deserved. As if something that was a source of true fear to me would only ever be a joke to him.

But he was the *only* reason I had anyone to talk to, and could potentially avoid some of my mother's disapproval for a short while. Some days I actually believed he wanted to help, and could. As if being friends with him would one day make everyone stop seeing me differently.

It took me too long to see the truth. It made me ache, the first moment he'd asked, "So, what are they like?" as if 'they' were an entirely different, dangerous species and not one of the very humans he had grown up admiring most of his life. He'd told me about the girl he was seeing, with pity, as if I'd had some interest in him like that.

My only interest had been in having a friend. Etta's treatment numbed me, as she planned it to. His was like a knife constantly cutting me back open, until I couldn't bear it.

It was why I tried to run, that one time. They had found me and punished me severely for that. I was terrified to leave my window for a week.

"I'm sorry."

It was said in the same way, wasn't it? Empty words. Meaningless ones. Kaiden coming up with excuses for why he couldn't tell me the truth. That I didn't deserve it. That I never would.

It hurt because deep down, I cared for people way more than I ever wanted to admit, and it made me a little more callous every time I lost someone. The innkeeper who let me stay the night my first week in Calest, despite my obvious heritage. The man who had been kind enough to give me a job, and bread from his table. My jewels went quick, and I didn't regret them, despite the hardship I faced. It made me stronger, in the end.

It was wrong, comparing Kaiden to a former friend. But the tiny, terrified part of my mind continued to cling to it, for protection. It was better than possibly being hurt. Being vulnerable was just...too scary. And though I'd promised Zarafel I'd still try, I hadn't worked up the courage yet. Even though a small part of me knew Kaiden's reaction to our fight was not at all what it seemed.

But...asking him about it would have been admitting, again, and I got scared. What if he didn't tell me and just shut me out? That was sure what it seemed like he was trying to do, by leaving as he did. Like the letter he'd left was a *Goodbye* rather than *See you later*.

And if I looked close enough at his eyes, I knew it *had* been that. Maybe not for the same reasons, but...he hadn't planned to come back. That, more than anything, scared me more than I wanted to admit. I wasn't brave enough to keep him here if he left again. I didn't know how.

Still, my feet reluctantly turned back to check on him, as much as it made my insides tense up to consider. I let myself get distracted, along the way, attending to a few things I needed to do and ignoring the tangled knot in my chest. A terrified part of me worried that when I finally got there...he would have left again. Like this was all a dream, or a brief detour, if nothing else. I sure seemed to be doing a good job at driving him away.

What a pair we made. What a mess it always was. And yet, for some reason I couldn't name, I never regretted it. Even if this all ended in fire, and he never spoke to me again. Even though we frustrated each other, and couldn't speak right. If anyone would understand, it was him. And that, if nothing else, was a good enough reason to keep going. Maybe one day, everything would settle down and lock into place, and we'd be able to speak our minds.

And maybe, I mused, I could just sprout wings and fly away like a dragon. It seemed just about as likely, at this point.

KAIDEN

Still shaking from the memories shooting through his mind, Kaiden drew himself to his feet, a noise too close to a sob fighting to break its way out of his chest. This was fine, he told himself. She hadn't really hurt him, after all. It had been mild, *so* mild compared to what he was expecting. The scars carved into his back. The fire raging in his memories.

Tell her.

But he couldn't. If he did, he would just fall apart. He couldn't acknowledge any of...*this* without bringing up his inherent failures, and things he didn't want to talk about. He'd done his best to write it down, before, and ended up burning the paper instead.

What was the point? He couldn't tell her what mattered most, and so she would never understand. And a part of him wanted that. The same one that had told him to leave, before, and he'd obeyed.

It was easier then. With so few memories to contend with, it was easier to twist his perception to see things as worse than they had been. To see her as angrier than she was, and hurt. To tell himself that there was nothing he could do to fix that, no matter *how* hard he tried.

Now, though, he saw it all, and if nothing else, he'd never stop wanting it. He'd never stop wishing and wondering what would have happened if he tried. If they managed to make things work. He'd never stop wondering what it would be like to have her as a friend, and that word to actually mean something.

She still deserved better. They all did. And yet, it was easier to understand now why they didn't *want* 'better'. Why, despite all their cracks and flaws, they couldn't just give up on each other, even if it would have been easier. Why Basil kept hoping, and Chan had dragged him back, and even Olive opened up in ways she never usually did.

They *were* friends, and no amount of separation would ever change that fact. They'd formed bonds that ran deeper than words, endured things together that drew them closer. Even when he'd smirked at everything she said and she'd thrown him annoyed looks, they still cared, on some hidden level. He hadn't wanted her to die. She'd kept prying, as if she already knew the sorrow he buried beneath everything.

The truth of the matter was, they were far too similar for distance to make any difference. When you found someone whose very being resonated with yours, even if it was in ways you didn't want to admit, you couldn't just let them go. They'd always be a part of you, because of the connection you shared.

For perhaps the first, most startling moment, he didn't hate what he had been through, if this was the result. Jade had been his only friend for so long...he hadn't even realized how much they meant to him. How much he'd think of all of them, and moments they'd shared, if he dared to leave again.

But just because they wanted it didn't make it good for them, and Lena was no exception. Deep down, she pushed him away because she *knew* that. Because she was trying to protect herself, and the rest of them.

It was the same with his siblings, he realized, swallowing down the lump forming in his throat. Even if they wanted him, they *shouldn't*. He'd just cause them more pain, all over again, because he was too broken to do anything else.

There were some things he just couldn't say, and some she couldn't forgive. He knew that. It was time to move on, and try to make it better.

Except, nothing he did was working. She hadn't even said anything about the carving. How silly of him to think that could make a difference. As if he could bribe her into trusting him again, with gifts.

It fed into the spiral his mind was dragging him down, the world washing out to a numbed, dull backdrop, a waterfall of white noise that he couldn't brush away.

He had to do something to get it off his mind. Something to try to dull the ache, even if it was pointless. He got up, not sure of where he was going, but hoping to run into someone anyway. Faces blurred, most of the citizens paying him no more than a passing glance as he walked on, his boots thumping on the hard earth.

The sound of people talking caught his attention. He slipped out into the open to see the twins together, with Fern sitting happily between them. They were laughing, sitting in a makeshift circle with their dragons lounging nearby.

Kaiden dropped down in an empty space as casually as he could, picking up a roll. He felt a tiny head peek out from the confines of his jacket.

Fern's eyes lit up when she saw him, the tiny bell on her crooked hat tinkling. "You're just in time!" she exclaimed. Tiny hyperactive dragons bounced around everywhere, fueled by whatever nonsense Fern had given them.

"They got into the sugar," she admitted, looking at the bag. "But it made them happy, so that's what matters, right?"

Basil looked at him carefully, eyes quietly hopeful. Kaiden ignored the burden in his chest.

"I made food!" Fern exclaimed, even as he got a wary look from Basil. 'Food', he mouthed with cautious emphasis. Kaiden stifled a chuckle, watching Fern with a smile. She was excitedly recounting an adventure she'd had with her kit dragon, and comparing it to one from long before, back in the Mountain.

Olive tossed him food that hadn't been made by Fern, and he ate it slowly as he listened, and nodded. Fern kept looking around every so often, stretching up to peek around, and then looking disappointed.

"Lena hasn't come in a while," she said sadly. "I was hoping she would."

It quieted something in him, seeing her expression. If he looked too closely, he could see the hurt beneath it all, the glances they kept casting his way as if worried he might leave.

Before he had to pretend further, Chan approached the group with Joss trailing him, looking like he had hardly slept. Instead of interrupting, though, he simply settled against the outer wall of a nearby building and folded his arms, watching them. The familiar action sparked many memories in his mind, again.

Fern's breath hitched audibly in the silence. "You're not leaving again, are you?" She searched his eyes, and then Chan's, as if asking them both.

"Not for a while," Chan replied, and Kaiden again heard the heaviness to it as he pulled in a breath. His eyes searched the ground for an explanation. "I can't go back."

"Why not?"

"I...lost control. Used my Gift."

Beside him, Joss frowned, in the same way that she did when Kaiden told her that cake was better than pastries. "He saved them."

Chan shook his head. "Talon..."

Basil's shoulders tensed. Kaiden wondered how he hadn't noticed it before, the way he reacted to that name. Quietly, but by no means calmly. "He *what*?"

Chan looked down, very near to frowning. Joss, stubbornly, continued on, gesturing to Kaiden.

"He messed with their heads and Chan threatened 'im and then he left." Her accent came out stronger when she was upset, Kaiden had realized. Basil was quietly stiff.

"Talon was there?"

Kaiden knew none of them had truly forgiven their former friend for his betrayal, or treatment of the others. But he didn't think any of them realized just how deeply it went with Basil, this resentment. It flickered in his eyes and twitched at his jaw, tightening the lines by his eyes. Very few things made Basil so mad, or so sad.

Elle, he realized with another breath. He hadn't realized how deeply Basil had cared for his sister.

Kinelly. Her memory was subtler, quieter, like the soft light on a painting, as if to lessen the blow of the memories there.

The grief locked behind his friend's eyes shone out as shame, and anger, though no one else seemed to notice or comment on it. Did no one else see it like he did?

Kaiden knew what he should do, now. But knowing and doing were two different monsters. And both of them loomed overhead, threatened him.

For a moment, Kaiden could have sworn he saw *everything* clearer, and it scared him. Chan's exhaustion. The dark rings under Fern's eyes. Olive's thin smile. It all clashed and screamed at him.

This was his punishment, then, and his salvation. Knowing exactly what would help, and choosing to do something else instead. It was far easier to think it than actually act on it.

"Yeah," Joss admitted with a shrug. "He ran away once Chan started shooting lightning ev'rywhere."

She grinned up at him, and Chan almost looked admonished for a moment as he shook his head. "Don't spread tall tales."

"Aw, but 'ow else are they supposed to travel, then?" She glanced over at Kaiden, something different to her eyes for just a moment. "They don't exactly have legs."

Chan rubbed a hand into his forehead, murmuring to himself. Basil looked amused, regarding the little girl. At his questioning look, Chan gestured to Kaiden.

"You explain," he mumbled, something suspiciously like a smile fighting at the corner of his mouth as he turned away. "I need to go talk to Sari."

Sari? She had returned, and he hadn't even known it. He supposed it wasn't surprising, considering how long he'd been gone. In some ways, it felt only like a few minutes. In others...

"I bribed him," Joss cut in mischievously, a smile making her eyes glitter. "He makes a good bodyguard."

Basil let loose a laugh, while Fern seemed more withdrawn, sitting subtly closer to Olive. The older girl didn't even appear surprised.

"It's true," Kaiden answered teasingly, just to see their reactions. Joss' grin widened, her eyes sparkling.

"We should do something," Basil said, sitting up suddenly.

Kaiden couldn't help but grin. "Got any bright ideas?"

Basil looked at him, and then laughed. "Not really."

"Aw, come on. Surely you can think of something to...lighten the mood."

"I could hit you to make you stop with the jokes," Olive said under her breath, teasing. Or so he hoped.

He raised an eyebrow at her. "Oh, just wait. They'll grow on you."

She stood coolly, a hand sliding the first inch of her sword free from its sheath. Kaiden laughed, enjoying the way she relaxed, a challenge in her eyes. "They get planted in your mind and take root, and then..."

Basil knocked his shoulder against Kaiden's, jokingly. "She's trying to challenge you. I wouldn't give her a reason to follow through with it."

"Why not?" A wild, reckless part of him thought that he might as well, as surely as he knew he'd fail. "She's not that good."

He was thunked on the head with a waterskin. "Next time, it'll be Chan's book," Olive warned, sitting back down with a smile. However lightly, the action flared something in him, his fire humming in his veins and begging to be let out.

"If you can pry it from his fingers," Basil added with a laugh. "He's practically attached to those things. Once he sticks his nose in, there's no way to get it out."

"You're one to talk," Olive replied, eyeing him over in a knowing way. "You and your flowers..."

With a noise of protest, Basil shoved her shoulder with both hands. Olive looked nearly smug, while Fern's eyes sparkled.

"Yeah, well," he tried to protest, as Olive leaned all of her weight against him, "you..."

"Like swords too much?" There was no mistaking Olive's forming smirk. "Secretly enjoy wearing dresses? Have an undercover plan involving dragons?"

Basil dropped his head on hers, making a face. "Stop it."

"You started it."

With another noise of protest, he lifted his head. "Do you see this?" he demanded, gesturing to Fern.

She hid her mouth with a laugh, eyes sparkly. It made something relax in Kaiden, even though he wanted to tense at the same time. Something kept churning inside him that he desperately shoved down.

"... Kaiden will agree with me," Basil was saying with a huff, his arm coming too close around Kaiden's shoulders.

"I'll do what now?"

Olive looked smug. "Face it, Basil. You're outnumbered."

Kaiden did his best to keep his face calm as he looked Basil over carefully, then nodded. "Yeah. You definitely started it."

Defeated, Basil sank his face into the grass. Olive choked back a laugh. Just for a moment, her eyes seemed to sparkle as much as Fern's, as she looked at them both and smiled far more fondly than Kaiden was comfortable with. He curled his hands in the grass to keep them from shaking, picking up a single blade of grass that he lit aflame, to control some of the energy in him.

"So," he interjected, clearing his throat, "before things get more heated..."

"I vote Kaiden decides what we should do. Since obviously he's the one with all the bright ideas," came Basil's muffled voice.

With his free hand, Kaiden patted his friend on the head. "I'd be proud of that one, if I hadn't already made it."

"Rude," Basil mumbled, though there was a smile to his voice.

"Hey, Basil." Kaiden stretched his mouth in a careful smile. "What do you get when you cross a joke with a rhetorical question?"

As Basil's forehead creased, Kaiden went back to talking with Fern, keeping his smile schooled.

"Wait. What's the answer?"

Kaiden's eyes twinkled, and Olive hid what Kaiden thought was a smile in her drink, not looking at her brother. Basil continued to look confused, until it hit him.

"Wait...!"

"That was the joke," Kaiden explained, trying not to burst out laughing. If he did, they would hear how wrong it was.

"As I said," Olive repeated. "He still seems very determined to get beaten in sparring. I think I should indulge him."

"I think not," Kaiden cut in, forcing his shoulder to shrug. "I'm rather rusty."

"Like a rusted nail," Basil added. Kaiden patted his head again.

"That's more of a simile. But we'll work on it."

Basil expelled a long sigh, though his shoulders seemed to relax further. Rolling onto his back, he grinned up at Kaiden. "Maybe I just want you to correct me," he teased, "so Olive will fight you."

Kaiden forced a noise of disbelief, a hand over his chest. "And I thought you were my friend."

"I am," Basil replied, his eyes crinkling softly, along with his smile. "Nothing's going to change that."

To disguise his reaction, Kaiden looked away, letting out a loud huff. For a moment, his face wanted to crumple, all the emotion spilling loose. How little he deserved it, and how much they shouldn't want him around.

It was easy enough to blink the shadows from his eyes, now. As natural as folding clothes and tucking them into a drawer. He could do this. He wanted to make them smile. They didn't need to see his distress.

Forcing a smile he didn't feel, he eyed his strange friends. "You don't make this easy, do you?"

"What do you mean?" Basil asked, looking up in innocence. "Being your friend?"

Kaiden couldn't stop his frown, rolling his eyes for good measure. "Yes. That's exactly what I meant."

Basil rocked back to a sitting position, his head tipped curiously. "Huh?"

"It was a joke," Kaiden muttered, rolling his eyes again. "I thought you were bright enough to understand those."

For a moment, something different crossed Basil's face, before he smiled a little less enthusiastically. "Who said I wasn't teasing, too?"

Kaiden let out an exasperated sigh. Basil gave him a little grin, shifting to glance over his shoulder at Fern.

It was too much. Watching them there, so relaxed, yet glancing at him carefully every so often, as if worried how he would react. Like he might lash out at them. It made him uncomfortable.

"I should go," Kaiden said abruptly, standing to his feet. "I...need to find Lena."

It wasn't quite a lie, though the rest of the teasing light faded from Basil's eyes. "Ah. Right."

He fiddled with his hands in his lap, quickly standing a moment later. "Hey." His hand fell on Kaiden's shoulder. "Kaiden?"

"Hm?"

Basil's smile was too hopeful, and a little worried, as he followed Kaiden a few steps away from the girls. "Don't leave me alone," he murmured teasingly, half-glancing over his shoulder at them. "I'm outnumbered."

Though he barely felt it, Kaiden forced a small smile. "You'll be fine."

"Hmmm. I'm not so sure about that." He wouldn't quite meet Kaiden's gaze. "I think I should stick with you."

"I think not," Kaiden replied, brushing his hand away and avoiding the slightest wince as he did so. Why couldn't they see how bad this was? He couldn't just...be normal. He was going to hurt them again. Like everyone.

"But you look like you could use the company too," Basil pressed, ever so subtly. "Right?"

Inwardly, he nodded. Outwardly, though, he shook his head. "I'm fine."

"Funny word," Basil murmured after a moment, "'fine.' Doesn't usually mean what we claim it does, yeah?"

Kaiden kept his gaze away, hand curled loosely at his side. "No. It means exactly what I said." Before Basil could stop him, he kept walking, and then hesitated. For a brief moment, it was terribly tempting to change his answer, and tell Basil the truth. Tell him how right he was.

But what good would that do, even if he could manage it? He would just break them, again. As he always did. He'd snap, or crack, and that would be the end of it.

"I'll be back soon," he said carefully, turning so Basil couldn't see the lie in his eyes. "I just need to take care of some things."

Finally having given up, Basil nodded, watching him walk away. "Just..." He hesitated, brow twisting for a moment before it relaxed. "If...you do need something, feel free to ask?"

Without looking back, Kaiden nodded, stifling a laugh that wanted to burn in his throat. "Of course."

Before Basil could dog him further, or actually get the truth from him, Kaiden slipped away. He went to find the one kind of company that wouldn't scold him. Dragons. Resenya rested calmly outside of his room, watching the many other dragons in the sky and on the streets before them.

With a weary sigh, he sank down beside her, pressing his face into her side. Despite the shifting metal of her scales, the warmth was oddly comforting, and he vaguely wondered if he'd done this before.

Though he wouldn't open his mind to her still, he practically felt the rumble in Resenya's throat, and her affirmative. It made sense, with how he felt at the moment. Like nothing mattered, least of all his actions.

What was wrong with him? He couldn't put it in words, or grasp it, or fight it off. It was just...there, looming, and its presence only seemed to grow with each day. A shadow he'd been trying to fight back that now he just...couldn't. Like swinging a sword at mid air. Being unable to touch his opponent, yet being struck by it all the same.

It dragged him down slowly, dully, into a quiet that almost felt like sleep, though he knew that wasn't the case. Resenya eventually laid her head next to him, and he wrapped his arms around her neck, choking out a laugh. Honestly, what was *wrong* with him?

Nothing felt quite real. It all settled on him now, knocked loose by the words and actions and his own failure. Nothing he did was going to make things better, ever. Nothing would be enough. He couldn't even smile at his friends without feeling like he was going to snap.

And he couldn't do that, because they wouldn't understand. They would take it so terribly, and then he would lose them, and...

Resenya huffed a breath in his face, cutting him off for a moment. What was he thinking?

That seemed to be what she was asking, as her dark eyes dug into his. He couldn't even muster a smile, a word — anything. It was all just too...much. He couldn't even let his dragon in anymore, because he was too afraid. Too broken. Too...

A tail lightly flicked his leg. It made a half-smile touch his face, just for a moment.

"Still looking out for me, huh?" He didn't like how heavy his voice sounded.

Resenya huffed again, as if he'd asked a ridiculous question. If he had any more energy, he might have let her in, just for a moment. Just to thank her. He didn't care what it did to him. He should have stopped worrying about that long ago.

But it was all too muddled, still, for him to even try. So he rested his head back against her and let out another quiet sigh, waiting for it to pass.

The kits all found him, soon enough, though even their antics couldn't pull a smile from him. Even as the red one squealed and tussled with Green, a flailing ball of colors amidst the soft grass. Eventually, their play drew the attention of other kits, until the clearing was full of them.

He couldn't even have guessed how much time passed, sitting there with his dragons, Jade settled by him with her hand on his arm. She hummed an offkey tune now and then, as if to distract him. Absently, his fingers played with the uneven stone he kept in his pocket, studying its surface. The past was painfully prominent in his mind, even the marks on his back feeling more present when he rubbed the lighter ones on his arms.

Eventually, footsteps dragged him back to the present. Raoul stood in front of him, his shadow looming far too much for Kaiden's liking as he slowly dragged his eyes up to the man.

"You look like you could use something to do," he said, and Kaiden reluctantly agreed. Though he didn't particularly feel like moving, a small part of him still knew he probably should, anyway.

Smiling, Raoul offered his hand. Kaiden curled his into a fist, before reminding himself that this was *not* a memory and letting the other man help him to his feet.

"What do you need?"

Well. As it turned out, 'something to do' was little more than negotiate with a bunch of rogues in one of the nearby villages – thugs with ugly knives and uglier faces. In light of her weakened source of support from the Cities, the Empress had employed whoever she could to carry out her dirty work. Men under Talon's command controlled them, just as despicable as Talon was with their dragons and misuse of their gifts to frighten others. But these thugs claimed to have a backway into the Cities, as well as valuable information on the Empress.

This was it, Kaiden thought with the smallest spark of hope. Maybe he could find some information for Lena, too, about her brother, and that would make everything right.

It still made his blood boil that they were simply going to *talk* to these men, rather than do something better about it. Though Raoul explained how powerful they were, with the Empress' Gifted backing them, it still wasn't right.

He shouldn't have agreed to go along, in his state. But Raoul had found him at the perfect time – or perhaps the worst one – and despite Jade's warning, he went along with it. This was his chance. His way to make it up to her. Whatever it cost him.

But he knew, deep down, that he was only pushing things aside. As long as he dodged around this, she would dislike him. He saw it in the cold glances she gave him when she passed him by, even as Basil got a protective frown.

"She's just grumpy." Basil had said earlier. *"She's worried about her brother."*

The only living family she still had and cared for. Kaiden remembered discussing them, what felt like so long ago. Her stepsister, and her older brother.

The thought only tightened his chest, thinking of Kelrin. How he had failed them, and was continuing to fail them.

And now, he was only adding to her hurt, too. Reminding her of his lies, and promises he'd never be able to keep.

I want to know, her eyes said, and he couldn't give that to her. He couldn't. It was an entire web of tangled, messy thoughts, and he didn't want to divulge that many of them.

Shaking aside the thoughts, Kaiden followed Raoul away, taking care not to step on any tails or wings, and brushing away the kits that attempted to follow him. This was too secret to have their noisy, nosy selves messing things up.

The mission seemed simple. They were to infiltrate a nearby village — one mostly populated by rogues and other such filth as would never be allowed in the Cities — and find what information they could, to aid the rebellion.

Surely they'd have news on what was happening in the Cities.

As luck would have it, he got his wish. Though not their intended target, he caught sight of two thugs each dragging a young girl against their wills toward the border of the city. When he informed Raoul, he was told that attacking such a large group would be too dangerous, and they'd attempt it at a safer time. But he couldn't just leave them there, to be treated like that. His blood flickered with fire that would not be quelled, coupled with a recklessness he couldn't shake. What did it matter if he got hurt? He'd dealt with worse. He could handle it. He should, because he wasn't weak. He couldn't let them think that. Not ever.

Kaiden's chest tightened, shoulders tensed as he watched how the men treated them. Raoul set a warning hand on his shoulder, which he shook off. They were here to help, right? This was how he could help.

He could get them out, he thought recklessly as a rogue eyed him over. Raoul wasn't paying attention, too focused on the negotiations to notice what else was going on around them. He moved away from the group, walking after the thug.

A knife was flashed in his face, steely eyes glinting. "Stay out of my way, *tava*."

He heard his name, called warningly, and Jade was saying *be careful*, but it hardly mattered to him. Something was stirring in his chest, a pressure built too hard from everything he had experienced, swirling together until...

It happened all at once. The man's buddy came around behind him, as the townspeople shrunk further from the irate rogue. A hand clamped around his wrist, harsh, a knife whizzing through the air by him and nicking his arm. He was shoved away, right into the grasp of the other man, who gave him a solid blow to the jaw. Kaiden would have fell if they hadn't caught him, bending his arm at a dangerous upward angle.

"Stay away," the man hissed in his ear, and Kaiden had to suppress a shudder. They released him, and he thought he saw Raoul relax, but they were still dragging the girls away. "Kaiden," Raoul called, but he wasn't hearing it. The rogue struck at him, only barely missing his cheek as Kaiden dodged away.

Raoul stepped between them, casting a disapproving stare at Kaiden. The rogue scowled and scampered after his buddy, who had already snuck out of the city. Kaiden shook off Raoul's grip, suppressing another, harder shudder. He waited until Raoul was preoccupied once again, breathing in hard, then followed after the men, out of the city.

A part of him said he should have told Raoul the whole story. A part just didn't care. Raoul wasn't listening to him, anyway. And if he waited, who knew what would happen to those girls?

He stayed just out of sight behind a tree, drawing his sword. Before he could act, though, a knife was drawn, the point glinting at him. Without so much as a pause for dramatic flair, the rogue in front of him struck, fierce and fluid in a way Kaiden was barely able to dodge. His blood flowed with adrenaline as he summoned his fire, keeping it just beneath his fingertips.

The blow was sloppy, and entirely unnecessary. He was too close, caught off guard by the harsh impact, and the fire that spread through his ribs soon after. The man let out a curse as he pulled out the knife and stepped away. Kaiden clamped his hand over his side, frowning. The girls were not let go.

He shoved the man away, and regretted it. A sharp pain hit his spine as he drew in breath, an unusual warmth spreading over his hand.

It was like having the wind knocked out of you. You didn't feel much at first, until you tried to breathe and it hurt and nothing worked quite right. His hand instinctively cupped over the wound, a feral grin still peeling his lips as he smiled up at his attacker.

"That the best you can do?"

He dodged the next hit and stumbled, his fingers starting to feel sticky. Dagging rogue. Why couldn't he have minded his own business?

"It *sword* of seems like you have a problem with me, huh?"

Teeth bared, the man swung at him again. Kaiden let his gift flare to life in his hands, responding with a wild grin. It was enough to throw the man off, so the blow glanced off of him. Out here, no one would see, and he could tell these men knew it. Galdanians might not be as in tune to others' suffering, but he was. He had no intention of letting him win this, no matter what it cost him.

Whether it was from his fire or the look in his eyes, the men decided they had enough. They spooked at the sight of it, encouraged in their decision to flee by the little flames Kaiden blew toward them. The girls fled as soon as they were able, sending him grateful glances as they scurried back toward the city. He didn't want to think about what the rogues might have planned for them, or whether they were as scared of him as the rogues were. Either way, they were safe now, and that was what mattered.

Extinguishing his flames, Kaiden looked down at the sticky warmth on his side, ignoring Jade's frown and slipping a hand back over the wound. Wrapping his arms around himself, he headed back into the city, until he saw the group searching for him.

Raoul took one look at him and cursed. "What did you *do?*"

Kaiden waved off their concern, a breathless assurance slipping past his lips. "I'm fine."

"That's not what I asked."

Why couldn't he stand straight? Kaiden let out a laugh that choked hot and bitter in his throat, stinging like the breath in his lungs as he leaned against a moving wall.

Raoul. What was he doing there?

"I'm fine," he murmured again, bracing a hand on his side and flashing them a weak smile. His bones were threatening to give way beneath him, the pain flaring in bursts of color that hurt his eyes. "Just fine."

Raoul didn't look convinced, his gaze going to the wound and narrowing. "Kid," he hissed. "You're *bleeding*. That is not fine."

The world tilted beneath him, but Kaiden held himself up with a hand against the tree, a touch of a grin on his face. He had to be okay, because that was how it went.

"Am I? Huh. Didn't even realize it."

Jade crouched down to examine the wound, that uncharacteristic frown still lurking at the edges of her lips. "Mmhm, sure, you're *just bleeding*. What have I told you about doing awesome stuff? It always results in bad things."

"Exactly," he muttered in response, ignoring the second part.

"Let me see it." She nudged his hand to try to move it away. Reluctantly, Kaiden pulled it back, and frowned. There was more blood than he'd expected.

Jade inspected it and huffed. "You've gotta take better care of yourself, Butterfly. Let's go get this bandaged."

Kaiden blew out a breath, brushing away Raoul's real hands and Jade's phantom ones. "It's fine."

"It is not," Jade responded. "You need some stitches."

Raoul cursed and caught him when the world suddenly tipped over. He tried to brush the man's away, shaking his head. He had to find something. He had to...do something.

"Don't make me carry you," Raoul growled, settling him against a tree. He barked orders to the others, whose words began to swirl in Kaiden's head. He had to move. He had to find Caleb...

He lifted a shoulder in a shrug, but let them support him anyway, so they'd stop worrying. "It's just a scratch. I've had worse." He tipped his lips in a teasing grin.

Raoul was trying to save him, and Kaiden knew with some shame that he had seen the reason Kaiden had done it. It didn't hurt, he told himself, although the sensation of his life slowly eking away, as familiar as it already was, was a little unsettling.

"Just because you've had worse doesn't mean you shouldn't get it fixed," Jade replied, exasperated, but gentle.

In order to not seem entirely insane, Kaiden just nodded, pretending it was in response to Raoul. Jade squeezed his hand, and, with a breath, he squeezed it back, letting a slight sigh escape. He was fine. He'd endured far worse for far longer. It wasn't going to kill him.

And if it did? He wasn't really sure that mattered, either. No one really needed him. He'd helped save someone. Sounded as good a way to go as any.

"You have to take care of yourself better, Butterfly," Jade persisted, though her voice was quieter than usual.

Holding back a wince, Kaiden shook his head. Raoul was trying to move his arm, and he sucked in a breath, pushing him away.

"You do," Jade insisted, tone still subtly softer, but also firm. "You have people who need you around. *I* need you around. You have to be more careful."

Raoul swore hot and sharp. Maybe it was worse than he thought. He took hold of Kaiden's shoulders, firm enough to hold him in place and jolt him back to the present.

"Do you *want* to die?"

It swept over Kaiden in a gray wave, a wash of memories that prompted only the feeblest of laughs from his lips.

"Do you want them to die?

"Well?"

"No," he whispered, and wondered why the simple action hurt so much.

"Then stay still and let me look at it."

Panic filtered through him, then, as Raoul tried to touch him again. He wrapped the jacket tight around himself, even as a gasp flew from his lips. "No."

"Kid." Raoul's eyes narrowed, though his hands stilled. "Either you let me bandage it, or do it yourself." Raoul frowned, his brow softened by concern. "I'm not having you bleeding out on me."

Kaiden's fingers were shaky as he took the bandages, too many memories knocked loose from everything. Dark rooms and burning grips, holding him captive. Too many voices, and touches, and screams. He thought they might be real again, for a moment, staring at his hands.

Raoul turned away, to talk with someone else. With Jade's guidance, Kaiden managed to get his mind under control enough to focus, breathing easier when no one else could see him.

Jade's hands helped him wrap the wound, gently, her forehead creased. Save for the gaping rip in his shirt, and the blood staining it, everything was normal. They wouldn't be finding out his secrets anytime soon.

Feeling dizzy, he pushed himself to his feet, leaning heavily against the tree for a moment before walking carefully over to Raoul, forcing a grin. "All set. I told you it wasn't that bad."

The world teetered for a moment, like it was trying to throw him off balance. He frowned at it, his vision flickering in and out of focus like a shutter adjusting, before he realized what was going on.

"Kid." Raoul's voice faded in and out of his hearing. "You okay?"

"Fine," he whispered, although he didn't feel it. He smiled at the other man, ignoring the ache in the action. "It doesn't even hurt."

Despite his insistence that he was fine, Raoul kept an arm around his shoulders, supporting him as they headed back to the city. "We'll have someone look at it there," he muttered, in a voice that didn't leave room for argument.

XX

LENA

Kaiden wasn't in his room.

I stopped by to see if he was there, to talk to him, but of course he wasn't. His little thief didn't seem to be around, either. Dez chirped from my shoulder, rubbing his little head against me.

I was about to leave when I caught sight of a drawing, set out on the little table. Though I shouldn't have looked, I couldn't help it. There was an entire notebook sitting beneath it, worn with use. Carefully, I cracked it open to find sketches of objects, assumedly from his memory, and scenes I didn't recognize. A short girl with a mess of curls around her face, leaning against a pillar in the Mountain. A fierce spark in his eyes and a light of delight as he sparred with an unknown opponent.

There were other images, too many to name, some of them more ominous than it seemed at first. One that made me smile, at first, was of him cradling a child, before I noticed the shadow looming in the background. He drew arms and hands and marks stretched across them, fingers intertwining, soft things that didn't seem to belong in the madness. Occasionally, there were scribbled notes at the bottom, with a series of lines and dots that I eventually recognized as his name.

There was another piece of wood sitting out on the table, a knife laying open next to it. A small jacket, a messy bed, a neat blanket on the floor that looked far too long for a child. There was a piece of cheese sitting out, and a tiny jewel that I realized, on closer inspection, was actually just a rock.

I couldn't keep being mad at him, as much as I wanted to. Seeing those images was like seeing a piece of me, laid out on the page, and more than anything, I just wanted to see him again. To talk, or joke, like everything was normal. Was that too much to ask?

A displeased squeak answered me. I looked in surprise at Dez, who looked just as wide-eyed back, and shrunk closer to me.

A tiny red dragon hopped onto the table where Kaiden's sketchbook was, hissing. Its little ears flattened, eyes narrowed, and Dez whimpered against me, hiding his little face against my neck. The red kit curled up protectively over the book, eyeing me suspiciously.

I didn't remember Kaiden having a red dragon. Though, I supposed, odder things had happened, as the tiny dragon bared her little teeth at me, a growl rolling through her. If she was any bigger than a kitten, I might have been concerned.

Somewhere in the room, another dragon chirred. I looked toward the sound, catching sight of Ril curled up tight in a chair cushion, watching the red kit. Red grumbled a reply, spreading her wings out over the drawings.

No, not Red. That was a different dragon, apparently, according to them, and he was hiding somewhere in the room. It wasn't his actual name, of course, but they were okay with that.

I began to wonder just how many dragons were scattered around Kaiden's room, and why. I mean, there were quite a few dragons in the drawing he'd done, but I assumed that was just from the influx of dragons we'd gotten in the Cities. It was hard enough not to trip and find a dragon in front of you, now, with all the new arrivals.

There was another squeak from somewhere too close to me, followed by Dez' terrified squeal. A tiny blue dragon perched on the back of the couch and watched us with wide, curious eyes, sidling closer to Dez. He dug his claws into me enough to make me wince, a little shiver running through his tiny body.

Another dragon – they just didn't stop coming, did they? – landed beside the blue one, a larger green kit with mischief in its eyes. Dez dove off my shoulder and plunked on the couch, curling up tight between my arm and side as if he could hide away from them all. I tried to stroke his head reassuringly, or at least some part of him, frowning at the other kits.

The little blue kit looked sad, her squeak getting softer as she inched forward, cocking her head at me. Dez' fear was starting to mess with me, just a bit, and I shook it aside.

"They aren't going to hurt you, Dez."

He whimpered his reply, and I scooped him up to my chest, to the dismay of the other kits, covering his little head. "I won't let them."

He peeked one scared eye out at the other kits and instantly hid it again. I was about to pick up the blue kit, to prove my point, but she hopped up onto my lap anyway, standing as high as she could on stubby legs to see Dez better, and chirped inquisitively. Slowly, I lowered Dez down closer toward her, even as he trembled more.

The green kit watched them from a distance, as if he was more concerned with Dez hurting her than vice versa. Blue reached out a tiny

329

paw to bop Dez's head, chirring curiously. When he still didn't move, she nudged her head against his, a tiny hum rumbling through her chest.

Dez watched her with wide eyes, though he had almost stopped trembling, looking up at me as if for help. In response, I moved my hands away, leaving the two of them to figure it out.

He squeaked in terror, hiding his face with his tiny wing-arms, but the little blue just paused, blinking at him for a moment, and then continued humming more. Red – sorry, the terribly overprotective one watched them both with an expression of satisfaction, as if she had somehow orchestrated this. I didn't even know kit dragons were capable of conveying that emotion so strongly.

Dez continued to look up at me uncertainly as the little blue flopped on her back, looking at him playfully. She was almost his same size, just the slightest bit bigger, and I wondered if that was the only reason he began to relax, hesitantly chirring in reply to her. She flicked him playfully with her spaded tail, squeaking.

I would have continued watching if the window had not slid open then, a small form slipping through it and then stopping, watching me with wide eyes.

"I didn't do it," Joss said automatically, looking around the room and keeping her hands mostly out of view. She cocked her head at the kit dragons and then laughed. "Did he adopt another one?"

There was something pleased and amused in her tone all at once, even though her eyes still seemed slightly nervous at my presence. Leaning against the windowsill, she cleared her throat. "Were you, uh, looking for Kaiden?"

"No. I was investigating a complaint from the bakery. Apparently they keep having goods go missing." Though I couldn't hold back a smile, I nodded to the kits, as if nothing was up. "They suspect the dragons are involved."

Joss' eyes widened and then relaxed in the same moment. She nodded in agreement. "Ah, yeah, you really have to watch out for those kits. They like eating *way* too much."

"Mmhm." I raised an eyebrow at Joss, glancing at her still rather hidden hands. She stayed still for a moment before her eyes narrowed.

"You're making that up, aren't you?"

I turned back toward the kits to avoid smiling again, watching Dez and his friend interact hesitantly. Arms folded over her chest, Joss stalked over to the couch, sitting down hard enough to make the green dragon beside her bounce. "I didn't steal anything," she muttered, eyes

330

fixed on the tiny dragons. "Everyone's too nice. They just...give you things when you ask for them."

"Such a tragedy," I agreed, smiling at Dez. Joss scowled.

"What are you doing here, anyway?" Her gaze swept over the dragons, landing on the mostly obscured notebook. "Ruby doesn't like people prying."

I had to stifle a laugh. "Ruby?"

"Oh yeah," Joss said, smiling. "The others are Blue, Green, Red, and Yellow." She nodded to a dragon I hadn't even noticed, half-buried under a blanket. "There should be a few more around here somewhere."

I must have looked disbelieving, for Joss laughed. "It's true! You should ask Kaiden. He'll tell you the same thing."

"Do you know where he is?"

Joss shrugged, eyeing the window that was still propped open. "Does it look like I do? No. He goes off on his own a lot. Usually to talk with his imaginary friend." She rolled her eyes, though there was a sparkle of teasing to them.

Deciding to ignore that last comment, I stood. "Well, if you see him, you should let him know I want to talk to him." I frowned, scooping Dez up in my hands. He made a dismayed noise, peeking down at his now new friend.

Joss laughed. "Ooh, is he in trouble? I still didn't do it, whatever it is. Thief's honor."

Shaking my head, I walked toward the door. "Mmhm. Sure you didn't."

BASIL

Basil liked long walks. They helped him to think, much like Olive's sparring helped her focus.

And today, especially, with everything that had happened, and the worry he kept trying to tamp down, it helped ground him. Although, he could have sworn Raoul's men kept giving him odd looks. They were probably wondering why the clumsy, barely-Gifted boy was hanging out with a bunch of warriors.

The short answer was: Olive asked him to. And the long answer was, well, *Olive* had *asked* him to. Olive, who rarely asked anyone for anything. Who had spent the last months putting her all into training not only herself, but anyone she could teach. The one person, Basil mused, who might have taken words more seriously than Raoul.

331

He was watching over one of the little girls who liked hanging around him, thinking once again of any potentially useful uses for his gift, when he caught sight of Raoul returning to the camp. His mouth fell open at the severe look on the older man's face, and the fact that Kaiden was leaning heavily against him, a hand clasped lightly on his side.

"Get help," Raoul said lowly, pulling Kaiden into the closest tent despite the boy's mumbled insistence that he was okay.

Before he could move, or even form words, something tugged at his shirt. The little girl beside him looked up with big, earnest eyes.

"I can help," she said hopefully, taking his hand.

Basil shook his head, but she was already wandering into the tent, and since he was supposed to be keeping an eye on her, he was forced to follow. Kaiden was breathing hard, laid out on sheets that his complexion too closely matched. And yet still there was a stubborn set to his eyes as he tried to keep Raoul's hands from touching him.

"I'm *fine*."

"You're not." The little girl, Daya, stood far too calmly for the scene before her, shaking soft curls around her face. "You need help."

For a moment, Kaiden's face turned sick as his eyes met Basil's, as if asking why she was there. He swallowed visibly, his gaze torn back to the ceiling as he covered his side with a red-stained hand. Basil opened his mouth to explain, but no words would come out.

Kaiden tried to sit up, looking at his side as if unaware that was even an issue. "I told you. I'm fine. It doesn't even hurt."

"Quit saying that," Raoul snapped, though not unkindly. "You are not moving." He pushed Kaiden back down, shooting a sharp look at Basil. His concern mirrored Basil's for a moment, and Basil could practically see the frustration trapped on his lips, the guilt from other lives lost, the hurt. Pain made it shine through, transparent, as it usually did with people.

But pain, it seemed, only made Kaiden shut down.

"Watch him," Raoul commanded, brushing past them toward the tent's exit. "I'm going to get help."

"I can help," Daya insisted, though Raoul was already gone. She advanced on the bed like approaching a wounded animal, sitting down next to Kaiden.

"Daya has a healing gift," Basil explained hesitantly, at the same time the girl tried to speak, and frowned at him for his interruption. "She...wants to help."

332

Panic twisted on Kaiden's face for a brief, unbridled moment as he visibly recoiled. "No," he whispered, trying unsuccessfully to back away.

Daya looked hurt for a moment, glancing up at Basil. "I *can* help."

Basil didn't argue. A part of him was just worried to see Kaiden look so ill, despite the fact that Daya was young still and didn't have as strong of a Gift as others would.

But there wasn't anyone else around, was there? Basil couldn't see how bad the injury was, but it was obviously serious enough to concern Raoul.

Daya let out a breath, eyes wide and serious as she regarded Kaiden solemnly. "It will hurt. But it will also help."

Before he could protest, she laid a hand over his and closed her eyes. Basil watched as Kaiden's eyes went wide, panic doused in a twist of pain and then brought back just as quickly as his face contorted, jaw locked shut to unsuccessfully keep back a cry. It was gone in a flash, but the terror remained, his face drained of color as he watched her.

"It's always the hardest first," she explained, as he looked down at his side. "Gotta pull it all together, in one place, to make it easier. So it hurts a lot at once, rather than a little for a long while." She sat down with a smile, holding on a little closer to the bedpost. "Whew."

Kaiden didn't say a word. Basil started to get concerned again.

Daya's brow creased as she rested a hand on his arm, suddenly uncertain. "You okay?"

Basil was wondering the same thing. Kaiden seemed...frozen, something trying so hard to claw its way out of him, his eyes a little too bright amidst the panic.

"Fine."

"Hm." Daya regarded him for a moment longer, her hand twitching a little, and then yawned. She rested her head on the bed next to him, smiling sleepily. Even if she had healed him, it would have taken a *lot* of energy out of her. It was a wonder she hadn't conked out already.

As much as he shouldn't have been proud, Basil was glad the girl had at least shocked some sense into Kaiden. She yawned again when Basil picked her up, rubbing her eyes with her hands as the tiredness descended quicker over her face.

"I helped," she murmured, leaning her head against him. Her words slurred together as she drifted off. "He's okay."

Her breathing evened out quickly. Kaiden's face was pallid as he watched them, stricken with horrified silence. He was hardly breathing, it seemed, his lips parted in a silent sound that was never heard. "Basil...?"

"She's okay." Basil smiled at him. "Promise."

Kaiden shifted his gaze down, his lips wavering, but nodded slowly. His hands tightened at his sides until they were as white as his face. Basil's brow creased, eyes going to Kaiden's side. He was looking down at it and breathing fast, still appearing panicked.

"Are you?"

Kaiden shook his head, fast and sharp as a sound choked from his throat. Basil set the sleeping girl on a chair and came over to sit next to him.

Kaiden's arms flew around him as best they could, soft and fierce all at once and shaking just barely, and more so as he held on tighter, his breath sharp and uneven. Basil held onto him, wanting to ask, but doubting he would get an answer anyway.

It was then Raoul returned, and Kaiden pulled away quickly, swallowing as he looked down at his side. Raoul had another healer with him, the one who had tended to Kinny – though her Gift was far from miraculous. Reluctantly, Kaiden let her look at the wound, which was barely there anymore.

Raoul's brow furrowed, until Basil explained. He looked over at the sleeping girl, disbelief warring in his eyes despite the proof in front of them. Eventually, he nodded.

"I'll stay with him."

Basil hesitated, watching Kaiden, but he did need to get Daya back to her parents, and someone had to tell the others. Including...Lena. That would go splendidly.

"What happened to him?"

Raoul narrowed his eyes, explaining the situation. Kaiden was back to frowning, though there was still the slightest spark to his eyes that he didn't seem able to shake.

Scooping Daya back into his arms, Basil sighed. "Well...just keep me updated." He glanced over at Kaiden, pressing his lips together. "Daya said he should be okay, though."

"As long as he doesn't decide that himself and get up before he's fully healed," Raoul muttered, casting a look at the bed. "Which is why I'm going to stay."

Basil nodded, shifting Daya better in his arms before he left the tent. Why did he keep trying to prove himself like this? Unnecessarily putting himself in harm's way, and then trying to brush it off as if it were little more than a scratch?

Basil sighed. He understood *why*, but it was still frustrating. Even though he hadn't been able to tell as much before, he could see now, since Kaiden wanted them to see, that he was trying. Even as he disguised it, and made an easy joke with a bright smile, Basil saw that spark behind it, that glimmer of hopefulness that it had done some good.

He knew the feeling. After their parents' deaths...Basil felt the need to make up for it, too. It wasn't his fault, and Olive would probably hurt him if she knew he thought it, but a small part of him still wanted to rationalize it. If he'd just been like the other boys, and learned to fight. If he'd scouted, or kept a better eye out, rather than playing with the younger kids. If he'd somehow managed to convince his mother not to sell her wares that day, or his father to stay with them. Maybe they'd still be alive.

It hurt worse, realizing how much all of them had lost. Basil had lost his parents, but he couldn't even imagine losing Olive. She was his other half, his *better* half, and without her, he thought he might feel as lost as Kaiden looked.

Even Chan had hinted at having a sibling, once. *Once.*

Such a painful word, when you thought about it. Once they had been happy. Once he'd had a family. Once...

Once, they had been whole.

They'd just have to make a new family, in its place. Even if it wasn't said, they needed each other, more than he thought any of them would ever put into words.

KAIDEN

Kaiden couldn't have slept if he wanted to. But Raoul wasn't going to leave him be until he at least seemed like he was. Using all his control, he shut his eyes and fought back the images that bombarded him, drawing on all his tricks to pretend he was asleep, before slowly, painfully evening his breath out. He hoped Raoul couldn't hear his heart pounding in his chest like it still wanted to rip out of him.

Kinny.

Once Raoul gave up, and left the room, Kaiden let his eyes fly back open, gasping in a breath. It wanted to choke and curl into a sob, but he held it back, forcing all the things in his mind into their proper places. Slotting memories back into place and locking them down, praying they wouldn't get back out. It left him exhausted.

"She has a healing gift."

Kaiden's mouth was a scorching desert, the dryness burning in his throat. He couldn't even speak when she came over, a small, gentle smile on her face as she laid a hand on his arm.

335

He couldn't stop seeing her collapse, chestnut hair turned a bright red as she laid on the ground, pale and unmoving. Because of him.

No. No, no, no...

The pain sucked a breath from him and gathered in one spot, finally ripping a cry from his throat. It sounded like a plea to him, but he was choking on it, and he could barely move. He felt chained to the bed, forced to watch it over and over again, like he did in his dreams. Like Damien had made him, again and again. Made him run through the scenario until he wanted to scream, because there was *nothing* he could do. Kinny always tried to heal him. He couldn't stop her.

He couldn't save her.

Just let me die, he'd whispered, holding her close. It was a cruel, cruel reminder that in the end, she still didn't survive. He couldn't save her before. And now, he never would.

And why? Because he was foolish, and weak, and couldn't fight against the Bane. Because he'd taken a chance and it had turned out to be terrible. It had cost her life.

He had cost Kinny her life.

And that wasn't even the end. The worst part, the twisted knife in the wound was the last words he ever said to her. He remembered them clearly, even though her written words seared in his mind assured him she wasn't upset. She knew it wasn't him.

It still didn't change what he'd done. It didn't change the fact that he'd hurt the one person he spent so long trying to protect.

He'd hurt them all, in one way or another. He didn't understand why they still wanted him around.

Please, he'd whispered, and Damien did nothing. He'd begged, screamed, made reckless promises that Damien didn't even deign to answer.

Just like with Gigi.

It left something sharp and hot in his chest, burning long after the girl left. He still felt pale, like he was shaking all over.

It doesn't hurt, he lied to himself. *It never does.*

The lashes never did. The blows, the words, the scars in dark places and open ones in the light. The ones on his skin, and the ones on his heart.

"Are you okay?"

Kaiden stilled, looking over at where Basil sat beside him again, concern creasing his brow. Hadn't he left? Had he imagined that?

"Of course."

Basil didn't seem convinced, a funny tilt to his lips as he watched Kaiden. "You got stabbed."

"So?"

For a moment, Basil just looked at him, until it clicked. "Most people aren't just 'fine' after that."

"I'm special," he said with a grin already slipping through, though he didn't feel it at all. "Besides, it wasn't very sharp. Sort of like me for letting it happen in the first place."

Basil sighed, looking away. His fingers tapped each other nervously. "Lena won't be happy."

"She never is," he replied quietly, and frowned at how vulnerable it sounded. "She's mad at me."

"Because she cares." Basil shifted in his seat, running through his words. Finally, he shrugged. "She was furious with me last week because I cut my hand trying to carve some...strange fruit Fern found. That's just what she does." He shrugged a shoulder, half-smiling as if trying to imitate Kaiden. "It's how she shows she cares."

Despite the fact that it wasn't bleeding anymore, Kaiden settled a hand over his wound, trying not to frown. When he didn't respond, Basil continued on.

"It's a funny way of showing it, I know. Much like...well, Fern makes cakes for people. And you...smile."

Kaiden was caught off guard by that, an unsettling feeling at being known so well. "I don't."

"It's in your eyes." Basil took a breath, quietly, looking away as if to gather himself, or give himself time to deliberate. He nodded to Kaiden. "Like that. That little...half thing, like you don't actually want people to know it's there."

Kaiden sat there quietly, watching the ceiling and contemplating it. Basil gave him a moment, which only made him more unsure. "I'm fine," he whispered again.

Basil gave him a half-smile, the edge of it slightly sad. "Are you?"

Too quickly, he knew, Kaiden shook his head.

"You don't have to prove yourself, you know," Basil said softly.

Kaiden turned his head so Basil couldn't see, swallowing. He hated to be confined here, in this bed, and interrogated. He'd almost rather have Lena yell at him.

"You don't have to hide it from me. I know she's mad."

"She is," Basil agreed. "But there's more to it than you think."

BASIL

Kaiden seemed supremely uncomfortable, rubbing a spot on his arm. It wasn't the first time Basil wondered if he had done all this on purpose.

What are you trying to prove?

That he was good enough? That he was sorry? Maybe the others couldn't see it, but Basil read it as clear as a book, right on his face. The wide grins and the endless jokes, the laughs and hopeful smiles, wishing they'd return them. Practically begging, with that expression. Like if they would just smile, too, everything would be right. He'd relax a little, just slightly, and that, more than anything, was what made Basil smile.

He wondered if Kaiden knew how much showed on his face. Intentionally or not, it was what had first convinced and relaxed Basil. The little smile and the earnest, pleading spark in his eyes. Maybe Chan couldn't see it, but Basil could.

And if he pushed too hard, he saw the change, and if not, the regret. The slight dismissal and softer grin, to assure them he was alright.

Basil couldn't help but smile, even as Kaiden frowned at him and refused to meet his eyes.

He didn't want to let Kaiden know, but Lena would surely be coming soon to yell at them both. Basil had gotten away purely with the excuse of caring for the little girl who had healed Kaiden. Now, he was just trying to keep his friend distracted, and maybe get him to smile.

And that was when Lena came storming in, their half-second of peace shattered by the low, furious look in her eyes.

He'd caught the approaching footsteps a moment before Kaiden did, preparing himself for the scolding he knew Kaiden was about to get. The more she cared, the louder she was. And she was definitely about to get loud.

Her eyes cut between the two of them, landing squarely on Kaiden. Her expression went rigid, as did her entire posture.

"What did you *do?*"

Kaiden still wouldn't look at her, though, and Basil winced inwardly at the hurt he saw sear across her face. She stifled it quickly, turning to look at him with a hard gaze. "Tell me."

He wouldn't, though his shoulders lost a little of their rigidity. She pulled his chin over so he had to look at her. "Kaiden."

His face was unreadable, a mask of quiet loss and defiance. But just below the surface and out of sight, his resolve crumbled.

Lena pulled away, hurt. "Fine," she said, though it was anything but. "Be that way."

His shoulders fell once she turned away, though he didn't look over at her, regret written across his face like a five page apology. It crumpled to desperation a moment later, something aching bright in his eyes before he brushed it away.

Basil stood up, throwing a little apologetic smile at Kaiden as he slipped past Lena out of the tent. They wouldn't get anything worked out with him there, and Lena was more than capable of keeping Kaiden out of trouble. He just hoped, for everyone's sake, that they'd be able to work things out okay.

KAIDEN

Once Basil left the room, Lena turned her barrage on him again. "What were you *thinking*?"

He looked down, frowning at the sheets. What *had* he been thinking? He didn't rightly know.

"You're an idiot," she said, scowling. He couldn't argue with that. "What did you think you were going to accomplish?"

I was trying to help, he thought, and frowned. "Nothing."

She turned away. "Idiot," she muttered under her breath. Then, she sighed. "How bad is it?"

He lifted a shoulder and let it fall just as soon. "It's fine."

"No, it's not fine. Did you even *think* about your actions?"

No, he admitted. But he wouldn't say it aloud.

"Of course you didn't," she continued on bitterly. "And I know what you did, so don't try to tell me you thought it was a 'good idea'. Did you even stop to think about the fact that they still need you? That I might need you?" Lena let out a hard breath. "Do you really think I want to explain to Fern how you went off and got yourself killed for *real* this time, all because you were being stupid?"

It confirmed a small, sinking feeling inside him. She didn't care. She never actually had.

He couldn't stop the words from slipping then, like sock-covered feet on a frozen lake. "You don't need me."

She laughed. "Shows how much you know. You can't go off and keep getting yourself injured and giving everyone a heart attack."

"I...didn't think you'd care."

"I don't," she snapped. Despite his reiteration of that, the words stabbed his chest. "But I still need you alive."

"I was looking for information on your brother," Kaiden forced out, too much of the desperation escaping with the bitterness. "I was trying to help."

His voice got hushed at the end. She looked at him as if she'd never seen him in her life before. "You what?"

Kaiden looked away, a slight frown on his face. "You heard me."

She shook her head, a laugh stuck on her lips as she blinked at him, then shook her head again. "You're joking."

He buried his fingers into his palms, jaw tightening. "Yes."

Now she frowned, turning to face him better. "It wasn't a good joke."

"I wasn't trying to make you laugh," he said bitterly, and noted how it made her shoulders go rigid. It wasn't his intention, but it happened anyway. She stood, her eyes flashing fire for a moment.

"I know what you did," she said lowly, trying not to spit the words out. "Basil told me the whole thing." Wincing, he braced himself. "How you recklessly risked your life...to save those girls." Frowning, she folded her arms tight over her chest. "Idiot."

He didn't know what to say. Lena took an unsteady breath.

"There were better ways, you know." She looked at him pointedly, and he again got the feeling that she was talking about something different. "Someone could have helped you."

And the way she stressed the words, ever-so-slightly, made it click. "I didn't...think they would," he admitted.

She looked away, hurt flashing through her eyes. "Of course you didn't," she bit out, words unconvincing. "Because you don't think about anyone else."

He bit his lip hard, looking down at the sheets. "I'm sorry," he whispered, eyes slipping shut. "I..."

"Don't bother," she replied, getting to her feet. "It obviously doesn't matter."

He held back a wince as she walked out, her words stinging more than he thought they would. *That isn't why.*

But he couldn't say any of it. She wouldn't believe him even if he did.

From her spot beside him, where she had been unusually quiet, Jade squeezed his hand. "I think you just scared her, Butterfly."

Finally, he let a frown show. "Yeah. Scared. That's why she wanted to yell at me."

"People yell more when they're scared. Why would she care if you got hurt otherwise? If she didn't care, she wouldn't have bothered to come in here and yell because you had gotten hurt."

His brow creased in discomfort. "Because..." A quiet laugh escaped, and he shook his head again.

"Because?" She brushed her thumb against his hand, cocking her head at him. When he didn't reply, she brushed his bangs from his face. "I can't help if you don't talk to me, kid."

He let out a sigh, shifting his arms closer to himself, and then rubbed the back of his neck. "You heard her. She's just mad."

"I'm sure lots of people have thought you were just mad when it was something more." Quietly, she shrugged.

He couldn't stop his shoulders from tensing, curling a hand in the sheets as he looked away. "She doesn't know that."

"And maybe you don't know all of what's behind her anger, Kaiden. Just talk to her. She might surprise you."

"I've caused enough trouble," he replied, quieter. Because it was true.

"Talking to someone isn't causing trouble, Butterfly. It's healing the rifts."

He rubbed a hand over his face, sighing out quietly. "That's gone well before."

Jade rested a hand on his arm. "Nothing will ever get better if everyone doesn't try."

"I can't." Ashamed, he shut his eyes. "It's too much."

Jade shifted to lay down next to him, looping an arm behind her head. "What is?"

Faintly, he shrugged, breathing out lowly. "Everything."

Jade moved her other hand to rest on his arm again, too gentle. "It'll work out. You'll see."

He breathed out a laugh. "You can say that." Quiet, he rubbed an arm over his face. "I...can't."

"Then I'll say it for you." Jade nudged his chin, gently. "I always want to be here to tell you stuff will get better when you can't think it for yourself. That's what best friends are for."

He let her words sink in for a moment before turning to hug her, overwhelmed.

Jade grinned slightly, slipping her arms around him gently. "Careful there. Don't agitate the wound or anything."

"I'm fine," he replied, half teasing, half out of instinct. The damage was mostly gone by this point, anyway, thanks to Basil's friend.

Jade didn't seem convinced. He shrugged a shoulder, smiling out of the side of his mouth. "I'm always fine. Obviously."

"I think I would lose best friend points if I believed that. No one is fine all the time."

341

He let a chuckle escape. "Guess I'm the first, then."

Though she shook her head, Jade grinned. "Mm. I don't think so."

LENA

It only took me a few minutes to realize my mistake, and head back to the tent. The last time Kaiden had gotten hurt, he'd tried to brush it off even when he was about to keel over. Though I'd been told it wasn't serious any longer, he *did* still need to rest to let his body finish the rest of the work. And he wasn't liable to do that if he was unsupervised.

I shook my head, frowning, and only half-brushed it aside. He was too much like a child sometimes. Too stubborn, and reckless. What if it *had* been serious? What if no one else had been around? I locked my jaw so tightly it burned, taking a moment outside the tent to compose myself. *Idiot.*

Kaiden looked surprised to see me again so soon, and then regretful, glancing away. I took a seat by the bed, my posture stiff.

"Someone needs to watch you," I muttered, cutting him a look. "Since you're so dagged set on acting like an idiot all the time. And I still need you alive, for the time being. So guess what? You get a babysitter."

He frowned, still not looking my way. Something flickered through his eyes that I had trouble naming, even as it made my chest tighten.

"I don't need one," he muttered.

"Obviously you do, with the stunt you pulled today. Do you think I don't know *why* you did it?"

He lifted glittering, wearily defiant eyes to mine. Unapologetic.

And it was then it hit me. He really *didn't* care about himself. His disregard for his own well-being was clear enough in his actions, but this took it to an entirely new level. His eyes almost challenged me, daring me to tell him differently.

"I still need you," I snapped, trying not to respond to the look in his eyes. "Caleb's trapped in the Cities, and I need a way in. I need someone who knows how to lie, and act like something they're not. You're the best liar I know."

A faint smile touched his face. "I'm not quite sure that's a compliment."

"It isn't. But it makes you useful."

He only nodded, a fraction of the burden lifting from his eyes. I frowned, continuing on.

342

"There's a ball that happens every year, a week from now. I can get us into it. You'll have to dress like a Galdanian, and act like one, so we aren't discovered."

He nodded again.

"It won't be fun. Or easy."

He smiled in a way that said it didn't matter. It made me want to scowl, a million words rising in my chest that I could never say.

"No one else can know about this, understand? With everything going on with Sari and the dragons...they don't need to worry further." Frowning, I looked away. "They'd only want to come along, and would get hurt."

Kaiden looked tired again, though I wondered how much of that was actually from the incident. "So you want *me* along instead."

"Don't turn this on me," I shot back. "You're the one who got my father killed."

From the look in his eyes, I might as well have struck him right across the face, though he rubbed at his eyes to disguise it. I frowned.

"Sorry. That was out of line."

"No," he replied, a smile tipping his lips. "You're right." He scrubbed at his eyes again, letting out a frustrated breath. "You have every right to be mad."

I kept silent, watching as he laid on his side, away from me. A million words pressed at my lips, wanting to get out.

"Why did you leave?"

He lifted his head to smile at me, a bitter, flickering thing that played havoc with his eyes. "I was scared."

I wanted to laugh, even as he shut his eyes. "Scared of what?"

But either he was ignoring me, or the sedative they'd given him had kicked in. Biting my tongue, I reached over to take his hand and squeeze it briefly, frowning.

"Idiot," I muttered. "You never should have left."

I wanted to be mad at him. I hated that it was failing. Now that he couldn't see, I was sure my eyes showed far too much, the fear flickering in me like a candle's frantic dance in a breeze. Even if I'd wanted to, I couldn't tell him how much it terrified me. How hard it had pounded through me as I made my way over here, not knowing what I was going to find.

He'd left just after our sparring match. By the time I'd gotten over myself and went to make sure he was alright.... Well. Obviously he wasn't.

"Don't you dare leave again," I muttered, looking away from him. Why did he have to be so stubborn? Brave wasn't even a good word for

343

it, considering his actions. He really didn't think it mattered. And I might have contributed to that. It made my stomach twist further, in a mess of guilt and anxiety. I couldn't just change at a snap of my fingers. I couldn't just push open a door and let him in. It was far messier than that. And though it hadn't gone badly with Basil, so far...it still worried me. Being myself. Not hiding behind...everything. Not snapping at people *because* I cared about them, not making them think I didn't care...

It got a little harder to breathe, the further it settled in. That I was the reason that he was hurting. That I kept making things harder on him, and blaming him, and using it as an excuse to disguise my own shortcomings.

Sometimes the words that aren't said hurt more than the ones that are.

Taking a deep breath, I squeezed his hand, doing my best to keep my voice from sounding too gruff. "Kaiden?"

He still didn't respond. I brushed a finger over the gem of my earring, gathering all my courage and squeezing his hand again. "Beanhead."

At his silence, I shut my eyes, warring with a frown. "If you're ignoring me, I'm not going to be happy." My shoulders sank a little as I looked over at him. "But even if you won't face me...I'm sorry. I'm still mad at you, but I'm sorry...I made you do it. I was..." I frowned, glancing away. "I shouldn't have done it, no matter the reason. I should have listened to my instinct. Shouldn't have just...left you, without making sure you were okay. Some friend I turn out to be, huh?"

Huffing a quiet laugh, I shook my head once. "I'm not good at this, if it wasn't obvious. But...I meant what I said. I do need you. Possibly...not just for the reasons I gave." I cleared my throat, glancing at him again. He still hadn't moved, which made it a little easier to speak. "You're a good person. Much better than I am. I'd hate to lose you. We all would," I added quickly, inwardly sighing. "So...if you've heard any of this, you should know...I *do* care. I just have a hard time showing it." Slipping my hand from his, I stood to my feet. "And if you haven't heard any of this...I guess I'll just have to tell you later. 'Cause you deserve that. We all need a little help along the way, right?"

When he still didn't respond, I took in a breath, watching him for a moment. "See you later, Beanhead."

XXI

KAIDEN

He hardly remembered falling asleep. The soup they'd made him drink must have been laced with something, he reasoned, trying to reopen his heavy eyelids. But they'd already taken care of most of the wound, and it wasn't like he needed it for the pain. Maybe it was just their way of trying to get him to stay put.

He looked over at Jade and couldn't help smiling, even though he was only half-awake.

Yeah. They definitely drugged him.

Jade grinned. "Hey there. You look sleepy."

"I'm not," he mumbled, rubbing at his eyes.

She laughed, a bright and happy sound. "Your face says differently."

Dagged healers. They didn't know what they were doing, obviously. He didn't need more sleep, and especially not like this.

A little blue dragon landed on him curiously, and he smiled at her too. "Hello."

Jade chuckled, amused. "You're cute sleepy, kid."

He shifted down so Blue could curl up next to him, rubbing her head absently. "No."

"You arrrre. You've always been cute, since you were a tiny kid. Duh."

"I'm not trying to be."

"I know you're not. That's part of what makes it cute." She smiled back, eyes sparkly.

He couldn't seem to stop smiling, even though a part of him wasn't very happy at the healers still. Blue squeaked, rubbing her head into his hand.

Jade grinned at him, eyes twinkling fondly. "You've always had a nice smile. You should smile like that at Lena and then she wouldn't scold you as much." She winked.

He shook his head, petting Blue and failing to hide his smile, ducking his head down. "I doubt it."

"Well, I still think it is."

He rubbed an arm into his eyes, his brow creasing. "Why?"

"Why do I like it? Because I like seeing you happy, kid. I've spent as long as I can remember trying to make sure you're as happy as you can be during all this insanity, and these brief moments where you just *smile* are why. I like seeing you happy." Jade paused and made a face, wrinkling her nose. "And yikes, that probably sounds super mushy and cheesy."

Kaiden smiled, looking down for a long moment before shaking his head. "No," he murmured. "It doesn't."

Jade returned the smile, softer. "No? Well good. I wouldn't want to be considered mushy and cheesy. That's like...cheese that's been set out in the sun for ages. Gross."

A laugh left his throat. "You're just getting more ridiculous."

Jade flipped her hair over her shoulder. "I do not get more or less ridiculous. I have been steadily ridiculous since the day I was born."

He couldn't hold back a laugh, fondness slipping into his tone. "Is that so?"

"Yep, pretty much," Jade replied, grinning.

Lena stepped into the tent then, a frown marring her face. He blamed the drugs that he didn't hear her come in.

"What are you smiling at?" She glanced around the room as if she was missing something.

Try as he might, he couldn't get it to leave, subtly nudging Jade's arm with his own. "Nothing."

Jade returned the gesture, teasing. "I'm nothing now, huh?"

Lena frowned, deciding to leave it be. "I got everything settled for our...trip."

He hesitated, briefly surprised she still wanted him along, but nodded. "That's good."

"It'd be better if you hadn't gotten yourself injured." She settled down in a chair by the bed, eyes going to his side. "How is it?"

He shrugged a shoulder, glancing down. "It's f-" On seeing her look, he stopped. "It's healing."

"How come she gets an 'It's healing' and I get a 'It's fine'? I think I should practice my looks more." Jade adopted an exaggerated version of Lena's expression. He coughed to disguise a laugh, flashing her a brief look. They did *not* need to repeat the incident with Chan. Especially not with Lena.

Speaking of, Lena was still frowning. "As long as it's good in time." She stopped, adding in a mutter, "I still don't understand why you had to be an idiot and let that happen anyway."

Jade looked at him innocently, which didn't help his composure. He rubbed the back of his neck, fighting off a smile. "It will be."

Lena followed his gaze for a moment, shaking her head. "Idiot," she muttered again, leaning back in the chair. He could see the tension still written in her posture, the worry faintly creasing her brow.

Hesitating, and hoping he wouldn't regret it, Kaiden picked up one of the drawings he had done earlier, holding it out to her. "This is for you."

With a look close to exasperation, Lena took it, a brief change flickering over her face when she looked down at it. Wordlessly, she folded the paper up and tucked it in her pocket.

After a moment, she pulled in a sharp breath. "I don't want to fight anymore, okay? There's too much at stake for that." Her voice almost sounded strained, getting quieter. She rubbed an arm over her eyes. "I don't need explanations. I understand, a lot more than you would think. Just...don't do it again. Alright?" She fixed her gaze on him, stern. "*Anything* like this. You're too important to lose."

Clearing her throat, she glanced away. "For the mission, of course. I couldn't do it alone."

He nodded, keeping his gaze down.

"I'm still mad at you," she clarified, frowning. "I just don't have time to waste on this. Help me get my brother back, and we'll call it even."

He pet Ril absently, thinking her words over. Lena shifted on her feet, looking uncomfortable for a moment.

"I should...get back to work."

He tried to read her expression, subtly, but it was clear she was still mad at him. He just...hoped he could make up for it, somehow.

"Okay."

At the entrance to the tent, Lena paused. "Don't make me regret leaving you unsupervised," she warned, just before she ducked out.

Jade shifted onto her back beside him, chuckling. "I think she liked it."

He rubbed the back of his neck, fighting down a small spark of hope. "She didn't...seem as mad, at least."

"She definitely didn't." Jade grinned widely. "I keep telling you stuff will work out."

"Hm. Maybe."

Jade chuckled. "Half-agreement. I'll take it."

"It's the best you've gotten."

"Yes, it is. I should throw a celebration." She winked. "With cake and confetti."

Embarrassed, he buried his face in his arm. "Because I partially agreed with you...?"

"Yes! It's celebration worthy."

"What would you ever do if I actually agreed?" he mumbled, mostly to himself.

Jade laughed. "Fireworks."

He peeked out at her, trying to appear unaffected. "And how, exactly, would I explain *that* one?"

Jade's eyes got mischievous. "You'd think of something."

"You just *want* me to look insane, don't you?"

"You could deny all knowledge and participation." She grinned.

"I could. They'd probably still blame me, though. Being, you know, *fireworks*." Jade looked thoughtful. He gave an exasperated sigh. "See? You *are* trying to make me look insane!"

Jade shook her head with a grin, changing the subject. "I think you should nap some more so you finish healing before Lena decides to come back and give you The Look." She recreated her expression from earlier.

He sighed, trying not to laugh. "I'm fine." Funny, how easily those words slipped from his mouth. He was too used to them. Shaking his head, he half-smiled at her. "They took care of most of it already." And he didn't have much desire to sleep, still. Lena's words kept playing in his head, refusing to leave him alone.

JOSS

Joss peeked her head into the tent just in time to hear her bodyguard talking to 'himself' again.

"Well, you didn't *say* that," he exclaimed to the open air, sounding huffy. "You said ornery in the most lovable way possible. Like ornery was somehow still a good thing."

Joss fought down a smile as she slipped in. He certainly *sounded* like he was doing better, at least.

Kaiden adopted a mock hurt expression. "How? I don't think you're ornery." He stuck his lips out in a pout, seemingly uncaring that Joss could see it. "Do *you* think I'm ornery?"

Joss raised an eyebrow, hopping up onto the bed next to him. "Hmm. Right now?" She looked around, wondering where Jade was, and schooled a grin. "Yeah."

Kaiden's shoulders fell, his expression turning dejected. "You're not supposed to agree with her."

Joss laughed, still not fully over how comfortable he was talking to thin air in front of her. He was a funny one, that was for sure.

As if answering her unspoken question, Joss felt a telltale breath tickle her hair, grinning. "Hey, Jade."

Kaiden collapsed on his back dramatically, sighing at the ceiling. "Betrayed." After a moment, he looked over at where Jade assumedly was. "Not you. You're the one who started all this."

Joss still had to grin, dropping down onto her stomach. "He means me," she said, even though she couldn't hear Jade.

The 'wind' tickled Joss' cheek again. Kaiden pouted more. "That doesn't make it any better!"

Joss briefly wondered if they'd given him anything for the pain, or just to make him cooperative. She knew some mixes had rather funny side effects. Like making you act like an overgrown child, apparently.

She propped her chin in her hands, laughing. "Of course it does." She batted her eyelashes adoringly. "I'm too cute to be mad at."

"Too ornery?" Kaiden replied, even though he wasn't looking at her.

"Hey!" Joss sat up, offended. "I'm not ornery! *You're* the ornery one!"

He hid his face in his hands, as if embarrassed. "Not *you*."

Joss huffed, though if he were looking, he would see the sparkle to her eyes. "Well it sure sounded like you were talking about me. And if you weren't, then you were talking about Jade, and that's not a very nice thing to say to your not-imaginary friend."

Kaiden let out a groan, burying his face further in fake despair. "They're teaming up against me."

Joss eyed the tiny kit dragons sleeping nearby, glancing where she assumed Jade was with a mischievous smile. While Kaiden was distracted, she picked up one of them, lightly dropping it on his side.

Kaiden startled, eyes wide as he looked up at her and the kit, and then relaxed. The kit squeaked at him, cutely confused, and promptly snuggled against him, falling back asleep.

Holding her stomach, Joss fell back on the bed, laughter pouring out of her as she pointed away. "It was her!"

Kaiden finally laughed, looking between the two of them before he reached over to tickle Joss lightly, smiling. Her laughs turned into gasps as she squirmed away, rolling into a ball. When she had an opening, she tried to retaliate, chest heaving with laughter.

Kaiden moved away from her reach, grinning, though there was something slightly different to his eyes for a split second. He gave her a moment to rest, looking over at Jade teasingly.

Joss clutched her stomach, gasping in breath and huffing at him for moving away. In one fluid move, she sprung up to tackle him, half-latching onto his back and attempting to tickle him again. There was something funny pressing into her arm from beneath his shirt, making it feel all uneven.

Just for a moment, her bodyguard tensed, though he grinned as he reached up to try to pull her off. Joss could have sworn she saw something different to his eyes before he tickled her again, smiling. "Hey."

She squirmed away, pouting up at him. "You're not ticklish?"

Chuckling, Kaiden laid back down. "No. Not really."

Something wasn't quite adding up, though she could tell at least that it made him uncomfortable. "How come?"

He looked away, shaking his head and half-smiling. "I dunno."

But he did, and just didn't want to tell her. Which was okay. People were entitled to their secrets.

"So, what are the scars from?"

His head shot up, eyes wide. Joss gestured at his arm.

"Unless those aren't the only ones."

Kaiden hid a laugh, as unsteady as it was. "Stupid things I've done before. Are you hungry?"

It was an evasive tactic, but a dagged good one. "Am I ever not?"

Kaiden grinned, doing an unnervingly good job at hiding his previous discomfort, as if it were never there. "You should go steal us some cake," he whispered, only half-teasing in his tone. "Since I am confined here and Lena might kill me if I try to get up."

Joss grinned. "Well, I doubt she'd kiss you for it, but I don't think she'd kill you." She looked up, eyes sparkling to hide her delight at the fact that he was *suggesting* she steal.

If Kaiden looked surprised, he shook it off quickly, chuckling. "I sent one of the kits to fetch some earlier, but all I got was a clawful of crumbs and a very sheepish dragon."

Joss wrinkled her nose. "That's why you don't trust kit dragons. Greedy little cake-stealers." She slid off the bed, headed to the door before he could admit he was joking. Being asked to steal was an opportunity Joss never took lightly.

Kaiden laughed, though whether it was at her or Jade, Joss wasn't sure. "No, she really isn't," he said.

"I heard that!" Joss called back as she disappeared out of the tent. Served him right for talking about her to a ghost person.

KAIDEN

Kaiden watched in amusement when Joss ducked back into the tent not too long after, part of the cake already in her mouth as she practically leapt up onto the bed. Situating herself nearly behind Kaiden, she set down two other plates. "Hide me," she said, voice muffled in his shirt.

From beside him, Jade laughed, reaching over to pull one of the plates closer to her. "Are there angry hoards coming behind her over a few pieces of cake?"

Most likely, Kaiden thought, grinning at the girl and the entrance to the tent. She shoved more cake into her mouth, watching it intently.

A moment later, he saw what the trouble was. A figure peeked into the room, immensely large and terrifying as it looked at them with wide, adorable eyes.

A kit dragon. Kaiden couldn't hold back a laugh, looking over at Joss. Of course that would be what she'd be concerned about. She could face down angry men twice her size and take on a storm like it was nothing, but she couldn't handle the cuteness of kit dragons.

"Oh yes, the most terrifying of all hoards. Horror of horrors. *Kit dragons.*"

The kit chirred hopefully, peeking up at Joss with droopy eyes. She elbowed Kaiden lightly, eyes narrowed. "It wants my cake," she grumbled, sticking a large piece in her mouth and looking to where the other plate vanished. "Remind me to add your not-imaginary friend to a list of potential cake-stealing suspects."

Kaiden wanted to add that *she* deserved a place on that list, too, but he didn't want to get hit again. He grinned as the little kit dragon flew over to them, orange scales glinting in the dim light.

"Hey now, I wouldn't ever steal her cake. Rude!" Jade leaned over to blow at Joss' bangs indignantly.

Kaiden laughed, taking a bite of his cake. Joss looked up, confused. "What?"

Trying not to grin, Kaiden leaned over to whisper to her. "Jade wants to steal your cake."

Though Joss eyed him suspiciously, she shoved the rest of her piece in her mouth, clearly not taking any chances.

After a moment, Kaiden held back a laugh, looking away from her. "Aw, don't pout, Jade. There will always be more cake."

Joss swiped a part of his, tossing a tiny piece to the dragon and stuffing the rest in her mouth, a too-pleased expression on her face.

"I'm not talking to you," Jade huffed.

Pouting, Kaiden drew Joss into a hug. She looked up at him, confused.

"Okay. What did you do?"

"Nothing," he huffed. Jade nudged him with her foot, but said nothing.

Joss raised a lone eyebrow. "If she's mad at you, I think you deserve it."

He held her closer, pouting more. "I didn't do anything."

"Ah-huh." Joss didn't sound convinced, shifting in his arms. After a long moment, she squirmed free, giving him a weird look.

"Okay, yeah, that's enough cuddling. I'm going to go make trouble." She gave him an only half-teasing look, slipping off the bed and out of the tent before he could stop her.

XXII

KAIDEN

He hated being confined to a bed. Despite the healer's insistence that Daya had only *helped* him, and not entirely fixed everything – therefore prolonging the time he needed to rest – the week still dragged on, agonizingly slow. He began to wonder if this was all part of Lena's plan, to keep an eye on him until she needed him. If she could tell how much he disliked it, it might have also been payback. He wasn't quite sure.

Lying around all day gave him way too much time with his thoughts, which was still a little terrifying. He became immensely grateful when Fern stopped by to 'bother' him, after her initial worry, or Basil just sat on the floor and kept him company. Olive threatened to soundly kick his tail at sparring if he did anything so foolish again, though she seemed busier than usual with training Gifted, often sending a message by kit dragon or via her brother instead. He got versions of the same scolding from all of them, in their own ways. Chan was also busy, but clearly worried.

Lena, too, stopped by every so often despite her busyness, on pretense of looking for Basil, or updating Kaiden on varying things. She still got a hard look in her eyes if anyone brought up why he was there. He tried to soften that by giving her more pictures. It wasn't like he had much else to do, stuck in this tent.

He wished they had better memories together. The best he could do for pictures of them was the rare moments in between everything, when there wasn't quite a smirk on his face, or almost a smile on hers. When they were just themselves, chatting over a meal and enjoying the moment. He spent a long time on those, to try to get them right. Getting lost in expressions and thoughts of the past...wondering if it was even worth it, with how little reaction she had to them. A part of him knew there was one, though – she just wouldn't let him see it. He wished she would. There was always the briefest flicker to her eyes, though none of them were as strong as for the one he'd done of her. He'd taken a long time to get that just right, and could only hope beneath everything, she did like it.

Along with pictures, and things he scribbled out beside them, he made a lot of carvings, and played with his pipes softly when others weren't around to hear it. Though they still checked up on him frequently, his lack of escape attempts allowed him a little time with Jade, when they all had things to be doing. He'd moved up from having a constant babysitter, at least.

Now that it wasn't a burden, too, he found some comfort in using his gift, rediscovering old wonders with it and training himself in new ones. He let it play around his fingers, sliding up his arms as far as he dared and relaxing at the warmth. The flickering flames on his fingertips drew curious looks and awed ones from the kit dragons around him. He made them into images, tweaking the fire carefully and painstakingly until it resembled one of the kit dragons. Though it wasn't the easiest to keep a handle on, the kits' reactions to it were worth it.

Oh yes, the kits. If he could connect with them, he might have actually learned their names by now, though he swore the numbers just sort of...grew with each day. There were two blues that liked to hang around, now, though his Blue was a bit paler, like the sky. And he definitely didn't remember seeing a grey dragon before this week. They liked to alternate, as if to keep him guessing on which of them would show up for the day.

They still refused to leave him alone, but for once, he felt grateful for that, seeking comfort and distraction in their scaly warmth.

Despite how much they loved the outdoors, the tiny dragons stayed close by him whenever they could, amusing themselves with games of hide and chase, or playful tussling. Ruby liked to sit on his head and glare at anyone who came in. The kit's expression when Lena glared back had been rather amusing.

As unreliable as these kits could be, sometimes – Kaiden remembered why they had not been chosen for message-delivering duties – he managed to persuade them to carry things to and from his temporary quarters, leaving little things for Lena to hopefully keep on her good side. She hadn't yelled at him since the first day, at least, though she still seemed rather tense when she sat by him, to 'keep an eye' on him. Sometimes she brought whatever she needed to work on, brow furrowed as she frowned at it in silence. She seemed less annoyed toward him as each day passed, though any mention of it made the tension return. So he let her pretend, hiding a relieved smile at her lack of yelling.

Even after he knew he would be fine, he stayed in the tent, to keep from being yelled at. Though one time, he did venture out of the tent to pick flowers for her, after the kits' attempt had provided him with a pile of chewed-on weeds. Lena had frowned more than usual that day. Despite all his best efforts, nothing truly seemed to help.

Yet he kept it up, all the same. Occasionally he turned to Fern for help, or Olive, and had to then explain to a very annoyed Lena that he hadn't gotten the things on his own.

It gave him something to think about, when his hands refused to do any more drawing, or carving, and he'd pet the kits so much his fingers felt numb. He had far too much time otherwise to hate himself, and rehash his failures, and fail at keeping memories at bay. It made that weight pull him down again, and he didn't want that. The kits didn't either, from the way they practically smothered him sometimes, sleeping in the crook of his neck and on his chest and in his hair, or curled up against his fingers. Even Jade's constant chatter couldn't always distract his mind.

Amongst it all, when he let them, Basil's words spiraled in his head, over and over.

"She's upset because she cares."

But that couldn't be. After everything he'd done, he was just going to cause her more pain again. She had no reason to care about him, no matter what she said.

It didn't make sense, anyway. Why *should* she care about him? What had he ever caused her but hurt and misery? Since the first day, he'd treated her horribly. Even when he'd been kind to her, it was only pretending. And every line of that was written across her face, as indelibly as the ones gouged in his back.

So why pretend? Why act like anything other than that had happened? It was little wonder she brushed him off, and made no sense why he kept trying. Why he couldn't just...let it go. Take what he could get.

He couldn't even make it up to her, confined here.

He wrote it all out many times, to keep his mind from nagging him about it. Letter after letter, each torn up, crumpled, burned until nothing but the ashes remained, scattered in the wind. Nothing would make it better. Nothing he said, at least.

But maybe, just maybe, this could negate the damage. He sent little gifts to the others, too, but they weren't the same. He drew whatever he could to possibly make her smile, even if he wasn't very good at it. Like the ocean, and the secrets in its depths. He certainly had time to practice, at least.

One time, he almost opened his mind to Ril, when nothing he wrote down was working. The tiny dragon couldn't have looked more surprised or delighted at the request, which only made him feel worse. He didn't know how to open up to anyone anymore, not even his own dragon. But if he could, he was going to try.

Lena's words had hit him hard, in a way he couldn't ignore. She was right about his recklessness being harmful. He didn't want to slip into that place again, if he could help it.

Despite all this, a part of him still hoped that Lena might relent and admit he was fine now, if he was good. But even though he didn't feel any pain, they still insisted on keeping him confined, 'just in case'. And Lena's gaze didn't broach disagreement. Kaiden wondered if she was aware of how much of a punishment it had become.

Beside him, Joss huffed a breath, her arms folded. "I don't know why I have to stay cooped up too because you were dumb."

He smiled, glancing between the two of them as an idea formed. "Why don't you ask Basil about his gift? Maybe he can help you with yours."

Joss frowned, but he could see the spark of interest in her eyes regardless, one that wasn't likely to go out anytime soon. "Fine. But only because you're boring."

"Bring me back a piece of cake?" he asked hopefully, and Joss made a face at him in response. Beside him, Jade chuckled, an amused smile on her face.

Though Joss didn't have to stay by him, despite her statement, she always came wandering in eventually, with complaints about people being too nice or her feeling bad about stealing from them, which wasn't okay. Kaiden stifled a smile and did his best to seem 'sympathetic' to her plight.

Then it finally came. The day where Lena unceremoniously tossed him a bundle of clothes, without so much as a hello.

When he looked up, he couldn't help but note how fancy she looked in her dress, in comparison with her usual. Unlike other days, her eyes were no nonsense, the tension in her shoulders showing as she gestured to it. "We don't have much time. Get changed and let's get going."

He was going to be free. Well...sort of. Looking down at the outfit she'd given him, it seemed a little like exchanging one prison for another. He wasn't very fond of Galdanian clothes. And despite the circumstances surrounding it, he remembered the other times he'd had to wear them. They were never comfortable.

It surprised him, then, when he unfolded the shirt from the pile, unpleasantly soft in his hands for how obnoxious it was. He might have to eat his words now.

Lena glanced down at it with a nod, muttering in acknowledgement, "You'll be in that for a while. Might as well make it comfortable."

He didn't know Galdanians actually *made* clothes that didn't make you stiffer than a rod to avoid discomfort. He'd always assumed that was part of why they did it.

Worst of all, it was red, in a way that somehow didn't clash with his hair. Lena, in comparison, wore a midnight blue that seemed to weave dreams in her eyes, the green hues sparkling in contrast like the ocean reflecting the sun. Her hair, short as it now was, she'd wrapped in a simple crown around her head, a silver pin securing it. It matched the earrings she always wore.

After giving him a look he didn't understand, she turned back to duck out again. "I'll be back in five. Whatever you're wearing then is what you're stuck with."

He couldn't help a little grin at the words, even if they didn't have quite the same effect as when he said them. "So, you're saying I shouldn't change, then?" he called back.

This time, he definitely *did* understand the look she gave him. "Yes, and then we can both get arrested for sneaking into the capital of Galdania and be executed for treason by the Empress, most likely being slowly tortured first," she said sweetly. "Good choice, Kaiden."

Hiding a frown, he stared down at the outfit until she left. Her argument there was a little too valid. Still, he did his best not to wrinkle his nose at the outfit, slipping the snug jacket on overtop the shirt – which was even softer than it looked – and buttoning the lapels. It pressed too closely to his back for his liking, but Lena looked like she might murder him if he refused it, so he said goodbye to his freedom with a sad sigh and finished dressing, only fighting a little with the pants to get them to behave. Finally, he buckled up the boots, admiring them with a thoughtful frown. They were a little tight for his liking, but well-made and sturdy, if too shiny and spotless for his tastes. He kicked the dirt with them, just to fix that.

When he stood up, though, it all came together in a very wrong way, like he'd been forced into a mold he was never meant to fit. Tight. Unfamiliar. Suffocating. It rushed over him in a wave that had him sitting back down just as quickly, kicking off the boots and slipping his back on until he could breathe normally again. There was just something about shoes he wasn't used to that left him feeling unbalanced, like he wasn't grounded properly anymore.

He must have taken too long, because Lena came back in a moment later, frowning. "I was kidding with my threat, you know. You have to wear it all."

Kaiden followed her gaze to his shoes, burying a frown himself. "I am."

"No, you're not."

He drew in a sharp breath. "They didn't fit. So I can't wear them."

"Don't lie. I had them made based on...those." She nodded again to his boots, sighing in exasperation. "Which you are *not* wearing."

"Why not?" he challenged, feeling something biting rise with his tone. "Too unsophisticated for your snobbish tastes?"

She narrowed her eyes at him, something glinting in her eyes. "Quit acting like a child."

"Nope." He dragged his boot across the ground in front of him. "This is where I draw the line." *Very literally.* It took him a moment not to snap out the words. "I'm not wearing those...things."

"They're called shoes," she said, flat and unamused.

"They're dagged uncomfortable is what they are," he muttered, scuffing the toe of his boot against the ground.

She frowned at him again, though there was something different to her eyes this time. "What's the *real* reason?"

He narrowed his eyes at her, hating how vulnerable the question made him feel. There were some things he didn't mind admitting. This wasn't one of them. But she was going to dog him until he snapped or gave in, so it didn't seem to be an option.

"I don't like them."

She rolled her eyes, slow and exaggerated. "Well. I wouldn't want to do *anything* that the great Kaiden Dyran doesn't like. It isn't as if I'm uncomfortable with the idea of walking back into a city I despise and pretending to be something I hate so I can find my brother. Or that I'm terrified of being found out. No. Gods forbid the *shoes* are uncomfortable."

"They...they make me feel..." Though it was also uncomfortable, with how tight the sleeves were and how the gold overlay dug into his chest, he crossed his arms over one another, frowning at a distant patch of ground to his side. Her words continued to mock him in his head, blending with other ones until he shook it. "Forget it."

Lena nearly sighed. "No self-respecting Galdanian would wear those hideous things, idiot. It's not just me." He felt her eyes on him, studying him. "But I know the feeling."

Do you? he wanted to ask, as other words spilled from his lips. "Just...until we get there. Until it's necessary." He hated how he could hear the pleading in his words, even if it was subtle enough she might not notice. "I'll still bring the other things," he added in a mutter, lowering his tone. "Wouldn't want to endanger you."

Lena let out a longer breath, still watching him. After a moment, she gave a little nod. "Fine. But you'd better not fight me when I do make you put them on." She raised an eyebrow, almost looking amused.

He tried to keep his frown from deepening. "If it's absolutely necessary."

"It will be," she said softer, as if hoping to persuade him. "Once we get there."

Letting out a careful breath, he nodded again. Lena stepped forward to rest a hand on his upper arm, brushing at it a moment later as if to get something off.

"You look the part, I suppose," she said teasingly, reaching up to tame his wild hair. "You can pass for a Galdanian. But leave the talking to me unless I tell you otherwise, alright?"

"I look ridiculous."

She barely hid a smile. "You look like a Galdanian."

"As I said." He gave an exaggerated roll of his eyes. "Ridiculous."

Lightly, she slapped his arm. "*I'm* Galdanian, you nit."

"I know."

Sighing, she stepped away, gesturing for him to follow her out. "The clothes will help you not stick out as much. Okay?"

Even the irony of the statement couldn't quite make him smile, given what they were wearing. "Right. Definitely not."

She pushed at his shoulder, shaking her head lightly. "Behave. And don't say a word to the others."

I wasn't planning on it, he muttered in his head. Lena took his arm, tugging him along lightly. She'd explained earlier that they'd disguise themselves further once they got near the City. For now, though, this would suffice.

The others were waiting to see them off, though Fern still seemed confused as to why Kaiden was going. As far as they knew, Lena was meeting with other leaders to discuss their plans against the Empress.

"To keep an eye on him," she'd muttered in explanation, dragging him along with her. "He's going to come sit with me through boring meetings. That should keep him out of trouble."

Basil didn't question it, even as Chan seemed slightly stiffer as he cast a glance at both of them. "Be safe," was all he said.

Fern hugged them both as if they were never coming back, burying her face in Kaiden's chest so it muffled her voice. "Yeah. Be safe, okay?"

LENA

They had no idea of where we were going. Or what we were attempting. They thought I was taking Kaiden with me on a diplomatic mission. And I was, in a way. It just wasn't to where they would expect.

Chan knew, though, for if anything went wrong. He agreed to allow it only after I gave him enough detail to assure him, and informed him Kaiden was going too. He seemed to relax at that.

"You balance each other out," he explained. "You keep him from being too reckless. He keeps you honest."

They waved us off, and I hoped our smiles didn't look too fake as I faced Kaiden. "Ready?"

He gave me one of those half-smiles, shifting the pack on his shoulder. "Are you?"

It was meant to be teasing, but my heart rate still spiked for a moment. To cover it, I frowned. "Of course."

We walked without speaking for a while, long after we needed to for any sort of pretense. Silence was a blanket, and I felt it smothering me the longer we walked on.

It occurred to me, not for the first time, that this must have been what he felt like. Leaving with little more than a vague indication of where he'd gone, and why.

"Why didn't you tell me where you were going?" I paused. "Before, I mean. When you left with nothing but a letter."

He stilled for a moment, but kept walking, shrugging to disguise the way he glanced away. "I didn't think you needed to know."

From anyone else, it would have sounded arrogant. From him, it just sounded sad.

He drew in a breath, staring at the sky. A thousand things seemed on his mind, and yet he didn't voice any of them. And I didn't bother to ask.

I missed Dez. Everything was too quiet, without our dragons or anyone to chatter on inanely. Just the two of us, walking through paths with lush fields, the wind whispering amongst us. But keeping one ridiculous troublemaker would be hard enough. I didn't need kit dragons added to that mix.

At one point, his hand brushed against mine briefly – though if he noticed, he didn't show any indication of it. I was still on edge, glancing at him every so often. He seemed lost somewhere in the distance, something almost longing on his face.

"Elle would have liked this."

I stopped, then, and took a moment to take everything in, drawing in a breath. "She would have." The flowers, the green everywhere – her favorite color, despite all the teasing. But beyond that, too, the peacefulness of it all.

Out here, I could almost appreciate the beauty, without it feeling tainted. Far enough from anything to be much of a reminder, other than of a few certain times.

Kaiden's hand captured mine, and the smile he gave me was too one-sided. "We'll find your brother," he murmured.

It was then I realized, as I should have before, what this meant to him, too. That a part of him understood better than I ever could how it felt to be separated from your sibling. Years apart were still nothing when there was still hope that you could see them again. He didn't have any of that.

I had to make conversation somehow, and the presence of his hand in mine was...comforting. It kept me tethered to the present, rather than being pulled adrift in a sea of memories. Though I hated it, I didn't want him to let go.

"We used to picnic there," I murmured, hushed, as my eyes caught on a familiar spot. A clearing with a little pond, and a waterfall that had seemed magic, when I was young, if the sun caught it just right. It spilled rainbows across everything, like fairies had decided to vacation there.

"If we weren't all prettied up," he teased, "I'd say we should jump in."

"Later," I murmured, then shoved him to make it seem like I was joking. He smiled, and I frowned.

It wasn't too far to the Cities, even without dragons. Despite my dwindling grudge against him, it took a while for either of us to speak again, me frowning at the plants and muttering about my dress while he toyed with buckles uncomfortably and fiddled with something small and round in his hands, making weird faces every so often or glancing over at me, as if he was talking to himself. I couldn't help but recall what Joss had said, even if it was in jest.

With the world quiet, the silence seemed to weigh heavier, begging for an answer. Save for the clink of the object in his hand and our soft footfall, there was no sound.

"You can speak, you know." Cursing inwardly at how harsh it came out, I frowned. "If you want to."

He looked up with that small, slight smile and shrugged one shoulder. "Whatever you'd like."

I nearly huffed in frustration, settling down in the grass to take a small break. That wasn't what I meant, and he knew it.

Just a few simple words, practically whispered between us, but it felt like it tightened the noose of silence once we stopped. Even with the rustle and clinking of sitting down, and him pulling something out of his bag, the pressure built until I couldn't contain it.

"You don't have to be afraid of me."

He hunched his shoulders, a little like he was embarrassed, letting out a short laugh. "Ah. Sorry."

I sighed, and he moved subtly away. "I don't bite."

He squinted at me, as if examining my teeth. "Are you sure about that?"

It took me a moment to realize he was teasing, and for a short laugh to escape my lips. "Fairly certain."

"Hm." He shifted away mock-warily now. "I think I'll still keep my distance."

He was smiling and I chuckled, before he added more to himself than anything, "Wouldn't want to do anything to upset you more."

Frowning again, I turned to face him. "Look, can we just...forget all of that right now? Have a normal conversation for once?"

Despite the solemnity to his tone, his words made his meaning clear as he nodded sagely. "Ah. The kind where we insult each other and I pretend to be offended because it secretly makes you smile?" His eyes gained a twinkle, just for a moment. "Or where you hit me for making too many jokes?"

"Either," I said without thinking, shoving his shoulder. He pretended to sway backwards exaggeratedly, clasping a hand over his chest.

"You're not supposed to hit me *before* I make jokes! Now I'll get hit twice! I don't think I can bear that, Lena Maye."

"Shut up," I said, and then added in a mumble, "It's Montellene."

"Yes, but if you want to forget everything, then that means I don't know that." His eyes got mock-solemn. "You should have asked for this when I *didn't* remember anything. That would have made it a lot easier."

"Shut up," I mumbled almost in a laugh. It was hard to be mad at him when he was making such a ridiculous face, an exaggerated earnestness covering his expression. And yet beneath it was a spark of genuineness that I couldn't deny, and didn't want to face. He really was trying to help.

"Maybe I remember more than I remember I remembered," he mused, affecting a serious face.

"Maybe you're just an idiot."

He wrinkled his nose in distaste. "You're still bad at insulting, Lena Maye." He filled his voice with disappointment, releasing a heavy sigh. "We'll have to remedy that."

"And why's that?"

"Because it's hard to have a battle of wits when your opponent isn't armed." He clasped a hand to his chest. "I am a gentleman, after all."

I shoved him again, mostly to disguise the smile I kept trying to fight down, and the flood of memories that made me want to just...relax. This was familiar. This I could deal with.

"Just let me know if you want me to...leave you alone," he said, picking up a stray leaf to drop on my head. Though he said it casually, there was no mistaking the amusement in his tone.

"What?" I looked up and let it fall on its own, as a grin slowly spread across his face. He ducked his head away, still smiling.

I poked his side, then. "*What?*"

He looked back, the shine still in his eye at my confusion. "You didn't hit me again."

I did so lightly then, purely out of principle, ignoring the slight flicker in his eye as he rubbed at it and grinned, softer. "I made a joke, and then you hit me. There. Normal conversation accomplished."

I let out a long sigh, to which he just laughed and shrugged. With a grin, he slipped his hands into his pockets. "You didn't think they were funny before, either."

"I still don't," I said, rolling my eyes. "They're awful."

"I know. I don't know how you bear them." He grinned. "You must be furry-ous with me."

I swung at him teasingly, and he laughed, dodging this time. There was an almost hopeful light to his eyes, just for a second. "There we go." He paused for a moment, then added teasingly, "Priss."

"Beanhead," I returned, shaking my head at him. He wouldn't stop grinning.

"What do you call a blonde-furred, stuck-up kitty?"

"I'm really going to hit you if you keep this up," I replied warningly, though I couldn't keep a smile from the edge of my lips. "What?"

He took a moment, stretching his legs out in front of him, and grinned. "A prissycat."

I smacked a hand against my forehead, and he chuckled, but hesitated, locking his elbows against his sides. "If you want me to stop, I can."

"You're fine," I said with a sigh.

He reached over to tip my chin up, lips quirked. "Now, none of that. This is normal conversation time, obviously. That means you're only allowed to act like you hate me. I might even smirk, if that would help."

I shook my head, even as he tried and failed to make the expression, eyes twinkling too much. "No, thank you."

The light faded just a little, his smile more subdued as he leaned back on his hands. "Whatever you want," he said, shrugging a shoulder a little.

I want things to be normal, I thought. *But not...fake normal.*

He looked away, drawing in a slow breath. "I don't appear to be that good at being normal anymore."

"No, you are." I frowned, even as he turned back to meet my eyes, carefully. "I never liked Blaze anyway."

"Right." He nodded, the last of the light dissipated as he looked down.

"You're not allowed to apologize again," I said, seeing the look in his eyes. "That's not normal."

His lips quirked a little bit. "What is?" He looked up at me, eyes seeing too far for my own comfort. *We both know we're hiding things.*

"I don't know," I answered tiredly, getting to my feet. "This, I guess. Arguing. That's our normal." I waved my hand, turning so he couldn't see my frustration. "We're wasting time. The sooner we get to the Cities, the better."

KAIDEN

They walked through the open countryside of Galdania, which seemed far too serene for his memories of this place. Though Lena didn't seem quite normal, he was glad to see there was a little less tension to her shoulders.

Something kept nagging him, though, that he couldn't push aside. "Why didn't you bring another Galdanian along, instead of me? Wouldn't that have been easier?"

Lena sighed, as if she was expecting this. "I don't trust them," she said simply, lifting a shoulder. "I don't know them well enough. And of the people I do know..." She frowned, shaking her head. "Well. I couldn't ask Fern or Basil. They've been through too much. Chan is always coming and going with his own plans. And Olive wouldn't leave Basil again." Eventually, she added in a mutter, "You're the only other one I trust."

The words made him far lighter than they should have, a smile slipping onto his face. "Thanks."

"Don't take it too seriously." She scowled, though he suspected it was mostly for show. She looked out at the fields, silent for a long moment. "You're my last chance."

He thought it was supposed to be insulting, but instead it came out soft.

"Last choice," she snapped, at his resulting look. "I meant choice. Don't turn this into a compliment."

A smile kept toying with his lips, though he tried not to surrender to it fully. "I wouldn't dare."

Lena narrowed her eyes at him. A moment later, she loosed a breath. "I don't know anyone else in the city that well, alright? I don't trust them."

"Not even your own people?"

"*Especially* not my own people." She narrowed her eyes, turning to him. "I doubt you remember it much, but Galdania is ruthless. They'll sentence their own to death if they consider them out of line." Her voice was bitter; the shine to her eyes showing she was thinking about her father.

"One more thing," she added, stopping to face him better. He didn't like the seriousness of her look. "We're going to have to have a mental link open, in case something goes wrong. I can't help you if I can't communicate with you." She sighed, her look seeming to soften a little. "Alright?"

He pushed down a spark of panic at the words, mentally scolding himself. This was Lena. She wasn't going to...

He didn't want to finish that sentence, with the memories already springing to mind. He swallowed, nodding. "Of course."

She gave him a half-smile, almost apologetic. "I won't use it to yell at you, if that makes you feel better. I'm perfectly capable of doing that out loud."

He let his lips quirk to the side, trying to imitate her. "Ha ha."

She pulled in a breath, looking at him as if asking permission. Her hand slipped over to cover his as she hesitated. "Let me know if I accidentally jostle anything."

He nodded, squeezing her hand lightly. It was less that he was worried about her messing with things, he realized, than seeing ones he didn't want her to. Everything felt so fresh in his mind still, floating near the surface rather than buried under layers of jokes and defenses and other, milder memories.

He scrambled to conceal what he could, still feeling too vulnerable as her presence nudged at the edge of his mind. *"Is this okay?"*

"Yes," he said quickly, hoping to distract her from everything and inwardly wincing at the fact that she could feel that, too.

She pulled back out, smiling a little at him. "Just for emergencies," she repeated, her hand curling around his. Drawing it away, he cleared his throat.

"Of course."

Her smile seemed almost fonder as she looked at him for a moment longer, possibly searching to make sure he was okay. He gave her a big grin in response, shrugging.

"Ready to keep going?"

Her voice was too soft, and he didn't like it. It set him on edge, thinking of what she might have seen. She couldn't seem to stop smiling, her shoulders relaxed as she waited.

He supposed, at least, that was a good thing. "Yep."

"It's nice to know I'm not the only one," she continued, and then hesitated. "Nervous, I mean." She rubbed at her wrist absently. "Aurillea...doesn't hold good memories for me."

"Does Galdania hold good memories for anyone?" he muttered, resisting the urge to fidget more. It bothered him to see how quiet she'd gotten, knowing the cause of it.

Lena lifted a shoulder, faintly. "I don't know," she admitted. "Are they all just pretending, too?"

He reached over to squeeze her hand, if only so she'd stop sounding so...fragile. "Most people are."

She looked over at him, and though he didn't meet her eyes for a moment, he could feel her gaze still, as he watched the ground. He *hated* feeling so vulnerable. It left him...unbalanced. He wished, once again, the kits were around to distract him.

"Any hobbies?" he forced out, trying to sound like he was just making conversation. Never mind that wasn't something they did, normal talking. He just needed the subject changed.

She stopped to look at him again, before moving to sit carefully in the grass instead of moving on. He wondered, if she had the choice, if she'd lay spread-eagle instead, the wind whipping freely at her hair.

"I love to ride," she murmured, staring up at the endless sky. "Used to do it all the time, to escape everything." She took in a breath that seemed too much of a burden for her. He felt bad about prying. He wished she would just go back to being mad at him.

She brushed it aside a moment later, clearing her throat. "It's not important what, of course. It just...made me feel free, for a time. Since nothing else did."

He took care not to dirty his uniform as he sat down next to her, as much as he wished to shuck it off and be done with it.

"I see."

She didn't ask about him, or anything, seeming caught in memories for a moment. He gave it to her, thinking back to Joss and what she might be doing.

"It's nice," she admitted after a moment. The unease in his chest resurfaced at her tone. "Being here...without all my responsibilities and such. So thank you," she said teasingly.

He rubbed an arm over his face, barely nodding. "You're the one who dragged me along."

"Because I was mad at you."

"Was?"

She raised an eyebrow. "Was doesn't mean I can't still be mad at you. I'm just taking a break from it so my face isn't all creased and scowly when we get to the party."

"Ah. I see."

She sighed, shifting subtly closer to him and pretending it was just to pluck a blade of grass off his leg. "You really don't like Galdanians, huh?" she murmured softly.

He tried not to tense, tossing another blade of grass at her. "Does it matter?"

"I just thought...it might bother you, when I'm acting more like one."

He let a frown slip through, shrugging. "No."

"Okay." She said it softly, and not fully convinced. But it was her undertone, the slight note of disappointment, that loosened his lips.

"My...father was killed by Galdanians." He frowned, thinking of how different that sounded from how it actually was. "They tricked him, and used him, and stabbed him in the back once they were done with him. Quite literally," he added unevenly, hating what the tension in his tone seemed to imply. "So no, I don't like them."

"I'm...sorry."

"Don't be," he replied, barely keeping his tone from turning sharp. "It wasn't your fault."

She frowned, looking down at the small distance between their hands. "I know. You just...never talk about it."

"It must have hurt," is what he heard hidden in the words, her own mind probably thinking of the General.

367

He must have waited too long, for she squeezed his hand, still looking away. "I...don't mean to pry. I just..."

"No," he replied, letting his eyes slip shut and hoping the word didn't sound too bitter. It tasted that way on his tongue. "I've kept enough secrets from you. Don't need to keep any more."

He squeezed her hand back, for courage, and found he couldn't say anything farther. She leaned against him lightly, looking up.

"Damien...?"

He had to choke down a laugh, feeling it burn in his throat. "What?"

"Olive said...he'd threatened you before. Is that why?"

He curled his free hand in the grass, to keep from gripping hers too hard. Her words were too vague for him not to fill in the blanks with the truth, even if it wasn't what she was asking.

She let out a soft sigh, closing her eyes. "I'm sorry." She swallowed, shrugging too swiftly. "I just...wanted to understand."

He turned to face her better, slowly, taking both of her hands in his. He hoped she could see the earnestness in his eyes. The words played through his mind, so easy to say. Or so it seemed, until he opened his mouth and they choked him. So much to explain, and so little he knew how to.

She looked at him expectantly, though, and he did his best to ignore the open look to her eyes. To pretend this wasn't as big of a deal as it was.

I want to tell you, he thought, warring with the words. Did he? In some ways...he supposed it was both.

"I don't know," he whispered, even though it was a lie. He couldn't bring himself to answer truthfully, glancing down. "He did a lot of things."

Lena bit her lip, not calling him out on his dishonesty, even if she could see it. She glanced down, her gaze taking in his hands. "I know."

He bit his tongue, following her gaze, and forced his mouth into a half-smile. "Do you?"

She hesitated, lips pressed together. He squeezed her hands gently.

"I guess not," she admitted.

"I'm not...ready to talk about a lot of things." He fought the urge to tense up, even as her eyes filled with quiet understanding. "I don't have it all straight," he lied again, pushing another half-smile. "It's still a work-in-progress. But yes, Damien was...involved."

She nodded, her eyes going down again. "I figured as much."

He squeezed her hands lightly, to disguise the need to tense at that. At everything that was still far too fresh, even if it had occurred years ago. He let her think what she would, rubbing a thumb over her hand.

"Thank you, for telling me." She met his eyes briefly, her lips quirking a little. "You didn't have to."

I did, he thought, but wouldn't voice it. He hadn't wanted to see the disappointment in her eyes, yet again.

She rubbed an arm over her face, her eyes focusing too much on his hands. He could see the wheels turning as she tried to sort it out.

"You've been...through so much and I've just demanded more of you. The Bane wasn't your fault. Nothing...Damien did was, either." She shifted slightly, adjusting her hold on his hands. "I might not have known it at the time, but...I still didn't need to yell at you. You were just trying your best."

He shook his head, hating the burn that sparked in his eyes. "No. Best means they wouldn't have died. It means..." He bit his lip hard to still it, a breath trembling through him. He couldn't finish the sentence.

"Hey." Her voice was too soft, and he hated the way it made the burn worse. He could taste blood in his mouth, swallowing slowly. "Kaiden?"

He couldn't do it. Just the thought of trying to swallow it again made him ache, more than he could put into words. He didn't want to make her upset again. He didn't want to lie. He just didn't want to tell the truth.

She pulled him closer, gently, wrapping her arms around him. The weight of her hands against his back only made it worse. "It's okay," she said uncertainly. "It's...okay."

He shook his head, choking down a violent sound. It wasn't, but she couldn't know that. The fear of hurting her mingled with the fear of *being* hurt, sealing his mouth shut.

One of her hands slid up to cup the back of his head, pulling him closer. His own stayed trapped at his sides, caught by indecision and trepidation.

"Shh," she said quietly, eyes closing. It soothed him, somehow. The way his mother would calm him, all without knowing what was going on. He didn't have to explain, it seemed to say, just...holding him. It didn't have to be okay, since it wasn't. If he wanted to speak, he could. But he wouldn't be faulted for remaining silent.

A tear escaped his careful hold, and he couldn't get his hand up to catch it before it hit her shirt. Lena blinked at it for a moment, quiet, and reached up to brush at where another was forming.

"It's okay," she whispered, even as they just kept falling. Every touch seemed to pull more and more free, silent sorrow showing itself in the only way he'd let it.

"*What's wrong?*" she would ask – his mother, that was – and he couldn't even answer. Even if he could, he wouldn't want to. But she didn't fault him for that, or look disappointed when all he could do was cry, and do his best not to tense up at her touch.

Lena pulled back to look at him better, the same expression on her face. He didn't understand it. He kept his gaze down, not daring to meet her eyes until she nudged his chin.

He swallowed, hard. It was so much harder, seeing it head-on. The faint, sad smile, her eyes seeming to understand too much for not knowing anything.

"We're a lot more alike than you think," she said quietly, half of the smile sticking. "It's okay if you can't tell me." She rubbed over one of the marks on his hand though, gently, as if she had a guess.

He scrubbed an arm over his eyes to get rid of the rest of the tears, drawing in a breath. "I can."

"Can you?" It wasn't accusing, just soft. This, he barely let himself admit, was why he hadn't wanted anyone in his head. Not out of fear of what they'd do, but what they'd find. She kept looking at him as if she knew him fully now, like every action of his made sense.

"No," he admitted, looking away. She reached up to brush his hair into order, nodding.

"I know you're scared." On instinct, he tensed at the words. She looked down, quiet. "To be honest, it's...relieving. You seem so put together. I guess that's why I get defensive." She shrugged faintly. "And you're a beanhead who won't listen to reason. That doesn't help." She lifted her lips in a teasing smile.

Now it was his turn to look away. *I'm not.* "Being Blaze was...a way to cope."

"I know that," she said softly, an almost smile touching her lips. "And then you were controlled by the Bane, or didn't remember anything, or..." She drew in a slow breath. "I guess it's just...relieving to know you're only human underneath."

His lips quirked. "What, did you think I was a dragon? Even though I 'tail' such horrible puns?"

She shoved his shoulder, smiling. "No. I just mean...I can finally see it all. I felt so alone for so long..." She drew in a breath. "I forgot what being understood feels like."

He laced his fingers through hers, squeezing lightly. "Oh."

She smiled, though there was a faint sadness to it. "You...understand more than most. What it's like to have...scars." She rubbed at her wrists absently, looking down.

The fact that she knew of them was almost relieving. She could form what opinion she wished, but the facts would stay the same. He did know. He knew it a little too well.

"My stepfather locked me up a lot," she continued quietly, still rubbing at her wrists. "If I did something...wrong, or just that he didn't like. I hated it." A shadow crossed her face. "When my father fled the country, they interrogated me, sure I was involved somehow, just because of my blood." Her lips quirked humorlessly. "I was six."

Before he could respond, she continued on. "I don't like chains. I'm...terrified of them, now. I refused to wear bracelets because it would remind me..." She drew in a breath. "Once they knew I was a 'traitor', it only happened more frequently. No one cared how I was treated. My mother was probably grateful." She let out a quiet laugh. "She asked me, sometimes, what she'd done to deserve me. As if having a daughter who wasn't pureblooded was a punishment, from the gods. She might have gotten rid of me, were she not so desperate to change me. To 'make up' for marrying a traitor. It was why she married my stepfather. He said he'd 'help' her regain her social standing." She lifted a shoulder, letting it drop after a moment. "I don't like Galdanians either. Every one I've met has been cruel and selfish. Talon was no exception." She bit her lip, shaking her head. "In fact, he is basically what all Galdanians are. Pretending to be nice, so you can't snap at them, but planning to stab you in the back."

"You don't sound bitter at all," he murmured, to try to lighten the mood.

She let out a quiet laugh. "And yet I still believed him. I believed every one of them, because I was so desperate for acceptance..." She pressed her lips together, cutting herself off. "You made me mad, when I first met you. But it was because I could *see* through it all, and I thought you could too, and it frustrated me. Because for as infuriating you could be, I understood it, and I just wanted you to understand me, too." She squeezed his hand lightly. "We both had reasons to hide, and so we could never be fully honest with each other. I hated that. I understood it, but I hated it. I wanted to see it slip. I wanted to know...*why.*" She released a quiet breath, looking down at their hands. "Because if you were just as lost as me, then maybe we'd get along." She quirked her lips up, half-sad.

He could only watch for a moment and nod, a million pieces sliding into place. She *had* known, already. She just...was showing it now. She didn't need him to explain.

"...to explain," Lena was saying, ironically enough. "I just...want you to show it."

He let his mouth quirk, teasing. "Does that mean no more jokes?"

She rolled her eyes, reluctantly. "No. Because that's when you're the most real, I think." She tilted her head, considering him. "I don't want you to change. I just want you to know I understand, and you don't *have* to hide it."

He almost laughed at the first part, but held it back. They had a ways to go still, he thought. Though she wasn't entirely wrong, she wasn't exactly...right, either.

"Jokes got me through a lot," is what he ended up saying, shifting so he was no longer facing her. "And others."

"Which is why they're such a big part of you." She gave him a little smile. "For good reasons or not."

He drew in a breath, absently rubbing his arm. "We should probably keep going, huh?"

"Yeah." Lena smiled, something indecipherable to it. She got to her feet, offering him a hand up with a teasing smile. He got up with a frown, sliding his into his pockets.

"I don't need a hand, Priss," he muttered, finding a small bit of comfort in the words. "I already have two."

"Ah, I see," she replied, still smiling. He switched to crossing his arms over his chest. "How about a leg?"

"Well, I guess I could break it then, and get good luck. That could come in handy."

She shoved his shoulder, shaking her head. "Funny."

He gave a mock, sweeping bow, trying to smile. "I'm here all day. And night. You'll never get away from me."

"Well, I wouldn't want to lose you in the City, so I suppose that's a good thing. Have to keep an eye on you, and all."

He rubbed his arm, faintly aware of the scar there, and tried to bury some of his unease. Maybe she hadn't seen anything, after all, and he was being paranoid.

XXIII

LENA

We kept going, for a while, the silence between us settled to companionable when it came, now, rather than uncomfortable.

As we neared the City, Kaiden hesitated, shifting on his feet. "Weren't you going to...you know..." He waved a hand in a vague gesture at our heads.

Right. Already he'd distracted me from the plan, by making me relax. I dug in my bag, coming up with a little bottle. "You'll have to get that all through your hair, and don't miss a spot. I'm not having you blow our cover because your hair looks like it's on fire," I muttered, handing the bottle to him.

He gave a mock-heavy sigh, looking it over. "You know, I hadn't known what to think of my hair at first. But then it grew on me." He kept his expression sad, only the slightest spark to his eyes betraying him as he sat down and started running it through his hair.

"Finding out about his Gift must have been a hair-raising experience for Chan, huh?" he continued after a moment. "With the lightning and all."

"I'm not dumb," I called back, working a different color into my own hair. It was relaxing, a small sense of security in the disguise that loosened the tension in my shoulders, just a bit.

Kaiden made a face at his hands, which were thoroughly black by now. "How long did you say it takes to fade once we get out of...hair?"

"Not long."

He grinned, even as his nose wrinkled. "Oh, that's good. I might 'dye' if my hair was this color forever."

I let out an exasperated sigh. "I've had it about up to 'hair' with your puns."

He grinned. "Hey, that was pretty good! Try insulting me, now."

I screwed up my face at him. "You make me want to step in a puddle of mud."

He chuckled, still making a face at his slowly blackening hair. "Okay, that one wasn't so good."

"Sue me."

"It just needs to be a little clearer," he explained, turning to face me better. "Like, 'I'd rather step in a puddle of mud than look at you.'"

I sighed through my nose, looking away. "Beanhead."

"Well...beans don't exactly have any brains, so I suppose that works. Though I think you can still do better." He grinned at me, enjoying this way too much.

"Why do you *want* me to insult you?"

He stayed silent for a moment, running fingers through his hair. "I thought it might make you smile."

Rolling my eyes, I got to my feet. "Why?"

"Because..." A hesitant look crossed his face, and he shrugged, looking away. "It seemed to...before."

I bit back the urge to tell him we were two different people then, dropping down by the river to wash my hands before the dye stained. "Well, it didn't."

He nodded, continuing to look up at his hair as he carded his fingers through it. "This smells awful."

"Almost as awful as you," I replied, and nodded to the river. "It'll fade."

He laughed, something bright sparkling in his eyes as he examined his hair carefully. I didn't understand why he was enjoying this so much.

"You're good," I said briskly, debating a moment before adding, "You need to wash that off before it stains."

He affected a look of fake horror, practically jumping to get to the river. I shook my head.

"Think about it. My hands might have been black forever. Horror of horrors." He widened his eyes in mock-terror, his voice overdramatic. "Then again, no one would ever catch me red-handed. That could come in handy." His grin widened considerably at the last part, as if he'd surprised even himself.

"If it wouldn't undo all your hard work, I'd push you in the river for that."

He stood up quickly, backing away from the edge as he shook his hands out. "Well, I'm grate-ful you didn't, even if it was a little....cheesy."

I turned away, hiding a groan. "Do you *ever* stop?"

"Nope," he grinned, only the slightest hesitation to his eyes. "You like them."

"And what makes you say that?"

"Well. Despite your excellent reasonings, I've yet to see you carry out a single threat against me."

I shoved him again, hard. "Just you wait," I warned. "It'll come when you're least expecting it."

"I'll be on my guard, then."

It was impossible to be mad when he smiled like that. Eyes crinkled, lips spread wide in a joyous, carefree expression. It took years off his face, and almost made me forget the things he did.

I punched his arm lightly in response, frowning.

"Beanhead."

"Priss," he responded with a grin. He was having way too much fun with this.

I shoved him in the grass, but he only laughed. Screwing up my lips to keep from smiling, I folded my arms over my chest, turning away from him all haughtily.

It was hard not to smile, seeing his laugh. It was so bright and free and relieved, like I had given him a gift that released all of his burdens.

It was so easy to see, then, why he had behaved as he did. Underneath everything...*he* was afraid. It was a different kind of fear, I thought, but it brought about the same result. And perhaps, at its heart, it wasn't so dissimilar after all.

He was afraid of me finding his secrets. I was afraid of exposing mine.

A part of me wanted, for the first time, to tell him. But that gap was so large, and I hadn't crossed it in so long...I was still shaking when I took that first step with Basil. It scared me to tell him those secrets, no matter how small they were.

I couldn't find the shadows in his eyes, when he laughed. It chased them away for the moment, and I think that's when I decided I liked this much better than the sadness. I wanted to push him away, but I also liked to see him smile. I wanted him to do it again. I wanted him to stay like this, carefree and unaware.

The shadows were a part of his expression, except for that moment. He laughed so joyously I thought my mouth might burst from trying to imitate him. I loved seeing him like this, far more than I enjoyed being mad at him. I shoved him in the side again, for good measure, though he remained sprawled in the grass.

"It's like a green pillow," he murmured, gathering a fistful in his hand. "Is it even real?"

"It's called grass, Beanhead." Despite the words, I couldn't stop grinning. "That's what it looks like when it's actually cared for."

"Mm." He closed his eyes, smiling up at the sky. "Why don't we just stay here for a while?" His voice was only half-teasing, slightly slower as he yawned. "It's nice...just relaxing."

For a moment, I was tempted to let him, even though we couldn't linger long. "It is."

He curled onto his side, his arms resting under his head. "I didn't sleep well," he murmured.

Holding back a sigh, I laid down in the grass near him, blinking up at the sky. "Okay. Just a few minutes."

KAIDEN

"Beanhead." Something tickled his ear, as the voice pulled him from sleep. "Hey. Wake up."

Something shook his shoulder. He shivered, pulling away from it. The presence moved away, a sigh following it.

"Get up." It nudged him in the side. "Kaiden. We need to get going."

He curled up further to avoid the touch, shaking his head. A mumble answered him, dying down as the person moved away.

A crash of cold water jolted him up a moment later, just in time to see Lena smirking more smugly than he'd ever seen before.

"Payback," she said, a smile stretching at the corners of her mouth.

It took him a moment, blinking against the wet strands of hair hanging and dripping in his face, and then a low laugh left his throat. "Oh."

His gift was already working to warm him up, which she eyed with a certain level of dissatisfaction. "Knew it would work."

He shook his head to spray droplets at her, which made her gasp and pull away. "Don't you dare get me wet."

"Yes, Your Highness," he murmured, pushing his hair back from his face. It took him a moment still to register where they were, and why.

Lena huffed, standing a ways from him. "You wouldn't wake up," she said, the slightest crease to her brow for a moment that almost resembled worry. "And we don't have a lot of time. We need to keep going, as soon as you're ready."

"Mm." He eyed his clothes, which weren't drying quite as quickly as he hoped. "Remind me why I'm here, again?"

"Because I asked you to come," Lena replied, holding out a hand to him. "And you agreed."

He used the momentum to wrap her in a still-wet hug, before she could stop him. The noise of protest she made was more than worth the look she gave him.

"Honestly. What am I supposed to do with you?"

"Feed me?"

She chuckled, shaking her head. "Oh, that's one thing you won't mind about Aurillea. The food may be unnecessarily fancy, but it's far better than chewy bread and dry...well, I shudder to even call those things 'vegetables'."

"Careful, Priss," he said with a smile. "Your roots are showing."

She frowned, a bit of the rigidity returning to her shoulders. "I suppose that's a good thing, considering we're about to be there again, isn't it?"

He reached over to squeeze her hand, with an apologetic but hopefully assuring smile. "We'll be fine."

She drew in a slow breath. "I hope so."

<><><>

Even once they reached the Cities, Kaiden decided to stay silent about his boots, in hopes that Lena would possibly not bring them up. To his surprise, she just looked down at them for a long moment and sighed.

"You know, this is going to be on you if this fails because I can't fool the guards into thinking those are as lovely as the rest of you." She almost sounded serious, until he saw her eyes. "This might be the hardest challenge yet. One wrong move, one glimpse of that ratty leather, and we will be doomed."

He nudged her shoulder, feeling relief flood him at the words. "Thank you."

"Don't thank me yet," she muttered, lifting her chin high. "You're still wearing them to the party. Now, stay quiet and try to look like you did when you first put that on."

Lena's entire demeanor changed, as they approached the walls of the City. She radiated a cold arrogance as she presented an empty hand to the guard – who would see some sort of elaborate seal that served as their ticket in. With a quick flick of her hand, she gestured him in, as if he was a servant to order around. Kaiden did his best to appear haughty at that, figuring this must be the way Galdanian culture worked. Look haughty and offended, no matter what you do.

He took her arm to hopefully relax the tension in her shoulders, which she allowed with a cool glance his way. They remained silent as she led him down the street, her heels clicking on the polished ground.

The capital held the odd familiarity of a dream, like he might have seen this before, but with a different set of eyes. The colors were more blinding, the tapestries hung over windows gaudy and nonsensical in

377

their designs. Everywhere you looked, something glittered, from the crystal water in the many fountains to the gemstones embedded wherever made sense, and also where they didn't. All the voices seemed to blend together in his mind, the same uppity tone resonating from all of them.

Despite her calm appearance, Lena walked like a woman on a mission, pulling him briskly along and directing as cold an eye at passerby as they did to her. Kaiden began to wonder if that was just the way these people greeted one another. Like a bunch of stuck-up dogs, all attempting to claim the same territory.

They entered a building that might have been a small palace, but turned out to be just a regular inn. They had a different word for it, as if such a simple word was too plain for them, but he wasn't quite sure how to pronounce it. Lena paid for their room with a handful of jewels as if they were mere copper coins, discarded and swept from view with no regard for their value.

And now he stood in a place too fancy to be called a 'room', waiting for Lena to return. Between the glittering gemstones and flawless fabrics of the interior, he was afraid to sit anywhere, let alone *touch* anything, lest he get it all grubby. Even the floor was probably protesting his shoddy boots on them, appalled to have anything less than perfect walking its surface.

He would have gone mad, living here. He would have ended up breaking something, and being indebted for the rest of his life to a woman who wore only blinding orange and owned a rare multicolored bird that insulted everyone else's fashion sense; all because the glass she'd offered him water in was actually made of a very old and rare crystal that cost more than he could ever hope to repay in ten lifetimes.

When he told Lena this, her laugh almost implied that he wasn't far off. She'd patted his arm and told him not to accept any water, then, and he'd be good.

Now he was pacing lightly and wincing any time his boots hit the floor. He would have taken them off, except there was a certain comfort to them that he couldn't quite explain. Gigi had helped him pick them out – or, well, she was *with* him at the time, and Rafe helped him turn down the various ridiculous possibilities she'd presented him instead. She had been in an odder mood than usual that day, he mused. It still made his chest tighten up to think about it.

But they were good boots, and they made him feel...safe. Though gloves made him worry about accidentally setting them on fire, by absently activating his gifts, he was more worried about someone *taking* his boots if he left them somewhere. Although, he supposed, the only place they would take them here would be to the trash.

This was ridiculous. Why did he *care* if everything was spotless, anyway? Maybe it was because he didn't want to draw attention to himself, or behave too out of the ordinary, but there was just something, too, about the impeccable nature of everything that made you feel as if the ground itself would turn up its nose at you if you walked on it wrong.

He wondered why Lena hadn't gone mad, growing up here. He wasn't sure he wanted to ask.

When the door opened, it did so without a sound, save for the latch clicking out of place. After a moment's tension, in which he wondered if they had been discovered already, Lena walked into the room, closing the door with her back. She let out a breath, tiredness seeping into her eyes as she dropped her bag.

"I hate this country," she muttered, tugging off her fancy shawl as if it were a poisonous snake. "They don't get the meaning of 'costume' at *all.*"

He had been about to agree, but closed his mouth. Right. That was why, for sure.

She bent down to pull something from her bag, dropping a black bundle in his arms. Although he supposed it was clothes, there were too many clasps and buttons to be fully sure. She added a feather-covered mask on top of it, giving a satisfied nod. "Try that on."

Kaiden tilted his head to the side, studying it. Not just a feather mask. A raven head, with small eyes and a large, curving beak. Sighing, he crossed into one of the bedrooms, shutting the door behind him.

Looking down at the clothes Lena had given him, he made a face. From what he could tell, it would be even *more* ridiculous than what he was currently wearing. Despite not wanting to admit it, the clothes she'd given him before were actually...comfortable. He could see why people would spend so much time and money on them.

Jade eyed the clothes like she was trying hard not to laugh. "Well, unfold them and let's take a better look." She grinned.

Huffing out a dissatisfied sigh, he did so slowly, wrinkling his nose up more. "I will never understand Galdanian... 'fashion'." He unfolded the top piece and held it out, examining it. It was made of similarly soft, almost stretchy material, but blacker than black. It clinked when he let it fall open. He shook it a little, wincing at the clatter it made from all the buckles and clasps attached to it. Looking up at his hair, he sighed.

379

A slow, wide, highly amused grin spread across Jade's face, setting her eyes sparkling. She coughed down a laugh. "Well, I think you'll look very... You know, tall, dark and handsome. You'll get to be your alias The Dark Butterfly again." She said it all dramatically, drawing a hand across the air as if displaying a sign.

"It's not even butterfly-themed. I don't even know what it is. It's...boring-themed." He made a face at her description, shaking his head. "No. *None* of those words should be used to describe me."

"I am calling you that every time you wear black now." She looked way too pleased, grinning.

Kaiden let the shirt drop, putting his face in both hands with a loud groan. "I am never wearing black again. After tonight," he added reluctantly.

Lena pounded on the door, obviously impatient with him. "It doesn't take that long to get dressed, Beanhead! I need to see if it fits!"

Jade burst out laughing. "It's a great alter ego!" She grinned at the door. "I don't think she's happy I am distracting you with awesome new nicknames though."

"It does when the 'clothes' might as well be alien!" Kaiden called back, and then made another face at Jade. "It's the complete opposite of what I am." He sighed at the outfit. "I guess I have to put it on, though, huh?" Reluctantly, he sat down to slip off his boots, eyeing the new pair with distaste.

"Alter egos are supposed to be the opposite of what you are. That's why they're *alter egos*." Jade flopped on her back in the corner of the room like usual, plopping her arm over her eyes. "Yes, so I can be surprised by how fabulous your Dark Butterfly outfit looks." She grinned.

With a dramatic sigh, he peeled his shirt off, fighting the urge to tense at the cool air on his back. He quickly replaced it with the undershirt, shrugging on the jacket thing and eyeing all the very unnecessary buckles. "I should have a cape then or something," he muttered, fiddling with the clasp on the pants. Stupid Galdanians couldn't even make that simple.

"Tell me when to look, oh great Dark Butterfly."

"Never." He said it mostly-teasingly as he messed with one of the straps on the jacket, sighing and leaving the rest unmanaged. With a dissatisfied examination, he picked up the boots, eyeing them. "You can look," he grumbled.

When Jade dropped her arm, she laughed. Making a face at her, Kaiden attempted to cross his arms over his chest, though the dagged buckles and clasps made it rather stiff, and uncomfortable.

"It's definitely a good disguise." Jade laughed again. "Very dramatic and not-you."

He huffed a sigh, looking away. "I suppose that's the point," he said unhappily.

Lena pounded on the door again. "*Kaiden!*"

With another face directed at the door, he shoved his feet into the boots, hating the feel of the unbroken leather and tight, tapered shape suffocating his feet. Everything else fit surprisingly well, despite the ridiculousness of it all. The boots, however, were *made* to be uncomfortable. He was sure of it. Taking a look in the floor-length mirror, he sighed. Everything about him was black, a dull silver glinting where clasps hooked needlessly and buttons sat glimmering for show. He didn't like it.

Jade choked down a laugh. "The Dark Butterfly is ready for takeoff." She gave him a thumbs up.

He let his shoulders slump forward, the jacket clinking when he did so. There was no stealth to the outfit in the slightest. He cast one last mourning look at his hair and opened the door, drawing in a breath.

And then he stopped.

Lena stood impatiently by his door, her head turned away from him. It was easy, in that moment, to understand the differences between them. Where he held his shoulders too stiff and high in imitation of a stuck-up nobleman, she exuded a cold, elegant indifference, a distance to her very being that gave the impression that she did not just *think* she was above you. She simply *was*, in the way a glass statue stood unmoved by anything around it, delicate and eye-catching in its intricacies.

Her hair was swept to the side with a silver pin to keep it in place, falling in loose waves around her face, and she wore a deep green gown that draped over itself near her waist and spilled toward the floor, seeming to shimmer with each movement. It brought out every hue in her eyes, like it was made for her. The silver hanging in clusters from her ears and glimmering delicately at her neck somehow completed the picture, long gloves covering half of her otherwise bare arms.

He thought, in that moment, he understood more about her than he had in all the time he'd known her. If joking was his default, this was hers, hidden and obscured beneath so many other layers. It was easy to pick it out, now, in all of her expressions. A biting glance, a stiffness to her shoulders, all to disguise the elegant disgust that had been bred into her. She was as uncomfortable in it as he was with giving a straight answer, despite how effortlessly she fit in the role. No one would dare accuse her of not being Galdanian.

It was easy to see the struggle in her eyes, and understand it, in a way he couldn't put into words. How she usually teetered between looking put-together and yet never too fancy, finding a balance between what she was used to and what she wanted. It had grown on her, as anything you were forced to wear for that long eventually would, and yet he knew she despised it, all the same. This was probably why. Elegance was as much a part of her as jokes were for him, and most likely only served as a reminder of very painful memories.

Her shoes, he also noted, from where they peeked through a slit on the side of her dress, looked far more comfortable than his. Which totally wasn't fair.

Lena's look turned scathing when he met her eyes. "Well?"

"You look lovely." The words left his mouth before he could stop them. It wasn't what he meant to say, or at least, not *how* he meant it, but there was no taking it back. Beside him, Jade did her best to smother a laugh.

Lena's eyes narrowed. "That's not what I was asking." She motioned for him to turn, swiftly fixing one of the buckles Jade had missed.

"But you do. You look way better than I do," he insisted, half-tempted to mention her shoes as well. He could still see the tension hidden in her eyes, and wanted to make sure she knew no one would suspect her. It just wasn't coming out right.

Jade grinned widely, watching them. "Don't turn red, Butterfly, that ruins the effect of the dark and ominous outfit."

I wasn't planning to, he thought, resisting the urge to scrub at his cheeks.

Lena's eyes sparked, and she shoved him roughly away. "I bet you wish I looked like this every day, huh?" Her eyes were cold, a sharpness to them accented by her appearance.

His mind sensed a trap about the time his mouth had opened, words slipping free on their own. "No."

She narrowed her eyes further at him. "I can't decide if that was an insult or a compliment."

He hesitated. "You don't...have to look a certain way, to look lovely." He was messing up his words again, gesturing aimlessly with a hand. "You just...you look *more*..." He winced. "You look...Galdanian," he finished lamely, his point entirely muddled.

The daggers in her eyes couldn't have been sharper. "I know," she snapped. "You look ridiculous."

In response, he folded his arms over his chest the best he could, ignoring the clinking. "You're the one that picked it out," he muttered.

"Aww, I thought you looked adorable, Butterfly." Jade grinned. He didn't appreciate it.

Lena eyed him for a long moment. "At least it fits you well," she said bitterly.

"I'd rather it didn't. I'm taking it off." Before she could veto the idea, or he could dig himself in a deeper hole, he stepped back into the room and shut the door,

Jade laughed. "Aww, you want to change back to regular Butterfly already?"

"Yes." Even before he shut the door, he started stripping off the jacket. "It's dagging uncomfortable. I don't like it."

"Well, I thought it was cute." Jade grinned, her eyes sparkly and fond.

Kaiden shook his head, kicking his feet out of the boots. "Cute is not the word I'd use to describe it."

Jade dropped down to sit cross-legged on the floor, chuckling. "No?"

"No."

"I guess we'll just have to disagree, then."

"I guess so." He sat on the bed, trying not to seem too relieved that he could fold his arms normally again.

Jade grinned at him, the expression fond. "It wasn't that bad. And it's only for a short while and then you can go back to your regular. Try to focus on that."

He stood to leave, then let out a loud sigh, deciding against it. "You didn't have to wear it. Galdanian clothes aren't really my 'thing'."

"I know." Her grin turned a bit softer. "Maybe if we removed some of those weird buckles they'd be more bearable."

"It's not that bad."

"Well, you just let me know if you want me to attack it with scissors or whatever." She made a cutting motion with her fingers, exaggerating it.

Kaiden chuckled, his face smushed in his hands. "I don't think scissors would do much to this. But alright."

Jade bent down to see his face, teasingly. "Yeah, guess not. Anything else I can do to help then?"

"Not that I can think of."

Jade grinned a bit back. "Well let me know if something pops up in your brain like 'hey, she could totally do this for me'." She winked.

Kaiden chuckled, leaving his elbows on his knees. "Alright."

Jade shifted to flop on her back in front of where he was sitting, so she could see his face. "Why are you hiding behind your hands?"

"I'm not hiding."

"It looks a tiny bit like hiding." She held her finger and thumb close together, then reached over to ruffle his hair.

"Well, it's not." He forced a grin, making a face at his hair again.

"If you say so." Jade thoroughly messed up his hair and then dropped her hand, looking satisfied. "It looks better that way."

He half-smiled. "Marginally."

"Are you doubting my hair abilities?"

"No. It's the hair that's the problem." He sighed.

Jade grinned. "Because it's black?"

"Yes," he huffed, a pout on his lips.

"Aww, but that means we match!" She picked up a strand of her wild hair. "Though I do agree. It's weird seeing it not-red."

"I guess that's one upside to it." He tugged at a strand of his own, chuckling. "Maybe *that's* why Lena's so upset."

"Nah. I bet she's just grumpy because she thought you looked nice too and she's not ready to stop being grumpy at you. Like, being grumpy about not being as grumpy." She grinned, winking at him.

Kaiden shook his head at her, wrinkling his nose. "No, definitely not." He paused. "Being grumpy about not being as grumpy...?"

"Yes! It's totally a thing. People who are now less mad about something act madder because they're grumpy about their anger over something fading faster than they wanted."

Huffing, Kaiden folded his arms back over his chest. "That makes no sense. She's less mad at me, so she's madder...?"

"It does so. This type of thing happens all the time. They're annoyed by their fading anger so they get mad about it fading. Duh." She folded her hands behind her head, shrugging.

Kaiden rubbed a hand through his hair, smoothing it back out. "People are confusing."

Jade laughed, nodding. "Yeah, they are."

He shook his head, brushing it aside. "I wonder what Joss is up to."

"I don't know. Probably eating all their food and scolding dragons or something."

Kaiden released a chuckle, letting the corner of his mouth lift in a half smile. "Yep, that sounds like her. Probably ranting about how mad she is at me for leaving, too."

"Hey, at least you know she wants you around. Confirmation." She coughed, adding teasingly, "Told you so."

Kaiden made a face at her. "Only because I fed her."

"I don't believe you." Jade grinned.

"Why not?"

"Because it's not true. She likes you."

He rubbed a thumb over his palm, shrugging. "Maybe."

"No maybe about it. I can tell." The grin lingered on her face, confident.

He shook his head, but smiled. "Alright."

Lena didn't come to check on him again, and he left her to do her own thing. He didn't want to upset her further, since he seemed to be good at that. She deserved not to be upset for a time.

"When do you have to leave for this big party again?"

"I don't know." He glanced out the window, fighting not to make a face at the too-bright colors and gaudy nature of the city and its people. "Soon, probably, by this point."

"Want me to come with?"

He chuckled, letting the curtain fall back into place. "Of course. I don't think I'd survive otherwise."

Jade laughed. "Hmmm. No?"

"No. Are you kidding? I'd die of boredom."

Another chuckle punctuated her reply. "Ah, right. I need to tag along to make sure you don't die of boredom while going to a party with a gorgeous date. That's definitely the reason I need to come." She nodded, affecting a serious expression.

Ignoring the spike of confusion at the words, Kaiden wrinkled his nose. "First of all...it's not a date. Second, no. I'd die of boredom because Galdanians are awful and their conversation is even more so."

Jade's eyes sparkled with her grin, the light in them teasing. "Alright, I'll come then to make goofy comments and you can try not to laugh and look insane." She winked.

"There we go." Kaiden grinned back at her. "Then it'll be bearable. And you can warn me if something starts to go wrong."

"Alright, deal." With a chuckle, she stuck her hand out to shake, goofily.

Laughing, he shook it back. "Perfect."

"Cool. In that case, you need to finish getting ready."

He let his shoulders slump again, sighing. "I don't want to."

"It'll be over before you know it."

"I hope so. Otherwise I'd have to be..." he looked at the mask he'd yet to put on, "a raven forever, and that would be awful."

With a mischievous smile, she shook her head. "No, you'd have to be The Dark Butterfly forever, obviously."

Kaiden let out a groan. "That's even worse. No thank you."

Another of her bright laughs followed. "Why is that worse?"

"Because!"

Jade pouted at him. "Are you saying you dislike my new nickname?"

"Oh no. That's *not* going to be my new nickname."

"Only for when you're on secret missions!"

"That's considering I even go on any more secret missions! Or that this one doesn't go wrong!"

"Well, you never know!"

He shook his head. "I'd rather it not."

"Okay, I amend my statement. I'm sure it'll go fine and you'll have a very boring, uneventful rest of your life."

He let out a sigh. "Well, I suppose that's better."

Jade hopped to her feet, holding out a hand towards him. "Up you come. I'll help you figure out all the weird buckles if you stick the jacket back on."

Expelling a louder sigh, Kaiden nodded reluctantly. "Alright."

Jade motioned to the jacket, which he shrugged back on, before she reached over to adjust it and get one of the buckles to start behaving. "I used to do this for my brother when he had to wear fancy clothes. He didn't dislike them as much as you do though."

"I think I have a pretty good reason to dislike them. Plus, I highly doubt he ever had to wear something this ridiculous."

Jade laughed. "True." She glanced up after fixing the last one, reaching up to ruffle his hair. "We'll try to make it as quick and less icky as possible. It'll be over before you know it." She grinned at him, attempting to be encouraging.

He gave her a half-grin back, turning as if to model the jacket. "How do I look? Ridiculous and stuck-up enough?"

"I don't know that you could ever adequately pull off stuck-up. But you'll pass their inspection, I'm sure."

"I think I could manage," he said, making his face as haughty as possible.

Jade tossed her head back in a laugh. "As if."

He shifted his arms to fold over his chest, the best he could. "I'd better be able to, for this."

"I'm sure you can fake it, but I know you too well to be fooled. Underneath, you're just adorable and sweet." Her grin widened.

Kaiden looked at the door pointedly. "Mmhm. I'm sure *everyone* thinks so."

As if in reply, Lena knocked loudly again, calling his name.

"They don't know you like I do," Jade answered.

A half-smile crossed his face as he held back a laugh. "Yeah...I know." Which, of course, was no one's fault but his own.

Jade reached over to squeeze his hand. "I was talking about the strangers at the party, Butterfly. I think your friends have come a long way to knowing you lately."

He breathed a sigh through his nose, returning her gesture. They had seen a lot, true, but they still didn't know him.

Jade looked up at him with a crooked grin, reaching up to nudge his chin with her knuckles.

"I think I might get in trouble if I keep you much longer. And don't say she can't scold me since I'm imaginary – we proved that was entirely possible with Chan already."

He let his mouth slip into a half-smile as he walked to the door. "Don't need her even more mad at me."

Jade grinned widely. "Yeah, let's not make your date grumpier."

Kaiden stopped to look at her, wrinkling his face. "She's not..." He shook his head.

Jade's grin was too innocent. "Ah, yes. I forgot."

"Forgot...?" he questioned, forehead creasing. She wasn't making any sense.

"That the gorgeous girl you're taking to a fancy party isn't your date." She shrugged nonchalantly, her eyes dancing. "Where I'm from, that's basically the definition of a date – taking a girl to a party."

He rubbed the back of his neck, trying not to frown. "It's not...like that..." The idea set him off balance, his free hand fiddling absently with the jacket.

"*Kaiden!*" Lena sounded more impatient this time, and almost worried. "Don't make us late!"

"Coming," he mumbled, turning a circle to try to find his mask – as much as he didn't want to put it on.

Jade laughed. "Come on, let's go appease your not-date with your presence before she storms in here to find out what's taking so long."

Not-date. Not-imaginary friend. Not-his kid. He had a lot of 'nots' lately, didn't he? Dragons that weren't his, siblings who didn't want him, friends he didn't let get close...

And yet that's practically still what they all were, right? He fumbled with a button, accidentally unlatching it and latching it again before trying to stick his hands in his pockets, before they flustered him further. They slipped down his thighs, and he stared for a moment at the outline of where pockets definitely *seemed* to be – or 'seamed', he thought jokingly – but...weren't. He switched to trying to fold his arms again, the jacket straining uncomfortably and clinking in a way that didn't help his already slipping focus. Clearing his throat subtly, and hoping his face wasn't as red as it felt, he reached for the mask, sticking it on before he made more of a fool of himself. Why would they *pretend* to put pockets without actually having them?

The mask itself felt funny, black feathers sticking out from the edges of it and a pointed beak sweeping out over his nose and mouth. But it didn't smell off like having something over your face usually did, as if someone had made even that pleasant so the wearer didn't have to deal with anything so terrible as an unusual smell.

Rubbing the back of his neck and taking a slow breath, he faced the door, ignoring Jade's likely grin as he turned the knob.

Lena had her arms folded over her chest – which was *easy* for her, he noted with no jealousy at all – and the pose somehow made her look even more regal, as she stood there tapping her foot. She stopped when she saw him, a laugh choking from her throat.

"Okay, now you *really* look ridiculous."

He affected his best haughty face again, trying to imitate her bearing. "How rude of you to say."

"Not snotty enough," she said dryly, slipping on her own, much simpler mask. It glittered silver around her eyes, accents of black in the feathers and intricate lacework sweeping up and out from both sides...almost like butterfly wings. He had to choke back a laugh at the thought. Lena wouldn't find it funny. "This is why you have a full mask."

"I think I might be insulted on your behalf at her lack of trust in your acting skills," Jade said, teasing.

He gave a little shrug, grinning behind the mask. It was sad that so much of it was obscured. Then again, he could probably make faces at all of the Galdanians, and they'd never know. They'd just think he was a very prideful...raven.

"Aw. I thought I made a pretty good impression."

"Just leave the talking to me when you can." For the briefest moment, she looked worried, before brushing it aside. "No bird jokes."

"There won't be any bird jokes from me," Jade said teasingly. "Just dark butterfly ones."

Kaiden fake-sighed, to *both* of them. "And I was all ready to spread my wings and fly tonight." He spread his arms out to the side. "Although I wouldn't want to ruffle any feathers."

"And this is why you're not allowed to talk unless it's necessary," Lena replied, shoulders slightly tense. "You'd get us found out faster than you can say-"

"Caw?" he suggested, before he could stop himself. She shot him a withering look.

"Shut up."

Jade cracked up, grinning widely. "What, she doesn't think stuck-up rich people like jokes?"

Kaiden grinned, even though she could barely see it, he was sure. At the look in her eyes, though, he hesitated. "I wouldn't do anything that could put you in danger."

Lena waved her hand in annoyance. "We need to go. I can't take you seriously in that thing." She hesitated, nodding to the mask. "You should be glad for that, though. Without it, I'd have to doll up your face, too. And then you'd probably give us away with clown jokes."

He affected an appropriately horrified look at her statement, to try to make her laugh. When it didn't, he waited a moment, wondering if it was a bad idea, but slipped her free hand in his, casting a brief look at Jade beforehand so she didn't tease him. "We'll be alright."

Lena pulled her hand away, frowning. "Not here," she warned, her shoulders tightening further.

Even with the disguise, there was something striking about her eyes. The vulnerability added a gentleness to them that he didn't think he'd ever seen before.

"I suppose I should warn you," she said softly, as if to her reflection, and not to him. "This is going to be dangerous. Not like before."

He didn't want to pry, but he could see that this was eating her alive. "It'll be alright."

She whirled toward him. "You don't understand." A hint of desperation entered her tone. "I'm... I'm sorry I dragged you along for this. You don't have anything to make up for." Disregarding the makeup, she scrubbed a palm over her eyes. "I don't know how this is going to go."

"It's alright." Whether it was because they were the only two in the room or something else, she didn't snap her hand back when he touched it. A smile tilted his lips. "I'll take the fall for whatever happens, okay? You can shove me at them and scream about how I betrayed you. It'll be alright."

She turned her face against him in one swift motion, letting out a shuddering breath. "She almost recognized me," she whispered. "The woman I bought the costumes from."

Carefully, afraid she might hit him for it, he slid a hand around her back, surrounding her loosely. She shuddered again, something wet touching his shirt before she tried to pull away.

In a sudden stroke of insanity, he tightened his arm a little, holding her closer. Lowering his head onto hers, he closed his eyes. "If anyone's going to get caught, it'd be me. You..." He still couldn't think of a way to explain it, without upsetting her.

She tried to pull against him, a small, high noise escaping her throat before she tensed, pressing back against his arms. But he could feel her crumbling, and he knew too well that was easier to handle with help.

"It's alright," he murmured instead, lips almost touching her ear. He squeezed her gently as her breath hitched in the start of a sob. "No one's going to know who you are."

"And what if they do?" she whispered back, desperation tinged with a note of fear. She gripped his shirt, choking. "I..."

His fingers moved to stroke her hair, gently. It was easy, in that moment, to imagine she was just one of his siblings, and he was comforting her. He drew her closer, resting his cheek against her head, and breathed out softly.

She still fought against him, half-heartedly, but eventually she gave in most of the way. He didn't dare let go, especially when she whispered for him not to.

He knew it wasn't for him, but he was okay with that. She could pretend it was her brother holding her, and he could pretend it was just his sister he was comforting. It brought about the same result. It's usually how they ended up doing things.

"I can't do it again," she finally admitted, as if she was ashamed. "I can't let them find out."

"They won't," he replied, squeezing her lightly. "I'll make sure of it."

She let out a quiet sigh, all the tension slipping out of her as she pressed closer to him. They stayed like that for a long moment, his fingers brushing through her hair. It seemed to relax her, for the moment.

"Kaiden." She pushed at his arm, gently. Her voice was hushed. "Let go before I hit you."

He didn't want to test whether or not she was serious, slipping his arms away from her. She wiped her eyes and attempted a half-hearted glare, though he could see past that, in the redness of her eyes.

"I didn't ask you to hold me," she muttered, rubbing at her eyes again. This time she frowned a little more. "I'm not fragile."

But he knew the truth, and she knew he wouldn't mention it. The same way she'd never divulge how much of a liar he was.

"You think I wanted to be cried on?" he replied instead, giving her a look. She smacked him in the arm.

"Shut up."

He was feeling smug and liked the way it cleared the shadows from her eyes, so he imitated her bearing the best he could. "Never."

Lena rolled her eyes, muttering about needing to fix her face as she crossed into the bathroom and shut the door, effectively cutting off his charade.

He couldn't help a little smile. Perhaps it wasn't the best to claim this situation was 'fun', but he couldn't deny, at least to himself, that he liked being around her. Their mutual agreement to allow each other secrets made for a much more comfortable time than around anyone else. She could insult him and he thought nothing of it; he could tease her and have her ignore the meaning beneath it.

It was peculiar, the feeling of comfort he had with her. He found himself smiling more and said it was just from being able to joke around with her for once. If she hit him, well, he could easily stand a couple more bruises.

XXIV

LENA

If it weren't for my paranoid side making sure we were ready even before we needed to be, we might have been late. Kaiden took longer than I expected to get ready – seriously, were buckles that hard? No. He should have been glad I didn't make him wear some of the *other* things I'd seen – and though I'd anticipated getting anxious about it, I hadn't planned on having a small breakdown. I hadn't planned on mentioning *any* of it, actually. He'd taken down my guard, somehow, and I didn't like it. Even with that ridiculous raven mask on. It made no sense.

Not to mention, despite my annoyance that he was apparently inept with buckles, I was starting to regret the costume choice, too. The buckles' stupid clinking wasn't helping me brush off my meltdown from earlier, tugging at memories I couldn't afford to think about now.

I was nervous all the way to the event, keeping my bag tightly clutched in my lap as we rode in a carriage. It wasn't unusual for a Galdanian to be so worried about their belongings, so I wasn't concerned about seeming suspicious. Kaiden, however, kept looking out the window with a mix of distaste and disbelief, which I caught only when he turned to look at me every so often. This was why his mask covered most of his face. The raven already had a regal angle to it, imposing and condescending, so it should mask any slip-up he might make. I grimaced to myself at the unintentional pun. He was not going to rub off on me like that.

"*Do they* really *live like this?*" he said incredulously in my mind, facing me once again. I bit down the urge to tell him to stop looking so much, though there was an odd bit of appreciation at the fact that he didn't say 'you' instead.

"*No. It's just an elaborate scheme meant to fool the world. The real City is underground.*"

I couldn't tell for a moment if his surprise was real or faked. "*Wow.*"

"*Mmhm. And I'm secretly a dragon.*"

"I knew it," he replied, squinting through his mask at me. *"You like shiny things too much."*

I fingered the gem of one of my earrings. *"My father gave these to me. Before he died."*

He fell silent, then, and I tried to tell myself that was a good thing. Better he be silent, and let the mask hide everything.

He fiddled with a little stone, though, that I didn't even realize he still had. *"Kinny..."* He paused, then continued, *"or, Elle liked collecting rocks. It didn't matter how ordinary they were. This was her favorite."* He held up the uneven pebble, and I could almost see him smile from behind the mask. *"So I get it."*

I gave him a cold look, while inwardly smiling. "Quit acting like a child."

His lips quirked from beneath the mask, but he seemed to get the hint. The carriage came to a stop, a footman opening the door for us. Kaiden let his shoulders stiffen, looking down his nose at the people outside as he stepped out.

It wasn't the best impression, for Galdania's standards, but he almost could have posed as a dignitary elsewhere. Certainly better than the grubby Calestan officials.

I frowned at my hands to avoid looking at him. Kaiden leaned his head close to mine.

"Keep frowning like that and it'll stick. Or you're bound to attract attention."

I was glad he couldn't feel the sudden spike of my heart at the thought. I pulled myself up as we approached the gate, holding onto Kaiden's arm. I almost could have sworn I felt him smile.

Presenting fake documents as real was a *lot* easier this time, even with several sets of eyes on it. I'd practiced endlessly for this situation. Kaiden even seemed impressed, if a touch confused. I held down a smile, willing my heart to calm itself down as the guard handed the papers back...and let us pass.

I held back a breath of relief, inclining my head to him briefly and briskly pulling Kaiden along into the Empress' fortress. She enjoyed showing off, for these kinds of events. I thought it might be a subtle offering, an attempt to get her people more firmly on her side, as well.

Kaiden was far too relaxed, both for a Galdanian and for the situation in general. My eyes scanned the hall on instinct, looking for any familiar faces to avoid. The real danger would be in the ballroom, but we couldn't be too careful.

Kaiden expelled a frustrated sigh, though it sounded more like a groan in my mind. "Shall we?"

He had the disdain down, at least. Luckily for us, there was little attention drawn as we entered the room – lower viyers and viyesses who weren't announced at the door tended to be ignored. They were also the ones you most often had to look out for.

"Stay close to me," I said lowly, and resisted the urge to smack the calm smile off of his face. It looked far too nice, being there.

What a pair we must have looked, him with raven black hair and mine the color of chestnuts. Red hair was just too noticeable if there was an incident, and I couldn't risk possibly being recognized, especially by my family. They were bound to be here, somewhere. I just had to hope I didn't run into them.

KAIDEN

Kaiden did his best to keep Lena from tensing up too much, however he could. He made quiet comments about his thoughts on the partygoers and couldn't ignore the way she turned her head to hide a smile. Occasionally she'd look at him and laugh just a little too loudly, when they were passed by someone else, or hold his hand tighter to steer him away from a waiting lady. Any time someone asked him a question, she supplied the right answer in his mind, if she wasn't already occupied. He began to think maybe he could help out, too.

"Leave the talking to me," Lena said in exasperation after he accidentally insulted a nearby lady – how was he supposed to know her costume was a *flower*? The man Lena had been talking with looked at him in disdain when he came back over. Lena airily waved a hand.

"Go fetch some food for us, will you?"

Food. Right. *That* he could do, and not mess up. Kaiden glanced around the room, subtly nudged by Lena in the right direction, and tried to nod in the same way a Galdanian would. "Of course."

Even the food was elaborate, unnecessarily fanciful where each item looked more like a work of art than something edible. He picked up a few things he couldn't even guess at, more colorful than seemed natural, and a couple of intricately decorated pastries, listening to Jade's teasing guesses at what some of it might be. Lena gave him a sideways warning glance when he came back over, and he waited this time while she chatted with her target, tones airy and self-assured. He wished he had that sort of confidence.

With his hands full, he couldn't even try the food while he was waiting, without finding somewhere to set it first. Did these people not believe in sitting down?

Lena waved a farewell to the man, a frustrated look in her eyes for just a moment before she smiled too pleasantly, pulling Kaiden to the edge of the crowds.

"Find anything?" he asked, handing her one of the dishes.

She was clearly trying to hold back a sigh. "No. They're all as airheaded as...air."

He tried not to choke on whatever he'd just put in his mouth. "Careful, darling. You could cut someone with words that sharp."

She gave him a withering look, taking a small bite of pastry. He eyed the little pastries, briefly hoping that's what they actually were. "What are these?"

"Dagens." She pronounced the first part like a note in a song – each syllable light and rich in its pronunciation. He nearly choked again, watching her for a sign of a joke. Maybe he was hearing it wrong. "They're basically just fancy little cakes."

No...he definitely heard that right. "Dagens," he ventured, feeling suddenly foolish. The word sounded wrong on his tongue, even though it should have sounded right. Lena looked amused.

"Calestans like to pronounce things wrong all the time. It's all short vowels and sharp sounds to you. So yes, it's actually dagens." She drew out the 'ah' sound, like someone humming. The word was as airy on her tongue as the pastry was on his, soft and lilting. "Or, as you seem so fond of saying, dag. Where did you pick that up from, anyway?"

He was ashamed to tell her it was something he'd heard in a market one day, years ago, and decided to steal. It sounded like a good word to say, and certainly better than other ones he'd heard. How was he supposed to know it meant *cake*?

Dagging dragon. *Cake*-ing dragons...

"You...knew that was the word I was using..."

She gave a delicate shrug. "It makes you sound ridiculous, yes." Her lips curved in a slight smile. "But I couldn't exactly tell you that you were pronouncing it wrong, could I? How would I have known what word it was?"

Her voice held too much innocence to be sincere. He let out a quiet laugh. "Dagens." It still sounded wrong. But he could hear the wrongness in the way *he* said it now, too. He didn't like it. Dagging... No. That just sounded wrong, now.

Lena hid a smile behind her fan. "*Dagging Galdanians, hm?*" she said in the Galdanian way. He fought not to make a face.

"*Shut up.*"

For a brief second, her eyes twinkled behind her mask. "*Never.*"

LENA

It was almost unnerving, how easily Kaiden slipped into the smooth tones of a nobleman after that, with all the obvious secrets beneath his casual words. The only difference, I supposed, was that his weren't likely to get people killed.

My pulse still spiked at any sight of blonde, or the familiar coat of a viyer, decked out as they were. My father would have worn one of those, were he still alive. He would have had the best costume, too.

I'd purposefully kept my disguise simple, as to not draw as much attention. Kaiden's almost stuck out in the sea of colorful jewels and elaborate feathers, needless straps pretending to hold things together and all manner of useless, flimsy fabric. It was all about the statement made, and each outfit could hold as much meaning as one's political stance – or none at all. Some were warnings, or codes, or subtle messages. A very few were memorials to times and lives long lost, demurer, but no less stunning.

I felt like I was amongst birds who had spilled paint everywhere to try to change their coloring, each trying to outdo the rest. It almost amused me, how regal it made Kaiden appear in comparison – were it not for the mask.

I was right to keep him close by. Though we couldn't keep it up for the entire event without drawing questions, it wasn't unusual for a Galdanian to be so controlling. Many of the women kept their partners nearby solely to order around, while they chatted in cordial tones about topics I knew were far from innocent.

Eventually, though, it happened. A young lady in colors of every kind sauntered up to Kaiden before I could stop her, waving her fan in a way I knew he would never understand.

"I'm Ourelle," she said, smiling from behind the elaborate lace. Her 'mask' was many tiny gemstones attached to her face and spilling down the side of her neck, as if they were falling away. It gave her a prism-like effect when the light hit them. "And you must be...?"

"Leaving," I said for him, pointedly taking his arm. Kaiden looked confused, even as I steered him away from her with a too large-smile at 'Ourelle'. She fanned herself, cold blue eyes now filled with contempt even as she smiled back.

Uncertain, Kaiden turned to me. "What was that for? I thought you *wanted* to talk to people."

"And *I* will, just not you." I gave him a pointed look. "She was trying to flirt with you."

He looked back in surprise. "She was...?" Then he paused. "Why does that matter, anyway?"

"Just trust me." I narrowed my eyes at him. *"We're posing as a couple, idiot."* Aloud, I said, "Obviously I'm not *okay* with you flirting with another girl."

He raised his eyebrows, glancing around. "Funny, that doesn't seem to stop anyone else."

"That's different," I muttered, waving my hand. *"Galdanian societal rules are way too complex for you to understand."*

It wasn't quite a lie. He cast a glance beside him, messing with the cuff of his jacket. "Right. Well, I'm going to get more food, then. Since that seems to be a safe course of action."

"Don't go far," I said coldly, adding after a moment, *"If you have trouble, let me know."*

"Yes, dear," he replied, and I could almost hear the grin in his voice. Drawing in a deep breath, I turned to a woman beside me, pasting on a smile. "Men can be so idiotic sometimes."

Kaiden seemed to enjoy the food more than he should have, chatting amicably with a young man there about it, and only getting a disinterested look rather than a judgmental one. Eventually, though, the man turned up his nose at him, and I could almost see his face fall from behind the mask. He didn't have a clue what he was doing, but he was still trying.

No one I talked to had anything worthwhile to say. There were jealous and dangerous comments about other partygoers, made under light talk of other events, but despite the unusual state of affairs, not one person seemed interested or concerned with what was going on. Either that, or I was losing my touch.

I kept the mental connection with Kaiden close and open, in case he needed any help. Occasionally, I'd prompt him with a word or suggestion to get a better response, but wasn't surprised when it failed. I'd asked him along more for moral support and to keep an eye on things than gathering information. The way Galdania was run was too complex for him to understand in a single day, or even a year. It had taken me several even after realizing there *were* secrets in what was said to truly decipher any.

Just knowing someone was there, though, did wonders for my nerves, even if I kept positioning myself so I wasn't ever far from him.

"May I have this dance?"

Speaking of...he'd somehow snuck up on me. I drew in a breath to calm myself at the words I'd been avoiding, of the thought of having to touch *anyone* at this party.

He must have been watching the others, to know what to say. I hated him for putting me in such a situation, taking his hand and stepping close enough to say, "You know this isn't going to work."

"All the same, people are starting to ask, and it's a perfect distraction. Plus," he added as he pulled me unwillingly toward the floor, a smile on his face, "you can always just claim I'm insane and that you humored me."

In any other situation... I let out a sigh, glancing around before lowering my voice further. "If that *were* the case, I should be terribly ashamed of you and disown you. Galdanians don't tolerate weakness."

The smile faded from his face. I didn't want to think about what he'd inferred from it. "I'm...drunk?"

"Have you ever had a drink in your life?"

A shadow crossed his eyes. Silently, he eased me onto the floor, imitating the posture of the other men and sliding into the steps of the dance.

"I promise I won't do anything to endanger you. Alright?" His eyes sobered to something serious. *"If we're caught, you deny any involvement in it. Turn me in faster than anyone else and get out of here."*

"No." How did I make him understand? *"They'd keep me, too. They'd find out. We'd both be caught."*

His eyes remained too serious to be comfortable, for the intention behind them. *"I won't let you get hurt."*

"Galdanians don't care who you are. They'd still question me, and possibly everyone else here."

He remained quietly serious for the rest of the dance, and I did my best not to seem uncomfortable with the arrangement. His steps were not quite right, like he was used to a different style of dance than the nonsense Galdanians bothered with, but his pace with the rhythm was flawless enough that I might not be scorned for this. He led me through it like a river's current, flowing from one step to the next in a way that might make others jealous.

However, it was unfortunately and undoubtedly not a Galdanian style. It was too smooth, unhampered by the stiffness affected by all the other dancers, like they were dolls being pulled through something they had no control over, and no passion for. Kaiden moved like a puppet whose strings had been cut, using the music for his own means as surely as it used everyone else. I had to remind myself to follow the routine, rather than break out of it and let the floor become a stage rather than a prison. I wanted to enjoy what I was doing, for once in my life.

As the dance ended, I noted the turned-up noses were mixed with a few envious looks, and the sort of disdain that only a Galdanian could hold upon seeing something so beautiful, yet despising it on sight because it wasn't their way. My theory had been right.

What excuse could I use if they asked? Perhaps I could say he was visiting from elsewhere. They'd be disgusted, but it would give them an explanation for his behavior – and more "proof" for their own methods.

A flash of purple caught my eye, a moment too late. Only one man would be arrogant enough to wear that color so boldly tonight. The silver cloak and matching thread confirmed it, even before I glanced at the river of black curls spilling down the back of his neck. My feet froze to the spot as I cursed my own stupidity. I couldn't even think enough to warn Kaiden.

A viyer. *The* viyer I had been working so hard to avoid.

"Sharalene," I heard my mother say coolly. My heart stopped before she went on, "has still not been found."

In the grip of his leather glove, Kaiden squeezed my hand, tentatively slipping into my mind. *"Are you alright?"*

"Of course," I snapped back, panic causing me to act irrationally. I turned away from the family before they could engage us, fanning myself and laughing as if Kaiden had made an entertaining joke. They hadn't seen us. Had they seen us? They were *right there* and my feet wouldn't move fast enough to get us away.

Kaiden was looking at me funny, through the holes of the mask. I was fairly certain my hand was shaking as I tried to pull him away.

I wasn't fast enough. Like I was trapped in a nightmare, Viyer Cloris Friedel was now approaching us, flanked by a woman I only knew was my mother by her voice. She was drowned in jewels and nonsensical decorations, in a display others could only pretend to fawn over while even she knew full well how terrible it was. I had to fight not to shrink back behind Kaiden, pretending not to have seen them despite the future trouble that might cause.

Without thinking too much, I opened my thoughts fully to Kaiden, hoping he would understand. He nearly tripped, eyes widening at the floodgate I'd just released on him, but recovered quickly, pulling me away from my stepfather with an almost devilish smile for anyone we passed, as if he couldn't wait to get me alone and free from prying eyes. It was almost chilling, with the narrow raven eyes, but appropriately Galdanian. If my mind weren't so frantic, I might have marveled at his quick thinking.

"Thank you," he teased, backing me against a far wall and standing almost too close for comfort, his palms resting flat against it on either

side of me as if to cage me in – or shield me. I forgot he knew everything I was thinking now. Keeping the smile on his face, he brushed a gloved hand over my cheek, while my heart pounded louder and louder in my chest.

"*In case anyone's watching,*" he murmured in my mind, leaning close enough that our foreheads almost touched. He lowered his head by my ear, words silky. "Should we take this elsewhere, darling?"

Maybe he could pass for a Galdanian after all – the most dangerous kind. Despite my fear, my instinct to smile no matter what was strong enough to keep things convincing. The Viyer despised public displays like these, almost as much as he despised being ignored. And my cheeks already felt flushed.

Before I could say a word, Kaiden captured my hand in his, one arm around my shoulders to keep me turned away from the other guests as he guided me to an obscured alcove of sorts – one made just for this sort of thing. My mind was still too open, dizzyingly so as everything began to settle more solidly on me.

"I need a moment," I managed to whisper, slipping my hand from his once I could. I saw my name forming on his lips, changed at the last moment as he stopped.

It was too much. Too much. He didn't pry. He didn't ask what was wrong or try to comfort me when I sat back in the corner, not far enough away from the glances and the comments and the past slowly creeping over me like a rising flood. He sat beside me in silence, one hand subtly open in an invitation, if I wanted it.

It hurt so much worse than I expected, seeing them all. *Knowing* if they were aware of who I was, there would be no smiles. Remembering, as I had before, those awful years of loneliness. The snide comments and the judgment, tearing apart every little decision I made as if it was theirs to control, and change, and demand more from.

"Lena..."

I held up a hand, cutting him off. He fell silent again.

"I don't want to discuss *any* of what just happened, Orlen."

My slip into his false name only seemed to concern him further. "It's just us, you know."

"*You* know." I couldn't take the harsh edge from my voice. "For all *I* know, they're already aware of who I am and are just mocking me. Biding their time." I knew it was agitated, and nonsensical, but my mouth was running away without me. "They could be *purposefully* playing along."

"Why?"

My hands flew in the air. *"To see if we know where the rest of Caleb's rebellion is? I don't know!"*

He studied me for a moment longer, before venturing. "Are you so sure this is a good idea?"

"Do you have any better ones?" I flung back. He rubbed the tip of his chin, unperturbed.

"I just think...you may be a little too close to this."

I let out a brittle, bitter laugh. "So, what? You think I should have dragged Chan into this? Olive? *Fern?*" I was aware of my voice rising, but couldn't bring myself to stop it.

Kaiden shook his head. "I just think...maybe I should be the one to do the talking now."

I laughed, but he was serious. I folded my arms, not bothering to mask the sarcasm slathered over my words. *"You. Imitating a Galdanian."*

"Your faith in me is overwhelming."

I let my head fall again, a low and shaky breath escaping. Slowly, carefully, I started tucking everything back in its place in my mind, closing him off to all but what was necessary.

"I'm sorry," I whispered, my head tucked in my arms. *"I'm putting you in danger, and you don't deserve that."*

His smile turned lopsided, smaller than usual. I raised my head, fixing him with a quiet frown. "I don't care what your mind tries to tell you, Kaiden. What you've done for me even just in coming here is...is huge. I've never had a friend who would do that."

His lips parted, but I cut him off. "I don't care if you believe it. It's still true. You...you're far better than I am. I shut everyone out *because* I want them to be safe." A laugh escaped my throat, too quiet. "Does that make any sense? I'm harsh because I don't want them to be hurt. And yet I do that all the same, all the time, by ignoring them. I'm not saving them. I'm just saving myself." I looked down at my feet, quiet. "That's all I've ever done."

Now Kaiden was shaking his head. "No. You're far better than I could ever be."

I released an unsteady laugh, before it broke into something worse. "Agree to disagree, huh?"

A smile lifted the side of his lips. "I suppose so."

I tried to imitate him, shifting to stand. "You really think you could pull it off?"

Taking my hand, he helped me to my feet, a hand gently on my back for a moment.

"I've managed harder things. Like doing up all these buckles." He touched one with a teasing smile, before his eyes went serious. *"You just focus on keeping out of sight of your family for the moment, alright? I'll find someone to talk to."*

KAIDEN

It was easier not being noticed. He'd assumed since everyone else was doing it, that dancing would help take suspicion off of them, but it only seemed to have drawn more looks. No one would *say* anything, either. That was the worst part, in his mind. Despite the disdain flickering in their eyes, you couldn't be fully sure of what they were thinking, or why. He understood why Lena had been so tense about coming here. Why she was in general, having grown up in this situation. He probably would have hit someone in the face, just to see a real reaction from them.

He'd had a bit of a selfish reason for wanting to dance, too, but decided not to dwell on that, considering where it got him. He'd thought, wrongly, it might help Lena relax.

Maybe this would, though. Surely he could find *some* Galdanian who would talk to him for more than a cold moment, right?

He decided to stay near the food tables, both for Lena's sake and his. It gave him a topic of conversation, as well as something to occupy himself so he didn't look lost. And perhaps, the kinds of people who would do the same would be easier to talk to than the ones gathered in groups he could clearly never be a part of.

Still, it was hard to mask his surprise when a girl came to stand by him, picking up one of the ridiculous dagens, and smiled at him. Not even in a predatory way, or even a – well, he didn't *think* it was flirtatious, but perhaps genuineness was a form of flirting, here.

"You're in the best part of the room," she murmured, popping the treat in her mouth. "Great view, best company you could find..."

He didn't have to force the smile that grew on his face in return. Finally, someone who got it. Even Lena didn't seem that interested in the food, although he supposed her nerves and the memories associated with everything might have something to do with it.

"I couldn't agree more."

The girl turned toward him more, surprised. "Really?"

He did his best not to seem too eager, picking up an odd pink square by the tiny stick coming out of it. Lena's scolding from the first time had taught him that, even though he still didn't understand the reason behind it.

"Of course. It's the whole reason I'm here."

The girl laughed, relaxing back against the intricate tablecloth. As soon as she did, she straightened back up, as if she might have dirtied it, or somehow offended it. Discreetly, she cast a glance around the room. "Is it, now?"

"Mmhm." Salt and sugar mixed in his mouth, dense and sticky if he tried to bite into the treat. Maybe that's why it was so small. "It's the only good thing about these parties."

Hesitating, the girl glanced away, though her eyes seemed to agree behind her dark mask. He couldn't decide whether it was black or a very deep blue, like the night sky without any stars. "Perhaps."

Silence fell between them like a heavy curtain, one he wasn't sure how to brush away. She affected a distant look, eyes shifting over the many party guests.

Maybe all Galdanians weren't that bad, after all. With her blonde hair half-pinned up, loose curls spilling from the end of it, and the elegant but not too showy costume of...whatever exactly it was, her mask curling out on one side to obscure half of her face, she almost could have passed for someone...normal.

Shaking her head, the girl gave him a tight smile. "I seem to have forgotten my manners. I do hope you'll excuse me. I'm Charise." After a beat, she added with reluctance, "Renelé Dolora Friedel, daughter of a viyer...but that's such a mouthful." Her eyes met his, hesitant and uncertain. "Don't you think?"

There was something hopeful about her eyes that made him want to nod. She extended a hand, and he took it, not entirely certain what to do with it. "I'm...Orlen." A very stupid name, in his opinion, and that was only a third of what he was supposed to say. Luckily, she'd already proved he didn't have to.

"A very Galdanian name. You should be proud," she said, and he couldn't tell if she was joking or not. At his indecision with her hand, she laughed. "You don't have to kiss it. I've had enough of that tonight." With a sigh, she withdrew it, eyes drifting to the rest of the party again. "Did you come here alone?"

"*Yes*," he wanted to say, but wondered if that would get them in trouble. What would Lena say? "To this table, yes."

Definitely not what Lena would have said. But it made Charise laugh again, a quietly restrained yet underlyingly mirthful sound. "Humor. Huh. That's a new one."

Before he could ask what she meant, Lena's voice filled his head, making him straighten up immediately. *"Get over here. Now."*

The tension in her voice worried him. "Actually, I need to get back, before I get scolded. It was nice meeting you." With a briskness he didn't necessarily feel rude for, given the people around him, he lifted a hand in farewell, ignoring the spark of sadness in her eyes as he turned away.

His mind raced with possibilities as he pushed his way through the crowd, muttering stiff apologies as he made his way toward Lena. Had something gone wrong?

Lena's arms were folded like she really *was* going to scold him, eyes sparking with something he couldn't identify. He looked her over, not seeing anything immediately wrong.

"What happened?"

Grabbing his arm, she yanked him further away with a cold expression. "Don't play games with me," she spat, while different words drifted through his head. *"That's my sister, you beanhead."*

It was a good thing she was pulling him, for he nearly stopped, confusion muddling his worry. "Your..."

Lena's eyes flickered as she pulled him mostly out of sight, her grip tightening on his arm. *"Sister. Stepsister. One of the people we should be avoiding."*

"I didn't know," he mumbled lamely, as her eyes danced between fury and worry she couldn't quite conceal.

"What did she ask you?"

It figured. The one person he actually was able to talk to...was the one he should have been avoiding. He was doing a fine job tonight, wasn't he? "Uh. If I came here alone?"

"And what did you tell her?"

His gaze drifted away at the whispers near them, a tittering laugh distracting him. "No?"

Letting out a frustrated sigh, Lena forced him further away from the eavesdroppers, brow furrowed. "What did you talk about?" she asked, voice lower.

"Food?" It came out as a question purely because of how silly it sounded. Lena eyed him, disbelieving.

"Food."

If they weren't at a fancy party, she seemed like she might smack herself in the face. *"Of course that's what you would talk about."*

"I was getting her comfortable first. Before you distracted me."

She narrowed her eyes at him, though inwardly she just seemed...tired. *"She didn't see you come over to me, right?"*

"Through that crowd? I doubt it."

Her shoulders relaxed, hand slipping down to cup his, instead. *"You know what? I'm fine, now. I'll keep searching. You just...stay out of trouble."*

A faint smile tugged at his lips. He should've just kept his mouth shut. *"Alright."*

Lena turned to go, her chin held stiff and high. He hesitated. *"She wasn't bad to talk to."*

Just for a moment, her eyes looked regretful. *"I know."*

Then she was gone, slipping off through the crowds until he couldn't see her any longer. What was he supposed to do now?

Stay out of trouble. Well, he tried that. Now he couldn't even hang out by the food without making things worse. What was he supposed to do, wander around and pretend to blend in?

People kept watching him, subtly and not, their judging looks feeling as invasive as hands on his skin. It didn't take long before they were too much, and his hands itched with the fire flickering through his veins. He had to do something, *anything* other than just...stand around.

As soon as he was able to, without drawing too much attention, Kaiden found a balcony and slipped out onto it, expelling a breath of relief. Cool air filled his lungs, no funny smells from whatever it even was that rich people wore, or feathers and the like brushing against him every time he moved. It was a wonder it hadn't given him a headache yet.

Jade followed him, eating a dessert she'd swiped from the table. He would have done the same, if people would have left him alone. No wonder Lena said to stay close to her.

But she was also talking with 'important' people to possibly get information, and especially after his little stunt, he didn't want to possibly endanger her by not being able to join the conversation.

Jade glanced around, grinning. "Aha, less crowded. Much better." She cut the dessert in half – even though it was already tiny – offering a part to him. Galdanians apparently didn't believe in normal portion sizes.

It wasn't hard to understand why Calestans so despised Galdanians. Everything they did spit in the face of Calest's marginal resources, flaunting how well off they were in comparison. Jewels for which his people had shed sweat and blood glittered uselessly in gaudy displays, deceivingly rich yet unsatisfying dishes made in portions only someone who was never hungry could enjoy. Flowers of colors he didn't know existed positioned wherever was possible, vibrant and flourishing from the health of the land. Untouched plates left to go to waste, unnecessarily intricate tapestries and garments made from fabrics that would take days or weeks to gather the materials for. It made him sick.

That was the excuse he'd give if someone came looking, he decided. And it would only be partially wrong.

"Yeah, definitely." Grinning back, he took the piece, considering his mask for a moment. "They don't really think this through."

Jade laughed. "Just tilt the mask up a bit and slide it under."

"I was going to do that." Were the piece much bigger, his mouth might have been full.

"Mhm, sure you were."

"I was! It's just weird with the mask."

"Lucky for me, I don't need one."

"Yeah. Lucky you. Don't have to wear awful clothes or try to follow all the rules or listen to mind-numbingly boring and frustrating conversation. I'm pretty certain these people just really like hearing themselves talk."

Maybe that's why the food was so small, he mused, so Galdanians could never stop talking. Then again, they were too proper to speak with anything in their mouths.

Jade laughed. "I suppose being invisible has its upsides."

"Tell me about it. Especially at parties with lots of food."

Leaning back against the wall, he took a moment to survey the City. "It looks a lot prettier from up here," he admitted. There was a certain beauty the darkness drew out, accenting what was necessary and obscuring what wasn't. The streets glimmered in varying hues, buildings and signs seeming almost to sparkle in the moonlight. Too bad it was all so...wasted.

Before either of them could say more, though, footsteps made him straighten back up. Kaiden braced himself for another boring conversation, stopping at the sight before him.

Two of the Empress' guards stood just outside the doorway, even their uniforms glinting in the light with golden buttons and useless tassels, like a more formal version of what any other guard would wear. Thin black masks swept around their eyes, as if even they had decided to participate in the event.

The taller of them nodded to him, his voice gruff. "You shouldn't be out here."

He was about to apologize when the smaller guard folded her arms, voice sharp. "No, he shouldn't. What *are* you doing out here?"

Kaiden put a hand to his mouth, faking something between indignation and ignorance. "Well, there wasn't a *sign*..."

The female regarded him for a moment, eyes narrowed. "Come on."

He expected to be escorted back inside, and was. He breathed out in relief, until the guard nudged him further, through the outskirts of the room.

"Keep moving."

Fighting down a spike of panic, he turned to smile at the stone-faced officials. "May I ask why?"

The woman took hold of his arm, her smile too sweet. "I have a question I'd like to ask you. Elsewhere."

Though the other guard walked off, the woman was more than strong enough to pull him along, even if he did decide to fight. Her grip kept his mind subdued, and he wondered if any of the other Galdanians even noticed what was happening, or if this was just...normal.

"Lena?" he asked, reaching out, and prayed she'd answer.

"Galdanians love jewels," she answered, clearly distracted. *"Compliment them on those. Throw in some subtle insults and you should turn them away pretty easily."*

Maybe she'd found something out, he thought hopefully. Either way...they hadn't 'found' her. That was good. They still had a chance, then.

"Kaiden? Does that answer your question?"

"Yes," he replied, forcing relaxation into his tone. *"Thank you."*

The guard guiding him opened a door he hadn't even noticed, leading him away from the party. He felt his connection to Lena grow fuzzy as they walked down the hall, his absurd boots clomping loudly in the silence. At least she was still safe. That was what mattered.

The guard took him down one flight of stairs, and another. A worrying familiarity crept over Kaiden as they went.

"You like the dark, huh?"

The woman gave him a biting smile, digging the point of a knife into his back. "Shut up." At the bottom of the next set of stairs, she pushed open a doorway, leading him inside. The ground they walked on turned to cold stone, the walls looking less like an elaborate mansion and more like a gloomy cave. He didn't need his memories of this place to know that wasn't a good thing. He fought off a shiver as the woman released him, shutting the door behind them.

He was about to demand to know what was going on when she yanked off the mask, tossing it aside. She squinted at him, the knife still in her hand. "What do you think?" she asked.

Confused, Kaiden hesitantly opened his mouth to reply, when something shifted in the shadows. Or, some*one*, he realized, as they

407

stepped into the dim light. A wide scar cut through the man's dark face, his mouth grim and narrowed as he took in Kaiden's appearance.

"Oh, we've found them, alright."

XXV

Basil

Basil didn't know what to do. This was more chaos than he'd ever seen before. Sari had told them to be prepared, but...this was something he didn't think any of them could have ever prepared for.

Fern hid behind an upturned table, looking far too calm for everything going on. A pot crashed near them, and Katya flinched. Chan was already tending to the situation, but it was quickly getting out of hand. Angry dragons were not easy to deal with, especially when there were so *many* of them. It made taking down the monstrous one in Danten look like a piece of cake. No pun intended.

There was another crash, and Basil saw Chan duck, scolding one of the dragons like it was an oversized child. Olive fought to restrain another one, vines growing around its limbs and slowly tightening, trying to stop it before it could shake them free. Basil had tried to distract one with his light, which often worked at other times, but these dragons weren't having it.

Chan smacked a dragon on the nose with a heavy book. It howled, drawing back from him with a mix of rage and hurt in its eyes.

The dragons, Sari explained, were still under Shedim's influence, even if it wasn't as strong as the ones in Calest. They hadn't set fire to anything *yet*, but Basil worried it was only a matter of time.

And of course, Lena wasn't even there. The one person who would have been best at this, considering her gift. Shouldn't they be back from that meeting soon? Although by then, it may be too late, anyway.

Fern huddled closer to the underside of the table, looking worried. "What are we going to do?"

Get them to safety, Basil's mind urged, scanning the remains of the room. There was an ugly hole bashed in the back wall, from a dragon with a particularly blunt and powerful tail.

A part of him desperately wanted to stay and help. But what could he do? This wasn't his role. Chan and Olive would be okay for a few minutes.

"This is my fault," Fern whimpered, her eyes sad. "I didn't know..."

Flames hit a nearby table. Basil pulled them both away from it, ignoring the fright in Katya's eyes at the action. He motioned to the hole, helping Fern through, and then let Katya go next.

Flames *and* angry dragons. And their two experts on those gifts were not currently available. This was turning into quite the disaster.

Fern huddled against the outside of the wall, looking up at him with wide eyes. "Do you think they'll calm down?"

Basil hesitated, glancing back through the wall. Chan muttered a curse, a tiny rainstorm forming near him to help put out the fire. He tossed aside a book that had gotten ruined, something twisting his features as he did so.

"I hope so."

Fern buried her face in her hands, almost laughing. "This wasn't supposed to happen."

"I know," Basil replied, urging her to her feet. "Don't dwell on it too much."

Fern shivered visibly, wrapping her arms around herself. "Do you think they'll destroy everything?"

He stopped to look at her. There was a reason Fern had rarely come with them when dragons were making trouble. She'd seen an entire village burned down...twice. He gave her shoulders a brief squeeze.

"No. We'll get it figured out."

She sniffed, rubbing the arm of her too-big jacket – or his jacket, he supposed – over her face. "I want to help." Her eyes took on a strange shine. "And I think I have an idea."

LENA

I began to wonder where Kaiden was, and how he was doing. I hadn't heard from him since he asked me a question. I just hoped he didn't get caught. Some of the people here had made me rather uneasy.

One of us had to make it out, though. Despite his insistence that it be me, I wasn't going to let them drag him away, too.

I thought through the conversations I'd had, as if I might have missed something. No one seemed to know or care about the rebels. Typical Galdanians.

I shifted my wrist, wincing instinctively at the soft clinking. Kaiden *had* to be okay. Maybe he would figure out something I couldn't. Futilely, I tried to reach out to him. This far away, we didn't seem able to keep up a steady connection.

It could be worse, I tried to tell myself. We could have *both* been caught, and then...well, I didn't think there *was* an 'and then'. No one knew where we were, save for Chan, and even he was aware of how helpless he'd be, even if he somehow found out about our capture.

It didn't mean I was giving up by any means. It just meant this would go a little differently than I'd originally planned.

They'd left me down here for 'questioning', I was told, and then been ushered away elsewhere, to check on something else. I assumed they knew the chains were enough, or would at least keep me restrained. They were bolted to the wall, above my head, and the position combined with the restriction of cold metal kept me tense and unmoving. I drew in another short breath, thinking back to Kaiden. I couldn't start panicking now. I just had to hope...maybe fate would decide to smile on me, somehow.

I wondered what would happen when he started looking for me. He wouldn't be stupid enough to try to break me out, right?

No. He would. I let out a deep sigh, letting my head sink down. Why had I thought this plan would *work*?

The worst part of the whole thing was...I didn't know *what* had tipped them off. There was just this woman in a guard uniform, a black mask around her eyes, asking others questions and mingling with the crowd. I wondered if some of more simpleminded ones thought she was another partygoer.

But she'd pulled me away, specifically, asking a question, and then gestured to a door. To 'talk', she said, and I couldn't exactly just say...no. It was possible the Empress was just being paranoid, after her recent failures. I'd heard talk of displeasure with her in some of the conversations. Maybe they were just looking for the disbelievers.

But then Talon showed up, and all hope for that disappeared out the window. Even if they *hadn't* found me out to start, there was no way he wouldn't recognize me, especially after taking off my mask.

My heart sank as I considered it. He'd probably sent someone back out to look for anyone else who seemed out of place. I hadn't told Kaiden at the time, because I didn't want him to get caught, too, by doing something rash.

I should have warned him.

At least my months of training with my Gift had paid off. Talon hadn't been able to get into my mind, despite worryingly skillful attempts. Then he was called away, and said we would 'continue later'.

I wasn't going to break. I *wasn't*. Tired and hurting, every movement made the room twist in my mind into one far too similar, and far more terrifying. When all I'd been able to defend was the smallest part of myself, the one I'd been told never to let anyone know of. I knew what they'd do to me if they found out. Being Calestan was mild, compared to being Gifted. Being both...that was more than a death sentence. The Empress loved to make examples of traitors and the 'impure', Gifted even more so. Sometimes she tortured them first, for varying periods of time, before finally ending their lives.

A shudder rippled through me, making the chains clink. I cringed, hating how such a small sound could steal all of my bravery.

Footsteps filled my ears, the door creaking open. I braced myself for further questions, fighting down a spike of panic. They were back.

BASIL

Fern took his hand, tugging him along through down the street toward an empty building. Ducking inside, she made her way toward a desk, carefully pushing aside flower pots and intruding vines to climb up to one of the cupboards.

Basil looked around, confused. "What is this place...?"

Fern blushed, retrieving a few bottles and slinking back down. "I...thought Elle would like it." She fiddled with a lid, eventually unscrewing it and giving it a cautious sniff. "She...always had lots of flowers, so I thought I'd keep some, for her." She nodded to a corner of the desk, setting aside the bottle. "Nyx and Rox seem to like it, too."

It struck him, then, that this was exactly this what it looked like. A pang thudded through his chest, and he swallowed. "That's..."

"Silly. I know." Fern wrinkled her nose, capping a jug and pushing it aside before reaching up for another one. None of them were labeled. "It gives me something to do."

"It's lovely," he choked out, taking a careful breath. This wasn't a good time to get emotional.

"It's like a memorial or something," Fern said simply, cautiously dipping a finger in white paste of some sort. Grinning, she held it out to him. "Except it's still living, since she can't."

He stared at the container, his throat feeling tight. Elle usually worked with anything plant-related, many of them very gross, but effective, especially when heightened by her gifts.

"It's frosting," Fern said brightly, eyes twinkling. "I forgot I brought it in here."

"Frosting...?"

"Yeah. The stuff you ice cakes with? Duh." Her grin widened as she put it in his hands. "Taste it and make sure I'm right."

As he dipped a finger in it, she continued scanning jars, commenting offhandedly, "I sometimes mix up where things should go." She grinned ruefully. "Those cupcakes might have had – um...berry juice? Except...less of a yummy kind and more of a makes-your-nose-run kind. It's kinda spicy. I dumped in a bunch of sugar, but I think it still came through."

His finger was in his mouth by then, and he was immensely glad to discover it was indeed frosting and not like...artist's paste. He knew exactly which cupcakes she was talking about.

"We came in here...for frosting."

"No, silly!" Fern shoved aside a heavy rock – who knew what it was doing there – peering into the alcove behind it. "Nyx! Do you have my jar in there?"

The blue-white dragon glared at her sleepily, the feathery spines on her head raised. Fern huffed, reaching past her to pull something out.

"I *told* you not to take that one! I know the lids are shiny, but that doesn't mean you can just hoard all my jars." She frowned, peering further in. "Is that my cookie tin?"

"Fern." Though Basil still didn't know what they were doing, he knew she might never get back on track on her own.

"We came in here for this!" She held the jar up triumphantly. "The frosting is just an added bonus. Now we don't have to make any, see?"

Basil rubbed a hand over his face. "You're not making any sense."

"You wouldn't understand my genius anyway," Fern huffed, taking the frosting from him and dumping the mystery liquid in it. She added a few heaping spoonfuls of a powder she'd gotten down, wrinkling her nose at its thickness, and added a little water. "There! Can't have it not looking like frosting, or they might get suspicious." She added a drop of bright liquid, mixing it in until the mixture was pink. "Want to try it now?"

She offered the jar to him, teasingly, pulling it away just as quickly. "Don't actually," she said seriously, capping the jar. "I don't know what it'd do to you."

"That...isn't reassuring me any, Fern."

"Well, dragons are a lot bigger than us, see?" She cocked her head to the side, eyeing a sleeping Rox. "Other than kits, of course, but they're a different case. So I added a lot more than usual." She furrowed her brow. "Hopefully it was the right stuff. Chan was right. I really should have labeled it." She huffed out a loud breath. "That's just so *boring*."

She turned to leave the room, and Basil wondered if he should even ask, at this point. "So...this is for the dragons?"

413

"Well, duh. Weren't you paying attention? I don't know what it'll do to humans. But I'm reasonably sure about what it does to dragons." She paused, frowning, and bent down to retrieve something from a cupboard. "I don't know where the other kits are," she explained. "So it's probably better to do this here."

Basil found he wasn't all that surprised when Fern set out a giant box of...cookies. "Fern," he ventured as she started spreading pink frosting on them, "you do know what got us into this mess, right?"

"Uh-huh!" She continued slopping frosting on, splattering a bit on her and reaching to wipe it off. She stopped, giving an awkward laugh. "Oops. I guess I can't taste it this time."

It was hard to get a straight answer out of her when she was focused like this, so Basil just went with his gut and started helping her, hoping she wasn't thinking *more* sugar would just...placate the dragons.

"...is made with the seeds, see?" Fern was saying as she filled the box with now-frosted cookies. He hadn't even realized he'd tuned her out. "So when you mix the two of them, you get this hybrid that, well, you know." She gestured to the cookies, grinning.

He didn't know, but nodded anyway, grabbing a nearby cloth to wipe the frosting off Fern.

She wrinkled her nose, shoving it away. "Eww. I cleaned the floor with that, you know." Proudly, she picked up her box of sweets, eyes twinkling. "Ready?"

Basil nodded, scribbling a note that said *Don't Eat* and hesitating, but left it at that, sticking it on the jar. "Guess so."

"You might have to figure out how to get me close to them," Fern said seriously, her voice more subdued. "I didn't quite get to that part. That's why I was stalling."

I had no idea, Basil wanted to say, but her face was already screwed up in concentration again.

"I don't suppose they'd understand me if I just shouted 'Cookies!', huh?"

"No, I don't think so," Basil said quickly.

"That was my plan," Fern admitted, looking sad for a moment. Then, she perked up. "Of course!"

She proceeded to explain her plan, in rambling detail, and Basil rubbed his chin.

"...Of course, I'm *reasonably* certain they won't..."

"Let's try it," Basil replied, before he could doubt it further. Kit dragons were smart, right? Maybe...it would work.

414

From somewhere nearby, Qui huffed, offended. He got the impression that she had just woken up, and hoped that would help them out.

"Nyx says we should do it ourselves and not bother her," Fern said, poking her head out from back inside. "Rox would just eat them."

On his shoulder now, Qui gave him a look, as if they expected anything differently. He chuckled, rubbing her head. "That's okay. Qui's got it."

Fern eyed the dragon skeptically, making Qui fluff out the feathers on her tail. Her tiny angry thoughts on giving Fern a piece of her mind almost made him laugh.

"Okay," she finally said, closing the door behind her. "But it's not my fault if something goes wrong."

They headed back toward the disaster area, Qui continuing to rattle frustrated thoughts at him. She seemed more annoyed when she saw the mess, looking at him like *"You haven't taken care of this already?"*

"There," Fern said, holding out a cookie. "Don't eat it."

Qui squeaked in indignation at her, still grumbling as she flew toward the irate dragons. Chan caught sight of them, looking more worn than before, his hair slightly on end. He must have forgotten to cut it recently.

One of the dragons eyed Qui, growling. She chittered back, dropping the cookie in front of it. It snatched it out of mid-air in one gulp.

Fern furrowed her brow worriedly. "Do you think it'll be enough?"

Basil watched as Qui flew over, huffing, and grabbed another cookie. The dragons started watching her from the side now, still fending off Chan and the other Gifted that had joined them. She dropped one in front of a different dragon, zipping back over with a huff as she took two this time. Chan smacked the dragon in front of him with the leg of a chair, to distract it, looking at them in disbelief. "Fern!"

She pouted at his exasperated tone, as the dragons started to eye her. With a shrug, she tossed the contents of the box up and out, calling to the others, "Don't eat them!"

Olive leaned on the hilt of her sword, watching in a tired mix of amusement and uncertainty as the dragons started snatching cookies from the air and ground. Fern tossed her shoulders up in a dramatic shrug, hands splayed to the side. "Hopefully that works?"

Basil watched, surprised as the dragons grew *less* aggressive, eyes narrowing as they slowly searched the ground for more cookies. Their growls grew lower and more subdued, as the first one Qui had fed sank

415

down and closed its eyes. Qui landed on Basil's shoulder with a huff, eyeing Fern like *"Well, why didn't you do that in the first place?"*

Fern let out a loud exhale as the dragons began to curl up, rumbling in contentment and dragon snores while everyone stared. "Well, I'm glad that worked!" When their gazes turned to her, she lifted her shoulders, sheepish. "They were just hungry. And...being around the Bane didn't help their tempers any. So I made them go to sleep."

Chan rubbed a hand over his forehead, leaning against the remains of a table. "Please tell me you couldn't just do that before."

She made a face at him. "No, silly. I had to get the stuff first, obviously." Understanding crossed her eyes a moment later. "Unless you mean *before* before, in which case, didn't Elle teach you anything? We *tried* that with the infected ones, remember? They weren't hungry. They just wanted to destroy stuff. Cookies wouldn't have stopped that."

Chan nodded, looking too tired to say more. "Of course."

Fern twisted from side to side, sheepish. "So, since I fixed the mess, does that mean I don't have to help clean it up?"

XXVI

KAIDEN

Kaiden bit back an unpleasant comment. *Talon.* How had he known they were here? Was it his blunders? Going out on the balcony? He didn't remember Lena saying anything about that, and she had expressly reiterated all the important no-nos of parties until he could recite them back.

Whatever the reason, though...this was definitely his fault.

Talon laughed, eyeing him with a glint to his eyes. "You really *do* look like a child in that outfit. How funny."

In comparison, Talon's ensemble was simple, but by no means less elegant, a deep gold that accented his eyes and complimented his skin a little too well. He pulled on dark, studded gloves, a dangerous smile on his face.

"Restrain him."

The woman pushed him down into a chair, cuffing him to it. Talon walked around him slowly, still smiling. "You just don't give up, do you?" He eyed Kaiden's back, a near-smirk touching his lips. They'd stripped off his jacket, searching it for hidden surprises – why hadn't he thought of using it for that? Although, he supposed, that would have been pointless now. The thin undershirt was what was left, a soft material that provided very little protection. "Who are you here with?"

Something pressed against his mind, trying to get in. He was relieved to find it wasn't able to. "No one."

The woman struck him in the face. He shut his eyes at the impact, flicking them back open a moment later to avoid a flash of memories. Talon stood behind him, his fingers ghosting over one of Kaiden's scars through the chair's open back. Muscles tensing involuntarily at the action, Kaiden fought down a shudder. He was vaguely aware of Jade kneeling beside him, her phantom hand curled around his arm gently, and her expression tainted by an uncharacteristic scowl.

"Wrong answer." As he said it, Talon ran his fingers slowly down the length of Kaiden's back, eyes glittering as he took in the resulting reaction. He pressed harder against Kaiden's mind, feeling along the edges as if looking for cracks. "I have to admit, I didn't think it would be you. I didn't think you had the spine for it." Kaiden fought for control, tightening his jaw as he did his best to shift away, just slightly.

"This would be so much easier if you just let me in." He smiled wider, pressing hard on one of the scars. Kaiden took in a sharp breath. "I will get it out of you one way or another, anyway."

He was constantly readjusting his defenses, trying to make up for the memories threatening to break free.

"Tell me who is with you," Talon added smoothly, "and I might even make this easy."

Kaiden shut his eyes, glad Talon couldn't see, and drew in a slow breath. Talon only grinned, malice shining in his. He dug his fingers in until Kaiden flinched. "Lie, and you'll see just how painful this can get." His eyes glinted with satisfaction. "What are you doing in Galdania?"

Kaiden felt something press against his mind, the hand on his back throwing him off again. "You know...I won't just let you in." He let his eyes fill with certainty, lifting his head. "I won't tell you anything."

Talon chuckled, the sound low and far too ominous. "Oh, I *was* hoping you'd say that. It's going to be much more fun to break it out of you."

Thinking of Lena, Kaiden forced a smile. "You can't break me."

Talon leaned in close to Kaiden's ear, his breathing slow and assured. "You forget, Kaiden, that I know all your darkest secrets. I *have* gotten in before. And I know exactly how to make you suffer." He smiled. "You're so fragile." He pressed his fingers into a scar, eyes laughing when he stiffened. "Do you really think your defenses will hold against me?"

They have before, Kaiden thought, even as a low sense of dread settled in him. "Yes."

Talon laughed again, his hand sliding up to the back of Kaiden's neck. As his fingers tightened around it, ever-so-slightly, Kaiden clenched his jaw to hold back a shudder. "You're pathetic. You can't even stand me touching you." Lowering his voice, Talon smirked. "What do you think would happen if I hit you? Would one blow be enough to make you crumple?"

Kaiden didn't reply, focusing on his mental walls and the vague feeling of Jade's hand around his arm, anchoring him to the present. Talon was just trying to distract him. And doing a terrible job of it.

"Face it, Kaiden." The man's smile was too wide. "I will get through eventually. I *will* break you, if I have to break every bone in your body first." He stood so he faced Kaiden again. "Now, let's try this again. Where are the others?"

"There aren't any."

Talon backhanded him, hard. "Wrong answer. You wouldn't be stupid enough to come alone, and I already have Lena in another room."

Kaiden felt the color drain from his face, wishing it would stay where it was. *No.*

Talon's eyes glittered with satisfaction. "Lucky for you, I can't do anything *too* damaging to you or you'll just pass out and be no use to me. Unluckily for you, I am very creative." He leaned forward, a wide smile crossing his face. "And we can take as long as we need."

He took Kaiden's chin in his grip, as fingers lightly trailed over his back.

"You're so weak." Talon laughed, watching him with glittering eyes. "This is way more satisfying than I thought it would be. You look so ashamed by all this, too. How pathetic is that? Not only can you not stop me, but you're too weak to hide your reactions. You let *all,*" he dug his fingers in farther with each word, "of it get to you."

White flashed through Kaiden's vision. For a moment, he couldn't breathe normally, shutting down his walls so Talon couldn't take advantage of his distress and creep in.

The words broke him down more than he'd ever admit, even Jade's quiet words almost drowned out by Talon's. But to give in that way was to risk losing everything else that was important to him. If he suppressed what he felt, then he wouldn't care if Lena was hurt, until it was too late. And so he let the words barrel through him, shutting his eyes and flinching them open again when something struck his back.

Talon's expression made him sick. "Oh, don't worry, I can't do as much as they did. Too messy, you know. But then again, neither of them knew what I know." He smiled widely, voice lowering in a secretive way. "I don't *have* to break you, to get what I want."

There was the sound of a knife flicking open, making him still. Talon laughed, the delight in it mocking him. "Did I trigger bad memories, Kaiden? Such a shame. But you needn't worry. I don't intend to use it on you." He moved around behind him anyway, the thin blade catching the light. "You know what's one of the things you fear most?" He traced the tip of the knife lightly down the back of Kaiden's shirt. "Reminders. You won't tell anyone because it lets you pretend they don't exist. You'd rather hide away from the truth, ashamed because of what it proves. How *weak* you are. How useless to defend yourself, or anyone else, because you just lie down and take things instead of fighting back."

He let out a low chuckle, moving back around to see Kaiden's face. "Scars are such lovely reminders, aren't they? Of strength, some say, but we know the truth. They're signs of *failure*."

"He's wrong, Butterfly," Jade whispered, but her words were lost under Talon's, and another voice from his memory, so he almost didn't hear them.

Talon's voice edged toward menace as he continued. "Not only are your own scars signs of your failure, but your friends' are, too, because you didn't protect them. I find that rather fitting, don't you?" His eyes gleamed. "I would love to return the favor, but we both know that won't *really* get to you. One more mark. One brief sting before you can bury it again. I prefer the kind of hurt that keeps digging in, like a thorn under your skin that throbs constantly and is impossible to get out. You know what I mean, don't you?" He laughed, as if he'd said something ridiculous. "Of course you do. I know your thoughts, after all."

Kaiden shut his eyes, though he was unable to keep them that way for long when the knife point returned to his back, shallowing his breathing.

"This part is all for show, by the way. A 'gift' back to you for the one you gave me." His breath rested hot by Kaiden's ear. "Lena's not fully seen your scars, has she? Brief glimpses don't count. It's such a work of art; it's a shame not to let it show." He paused, smile widening. "Don't breathe too hard, or I might just cut you."

Kaiden held his breath, ignoring Talon's laugh as the knife ripped down ever so slowly through the soft fabric of his shirt. His lungs felt too empty by the end, and he had to force down the urge to breathe in until Talon was finished. He stopped most of the way down, slashing it wide on both ends so it left a gaping hole that couldn't be concealed.

"There we go. That's much better." Smiling, he came back around to meet Kaiden's eyes. "You'll thank me for it later."

He forced himself not to think about it, even with the cool air from the dungeons now whispering freely across his back. Trying hard to will his heart into beating normally again.

He thought maybe Jade was murmuring to him again, but he didn't hear any of the words.

"So 'heroic'," Talon mocked, eyes glinting. "You think so you're clever for taking it all on you. But I know that tactic. Better yet, I know what will work much better. The only question is," he bent down by Kaiden's ear, "just how far will you bend over to keep me from hurting *her*?"

Kaiden pulled on his restraints, which only made Talon laugh. "Oh, fight all you wish. It won't do you any good." He grinned wider, eyes glittering with the kind of malice only someone given a guidebook on the best ways to hurt their enemy could. "You can't hide a *thing* from me. I see it written all over your face, because you were too weak to keep me out before."

He pressed harder against Kaiden's mind, taunting him. "You wouldn't even know if I've hurt her. For all you know, she could be dead right now and you did *nothing*. You let her get captured. You didn't even try to check up on her. Maybe if you had, you'd both be free-"

"Stop it," he muttered through gritted teeth.

Talon let out a long, pleased laugh. "Oh, this is really too easy. Do you know how pathetic you look right now? How weak and scared and utterly worthless you are? It's written *all over* your face, clearer than daylight. No wonder your father hated you."

"Shut up," Kaiden breathed. What did it matter, at this point? Talon knew everything. He would look smug whether or not Kaiden showed it. But maybe, just maybe, he could still fool him if he played along.

Talon dug his fingers into Kaiden's jaw, forcing his head up. "All I have to do is say *one thing*, and you fall apart," he said, his voice turned menacing. "You've failed even at that, every single time. Even now, you're failing. And you *still* let it get to you, no matter what the consequences of it are. Look at you!" He scoffed. "You're never able to do anything because you don't *try*. If you had, people wouldn't have gotten hurt." He smirked. "Gigi wouldn't be gone. She trusted you, too, and you let her down. You let them *all* down, just like every other time. And now you got Lena captured because you aren't smart enough to keep your mouth shut. I bet she hates you for that. She *hates* being locked up, don't you know? And it's your fault she has to endure that again."

He tried not to listen. He *tried* to focus on keeping his mental walls secure, despite the bombardment. He hated how right it was.

"Clever," Talon murmured, though it wasn't a compliment. "You may as well hide behind your fake identity now, and run from everything. Because you're too much of a coward to face it head on. You can't take the *slightest* criticism without breaking down. You won't even look at me," he snapped, digging his nails into Kaiden's chin, "because you're too weak to accept the truth. You won't tell your friends the truth, because you're *scared*." He let out a low laugh. "And so you lie to them, and hurt them, because that's all you've ever been good at. I bet Lena wouldn't even be surprised that you didn't come for her. It's just like you."

No, he thought, drowning it all out. Talon backhanded him, hard. He hated how his body recoiled inwardly, his mind flickering with images he quickly shut down. He almost couldn't even feel Jade's hand anymore.

"Look at me," Talon snapped. "You *won't* win this fight, and we both know it. It's because of you that I got this." Bitterly, he pointed to the scar on his face. "Because you took the Bane from me, and made me lose trust with the Empress. I fought hard to get that back. I won't let you take that from me again." His eyes glinted with a dangerous light. "So you had better understand that I will do *whatever* I have to to get this information out of you. I won't fail her again."

Kaiden took in a slow breath, willing himself to focus on the words so they didn't meld into other ones, the past slipping over him like murky waters to drown him. Talon wasn't right. He wasn't.

His grip on his walls was slipping, no matter what he did. "We came to find Caleb," he finally said, hoping to distract Talon. "She misses him."

Talon laughed, an incredulous, almost amused sound. "I really hope you don't expect me to believe that."

Kaiden sucked in a breath, willing his racing heart to calm. He *had* given him the truth, and Talon didn't believe it. He wouldn't, unless he could see it for himself.

But he couldn't let Talon in his head, either, knowing how he could twist things. He might never forgive himself if he ended up hurting Lena again.

"It's true," he said, as Talon's smile only widened. "We were searching for a clue to his whereabouts."

Talon's eyes glinted in an unpleasant way. "Fine. If you want to keep your secrets, it's going to cost you. *And* her. Would you prefer I torture her instead? That could easily be arranged. I could make you watch, knowing that this was *your* fault, and yours alone."

His smile widened, a spark to his eyes that Kaiden did not like. "Did you know, she's a lot stronger than you? She didn't even falter when I tried to get into her head. You started crumbling at the slightest resistance." He paused, eyes glinting. "That gives me an even better idea. I'll make *you* hurt her. Oh, now *that* would break you, wouldn't it?"

"Don't touch her," he said quickly. Anything but that. Anything to keep this on him, and away from her.

"What will you let me do if I don't?" Talon's face was mad with glee. "What will you give me?"

I'll do it, he thought tiredly. He'd give Talon access to his mind, if it would only save her. He could keep the details of her plan secret. Talon could know everything else.

"I could make you hurt her. Torture her. Beat her until she was black and blue, or watch me do it. You could make *her* scream. That would break you, wouldn't it?" His smile widened. "Knowing you *let me* do it. That you couldn't stop me, or I'd start again."

"Don't," was all he could choke out, his entire body tensing as fingers danced over his back again.

Talon laughed, soaking in his reaction. "Well. Now that we both know what will happen otherwise, I'll give you a chance to make it right. Let me in, and I'll leave her be," he said softly. "You don't have to say a word. I can find everything easily enough myself."

At his lack of response, Talon's eyes flashed with something dangerous. "You really think I can't break you, don't you?" He nodded to the guard, who moved to uncuff him from the chair, yanking him to his feet. "You thought you were *winning.*"

Talon slammed a fist into Kaiden's stomach, knocking the wind from him. Before he had a chance to recover, he took the collar of Kaiden's shirt in hand, cracking his fist into his jaw. Kaiden stumbled, tasting blood as he tried to regain his balance. Talon pressed against his mind, and for a moment, Kaiden almost let him through.

"You're pathetic," he mocked, as the guard knocked his legs out from under him. He kicked Kaiden in the side, hard, laughing when he flinched. "This is just for fun. Because you deserve to feel all this pain. You *deserve* to be beaten, and yelled at, and treated like the worthless person you are, and you *know* it."

He couldn't focus, feeling a dull stab of panic as Talon continued to hit him, pressing further in against his mind. He tried to get up, but the guard held him fast, as Talon drove another fist into his ribs.

It was too hard not to see a different face, and hear different words, his voice choked in his throat. What if he was right? His mind was spiraling too much to refute it. Talon was right. He had won.

He couldn't let that happen. He wouldn't let himself be twisted and used, ever again.

"You're infuriatingly stubborn," Talon spat, throwing another punch at him. "You can't stop me from breaking through your defenses." He stopped for a moment, his eyes dark. "You could have made this so much easier, for both of you."

Stepping away, he jerked a nod to the guard. She yanked him back to his feet, the sudden movement dizzying and painful when he breathed in. Talon's eyes glittered as he watched.

423

He swung at Kaiden, making him flinch. The blow passed right by him, and Talon laughed. "So *jumpy*. Honestly, how does anyone put up with you?"

He swung again, and Kaiden bit his lip hard enough to make it bleed.

"How loudly do you think I can make her scream, do you think?" Flicking open his knife again, Talon tapped the flat of the blade against his lips, curving them into a slow smile.

His blood was boiling, flames flicking hungrily through him stronger than the sharpness that struck when he tried to breathe.

"Go on," Talon dared. "Hit me, if you're not too weak. You have an open shot. *Hit me.*"

Kaiden swung, instantly regretting it. Talon dodged far too easily, returning the blow hard enough to cut into his cheek. His laugh rang out, low and delighted.

"I will admit, I was hoping it would come to this. You had your chance, Kaiden. You only have yourself to blame for what happens next."

His entire body went numb as Talon grabbed his arm, pulling him from the room. The pain humming through him was old and too familiar, settled in his chest as normally as his breathing.

Talon tightened his grip, bringing his mouth unpleasantly close to Kaiden's ear. "Oh, and if you try to get away? I'll take it out on her." His voice was close to sing-song. "Wouldn't that be a fitting end to all of this? You'd get to let her down one last time before you both die."

More than anything, Kaiden hated that he couldn't stop it. *Any* of it. Couldn't fight back, couldn't stop reacting, couldn't do a single dagged thing right. His only consolation was now he'd get to see Lena and if she was alright. It was killing him inside, not knowing if what Talon said might be true.

Talon pushed him into a different room, shutting the door. Lena was chained to the wall, a noise choking from her throat as her eyes fell on him. "Kaiden...?"

Talon undid her bonds, forcing her to her knees with her back to them, which was bare above the edge of her dress. She fought against him, which he seemed to expect, latching her wrists to a short chain attached to the floor. She quit struggling, then, letting her head hang as she breathed in heavily.

Talon held a narrow, flexible strap out to Kaiden, his smile growing. "This should be easy, don't you think? I'm sure you want to hit something after all of that. You're practically shaking with it." He smirked. "So here's your chance."

Lena was on her knees, silent, her back bared to them. It made bile rise in his throat that he had to choke down. He couldn't do it. She couldn't even turn to see the look in his eyes.

His split second of relief that she wasn't already hurt was swallowed by the gaping knowledge of what was going to happen. Of what *he* had to do, to...

"All I have to do is clink some chains and she starts screaming," Talon mused. "But *you*, you're a far more interesting case. I'm going to enjoy watching you break."

Kaiden's fingers wrapped around the strap, just enough to keep it from slipping. If he could make it convincing, maybe it wouldn't be as bad for her.

"You're going to beat her, now," Talon said slowly, savoring every word, "And if you don't, then I will. And I can promise you it will be *much* worse for her if that's the case."

Lena made a noise in her throat. Kaiden swallowed, tensing his arm to keep it from shaking. He couldn't do this. He couldn't.

"Every moment you hesitate, I'll add another strike."

Kaiden cringed, every fiber of his being screaming at him. If he didn't do it, things would get much worse. If he kept stalling, it would get much worse.

But something broke in him when he did bring the strap down on her back, as convincingly as he possibly dared. The crack echoed through more than just the air, as if in the silence, part of his soul was shattering.

"Again."

His mouth was a desert, his arm numbed and yet still shaking as words rang through his head, again and again: *I'm sorry*. He couldn't tell her himself, with their Gifts dampened and his tongue too leadened to speak. He brought the strap down again, his hand faltering too much for it to even make a sound.

Talon tsked his tongue. "Honestly. It's like you *want* me to hurt her."

The weapon slipped from his trembling fingers, a sound choking his throat. Talon stooped to pick it up, admiring it for a moment. "This is on you," he said, casual and far, far too pleased.

And then he struck her with it, far harder than Kaiden ever could. He flinched at the sound, turning his face toward the wall and leaning against it heavily as bile crawled far up his throat. His stomach heaved, the audible *crack* seeming to split the hole inside him wider as his knees slowly gave way, bringing him numbly down to the ground. Talon continued to hit her, again and again. Lena hardly made a sound.

425

Kaiden's breath still quickened as his head spun, dizzied and *screaming* at him for letting this happen. Though he hated himself for it, vehemently, he couldn't look. It was impossible to get the voice out of his head now as it taunted him, the screams from his memories piercing and tearing through him. His mind filled in the blanks between the sounds of the strap falling, his entire body cringing.

The weight of it all settled on him heavier and heavier with each blow. His arms came up to hide his face as a sob choked from his throat. He'd *failed*. He'd...he'd...

Nausea rolled through him in building waves as he fought for control. He choked on another strangled cry, burying his fists in his closed eyes. He hadn't contributed to this. He *hadn't*. His breath came sharp and burning in his chest, eyes stinging as he pressed himself closer to the wall. He didn't even know when Talon stopped, the sound continuing to echo on and make him cringe like a kicked dog.

He couldn't even move when Talon pressed against his mind again, slipping in with the ease of a slithering snake. Talon's quiet triumph flooded through him like poison, overshadowed by something almost like amusement. With too-light fingers, he brushed at Kaiden's bangs, smiling.

"So you were *telling the truth, after all.*"

Kaiden didn't dare open his eyes, fighting down another shudder at the intrusion. Talon touched the back of his hand to Kaiden's cheek, gently. He didn't have the strength to pull away.

"I told you I would get through," he said softly, before standing to his feet. "You didn't have to make it so hard."

Talon tossed the strap down by him, satisfaction flooding his face as Kaiden flinched. "You should be glad the Empress asked me to keep you mostly intact. I would love to twist that mind of yours again." A slow, dangerous grin crossed his face. "Who knows? Maybe she'll still let me."

He unlatched Lena's chains from the floor, leaving them attached to her wrists, and strolled toward the door. "I'll leave you two alone for a while. I'm sure the Empress will want to hear about this." He smiled at them both. "Enjoy yourselves. It will most likely be your last time together. And if it isn't...you'll wish it was."

He left, locking the door, and Kaiden's eyes squeezed tighter shut until thy burned, his mind continuing to play back that wretched sound and the images he couldn't escape. His stomach heaved as it tried to empty its contents, his hands shaking uncontrollably. He felt too hot, his gut twisting and caving in on itself as he tried to take a breath, and failed.

"Kaiden?" a voice whispered.

Despite the awful burn in his chest, he forced himself to look up. But he could only hold the person's gaze for a brief second before he dropped it again in shame. He couldn't even say her name.

Gently, Lena wrapped her arms around him, closing her eyes. "I'm sorry," she whispered again.

He pressed his fists into his eyes, trembling. He couldn't face her. Not yet. Not with a million memories screaming through him and-

"Shhh." She let it out on a tired breath, and it was then he realized he was sobbing. "Shh. I have you."

It broke from his throat like it wanted to tear him open, his mind split between being a million miles away and suffocatingly close, reliving every moment. He nearly choked, a horrid taste from somewhere deep down now coating his tongue as it mixed with salty tears. Sobbing, he held onto the closest thing he could find and gasped for breath, his voice slowly rising in hysteria.

"I've got you," the person murmured again, holding him against them as he shook in their arms. He buried his fists in closed eyes, fighting down a scream that wanted to work its way out of his throat. Why was *she* comforting him? Nothing had happened to him. And yet he couldn't stop sobbing anyway.

Her hands gently examined his arms, concerned, trailing down his sides as if searching for something. Hesitant, she slipped them onto his back, stopping when they brushed the tear in his shirt, and the bare, raised skin beneath it. "Are you okay?"

He tensed, choking down a painful sound as he forced himself to lift his eyes and meet hers. They were too gentle. His filled with tears again. Shaking, he reached a hand up to touch her face, desperate to convince himself she was actually alright, even though he knew for a fact that she wasn't. She looked confused by the gesture, eyes soft as she rested her hand on his.

But then the images slipped back in, and he pressed his face tightly against her, shoulders wracked by a shudder. He couldn't hold her, even if he could bring his arms to move. He didn't want to hurt her further.

"I'm sorry," he choked, each word shaking from him. His lips trembled too hard to repeat it.

"Don't be," she said, holding him closer. "That's how they win."

It burned in him, another sob ripping through his throat. He pressed a shaky kiss to her hand, as if such an insignificant gesture could fix what he'd done. He held it against him as she brushed her

427

other hand through his hair, gently. Too soft, like he was the one needing comfort.

"Shh. It's okay. We're okay. I promise."

She held him close against her until he stopped breaking down, until he could breathe without it shaking through his whole frame, despite the images that refused to leave. Carefully, she pulled him back from her just enough to meet his eyes.

"Did he hurt you?"

A choked sound was all he could manage, shaking his head as he fought not to tense, or flinch. The irony was so painful, it made it hard to breathe again. *No.*

"Kaiden." Lena nudged his chin, making him look up at her. "This wasn't your fault. Please don't take this on yourself." She looked away, pained. "It wasn't your fault."

"I can't..." He choked on a sob, but it came out anyway, tears burning his eyes. "All I do is mess things up..."

"No." She brushed away the tears, quiet. "You don't. You've..." She took in a sharp breath, looking away. When she met his gaze, her eyes were soft and sad. "I haven't helped you, feeding into everything, have I?" Her gaze dropped away, pained. "You can't see... how much you've done. You're sitting here apologizing to *me*, and you can't even see..."

Swallowing, she rested a hand lightly on his cheek. "You know...how much this means to me, right? I've never had anyone do all this for me."

A quiet laugh choked from his throat. "Gotten you tortured...?"

Her eyes turned sad, and she shifted back to a sitting position, gently helping him up to hold him closer against her, taking care not to touch his back too much. "No. All of *this*. Coming here. Apologizing. Doing your best to protect me, no matter what it cost you. The...pictures, and the carvings." She tucked a strand of hair behind her ear, swallowing. "Smiles," she murmured, "and jokes, and...everything you do...to 'make up' for things. But you never had anything to make up for." She looked down, her free hand in her lap. "I just made things difficult for you, because I was scared."

"I hurt you..." he started, even as she shook her head.

"Most people would just apologize and move on. Maybe they'd be slightly nicer for a week." A smile played on her face. "You tried to erase it entirely. I know it wasn't you, with the Bane. And I was just as wrong as you were, before, so I'd say that cancels things out." The smile grew a little. "In which case, I'm the one who owes you. A lot."

He shook his head, drawing in an unsteady breath. Her smile turned different, something he couldn't read lingering in it.

"Kaiden." Even her eyes were gentle as she tugged his hand gently, urging him. "Come here."

She let go to take his face in both hands, thumbs stroking below his hairline for a moment. He shut his eyes when her lips gently brushed against his forehead. For a moment, neither of them spoke. She settled back, eyes resting softly on him.

"Thank you."

He swallowed, feeling glad he didn't have more tears to cry. "Why?"

Quietly, she smiled at him. "I didn't make that clear enough?"

He rubbed his arm over his eyes, taking in a ragged breath. "No. You did. I just..." The words whispered away to nothing as he swallowed again, his throat burning. "I don't...understand," he choked out.

"Why I would want this?" she asked, taking his hand gently away from his face. She let out a soft sigh. "Kaiden..."

"Why do you...care?" The words hurt his throat, already raw from all the sobbing.

"Because... I've given myself excuses for years on why my actions are justified. Why...I was allowed to be hurt, and rude, because of what had been done to me." Her mouth slipped in a faint smile. "Because I wondered if there was any hope for the world. And then I met a boy, just as messed up as I was, who taught me the truth. We might not be healed, yet. But we can be."

A million words clamored to fill his mouth. *I'm not worth it,* he thought. And it was true. He was too much trouble. Too...*much.*

He must have said something, for her brow creased. She took his hand again, squeezing it gently, but tightly. "Because I care about you. A lot more than I should."

His lips quirked in a sad smile. "You shouldn't."

"I shouldn't do a lot of things, but I do anyway. Call me stubborn." She mimicked his expression, quieter. "Maybe I just see a lot more than anyone thinks I should."

He didn't understand how that could be, when there wasn't anything to see. A shaky laugh left his throat as he tried not to wince. "Y-Yeah. How...worthless and..."

"Kaiden."

She squeezed his hand again, even as he continued on, "weak, mean, helpless, selfish..."

She winced, putting a finger to his lips to stop him and shaking her head. Her eyes looked just pained enough to make him hesitate, wondering if he'd again brought up something he shouldn't have. But she deserved to know the truth. She deserved to know that he knew how pathetic he was. She was right. They all were.

"*Kaiden.*"

"You've always seen it," he continued on unsteadily, a ragged laugh wanting to escape with his breath. He pushed it back for the moment. "I know."

Drawing in a sharp breath, she looked away, eyes hurt. "I was *scared*. I didn't mean..." She bit her lip as it wavered, her forehead creasing. "I took what people said and turned it against them, to protect myself. I was wrong." She nudged his chin again gently, something too-bright glinting in her eyes when she met his.

"You're not a bad person pretending to be good. That wasn't what I saw. You're a good person who's been hurt badly enough that you don't believe it anymore. But that doesn't change the truth of who you are. You're brave and gentle and selfless, no matter what it costs you. I don't know...who made you stop believing that, and I'm so, so sorry that I helped contribute to it, but...that's why I was scared. Because you could see past my walls. You *understood* me, and carried your pain better than I ever could." She brushed her thumb over his cheek, gently. "I knew that. And I was terrified what that meant. Because...you were someone I could actually get close to."

She looked away, quiet. He realized just how terribly he had messed up, making her think these things. Hurting her further, like he always did.

"You never hurt me with your words," she said quietly, as if she'd heard what he was thinking. "I blamed you for...a lot, because it was easier than blaming myself. It was easier to be mad at you than to admit..." She pressed her lips together tightly, meeting his gaze for a moment as a spark of pain swept through her eyes. "You have never been the problem. Okay? No matter how you see it, it's...not true. Even now..." she drew in a short breath, squeezing his hand, "you don't even know how much it means that you would even *try*. That you showed me any bit of kindness, even after I hurt you." She bit her lip, something flickering through her eyes. "You don't know...how much *you* mean to me."

He kept his eyes on her – since it seemed to bother her when he looked away – even as he shook his head.

"Don't deny it," she breathed out, squeezing his hand tightly. "You can't tell me how I feel. You can't tell me I'm wrong to care about you just because you can't...see it." She lifted their laced hands to her lips, holding them there quietly as her eyes shifted elsewhere. "I'll find a way to show you, somehow. You never gave up on me, no matter how much

430

I pushed you away." She squeezed his hand lightly, taking in a shaky breath. "Well, you're not going to get rid of me that easily, either."

"I deserved it," he choked out, and wondered if it was true. Why else would it have happened? What could he have done?

The look that crossed her face was one he didn't think he'd ever seen before. "No. You didn't."

How do you know? he wanted to ask, as her fingers curled around his trembling ones, tight.

"No one ever does."

But what if you're wrong? he wanted to say, even if a terrified part of him thought she was right. He was too young, he'd messed up, he'd...

She'd backed him into a corner. As much as he searched for excuses, he couldn't find any that seemed strong enough to justify it.

She brushed at the edge of his hair, too gentle, as she let him process. "You don't have to believe it," she said softly. "But it's true."

It took him a moment to place the warmth rolling down his cheek, and realize it was a tear. She caught it with a hand, her own eyes spilling over as she brushed at his cheeks. He lifted his hand to do the same for her, and ended up cupping the side of her face, catching the drops gently with his thumb.

"Look at us," she whispered, and closed her eyes. "Two hopeless messes."

He was shaking his head, even as he drew in a quiet breath. *Not hopeless*, he wanted to say. *Not together.*

Instead, he drew her closer and let the tears fall, circling his arms around her as she did the same, and he felt the moisture on his shirt. He wondered if he had said the other part aloud, with how she started to sob and held him tighter, keeping her cries quiet as she pulled in breath. He rubbed the back of her shoulders, soothing her as tears continued to intermittently fall from his eyes, like water in a leaky pipe. He wished he could wrap her up and keep her safe here, forever.

"I'm scared," she whispered, and he shouldn't have been so relieved by her admission. He held her closer and nodded, stroking fingers through her hair.

"I know," he replied, almost too hushed to be heard. "So am I."

Her arms tightened around him, shaking for the moment as she held on as if she could keep them both together. They stayed like that for a while, quiet, holding on to each other as if it could delay the inevitable.

He swallowed, rubbing his thumb over her hand. Everything hurt too much to sort through at the moment, but he knew what to say. "Thank you."

She brushed a kiss against his hand, closing her eyes. "I'll find a way to tell you," she repeated, determined. "I'll make you see, somehow, just how much you're worth."

Her voice got too soft at the end, and he felt the words prick something in his throat. She wrapped her arms around him tightly, closing her eyes, and took in an unsteady breath.

"I'll repeat it a thousand times, if I have to. Until I erase those words from your mind, both mine and anyone else who's ever told you you're not worth anything." She squeezed him tightly, her voice choking off. "Okay?"

He didn't understand. Though it hurt, seeing how it upset her, he didn't know how to fix it.

She continued to hold him, quiet, his mind frantically trying to sort out what she meant, and how to make her happy. It played through his mind, the pieces slowly clicking into place. It choked him too much to be able to reply.

She *saw*. She didn't...blame him. She didn't hate him. Somehow, even after everything she'd seen, she'd still decided to stay.

He wrapped his arms around her, careful of her back, and buried his face in her shoulder, aware of the tears slipping steadily down his face. It took with it a burden he hadn't thought he'd ever be rid of.

She stroked the back of his head, murmuring to him reassuringly. "I won't leave, okay? No matter what happens. Even if it takes my whole life to convince you...I'll gladly take that time. I swear. Because you're worth that. And you deserve to have someone fight for you." She nudged his chin up, gently, brushing away his tears. "Even if that means fighting against yourself some days."

He scrubbed an arm over his eyes, taking in a breath. She smiled at him, softly, and it made his chest ache, but...not in a bad way.

"I care about you too," he found himself whispering, the words spilling out all on their own. "I have, for a long time. I never meant..." He swallowed. "I never wanted to hurt you."

"Shh." She brushed his bangs with her fingers, a quiet smile on her face. "You don't have to apologize."

"I want to," he choked out, tears threatening to burn his eyes again as he reached out to stroke her cheek. Shaking, he raised himself up quietly, shifting to press his lips to her temple and keep them there for a moment, closing his eyes. He could feel the tears slipping down his face, but couldn't bring himself to feel ashamed of them. "Does...that work?" he whispered, opening his eyes to meet hers.

She nodded, something too soft to her eyes that he couldn't look away from as she took his hand in hers, lightly. "Yeah."

He kissed her hand, too, unable to put into words just what was swirling through his mind now. Something new and scary but far too familiar, like a secret he'd just discovered buried deep in him.

"Lena?" He swallowed, carefully. "I... I think I might be in love with you."

At the same time as him, she murmured, "What a pair we make, huh?" Then, surprise crossed her face as his words set in.

Hesitant, he looked away. "If...if that's...okay...?"

"Kaiden." Breathing out quietly, she rested the back of her hand to his cheek. Now it was her turn to look uncertain. "Are you...sure?"

Nodding, he leaned into her touch. "I think so. I haven't..." He hesitated, carefully clearing his throat. "I've never felt like...this, with anyone else."

He didn't know how to put it in words, or even when it started. No – if he thought about it enough, he could. But for right now, that wasn't what mattered. All he knew is he wanted to spend as long as he could to let her know what she meant to him. What she clearly meant to anyone who had half a mind. She might have been hurt, too, but at least she could voice it. She spoke her mind regardless of what it would mean to others, no matter how disguised it sometimes was. He understood that more than he thought anyone ever could.

There were just some people that were meant to be a part of your life. Whether she thought it was due to a god, or fate, or anything she wanted to think, there was a connection between them he didn't think either of them could truly avoid. He thought that even had they not met when they had, they would have somehow found each other anyway, because it was meant to be. *This* was meant to be, somehow, in a way he couldn't explain, but just...knew, as easily as he knew how to breathe.

She looked away for a moment, taking in a breath, and blinked. "You're sweet," she finally murmured. "But I don't deserve that, just because I said I'm sorry..."

A faint smile touched his lips, a bit of the irony rubbing off on him. "I thought that was my line."

She hesitated, eventually letting out a quiet laugh and looking up at him, eyes worried. "You wouldn't want this. I said I'd try, but I-I don't know how I'd do with it. I might still hurt you."

He shook his head, resting his hand on her arm. "I don't care."

"You *should*," she replied, looking away. "You've...been through enough. You don't need that on you, too."

"I'm stubborn," he said, feeling a smile slip onto his lips. "I don't listen very well."

She let out a quiet laugh, almost smiling back. "You're really something. You know that?"

"As long as you mean that in a good way," he murmured, mostly teasing.

The smile spread to her eyes as she nodded. Her eyes took on a soft shine as she took his hands, breathing in like preparing herself.

"I think I might be in love with you too," she admitted. Her gaze glanced away for a moment. "I'm not very good at it, and I'm sure I'll mess it up, but..."

He squeezed her hand gently, letting a quiet laugh free. "You do know who you're talking to, right?"

"Mmhm. A very sweet boy who's too stubborn for his own good."

His chest squeezed at the words. "What can I say? I've never been very good at listening."

"I know." A smile lifted the side of her lips. "Maybe you should try harder."

"Maybe," he admitted quietly, watching her for a moment.

She hesitated, linking her fingers with his. "But, if you're really serious..."

Despite everything, her words made doubt flicker through him. Did he love her, really? Maybe he'd just misunderstood. He didn't really...have much experience. What made him think he had any right to claim such a thing?

She squeezed his hand, gently, and his thoughts stilled.

"I am."

Though he didn't know how to put it into words, he knew, the moment he said it, how true it was. Nothing anyone said or did would change it.

It might have been the truest thing he ever said.

He wanted to find some way to show her just what it meant to him. Words weren't enough. Pictures wouldn't do it. The only thing that would suffice, he thought, was little reminders, every day, piling up and building until one day they would show her exactly how much he cared. He wanted to be the one she stood by, and turned to, the one who could make her laugh even when it was the last thing she wanted to do, and share in her tears. He wanted to find a way to give back even a fraction of what he could to her, because she deserved it.

He might spend the rest of his life trying to figure it out, but it would be worth it. Lightly, he squeezed her hand back, lifting it to brush a kiss to her knuckles. "I mean it," he whispered. "Every word."

Though she took in a soft breath, she disguised it by nudging his shoulder, lightly. "You do realize, though, that I'm never going to stop insulting you."

"Trying to insult me, you mean." He couldn't help the bit of smugness as he rested his head on her shoulder, holding her hand close to his chest. "Maybe with time, I can actually teach you."

"Hey. Beanhead is an entirely valid insult."

"Whatever you say, Priss."

Lightly, she shoved him away, a laugh escaping her lips. "Shut up."

He couldn't stop himself from smiling. "Never."

XXVII

LENA

You can't see the way you look when you smile at someone. You can feel it, but you can't really *know* what it's like to see it through their eyes, for it to be a surprise rather than a planned reaction. You can't see how vulnerable you get when you talk about things that make you sad, or the shine when it's something you love.

You can't see how you look through other's eyes. I think that's why so many people like to say what they're not, rather than what they are. Not brave. Not strong. Not *enough*.

I supposed the same could still apply to me. But I couldn't stop thinking about how he looked, now, and how little he was aware of it. How he couldn't see the light in his eyes, the way his shoulders had untensed as if they had finally, just for a moment, dropped their endless burden. He couldn't see any of it. Even with the bruises forming on his skin and a redness to his eyes that hadn't quite faded, and the long, raised scars stretching across his back, he still didn't think he'd done anything...meaningful. And I didn't know how to explain it to him. So I settled for holding his hand, letting him slowly shift closer as if the nearness helped him relax. There was still a brief flicker to his eyes, every so often, but I did my best to keep that away.

The words hadn't quite...settled yet, drifting in the air like they weren't certain it was alright to land. Kaiden slumped against the wall with a labored breath, though none of the strain showed on his face. Though the bruises were showing, he wore them with no shame this time. He didn't flinch from them, though I saw the sharp intake of breath at a particularly sensitive one. Despite the tiredness playing in his eyes, he looked...content.

"If...this is..." He faltered, his fingers brushing gently against mine. He was practically curled up against me, now, his head resting in my lap as I played with his hair. "If we don't...make it out of this..."

"Shh." That was still a thought I didn't want to consider, but he shook his head, continuing on stubbornly.

436

"I want you to know I meant it. Every word." He swallowed, looking up at me. "I'm not going to change my mind, or take it back, or..." He hesitated. "I didn't just say it because...we might not get out."

I let a faint smile slip onto my face, though he was still looking at me in earnest. "Okay."

He bit his lip, momentarily looking frustrated. "I just...wanted you to know."

I squeezed his hand, smiling. "I know. Thank you."

He stayed quiet for a moment, sitting up a little more against me and fidgeting with the sleeve of his shirt. "My father wasn't a good man," he said quietly, messing with it more. "He's... I didn't..." He swallowed, letting out an uncertain laugh. "I think that's part of why."

I stopped to look at him, trying to keep my gaze from drifting to his back. "Why...?"

He fiddled with the fabric, not meeting my eyes. I let a faint smile touch my lips.

"I may technically be a mind reader, but I wasn't planning on reading your mind."

"I know," he said quietly, taking in a deep breath. "I just...I want to tell you, but it's..." He let out a quiet laugh. "Hard."

I laid my hand on his shoulder, rubbing it gently. "Would it be easier if you showed me?"

He kept his gaze averted, eyes shifting like they couldn't decide where to settle. "I don't...know," he admitted, biting his lip and consequently wincing. "I don't...talk about it. Ever."

"You don't have to," I murmured, squeezing his arm gently. "If it's too hard."

He shook his head, swallowing quietly. "You've seen it anyway," he managed to choke out, curling up tighter as if it might hide what Talon did, even as it made the gap in his shirt pull wider. "I want you to know." He averted his gaze again, almost as if he was ashamed. "If only so it...explains things. I don't want pity," he said quietly. "I just...don't want to keep secrets any longer."

I nodded, giving him a moment. He rubbed one of the scars on his hand, pulling in a deep, slightly unsteady breath. "He...ah. My...my father gave me these." Quietly, he pointed to a longer one on his arm, the corner of his mouth lifting faintly. "That one was from Gigi. She got into a lot of trouble. I had to pull her out of it, most of the time." He shook his head, even as a slight shadow crossed his face. It seemed to take him a moment to collect himself, taking in a short breath. "Most of the others, though..."

He shut his eyes for a moment, quieter when he opened them. "Well. Damien...knew, and used a lot of it against me." He swallowed quietly, his eyes flicking to mine for a moment, and then away. "Which is why...he..."

He gestured a little toward his back, wincing again. I couldn't help but follow the motion, my chest tightening at the implications, and the ugly marks poking through. It still hurt to look at them, even with the brief glimpses I'd seen before. Somehow it was worse like this, when there wasn't anything to clean up. No way to fix the damage seared into him from the past.

His eyes flickered a little, as if seeing something I couldn't. "Damien worked with my father for a while. Which is how I met him." He averted his eyes, tense for a moment. "He was also... 'fascinated' with my 'strength,'" he mumbled, drawing his arms around himself. The corner of his lips twitched a bit. "Kaiden means 'warrior' or 'strong one', ironically enough. I always thought it was a cruel joke." He drew in a slow breath, eyes slightly distant. "My mother liked it. My father wanted to name me something different. Maybe *that's* why he didn't like me."

His lips twisted up wryly, in a poor attempt at a joke. It faded a moment later as he rubbed at his wrist again. "He liked to say they'd been happy, before I was born. So I guess I ruined that, somehow." His lips lifted faintly again. "I mean...my mom came from a very well-off family. They practically disowned her for marrying my dad, and he didn't have a lot of money. So I guess I did, then, since they hardly had enough money to support the two of them." He rubbed his wrist again, continuing on before I could interject. "And then he lost his job not long after, and my mother found one instead. Guess he blamed me for that, too." He took in a slow breath, shifting to disguise a little shiver I still felt run through him. "So it was just us a lot, or us with my siblings. He'd...go off and do who-knew-what, when I was a little older, and come back in a very different mood. Usually a bad one."

Though I didn't want to interrupt him, I slipped an arm around his shoulders. He messed with his sleeve again, quiet. Slowly, he swallowed. "He– Ah. I don't...remember when it really...started." Rubbing his thumb over his wrist, he drew in a quiet breath. "Other than..." he dug a nail into the skin, blinking at it, "when I...got my gift. It...it helped, since he..." He shook his head, blinking fast. "He pretended they were accidents, or said it was my fault. I couldn't...tell my mom, either." He looked away, quiet. "He wouldn't let me."

I squeezed his arm lightly, and he tensed. Blinking it off a moment later, he shook his head. "Sorry. It's a lot." He rubbed the back of his

438

neck, eyes flickering a little. His hand slipped a little lower, just barely touching the scars that curled up there. "My mom wasn't very strong, physically. He said I wasn't allowed to worry her. Or that he'd hurt her, too, if I did." He let his gaze drop down, with his hand, voice near a whisper. "And I didn't want to upset her. She loved my dad. She said he was trying his hardest." He scrubbed a fist against his eyes, a quiet laugh escaping. "So I kept it to myself."

He bit his lip, his eyes going distant again for a moment before he shrugged. "It wasn't usually that bad, until later. He'd tell her I'd gotten into a fight, if it was particularly bad. Sometimes, he even used that as justification to hurt me again, as 'punishment' for acting out." Quiet, he shook his head. "He couldn't hurt the other kids, though. I didn't...I wouldn't...let him."

Shrugging faintly, he rubbed at his arm. "He didn't seem to hate Kel or Katana as much, anyway. Maybe because they didn't look like Mom." He paused, looking up at his own still-black hair with a faint, humorless smile. "And the one time he tried, with Kinny, I made him stop. He didn't like that." He rubbed at his arm again. "He'd hurt me worse if I showed it too much, or started crying. He said I was weak. And a million other things."

Rubbing at his throat lightly, he cleared it. "But it wasn't that bad. He kept most of it out of sight, or just got...creative." Shaking his head again, he took in a slow breath. "And then...I don't know what happened. My mom was always tired, but...it got worse, one day, and she didn't really get better. I found jobs where I could to keep us fed, since my father still didn't have one. He left during the day a lot. Sometimes he came back drunk, later." He lowered his gaze, mumbling, "That was usually...easier, because he wasn't as..." a small laugh choked from his lips, "coordinated."

Swallowing, he shifted to sit up against me a little better and drew his knees up, partially hiding the scars. "One day I came back, and he was...crying. I knew right then that something had gone terribly wrong."

He rested his arms on his knees, dropping his head down on them, his shoulders growing tense. "He wouldn't explain what happened. She was just...gone. I really thought he might kill me that time," he admitted quietly, "when he found me afterward. He didn't really...have a reason to show restraint any longer." He shifted, swallowing slightly and rubbing a hand over his eyes. A breathless laugh escaped his lips. "I barely remember that night. Or a lot of them after that." His hand brushed the top part of his back again. "I just know if Kinny hadn't gotten help, I...would have..."

439

He looked away, not even needing to finish the sentence. I rested a hand on his shoulder, gently, and he laid his over it, quiet for a long moment. He fought down a long shudder, his lip trapped between his teeth to keep it from wavering. "That was one of the worst...times," he choked out hoarsely, blinking. "My father didn't come back for a while, after that. I wasn't even sure he would. I was terrified every time I left the house that I'd come back to find he had, and I wasn't there.

"When he did come back, eventually, it would be at night. I still...let him hurt me, rather than risking finding he'd taken it out on them, instead. I...I let him do whatever he wanted, as long as he left them alone. I thought...that would be enough."

He expelled a long breath, resting his head gently against our hands. "Then Damien really took an interest in me. He paid me, at times, to do things for him. Test...well, let him test things." He rubbed his wrist again, shrugging and glancing over to the side away before continuing. "I found out my father was working with Galdanians, on dangerous and underhanded things I didn't care to know about. He must have betrayed them, or was no longer useful to them, because they stabbed him in the back." He let out a humorless sound. "As in...I found him dead with a knife in his back, one day."

He went silent for a long moment again. "Apparently I should have cared, though, because two men tried to kill me less than a week later. Damien claims he rescued me. All I know is they beat me until I passed out, and then I woke up in the Mountain. With Kinny." He averted his eyes again. "Though, recently found out he lied about what happened there. He forced Kinny to use her gifts, beyond her breaking point, to try to heal me. He manipulated her, and me."

He shook his head, another quiet laugh leaving his lips. His fingers curled into fists, and I slipped mine between them, smoothing my thumb over his knuckles. "And then *he* threatened our siblings, and said he had them elsewhere. He must have known I wouldn't leave them otherwise. He made us stay at the Mountain...and used whatever he could against me. I didn't have much of a choice." He smiled faintly, eyes going to mine. "Which is why he hurt me like that, before. Because my father had. So he knew it would get to me."

He was still smiling a little, like it was stuck on his face. "My mother, though, she was...wonderful." He murmured the word like a treasure. "She comforted me even when she thought I'd gotten in a fight. She held me, or sang, and told me how much she loved me." The smile wavered, eyes too bright moments before he blinked it away. But, hearing the opposite all the time, that it was my fault and to choke it down because I was weak and that wasn't allowed, it...it just became a part of me. Easier to believe it, to try to justify it all. I thought, in the beginning, I really *had* done something wrong. Nothing I did made him look at me differently. I thought I'd just...failed."

He glanced over to his side again, a sad smile on his face. "Still think that, a lot," he admitted quieter. "It's...hard to get rid of it." The smile disappeared as he looked back down. "So it's not that I don't believe you. It...I just have a hard time believing in myself."

I waited a moment, as he finally met my eyes again, and then pulled him into a hug. He swallowed, but returned the gesture, squeezing me tightly as a sharp breath escaped his throat. "It doesn't bother me."

"It's okay if it does," I answered, squeezing him lightly again. I rested my head against his, breathing out quietly. After a moment, I pulled back, just enough to brush the side of his face. "Some things just...take time."

He watched me quietly, something heavier behind his eyes before he finally nodded. "Yeah. They do."

Fear exposed the best and worst in people. It tore us apart, and brought us back together. I squeezed his shoulder, pulling him gently down against me. He let out a quiet sound, pressing his face into my shoulder.

"Thank you."

I squeezed him gently, shifting to cradle him against me. "What for?"

"Listening," he whispered. "And...understanding."

"I fight with memories all the time, too," I said softly, wrapping my arm more fully around him despite the way it made him tense up for a moment. "I know what it's like."

He nodded, quiet for a moment before glancing at the side again. "I don't...like people seeing."

"Seeing?"

"Scars," he choked out, eyes pained. "The...reminders."

"I won't look, if you don't want me to."

His gaze fell, shame smothering any other emotion. After a long moment, he added, "That's why he did it."

"Your dad...?"

He shut his eyes. "Talon."

"Oh." Hesitantly, I rubbed his shoulders. "You don't have to be ashamed, Kaiden."

"I know," he cut in, regretfully. He still wouldn't look at me. "But I am."

Hesitating, I reached up to brush his cheek, softly. "Why?"

441

He kept his gaze away for a long time, things warring in his eyes that I wished I could help him fight. "They're...my failures."

I shook my head, shifting to hug him better, and squeezing him lightly, despite how that also made him tense up. "No. Scars aren't reminders of your failures. They're testaments to your strength." I pulled in a soft breath, wishing I could hold him closer. Hesitating, I shifted my hand to rest against them, gently. "Especially these."

He pressed his face against me, as a shudder ran through him. "No..." he murmured, though he didn't sound convinced. "I..."

"It doesn't matter what Talon said, or your dad, or anyone else. They're not right. I promise," I added softly, leaving my hand against his back. "Because the reasons for them? That is *brave*. I don't care what you think. Just because you couldn't stop it doesn't mean you didn't make it better – in the most selfless way possible." Expelling a quiet breath, I rested my cheek on his shoulder. "I couldn't have done that," I murmured. "Few people would."

He shut his eyes, pulling in a slow, unsteady breath. "You would."

"No." I shook my head, pulling away just enough for him to see the honesty in my eyes, sad as it was. "My stepfather...wasn't *half* as bad, and I still wouldn't..." I swallowed around the ache in my throat. "I couldn't have...faced him."

Clearing his throat, he lifted his shoulder in a faint shrug. "What else was I supposed to do?"

I let my eyes drift shut, settling my chin on his shoulder so my lips were close to his ear. "One day, you're going to see it. Just how incredible you are. And I hope I'm there for that."

"You should be," he whispered back, as if only to himself. "I'd never get there without you. Or-" He cut himself off, hesitating as he pulled away, just enough to see my eyes. "There's...one other thing I need to tell you."

"You're secretly a dragon. I knew it."

He looked away, smiling. It made my shoulders lighter to see it. "Hm. Not quite."

"No? You've already got the fire part down. All you need to do is learn how to fly."

His shoulders tensed a little. "I don't like flying."

"Scared of heights?" I teased, regretting it as he looked away.

"My dad..." He shook his head, swallowing, and then nodded. "He used that against me, too."

"I'm sorry." I brushed my fingers through his hair, watching how it made him relax, just a little. "What were you trying to say?"

His gaze drifted to the same empty spot again, which was starting to make me wonder. "I have...a friend. But you can't see her."

I raised an eyebrow slowly, remembering his little thief's comment. "Meaning... you have an imaginary friend?"

He shook his head, but looked down. "Not...quite." He hesitated again, glancing at that spot for a long moment. "If we get out of here, I'll have to introduce you."

"Well, now we really have to get out, huh? The suspense might kill me otherwise, before anything else can." I let out a quiet chuckle, teasing. "So you're *not* crazy, after all."

A faint smile touched his lips. "No. And you don't have to worry." He scanned the panels of the ceiling, as if searching for something. "I have no intention of losing my head today. Literally or otherwise."

Though he grinned, I felt sick to my stomach. Would I have to watch, if that happened?

To avoid that thought, and the severity of the situation we'd both been avoiding, I settled against the wall, letting my shoulders relax. He stayed pressed against me,

"Any other crazy secrets you want to share with me?" I asked quietly.

He fiddled with the edge of his shirt. "I could tell you more about Gigi."

"It sounds like you have a lot of stories there," I mused, and then made a face. "I don't have any wonderful stories worth telling. Just odd days of traveling to seaside towns and beaches and playing hide and seek with my brother."

He was smiling again. I stopped, looking at him. "What?"

"It sounds...nice."

I let out a quiet laugh. "Caleb, maybe. Most of my days were not worth mentioning." I stopped. "And...Caleb left when I was young, anyway. With my dad. It was just my mom and I, until she remarried."

He laced his fingers with mine, squeezing tightly.

"Anyway," I said, forcing another laugh, "You were going to tell me about Gigi?"

He was about to speak when footsteps cut us off. His hand tightened in mine, his face coming against me for a brief moment as he took in a tight breath.

"Together," I murmured quietly, squeezing. Whatever happened, we would face it together.

He wouldn't let go of my hand, watching the door. "Together," he echoed, quiet.

I hesitated, leaning over to briefly kiss the top of his head. "If this *is* how it ends," I said softly, "then I'm glad it's with you."

He smiled quietly, though it was replaced by tension when the door opened. It wasn't Talon that stepped in, but several of the Empress' guards, the majority of their faces concealed by their helmets. Kaiden gripped my hand tight enough it hurt. The guard in front narrowed his eyes on Kaiden, glancing at our linked hands before he grabbed Kaiden's shoulder to yank him away. "*Move.*"

He held his ground, though, something unwavering in his eyes as he kept his hand over mine. "Tell Talon to come get us himself."

The guard snorted, eyeing him derisively. Something about it struck me as different, even as he leaned in close and hissed, "Don't test me, kid." He shot a sharp glance at me. "Just be good, sport, and things will go smoothly."

Sport. My brow furrowed for a moment at the word, as seemingly out of place for a guard as everything else about him seemed to be. The guard narrowed his eyes, as if warning me to stay quiet. Did that mean...was my suspicion right?

Taking a chance, I let go of Kaiden's hand when the guards tried to pull him away again. We couldn't fight forever, anyway. Confusion mixed with hurt as he fought against them, earning him a solid blow to the stomach. The first guard unlocked my chains and yanked me out of the room, Kaiden shouting at them as we left.

"He's my *friend*," I snapped at the guard, once we were out of earshot. His voice was too gravelly, his face too concealed to truly be sure of my theory. If I was wrong, my words wouldn't give me away. But if I *was* right, I had to take this chance, or they'd just leave Kaiden there.

The guard stopped, pulling up his facemask just enough to confirm my suspicions. *Caleb.*

He was alive. Not only that, but he was *here*. We hadn't failed, after all. Even though I didn't get any information, or keep Kaiden safe, or...

"Your *friend*?" he retorted, lowering his voice so only we could hear. "He got our father killed. He's working with the *Empress*. He's not your friend, Lena."

"That wasn't his fault. You don't know him!"

He let out a laugh, his eyes sad for the briefest moment as he pushed the mask back in place. "I can't let you get hurt again, even if you somehow think he's right. I'm getting you out of here."

I tried to pull my wrist free, fighting down a spike of panic at the action. "If you take me, you take him, too."

"We don't have *time* for games, Lena!"

"Exactly." I yanked my wrist again. "So you have to bring him with."

Caleb cursed, not letting go of my hand, but barked a command back to his companions once they joined us. After a moment of hesitation, they complied, bringing Kaiden out with them. His cheek was cut and reddening, his eyes filled with a barely suppressed fire from his gift. The Empress kept them dampened, somehow, throughout her dungeons. "Keep a close eye on him," Caleb warned them. For a moment, with the determination alight in his eyes and tension coiled in him, I couldn't blame them. He *looked* dangerous.

I reached toward him, but Caleb kept a hold on my wrist, tugging me along. "We need to make this convincing if someone stops us," he muttered, his back now rigid again as he walked.

One of his guard friends frowned. "How will this affect...?"

"I'll figure it out," Caleb snapped, keeping a brisk pace. "They're still distracted. It'll work."

"You'd better hope so," the other said, her voice low as she kept a tight hold on Kaiden's arm. "I didn't risk my life just to rescue one prisoner."

"She's my *sister*," Caleb growled, "and the Empress would have killed her if we didn't."

"She might anyway," the woman muttered, "if we're *all* caught."

Caleb shook his head. "The plan will still work. I know it."

I furrowed my brow at them, sending a brief assuring look at Kaiden despite his expression. He stayed behind where no one could see his back, the lines of his shoulders tense.

"Yeah. How *did* you know we were down there...?"

Caleb looked at me, a breath escaping through his nose. "I didn't, until we heard the guards talking about it. You unintentionally helped us, by getting caught." He cast a sharp look either direction down the corridor we passed before continuing on. "We knew the Empress wouldn't leave herself unguarded just because there was an event going on. But it provided a distraction, and chaos if we needed it." He lowered his voice, to keep things secret. "With you being found out, they think the danger is contained. It's the perfect time to strike."

"Which we're currently wasting while being down here," the guard holding Kaiden added under her breath, and cast a glance at me. "No offense to you."

I shook my head. "Wait. You're..."

"Going to kill the Empress. Yes." He smiled, a sharp, calm thing like the balanced edge of a knife. He only got that look when he was completely committed to a plan, no matter how terrible the odds. "We just had to get you first."

I stared at him, silent for a moment. "*What?*"

Caleb started up the stairs leading out, tightening his hold on my wrist. I fought down a wince. Kaiden kept his gaze away, frowning at the wall. "We draw her Gifted away, once we get close, and then take her out when no one suspects it."

"This is the *Empress* you're talking about. She's-"

"Human. And vulnerable. Most of her guards aren't even certain she's meant to lead anymore," Caleb said briskly. "Their loyalty is shaken. As long as Talon and the others aren't around, it won't be hard."

I shook my head. Caleb put a finger to his lips before I could speak, pulling us up the next flight of stairs. "When we get back in the fortress, split up," he said, nodding to his friends. "Find Talon. Tell him you've found another guest to interrogate. Get him away from the Empress, and keep him busy. He's our biggest concern right now."

The taller, thinner one shifted uneasily, eyeing Kaiden. "What about him?"

In one fluid motion, Caleb let go of my wrist and caught Kaiden's shoulders, pressing him harshly into the wall. I bit my lip hard at the action.

"Well. If he so much as touches her or does a *single thing* to endanger her or any of us, I will make sure he's barely alive to regret it. Got that?"

Kaiden nodded, only a hint of a wince crossing his face. Caleb released him, shoulders rigid as he pushed open the door. No one dared question him, most of the guards we encountered seeming too at ease with what was going on.

The others split off as they'd been commanded, leaving just the three of us alone. Caleb took my arm this time, pulling us along. I wrapped Kaiden's hand in mine, sending reassurances through the mental link now that it wasn't suppressed. He was tense, like he thought he might be hit for it, but I kept a stubborn hold.

"It wasn't him," I insisted to Caleb, as we walked down a surprisingly empty hallway. "The Bane was just controlling him. It wasn't his fault. He's been protecting me." Kaiden turned his gaze away, as if he hadn't heard.

"Forgive me if I'm not so trusting," Caleb muttered in response, shoving open a door.

"Sir." The guard approaching us gave a salute I'd never seen before. Caleb seemed to relax. "Everything is in place."

Caleb cast a warning glance at Kaiden as we slipped into the next room, much nearer to the throne room. "Keep an eye on him," he warned me.

I suppressed a sigh, squeezing Kaiden's hand lightly. "You're really going to kill the Empress?"

"The Cities are fragile enough right now. If we take her down, the entire system will collapse. The people won't fight back, even if they knew how to. We take the Cities, through force if necessary, and establish a new rule, where Gifted aren't executed just for existing." His jaw tightened. "Some of them won't listen. But I believe some will, given the choice. Which they won't have, anyway. So, yes. We're going to kill the Empress."

I held tight to Kaiden's hand as we followed Caleb. He frowned.

"Once it's done, you're going to need to get out of here. There's no telling what kind of backlash we'll encounter. If nothing else, there will be chaos."

"I'll get her out," Kaiden said beside me, even as Caleb shot him a cold look. He held it silently, unafraid. "I promise."

"You'd better."

A feeling of unease crept up my spine as we grew closer to the Empress' location. "Even if you get the Gifted away in time, the Empress isn't...helpless."

"I didn't think she was all that Empressive," Kaiden replied. He paused. "Wait, I said that last time, didn't I?"

Caleb pulled us into a side room, searching for and then shoving spare guard uniforms at us. "Put those on."

"Yes, you did," I answered Kaiden, burying amusement as I pulled on the armor. It was surprisingly light, but bulky for me and smelled funny, the facemask providing me a too welcome sense of relief as I slipped it on. Kaiden pulled his on, brow furrowing as he tried to figure out the mask. I turned it around, giving him a smile he could barely see as he put it on. Caleb stood by the door, hand on his sword as if watching for intruders.

"The Empress will be able to tell if something is off with three of us. But the two of you can hide in the back of the room and keep an eye on things in those." He nodded to the uniforms, crossing his arms. "Your belt is crooked," he told Kaiden.

He looked down at it and quickly fixed it, almost looking embarrassed. I hid a smile. "Yeah, can't have that, can we?"

"No." Caleb walked to the door, pulling in a breath, then paused, motioning to us. "Go in that way," he said, motioning to a less grand version of the main doors. "She won't be able to see you from there.

447

Stay low and stay *quiet*." He narrowed his eyes on Kaiden, and then me, muttering, "You might be my sister, but I'm not letting you botch this opportunity with your clumsiness."

I rolled my eyes. "Well gee, thanks for the vote of confidence." I did feel *slightly* unbalanced in the armor. "We'll stay out of the way."

An almost smile crossed Caleb's face before he nodded. I pulled Kaiden through the doors quietly, settling behind an intricate statue to watch. Would this actually work?

SARI

Something wasn't right. Shedim should have attacked the city by now. Ru'ach was unusually quiet, which Sari chose to see as a good sign. Perhaps she had made progress with her brother. Perhaps she had merely prevented the whole thing.

But no. The truth was far more worrisome than that. Raoul paced in front of her, agitated. They'd kept the news from most of the city still. There was no need to worry them all, when they didn't even know what to prepare for.

She knew it had been a bad idea, telling so many the truth. They had *needed* the Gifted, and they needed the truth, and yet...she had known the risks, too.

It had only been a matter of time, she repeated to herself. Shedim would have discovered the information somehow.

Just...perhaps not this soon.

"Let him have them," Raoul muttered finally. "I don't see how it's our business."

But the way he was pacing, restless since discovering the news, said otherwise. Ru'ach's return ensured that Shedim would leave them be – for the moment – but it turned out he had his eye on another target, now. Somehow or another, they had been betrayed. A spy or defector had relayed the secret of Gifted to one of Talon's men. Not knowing the consequence of the knowledge, they let the secret spread, until Shedim found out.

She'd been afraid this was coming. Now that Shedim knew that *all* humans were capable of manifesting Gifts...there was no need to be so selective about who he slaughtered. Ru'ach's return kept them well-protected, but left the arrogant Cities entirely defenseless, and unaware. Even if they knew the scope of what was coming, they couldn't possibly prepare for it. Raoul's Gifted would have hardly stood a chance were it not for the dragons.

And now, they had a choice. Sari knew, as well as Raoul did, that many of his people wouldn't care about the Cities. The people there had certainly never cared about anyone else. Why shouldn't they be left to their plight?

But they were *people*, and they were defenseless. It was an easy decision, in Sari's mind, and one she knew Raoul would soon come to. The only question, then, was who to tell.

Dragons did not need humans to fight, or make decisions of their own. It was as ridiculous a notion as claiming that Sari couldn't act without Ru'ach's permission. Despite the grudges many held against the Galdanians, dragons were honorable creatures, far deeper down than they wished to admit. They couldn't willingly turn a blind eye to human suffering, when they could stop it. Many had retreated because the Galdanians treated dragons as useless – little more than pets, or ornamentation for their own wealth. But if they stayed here, and didn't act, the Cities would be destroyed, and precious life lost.

With or without the humans, the dragons had made a choice. Sari was simply waiting to see what Raoul's was.

XXVIII

BASIL

Something wasn't right. Other than the small fiasco they'd dealt with...there hadn't been any *real* attacks. Had Shedim changed his mind? Had Ru'ach stopped them?

Basil was almost relieved when Sari called them together. She had to know what was going on, even though she seemed...distracted, and not quite herself.

"Shedim is not coming."

He would have relaxed, were it not for her troubled expression. There was something she didn't want to say. Something she hadn't informed the rest of the city of.

"I was right. Ru'ach protected the city." There was a hanging '*however*' in her words, though, and he could tell they were all braced for it.

"He knows," she said quietly. "Shedim...knows the secret of the Gifted."

Silence fell over them, as the implications set in. Sari drew in a quiet breath, some of the calm returning to her face. "He isn't coming, because there is no need to pick and choose anymore. And so, he has chosen the easiest target. One very few would stand to protect."

The Cities. Chan swore sharply under his breath. Basil startled, wondering if he'd heard something wrong.

"This is...good, right?" They weren't in any immediate danger. It was an immense burden off his shoulders.

"It would be," Chan muttered, looking torn for a moment before he scrubbed a hand over his face, "if Kaiden and Lena weren't currently *in* the Cities."

At their shock, and confusion, he explained the truth of their friends' mission, to open mouths and tightened jaws. Olive looked about ready to hit someone over the head with a staff, her lips a tight, dark line.

They all fell silent at the explanation. Basil's throat tightened. "We have to *do* something. Right?"

450

Sari's gaze was distant – worryingly so. "Ru'ach..." She shook her head, the submission on her face slipping off like an unwanted mask. "It is up to you. Ru'ach believes she can still stop her brother." She cast a gaze at Chan, her face unreadable. "I do not know how long that will take."

Galdanian or not, they couldn't just let that many people be slaughtered. Basil glanced around the group, relieved to see the same determination reflected there. Whether it was simply for their friends or for everything else, he knew they would agree.

"I do not know who among the humans will join, but you have the support of the dragons," Sari said. "Shedim is sure to make his move very soon. We should attempt to cut him off before he does."

VERENE

Verene was tired.

All her life, she had been told what to believe. What to do, and say, and think. It made things easy, and incredibly stifling. It also made forming her own path near impossible.

You are destined for greatness, they would say, as they dusted a stray speck of dust off her circlet and forced a smile on her face. *Act like it.*

Her own parents had been killed for their foolishness. A curse, anyone else would have called it, but Verene knew better. It was amusing, the number of things that could be covered up by the pretense of it being the hand of gods.

Now, that power was gone. Shedim had failed her, and Verene found herself slipping again, nearly caught in the cracks between what she believed and what she used to. Doubting herself, once again, as she swore she never would.

Curse her parents a thousand times, from wherever they rested, for drilling it into her. They had been a nuisance she simply couldn't allow. It was a marvel how blind their devotion was, that an entire country would turn a blind eye to the death of its rulers in belief of their 'disobedience'. It was far too easy to frame them.

They had gotten in her way. She never wanted to believe what they did, and yet it would have been her head otherwise if she disobeyed.

Her head, or theirs.

Once the queen-regent was old enough to assume command, it only seemed natural that the cycle should continue, as it always had. The strong rising up to take what they yearned for, through whatever means necessary. For the greater good.

Verene was always hungry for more. She envied those that harnessed the power of the gods. She used it to challenge their own beliefs. She'd studied and pressed at those she found, tore them apart in hopes of discovering the secret.

Before today, she'd had no success. Now, it seemed she might have found the key.

And it was so frustratingly easy, it made a bitter laugh leave her lips, harsh as sour wine. It was like telling a child they need only believe they could fly, and they would magically lift off the ground.

Verene envied her Gifted, who stood unaware how precious a power they had. The kind to defy the gods. No wonder the Bane kept Gifted under wraps.

But Verene was not foolish enough to simply defy the gods. No, she had decided to usurp them, subverting their power by turning it against them. Gathering her army, so none could stop her.

Verene was not childish enough to believe that all should have access to this pool of knowledge. Only those deemed fit for it. And if she had to kill others to make that the case, well, there was little problem to that.

She held back a sigh as one of her guards entered the room. Once, their loyalty had been something she treasured. Now it was only tiring, as they insisted that she get to safety at the slightest alarm, as if she was some weak thing unable to fend for herself.

Verene had sworn to find a way to harness a gift of her own, or die trying. It was the only way they would ever view her as more than a liability. A figurehead, the crowning piece on her gameboard, meant only to be protected.

But Shedim had left her. Her own people were turned against her, waiting for her to earn back their trust. As if she were the one who had broken it, somehow, rather than the 'gods' they so admired.

It was then it had become perfectly, startlingly clear to Verene. She was never meant to win. She had clawed her way through life thus far, if one could call it living, but this was never meant to be hers.

It was theirs. And that was a gift she freely gave.

She allowed herself a moment to contemplate a day ages past, when the largest concern on her mind was how tart the juice she was given tasted on her lips, and that she said each of her many prayers before her eyes drifted shut for the night. Verene had always felt empty, even then. Lacking in the one thing that seemed to fuel all the other useless shells in this country. Belief.

And yet she knew, as clearly as day, that to defy the gods was to invite ruin on them all. She had to be cleverer, and fool the beings posing as them into believing she was playing along.

It was easy, directing her hate toward those unlucky few she found. How she would have liked to pick their minds, instead, but it did give her a flicker of satisfaction to watch the light slip from their eyes, to steal from them what should have been rightfully hers. Even more so now, knowing how long it had been taunting her.

Verene was never satisfied. She wanted *more*. She wanted to explore the depths of these abilities, and the forbidden nature of them only made them that much more tempting.

In the beginning, she may have still harbored some fear as to her actions. It was a thrill, defying those she had served for so long, and wondering if she might be discovered for it.

But she never was. And so she grew bolder and bolder, employing Gifted for her own purposes. They were the only ones who could stop her. They were a danger, and an asset. A lit flame, sparking in her fingers. Kept too close, they would burn everything down. But at the right distance, she could fuel her greatest dreams with them.

And what a perfect opportunity, then, to prove them all wrong and silence the voice in her head. Despite Shedim's disappearance, it was always warned that he would see their actions, and even Verene found herself keeping to shadows in hopes of hiding them.

She surveyed the damage from the highest window, a breath of calm rushing over her. If this was her punishment, so be it. If this was the way she gained her wings, she would pay that price.

All she wanted was to be *free*.

LENA

The Empress looked too...regal, as if she had been expecting this. Perhaps she was, with Caleb, at least. I had no idea how deep his cover went.

"Say your piece."

He gave her a salute, in the way I was more familiar with seeing, armor scraping as he bowed. "All the imposters have been caught, your Majesty. Talon is...dealing with them."

Her lips spread in a slow smile. Caleb cleared his throat, gesturing to his companion, who had rejoined him. "Nevertheless, we will continue to protect you, until this matter is settled."

The Empress was a clever woman, and yet I saw a smile curve onto her face as she regarded him. "I am perfectly capable of taking care of myself."

"Of course, Majesty. I meant no disrespect. But it would be our honor, anyway." He lifted his hands in a reverent salute.

If I admitted it, she simply looked...amused. "If you're going to kill me, I suggest you get it over with."

Caleb's face twisted in shock. "How could you suggest such a thing?"

The Empress sighed, sinking into her enormous throne as she rested a hand on her eyes. "You don't think I've heard the rumors? I am quite certain there is at least one person in this fortress who would see me dead, either by their hand or another's."

Caleb's shoulders tensed just slightly. He disguised it brilliantly, taking on a tone of indignation. "I would stop them, Majesty."

"Would you? Or would you simply let them strike?" She smiled at him, something playing in her eyes. "As I said. There will be no need for guards. If someone wishes me dead, they may face me themselves."

He hesitated. "And, what do you plan to do against such intruders, Majesty?"

"Flee. Dispatch of them myself. Let them come." She waved a hand, seeming distracted. "I don't appreciate such questions. I am not helpless."

"We have word," Caleb continued, "that the rebels are growing stronger. They *will* strike at some point, Majesty, and if they managed to take you out, the Cities will crumble."

"Such little faith you have in them," she replied, musing. "And so much placed in me."

Before he could respond, she took a sip from the wine sitting beside her, one hand delicately curved against her cheek.

"I had always assumed," she mused, "that there was simply something I was missing. An element to complete the puzzle. But now I've been informed that anyone can manifest these Gifts. It's no wonder they were kept so tightly under wraps. Can you imagine the chaos that would breed?"

She rose from her chair, pacing in a slow, graceful manner. "I cannot unlock the mysteries of these abilities, nor do I know any who are capable of them. I am beginning to believe I truly am cursed by my ancestors, never to find the thing for which I wish most. Searching for riches is easy when you have a kingdom at your command. But if even they cannot provide it...what is the point? I have failed. I begin to wonder if I made a mistake, and doubt myself. Perhaps...this is their way of telling me it is time to step down. Perhaps if I shed this mortal skin, I shall finally be able to fly.

"It is never inquired, you understand," she continued with fervor, "whether or not you wish for this job. It is simply handed to you, ruins and boxes of baggage from your predecessors, and you are expected to carry it. There is no alternative."

Why hadn't he struck yet? Caleb seemed determined to discover the Empress' secrets – even if most of those were likely from too much wine. "And?"

"As I said. I only ever wished to fly." She took another drink of her wine, savoring it. "But this city demanded a hand to push them, and so I complied. And what have I received in return? Not gratitude, but suspicion." She shook her head, her eyes thin slits as she eyed the glass in her hand. "These people are too mired in worthless superstitions to be of any use." She sighed, setting the glass aside and folding her hands in front of her. "And yet I still wished that they might see. It would appear that is not meant to be." Her eyes glinted as she looked back at him. "The gods rejected my help; I am no fool. I understand the dangers of Gifts being rampant. But under the right hand..." She raised hers in front of her, slowly closing it into a fist and then letting it slip away, shaking her head. "I truly believed I could change them."

Caleb watched her, seeming caught between his own wondering and searching for an opening to strike.

"Let their chaos destroy them," she said bitterly, that light back in her eyes as she examined her hand, and the many jewel-laden rings on it. "My chosen will continue forth with their task. Mine, it seems, has drawn to a close." She eyed Caleb. "And I presume you shall be the one to carry it out."

None of this was making sense. The Empress was...giving up? I wanted to call out to Caleb that it must be a trap. She knew what she was doing. She was far too clever for this.

"It doesn't matter who attempts to take my place. My Gifted will assure it is who I wish, and that my plan will continue on."

She smiled, a wide, unpleasant thing. "I was never meant to have them, was I? I see it now, clearer than I ever had. My true role in all of this. The sacrifice, for our dream to live on." She tilted her head at him. "Perhaps then, at the end, they will see fit to grant my one request, if only to be rid of my incessant questions."

Caleb took a step toward her, shaking his head. "Your 'Gifted' will never rule."

Her smile only grew as she watched him, reaching to finger the stem of her glass again and lift it up. "So you assume. But time may very well prove to you otherwise." She examined the edge of the glass, something certain filling her eyes. "This is not over."

Caleb drew his sword, placing the tip of it to her neck. "Give up."

The Empress nearly looked amused, not at all concerned with his sword. "Is that not what I am doing? Would you prefer I snivel and beg for my life?" Her eyes glinted with a hint of danger. "I can assure you, this is not your victory. It may take years, but they will come, and they will carry out my vision. You shall see it." She lifted her chin proudly. "They all will."

Caleb drew his sword across her throat even before she had finished, red weeping from the wound as she sank against her throne. The glass in her hand fell and shattered, sending a spray of wine across them both. It made the picture more gruesome than it actually was.

And so it was that the Empress of Galdania died with a smile on her face, having defied her 'gods' for better or worse, and won. And the world would never be the same.

It was unsettling, seeing her smile in her death. As if we'd done her a favor, sealing the final act of her devastating plan. As if this were simply the crowning glory of her grand scheme, and we had played right into her hands.

"That was for my father," Caleb said unevenly, watching the blood seep off of the seat. "And for the million other innocents you've murdered. I don't care how you wanted to justify it. It was *wrong*." He pressed the tip of his sword into the floor, leaning on it. "My actions were honorable."

He still looked troubled for a moment, looking at the blood on his sword and tossing it aside. "Lena?"

I pulled Kaiden out from our cover, watching his grim face. Surprisingly, Caleb focused his eyes on Kaiden.

"Get her out of here. Whatever it takes – *keep her safe*." He looked over at me, drawing in a breath, and then turned away, muttering as he went, "If you don't..."

"You'll flay me alive. I get it," Kaiden murmured, shaking his head slightly and turning away from the Empress' fallen body. His smile was almost apologetic at the look on my face. "Not that you need protecting."

"You have that right," I muttered, following him out of the room. I couldn't shake the image of the Empress, or what she'd said. She was right, wasn't she? This wasn't how it should have gone.

The fortress *shook*. I held onto Kaiden's arm, my eyes widening. His expression matched mine as he walked over to the nearest window, peering out of it.

"What..." The dread was growing as I followed him over, taking in his grim expression. It had to be huge, to shake a place this big. As if the building itself was crying out in protest of the blood spilt.

I followed Kaiden's gaze, my mouth slowly dropping open. Outside, wreaking havoc and breathing flames everywhere, were *dragons*. Far too many dragons, like...

Like they had decided to attack here, instead of elsewhere. My mouth went dry at the implication. Had they already crushed our city? Ru'ach said she would protect them. Was she wrong?

Whatever the reason, Kaiden took ahold of my hand, tugging me along down the hall as swiftly as he could. Further down, party guests were beginning to panic, and he headed for an empty stairwell, hoping to avoid them. His knowledge of the layout surprised me, until I remembered the time he had spent with the Bane. Maybe that was still in his memories, somewhere. Or he was just very, very lucky. He found a back exit and tugged me out, past stables that left a pungent smell in my nostrils. Smoke wafted in the air nearby us. With the number of dragons Shedim had, it wouldn't take long for them to lay siege to the City.

"We have to help them," I murmured. They might have been horrible, but they were my *people*. They didn't deserve to die just because they were...stuck-up.

Kaiden looked grim, pulling me beneath a sheltered alcove and turning to face me. "We can't take on that many dragons, Lena."

Was the Empress involved in this somehow? Was all of this part of her scheme? My mind spun with trying to interpret her words, and matching them to what I saw. That might have been her intention too, though.

"They'll destroy it," I whispered. "They won't leave anyone alive. We can't..."

Kaiden looked away, lips pressed in a thin line. "I know," he said quietly. He took a deep breath, releasing it as a sigh.

"The others should hear about it, right? They should come."

If they're alive, I added to myself, grimly.

If Kaiden was thinking the same, he didn't say it. "You're right. We just have to hold out...until then." He sounded uncertain, but took my hand, pulling me along again. Then, he hesitated, looking at me sheepishly. "You lead."

I quirked my lips. "You were doing a good enough job of it back there." But I started pulling him around toward the front of the fortress, while he shrugged a shoulder.

"I...remember some of it."

I was right, then. I tried not to dwell on that, or anything else, keeping a lookout as we ran. Dragons filled the skies and nearby streets, but I did my best not to focus on them, or the screams. *We can't save them all*, I reminded myself.

At the front of the fortress was chaos. The dragons seemed to have focused their attack there, bashing their tails against the bricks and breathing fire on anything that would catch. Hysteria sounded from within the walls, a few foolish Galdanians who had tried to escape crumpled outside the gates, unmoving.

"We have to draw them off," I whispered, as foolish as the idea was. Kaiden was already nodding, surveying the situation. There were still too many for this.

"They're going to destroy it otherwise, and everyone in there." My breath hitched. "My mother and sister are in there."

Kaiden squeezed my hand quietly, nodding. There would be no reinforcements to help us out here. No one even partially adept with a weapon. Just a bunch of screaming, crying men and women in masks. Some of them had taken them off, but most still hadn't, begging on their knees in fruitless prayer, gesturing toward the sky. None of them did anything useful.

We both knew what drawing the dragons away would do. We had to find a place to defend from, without trapping ourselves in.

Both of us ducked as a dragon swooped overhead, soaring up to land on one of the fortress' parapets and snap it under its weight. Intentionally or not, the action made it screech, flying up as the tower crashed down below. We had to draw the dragons to us, somehow.

Kaiden sent a fireball at the dragon, which did little but light up its eyes with a reddish glow as it stalked toward us. I reached for its mind, pulling myself in with a wince and commanding the dragon to sleep. It bucked against my control, and Kaiden kept it occupied, just enough for me to take it down.

How long would it last? I had little idea, and neither of us had much desire to try killing a dragon by other means. We left it there and moved on quickly, keeping an eye out.

Two dragons landed in front of us and screeched, eyes hungry with something dark and foreboding as one breathed fire at us. Kaiden pulled me behind him, shielding us from the flames, and I barely had time to breathe a thank you before the other dragon lunged.

The black was fading from his hair, between the sweat and everything else, and there was a look of quiet determination on his face. He waved with quiet fury toward the party guests, and they hurried out with frantic squeaks at the tone of his voice. His hair was plastered to his head, the armor affecting little protection except against their claws. He let them scratch at him, and I felt my heart jump in my throat at each strike. Luckily, there was a sword with the outfit, and I saw the grudging admiration on his face despite his muttered comment about it not being the same as his sword.

There were too many dragons, and they didn't stop coming. I felt him grip my shoulder and realized I was wavering, my energy draining much faster than I would have hoped.

"Lena..."

We had to keep fighting. There wasn't time to recharge, and the dragons kept coming. I felt a flood of energy fill me and nearly gasped. Kaiden gripped my shoulder unsteadily, staying further behind me and doing the best he could. He threw rocks and insults at the dragons with tired and taunting flippancy, laughing and doing whatever he could to draw their attention away.

And *still*, the dragons kept coming. Exhaustion pricked at the corner of my eyes as Kaiden squeezed my hand, tightly.

We both knew what we'd gotten ourselves into, and yet, he didn't look like he regretted it, either. I felt...at peace, far more than I would have expected.

We were going to make it. We...

Kaiden took in a sharp breath, nearly stumbling against me. He was breathing too hard, his eyes flickering with something unnatural for a moment before he shook his head.

"I can't..." He held back another cry, his hands shaking with contained flames even as he forced them back at the dragon. It seemed to leave him even more exhausted. "It..."

His voice cut off as he wrapped an arm around his chest, sucking in a sharp breath. "Lena," he breathed, his voice turning desperate. "It's...t-too much..."

The flames. He could absorb them, but even that put strain on him. Even with the extra reserves he gained from it, it still took its toll on his body. He transferred some of the energy to me, desperate.

What would happen if we kept going? I remembered Elle's warnings, from what felt like so long ago. Overexertion didn't *just* come from depleting your gift. It also came from using it in excess, without a chance to recharge. With power or not, it still put a strain on the body. You could burn yourself out from using it too frequently, with or without an energy source.

I felt it strain at my mind, but refused to accept it. I wasn't going to let him die, here, after this was *my* decision. I remembered what they said, last time, about my gifts. How I nearly died from using it all at once.

And yet...if I could just take out these few, it would give him a chance to escape. I'd have saved my people, *and* him. I couldn't think of anything more worth it.

He must have figured out what I planned to do. I couldn't call out a warning before he flooded my mind with energy.

He gripped my hand tightly, though I couldn't tell if it was from my plan or the exhaustion on his face. Taking in the dragons' fire seemed to drain him even more so, even when he used it as a shield or shot it back at them. His foot caught on midair and he pitched to the side, barely catching himself. He was going to burn himself out, protecting me.

And if he died, how was I supposed to stop the dragons?

"Kaiden. Hold on."

He pried open his eyes, barely clinging to consciousness.

"I'm sorry I dragged you into this."

Too tired to reply, he gripped my shoulder. A gentle squeeze, confirming what he already knew.

"Everything...has to end sometime."

And for some reason, in that moment, I felt at peace with it.

"Thank you. For everything," he murmured, his hold already shaky. He fought to stay awake, conscious for just a few more minutes. "It's been fun," he teased, "fighting dragons with you."

They wouldn't stop coming. The moment I took down one, another rose to take its place. But if I could stun them all at once...I could give him a fighting chance.

I also knew how likely it was to kill me. And I wasn't afraid. If my last act was giving him a second chance at life...well, he deserved it. And I knew he would use it well.

"Don't give in," I murmured in his mind, jolting him just enough to keep him awake. *"You have to keep fighting."*

With one last breath, I gave him enough energy to wake him up and sent the rest at all the dragons, like a final gust of air leaving me. Blinding white filled my senses, darkness screaming through me, and then...nothing.

TALON

Talon swore under his breath, hands tense at his side as he shoved past a couple of stray partygoers. The fortress *shook* again, and he gritted his teeth. They'd distracted him. He'd been so eager to please the Empress, so willing to believe they had found something...

He cursed every god he could think of, and even beyond that, stalking toward the throne room. Of course it had been a diversion. He was so *stupid*. Whatever they were doing, they obviously wanted to draw him away.

But the Empress was strong. She would be fine. He was more concerned about his head when she realized how badly he'd failed.

No. No, no, *no*.

His blood ran cold as he pushed open the doors and saw her sitting on her throne. Were it not for the unnatural angle, and the pool of red surrounding her, he might have thought she was simply lost in thought. Instead, rage boiled inside him as he moved closer, sinking to his knees and letting out a fierce sound as it overtook him.

He'd never even *wanted* much. He was perfectly content to serve his Empress and see to her wishes. He didn't want fame. He didn't want power. All he'd wanted was recognition.

Talon Isreld, son of one of the most powerful men in the three Cities, had wanted to be noticed for once in his life.

It had always been Katya with the gifts, Katya with the charming smile and the grace that put even the sternest men at ease. Katya who would take over, they said, when their father retired.

He couldn't have that. He was jealous, and so he took it from her, framing her for their parents' murder and planning to have her shipped off to the Mines. It was only the Empress – and a man named Damien – who made him reconsider. How Damien had come to be on the Empress' side, Talon didn't know, but the man had valuable knowledge, and a clue to the Bane's whereabouts. He wanted to study Katya, and keep her wrapped up in secret, while Talon joined Damien in Calest.

It was easier than expected, assembling a group with promising Gifts. He had kept up on them and sent reports back to his Empress, and his hard work had paid off – until someone else stole that from him, too. The scar he bore burned worse than any fire, a constant reminder every time he so much as shifted a muscle in his face that he had failed. And she had made sure he'd known it. It was a wonder, even, that she hadn't killed him right then.

The Empress *had* noticed him. She had made him the head of her Gifted, a secret group to do her bidding. She had trusted him with duties of which few even knew.

Talon knew how self-absorbed Galdanians were, and yet he still resented his father for never commemorating him. It was never enough, to the Cloren. Never worthy of praise.

Well. The Empress thought him worthy of praise. She filled an ache he'd hardly been able to put into words, fueled by jealousy from his gods-charming, sniveling sister.

To their father, only the eldest ever mattered. Superstitious nonsense and all of that. Talon followed the Empress, not some archaic rules. He longed for the day that Gifted could *rule*, as they were meant to, and take the power he had been given. That *he* had been given.

It was part of why he'd always admired the Empress. She carried herself with unerring confidence. She took the power she had and wielded it like the sharpest blade, angled at the throats of those who dared defy her. She never let herself be pushed around.

Talon was the son of a Cloren. He should have been *powerful*. But his father always kept that from him, never even letting him try. Just like every other coward in this country, shunning those with power because they feared it.

His mother was hardly better. She never did anything to stop it. Worse yet, she'd simply enforced it by scolding him for not supporting his sister or remaining in the shadows like he was 'meant' to. Katya had everything he'd ever wanted, and she'd never done a thing to earn it other than be born first.

Their talk of her meeting the Empress had been the final straw.

And in the end, she'd broken so *easily*, she wouldn't have been fit to work with the Empress, anyway. Sure, she'd resisted at first, and wouldn't believe him, but eventually he made her see. In a country filled with lies and backstabbing, he showed her *his* version of the truth, and she'd agreed that it was right.

Yet they still wouldn't side with him. They tried to get her help and excused her fits; even the suitors who came weren't driven away. He broke her to the point that she could hardly speak, yet clung to him anyway like he was her savior, and they simply insisted that it would pass. Things went on as regularly as they could.

Even once Katya *should* have been out of the way, his father wouldn't recognize him. Ever. It was enough to drive someone mad, if that someone weren't as strong as he was.

It became perfectly clear, then, what he had to do. The Empress would have approved. Though there was no *proof* that she had killed her parents – if one clung strongly enough to beliefs about gods 'cursing' the unfaithful– he saw the implications clearly enough. They had been in her way, and so she'd gotten rid of them. Just as he did. Blaming his mad sister for it was pure brilliance on his part.

The Empress did not shy away because of archaic laws. *She* had sought him out, through a messenger, seeking those with Gifts. And since a half-mad Gifted was no use to anyone, he had stepped up to answer that call. As he was always meant to. He had thrown himself at her feet before any of the others could claim it and sworn his life to her. She'd given him freedom, and recognition. She admired his ambition, she said, and his loyalty.

She had given him the one thing he longed for most in the world, and in return, he sold her his undying loyalty. Even now, he would fight for her until his last breath.

It hadn't been just handed to him, either, on a diamond-studded platter like everything Katya had. She'd made him earn it, and oh, he had. He'd overcome every challenge, fought every contender who might steal his beloved place. He would not remain merely in the Empress' shadow, unseen by her as he carried out her work. He needed to *see* her, and hear her words.

As fluid as a knife slipping into a man's ribs, Talon rose from his seat. The Empress had warned him about this possibility, but he never wished to accept it. She had a grander plan. She always did.

And so when the guards came, and told him that *dragons* were attacking, he simply laughed, believing them sent from the gods to smite those who dared touch his Empress.

They wished to destroy her greatest works. Even if she no longer drew life in this world, Talon could fight for her legacy. He wouldn't stop until those responsible had been punished.

As the fortress shook again, he forced himself to lock it all behind cold, unfeeling walls and gathered all of his loyal Gifted. He sent them to try to stop the dragons, however they could.

Talon ascended further in the fortress until he emerged out onto the rooftop. The sky curled with smoke and silhouetted wings, screams and hisses of fire greeting his ears.

You did not make a mockery of the gods. And yet that was what they did, by destroying her. The gods had appointed her as the ruler, and they thought themselves high enough to take that away.

Surely even now, his Empress wouldn't fail him. Surely the gods would endow him with the strength to avenge her.

Dragons struck at the walls of the fortress with tails like battering rams. It shook beneath with the impact. They were destroying her home, brick by brick, and he couldn't allow that.

And yet, Talon knew how strong corrupted dragons were. This wouldn't be an easy fight.

He laughed at the first dragon to land on the roof with him, even as it broke off one of the parapets in doing so. It had no idea what it was facing. *Who* it was facing.

The dragon struck at him, and he dodged out of its way, fluidly. He let it strike at him again, laughing. He was Talon Isreld, chosen by the Empress, blessed by his gods. They would not fail him now.

He kept the dragon occupied while the others threw everything they had at it. He toyed with the dragons as more flew near them, or landed, letting them think they might hit him, and then twisting their minds as easily as any others. They fell from view, unable to stop his attacks, minds drawn blank and silent.

Even still, he couldn't fight forever. Already he could feel it tingling in him, the warnings both from Damien and that Gifted healer girl echoing through his mind. Overexertion. What a pathetic thing to die from.

If only he had the Bane. He knew he could have harnessed it, if Damien hadn't been so fixated on Kaiden. Yet again, he was swept aside, as everyone seemed eager to do. It made his blood boil.

One dragon lingered nearer the edge, as if taunting him. It was easy, with the grief and anger locked away in a deadly shield, to assume himself invincible. He would fight for his Empress' legacy, or die trying.

What good would he be past this, anyway? With the Empress gone, he would return to being nothing again. A shadow, unseen and unrecognized. Even if another leader rose who would carry on with her vision, they would never be his Empress.

He'd sought to serve her, and failed. When it mattered most, he had failed the one person he had sworn never to.

Were it any others' death, she would have him executed for it. He should do it himself, for failing her. But he wanted to defend her home, first, as one last apology.

Grief was blinding, and anger narrowed your focus. Perhaps it didn't matter all that much, anymore, what he did. No ruler would be as wonderful as the Empress. None could replace her.

He had adored her. They had *murdered* her. He would never again hear the approval in her voice at his deeds.

He imagined it in his head, all the same. He *craved* it, the way a starving child craved food.

The dragons were unstoppable. Even with his army gathered on the rooftop, fighting them off, they simply kept coming.

And yet, he had an odd peace that even if it did go all wrong, the Empress would still win, in the end. She was far cleverer than anyone ever thought. She had contingencies on top of her contingency plans, and in that moment, Talon was grateful for them. Even if he were not the one to carry them out, he had done his duty, to the best of his ability. And now, he would die avenging her. He couldn't think of a greater honor than that.

He left his fate up to the gods, serving as valiantly as he could to defend her home. Ultimately, though he gave it everything in him, he knew they would fail without help. *No one* could stand against this many dragons for that long. And with the assault they had wrought and continued to wreak on the fortress...it too, would not stand forever.

But perhaps, if the gods favored him right, they still had a chance. If the Empress wished him alive, she would assure he survived. If not...he could only hope he might see her again, and make it up to her in a world beyond the living.

He wasn't sure, any longer, what the shaking was from. As effortless as it still was to twist the dragons' minds – how it had *killed* him to pretend he wasn't capable of it before – he felt the toll it took on his body. Weak thing. Maybe if he made it to another life, he would have one that was actually capable of something.

The gods had to look on him kindly for this. Sacrificing his life in a valiant defense of his Empress and her home. How could they *not* reward that?

And if they didn't...Talon would *not* die simply because his body couldn't handle the strain. That in itself would be failure.

He felt recklessness tighten its grip around him, his distraction attempts growing bolder, his shouts increasingly louder. His Gifted started to look worried, slowed by the same inevitable fate he felt creeping in on them. He drew from their energy to support his, and didn't regret it for a second. The Empress wouldn't have. She wouldn't let herself die so pathetically, either.

His mind flashed back to the throne room, and the pool of red. Even just the way she sat there, barely limp against the seat, showed that she had been in control. This was her plan. Hopefully, he was part of it too.

And so, it was hard to say what had caused it, when it happened. It was an honorable sacrifice, either way, and one he was proud of.

But it only took one misstep – an inevitable misjudgment. One loose stone beneath his feet, the structure weakened and crumbling from the dragons' many blows. One last act to defend her fortress. One risk too many.

And from the heights that he had killed his way to reach, the boy with a scar on his face fell to his demise.

XXIX

RU'ACH

She shouldn't have kept stalling. It was selfish and *foolish* and...

And she couldn't stop hoping, even if it broke her. Couldn't stop extending her hand in a silent offer, waiting for the world in which her brother took it, and everything worked out. Where happily ever afters weren't just fairytales of ink and dreams. Where she could turn back time and keep those she cared for safe, no matter what.

People would die. People *had*, already, and yet she couldn't quit. She could fix it all with the Essence, right? Wipe the slate clean and scrub the blood from her hands – or claws.

Wasn't it worth it? Wouldn't it be, if she made it all work?

Wouldn't they, too, go to the ends of the world and back to save their family?

It wasn't fair to any of them. It wasn't right for her to hold so much power over how their lives would go. And yet, if they were in her place, surely they would do the same. Surely they wouldn't give up, no matter the odds.

"Brother." The word murmured from her lips like a prayer. "You can't win this."

He was just confused. He'd been fooled, as all of them were. He hadn't *meant* to use the Bane against her. She knew this as strongly as she understood his guilt, emanating from him so much clearer in that small form he stood across from her in.

Here, on the field of a battle greater than any human eye could understand, it all came to a head. The dragons had abandoned it, to fight for and against the humans. Ru'ach had done her best to keep her brother occupied, in hopes that he would finally see. That it would all just...*click*.

Now their fate was sealed, but not as she wished.

There was a light to the child eyes of her brother that saddened Ru'ach. Fury, misplaced and grown by years of misuse and misunderstanding. Held together by two simple words, whispering in her head over and over.

467

He knew. She'd failed. They'd lost.

"It doesn't have to be this way," she urged, even as she knew what the response would be. "Please..."

"You *made* it this way," he spat back, the anger alight in his eyes alongside a touch of fear. "When you tried to use your power-"

"That was a dream," she replied, gentling her voice.

"It was a *vision*, and it would have happened if I hadn't stopped you!" His scowl twisted too fiercely for the young face he wore. "Regardless of what you say, sister, I know what I am doing. We were much better off before humans ever had this 'gift'. *No one* should have that kind of power."

"Not even you?" she asked quietly.

"Not even me," he replied, low and subdued. The evenness to his tone betrayed his determination. "It's never been a burden I wanted to bear. But I know what I must do with it. Whatever the case, *you* are the ones who taught them how to use it. And I must take it away."

This was why she had to save him. Because he never intended to save himself. Even if she let him win, she would still lose him. His ultimate victory, he said. Leaving her aching and alone.

But he wouldn't truly wish that on her, when the time came. She was sure of it. She *had* to be, or this quest of hers was doomed to fail from the start.

And not only for her. For the entire human race.

"Would you rather we both leave?" she murmured, not for the first time. He never understood what she meant by it, though. "Would you like to go home?"

For a moment, uncertainty flickered over his face, though it was hard to tell if it was just from his diminutive form. Moments later, it hardened to a scowl.

"I know what your plan is. You're trying to distract me!"

In truth, she wasn't quite sure what would happen if they *did* leave. And that fear had kept her lying, and 'struggling' against him, wearing him down until he might give in.

Destroying him had never been in her plans. She would hardly be better than he'd become, then. Was it truly heroic to end a battle as swiftly as possible, if there was a different path that could be taken? Was it truly brave to take the easy way out, and not even try?

Despite the wells of knowledge she possessed, there were some questions that simply had no good answers. So Ru'ach stuck to her instinct, taking responsibility for the consequences of it.

And that was why this *had* to work. The price had already been paid. She owed it to those she'd borrowed from to make it worth it.

"I've never been against you, brother." She wondered if her voice sounded as tired as she felt. "Mistakes were made. They can be fixed."

"You don't need to tell me that," he shot back, a flicker of the guilt returning. "I'm the one doing my best to fix them."

"I can help you."

He let out a harsh laugh. "*You*? All you've ever wanted to do is *preserve* them. Protect them, so you can use them against me later." He spat the words out, eyeing her with suspicion and hatred. "Don't deny it."

A deep sigh broke from her, as she rested her scaled head on the stone beneath them. Laying down, while he stood rigid and wide-stanced before her in his dirty, torn human clothes, small fists clenched. "I do not know what I can do to convince you," she whispered.

"Nothing you say will sway me. I *will* destroy the humans, right under your very nose." His eyes were ablaze, like glimmering embers amongst the coals. "You knew, didn't you? You *knew* they were all cursed, and you kept that from me."

Ru'ach remained silent, long enough for him to hurl curses at her in a tongue no others would understand.

"Did you really think you could *protect* them? Really? I am the Bane." He let out a bitter laugh at the words. "They fear me, and rightly so. They *know* they can't stand against me.

"I have been merciful, for their sakes. I've only targeted the ones who could spread this plague. And now I find out," his voice turned low and furious, "that *every one of them* is a curse on this world. Every one of them corrupted by your meddling. If you had any chance to make me trust you, you've lost it.

"I *won't yield*. No matter what you say or what you throw against me. You'll have to kill me to stop me." His eyes glittered, monstrous even through a child's simple eyes. "And you don't have the stomach to do that."

It hurt more than she cared to put into words, watching him. Knowing that despite all her best attempts, there was only one way this would ever end now.

How she wished to turn back time. Perhaps it could unravel the knot tied tight and messy in her chest. As much as she hated to admit it, he was right. And her denial was no longer worth the cost.

She had done her best. She had fought, valiantly, knowing it might come to this. Knowing, if none of her attempts worked, that the price to pay would be far higher than the one that had already been exacted.

But she owed them all, now. As much as it ached through her entire being to consider it.

"I can't let you do this."

"You don't have a choice, Ru'ach. You threw that away when you betrayed us."

She whispered a word, then, in their native tongue, and he went still.

"You wouldn't. You'll kill us both." Despite his attempts to keep it hidden, his eyes flashed with anger, and an edge of fear.

"That's what you wanted, wasn't it?" Her eyes were tired as she watched him. "To see me dead?"

He bared his teeth at her, unthreatening as they were in his current form. "The humans must pay for their sins, too."

Ru'ach stood to her towering height, looking down at him. And though they were worlds apart, in these forms, she wrapped him in her wings like they were arms, and he was too small to fight her. Though, it didn't stop him from spitting endless curses at her, even as a long sigh escaped from her.

"I never wanted it to end like this." Her eyes slipped closed, the weight settling heavier in her immortal chest.

He must have felt it grow between them, the energy that shouldn't ever be unleashed. A hysterical laugh burst from his lips, though he'd quit struggling.

"You know you're *letting* me win? The dragons will destroy the humans, and you won't even be there to stop them. They'll still carry out my will, even if I'm gone." His eyes gleamed with triumph. "You can't beat me. Not without destroying everything you've worked for."

She opened hers, too wise and deep. "And that, brother, is where you've always been wrong." Gentle, but sad, she let the words spill out. "They will be fine on their own. They no longer need me."

His eyes turned angry, flashing with fury and hatred toward her.

"Please." She let the word murmur through the air as she shifted back to see his eyes, extending a claw to him in one last hopeful attempt. "Let's just...go home?"

He eyed her with a mixture of disgust and anger. "With *you*?"

She had done her best to convince him. She'd bared her soul to him, and he still called it a lie. No matter how gently she put it. No matter how far from accusatory her tone was.

She'd had to try. But now...it wouldn't be fair to any of the humans to keep going. She had hoped Shedim would never find out their secret. But there was no taking it back. He was lost to her, as surely as he had been that first day when everything went wrong, when none of it should have.

There was one thing left. Just one.

A quiet laugh rolled through her. For a moment, despite the energy it took, she shifted to her other form, that of an older girl with fiery red hair and deep eyes. Then she could wrap *real* arms around him, even as he shoved against her.

"Please."

And though he fought against her, and screamed, Ru'ach closed her eyes, flooding her power through both of them. She felt his own rise in response, crashing against hers, and for a moment imagined this was just the beginning, rather than the end. What would she have done differently? Could she have prevented this?

Perhaps there was still a chance. Perhaps...this wasn't the end of their story, after all.

But as was more likely...this was how it was always meant to be. They were too much for this world. In a way, he was right. Their meddling had only caused pain, even if hers was merely to balance his out. He wouldn't be stopped any other way.

She only hoped he could at least feel, as it all ended, her last, final truth.

I never blamed you.

Even though they both knew how much she *should* have, she hadn't. He'd never wanted to ruin everything, no matter what happened. And he already hated himself for doing just that, she knew. He didn't need it strengthened by anyone else.

She held to him tighter, even as she lost the ability to do it in any visible way. Already she felt their tether to the world slipping, as their physical forms gave way under the strain of so *much* power, combined now in a way this world simply could not handle. They were glowing, she thought, and yet that might have been how it always was, simply indiscernible from the rest of their realm before all of this.

This, however, was a different kind of death. A slow fall from a cliff, rather than the violent crash that had happened the first time. Then, they had been ripped away from their own realm, crammed into physical bodies as was required in this one.

This, however, was more like thread unraveling, their story flowing backwards, in a way, to where it always should have ended, or stayed.

She only hoped it would stop, once they got there, rather than pulling them further apart. Stitch by stitch, eon by eon, until nothing was left. Nothing to connect them together, ever again.

It was part of why humans fascinated her, she thought. The *permanence* to their form, like a mold set and destined to remain that way until it fell apart back into the dust it was created from. The solidity of a hand, and a hug, and the way they could express things which words only ever danced around.

Sari would know of her plan, soon, if she did not already expect it. It stung worse than Ru'ach expected, the extent of the price her decisions would enact. The depth of separation she would have to endure. Ru'ach had always loved the humans, and the world they lived in. She'd hoped, back when things were simpler, that they could stay there as long as they wished. Forever, in human terms.

She'd hoped for many things. But hope was not solid, like this world. It slipped through your grasp without ever being there in the first place, a construct of thought and wishing that gave the illusion of something to hold onto. Sometimes, it remained steady. Other times...

Well. Theirs had run out now, despite the immortality they had and would always carry, in another realm. For now, this human world, with its decided constraints and fabricated constructs of seasons and ages and ends had caught up to them, after all.

And now? It was time to say goodbye.

Forgive me, she whispered with the last of her voice, before that, too, became something unknowable in this world. *For bringing it to this.*

Shedim was slipping from her arms, speck by speck, and yet she clung to the hope that soon, she would be able to hold him again, in a way she never had to let go.

With one final breath out from both of them, their bodies turned to dust.

WINTER

In a lone patch of sunlight falling through the window, a girl named Winter crouched down, peeking at the tiny sprout she'd planted. Her mother said it couldn't grow here any longer, but she still had to try. The Galdanians had such lovely flowers. Why couldn't she have one, too?

She'd knelt in the dirt, sprinkling water over the tiny plant, and folded her hands in a prayer. Maybe, if she wished hard enough, it would be able to live.

That had been weeks ago. Mama said her plant would be dead, now, and she should get rid of it. They couldn't grow in Calest anymore, she said. Even with her gift, she couldn't make miracles happen.

But it was that little word, *anymore*, that had first planted a spark of hope in her, and determination with it. *Anymore* meant it had happened once. That meant it could happen again.

And it did.

Her mama was just as astonished when Winter came running in with delight sparkling in her eyes and a small white flower cupped carefully in her hands. She'd made it *grow*. She'd...

Winter had to stop, then, for the same reason her mother had, both of them watching the ground as if they were caught in a dream.

Her other flowers had sprouted, in the exact places they'd once died. Winter nearly dropped the one she'd just grown, looking up at her mother with wide eyes.

They only grew rounder as she watched her mother kneel, breath stilled in a sort of nervous hope as she brushed a hand through the dry, prickly grass. Her fingers curled into the dirt, stopping just as quickly when it gave, crumbling in her fingers. She turned up her palm to stare at the soft, dark soil, somehow moist despite what little rain Calest ever got. Her mother's eyes took on a sort of shine as she pressed it back in its place, a whisper leaving her lips.

And just like the flowers, the grass came to life beneath her fingertips, vibrant and green in a way that almost hurt Winter's eyes. She'd never seen her mother actually *use* her Gift.

Every house they asked at, in their excitement and disbelief, the story was the same. Farmers who broke their backs to try to lay down seed of any kind in the earth and get it to bear a harvest, thinking they must be dreaming when the soil just...gave way, as it was meant to. Mothers searching for herbs in the rocky hills, finding ones that couldn't possibly and hadn't ever grown there. People who thought they were dreaming, or delusional, even though they swore they could *feel* a difference in the ground beneath their feet.

Winter didn't understand it much, when her mother explained. She knew the old stories, and the curse that had been put on their land. She had heard her mother murmur a funny name, sometimes, though she wouldn't tell Winter what it meant. A savior from a story, a hope others thought her foolish to cling to, but she did, all the same. A being so unlike them, they couldn't comprehend what exactly she even was. A spirit. A god.

Now, it was that name her mother murmured again, as she looked up at the sky with eyes hopeful and wide and bright as spring should always feel. And though she didn't understand all of it, Winter knew it was a very good thing when a smile stretched across her mother's face, even if her eyes shone like she might cry.

"She did it." Drawing Winter close in a hug, the words whispered from her in disbelieving awe. "The curse is broken."

BASIL

Though it wasn't far to the Cities, every step felt like a million more than it should have been, in his mind. What if they were too late? What if Sari was wrong? What if...?

The fire made his heart stutter. They *had* to be okay. Despite the ruin twisting his gut, broken crystal and smoldering canvas carrying a blaze wherever it touched.

Chan said Kaiden and Lena were at a party. But the only party guests he saw were...

Well. He did his best to put that from his mind. They'd left Fern behind, to 'watch over' the dragons, but Basil was tired of hiding. He wanted to help, however he could.

And the dragons were...calm? Despite the destruction everywhere, and the low simmer still in some of their eyes, most simply looked tired, or annoyed. The Galdanians that tried to attack them were brushed away like flies.

Where were Kaiden and Lena?

It took far too much simpering on the guests' part, when they reached the chaos by the fortress, to decipher what had happened. Several of the Empress' guards helped usher people to safety. When one of them caught sight of them, he stopped, shoulders rigid.

The man looked familiar, though Basil almost didn't recognize him. He had the same eyes as Lena, with bluer undercurrents. Basil had only met him once that he remembered.

Beside him, Chan's eyes were grim, to disguise a hardness beneath it that they all knew he was doing his very best to keep at bay. It was leashed in his words, though, the potential for a storm in the low rumble of his tone.

"What happened?"

Caleb's eyes were already steel, hardened and sharp with something Basil couldn't name. Triumph, he thought, but something else as well. "The Empress is dead."

Basil could hardly contain his surprise. Olive's mouth pulled into a thin, unpleasant smile. They all eyed the nearby dragons uncertainly, like they might get up and begin killing again. Some were draped on the ground, as if they had fallen there. Others had simply laid down, eyeing the wreckage amongst them with something in their gazes that tried hard to seem repentant.

Caleb glanced at the other men, who lead hysterical Galdanians away from the mess. He waved a hand, curtly. "They were attacking, and then they just...stopped." His own hand settled close to the hilt of his sword. "I don't trust them."

Basil didn't understand, either, until Sari came into view from behind them, her eyes more mournful than he had ever seen them before. Years of loss seemed etched deep in their depths.

"Ru'ach sacrificed herself," she whispered. "To stop the Bane. Without his influence... these dragons have little reason to fight." She cast a glance at the resting dragons, something heavy in her eyes. "They must have been struggling against his power, to be so affected by this."

Caleb still looked like he wished to take his sword and stick it through their hearts, just in case, but he also looked regretful, and conflicted.

"I killed the Empress," he admitted, and there was something subdued to the way he said it. Steadily, he met all of their eyes, as if searching for their answer. "Do you think I did the right thing?" he murmured. "Did I *cause* all this?"

Basil shook his head, fighting the urge to rest his hand on the other man's shoulder. He might get it snapped off if he did. "No. They were already going to attack, regardless of anything you did." To the best of his ability, he explained what they knew, hesitating at the parts with Sari and letting her tell them better.

Caleb still looked troubled, at the end. Basil supposed that was the price to pay for toppling an empire.

For his part, Basil couldn't keep in his own anxieties anymore. "Lena?"

Caleb's eyes grew wide for a moment, and then stern. "She isn't with you?"

When he shook his head slowly, Caleb spun on his heel with a curse.

"I told him..." The muscles in his jaw tightened as he fought with his words. "They should have gotten to safety."

Olive had already slipped away from them the moment Caleb's eyes widened. Not long after, her shout echoed across the clearing. "Here!"

Basil moved away from Perell as quickly as he could, for once grateful for his long legs as he strode in the direction of Olive's voice.

There, near the side of the fortress. Basil almost didn't recognize their friend at first, dressed like a Galdanian guard in glinting armor, flames flickering hungrily in front of him. Kaiden seemed to glow with it, despite the disorientation and exhaustion on his face. He...*absorbed* it into him. Holding the blaze at bay with an unsteadily outstretched hand, fire licking at the tips as he kept them back by sheer willpower. A body lay by his feet, also in armor.

On seeing Olive, and hearing his name, Kaiden looked confused, eyes darting about as if he couldn't find her. He drew his hand toward him in a fist, pulling the flames with him and gritting his teeth. His breath caught with the action. He stumbled to one knee, eyes flickering with fire and exhaustion as he fell so only his hands were supporting him, breathing hard. Before he could fully collapse, Olive had a hand on his arm, urging him up.

"Stay with us. Don't...*Kaiden.* You have to stay awake. Don't..."

He didn't seem to hear them. His eyes flickered like burning embers as he tried to draw in the power again, flinching at the contact. His lips whispered a name, though it was too strained and weak to tell what it was.

From behind Chan, Joss pushed her way through, dropping to her knees beside them. "Bodyguard?"

He looked toward her, somehow, and smiled tiredly, cupping her face with a hand though his gaze seemed to look right through her. A moment later, he flinched, his entire face pinched in pain, and withdrew it.

Joss took his hand when he lowered it, murmuring something with her eyes closed. When she opened them, Kaiden shuddered, his eyes almost lucid for a moment and filled with tired relief before they closed, and he slumped back against the other body.

Slowly, Joss stood, not turning to face them as she said in a voice that sounded too old for her, "That might help."

Olive slid an arm under Kaiden's back, gently, pulling him to his feet. He shifted, just barely, but didn't open his eyes, just dead weight that Olive somehow managed to support. Chan tried to help her, but she snapped at him, pulling him away.

Caleb swept the other guard into his arms, despite so little of their face being visible through the mask. Gently, he slipped it off, eyes indiscernible at Lena's lack of expression beneath. She didn't stir, even as he followed them away from the fire, something resolute in his eyes and every step. Eyes narrowed, he glanced over at Kaiden, as if he were somehow the cause of this.

None of them said a word. What could they, in the moment? They had Kaiden and Lena back. That was what mattered, right? That was who they had come for. They could deal with everything else later.

Once they were away from any wreckage, despite the smell of smoke still drifting through the air, Olive propped Kaiden against a tree, looking him over properly with a tight expression Basil didn't want to acknowledge. Exhausted, he collapsed beside his dragon's gold side, watching them. The air was full of sobbing, though unlike the kind on any regular battlefield. For the most part, it sounded more like children wailing for a toy that had been taken from them, though there were undercurrents of true shock and grief scattered amongst it.

Joss kept her gaze low and away from them all, as if ashamed. Basil caught the glow to it and urged her over, until she was pressed against him. An arm loosely around her shoulder, hiding her, he looked back at his sister.

The question lodged in his throat refused to stay put, even though he knew none of them truly wanted the answer. "Will they be...?"

"I don't *know*," Olive snapped. Then she stopped, narrowing her gaze at the ground. "I'm sorry. I just...we can't risk messing with their minds, now, to find out what happened. So I don't know. There's no way to tell..." She trailed off, sounding frustrated despite all her efforts, and shook her head. "They will be *fine*."

And whether or not it was truly the case, she pulled Kaiden back to his feet, this time allowing Chan to help her and relaxing a bit when he did, as if the burden had suddenly become too much to bear on her own. When no one else spoke, she nodded to their waiting dragons.

"Please," she murmured. "Let's just...go, before something worse happens."

RU'ACH

With indiscernible eyes, Ru'ach watched as the results of their meddling were slowly undone. Balance restored, hope injected like a saving grace into the eyes and hearts of those who had waited, so long. Dragons calmed, the lands balanced out again. Shedim's 'curse' broken as his hold over the countries shattered, nature returning to its normal state.

She couldn't feel him anymore. She couldn't tell where he was, in this state between restoration and destruction. His influence on the human world had broken, and his physical form with it. They could never return to that.

And perhaps that thought would not have been so terrible, if she had something to show for it. Whether Shedim was avoiding her, or simply not...there, it only amplified the loss she still felt flowing through her.

The humans would be fine on their own. That had never been her concern. But she had grown fond of them, and now.... where did they go? *Could* they go anywhere?

They had been trapped for so long, Ru'ach almost forgot what it was like to just...be. No sensation, no seesawing emotions. Just existing, unable to be affected by anything.

It would be worth it, if only she had her brother. If they could finally make things right, without so many obstacles in the way.

He might never make himself known, or forgive her. He might never forgive himself either, despite the situations. He couldn't kill her here, so that had become pointless. Anything was but working through it. What did any of it matter, now that they were apart from that world?

It could take her years – lifetimes, even, by human standards. It might take until she forgot what it felt like to be able to touch things and hold her breath until her fragile lungs felt like they might burst.

But at least she had her brother back, wherever he was. He was safe. *They* were safe. And it could take as long as it had to beyond that – to find him, to make things right. She would not give up. Not ever.

And that, more than anything, was what mattered most.

CHAN

He should have been out helping the others. He should have been with Katya, if nothing else. They'd found her brother's body broken near the base of the fallen fortress, and though he knew that might come as a relief more than anything, he also knew how complicated such things could be.

But Chan had always been far more comfortable in Calest, and so he was content to let the others discuss what should be done with the Cities and all of the political decisions to be handled, while he kept an eye on his friends.

Lena was unmoving, looking peaceful in her sleep, but Kaiden had stirred not long after they got him to a bed, and wouldn't stop. He curled in on himself with a wince -- and Chan had checked him for injuries several times, despite Olive's assurances -- or choked on a quiet sound, mouth parted in a silent cry. Restless. Even when he opened his eyes, they didn't seem to see anything, his eyes contorting in panicked and upset expressions. He didn't respond to his name and only barely to touch, flinching away from it and biting his lip.

They didn't wake up for far too long. Chan couldn't get Kaiden's look out of his head, the glow to his eyes and way he barely seemed to recognize them.

It reminded him too much of Gigi, and how she'd acted just before...

No. He *had* to wake up. Chan hadn't forgotten the look on Gigi's face, years ago, when Kaiden had brought her back, or the slight glow to her eyes that wasn't quite...natural. She wouldn't sleep, tossing and turning or staring sightlessly at the ceiling, murmuring to herself.

Kaiden was equally restless, sucking in a breath at times as if it pained him, and whispering under his breath. When he did open his eyes, he barely seemed to see Chan, staring at something with a furrowed brow and barely responding if Chan spoke.

Lena had woken up after a while, at least, and had to be assured that he was okay before she would rest more. She watched him, holding onto his hand, but eventually slipped back into sleep, exhausted.

A small cry recaptured his attention. Kaiden was curled in on himself, breathing sharply, his eyes watching some distant spot on the wall. They flicked over when his name was said, but couldn't seem to figure out where to settle, confused.

Lena was okay, at least. Or so it seemed, despite the fact that she'd fallen asleep next to Kaiden again, after determining to stay awake until he was. Kaiden shifted again, brow creased in distress as he curled in further on the bed, sucking in a quiet breath. The few times he'd opened his eyes, they'd never been quite...lucid, and he wouldn't respond to anything Chan said.

Chan tried not to be worried, despite the obvious signs. From what little he'd been able to drag from Lena before sleep reclaimed her, Kaiden had used his gift about as much as she had -- if not more, given he was still fighting flames when they found him. Joss looked worried, and did her best to hide it, trailing off anytime she started to admit that she didn't know how bad it'd been.

Kaiden's back arched, mouth open in a silent scream. Lena was out cold beside him again, no matter how he moved around. Outside the room, the others worked on restoring order to the terrorized country. The Galdanians put up such little fight, even if they knew how to, that it was more a matter of assuring them they weren't all to be executed for 'disobedience' by the Gifted.

Everyone he cared for had died for selfless reasons. His sister, braving a dangerous trip for needed medical supplies the officials wouldn't give them. Gigi and the others, protecting Kaiden. Elle, saving whoever she could.

He didn't need two more names on that list.

It wasn't fair, because their sacrifices were so noble that he couldn't even blame anyone. But that didn't make it hurt any less. It was part of why he went so readily with Sari when she asked. His hometown was too small that every brick was packed with memories of his sister. She'd taught him to read, and write, and do dangerous stunts with ordinary tools.

Maybe now, at least, the sacrificing could stop.

Lena stirred, mumbling in her sleep before she blinked bleary eyes at Chan. "Chan...?"

He gave her a little smile. She stifled a yawn, looking down on Kaiden with her brow furrowed.

"He's...not woken up."

"Well, that's silly." Jokingly, she rapped knuckles on his arm. "Hey. Beanhead. Get up."

But he didn't respond, other than to shift beside her. Lena's brow furrowed with worry, followed by recognition as it came flooding back, and her voice got smaller.

"He'll be okay, right?"

Forcing a smile, Chan nodded. "Of course."

Several days passed, and Kaiden still didn't fully wake up at any point. Chan started to get worried. Lena stirred briefly at times, half-aware for a short time as she tried to answer questions or kept an eye on Kaiden, ending up very quickly asleep again beside him. But she would be okay, given the headache complaints and irritated responses he'd gotten to a couple odd questions.

Sari had warned him, gently, that recovery was not guaranteed for them. Even with Kaiden having survived the Bane as long as he did, his body still tried to shut it down eventually. And with everything he'd already been through...well. It was little wonder he was having a harder time than Lena was, even if she didn't seem quite functional yet to understand how bad it was. She mumbled to him in exasperation over the fact that he was still sleeping, in the short times she was actually awake.

And if he didn't wake up...?

Chan forced the thought aside. He had to. Right? It couldn't end like this. Not like everyone else. Not even for such a good reason. That just made it worse, in Chan's mind. There would be no one to be mad at. No one to blame.

What would he tell Lena, when she was aware enough? What would he tell any of them?

They didn't understand like he did. Basil hadn't been close enough to their first team to really bond with them. They'd *heard*, but they hadn't seen. They didn't know how bad the situation had been, even before Gigi's death.

Chan pushed the thought away, hard. He was well aware of how far they'd overextended themselves, and how precarious the situation still was. But he wasn't going to give up hope.

Not yet.

"Chan...?"

Kaiden's disoriented voice cut through his musing, as he shifted to prop himself up on a still-shaky arm, blinking down at it. Chan sat up straighter, setting his book aside.

Kaiden pressed a palm into his forehead, holding back a groan. "What...happened?"

He couldn't help a smile, even as Kaiden leaned heavily on the wall, breathing in slow and labored.

"Well. If I'm not mistaken, you nearly died from being too heroic and saving the day." He looked his friend over carefully, searching for any signs of anything else wrong. "You should really stop doing that."

<><><>

Days slipped by, bringing ups and downs that left Chan exhausted, as far as his friends' recovery went. Kaiden was awake even less than Lena before he drifted off again, more time passing than Chan was comfortable with before he even opened his eyes again. Lena did much better, though her eyes reflected Chan's worry as she sat by him and held his hand. Despite her improvement, and Olive's relief at it, they kept her confined to the room with him, just in case.

Lena had been hesitant to explain what had happened, even with Kaiden's eventually waking. He *had* used his gift even more than before...pushing himself until he couldn't go any longer, as Kaiden was prone to do.

At least, with all the time that had passed, they'd managed to get things mostly settled back to a semblance of 'normal' again. Olive had convinced the Cities to let the dragons help clean up the wreckage, and Raoul was acting as a leader for them, taking charge so chaos didn't break out again. The Galdanians had nearly panicked when they realized that they would actually have to *work* to restore their Cities to their former beauty. Or at least, somewhere livable.

But now, with most of that all falling into place, they could finally sit back for a moment and just...live.

Chan cast a glance to his side, a wry smile twisting his lips. Kaiden was half-slumped against Lena where they sat in a clearing with the others, eyes drifting toward closed despite his prior insistence that he was awake enough to eat. Lena wasn't doing much better, exhaustion written deep in her eyes as she curled her hand around his and stroked it lazily with her thumb. Kaiden rubbed his free hand hard into his eyes, the barely-touched bowl Fern had gotten him sitting forgotten by the side as he gave her a slow, tired smile. There was something different to the two of them since waking up, other than just lethargy.

"We match," he mumbled for what must have been the fourth time, holding their hands up a little to show the gift-suppressing bands they both wore. It was a testament to Lena's exhaustion that she didn't even look concerned, simply nodding with a little smile back and trying to laugh.

"Yeah. We do."

"Matching bracelets." He chuckled as if it was the greatest joke, eyes briefly meeting the others' as well as they nodded. Olive simply shook her head, but Chan saw the hint of amusement in her eyes, disguised by relief.

It didn't take long for Kaiden's eyes to slip back shut, and Chan would have suggested moving them if they weren't all so tired. Not as much as those two, of course, but still... They had done a lot today. Chan had spent the better part of the day working with Caleb and arguing the best way to situate the Galdanians. Finding places to temporarily house those without homes without causing hysterics had given him quite the headache. The dragons had assisted in helping pull away what rubble blocked the streets and clearing buildings. Raoul had taken charge the best he could, but it was like controlling an entire city full of temperamental five-year olds throwing a fit.

Right now, though, they were taking a much-needed break. Chan looked around at the circle at his friends and smiled. Katya had wanted to sit near Kaiden and Lena, to watch over them, so Chan sat beside her, lightly touching her hand with his. Olive had a leg in front of her, one drawn up with an arm draped over it as she talked with Basil, casting a glance over at Kaiden and Lena every so often. Fern and Joss were off somewhere getting into who knew what trouble together, and Caleb was still discussing plans with Raoul, a ways away. There was a sense of peace over the group, shrouded only with a shadow of worry that he thought might linger over them for a while. There would still be challenges, and days that stole his breath away, and obstacles Chan knew none of them would be able to predict. There would be conflict, as new trade was arranged between the countries and they learned to work together for the first time in a long time. It wouldn't be easy, and it wouldn't be quick. But the worst of it was over, and they had each other to lean on, and turn to.

They were all going to be okay.

XXX

LENA

"She just...sat there. As if it was all part of her plan." Caleb's voice sounded numb. "Do you think I...did this?"

From where I sat on the bed, lacing my boots, I shook my head. "Shedim had this planned long before you turned against the Empress. It was just a terrible coincidence."

He still looked troubled, though. "Should I not have killed her?"

"The people need a strong leader," I said gently. "One that can help them rise out from under Shedim's shadow and learn to *be*. The Empress would have hindered that."

He nodded, still looking disturbed. I slipped my hand into his.

"I think it would be wrong if you didn't feel conflicted about it. But..." I drew in a breath, weighing my words quietly. "I do think...it needed to be done." Whether or not she needed to die for that to happen, I didn't think I could accurately judge. I couldn't deny the relief I felt at knowing she was gone, or how I had wished for it.

"I can't lead," he said quietly. "I never wanted to."

"There are other people that need you. Dad organized an entire rebellion in Calest. They need someone to lead them. The Empress may be dead, but that doesn't mean Calest will be receptive to us still. They need someone who's on their side."

Though he nodded, he still didn't seem quite convinced. I tugged him out of the room with me, to join the others.

It was time. We were all heading back to Calest, together, for various reasons. I slipped away from my brother to find Kaiden, staying close by him even after our dragons took off. He still looked uneasy, but there was a slight smile on his face anyway, despite it all.

After the others stopped at the rebel camp, Kaiden and I continued on alone, heading for the place where his siblings now lived. The forest was so dense, we had to land a ways away and walk through it, leaving our dragons behind.

Kaiden seemed slightly tense as we stopped in the clearing, his hand slipping into mine. He hadn't told me much about his siblings, and I hadn't wanted to pry, so I wasn't quite sure what to expect. His hand squeezed mine, lightly, and he let out a small breath, a smile slipping on his face.

"Ready?"

I eyed him, trying not to smile. "I feel like I should be the one asking you that."

A half-grin touched his face as he glanced up at the house, just visible from this distance. "I guess you're right."

In response, I squeezed his hand back lightly. It shouldn't have surprised me by this point, but it still did, when he asked me to come along. Whether it was to have someone else there or what...I didn't care. He'd actually *asked*. And I don't think he realized how happy that made me.

Kaiden rubbed a hand against the back of his neck, smile fading. "This didn't...go so well last time," he admitted quietly. The smile stuck half on his face, a bit of worry in his eyes that he tried to brush aside.

"It will this time," I said. *I'll make sure of it*. Whatever misunderstanding might have occurred...I'd set the story straight for him, if I had to.

"Thanks." He paused, then added, "Thanks for coming with me."

"Thanks for asking me," I replied, smiling.

He looked down, nodding quietly. "Sorry I didn't before."

I squeezed his hand, giving him a half-smile. "It's in the past, okay? We can't change what we've already done, but we can choose what we do as a result of it. The present is what matters."

He nodded, quiet for a moment. With one last deep breath for courage, he led me up to the house, pausing in front of the door.

I gave him a little smile. "Go on."

He curled his hand into a fist, then raised it and rapped lightly on the door, dropping it as soon as he was done. I tightened my own hold on his hand for a moment, before he slipped his free.

A girl near Fern's age opened the door, dark hair gathered in a thick braid wound around her head like a crown. Her eyes widened, lighting up as a hand came up to her mouth.

"Kaiden?"

Before he could speak, or even move, she'd flung her arms around him, holding on tightly. He returned the gesture, closing his eyes.

"It *is* you," she breathed.

"Katana!" A rougher, deeper voice cut through the silence. "What are you doing?"

Both of them stilled, Katana glancing back at the house before pulling away from Kaiden with an apologetic look. "It's okay," she mouthed, though she cast an uneasy look in my direction.

"Nothing!" she called back to the house, the smile on her face just slightly strained. It turned to worry as she watched Kaiden. "He said you weren't going to come back. That you...shouldn't." Her gaze turned sad as it drifted back to the door. "He does miss you. He just won't admit it."

Kaiden smiled back, though his eyes betrayed the weight of it. "I shouldn't have left."

"Why is the door open?" A boy about Katana's height – with the same dark hair and piercing eyes – came to stand by the door. When he saw Kaiden, he stopped, eyes going cold. "What is *he* doing here?"

Kaiden cleared his throat, nodding at me. "Lena, this is Kelrin, and Katana."

Katana folded her arms over her chest in what I could now tell was a protective gesture, frowning. "He came back, Kel. Just like he said."

"Well, he shouldn't have," Kelrin spat back. My spine stiffened at his tone, and the look he then directed at me. "He causes nothing but trouble."

"He's your brother." Katana's eyes turned sad. "He-"

"The Empress is dead," Kaiden said quietly, cutting them both off. His gaze lifted slowly to meet his brother's, something indecipherable slipping through it. "You're not in danger anymore."

Kelrin frowned, but I could see from the look in his eyes that he'd already heard the news. "Well, good for you. You finally did something right for once. Considering you're even the one who did anything, which I highly doubt."

Kaiden barely hid his wince at the words. I reached over to lace my fingers with his and squeeze them for a moment, smiling sweetly at Kelrin.

"Kaiden, I'd like a word with your brother, if that's alright?"

Katana was on my side, at least, for she looked between the two of us and then tugged Kaiden through the door. Kaiden hesitated, but let himself be pulled along as she continued talking, gesturing at the house.

I put my best smile on for Kelrin, waiting until they were fully out of sight to start. "Kaiden's told me a lot, you know. About you, about..."

"A lot of lies, you mean," Kelrin muttered.

I let a frown show, just for a moment. "Look, you may not know me, and I don't know you, but we both know Kaiden, so you can cut this act. I know you're bitter because your father was an awful person.

486

But that is *not* Kaiden's fault, and I'm not going to let you stand there and tear him down in the same way he did."

Kelrin looked away, a scowl on his face. "Then he should quit-"

"No." I barely held the ice back from my words. "You don't have any right to blame him for any of this. You don't even know what he's done, do you?" Before he could retort, I shook my head. "But you and I both *know* he is nothing like that man, so don't you even dare say that he's in the wrong here. You don't have any idea what he's sacrificed to keep you safe."

Kelrin scoffed. "What do you know, anyway? I've never even seen you before. Why do *you* care what he does?"

"I'm his friend," I said evenly. "And if you were a good brother like he is, you would quit hurting him for trying to help. He's been through enough already. He doesn't need more of it from you, too."

Kelrin's eyes were steely as they held mine. "He *left*."

"He was *kidnapped* by the man you think 'saved' you. He used you all to threaten Kaiden into doing what he wanted. He didn't come back because he *couldn't*. But he tried anyway. And he let Damien do all sorts of awful things to him in order to find you." My voice turned cold again. "Kaiden risked his life to take down the Empress, so you would be safe. So don't you dare tell me your brother doesn't care for you, or that he left because he's 'just like your dad'. I won't buy it. Your fear doesn't give you the right to put him down.

"He loves you, and he just wants to keep you safe, more than anything else in the world. More than his own safety." I drew in a breath. "You should ask him about it sometime. Tell me then that he 'doesn't care.'" I let my eyes narrow in warning. "But you will not go in there and throw his words back at him again like they're nothing. I won't let you."

Kelrin snorted, looking away in disdain. "I see why he keeps you around," he muttered finally, shoving away from the wall of the porch. I watched him head down the steps and away from the house, letting him sulk, and then turned to slip in the door after the others. He'd see the truth, eventually.

Bright laughter rang through the hall as I stepped inside. It took me a moment to recognize it was Kaiden's. I followed the sound silently, pausing to smile at the picture before me. Kaiden was sitting cross-legged on the ground, a black and gold dog with a line of white fur down its muzzle enthusiastically licking his face while several kids with hair as bright as his stood around him, grinning. He rubbed the dog's face affectionately, answering something one of his siblings had said.

Katana stood off to the side, the youngest of the girls looking over at Kaiden and then up at her hesitantly.

I shifted back a step, to give them privacy before he noticed. But Kaiden decided to look up then and smiled, gesturing me over.

"Lena...these are my siblings." He nodded to two girls who looked too similar to tell apart, save for their expressions and clothes. Both thin, tall, with narrow faces and cheeks smattered with freckles, one wearing a simple white skirt and the other in bright yellow with colorful ribbons in her hair, both with straw-straight red hair that matched Kaiden's. "Kyra, and Kyla." Next, he gestured to a slightly younger, similarly-statured boy beside them, his hair cropped in close curls on his head, the faded vest and buttoned shirt he wore closely matching Kelrin's in style, but definitely not color. "Kellen." His eyes went to the shortest girl glued to Katana's side, softly-curved like she hadn't lost all her baby fat, red hair curled in a cloud around her sweet face and contrasting with the green jumper and wide blue eyes that watched him silently, waiting. "And Kaylissa."

She withdrew further behind Katana at the eye contact. A different sort of look passed Kaiden's face before he brushed it aside, smiling again. "And you've already met Katana."

One of the twins huffed, crossing her arms over her chest. "You still got it wrong. *I'm* Kyra."

He looked startled for a moment, glancing between the two of them. The indignant one burst out laughing, throwing her head back toward the ceiling.

"You forgot! I knew it!" She grinned widely, prattling on teasingly to her twin. "I told Katana he'd have forgotten. And then he actually did! I mean, 'Lissa was too little, of course, so she doesn't know. But...'"

"Kyra," the other girl said pointedly, her voice gentle in comparison. Kaiden blew out an unsteady breath, shaking his head, and grinned, despite the odd look still in his eyes.

"I was joking, obviously. I would never forget that."

"Good," Kyra replied, even as she was lightly elbowed by her twin. "Ow! Hey! What was that for?"

"Girls." Katana's tone held a hint of fond exasperation to it. "Why don't you come help me make food, alright?" She looked over at Kaiden, almost grinning. "You're welcome to join, if you'd like."

"Seeing as I'd imagine you'd prefer unburned food, I think I'll stay here."

"Mmm. You're right, that's probably for the best. Someone needs to keep Molly occupied, anyway."

He rubbed the dog's head fondly, though an odd look crossed his face. "Molly?"

"Yes." Katana raised an eyebrow at him. "The dog you're currently petting."

His hand slowed, uncertain as he looked at the dog and then let out a little laugh. "Oh. Of course."

"Goofy as always." Katana grinned, ushering the children into the kitchen. "If you need anything, just ask!"

"Will do," he replied, settling against the foot of the couch.

KAIDEN

Everything was so...different from how he'd imagined it. He'd known it wouldn't be the same, and yet...somehow he'd forgotten how old most of his memories with his siblings were. How long ago it had been since...*everything*. It made the ache just a little bit worse, realizing how much time he'd missed.

Lena settled down beside him, slipping her hand into his with a little smile. "I like them."

He did his best to smile back, his gaze drifting back toward the kitchen. He could hear them arguing playfully still, imagining Kyra with bright braids and a mischievous smile, wielding a spatula like a weapon. That, he didn't think she'd ever grow out of.

Some things stayed the same, even over the years. Kyla was still quiet, helping balance out some of her twin's wildness – when she didn't join in on it. Kellen and Kaylissa, though... he wasn't even certain they remembered him. Kaylissa certainly wouldn't, and didn't seem to. She was so small the last time he saw her. He hadn't been expecting her to be so...tall.

Kelrin still hadn't come back yet, either, since talking with Lena. Kaiden briefly wondered what had happened then, or if Kelrin had just...left. He hadn't exactly been enthusiastic the last times Kaiden had come back.

Now that the children weren't in the way, Molly proceeded to try to sit in his lap. He shook his head, blinking back a barrage of memories that barreled over him.

Of course this wasn't *his* dog. She might have looked the same, but...they'd had Beauty from when he was young. It was stupid to think she'd still be alive. Which hit him a little too hard, settling alongside everything else that was too different. The similar mannerisms must mean this dog had been Beauty's pup. As he looked closer, he could see the small differences, a patch of white missing from the dark fur on her side, one paw black instead of gold. He choked back a laugh as she flopped over his legs, as content and ridiculous as her mother, pink tongue lolling happily. Beauty hadn't been the largest dog ever, but she'd still tried sitting on him since he was hardly bigger than her, and never stopped past that point. Seemed it ran in the family.

"Your siblings are better at naming than you," Lena said, a teasing smile on her face.

For a moment, he tried not to stare, feeling a prick in his chest again. "What do you mean?"

She nodded to the dog, smiling. "Molly. You probably would have named her 'Dog' or something."

"'Dog'?"

"Yes." She buried a smirk, settling her hands on her lap. "It seems like something you would do."

His head was still spinning, the implications of everything striking a little too close to home. "What do you mean?"

"Nothing." Lena looked away, affecting innocence. "But I have heard stories..."

He managed a cough of a laugh, glancing at the kitchen. "From...?" Shaking his head to clear it, he forced his mind to focus, thinking as to what she might have meant. "Joss?"

Lena laughed, reaching over hesitantly to scratch behind the dog's ears. "Maybe?"

He forced a grin on his face. "And you really think... you can believe her?" He rubbed the dog's head, taking in a small breath. "She's not exactly reliable."

"Your mother, too." Her grin widened. "Not that I heard stories *from* her, obviously, but..." She gestured to the kitchen, a light playing in her eyes. "Kaiden. Kelrin. Katana..."

"Oh." He rubbed the back of his neck, a hint of a grin trying to play on his lips. "Well..." He took in a breath, trying not to shake his head. Everything was built up too closely that the slightest mention felt like it might make it all spill out. "She...they both had K names," he mumbled, ruffling the dog's fur. "Karah and..." he forced the name out carefully, "Kendel. And then there was me, and...I guess she wanted to continue the trend." He turned his lips up in a grin he didn't feel. His father hadn't even wanted him to have that name.

Lena laughed. "*Oh*, I see. So you would have named her...Kibble or something."

"Kibble."

She pressed a hand to her mouth to hide a smile, though it still shone through her eyes. "Fine. What *would* you name her, then?"

He looked away, so she didn't see the flicker in his eyes. "According to your confidence in my naming skills, nothing."

She leaned over to see his face better, grinning. "Aw. Are you embarrassed?"

He shook his head, pressing his lips tightly to hide a frown. "I had a dog. Before."

Lena shifted to face him better, her hand resting on the dog's head. Molly let out a soft woof. "Had?"

"She looked like this one." He managed to push the words out without choking, though the rest stalled in his throat.

"And her name wasn't 'Dog', I take it," Lena replied, teasing but somehow also still gentle.

Glancing briefly at the kitchen, he shook his head. "Beauty. Which is a perfectly good name for a dog."

"I didn't say it wasn't."

Trying to add levity to the weight he still felt, he squinted at her. "You wanted to." Before she could agree, he pulled in a breath. "My mother came up with it."

Her hand settled on his knee as she nodded. "I see. So *that's* why she wasn't named Dog."

He shoved her shoulder lightly, cocking a smile. "Shush."

Her eyes turned twinkly. "Never."

Pausing in his petting of the dog, he let his jaw fall. "Hey. That's my line."

"So I can't use it, either?" She raised an eyebrow challengingly.

"No! I'm supposed to be the one being annoying. It doesn't fit you."

"You're never annoying. Exasperating sometimes, maybe." She winked. "But never annoying."

"I feel like that was still an insult, somehow." He folded his arms over his chest. "I think I should be offended."

She shrugged. "Go right ahead, then. See where that gets you."

Making a face, he took the dog's head in both hands, though he was trying to hide a smile. "See what I have to put up with?"

Molly woofed, nuzzling her nose against him. He let out a little laugh, triumphant. "She agrees with me."

"She's a dog."

He poked his tongue out at her. "Why must you ruin my fun?"

"Because that's my role, apparently. Telling people to shut up."

He pushed out a breath. "That wasn't what I said."

"I know." She smiled, something he didn't want to name playing through her eyes. "You're too sweet for that."

Before he could respond, the door creaked open. Kaiden looked up as Kelrin walked in, a bag in his hands that he took straight to the kitchen. He didn't even look at them as he passed.

Kaiden held in a sigh. What *was* he doing here, anyway? Had he thought everything would magically change because he – as Kelrin so succinctly put it – 'did one thing right'?

"It's just going to take time," Lena said, seeing where his gaze went. She cast a glance at the kitchen and then stood up. "I'm going to go see what they're up to, if you don't mind...?"

He shook his head, watching as she walked away. Molly nuzzled her head against his jacket, looking for treats.

He chuckled. "Sorry, girl. Joss ate everything I have."

The dog let out a low woof, plopping her head in his lap. Despite not being the same, he shifted to hug her neck, burying his face briefly in her thick fur. The sensation was as grounding as he remembered, and he pulled in a deep breath, letting the smell and tickle in his nose brush away the rest of his uncertainties.

"Why did you leave?"

Surprised, he looked up to see Kelrin standing in front of him, staring. Pulling himself away from the dog, he cleared his throat.

"Take your time. But tell the truth." Kelrin looked away, his voice a mutter. "No half-baked excuses."

Closing his mouth, Kaiden drew in a quiet breath. "It wasn't my intention..."

"No apologies, either," Kelrin cut in, eyes slightly hard. "Just tell me *why*."

Kaiden swallowed down the lump building in his throat. No matter what he said, it was still going to sound like one. An excuse. A wild story to avoid the truth.

But he explained it anyway, as much as it hurt, and Kelrin just...listened. By the end, he was frowning, though it seemed different than before.

"That's what your girlfriend said, too."

At Kaiden's responding expression, Kelrin raised an eyebrow. "Despite what you might think, I'm not stupid." He looked away, eyes narrowing a little. "Are you actually sticking around this time?"

Just for a moment, Kaiden hesitated. "Do you...want me to?"

Kelrin snorted. "I'm pretty sure Katana might hit me if I said no." Frowning, he looked over at the kitchen. "Better they grow up actually knowing you than not, I guess."

Despite everything, and the grudging way it was said, Kaiden couldn't help the relief that washed through him, or the smile it tugged onto his face. It was like dipping into a cool lake after being sticky with sweat and dirt all day.

Kelrin rolled his eyes. "Don't expect me to start hugging you or something stupid now." He drew his arms to his chest, folding one over the other. After a long moment, he muttered, "Guess you're not as bad as him after all."

Afraid to try to speak for a moment lest he choke on the words, Kaiden rubbed at his arm, and the scars there. "Thank you."

Kelrin narrowed his eyes again. "Don't make a habit of it. I didn't do anything worth thanking."

"I just..." Kaiden looked down, releasing a breath. "It means a lot."

"Yeah, well, it seems I might have been...wrong. So." He frowned, gaze straying back to the kitchen briefly before he caught himself. "Figured I should say something."

"Thanks."

Kelrin released an exasperated breath. "Yeah, fine. Whatever. Thank your girlfriend, not me." Shaking his head, he turned and walked from the room.

Kaiden pressed his face back into the dog's neck, hiding the wide smile spreading across his face. He felt lighter than air. Like he might just float away if something didn't keep him there.

Lena's chuckle brought him back to earth. He peeked up to see her smiling in amusement, dropping down beside him.

"Hiding from your brother?"

Kaiden shook his head, although the irony did pull at his smile a little. "Did you..." He hesitated. "Do I even want to know what you said to him?"

"Probably not." Lena returned the smile, sitting close enough for their shoulders to touch. "I can be quite persuasive when I want to be."

"The girl with mind gifts, able to persuade people. I never would have imagined."

She rolled her eyes, shoving his shoulder with a hand. "Oh, hush."

Much easier this time, he grinned. "Never."

They sat down to eat once the food was finished, each of the younger three fighting for who got to sit next to Kaiden – and Lena refusing to give up her spot for them. Katana settled it by placing Kaylissa in the seat, despite the fact that she hadn't spoken a word to him since they arrived.

Across from him, Katana smiled, looking to their youngest sister. "It might just...take time. It's been a while, after all." She hesitated, seemingly to ask something, then brushed it aside, passing him a bowl. "I hope you're hungry."

Lena ended up with the endlessly chatty twins beside her, Kyla curiously prodding her with questions while Kyra simply exploded with them, nearly drowning out her sister. Kellen stayed quiet, glancing up at Kaiden every so often and then down, sadly.

"So, when do you leave?" Katana asked conversationally, glancing up at him. Kaiden met Lena's eyes for a moment, taking in a deep breath.

"I'm...not. I'm staying."

Katana dropped a fork, the clatter seeming to startle her as much as the statement. She blinked at him. "You are?"

He nodded, looking down at his food. "If...you want me to."

"Yes." Katana breathed out the word like she'd been waiting to say it her whole life. "Of course we do." She cast a glance at the empty chair beside her, hesitating.

"Kelrin's okay with it," Kaiden said quietly. "I talked to him."

A grin lit up Katana's face, her eyes dancing in its light as she picked up the fallen fork. After a moment, it faded, her eyes slowly going to his. "And Kinny?"

Kaiden's throat tightened. They didn't even...*know*. He'd been in such bad shape before, and Kelrin hadn't stopped yelling... Guilt constricted his chest, despite his attempt to choke it down. How had he not told them? And how would he now?

Katana looked worried. "She... she *is* coming too, right?"

Under the table, Lena's hand found his and squeezed. Swallowing, Kaiden slowly shook his head. "No. She's not."

Katana took in a sharp breath, nodding slowly. All her previous joy was sucked away, replaced by well-disguised dread. "Ever?"

Kaiden shook his head again, closing his eyes. It didn't block out the small noise that left Katana's throat, or the fact that the rest of his siblings were staring at him, confusion written across their faces.

Katana stared down at her hands, watching them shake. "I...I should go find Kel." Distracted, she pushed herself up with an only slightly unsteady breath, smiling at all of them. "Eat up. There's plenty."

Lena left her hand on his, glancing over at him before slowly slipping into his mind. "*Are you okay?*"

Kaiden stared at the wooden table, trying to remind himself it wasn't his fault. He hadn't brought it up. He hadn't...caused it. He couldn't get caught in that, again. Kinny's letter to him burned in his pocket. He pushed away from the table, mumbling distractedly to himself.

Bad timing. But was there ever good timing, for such a thing? He couldn't believe he hadn't told them, before. Showed how badly he'd been doing then.

Lena's hand wrapped around his arm, lightly. He just needed a moment. He needed to get out of there, before they realized. His head was spinning – or was that the room? – and he thought someone might have said something, but he wasn't sure.

Somehow, he ended up outside on his knees, breathing in deeply and gripping handfuls of long grass. It was like a blow to the chest, stealing his air all over again. It hit hard, and unexpectedly, his lungs burning as he clawed for oxygen.

"...Kaiden. *Kaiden.*" Lena was shaking him lightly, worried. "Please. Kaiden?"

His legs felt flimsier than jelly. Drawing a breath that hurt far too much to take in, he managed, somehow, to find her hand and squeeze it.

"...Hey, it's okay. Shh." Something brushed at his face, lightly. "It's okay."

It took him far too long to realize that there were tears on his cheeks, and he was shaking. Lena rubbed a hand over his shoulders, gently.

He couldn't face his siblings like this. He couldn't...let them see him crying like this. Not when...

"...okay? You're okay. I promise."

Gently, Lena's arms came around him, looped loosely behind his neck. "Shh." She whispered it by his ear, her eyes closing. "Shh."

He pulled in a deep breath, avoiding the way it burned in his chest. Words refused to work, no matter what he did. *Kinny...*

"I know." Lena rested her forehead lightly on his shoulder, nodding. "I know."

Shakily, he slipped his arms around her, holding closely to her until he could see clearly again. It still hurt to breathe, and his throat felt raw by the time he was done, but he wasn't shaking, at least.

"It's okay. Shh. It's okay to be sad."

He pressed his forehead against her shoulder, breathing in as deeply as he could. It still felt like a stab in the ribs, every time he did. "They don't know," he whispered, presumably repeating himself. He pulled a little closer, taking in a sharp breath. "I didn't tell them."

"I think they do, Kaiden," she said quietly, cupping the back of his head for a moment. "It's okay."

But it wasn't, and neither was breaking down in front of them. Old habits died hard, it seemed, and this one slammed into him like an angry dragon. He was still trying to catch his breath, braced for another emotional onslaught.

"I'll talk to them, if you'd like." She rubbed his shoulders gently. "Give you a minute to rest."

He shook his head, breathing hard at the knot still trying to force its way into his stomach. "I'll tell them."

She brushed her fingers over his hair, quiet. "You sure?"

Drawing in a small breath, he nodded, pulling away. "I think so."

She lifted his chin enough to see his eyes, watching for a moment before she nodded. "Okay."

Bracing a hand against the ground, Kaiden pushed himself to a crouch, using Lena's outstretched hand to help him to his feet and over to the house.

He couldn't stay, after all. He thought the circumstances being so different would make it easier, but now...

Kelrin stood outside, looking at him with something almost like concern. Katana's eyes were bright and worried. "I told you," she whispered.

Kaiden wished there weren't still daggers cutting his air to ribbons when he tried to breathe. The younger ones were still waiting, though Kaiden wasn't thinking clearly enough to know what to tell them. So he focused on what he had, nodding quietly when Katana asked questions and pulling in a small breath.

"Kinny died...protecting others. The way she always wanted."

It took a while to get out, and Kaiden was immensely relieved that Kelrin didn't just start yelling at him. He stood and waited quietly when he was done, still trying to calm his own breathing.

"I...need to go take care of a few things. I'll be back, after." He hesitated, but couldn't hold the words back. "I'm sorry."

Katana gave him an unsteady, teary look. "It wasn't your fault." Her brow creased as she brushed an arm over her eyes. "Just...come back soon?"

He shook his head, quiet. "I know." Hesitating, he looked up at Kelrin and then nodded. "Of course."

Kelrin folded his arms over his chest, frowning. Katana wrung her hands together, pulling in too deep of breaths. He felt awful for leaving them, again, but also knew there was no way he would be able to handle this either. It was too deeply ingrained in him not to let them see... and with everything being so *different*... what was he going to do? It felt wrong. Kelrin and Katana had everything handled, and lovely, and... they'd probably do it a lot better than he would. They didn't need to deal with his mess, too.

Lena waited for him away from the house. She wrapped her arm around his when he sat down, leaning lightly against him.

"You're going to stay here, then?"

Kaiden hesitated, looking up at the house and then shaking his head. "I don't...think that would be a good idea, actually."

She smiled at him, quietly. "You have family who cares about you. Don't let that go, okay?"

"I wasn't planning to." He took in a slow breath. "I was just...thinking..." He hesitated, looking down.

"Thinking...?" she prompted gently.

He let a half-smile show, lifting a shoulder and dropping it. "There's a lot of bad memories I still struggle with. Seeing them... " He paused, looking away. "It brings it all back. And yet it's too... different still. I feel like I'm... encroaching. I don't... belong like that anymore. I don't know what I'd do." A quiet laugh slipped out of his chest. "Where'll you go?"

Hesitating, she looked at her hand. "I guess... wherever Caleb is."

He nodded. She rubbed her wrist. "He's going to take Dad's position with the rebels and try to make a difference however he can. I figured I'd stay with him." She paused. "You could come with, if you want."

He looked down, thinking, and slowly nodded. Drawing in a breath, he glanced at the house. "They... don't *need* me anymore. But others do. And I could still be close, and keep in contact..." He hesitated, looking down. "It's... what I wanted to do, before..." he admitted. "What I tried to do, even after..." He shrugged a shoulder, trying to brush it off. "It wasn't the easiest, being Blaze and Kaiden in the same two breaths. Figured... I could help make some things better, without having to worry about everything else."

She nodded, resting her hand on his arm. "I think it's a good plan."

He stood up, blowing out a breath. Hesitating, he rubbed the back of his neck. "I... could use a moment alone, first, though."

"Of course. Take all the time you need."

He made sure to let the gratitude show on his face, lifting her hand to kiss it gently. "Thanks," he murmured. "I'll be back, soon."

She nodded, smiling at him softer than he would have liked. Standing to his feet, he crossed over into the trees, putting himself far enough out of anyone's sight, or hearing. Jade reached over to slide her hand into his, giving it a squeeze.

He managed a half-smile at her, squeezing her hand lightly back. "It's...different." A little laugh left his lips at the simple words. "Seeing them."

Jade nodded. "Yeah I can tell. They're a lot older now than when we left."

"Shoulda thought about that," he murmured, the smile turning odd on his lips. "Remembered them differently, so..."

"You didn't have a lot of time to think about it, Butterfly."

He rubbed the back of his neck, another quiet laugh escaping. "Yeah. Guess not."

Gently, Jade tugged him toward the little creek. "That probably makes it harder to see, huh?"

"I've...missed a lot." He rubbed an arm over his eyes, drawing in a breath. *A lot more than I expected.*

Jade nodded. "I know. So much time as passed. But there will be a lot more time in the future. You can be a part of their lives now."

He ran a hand into his hair. "It's still hard." He bit his lip to stop a frown, shaking his head. "It's a lot."

"I know. This would be hard for anyone to come back to. It's not easy to miss out on years with the people we love."

His hand curled in a fist at his side, the odd smile returning. A little laugh left his nose this time, though there was little that was funny about it. "I wasn't really... mad about everything that happened, before. Until now." He pressed the fist to his lips.

Jade tilted her head up, squeezing his other hand. "Yeah. That's not really surprising."

Slowly, he released a breath. "Mm."

"It's okay to be upset or angry about it. I think anyone would be." She stopped on the creek bank, looking up at him. "Did you ever imagine what it would be like when you came back?"

He let the air leave him in a rush, the sound weighing on him as he looked up at the sky. "Not all that much. I just wanted to... get back, and didn't think about how long it'd been. How much would have changed." Shaking his head, he frowned. "With how confusing everything's been..." A half-laugh spilled from his lips, his fingers combing through his hair. "I mean... I just got everything back, not that long ago." In a mutter, he added, "Which was a relief in and of itself. So I guess I didn't really think about it, no." He heard annoyance creep into his voice, directed solely at him, and bit his lip. "Should have."

Jade tilted her head at him. "Nah. With how insane it's been since you left, it's not really surprising that you didn't think about it much. In those situations, people usually don't." She stooped to pick up a handful of pebbles, holding them out to him with a smile.

He couldn't help the start of one too as he took a stone, fingering it quietly. So many memories wrapped up in such a small thing.

Jade skipped hers all the way across the creek. "They're still the same people, and they're going to have a long time to live a happy, full life now. You've made sure of that. You'll have years with them. It might not be the same, but it can still be happy."

Kaiden nodded, throwing his rock into the water. It sank with an unsatisfying plunk. "Yeah. I know."

Jade handed him another pebble, despite her smile being a little sad. "Looks like you need another."

He rubbed his thumb over the smooth surface before chucking that one, too. Plunk.

In comparison, Jade's went so far it was hard to tell when if it even stopped. "The twins haven't changed much. As ornery as ever." Grinning a bit, she glanced up at him.

"Mmhm. Ornery." As best as he could, he lifted his lips. They didn't stay like that very long.

Jade nudged her shoulder against his. He copied her, then bent to pick up another pebble, rubbing it between his fingers. "Remember the first time we did this," he said, looking down at it.

Jade skipped her rock way too skillfully. "Yeah. You were angry and needed somewhere to funnel it."

"Maybe that's why I'm not good at it," he murmured, a half-laugh escaping as he tossed his at the creek. Predictably, it sank.

"It does its job either way," Jade said with a grin.

He rubbed his thumb over another stone, checking the smoothness of it. "Yeah. Guess so."

Jade set her hand on his arm. "Do you need a hug?"

Just a little, his shoulders fell. "I don't know." He looked out at the water, lost in its surface for a moment. All the memories, and everything he'd missed. His siblings... even his dog was gone, already. Like the years he'd been torn from them, missing *everything*.

"What is it, Butterfly?"

Touching the back of his neck, he smiled, even knowing how off it would look on his face. "It just seems silly to be mad about. Like... it took something from me, and I can't get it back, but I should just... be focusing on what I do have instead." He shrugged, throwing the stone with less force than before.

"I don't think it's silly at all. There would probably be something wrong with you if you weren't upset over it. I mean, it's not one or the other. It's both. You can be grateful for what you do have and angry about what was stolen. Most people are both, especially at first."

"I don't like being angry." He squeezed the back of his neck, the gesture oddly grounding, despite the implications of it. "Bad reminders."

Jade nodded. "But this is different."

"I know." He let his hand fall, wishing there wasn't such a strain to his voice. "That's why it's hard."

In response, Jade stepped closer, wrapping her arms around him. He felt the tension leave his shoulders again as he turned to hug her back, burying his face in her shoulder.

Jade rested her head against his. "It's okay to be angry. You're allowed that. after everything."

He forced in a slow, tight breath. "I know." His voice grew hushed. "Don't really want to be."

Jade squeezed him lightly, before moving back a little to see him. "But it's okay. It's not a bad kind of anger."

"I know. It's just... more prominent right now, I guess." His hand curled into a fist again. It was hard to keep it from shaking.

Jade rested her hands on his arms, lightly. "Because of seeing them all changed so much?"

"I guess," he said quietly, not liking the way his voice felt heavier, and then sighed out, changing his answer. "Yeah."

"But you wish it didn't make you angry anyway."

He nodded, failing to smile. "Yeah."

Jade gave his arms a light squeeze. "Sweet Butterfly, always trying to have the best reactions to everything." Her eyes turned fond, amidst the sadness.

He looked away, shaking his head. "It wouldn't be right. I won't be like that."

"You've never been like that, Kaiden. You've never been anything but sweet and kind. Everything else was a twisted game played by people who shouldn't have ever had the power they did. But *you* – you've always been different." She smiled a little. "Even your anger is like this– softer and tucked under your wish to be kind and careful and *better*."

He swallowed, the words barely coming out. "I don't want to take the chance."

Jade rested her palm against his cheek, gentle. "There is no chance. There never has been. You'll never be like them. You're my butterfly, remember? If anyone should know, it's me. You're different, Kaiden.

Worlds different than any of the people who hurt you. Your anger won't spill over and harm them. I promise."

"It already did, though." He fought not to look away, pulling in a slow breath. That was exactly what had happened, before. What he didn't want to happen again.

"That was different," she said quietly.

"It was still my decision." His voice kept growing heavier, each word weighing on him. "There could have been a different way."

"Maybe. But it's over now. There's no going back, and you have no way of knowing if doing something different would have ended better or even worse. You don't know if we would be standing here with you saying 'If only I'd used the Bane when I had the chance' if you'd picked differently. All we can do is move forward." She squeezed his arms gently again. "But this is different. There is no Bane to manipulate you. No evil force to take over and force you to do things you would never do otherwise. This time will be different. You'll see."

"Before that, even." He tried to force a smile, as much as it hurt. *Being Blaze. Shutting them all out.* "That was still my decision. No one forced me into it."

"You were damaged, Kaiden. Not because you were weak or pathetic, but because for as long as either of us can remember, people had been hurting you, and no human anywhere in the universe can hold up forever under those circumstances. You closed off and used your anger because it was the only way for you to survive what was happening. No one can fault you for that. Most people would have done a whole lot worse under that kind of pain." She shook her head. "You don't need to keep beating yourself up, because the way you reacted? That's normal. No, it's *better* than the normal way people react to that much hurt and pain and loss."

Damien's words, in his head. *"You were damaged long before I ever laid hands on you."*

"It doesn't seem normal," he said quietly, closing his eyes and trying not to imagine too much. Fire and twisted laughs, Damien's voice mocking him. *"Try not to damage the ferns this time."* Smoking, charred wreckage, all from his hand. He couldn't hold any of it back. It burned too fiercely, too hot in him to have resisted it.

"I just...don't want it to happen again."

"It is normal, though. How we feel isn't usually how things are." Reaching up, she messed with his hair. "And it won't. Things are going to get better now. I've been telling you it would, haven't I? I'm always right."

Seeing no point in arguing, he glanced back in the direction he'd come. "Yeah. You are."

"Exactly." With a small smile, Jade nudged his chin. "It's not going to be like before."

Feeling overwhelmed, he slipped his hand around hers, squeezing it tightly. The familiarity was grounding, which was exactly what he needed at the moment, with flames still licking through his mind and under his skin, pulling at him, begging to be let out.

"You'll see. This time will be different." Her fingers curled around his, gently. But he couldn't stop thinking, and letting them tug him in deeper. He *knew*, far down, that she was right. He knew it wouldn't have gone well if he hadn't...done something. He would have broken, or snapped in a much worse way if he hadn't...pretended. It had been building for a while, with everything Damien did. The grief and guilt mixed with a swirling anger he tried so hard to keep down, turning deadly when they interacted. It was a wonder, in some ways, that even that had worked for a time.

But it still had bad reminders, at the thought of letting it out. He couldn't stop picturing... and thinking about how it felt, seeing it himself. Couldn't dare imagine standing in a role he swore he never would, laughing at someone else's pain. Causing it, just because he was mad and didn't know what else to do with it.

"I don't know why," he finally said, quiet. "I'm just as damaged and messed up as then." What was to say it wouldn't happen again?

"Because you know more than you did then, and you have people who love you and are here for you. You don't have to face any of it alone anymore." She looked up at him, smiling a little. "And because you're free now. You're not a butterfly trapped in a jar any longer. There's no one keeping you somewhere you hate being, forcing you through things that hurt you. It's over – the jar is open and you're free to fly away."

Jade reached up to brush his bangs with her fingertips. "So, Butterfly, what's it like to be free?"

He closed his eyes for a moment, letting himself think about that. *Free.* It was a funny word, more like he was a butterfly looking up at the open air and trying to figure out how to get up there.

"It doesn't... feel real yet." He rubbed the back of his neck. "Feels kinda like losing my memory, again. Like I should know what to do, but... don't."

Jade held out a handful of pebbles to him. "Then throw a few more rocks. That's always a safe bet when you don't know what to do."

His shoulders relaxed as he took them. "It is familiar," he murmured, curling his fingers around them for a moment.

Jade grinned. "Only because I shove rocks at you every time you're sad or angry." Her eyes sparkled. "It's my fabulous Best Friend Fix-All."

Chuckling, Kaiden tossed his rock, watching it sink in the water. "Wow. Ten thousand points to me."

Jade laughed. "You weren't ever very good. Try again." She held the handful out again.

A smile curved the edge of his mouth. "Why am I not surprised?" And why did she think throwing another one would make him improve? But he did it anyway, listening to the plink of it...just falling beneath the water.

Jade grinned, looking mischievous. "I like it, though."

Slowly, he raised an eyebrow at her. "You like how pathetically I can toss a rock."

"Yep."

Hiding the ghost of a smile, Kaiden shook his head, trying to imitate her movement and actually skip the rock. Even when he tried, though, he failed. Oddly fitting, for him.

He let out a long, fake sigh as Jade showed him, up yet again, her stone skipping effortlessly and merrily across the creek.

Jade grinned at him. "It's therapeutic."

"Is it?" He chucked another one harder, as if it might get out some of the fire whispering in his mind. It still sank.

"Sure it is. Chucking rocks at stuff is always helpful. Obviously," she said, with a healthy dose of teasing.

Letting out a breath that could almost be a laugh, he threw another one. "And why's that?"

Jade looked over with an innocent grin. "Because I said so."

"Well. That's sound logic right there."

"Why thank you."

Chuckling, Kaiden tossed another rock. "It's a funny statement, out of context. 'Oh, you're sad? Here. Have a rock'." He mimed shoving one at her, then threw two at the creek in succession, as if it might somehow increase their chances of making it.

Unsurprisingly, it didn't.

Jade threw her head back in a laugh. "I'm pretty sure *everything* with me is weird out of context, Butterfly. Even *in* context, I'm odd."

"The best kind of weird, though."

"Hm." She showed him up by skipping another rock. "I don't know about that."

"I do." He threw his doomed-to-fail stone, grinning at her.

Jade wrinkled her nose, sticking her tongue out at him. "None of that cute stuff."

He huffed out a breath. "And why not?"

"Because then I'll have to scold you. Duh."

He let his shoulders fall, the corners of his mouth drooping in a comically sad way. Jade stifled a smile when he turned to hug her.

"Don't be sad, Butterfly."

He released a long, dejected sigh. "How can I not be? You said you were going to scold me."

"Only if you keep calling me sweet things." After a moment, she sighed out, long and heavy. "But I wouldn't want you to be sad, so I guess I can forgo the scolding just this once."

He lifted his head from her shoulder, lifting his lips in a fond and grateful way. "You're the best."

Sighing at the word, Jade shook her head. "No, Butterfly, I'm far from the best."

"You're the best to me."

Jade smiled a little, crookedly. "I don't know why."

"I don't know why you think I'm so great, either." He slipped his hand down her arm gently to squeeze her hand, letting warmth soften his tone. "But that's what best friends are for, right?"

Jade shifted her hand in his, smiling a little less than usual. "Yeah, it is."

He tilted his head, just a little. "What is it?"

Seeming off balance, Jade reached up to touch the side of her neck, attempting to cover it with a smile. "Ah. Nothing, it's just..."

When she trailed off, he let his voice get quieter. "Does that...bother you?"

"No." Jade shook her head, and then laughed. "It's going to sound stupid and confusing. So, sorry in advance. It's just that I'm not very used to being touched." Shifting, she glanced away. "I'm used to being the one to initiate it, I guess. People don't really touch me if they can help it. Or not like, you know, in that kind of way."

He hesitated. "Why...?"

Jade shifted on her feet, not looking at him. "I'm...not liked where I'm from. I'm 'tainted'. A halfbreed, they like to say." She shrugged. "So yeah. I'm pretty sure most of them would rather have their hand cut off than touch me like that."

Doing his best to hide a frown, he nodded. "Well. I'm happy to be the exception."

Though she wouldn't quite meet his eyes, Jade smiled. "You're always my exception, Butterfly."

"I'm glad. I like doing things for you."

Jade blinked at him, shaking her head. "You're one of the few who would say that."

"Few people would have done all you have for me. So..." He squeezed her hand lightly again.

Glancing down at their hands, Jade shrugged. "It wasn't like it was a difficult thing for me to do. I like being your friend, Butterfly. I always have."

He let out a quiet breath. "Well, I don't really know where you're from, but given what I do know, I still don't think most people would drop so much to spend time with a broken, messed-up kid with a terrible sense of humor." He smiled, trying to make it soft instead of sad. "I like being your friend, too."

Jade rubbed her free hand against her pant leg, finally meeting his eyes. "Thanks." Her voice was quieter than usual as she lifted her hand to brush his hair aside, half-smiling. "I came here because I was lonely. I stayed because you needed me. But I *wanted* to stay because I see a thousand good things in you, Kaiden. You give me hope."

He returned the smile, tugging lightly on her hand. "I still don't know what you see. But I'm glad for it. And that you didn't have to be lonely, then." When she didn't resist, he drew her into a hug, resting his head on her shoulder. "Can't imagine anyone better to have as my best friend."

Jade dropped her forehead on his shoulder, quietly chuckling. "That sounds kinda mushy."

"I think you've been 'kinda mushy' with me for a long time and I've not complained, so." He smiled, leaning his head against hers.

"Hey now," she mumbled into his shirt. "That's going a little far, calling me mushy."

"I said *kinda* mushy."

Jade chuckled. "Is that better?"

"I don't know. You tell me."

"I'll have to think about it." She drew in a breath, quiet for a minute. "I'm glad you weren't scared away. You know, by my weirdness."

"I don't see how that would happen. If weirdness scared me, I'd have to be perpetually terrified from always scaring myself."

Jade chuckled. "That would be sad." She pulled in a breath, half-smiling at him again. "And I don't mind if you're sweet or whatever. It doesn't bother me. I'm just not used to it."

I can change that, he thought, unable to help a smile. "I wasn't used to you being kind to me for quite a while, either."

Jade laughed. "Yeah. What a pair we make."

"Mmhm." He squeezed her lightly. "Though for the moment...we should probably head back so Lena doesn't think I ran off or got eaten by a bear or something."

Jade squeezed him too, and then stepped back, grinning. "Yeah, probably. Wouldn't want your girlfriend to come track us down and scold us." She winked.

He rubbed the back of his neck, grinning a little too. "Yeah. I don't think I could...bear that."

Jade tossed her head back in a laugh. Kaiden grinned wider.

"I might bear-ly survive. Which would be unbearable."

Taking his wrist, Jade tugged him back toward the house. "How you always have so many immediately on your brain is the real question. We should get you a crown and name you King of Puns."

"I practice, obviously. I try to think of at least twelve puns when I wake up, so I'm always prepared. I tried just doing ten, hoping one of them would make someone laugh. No pun in ten did." He held back a laugh, pleased. "Yes. Then it truly could be my crowning glory."

Laughing again, Jade patted his arm. "Very funny."

He couldn't stop grinning, feeling his eyes slowly light up with it. "Do you think Lena will smack me if I tell her a joke? I've got a *grate* one, but she'll probably say it's too cheesy."

"If you keep telling cheese jokes, maybe." Jade's eyes sparkled.

"I'll just have to get cheddar at telling them, then."

Jade nudged his chin. "Well you can tell them to me anytime, whether you're 'cheddar' at them or not." She tossed him a wink.

His grin widened. "At least I'll have company when I get kicked outside for my bad jokes."

Jade nudged her shoulder into his. "You'll always have my company, Butterfly."

"Even when we're old and gray." He stopped, the smile replaced at a sudden thought. "My hair...won't be red anymore then..."

Jade burst out laughing. "Well, mine won't be black either, so... We can be gray together."

"That makes it marginally better." His lips still stuck out in a pout. "It's going to look like ashes." He paused, thinking it over and nodding slowly. "There we go. I can just tell people I accidentally burned it and it was never the same."

"Well there's *your* excuse. But what will I say about mine to be clever? There's already no excuse for it." She picked up a strand, which tangled around her finger.

"You can say someone drew a monster on your head and that's why it's so insane and wants to eat everything." He grinned at her. "And the ink has just faded over time."

Jade slowed, turning to look at him for a moment before she burst out laughing, bent over at the waist with her hands against her knees, the sound loud and hard.

His cheeks stretched wide in a smile. "It would fit!"

Jade gasped in breaths between laughs, taking a long time to collect herself while Kaiden's face hurt from all the smiling. "That's actually a pretty great explanation. I'm using that now whenever people ask why I have a monster on my head."

"Perfect. Then they can't look at you like you're crazy!"

Jade laughed. "Well, they probably still will, but at least I'll have an excuse." She rubbed the palms of her hands into her eyes to clear the moisture away, chuckling.

Kaiden couldn't stop grinning. "Exactly."

Jade shook her head, looking over at him with a grin back, and then grabbed his sleeve, tugging him along toward the house.

The smile stayed stuck stubbornly on his face, only quieting when they slipped in the house and he remembered everything that had happened. He was sure his eyes were way too warm, though, as he went to find Lena.

She looked up from where she was talking with Katana on the couch, smiling. "Ah, see? I told you he'd return." Her eyes twinkled teasingly. "Katana was worried you ran off again. I figured you'd gotten lost."

He pulled her to her feet, shaking his head. "You have no faith in my abilities."

Katana watched them, biting her lip, and then pressed herself into his arms once she was able. "Are you really leaving...again?"

He held her close, cupping the back of her head. "Not like before," he murmured, tipping his head down to see her eyes. "I promise."

Katana let out a quiet sigh, but relaxed against him. "I know. You have to go be all heroic and stuff, as usual."

A quiet chuckle left his throat as he brushed some of her hair aside. "You could come with us. Then you really wouldn't be far."

She looked up hopefully for a moment, then back down. "Kel likes it here," she murmured.

"Then you'll just have to come visit often, too." He squeezed her lightly, resting his head on hers. "Whenever you want. We'll make it work, okay?"

She shifted against him, hugging him tighter for a moment. "Okay," she finally whispered.

He smiled, pulling back enough to see her face. "See you soon, 'Tana."

Her eyes looked relieved. "See you soon."

He said goodbye to the rest of his siblings, crouching to Kaylissa and waving since she still didn't seem eager to touch him. "Bye, 'Lissa."

She frowned at him, brow creasing in confusion, but eventually waved back like she was thinking *"maybe this weirdo will leave me alone if I just give in."*

Kelrin watched them all with his arms folded, the start of a frown on his face seeming a permanent fixture for him. Kaiden hesitated, slipping his hands in his pockets for a moment as they faced each other. He let his shoulders relax, stepping closer to touch Kelrin's lightly.

"If you're going to hug me, just be quick about it," he muttered.

"You're doing great, you know," Kaiden said in reply, quiet enough for only them. "Taking care of them. So...thank you."

He let out a quiet snort, pushing Kaiden's arm away. "That's what siblings do."

A smile slipped onto Kaiden's face as he nodded. "Yeah. It is."

As he turned away, Kelrin sighed, muttering under his breath. "Kaiden?"

When he stopped to look back, Kelrin's gaze was firmly elsewhere. His brother tightened his arms over his chest. "Take care of yourself. I don't want to find out..." He frowned, eyes flicking to Kaiden's arms for a moment. "Just be smart, okay? Katana's going to kill me if you get lost somewhere again. They've missed enough time with you as is."

Kaiden's mouth tipped up in a little smile as he nodded. Snorting, Kelrin looked away.

"Go do that to your girlfriend. I get enough of cute smiles from these crazies as is." He waved a hand away from him, shaking his head.

Kaiden turned it into a grin instead, knocking his boot against Kelrin's. "See you later, Kel."

"Yeah, whatever. I'm probably going to see you way too much now."

Shaking his head, Kaiden turned to Lena, unable to hide the smile on his face. "Ready?"

They walked out the door, Lena wrapping her arm around his. As the house grew smaller and smaller in the background, she turned to him, smiling.

"You know, it's going to be a lot easier to tease you, this way. Having you in easy reach and all."

He hesitated, pulling on a little grin. "Yeah. You might get sick of me, though."

"If I do, I'll let you know." She returned the grin, looking down as it softened. "It'll be nice, being close. Considering..." She let the words hang, looking up at him.

"Considering...?"

Amusement played across her face. "Beanhead." She said it fondly, though, shaking her head. "It's usually considered normal to want to be close to the people you love."

His hand found the back of his neck, rubbing it even as he nodded. "Right. Of course. People...people you...love."

Her eyes held a laugh as she watched him. "Does that fluster you?"

"I'm not really...used to it," he mumbled, trying to rub away the heat that, as far as he knew, wasn't from his gift.

She leaned over to press her lips against his cheek, eyes soft. "Well, we can change that."

He had to fight not to rub his now-hot cheek, too, like her kiss had left fire under his skin. His fingers ended up tangled with hers, looking for something to occupy themselves with instead. "Oh...o-okay."

She smiled at him, fond and amused. "Shall we be off, then?"

"Yeah." He rubbed at the back of his neck, wishing it didn't feel so hot. "Chan is probably silently begging someone to take Joss off his hands, before she drives him crazy."

Lena laughed. "Alright. Rescuing Chan it is."

CHAN

All children could be bribed. Some, it was just easier than others.

Children, Chan thought, were easier to handle than dragons. Rena still refused to listen to him, and chittered sassily if she did. He'd all but given up on her ever actually delivering a message, despite Katya's wish to try. If anyone had the patience for it, it was her. And the tiny dragon, disgruntled or not, didn't nip at her or pull her hair as much as with others, or screech loudly in her ear. Probably because Rena knew how sensitive Katya was, despite the little kit's insistence that she just liked Katya better.

Joss, in comparison, was incredibly easy to keep occupied. She ate like she planned to make up for all the meals she'd missed in her lifetime, and occasionally could be persuaded to work for them, too, if the reward was high enough. She'd grumble that it was less effort than trying to sneak something out from Chan's watchful eye. If need be, he just hid the food, which at least discouraged her.

All that said, he was still grateful when Kaiden and Lena showed back up at the house and neither of them looked injured or in need of a hug. They were smiling, hands twined together in a way he couldn't quite ignore. Though it wasn't as if it was the first time, there was something...different about it. Probably because Kaiden was actually smiling.

Kaiden craned his head in all directions, inspecting the place. "Hey, she didn't burn it down." He grinned, eyes twinkling with teasing. "Where is the little troublemaker, then?"

"Kaiden!" Joss came flying out of the next room, barreling into his legs. Her eyes sparkled with delight for a moment, before she frowned. "No. Bodyguard still sounds better."

He chuckled, wrapping an arm around her. "You can call me by my name."

"Nope." Joss pulled back, examining his jacket. "Did you bring me food?"

As if she hadn't eaten enough, Chan thought, shaking his head. He couldn't help a smile, though, as he picked up the book he'd set aside. As much as he loved his friends, he was much happier sitting off in a corner, reading and keeping an eye on things from a distance. There would be plenty of time in upcoming days to talk. Right now, he wanted to relax.

The thought made him smile, as did Katya slipping over quietly to sit beside him. He pushed his glasses up his nose, cracking the book open, and spread the pages far enough that she could read too, if she wanted to. It depended on the topic, and sometimes the day, but he still left it as an option for her.

Today was a good day. She shifted over close to him, curious eyes scanning the pages, and rested her head on his shoulder so she could see better. He angled it toward her, resting a hand lightly on her dress-draped knee. She wasn't fond of intense things, and from experience, having it there gave her something to hold if she got jumpy.

Kaiden laughed loudly, drawing his attention away for a moment. Joss was making a face at him, though whether it was the cause or result of his laugh, Chan wasn't sure. He smiled, though, giving Katya's knee a gentle squeeze.

She looked up, too, and though there was no smile on her face, he felt it all the same, through her thoughts. *"They're happy."* She sounded relieved, as if she thought they might be terribly upset, instead.

Chan nodded, fingering the page for a moment before turning it. *"Yeah. They are."*

He knew what she meant, though. For once, there was no deadline weighing on them, no secrets or agendas kept to protect others. They could just...be, like this, relaxing in a house and taking moments to enjoy life. It was a wonderful feeling.

The dragons, too, were free to be themselves again. Without the threat of the Bane, they didn't have to suppress their gifts – though many were discreet about breathing fire, even harmlessly or merely in excitement, with how jumpy it made some people.

At least Rena hadn't figured out how to use hers. He didn't need a temperamental, *fire-breathing* dragon child to care for. Kits were a different kind of dragon altogether, and not necessarily children, but the way Rena acted...she might as well have been.

In some ways, though, their work had just begun. But it was less of the death-defying kind and more of the mending-countries one. Though he didn't fully understand *why* it was, Sari had explained to them just what had happened.

Ru'ach and Shedim were gone. And with them, a curse few had even known was on the land, destroying the balance between the countries. Calest and Galdania had been two halves of the same whole once, he knew, two settlements coexisting peacefully on either sides of a river. Somehow or another, by what the Galdanians claimed was a god, Calest was made barren, and Galdania 'blessed' for their willingness to follow this ancient being. As with any old story, there were many gaps, made worse at times by the destruction and loss of knowledge caused by the dragons, and the hatred Calestans had for anything Galdanian.

It made sense, when he thought about it. Shedim and Ru'ach had shaped so much of their world, intentionally or not. It all started, and ended, with them.

But now, that war was over. Now, they could start to rebuild, and heal, and work toward restoring the world to what it was meant to be. Together.

EPILOGUE

TIETO

Tielieto sat on the tallest shelf in the kitchen to watch the proceedings, proud of his work. It had been a long journey, and tested the limits of his patience many times, but it was worth it.

Honestly, how had humans ever managed to get along before kit dragons came around?

"Tieto!" A sharp chirr from below cut off his reflection. *"Quit preening like a pea-brained featherscale and come move this!"*

Huffing out, and watching the smoke curl from his nostrils with no small measure of delight, Tieto spread his wings and glided gracefully down to help his brethren.

Feli looked ready to breathe more than just smoke if he wasn't careful, red scales already glinting like it in the morning light. It had been a long time since that happened. *"Honestly, you're such a lazy sack of nothing. Why do they even keep you around?"*

For his looks, obviously. Who didn't love green dragons? It was a classic color, and obviously the best, considering how much of the world strived to be like it. Green was a sign of health and beauty, both of which he radiated in abundance. It was a wonder all the other dragons didn't want to be like him, really.

"It's too late," Xerilt remarked solemnly, his golden scales glinting as he assisted his friends. *"His ego is inflated way too far to ever return to normal. There's nothing we can do."*

"You're all just jealous," Tieto huffed, making sure to let the light catch his glorious scales as he turned to view the problem. Though he was bigger than most of them, by a small margin, that didn't mean they weren't perfectly capable of handling this *without* him.

Pari let out a squeal and wailed, shaking a frosting-covered claw. *"It's so stickyyyy!"*

Tieto attempted to roll his eyes, his head moving with the motion. That's how it was done, right? *"It's always sticky, featherhead. Nitl's person makes messes everywhere she goes."* He eyed their prize with delight. *"But they're usually lovely ones."*

"Other than paste," Zvi cut in softly, peeking her blue head out from behind the box. *"Don't ever eat the paste."*

512

Several other kits bobbed their heads in agreement. Pari continued trying to fling the goo off, silver scales glinting with the movement. *"I don't like it!"*

Feli huffed, eyeing the puff of smoke it made, as they all did, with satisfaction. *"Well, I like it. It tastes better than this sugar cloud stuff."* She narrowed her eyes at Tieto, baring small teeth. *"Now would you all quit being lazyscales and help me out?"*

Zvi's ears drooped, tiny tail curling around her. *"I'm sorry. I'm too small to be much help."*

"You don't have a lazy scale on you, Zvi," Feli replied, shoving against the box. *"Tieto!"*

He let out a dramatic huff, watching in satisfaction as each kit's eyes followed the lazy curl of smoke. It was the perfect way to get their attention, and Tieto had always made the best smoke trails. He was very pleased to discover he hadn't lost that ability. *"Don't you ever get, I don't know, bored of doing the same old thing?"*

An unhappy laugh rumbled through Feli. *"Oh, like you're one to talk, featherscales. Sitting up there thinking about how great you are."* She tipped her head up to look at the box, teeth bared. *"You don't even know what's in there."*

"I'm glad you agree," he replied, chirring in laughter when her nostrils flared. He gave the box a lazy look. *"And from the evidence scattered about as always, I'd say it's that crumbly sweet stuff everyone adores."*

"It could be something else," Feli snapped, watching Xerilt attempt to fly up and push the flap loose. He fell back to the table with a thump. *"You can't have too much cake."*

"It won't come off!" Pari cried again, falling over in her attempt to free herself. Xerilt eyed her for a long moment, sighing out a thin trail of smoke.

"I prefer jam myself," Tieto replied, eyeing their failures in disdain.

"I'll jam you in something if you don't stop," Feli hissed, ears flat as she tugged Xerilt back to his feet. *"Besides. Cake is Zvi's favorite."*

A squeal from above drew all their attention. D'sidi poked his head down over the box's lid, eyes lit up. *"Looklooklook!"*

He dropped a thin and glittery rope over the side, both sides of it flat and the length curling as it fell. His eyes sparkled with the reflection of it.

Some dragons, like D'sidi, gave them all a bad name with their obsession over mundane things that happened to reflect light well. From atop the box, he bobbed up and down in delight as the ribbon continued to fall over the edge, forming a sparkly pile near Zvi.

513

"It'ssoprettyandshinyandthere'smoreandmoreofitovertherethatId efinitelydidn'talreadystealbecauseit'stooprettytoresistand-" He let out a long squeal, jumping up and attempting to do a flying loop in the air.

"Someone's hyper," Xerilt remarked, and then stopped, making a dismayed sound. *"D'sidi, did you...?"*

"IdefinitelydidnotcrawlintotheboxbecauseI'msmallandeatsomeoft hecake,nope. ItwasverydeliciousandIdon'tregretanyofit."

"D'sidiekenethylyl!" Pari cried out, using his full name to scold him, the feathered tip of her tail thumping against the box. Her squeal sounded far too much like a wail. *"You got some and didn't tell us?"*

Tieto wondered sometimes if the humans had longer names that they just kept to themselves, too. Names held a lot of meaning, of course, and the implications of all humans having short names – well, it wasn't very flattering.

"You don't even like cake, Parizerarteisa." He wouldn't admit it, but he used her full name just to bother her. *"You can't stand it on you."*

"I like it in my mouth, which is the only place it should ever be." She sniffed, eyeing a dot of frosting still on her foot like she was deciding whether or not to go to war with it again.

D'sidi squeaked, falling off the box into the pile of ribbon. He scrambled back to his feet, clutching it close in his claws. *"They'recomingthey'recomingthey'recoming!"*

Feli let out a discontent sound, turning in a swift motion to tackle Tieto. *"This is all your fault!"*

"Oh, hi guys." The green-haired human looming above them waved, the edges of her eyes crinkled in a way Tieto had never seen a dragon achieve. Feli, unbothered by the interruption, bit his ear, claws scraping and tails tangling as she tried to pin him.

"Aw, look at that. Kaiden!" the girl called behind her. "Your dragons are playing again!" The corners of her mouth spread way too wide, eyes twinkling as much as D'sidi's as she reached down to pet Zvi with a messy hand. "Cuties."

Zvi squeaked in delight, licking at the white splatter on the girl's hand. Tieto kicked at Feli with a huff, breathing smoke in her face. She growled, tugging his tail until he yelped. D'sidi bounced in his pile of curly ribbon, the others watching but not interfering.

The girl just grinned as if they were humming in delight, rather than fighting. She reached down and lifted the box off the table, causing them all to still.

"This one isn't for you," she said with a laugh, then lowered her voice. "If there's leftovers, though..."

Feli nipped Tieto's ear with one last growl while he was distracted, getting up with a huff. The other kits let their ears droop, watching the box disappear. Zvi looked the most disappointed of all, her ears and wings hanging low.

"*It wasn't even frosting*," she said dejectedly. "*It was paste.*"

D'sidi perked up, looking over at her. "*Paste?Isthatshiny,too?*"

"*Not everything is shiny, D'sidi,*" Tieto snapped, shooting a glare at Feli. "*If you had had a better plan...*"

D'sidi squealed in delight again, flapping his little wings. "*Zvizvizvilooklooklook!*"

The little blue dragon perked up as she followed his lead. "*They're back!*"

All the dragons looked up, exchanging excited glances.

"*Well, finally.*" Tieto swept his tail at Feli for good measure, flying into the air. "*Bet I'll get there first.*"

But it was Zvi who landed first, nuzzling her head against Kaiden's neck happily. He laughed, rubbing a hand over her scales and smiling at the rest of them.

The dark-haired girl by his side stepped back, hands held up as if to ward them off. "They're attacking! I told you they were feral!"

Tieto changed his trajectory to land on her head, chirring a laugh when she shrieked and tried to bat him off. "Bodyguard!"

"Behave, Green," Kaiden said, brushing him off with a smile. Tieto nipped lightly at his hand, sending his displeasure through their bond. It might have been cute before, but they both knew full well that Kaiden knew what his name was now, and just refused to use it. He said Green had 'grown on him', whatever that meant. Zvi chirred a laugh, flapping her little purple wings.

The rest of the kits followed in the air, settling on his lap and near him when they finally sat down. D'sidi still had part of the ribbon in his mouth, squeaking happily.

Some human traditions still seemed odd to Tieto. This sort of thing was one of them. Since humans didn't live as long as dragons, they liked to mark the passage of time whenever and however they could. It had taken him a long while to realize they looked up at the sky to see how long it would be until the shiny light there disappeared from view again. They had all sorts of funny terms for time, and often spoke like it was a physical thing they could 'lose' or 'run out of'. It was as if they thought the world would quit working if they didn't constantly check up on it. Whether a passing remark or a long celebration, they treated it like a deity that deserved their worship.

Tieto was glad he'd had a long time to learn the intricacies of it all. He might have been confused, otherwise, as to why they had decided to celebrate the passage of time for just *one* human today, rather than all of them. As if it were some miracle that they had managed to make it this far without dying.

Although, given his human's track record so far, maybe that was something worth celebrating, after all.

The other dragons watched in delight and curiosity as the humans brought out boxes wrapped in colorful papers. This, most of all, Tieto had never understood. They watched with anticipation as if the box presented some wonderful challenge, though it never did. What was the point of concealing what was in it, then?

Still, even he had to admit that whatever the reason, it was nice to see their human happy again – even if Tieto was still jealous of his ability to smile so well. All of them wore that expression today, as if they couldn't make themselves stop. It made him relax against Kaiden, even letting Feli curl up next to him despite the disdainful look she pretended to give him. Quialilli and Chaertierena sat contently with their own humans, while Choril sat protectively on Kaiden's other shoulder, opposite Zvi. None of the kits even attempted to pronounce Ril's full name. It was too complicated.

Nyxetyen and Roxilelideth sat with the green-haired girl, since their human wasn't around anymore. Tieto couldn't tease them about their nicknames as well as the others, though, because 'Nyx and Rox' just...worked. Besides, the humans wouldn't be able to say their full names, anyway.

Zvi's ears perked up as the humans started singing some song – all but their human, that was. Tieto rumbled in contentment, the catchy little tune practically begging to be imitated. Zvi picked up on it and started humming along, the other kits absently following along with the humans. The green-haired one gasped in delight, hands clasped near her very messy blouse as she watched them with sparkly eyes. "The kits know it, too!"

There was a word that kept being tossed around that Tieto still didn't understand. Another of the humans' ways to mark time, he assumed. They repeated it several times in the song, as the green-haired girl brought out the cake they had tried so hard to get to, odd sticks poking out of the top of it. Even Pari's ears perked up, as much as she liked to complain about the mess.

"*Ohboyohboyohboyohboy,*" D'sidi squeaked, bouncing up and down with little happy wing flaps.

516

The darker-skinned girl across from them chuckled, watching the kits. "May I suggest keeping all sugar *away* from the dragons this time?"

Zvi hissed in dismay, ears drooped, even as the sunshine-haired girl beside their human laughed. "Yes, that would probably be wise."

"I'll keep them away," the smaller dark-haired girl muttered, giving them suspicious looks. At least her wyvern was off somewhere, rather than ruining their fun. Tieto had never gotten along with wyverns. The sun-haired girl's dragon, though, he didn't mind, even if he didn't actually know the kit's name.

"We decided you can light your own candles," she explained sassily, though there was laughter in her tone, "since that's your thing and all."

He laughed, too, which always made Tieto happy. He couldn't help flapping his golden wings a little as their human's hand created *fire*, without breathing it or anything, tiny flames flickering on the end of his – well, they weren't claws. What were they called? Oh, right. Fingertips. The flames stuck to the sticks when they touched, multiplying until they were all dancing happily in alternating rhythms. Then, odder still, he blew on them, and the flames went *out*, like he absorbed them into him or something. Tieto had never seen anything like it.

D'sidi wouldn't quit bouncing, but even he knew they wouldn't get any cake if they didn't wait. It was tempting, though, seeing it sitting there with colorful gobs of yumminess and crumbly, sticky sweetness everywhere. Tieto's stomach rumbled at the thought.

"Go eat a cricket," the dark-haired child said, eyeing him. "Cake isn't for dragons."

"Cake is good for the soul," the green-haired girl replied happily, her long braids swinging behind her as she moved to a song none of them could hear, humming.

The dark-haired girl's eyes narrowed as she bared her teeth at the kits, in a surprisingly scary snarl. "For yours, maybe. Not for dragons. And I'll be dagged if I let any of them steal it."

Kaiden stopped to look at her and burst out laughing, exchanging a look with the sun-haired girl before repeating *'dagged'* under his breath. His eyes looked too mirthful for the entire situation. At the looks he got from the others, he cleared his throat.

"The cake is good." Turning, he held one of the little sticks out toward the sun-haired girl. "Although, it can't hold a candle to you. But I can." His eyes twinkled with a look that was bound to get him smacked.

Surprisingly, she just rested her head against his shoulder, sighing. Zvi blinked down at her, though she was tiny enough not to be

517

squashed, and the sun-haired girl adjusted to sharing the perch fairly well.

Were it not for how much she made their human smile, Tieto might have resented her taking up so much of their space. He'd been theirs long before she came along, and if she ever left, they'd still be there. Although, the way they hung so close to each other, so often, that didn't seem likely to happen.

While the humans started talking about something other than food, the green-haired girl lifted the platter of remaining cake to carry it away. Trying not to seem too eager, Feli kicked him with her foot and took off with a squeak of laughter, following after. A game of race and chase ensued as all the kits followed suit, zipping around and underneath each other until the humans stopped watching them. The green-haired girl smiled knowingly, bringing the plate back into the kitchen and setting it within easy reach.

"Just don't show yourselves again until it wears off, alright?"

Zvi had already snatched a piece and held it close to her, thrumming happily. D'sidi landed *on* the cake and dug inside for the creamier goo, his tail thumping and flinging bits of sugar everywhere.

And even Tieto had to admit, as he joined them, that humans had done at least one good thing, inventing cake.

KAIDEN

"Kaiden!"

Stretching a bright grin onto his face, he turned in the direction of his name, letting his eyes sparkle as Fern came barreling against him. It felt good, having her squeeze him and relax like she'd just come home.

"Hey there, kid," he said, careful to keep his voice gentle as he ruffled a hand through her hair.

Fern made a face up at him, stepping away. "I'm not a kid."

He laughed. "You are to me."

She peered up at him, suddenly curious. "How old *are* you, anyway?"

It took him a moment too long to process and realize he didn't know the answer, even as Jade cheerfully supplied it.

"A hundred and thirty-seven."

Fern's nose wrinkled up like an unironed shirt. "That's impossible!"

"Is it?" For a moment it felt dreadfully fitting, like there were endless swathes of memories laid out behind him, so far he couldn't see them anymore.

"How old are you, *honestly*?"

Age was a silly indicator of time, Kaiden thought. The years people lived on this earth were not equal, no matter what anyone tried to say. One person might spend ten years in ten seconds, while to another, it stretched on for ten lifetimes. One person's year could feel like a blissful month of spring, while another remembered only a biting, endless winter. One person's year was peppered with smiles; another's drowned in tears.

"Twenty-three."

It felt odd to say, for whatever reason. Acknowledging just how much time had passed, and what all had changed.

Not all of it was bad, though. Lena didn't seem to want to be rid of him any time soon, despite the exasperated looks she still gave him when he tried to do something nice for her.

Everything was odd, being out in the open. His smiles, his... emotions. Being able to laugh with his friends, but also indulge the silence that sometimes overtook them, and simply let it be, rather than burying it. So much had happened – it was impossible not to just sit back and acknowledge it, sometimes. From a passing comment about Gigi to catching sight of Elle's favorite flower... or even just when one of them used their gifts, sometimes.

But that was alright, he was learning; all things had their place. Perhaps he kept more in when they found a new Gifted to help out, or brought supplies to needy districts and something sparked his memory, but here, with his friends, it was safe.

Fern wrinkled her nose, teasingly. "Okay. You *are* old." For a moment, the honesty showed on her face, too, a little smile that said all the things that words couldn't. Then she tucked it away, eyes twinkling as she clasped her hands behind her back. "I hope you like your present."

He looked down at the scarf she had made him, a lumpy, multicolored thing she had stitched together with little instruction. To keep him warm, she'd said teasingly, though he knew it was just because it was her latest experiment and she needed a test subject. Or, so she had confided in him the *last* time he got something new from her.

"It's perfect," he said, grinning back. Fern's eyes twinkled, like she was aware of the subtle joke to it, before she took off to 'see what Joss was up to'.

For a moment, he felt that twist in his chest again, a sort of uncertainty at everything, as if this all might just be... a joke or something. His last birthday, once he'd stopped to think about it, had fallen right in the midst of everything chaotic. While he was still under the Bane, and not actually himself.

In comparison, this was all just so... sweet that it was slightly overwhelming. It left him feeling full, and then some, where it now spilled over so much he thought it might drown him.

And though it wasn't necessarily a bad thing, he still felt himself relaxing when he found an excuse to slip away, and spend a little time with his best friend where he could actually talk to her, openly. He would have said 'alone', but the kits rarely granted that to him nowadays, even if he wanted to talk with Lena or anything like that. Not that he could truly mind, when they were so attached to him. Joss teased him about the hoard he'd end up collecting by the time he was old. He'd have so many dragons he wouldn't know what to do with them.

As long as he also had her, he'd added, and she'd wrinkled her nose at him, before reluctantly admitting he probably would. Just because he seemed determined not to let her go, of course.

A soft grin on his face, Kaiden rubbed Zvi's head, looking over at Jade.

She grinned back. "So, what do you think – are you a birthday person?"

Rubbing the back of his neck, he smiled. "I don't really know. I haven't really... done anything like this for it before."

"I guess we'll have to do it for a few more and see what you think then." Jade winked, slipping her hand into her pocket.

Kaiden grinned, trying not to let it look all funny. It was all so unfamiliar still, and yet... it was kind of wonderful, too.

"Last time I remember celebrating one, I'm pretty sure Gigi just used it as an excuse for a food fight and then blamed it on me. And then we got lost because she was looking for something and forgot what and got distracted, unsurprisingly." He chuckled. "We ended up way far away from where we were supposed to be. Rafe probably would have scolded her if it would have done any good."

Jade laughed. "I remember that." She shifted to sit on the floor, patting the spot in front of her.

He sat down where she indicated, grinning at the memory. "That was an interesting day."

"Mhm. It was. Birthdays are supposed to be interesting." From her pocket, she pulled out a little object, wrapped in blue paper with white dots on it, and held it out to him.

Kaiden laughed. "Well, she definitely succeeded there, then." He tried not to look surprised, taking the gift and grinning a little as he peeled back the paper, careful not to tear it.

Jade laughed, teasing. "You don't have to save the paper."

"No?" He smiled at her, but folded it open slowly anyway, as if he'd ruin something if he didn't. "But it's so pretty."

Jade laughed again. "Well, you can keep it if you like it."

Would that be weird? He glanced up at her for a moment, then down at the unwrapped object: a small, white-wood box. Inside, pale fabric formed little round holes, a couple with pretty, smooth stones resting in the first few.

"It's to keep all the rocks you're always collecting in," Jade said, grinning a little. "You know, so you have a safe spot to put them and stuff."

He couldn't help a laugh, looking at it. "I do have a little collection of them growing, huh?" He smiled at her, hoping it conveyed everything he wanted it to. "One thing Calest has always had a lot of: rocks."

Jade grinned back, leaning on one palm and looking rather pleased. "Yeah and you seem to like collecting them, so I thought it was fitting."

He nodded. "They usually hold meaning, and..." he chuckled, "for a kid with no money, it's an easy reminder for things."

She grinned a little. "Yeah. And this'll give you a good place to keep them."

Kaiden smiled back, letting it relax into something grateful and fond. "Thanks."

"Sure, Butterfly." She smiled. "Happy birthday."

He set the box aside, pulling her into a hug. Her arms wrapped around him, and he squeezed her lightly, staying there for a moment before pulling back just enough to smile at her.

"I think I like birthdays."

Eyes fond, Jade grinned back. "Yeah?"

He ducked his gaze away for a moment, unsure. "Yeah."

Jade grinned a little. "I'm glad you've liked it. Birthdays are meant to be enjoyed."

"It's a lot nicer than I'm used to," he admitted.

"I know. But this is your new normal." She motioned around them, smiling. "Fun birthday parties and gifts and surrounded by people who love you."

Glancing back where they'd come from, he rubbed the side of his neck, pushing his lips up in a smile. "You're sure I'm not just dreaming...?"

Jade rested her hand on his arm. "I promise. You're not dreaming."
He let out a chuckle, smiling teasingly. "Just checking."

Soft footsteps interrupted them, Lena smiling down when she saw
him. She was dressed prettily in a simple, sparkling dress, which she
claimed she was only wearing 'for the occasion'. He liked how it made
her relax, though, finding a balance between plain and gaudy that
just...fit her.

"There you are. Hiding from everyone already?"
Jade glanced up. "Whoops, we've been discovered."

Kaiden laughed. "Hiding? No. Just needed a moment to myself
without being attacked by dragons who want my cake."

"Mind if I sit with you, then?" Lena smiled, eyes twinkling with a
laugh. "They do love their cake."

"Yeah." He grinned, and then paused, shaking his head. "I mean,
no, I don't mind."

With a laugh, Lena settled next to him, slipping her hand into his.
"There was something else I wanted to give you, earlier, but I thought it
might be better when everyone else wasn't around." Her eyes softened,
as did her smile. Jade leaned back on her palm, watching them with a
grin.

His eyes traveled down, waiting for whatever she might hand him.
Lena tilted his face back up with her hand, eyes warmed by
amusement. Softly, she reached to cup his face, thumbs brushing
lightly against his cheeks. He smiled back, doing his best not to look
sheepish. She hadn't actually said it was a physical gift.

When she leaned in, he only had a fleeting moment of thought
before his brain shorted out. Lena's lips met his, soft and gentle, and
surprise coursed through him at it all. Near them, Jade nearly fell, her
hand slipping from underneath her.

"Whoa, hey, give a girl some warning before getting all mushy!"
Kaiden choked on the laugh that erupted deep inside him, his
shoulders shaking with it as Jade threw up her arms to hide from them.
Before he could ruin everything further, he pulled away, pressing his
knuckles to his lips and giving them both what he hoped was an
apologetic look.

Laughing in surprise, Lena eyed him. "Well. That wasn't quite the
reaction I expected."

In comparison, Jade groaned. "Scarred for *life*."

"Jade." He coughed the name into his hand, trying to disguise it as
he looked back up at Lena, taking in a slow breath. "Something... got
stuck in my throat."

Lena eyed him, smiling teasingly. "If it makes you nervous, you can just let me know."

"Well!" Jade exclaimed. "It's not my fault. Goodness, warn a girl." She scooted away from them. "Fine, I'm not looking now. You can kiss her properly."

"I didn't know either!" he wanted to say, casting a glance at Jade briefly, then rubbed his neck as he smiled at Lena. "It doesn't."

Lena laughed, raising an eyebrow at him teasingly. "Okay." She waited a moment, watching him, then lifted her hand to cup his cheek again, carefully, like she might set him off again.

Jade facepalmed into her hands. "Well, have you kissed her yet? I can't stay like this forever."

He hesitated, watching Lena's eyes. She seemed to be waiting for something now, so he reached up to mimic her and cup her face with both hands. Slowly, he leaned in toward her, until his lips brushed hers.

Lena was much better than he was. But he tried to make up for ruining her last gift, sliding his fingers into her hair and locking his lips with hers for a long moment, hoping he was doing it right. He felt like he was melting, his entire body relaxing with hers at the rightness of it all and the fire it sent rushing through him, somehow so different from the one he'd grown up carrying everywhere. When he pulled away this time, to see her eyes, he was nearly breathless, though whether that was from the kiss or the lights in her eyes, he didn't think he'd ever know.

"Better?" he asked, feeling a smile spread up his cheeks. She returned the expression, a soft chuckle leaving her lips.

"Than choking up in the middle of it? Yes."

He had to look away, pulling in a small breath. "Oh, good. Although, I suppose that isn't a very high standard to beat..."

Lena followed his gaze, laughing. "Well, you *did* get something in your throat. So." She didn't quite sound like she believed his excuse, as she shifted closer to him. "There's just one problem with it."

Jade peeked over at them. "Is it over? Thank goodness. I don't care if you two want to get all cute and mushy, but I'd rather not be the third wheel while you do. Ew, mushy."

Kaiden couldn't help smiling, both at Jade and from...everything. "What?"

Lena took his face in her hands again, eyes warm as they held his for a moment. Her mouth brushed against his again, the surprise jumping through him quickly burned away by the flickering heat it left in him. She pulled away after a moment, smiling up at him.

"I was supposed to be the one giving *you* a gift." Her fingers lifted to brush at his hair, gently. "Happy birthday, Beanhead."

Jade was flopped on her back to hide from them, an arm draped over her eyes. Even though she couldn't see it, Kaiden cast an apologetic glance her way. "Thanks."

Once again, Lena followed his gaze, her eyes twinkling knowingly. "So, can I actually meet this 'imaginary' friend of yours?"

Now that the danger was over, Jade stood up and dusted herself off, eyeing Kaiden. Reaching over, she poked his shoulder with her fist. "I'm ecstatic you have an awesome girlfriend and you two are all cute and attached now, but let's keep the mushy between you two, m'kay? I do not need to be involved in your cute intimate moments." Her nose wrinkled up. "I want warnings so I can get out of here and not be all stalkerish."

Hesitating, Kaiden glanced at Lena. "One moment." Then he turned back to Jade, doing his best to hide his rising embarrassment. Rubbing the back of his neck, he gave her a sheepish grin. "It wasn't *my* fault!"

Lena's eyes filled with amusement as she watched him, teasingly. "If she didn't want to see, she shouldn't have been here."

Folding her arms, Jade stuck her tongue out in Lena's direction. Despite her pout, her eyes sparkled. "Well it's not like either of you warned me. I was just minding my own business, hanging out and *boom*. Kissing."

Kaiden huffed. "As I said. Not my fault." He tilted his head mock-haughtily, looking over at Lena. The look melted to something apologetic again, in case she though he was accusing *her*. "She's not very fond of kissing."

Lena laughed, propping a hand on her hip. "Well. If you'd told me that before, I could have warned her."

Jade huffed. "It's not so much that I'm not fond of kissing. It's more that it's incredibly awkward being thrown into the middle of an intimate moment unawares. I'm all over here like 'Yo, peeps, I'm just gonna chill in the shadows over here and watch y'all get cute and mushy. Don't mind me.' It's creepy. And do I look like I enjoy being creepy? No, no I do not. I'm perfectly un-creepy." Dramatically, she huffed out another breath. "I'm chill with y'all being cute. I'm just not chill with being here *during* the cute."

Kaiden laughed. "Okay, I've been corrected. She doesn't mind kissing, she just doesn't want to *be* here during it."

"Which, again," Lena replied, "could have been prevented if I'd been told this. How was I to know any of this incredibly important information?"

Jade huffed. "Well, so long as this isn't repeated."

"Okay, okay." Kaiden hunched his shoulders, shielding his face with his arms. "We've been...busy, and I didn't think..." He bent over to hide from them both, making his voice sad. "I'll fix it. Just don't be mad."

Jade laughed. "When have I ever been mad at you?" She nudged his chin, then sighed. "Right. Meeting the girlfriend. You'd better warn her though. This'll feel weird when I let her in."

"I feel ganged up on," Kaiden mumbled, covering his eyes with his hands. He peeked out between them at Lena. "I've been told to warn you that this'll feel weird. If that's alright."

Chuckling, she raised an eyebrow at him. "Alright."

"Nothing like being put on the spot," Jade said teasingly, moving in front of Lena. He wondered what she would think, given Jade's unordinary appearance. Bright green eyes, wild hair, and arms filled with swirly scars he'd never seen anything like before, even with being way more familiar with scars than he had any right to be. He watched as Lena waited, intrigued, and then choked back a laugh once her eyes focused on Jade.

"Oh, I see why you thought she was imaginary."

Jade pouted. "Hey, what's that supposed to mean?"

It took him a moment to get it, a little grin crossing his face as he nodded. Jade didn't exactly look 'normal'.

Innocently, Lena smiled. "Nothing. Nothing at all."

Jade folded her arms, huffing. "I'm not really from around here. It would be weirder it I *did* look normal. Right, Butterfly?"

He rubbed the back of his neck, grinning a little. "I don't know. Are you saying everyone where you're from is that weird?"

A sigh. "No, I guess not. I'm considered pretty weird there too."

Lena gave him an odd look, mouthing the word 'Butterfly'.

"Aha. See? So your excuse doesn't work." He grinned.

"I guess not." Jade sighed, then stuck her hand out to Lena. "Nice to meet you officially. I'm Jade."

Lena shook it in her usual proper manner. "Nice to meet you too. I suppose you already know my name." Chuckling, she glanced between the two of them. "Should I be concerned that you're calling him Butterfly?"

Jade tossed her head back in a laugh, bright and loud. "Why would that be concerning?" She affected an innocent expression.

"I don't know. 'Butterfly' isn't really a usual thing to call people."

Jade laughed again. "We met when we were little kids, and I started calling him that way back then and never really stopped. At eight, I wasn't aware of what was or wasn't normal to call people, I guess."

Lena chuckled, glancing between the two of them teasingly. "Ah, well that explains it. What does he call you then, 'Birdie'?"

"Please don't get us started on that conversation." Jade screwed up her face, looking disgruntled. "His nickname for me is total nonsense and better left undiscussed."

Kaiden looked away, holding down a laugh. "Mmhm. Totally."

Lena raised an eyebrow. "Oh?"

"I've been begging him to change it for years, but will he? No, no he won't." A slow, mischievous grin spread over her face. "Heyyy, you're his girlfriend. Maybe you can convince him to change it. Girlfriends have lots of pull." She rocked back on her heels, looking pleased.

Kaiden made his voice sing-song. "Because it *fits* you, and you *know* it."

Lena propped a hand on her hip. "I think I need to know what it is first to know why I should change it, hm?" A brief smile crossed her face at the second part, though she quickly dismissed it.

"So if we tell you and you think it's ridiculous too, you'll change it for me?" Jade grinned over at Kaiden triumphantly. "I think I should have encouraged your romantic life sooner."

Lena folded her arms, looking mock-stern, but amused. "I'll think about it."

Kaiden made a face back at Jade. "You're trying to gang up on me."

Jade laughed loudly again, eyes sparkly. "Too bad you can't take back the introduction." She rocked on her heels, imitating his sing-song tone.

Lena eyed them both. "I'm curious why you don't want to tell me. Is it really that embarrassing?"

Kaiden let out a huff. "I never said I wanted to." He eyed Jade. "Better than her thinking I like to talk to rocks."

"Not 'embarrassing'. Just very unfitting. I'm still trying to figure out how he came up with it, other than trying to think of the most opposite thing possible." She shifted to sit on the ground, cross-legged.

Lena let out a fake sigh, raising an eyebrow at him. "So... 'tame'?"

Kaiden shook his head. "It doesn't *need* to be changed."

"Hey now." Jade eyed Lena teasingly. "Are you saying I look wild?"

"Possibly." Grinning, Lena nodded to her hair. "Or at least that is."

"That I can't argue." She reached up to try to flatten it, getting her hands tangled by accident. "I'm pretty sure it terrifies little children."

Lena laughed. "Oh, I bet."

526

Jade tried to untangle her hands, laughing, too. "Yeah, I'm used to the screams of terror as I pass."

"I'm sure it's not that bad." She paused, looking at Jade's hair. "Do you need help?"

Something passed through Jade's eyes, though she brushed it off with a grin. "Nah. Pretty sure there has been lots of terrified screaming. And thanks, but I'm used to this. It'll release me after it realizes I'm not tasty."

Lena chuckled, glancing over at Kaiden. "I still want to know what this top-secret nickname is."

"It's not top-secret." Jade cupped her chin in her hand, which was still partially tangled in her hair, and grinned at Kaiden.

"Says you," he huffed.

Lena watched them both, amused. "So this is where you get your weirdness from." Her eyes twinkled. "Or at the very least, amplified."

Jade laughed. "Ah, yeah. I'm probably ninety nine percent responsible for his strangeness. Not even going to deny it." She bumped her shoulder into Kaiden's, teasing.

Kaiden returned the gesture. "Excuse you. I'm perfectly capable of being weird on my own."

"Says you. But how would you know? I've always been around to influence your weirdness."

He wrinkled his nose at her, reaching over to lace his fingers with Lena's. "Because."

Jade eyed their hands, cocking her eyebrows. "Is that the beginning of the mushy? Because if it is, you're never going to get to know my horrible nickname."

Lena ran her hand lightly over his arm. "Is that a threat? I'm sure I'll find out, one way or another."

"Not so much a threat as an 'I am leaving as soon as this gets cute'. I don't do the whole third wheel thing, as thrilled as I am that Kaiden is happily attached."

Lena laughed. "I see. Well, I think I'm going to have to be more persuasive to get him to talk, so." She winked, eyes teasing, and leaned over to kiss the side of Kaiden's head.

"Quite literally attached," Kaiden added, grinning a little and pretending to look surprised.

"Ew. Yeah, there's that mushy, sappy stuff I was talking about." Jade wrinkled her nose at them.

Lena laughed again. "Well. Someone doesn't want to talk to me, so." She looked over at Kaiden, amused.

Jade grinned at him, flopping on her back on the ground. "He can clam up when he wants to."

"I'm right here, you know." Mumbling, he dropped his head on his arms.

Jade chuckled. "Well, I would hope you hadn't suddenly become the invisible one."

He leaned his head against Lena. "You couldn't make fun of me, then."

Jade grinned, shaking her head. "Crazy Butterfly."

"I can't deny it." He glanced at Lena briefly, then added, "Beautiful."

Jade let out a long, loud sigh.

"Again. We were little." He grinned a little at Jade.

"And it doesn't fit." She huffed at him.

Lena smiled. "He probably did it to be sweet."

Jade wrinkled her nose. "Don't remind me. He's too sweet for his own good."

Kaiden dropped his head against Lena's shoulder, shaking his head.

"Mmhm." Lena watched him, smiling. "He is."

Not bothering to pick the grass out of her hair, Jade sat up, eyeing them. "In that case, I should be going."

Kaiden pouted at her. "And why is that?"

"So you and your cute girlfriend can be mushy without me interrupting. Plus, I probably should actually go home and make sure nothing has imploded or anything." She cocked a grin, though it was slightly different for a moment as she brushed hair from her face. "I'll see ya tomorrow."

Sighing, Kaiden shifted to his feet. "Okay."

Jade smiled over at Lena. "It was nice meeting you. But I'm going to steal your boyfriend for a minute before I go if that's fine." She tossed her a wink.

Lena chuckled, eyes teasing. "Of course."

"He'll be back in a sec." Jade grinned, taking Kaiden's wrist to tug him away. When they were out of sight, she stopped, turning to grin at him. "You look happy."

Happy. It seemed a funny word, considering...everything. "I think so."

Jade nudged his chin. "It's nice. I'm glad she makes you happy. I'll have an ally in keeping an eye on you."

He made a face at her. "Because I'm so much trouble. I know."

Jade laughed. "No, not because of that."

When he raised a questioning eyebrow, she shrugged. "Because you're sweet and you need people in your life to make sure you're happy and not alone."

His hand caught the back of his neck, rubbing it as he thought about that. "Oh. I didn't... That's not what I was thinking..."

Jade smiled. "I know. But that's what I meant."

He took in a breath, quiet. "Ah."

Jade studied him for a moment. "You know I'll always be here when you need me, right?" She smiled at him. "I'll still be here. I'm not going anywhere. But you have her now, and she'll be able to help you, too, maybe even in ways I can't. I've heard that's a nice part of having a partner. And I'm glad for that, because it means you'll always have one of us around."

He rubbed the back of his neck again, breathing in quietly. Jade reached over to squeeze his arm, continuing.

"And while she is with you, I might not be around quite as much." She cocked a grin. "I mean, like, still enough to annoy you to death and probably groan about you two and being totally mushy constantly." She tossed him a wink. "But there's some stuff I have to take care of at home, now that things are better here." She rubbed her hand over the scars on her arm, a little quieter. "I'll be here a lot. Whenever you need, and just for fun, too, now that things are calmer. But there are things there that I can't put off anymore." She smiled a little, shrugging. "Okay?"

He nodded, quiet. The words weren't quite sinking in, everything too...unfamiliar at the moment. Like she was talking about someone else, far from here.

Jade laced her fingers with his. "I don't want to press if you don't want to talk about it. But with this... I need to know it's okay. *Really* okay, not saying so because you're being sweet like you always are." She grinned a little. "I need to know you're okay – that we're okay."

He managed a little nod, holding up a finger for her to give him a minute. Everything was spinning a little too fast, pieces clicking into place that he didn't know what to do with.

He'd...found his siblings. Lena wasn't mad at him. The thoughts were at once relieving and confusing. Like waking up from a nightmare and still being caught in the haze of it, understanding it's over but still feeling... trapped.

"It's just... a lot," he whispered, trying and failing to manage a smile. Jade shifted her arms around him, resting her head on his shoulder.

"I know. And I'm not leaving. I promise. Cross my heart and all that. I'll be here, whenever you need, as often as you do, plus some. Often enough you'll be wanting to kick me out so you and Lena can have some alone time." She gave him a little squeeze. "I'm not going anywhere. I'm just taking care of some things, in between annoying you and being your crazy imaginary friend."

He nodded, swallowing down the feeling trying to choke his throat. There wasn't anything wrong with this. No reason he shouldn't be smiling and encouraging her not to worry about him and take care of what she needed to.

It was just... so much. So different, all at once. He didn't realize how little he understood it until they started putting it into words. Until it clicked that this was actually happening, and not... a dream. Not wishful thinking or some wild fancy that he'd never actually attain. It was here, right in front of him, and he didn't know how to grasp it.

Jade turned her head to see him better. "You don't have to hide things with me, Kaiden. I won't be upset if something is bothering you. You don't have to hold things back."

He rubbed a hand over his eyes, taking in a sharp breath. "I know." Even the words felt choked out of him, as he tried to smile again. "It's not bothering me."

"It is, though, isn't it?" Her tone was too gentle. Too... understanding.

He didn't even understand himself. How did they make it look so easy? How did they look at him and not see... everything wrong with him?

It didn't make sense. It never did. He swallowed quietly, looking away.

"You really are ganging up on me," he murmured after a moment, trying to smile a little. Hoping she'd understand what he meant.

She nudged his chin lightly, to meet his eyes. Her tone was still far, far too soft. Like he was worth trying to understand, or be gentle with. "I'd never gang up against you, Butterfly. Not for real. I'm always on your side. Always."

A quiet laugh broke from his throat, the smile sticking. "Mm. Except in this, you'll always be against me."

"If you mean against you by wanting to know what's bothering you and how to help, then yeah. I can't deny that." She cocked a lopsided smile at him. "But that doesn't mean I'm against you. I'm still fighting for you, in ways you refuse to fight for yourself. That's what best friends do."

He rubbed an arm over his eyes, pulling in a quiet breath. "I think it was easier... when everyone wanted to yell at me."

"'Everyone' meaning anyone else who wasn't my fabulous self, since obviously I'm way too nice to yell." Jade rested her head on his shoulder, the words teasing. "Is there a reason it was easier?"

He held back a little laugh. Wasn't it obvious, or was that only to him?

"I'm...used to it."

Jade nodded. "I guess things are usually easier when they're predictable. But that doesn't necessarily mean they're the best. 'The easiest road isn't the best road.' That's one of my rules. Or I guess, not so much rules as reminders for myself." She dropped her forehead back onto his shoulder with a laugh. "I'm rambling again. Oops."

"I like your rules," he replied quietly, managing a little smile despite how much it hurt. It all hurt, just a little too much. Too strong of a contrast to what he'd gotten used to.

After a moment, Jade returned to her question. "Why would you rather we were all yelling at you now, specifically?"

Because... "Because, it's easier..." he mumbled under her breath, "to...accept. Or...believe. Agree with." He closed his eyes, swallowing. It was closer to the truth, in his mind, even if he knew it wasn't...true.

Jade nodded a little. "I know. And I'm sorry it's easier," she said quietly. "Yelling never should have been easier for you." Reaching down, she squeezed his hand again. "But we do mean it. All of this."

And that was the problem. He *did* know. He just didn't... understand it. It didn't make any sense, and he couldn't even pinpoint why. He didn't deserve it. He didn't...earn it.

He swallowed, looking at her quietly. It was easier...when there was a reason. When it was the result of something, rather than just...given. He didn't know what to do with that. He hadn't even thought about it, before. He was making up for things. They were just...much better than him. Doing things just because they wanted to. Just...because they cared, even if they shouldn't.

He pressed his free hand into his face, drawing in a shaky breath. "I...I don't know," he looked down, ashamed, "how to say it." Quietly, he let his hand fall. "Having...having someone..." He swallowed, hard.

"It's okay, Kaiden." Her fingers curled tighter around his. "Take your time. It doesn't have to come fast or all at once."

It hurt, trying to say, because it was so unfamiliar to him, and that didn't seem right. He always justified it, instinctively. They wanted to keep on good terms because they were teammates. Lena helped

531

because she wanted help in return. He wanted someone to protect. They needed something from him. Wasn't that how it worked?

And yet...by that logic, they should have just left him already. Maybe Lena was still getting over some things, and figuring herself out, but she didn't have to be so...gentle. She didn't have anything to make up for. She didn't have any reason to...care.

But she did. And that's what tripped him up, choking the rest of the words so they stayed in his throat, wanting to come out but hesitating, again and again.

"Someone...who cares," he finished quietly, even though it wasn't the full story. Jade nodded, smiling at him.

"It's hard to get your head around?"

He gave her a faint smile in return, choking back a laugh. Hard felt like way too much of an understatement. Impossible might have fit better.

"And the differentness of it is bothering you because it's hard to adjust to it?" She squeezed his hand again, gently.

"I guess so." He took in a painful breath, looking away. *Especially when it's...*

It just didn't make sense. He didn't think it ever would. Why they *would* care, without any reason to. Why anyone would want the messy, scarred, broken-and-pieced-back-together self he carried, or try to make it better. Why they didn't just give up.

"I don't understand it," he eventually said, quiet. "I didn't earn it."

Jade smiled a little, reaching up to cup his cheek for a moment. "Real love isn't earned. It's given freely, unconditionally, by both sides. You're just not used to the real thing yet. It'll come with time."

He looked away, hiding his shame at not understanding something so...simple. "I know. Didn't...think about...the other side of it, I guess."

"I know. You're too used to giving unconditionally, but getting nothing in return." Jade cocked a lopsided smile, eyes shifting a little sad when he looked away. "And that's okay. That wasn't your fault. You're so used to giving constantly. But it's time now, for you to be given back all the love you gave away." She squeezed his arm. "I think Lena wants that for you, too. Lena, and Joss, and all the others. It's your turn, Butterfly, and it might feel scary and overwhelming, but that's okay too."

He tried to smile back faintly, though it still hurt, squeezing her hand a little. "I think so," he said, quiet.

"I told you it would all work out okay." Jade nudged him a little. "And I'm always right, aren't I?"

He let out a little laugh, despite how it made his eyes burn, nodding a little. "Yeah, you did."

Jade shifted to hug him tightly, dropping his hand. He wrapped his arms tightly around her, squeezing.

Jade tucked her face into his shoulder, mumbling after a moment. "There are days I wish I could just stay here forever. Which is all your fault, for being the best friend ever."

Kaiden drew in a quiet breath. "Well, you're welcome whenever, still."

She chuckled. "You should know by now that I'll never stop." Letting out a quiet breath, she mumbled into his shoulder, "Thanks."

"I would hope not. What was it you said, I'd be an old man and you'd still be 'annoying' me?" He squeezed her lightly. "Think I should be the one thanking you."

"Mm-hmm. You'll be half-blind and half-deaf and I'll be yelling random annoying stuff in your ear. It's fated." She grinned, then shrugged. "Nah. I don't need any thanks."

A laugh broke from his throat. "Perfect." He copied her gesture, smiling. "Well, I don't either."

She smiled against his shoulder. "Don't steal my lines."

"Why not?"

"Because I say so. And because I probably shouldn't rub off any more on you than I already have."

"I think it's good if you rub off on me."

"Nah. No world needs another one of me. One is more than enough for any universe."

He chuckled. "Well, I could never be as wonderful as you, obviously, so there's no concern about that."

Jade sighed. "'Wonderful', he says."

"Well, I didn't say awesome, at least. I know better. Or, remember better."

"At least wonderful is better than awesome, yeah. But even still."

"Even still, it's true. I know." He did his best to hide a smile.

"No, it's not. How about 'strange'. I can do strange. Or 'weird'. I get that one a lot. Or even 'crazy'. I can get behind crazy."

His smile widened. "How about stupendous?"

"No. Because 'stupendous' means nice things."

"Exactly."

She stuck her tongue out at him. "Yes, that's 'exactly' why it doesn't work."

"You mean *why* it works."

"No, no I don't."

533

He pulled her a little closer, leaning his head on her shoulder. Jade let out a sigh. "Crazy, sweet Butterfly. What am I to do with you, hm?"

"Keep me, hopefully," he said quietly.

"Always." Jade closed her eyes, her voice softer. "We've been together too long, you and I. I wouldn't let you go now."

Squeezing her lightly, he nodded.

Jade took a breath and pulled away, grinning slightly at him. "Lena might come looking if you don't come back soon. You should go find her."

He smiled back, nodding. "Okay."

"Wish me luck?"

"Luck?"

She grinned, tucking her hands in her pockets. "Yeah, with my home stuff."

He reached over to squeeze her arm lightly, chuckling. "Ah, of course. Good luck."

She looked down at his hand, her smile softening. "I'll see you later then, Butterfly."

He let his soften, too. "See you later, Beautiful."

Her eyes sparkled with fondness as she held his eyes for a moment. And then, she vanished.

And though he knew she couldn't see it, he stood for a moment and waved at the empty air, a little smile on his face.

SARI

Sari had thought she'd known what it would feel like to be without Ru'ach.

She'd *known*, when Ru'ach pulled away, just what she'd intended. She'd felt the panic, the severing of the tie, the hope that it wasn't the end, and then...nothing.

The look her purple dragon had given her had sent Sari's insides spinning in a most unpleasant way. She knew that smile, and the gentleness meant to both soothe and reassure her. When they had sat in that hold, so long ago, joined together, and the dragon's warmth comforted her as much as the words whispering through her mind, that they *would* get through this, and she had nothing to fear.

Sari hated how effective it had been, in that moment. She'd *known* what her friend was about to do, and she was too calmed to even fight against it. She could only watch, dumbfounded as before, as Ru'ach rose up and used her power in the same way she had torn that ship to pieces so long ago, leaving the condemned to float stranded in the sea, and had carried Sari to safety.

Except this time, there was no land, and Ru'ach was not coming with her. It was a terrifying thought, watching her friend slip beneath the waves and not return, still within reach but not ever present, as she had been. Without that constant reassurance, she had to rely on what she knew, from Ru'ach's presence.

But this was what her friend had wanted. And Sari couldn't help a breath of awe when she walked amidst Calest and heard the stories, saw the *colors* blooming as the people caught on, united in the simple goal to restore their lands. Their awe as mysterious beings returned, stories of sprites amongst gardens and shadows in the sky that didn't look quite dragon-like enough to be familiar.

Now that the curse was gone, and Gifted were not hunted down, more than just the dragons would return, she knew. Many other beings had gone into hiding because of Shedim that most of the people would not have even known of.

Even the river was restored. The symbolism of it filled her with hope, as both countries, Calest still damaged by attacks they couldn't restore themselves from, sought to rebuild and reshape their world.

The balance of power had shifted, back to its intended place. Now that food was not near-impossible to grow in Calest, the Galdanians couldn't hold that over their heads any longer. Better yet, their land had been returned to a natural, unenhanced state, where growing things became more complicated than simply dropping seed in the ground and waiting. Even those who farmed in Galdania had never dealt with any of these normal farming troubles. They needed help, and what better place to get it than from people who had spent their entire lives fighting to get anything to grow?

It was still terrifying being without Ru'ach, some days. It felt like missing a part of her, and even now, Sari wasn't quite sure what to do to make up for it. She admired Kaiden all that much more, watching him face his demons with only the barest flinch and an unsteady breath, before a smile came creeping back in to shine a light on it. That, Sari mused, was also her friend's doing. The things Ru'ach could do now, freed from her physical form, were wondrous. She'd had the power, before, but now...not just Sari could feel it.

She had to rely upon her friends more, as well, for the reassurance she had usually sought. Ru'ach's presence felt stronger when she was in the midst of them, the warmth from it soothing some of her buzzing fears. They didn't consider it all that odd that she was so...different from most humans; even Kaiden brushed it aside with a joke that he'd 'seen stranger things.'

Sari was just as broken as they were, but she had help. And now, after so long in her friend's constant presence, Sari felt the tears in her soul beginning to mend. She felt the gentle nudge, at times, for her to join them, and set aside her previous solitude.

Had it just been a dream? It felt like it, some days. Was she only waking now, after so long trapped in a place she couldn't pull herself from, only to see the world around her changed? What was she to do, now?

The answer, of course, came as clear as if Ru'ach were sitting right beside her, and smiling all the while. *"Carry on with our work, of course."*

It was terrifying, going on without a part of her soul, but it was also freeing, being able to become herself again.

"Thank you."

And though she did receive odd looks from time to time, over her less-than-perfect calm that caught them off guard, they quickly laughed it off, and she was still invited in with open arms. Though she was so much older than them, she felt a kinship that went beyond words, deep into their souls. She knew, somewhere, that Ru'ach was connecting all of them.

Lena still had trouble like she did, at times. Sari watched her struggle for control, again and again, breaking down only once the rope she held onto had slipped entirely from her grasp. But she got back up again, every time, and eventually, she learned to let go on her own. She clung to Kaiden more than seemed necessary, but he was good for her, now. Despite the games he still played with himself at times, and with everyone else, he was more alright than he had been in a long time, and that gave Sari an inexplicable sense of peace. He might recall his past more than necessary, but it would not crush him like before.

Basil was the symbolic 'light' of the group, lifting them up when they needed it and always ready to suggest a new way or that they stop and relax. Chan kept a close eye on all of them, as usual, always the first to come check in if it had been a while.

The friendships that had been forged in the fire of their trials was stronger than any metal Sari had ever seen. They worked as a team, not because they were forced to any longer, but because they wanted to. After all the separation they'd endured, it was no wonder they wanted to stay close. Chan sought to educate the people from Galdania's vast store of knowledge, and watched over Katya however he could. Olive and Basil traveled the most, together, seeking out Gifted not only in

Calest, but Galdania and its protectorates as well, helping hone and awaken Gifts when they could. Lena worked with her brother to restore relations between the districts, and those with and without gifts, Kaiden helping them when he could.

They could stand on their own, now. They didn't need Sari, and, truth be told, she wasn't quite sure what she would do if she stayed. She had traveled around, checking on the other protectorates and helping them adjust to everything. There were many changes she doubted any of them expected, like the creatures that were slowly coming out of hiding now that Gifts were allowed freely, who thrived on the same energy that fueled Gifts. Creatures of legend, and children's stories, ones long forgotten by most everyone.

She debated staying with them, and did so for a time, at their urging, though she remained looser in her contact, resolving to ensure they were alright before continuing on. Raoul needed help adjusting to running a country, not yet realizing his lack of desire for power was actually a very promising sign. She used her knowledge where theirs was wanting, answering questions and helping them discover what to do with their lands back to normal.

But now, as things settled down and she was no longer needed, she felt herself being pulled elsewhere, a way she had felt a subtle tug toward for quite a while, but had dismissed in favor of saving the world. Back to a place she hadn't visited in a long time. They all had their roles, and filled them perfectly. They would do wonderful things for the world.

And as for her?

It was time to go home.

ACKNOWLEDGEMENTS

Contrary to what many would assume, writing a book is not a solo act, and I never could have finished this without the help of many amazing people.

To Miranda Marie, my official editor and word-conquering buddy, who cameoed her character, Jade, so Kaiden could have his best friend with him throughout the books.

To my wonderful book dragons, who are always encouraging and entertaining in their feedback of the book. Their petition to throw a certain character off a cliff actually became my inspiration for his eventual death. @fawnberrys_books, @ly_brary, @womanon, @ernest.bookingway, @gcreads04, @booksontheknightbus, Berlyn Mcgriff-Ramirez, Chelsea Girard, and Remi: You guys are superstars. Thank you all so much!

To Emma Tennant, my favorite grumpy raincloud, for letting me ramble on about this book in the least spoiler-filled way possible and bouncing ideas back and forth when I hit an inevitable snag.

To my beta-readers and everyone else who has offered feedback on the book, from excited fangirling reactions to suggestions about pacing and other such things. Your comments never fail to make me laugh or smile.

And to everyone who has stuck with me through this wild story from start to finish. I hope you've enjoyed the ride (and are ready to see where these crazy adventures will take us next!)

Once again, thank you all from the bottom of my heart. It means the world to me that I get to share my stories with you, and I hope you've enjoyed the journey as much as I have.

-Melody

EXTRAS

Songs listened to while planning/writing this series, and ones that fit certain characters too well not to mention.

(Kaiden and Lena)

Birds of a Feather – The Civil Wars

All Of Me – Matt Hammitt

All You Ever – Hunter Hayes

Dust to Dust – The Civil Wars

Hate Me – Eurielle

Please Don't Say You Love Me – Gabrielle Aplin

Little Do You Know – Alex and Sierra

Broken Together – Casting Crowns

Beneath Your Beautiful – Madilyn Bailey

I Feel Like That – Jason Walker

Poison and Wine – The Civil Wars

Fix You - Coldplay

(Lena) Human – Christina Perri

Gone – Beth Crowley

(Kaiden) What If I Told You – Jason Walker

I Am Not Nothing – Beth Crowley

Let It Burn – Red

(Series)

We Fall Apart – We As Human

Letting You In – Kris Allen

Inside Out – Madilyn Bailey

Daughtry – Home

Stand By You – Rachel Platten

True Colors – Anna Kendrick

Oh My Dear – Tenth Avenue North

In Time – Kris Allen

CHARACTER LIST

(In alphabetical order. To prevent spoilers, the description of each character relates to their status before the beginning of this book, rather than after.)

Humans

φ   Ashalee Shale (deceased) – Dailen's adopted sister who loves dragons and drawing. Died years ago during a dragon attack.

φ   Basil Greenleaf – Empathetic and gentle, has a secret love for flowers and the open sky. Gifted in manipulating light.

φ   Caleb Montellene – Lena's brother and leader of a rebellion within the Cities. Loves the ocean and his sister more than anything.

φ   Chanis Tiel – Peacekeeper, book lover, and all-around nerd excited by research, logic games, and anything blue. Gifted in storms.

φ   Charise Friedel – Lena's stepsister, a sarcastic and withdrawn girl afraid to rock the boat too much.

φ   Cloren Tyce – One of the overseers of the Cities, and Talon's father.

φ   Cloris Friedel – Lena's stepfather, a manipulative man loyal to the Empress.

φ   Dailen Shale – A timid but sweet boy who doesn't know how to make anything but soup. Gifted in controlling smoke.

φ   Fern Cabeswater – Loves everything artsy and messy. Bright and enthusiastic about just about anything she sees, and gifted in growing things.

φ   Gissina "Gigi" Gilford (deceased) – A bouncy, loud-voiced girl who was a member of Kaiden's team, and one of his first friends.

φ   Hanen Ramerien – A pompous man who betrayed the rebels to the Empress.

φ   Jade – Kaiden's not-so-imaginary best friend who loves hot foods and traveling.

φ   Jocelyn Rees – A mischievous girl from the Isles with a fondness for grumpy animals. Gifted in stealing things.

φ   Kaiden Dyran/Blaze Montego – Loves jokes, music, and making others smile. Gifted in fire and hiding how broken he really is.

φ   Karah Dyran (deceased) – Kaiden's mother, a kindhearted woman who died from an undiagnosable illness.

ϕ   Katana Dyran – Motherly, fun-loving, and secretly worried for her siblings a lot.

ϕ   Katya Tyce – Secretly loves kit dragons and soft things like pillows and hand-holding. Has the misfortune of being related to Talon.

ϕ   Kaylissa Dyran – The youngest Dyran sibling, slow to open up, but near impossible to calm down once she gets excited.

ϕ   Kinelly "Kinny" Dyran/Elle Rydell (deceased) – Warm and compassionate, always putting others' needs above her own. Gifted in healing remedies.

ϕ   Kellen Dyran – Shy, soft-spoken, and very passionate about building things.

ϕ   Kelrin Dyran – Took over caring for his siblings after Kaiden's capture. Despite appearances, he really enjoys talking to other people.

ϕ   Kendel Dyran (deceased) – Kaiden's father, though only by blood.

ϕ   Kyla Dyran – The quieter of Kaiden's twin sisters, who loves baking and creative things.

ϕ   Kyra Dyran – The wilder of the twins, most likely to get scolded for her adventurous shenanigans.

ϕ   Lilianne "Lil" Retters (deceased) – Was one of the members of Kaiden's first team. The mom friend of the group.

ϕ   Markus Alejandre Montellene (deceased) – Lena's father and the former General of the rebels in Calest.

ϕ   Samar Revez (deceased) – Was a member of Kaiden's first team and basically an honorary younger brother of the entire group.

ϕ   Sharalene Montellene (Lena) – A distrusting, snarky girl who loves cats and dresses, hates lies, and cares for others too much. Gifted in mind manipulation.

ϕ   Shalura Friedel – Cares more about her money and title than her own flesh and blood. Lena's mother.

ϕ   Taisha Fields (deceased) Was a member of Kaiden's first team with a rather fiery temper.

ϕ   Raoul Jinel – The leader of the Galdanian rebels. Cares deeply about his people and wishes he could make things better for them all.

ϕ   Rafe Tomassi – Was a member of Kaiden's first team. The level-headed one, even while dealing with his own struggles.

ϕ   Ru'ach – An ancient being with mysterious powers, and older sister to Shedim.

ɸ   Shedim – Also known as the Bane. An ancient being trapped in a child's body, and younger brother to Ru'ach.

ɸ   Sylen Tiel (deceased) – Loves mud puddles and teasing her younger brother. Chan's older sister.

ɸ   Saria e'Denan – A mysterious older woman who bonded with Ru'ach after being saved by her.

ɸ   Damien Cheaux (deceased) – A power-hungry man who shouldn't have been allowed to supervise children.

ɸ   Talon Isreld – Gifted in mental manipulation, and unwaveringly loyal to the Empress. There is a roll of tape somewhere with his name on it expressly for tying him up and tossing him off a cliff for what he's done, courtesy of readers.

ɸ   Olive Greenleaf – Is loyal to a fault, hates form-fitting clothing, and is always up for sparring. Gifted with manipulating plants.

ɸ   Verene Vi'dalla – The Empress of Galdania. Hates mismatched curtains and has a penchant for publicly torturing those who don't support her.

Dragons

א   Chaertierena (Rena) – A wild brown kit dragon with a rebellious streak and excellent sense of direction. Bonded to Chan.

א   Denizor – A fearful white wyvern-kit dragon hybrid given to Lena after Dailen rescued him.

א   D'sidiekenethylyl (D'sidi) A hyper orange dragon with a love for anything shiny or pink.

א   Felisyiedee (Feli) – A fiery red dragon with a fierce temper and a heart of gold. Will fight anyone who threatens her fellow kits or her humans.

א   Giltientitl (Nitl) – A stout brown kit dragon with an endless appetite for any kind of food. Bonded to Fern.

א   Indigo – A reclusive blue dragon, and Olive's companion.

א   Lyss – A gentle purple female, and Chan's companion.

א   Nyxetyen (Nyx) – A curious blue-white kit dragon who likes sleeping on people.

א   Paritzerarteiesa (Pari) – A vocal, silver kit dragon who prizes cleanliness and order.

א   Perell – A shy gold dragon, and Basil's companion.

ℵ Quialilli (Qui) – A sassy purple kit dragon bonded to Basil. Will fight anyone who upsets him.

ℵ Resenya – A protective green female, and Kaiden's companion.

ℵ Ril (full name unknown) – A sassy, bright pink kit with mother hen tendencies. She loves fire.

ℵ Roxilelideth (Rox) – A lazy green kit dragon, formerly bonded to Olive.

ℵ Serenya – A calm brown female, and Fern's companion.

ℵ Tielieto (Tieto) – A mischievous green kit dragon who's a little too full of himself, especially when it comes to flying.

ℵ Tsalel – A fierce red dragon, and Talon's companion.

ℵ Xeriltegthn (Xerilt) – A wise gold kit dragon with a dry sense of humor and a penchant for pranks.

ℵ Zarafel Stormfire – A grumpy white-blue dragon with a rocky past and a flair for sarcasm.

ℵ Zvinsiveitei (Zvi) – A sweet blue kit dragon with an extreme love for cake and cuddles.

kit dragon art by Hannah Williams

DRAGONS' HOPE

ABOUT THE AUTHOR

Melody Jackson is a young "crazy dragon lady" and a lover of all things geek. She resides in the rainy state of Oregon with too many books and not enough time to write (or read) them all. When she's not spinning the tales in her head into stories, she can be found working undercover at a grocery store or gathering intel for her next stories, and food for the dragons.

See more online at melodyjacksonauthor.wordpress.com, and get a glimpse of what I'm working on next! Or find me wherever there's social media, usually under Melody Jackson, Author or melodyjacksonauthor. I know, I know; I'm so creative. No need to applaud.

I hope you enjoyed the book!

Made in the USA
San Bernardino, CA
17 February 2019